Collected Stories

By the Same Author

Family Dancing
The Lost Language of Cranes
Equal Affections
A Place I've Never Been
While England Sleeps
Arkansas
The Marble Quilt
Florence, A Delicate Case

Collected Stories

David Leavitt

BLOOMSBURY

Published by Bloomsbury, New York and London
Distributed to the trade by Holtzbrinck Publishers

Library of Congress Cataloging-in-Publication Data

Leavitt, David, 1961–
[Short Stories.]
Collected stories / David Leavitt. – First U.S. ed.
p. cm.
ISBN 1-58234-348-9
I. Title

PS3562.E2618A6 2003
813'.54-dc22
2003060266

First U.S. Edition 2003

1 3 5 7 9 10 8 6 4 2

Typeset by Hewer Text Ltd, Edinburgh
Printed in the United States of America by
R R Donnelley & Sons, Harrisonburg

CONTENTS

Collected Stories

Introduction

These stories were written over the course of twenty peripatetic years during which I lived in many of the places where they are set: Northern California, New York City, Long Island, London, Rome. "There is a long time in me between knowing and telling," Grace Paley has famously observed, and for me that gap usually amounts to four years or two domiciles. Thus, though "Danny in Transit"—one of the earliest stories in this collection—takes place in a New Jersey house very much like the one at which I visited my aunt Pat when I was a teenager, it was written in Rome, while lying on the floor of a tiny hotel room, the summer after my junior year at Yale. A more recent story, "The Marble Quilt," is set in Rome, where I lived for three years in the nineties, but was written in the house near Semproniano, in Tuscany, to which my patner, Mark Mitchell, and I moved a few months after our friend Lou Inturrisi was murdered. (His murder was the event on which the story is based.) What is surprising to me about rereading these is that in almost every case, the world to which I am returned is the one in which the story was written, not the one in which it plays itself out: instead of the vivid blue of Aunt Pat's swimming pool, the dirty tiled floor of the hotel room; instead of the chilly marble floor of the church of San Clemente, the light through my study window in that Tuscan house we sold in 2002 after returning permanently to the States.

Or perhaps it shouldn't surprise me that the situation in which a story was written should be bound up with the memory of its genesis. Consider "Territory," the first of these: It is very much an homage to the Palo Alto of my childhood, yet I was able to write it only once I had hopped across the continent to New Haven and was sufficiently far from my parents to confront certain fears and hopes. I have described the birth of that story—which I wrote over the course of a weeklong spring break, in the smoking section of Yale's Cross Campus Library—in my novel *Martin Bauman; or, A Sure Thing*, attributing my ability to write it at all to "the solitude of that spring break, that ugly, empty library, which, in its tranquil amplitude, provided for my imagination a model of spaciousness it had not known since childhood: a blank page." The story was also, in a sense, prophetic; through it, I engaged "in one of those acts of literary palmistry by means of which writers so often predict or rehearse their own futures." For "Territory" is about a young man bringing his male lover home to meet his mother, and at that point I had not even admitted my homosexuality to myself, much less to my mother; never had a lover, much less brought one home. In retrospect, my bravura—the bravura of utter naïveté— astonishes me.

"Territory" came out in *The New Yorker* (as did I) in July of 1982. That summer I was in Italy, the first of many visits. (Being absent for my own great moments is something of a pattern for me.) At the time it was touted as the first gay short story to appear in that august publication—an honor (if it is one) that really belongs to Allan Gurganus's "Minor Heroism." Still, the story gained for me a degree of notoriety, and changed my life in one notable way: After it was published I got letters from half a dozen literary agents, all but one of whom insisted that I should begin my career with a novel. The one who didn't—Andrew Wylie—encouraged me instead to do what I felt like doing, and start off with a collection. He has been my agent ever since.

My first collection was called *Family Dancing*. I followed it with two further collections, *A Place I've Never Been* and *The Marble Quilt*, as well as a travel book, a collection of those strange hybrid creatures—long stories or short novels—known as novellas, and a bunch of novels. At first I wrote novels purely from a sense of commercial necessity; only later did I come to appreciate their possibilities, to approach the form, as one must, from the standpoint of an aspirant. Today the novel astounds and enthralls me—I am humbled and quickened by it—yet the story remains my first great love. This in part reflects the influence of Gordon Lish, my first writing teacher, under whose aegis I read some of the seminal story collections of the last century, among them Grace Paley's *The Little Disturbances of Man* and Raymond Carver's *Will You Please Be Quiet, Please?* A few months before I took Lish's workshop, at a rather miraculous summer writing conference at a junior college in California, I had the good luck to meet these writers, neither of whom, as it happened, ever published a novel. (Why? Paley was asked once. "Because art is short and life is long." Along with Deborah Eisenberg and Alice Munro, they are among the handful of novel-resistant story writers.) During the conference—which happened to coincide with Jimmy Carter's reinstatement of military draft registration—Paley hugged me and said, "Kiddo, I'll go to prison before you get drafted," while Carver took me aside and said, "If you understand one despair, you understand every despair." It is advice I have never forgotten.

Well, I kept writing stories. I thought about despair, and I thought about getting drafted. I tried to understand what made me love the stories I loved. The process was halting, usually exuberant, sometimes graceful. I don't think I ever wrote a single opening line that ended up being the opening line of the story for which it was intended. Some stories started short and ended long; one—"Gravity"—did the opposite, shrinking from forty pages to five. I switched regularly, sometimes frantically, between first and third person, past and present tense; changed the names of characters and their relations—if rarely the settings—on a daily basis. I also changed titles. "Territory," for the longest time, bore the dreadful title "Mothers and Dogs," while "The Lost Cottage" was "Lobstermen." "Dedicated" was "I Knew You When"—possibly a better title. "Gravity" was "The Bowl," "Black Box" "In the Event of a Water Landing." I labored over these titles, just as I labored over the ordering of the stories in the three collections. "Start with a pisser and end with a pisser," Lish advised on this front—wise words. Yet it was to record albums—particularly Joni Mitchell's—that I turned to find a model for how to arrange nine or ten seemingly unrelated pieces of prose into a coherent and meaningful whole.

My life these past twenty years has been a similar struggle to put diverse short elements into order, marked as much by restlessness as by the recurrent urge to settle. Indeed, if I see a common theme here, it is probably the (sometimes futile) effort to reconcile rival impulses: the desire to bolt and the longing to nest, the cheap hotel room and the house in which one invests one's soul. And of course—literary analogue to these polarities—story and novel. Novels are forged in passion, demand fidelity and commitment, often drive you to boredom or rage, sleep with you at night. They are the long haul. They are marriage. Stories, on the other hand, you can lose yourself in for a few weeks and then wrap up, or grow tired of and abandon and (maybe) return to later. They can cuddle you sweetly, or make you get on your knees and beg. And though betrayal by either party is a necessary risk with the story, less is at stake than with a novel, the renunciation of which usually has ramifications as complex and fatiguing as those of any divorce. Perhaps for this reason I seem to remember the writing of these as less anguished than the writing of my novels; less anguished, if more unsettling.

I think my favorites of the stories are the ones that include dogs among the principal characters: "Chips Is Here," "The Scruff of the Neck," "Spouse Night," "Territory." Also the ones that take place in Italy, most notably "Roads to Rome," which I wrote after making a brief visit to the thermal springs at Saturnia. At the time I had no idea that years later I'd end up living only a stone's throw from those very springs: one fewer place I could call a place I'd never been, and one further proof that stories are never really about the past. They're about the future. Having drunk the tea, we unmuddy the leaves, hoping for a glimpse, in Paley's words, of "what in the world is coming next." And sometimes, if we're lucky, we get one.

I would be remiss if I did not acknowledge here those friends and allies in whose company (and with whose guidance) I wrote these stories: first and foremost, Mary D. Kierstead, who published my first work in *The New Yorker*; my teachers, the late John Hersey, Gordon Lish, and Michael Malone; the agents I've been privileged to work with, Gillon Aitken, Jin Auh, Sarah Chalfant, Bridget Love, and (of course) Andrew Wylie; the editors who saw these collections to press, Bobbie Bristol, Colin Dickerman, Heidi Pitlor, and Dawn Seferian; Elaine Showalter; Joel Connaroe; Frances Kiernan, ever a source of shrewd wisdom to writers of short fiction; my closest writer friends over the years, Jill Ciment, Deborah Eisenberg, Amy Hempel, Padgett Powell, and Edmund White; my parents and siblings, especially my mother, Gloria Leavitt, who regularly checked out story collections from the library and then left them lying around for me to read; Gary Glickman; the late Giovanni Forti; Giovanna Marazzi; Mark Mitchell, my beloved companion for more than half of this journey; the editors of the journals and anthologies in which some of these appeared; and last, my students at the

University of Florida, whose enthusiasm for this sometimes beleaguered form keeps me from forgetting, semester after semester, that its potential has barely been tapped.

D.L.
Gainesville, Florida
June 14, 2003

Some of these stories were first published in the following magazines and journals: *The New Yorker, Harper's, Prism, Arete, The Boston Globe Sunday Magazine, Soho Square, Winter's Tales,* the *East Hampton Star, Mother Jones, Savvy,* the *Paris Review,* the *Southwest Review, Tin House,* and *DoubleTake.* "Counting Months" and "Speonk" appeared in different volumes of the *O. Henry Prize Stories* collection.

Territory

Neil's mother, Mrs. Campbell, sits on her lawn chair behind a card table outside the food co-op. Every few minutes, as the sun shifts, she moves the chair and table several inches back so as to remain in the shade. It is a hundred degrees outside, and bright white. Each time someone goes in or out of the co-op a gust of air-conditioning flies out of the automatic doors, raising dust from the cement.

Neil stands just inside, poised over a water fountain, and watches her. She has on a sun hat, and a sweatshirt over her tennis dress; her legs are bare, and shiny with cocoa butter. In front of her, propped against the table, a sign proclaims MOTHERS, FIGHT FOR YOUR CHILDREN'S RIGHTS—SUPPORT A NON-NUCLEAR FUTURE. Women dressed exactly like her pass by, notice the sign, listen to her brief spiel, finger pamphlets, sign petitions or don't sign petitions, never give money. Her weary eyes are masked by dark glasses. In the age of Reagan, she has declared, keeping up the causes of peace and justice is a futile, tiresome, and unrewarding effort; it is therefore an effort fit only for mothers to keep up. The sun bounces off the window glass through which Neil watches her. His own reflection lines up with her profile.

Later that afternoon, Neil spreads himself out alongside the pool and imagines he is being watched by the shirtless Chicano gardener. But the gardener, concentrating on his pruning, is neither seductive nor seducible. On the lawn, his mother's large Airedales—Abigail, Lucille, Fern—amble, sniff, urinate. Occasionally, they accost the gardener, who yells at them in Spanish.

After two years' absence, Neil reasons, he should feel nostalgia, regret, gladness upon returning home. He closes his eyes and tries to muster the proper background music for the cinematic scene of return. His rhapsody, however, is interrupted by the noises of his mother's trio—the scratchy cello, whining violin, stumbling piano—as she and Lillian Havalard and Charlotte Feder plunge through Mozart. The tune is cheery, in a Germanic sort of way, and utterly inappropriate to what Neil is trying to feel. Yet it *is* the music of his adolescence; they have played it for years, bent over the notes, their heads bobbing in silent time to the metronome.

It is getting darker. Every few minutes, he must move his towel so as to remain within the narrowing patch of sunlight. In four hours, Wayne, his lover of ten months and the only person he has ever imagined he could spend his life with, will be in this house, where no lover of his has ever set foot. The thought fills him with a sense of grand terror and curiosity. He stretches, tries to feel seductive, desirable. The gardener's shears whack at the ferns; the music above him rushes to a loud, premature conclusion. The women laugh and applaud themselves as they give up for the day. He hears Charlotte Feder's full nasal twang, the voice of a fat woman in a pink pants suit—odd, since she is a scrawny, arthritic old bird, rarely clad in anything other than tennis shorts and a blouse. Lillian is the fat woman in the pink pants suit; her voice is thin and warped by too much crying. Drink in hand, she calls out from the porch, "Hot enough!" and waves. He lifts himself up and nods to her.

The women sit on the porch and chatter; their voices blend with the clink of ice in glasses. They belong to a small circle of ladies all of whom, with the exception of Neil's mother, are widows and divorcées. Lillian's husband left her twenty-two years ago, and sends her a check every month to live on; Charlotte has been divorced twice as long as she was married, and has a daughter serving a long sentence for terrorist acts committed when she was nineteen. Only Neil's mother has a husband, a distant sort of husband, away often on business. He is away on business now. All of them feel betrayed—by husbands by children, by history.

Neil closes his eyes, tries to hear the words only as sounds. Soon, a new noise accosts him: his mother arguing with the gardener in Spanish. He leans on his elbows and watches them; the syllables are loud, heated, and compressed, and seem on the verge of explosion. But the argument ends happily; they shake hands. The gardener collects his check and walks out the gate without so much as looking at Neil.

He does not know the gardener's name; as his mother has reminded him, he does not know most of what has gone on since he moved away. Her life has gone on, unaffected by his absence. He flinches at his own egoism, the egoism of sons.

"Neil! Did you call the airport to make sure the plane's coming in on time?"

"Yes," he shouts to her. "It is."

"Good. Well, I'll have dinner ready when you get back."

"Mom—"

"What?" The word comes out in a weary wail that is more of an answer than a question.

"What's wrong?" he says, forgetting his original question.

"Nothing's wrong," she declares in a tone that indicates that everything is wrong. "The dogs have to be fed, dinner has to be made, and I've got people here. Nothing's wrong."

"I hope things will be as comfortable as possible when Wayne gets here."

"Is that a request or a threat?"

"Mom—"

Behind her sunglasses, her eyes are inscrutable. "I'm tired," she says. "It's been a long day. I . . . I'm anxious to meet Wayne. I'm sure he'll be wonderful, and we'll all have a wonderful, wonderful time. I'm sorry. I'm just tired."

She heads up the stairs. He suddenly feels an urge to cover himself; his body embarrasses him, as it has in her presence since the day she saw him shirtless and said with delight, "Neil! You're growing hair under your arms!"

Before he can get up, the dogs gather round him and begin to sniff and lick at him. He wriggles to get away from them, but Abigail, the largest and stupidest, straddles his stomach and nuzzles his mouth. He splutters and, laughing, throws her off. "Get away from me, you goddamn dogs," he shouts,and swats at them. They are new dogs, not the dog of his childhood, not dogs he trusts.

He stands, and the dogs circle him, looking up at his face expectantly. He feels renewed terror at the thought that Wayne will be here so soon: Will they sleep in the same room? Will they make love? He has never had sex in his parents' house. How can he be expected to be a lover here, in this place of his childhood, of his earliest shame, in this household of mothers and dogs?

"Dinnertime! Abbylucyferny, Abbylucyferny, dinnertime!" His mother's litany disperses the dogs, and they run for the doors.

"Do you realize," he shouts to her, "that no matter how much those dogs love you they'd probably kill you for the leg of lamb in the freezer?"

Neil was twelve the first time he recognized in himself something like sexuality. He was lying outside, on the grass, when Rasputin—the dog, long dead, of his childhood—began licking his face. He felt a tingle he did not recognize, pulled off his shirt to give the dog access to more of him. Rasputin's tongue tickled coolly. A wet nose started to sniff down his body, toward his bathing suit. What he felt frightened him, but he couldn't bring himself to push the dog away. Then his mother called out, "Dinner," and Rasputin was gone, more interested in food than in him.

It was the day after Rasputin was put to sleep, years later, that Neil finally stood in the kitchen, his back turned to his parents, and said, with unexpected ease, "I'm a homosexual." The words seemed insufficient, reductive. For years, he had believed his sexuality to be detachable from the essential him, but now he realized that it was part of him. He had the sudden, despairing sensation that though the words had been easy to say, the fact of their having been aired was incurably damning. Only then, for the first time, did he admit that they were true, and he shook and wept in regret for what he would not be for his mother, for having failed her. His father hung back, silent; he was absent for that moment as he was mostly absent—a strong absence. Neil always thought of him sitting on the edge of the bed in his underwear, captivated by something on television. He said, "It's O.K., Neil." But his mother was resolute; her lower lip didn't quaver. She had enormous reserves of strength to which she only gained access at moments like this one. She hugged him from behind, wrapped him in the childhood smells of perfume and brownies, and whispered, "It's O.K., honey." For once, her words seemed as inadequate as his. Neil felt himself shrunk to an embarrassed adolescent, hating her sympathy, not wanting her to touch him. It was the way he would feel from then on whenever he was in her presence—even now, at twenty-three, bringing home his lover to meet her.

All through his childhood, she had packed only the most nutritious lunches, had served on the PTA, had volunteered at the children's library and at his school, had organized a successful campaign to ban a racist history textbook. The day after he told her, she located and got in touch with an organization called the Coalition of Parents of Lesbians and Gays. Within a year, she was president of it. On weekends, she and the other mothers drove their station wagons to San Francisco, set up their card tables in front of the Bulldog Baths, the Liberty Baths, passed out literature to men in leather and denim who were loath to admit they even had mothers. These men, who would habitually do violence to each other, were strangely cowed by the suburban ladies with their informational booklets, and bent their heads. Neil was a sophomore in college then, and lived in San Francisco. She brought him pamphlets detailing the dangers of bathhouses and back rooms, enemas and poppers, wordless sex in alleyways. His excursion into that world had been brief and lamentable, and was over. He winced at the thought that she knew all his sexual secrets, and vowed to move to the East Coast to escape her. It was not very different from the days when she had campaigned for a better playground, or tutored the Hispanic children in the audiovisual room. Those days, as well, he had run away from her concern. Even today, perched in front of the co-op, collecting signatures for nuclear disarmament, she was quintessentially a mother. And if the lot of mothers was to expect nothing in return, was the lot of sons to return nothing?

Driving across the Dumbarton Bridge on his way to the airport, Neil thinks, I have returned nothing; I have simply returned. He wonders if she would have given birth to him had she known what he would grow up to be.

Then he berates himself: Why should he assume himself to be the cause of her sorrow? She has told him that her life is full of secrets. She has changed since he left home—grown thinner, more rigid, harder to hug. She has given up baking, taken up tennis; her skin has browned and tightened. She is no longer the woman who hugged him and kissed him, who said, "As long as you're happy, that's all that's important to us."

The flats spread out around him; the bridge floats on purple and green silt, and spongy bay fill, not water at all. Only ten miles north, a whole city has been built on gunk dredged up from the bay.

He arrives at the airport ten minutes early, to discover that the plane has landed twenty minutes early. His first view of Wayne is from behind, by the baggage belt. Wayne looks as he always looks—slightly windblown—and is wearing the ratty leather jacket he was wearing the night they met. Neil sneaks up on him and puts his hands on his shoulders; when Wayne turns around, he looks relieved to see him.

They hug like brothers; only in the safety of Neil's mother's car do they dare to kiss. They recognize each other's smells, and grow comfortable again. "I never imagined I'd actually see you out here," Neil says, "but you're exactly the same here as there."

"It's only been a week."

They kiss again. Neil wants to go to a motel, but Wayne insists on being pragmatic. "We'll be there soon. Don't worry."

"We could go to one of the bathhouses in the city and take a room for a couple of aeons," Neil says. "Christ, I'm hard up. I don't even know if we're going to be in the same bedroom."

"Well, if we're not," Wayne says, "we'll sneak around. It'll be romantic."

They cling to each other for a few more minutes, until they realize that people are looking in the car window. Reluctantly, they pull apart. Neil reminds himself that he loves this man, that there is a reason for him to bring this man home.

He takes the scenic route on the way back. The car careers over foothills, through forests, along white four-lane highways high in the mountains. Wayne tells Neil that he sat next to a woman on the plane who was once Marilyn Monroe's psychiatrist's nurse. He slips his foot out of his shoe and nudges Neil's ankle, pulling Neil's sock down with his toe.

"I have to drive," Neil says. "I'm very glad you're here."

There is a comfort in the privacy of the car. They have a common fear of walking hand in hand, of publicly showing physical affection, even in the permissive West Seventies of New York—a fear that they have admitted only to one another. They slip through a pass between two hills, and are suddenly in residential Northern California, the land of expensive ranch-style houses.

As they pull into Neil's mother's driveway, the dogs run barking toward the car. When Wayne opens the door, they jump and lap at him, and he tries to close it again. "Don't worry. Abbylucyferny! Get in the house, damn it!"

His mother descends from the porch. She has changed into a blue flower-print dress, which Neil doesn't recognize. He gets out of the car and halfheartedly chastises the dogs. Crickets chirp in the trees. His mother looks radiant, even beautiful, illuminated by the headlights, surrounded by the now quiet dogs, like a Circe with her slaves. When she walks over to Wayne, offering her hand, and says, "Wayne, I'm Barbara," Neil forgets that she is his mother.

"Good to meet you, Barbara," Wayne says, and reaches out his hand. Craftier than she, he whirls her around to kiss her cheek.

Barbara! He is calling his mother Barbara! Then he remembers that Wayne is five years older than he is. They chat by the open car door, and Neil shrinks back—the embarrassed adolescent, uncomfortable, unwanted.

So the dreaded moment passes and he might as well not have been there. At dinner, Wayne keeps the conversation smooth, like a captivated courtier seeking Neil's mother's hand. A faggot son's sodomist—such words spit into Neil's head. She has prepared tiny meatballs with fresh coriander, fettucine with pesto. Wayne talks about the street people in New York; El Salvador is a tragedy; if only Sadat had lived; Phyllis Schlafly—what can you do?

"It's a losing battle," she tells him. "Every day I'm out there with my card table, me and the other mothers, but I tell you, Wayne, it's a losing battle. Sometimes I think us old ladies are the only ones with enough patience to fight."

Occasionally, Neil says something, but his comments seem stupid and clumsy. Wayne continues to call her Barbara. No one under forty has ever called her Barbara as long as Neil can remember. They drink wine; he does not.

Now is the time for drastic action. He contemplates taking Wayne's hand, then checks himself. He has never done anything in her presence to indicate that the sexuality he confessed to five years ago was a reality and not an invention. Even now, he and Wayne might as well be friends, college roommates. Then Wayne, his savior, with a single, sweeping gesture, reaches for his hand, and clasps it, in the midst of a joke he is telling about Saudi Arabians. By the time he is laughing, their hands are joined. Neil's throat contracts; his heart begins to beat violently. He notices his mother's eyes flicker, glance downward; she never breaks the stride of her sentence. The dinner goes on, and every taboo nurtured since childhood falls quietly away.

She removes the dishes. Their hands grow sticky; he cannot tell which fingers are his and which Wayne's. She clears the rest of the table and rounds up the dogs.

"Well, boys, I'm very tired, and I've got a long day ahead of me tomorrow, so I think I'll hit the sack. There are extra towels for you in Neil's bathroom, Wayne. Sleep well."

"Good night, Barbara," Wayne calls out. "It's been wonderful meeting you."

They are alone. Now they can disentangle their hands.

"No problem about where we sleep, is there?"

"No," Neil says. "I just can't imagine sleeping with someone in this house."

His leg shakes violently. Wayne takes Neil's hand in a firm grasp and hauls him up.

Later that night, they lie outside, under redwood trees, listening to the hysteria of the crickets, the hum of the pool cleaning itself. Redwood leaves prick their skin. They fell in love in bars and apartments, and this is the first time that they have made love outdoors. Neil is not sure he has enjoyed the experience. He kept sensing eyes, imagined that the neighborhood cats were staring at them from behind a fence of brambles. He remembers he once hid in this spot when he and some of the children from the neighborhood were playing sardines, remembers the intoxication of small bodies packed together, the warm breath of suppressed laughter on his neck. "The loser had to go through the spanking machine," he tells Wayne.

"Did you lose often?"

"Most of the time. The spanking machine never really hurt—just a whirl of hands. If you moved fast enough, no one could actually get you. Sometimes, though, late in the afternoon, we'd get naughty. We'd chase each other and pull each other's pants down. That was all. Boys and girls together!"

"Listen to the insects," Wayne says, and closes his eyes.

Neil turns to examine Wayne's face, notices a single, small pimple. Their lovemaking usually begins in a wrestle, a struggle for dominance, and ends with a somewhat confusing loss of identity—as now, when Neil sees a foot on the grass, resting against his leg, and tries to determine if it is his own or Wayne's.

From inside the house, the dogs begin to bark. Their yelps grow into alarmed falsettos. Neil lifts himself up. "I wonder if they smell something," he says.

"Probably just us," says Wayne.

"My mother will wake up. She hates getting waked up."

Lights go on in the house; the door to the porch opens.

"What's wrong, Abby? What's wrong?" his mother's voice calls softly.

Wayne clamps his hand over Neil's mouth. "Don't say anything," he whispers.

"I can't just—" Neil begins to say, but Wayne's hand closes over his mouth again. He bites it, and Wayne starts laughing.

"What was that?" Her voice projects into the garden. "Hello?" she says.

The dogs yelp louder. "Abbylucyferny, it's O.K., it's O.K." Her voice is soft and panicked. "Is anyone there?" she asks loudly.

The brambles shake. She takes a flashlight, shines it around the garden. Wayne and Neil duck down; the light lands on them and hovers for a few seconds. Then it clicks off and they are in the dark—a new dark, a darker dark, which their eyes must readjust to.

"Let's go to bed, Abbylucyferny," she says gently. Neil and Wayne hear her pad into the house. The dogs whimper as they follow her, and the lights go off.

Once before, Neil and his mother had stared at each other in the glare of bright lights. Four years ago, they stood in the arena created by the headlights of her car, waiting for the train. He was on his way back to San Francisco, where he was marching in a Gay Pride Parade the next day. The train station was next door to the food co-op and shared its parking lot. The co-op, familiar and boring by day, took on a certain mystery in the night. Neil recognized the spot where he had skidded on his bicycle and broken his leg. Through the glass doors, the brightly lit interior of the store glowed, its rows and rows of cans and boxes forming their own horizon, each can illuminated so that even from outside Neil could read the labels. All that was missing was the ladies in tennis dresses and sweatshirts, pushing their carts past bins of nuts and dried fruits.

"Your train is late," his mother said. Her hair fell loosely on her shoulders, and her legs were tanned. Neil looked at her and tried to imagine her in labor with him—bucking and struggling with his birth. He felt then the strange, sexless love for women which through his whole adolescence he had mistaken for heterosexual desire.

A single bright light approached them; it preceded the low, haunting sound of the whistle. Neil kissed his mother, and waved goodbye as he ran to meet the train. It was an old train, with windows tinted a sort of horrible lemon-lime. It stopped only long enough for him to hoist himself on board, and then it was moving again. He hurried to a window, hoping to see her drive off, but the tint of the window made it possible for him to make out only vague patches of light—street lamps, cars, the co-op.

He sank into the hard, green seat. The train was almost entirely empty; the only other passenger was a dark-skinned man wearing bluejeans and a leather jacket. He sat directly across the aisle from Neil, next to the window. He had rough skin and a thick mustache. Neil discovered that by pretending to look out the window he could study the man's reflection in the lemon-lime glass. It was only slightly hazy—the quality of a bad photograph. Neil felt his mouth open, felt sleep closing in on him. Hazy red and gold flashes through the glass pulsed in the face of the man in the window, giving the curious impression of muscle spasms. It took Neil a few minutes to realize that the man was staring at him, or, rather, staring at the back of his head—staring at his staring. The man smiled as though to say, I know exactly what you're staring at, and Neil felt the sickening sensation of desire rise in his throat.

Right before they reached the city, the man stood up and sat down in the seat next to Neil's. The man's thigh brushed deliberately against his own. Neil's eyes were watering; he felt sick to his stomach. Taking Neil's hand, the man said, "Why so nervous, honey? Relax."

Neil woke up the next morning with the taste of ashes in his mouth. He was lying on the floor, without blankets or sheets or pillows. Instinctively, he reached for his pants, and as he pulled them on came face to face with the man from the train. His name was Luis; he turned out to be a dog groomer. His apartment smelled of dog.

"Why such a hurry?" Luis said.

"The parade. The Gay Pride Parade. I'm meeting some friends to march."

"I'll come with you," Luis said. "I think I'm too old for these things, but why not?"

Neil did not want Luis to come with him, but he found it impossible to say so. Luis looked older by day, more likely to carry diseases. He dressed again in a torn T-shirt, leather jacket, bluejeans. "It's my everyday apparel," he said, and laughed. Neil buttoned his pants, aware that they had been washed by his mother the day before. Luis possessed the peculiar combination of hypermasculinity and effeminacy which exemplifies faggotry. Neil wanted to be rid of him, but Luis's mark was on him, he could see that much. They would become lovers whether Neil liked it or not.

They joined the parade midway. Neil hoped he wouldn't meet anyone he knew; he did not want to have to explain Luis, who clung to him. The parade was full of shirtless men with oiled, muscular shoulders. Neil's back ached. There were floats carrying garishly dressed prom queens and cheerleaders, some with beards, some actually looking like women. Luis said, "It makes me proud, makes me glad to be what I am." Neil supposed that by darting into the crowd ahead of him he might be able to lose Luis forever, but he found it difficult to let him go; the prospect of being alone seemed unbearable.

Neil was startled to see his mother watching the parade, holding up a sign. She was with the Coalition of Parents of Lesbians and Gays; they had posted a huge banner on the wall behind them proclaiming: OUR SONS AND DAUGHTERS, WE ARE PROUD OF YOU. She spotted him; she waved, and jumped up and down.

"Who's that woman?" Luis asked.

"My mother. I should go say hello to her."

"O.K.," Luis said. He followed Neil to the side of the parade. Neil kissed his mother. Luis took off his shirt, wiped his face with it, smiled.

"I'm glad you came," Neil said.

"I wouldn't have missed it, Neil. I wanted to show you I cared."

He smiled, and kissed her again. He showed no intention of introducing Luis, so Luis introduced himself.

"Hello, Luis," Mrs. Campbell said. Neil looked away. Luis shook her hand, and Neil wanted to warn his mother to wash it, warned himself to check with a V.D. clinic first thing Monday.

"Neil, this is Carmen Bologna, another one of the mothers," Mrs. Campbell said. She introduced him to a fat Italian woman with flushed cheeks, and hair arranged in the shape of a clamshell.

"Good to meet you, Neil, good to meet you," said Carmen Bologna. "You know my son, Michael? I'm so proud of Michael! He's doing so well now. I'm proud of him, proud to be his mother I am, and your mother's proud, too!"

The woman smiled at him, and Neil could think of nothing to say but "Thank you." He looked uncomfortably toward his mother, who stood listening to Luis. It occurred to him that the worst period of his life was probably about to begin and he had no way to stop it.

A group of drag queens ambled over to where the mothers were standing. "Michael! Michael!" shouted Carmen Bologna, and embraced a sticklike man wrapped in green satin. Michael's eyes were heavily dosed with green eyeshadow, and his lips were painted pink.

Neil turned and saw his mother staring, her mouth open. He marched over to where Luis was standing, and they moved back into the parade. He turned and waved to her. She waved back; he saw pain in her face, and then, briefly, regret. That day, he felt she would have traded him for any other son. Later, she said to him, "Carmen Bologna really was proud, and, speaking as a mother, let me tell you, you have to be brave to feel such pride."

Neil was never proud. It took him a year to dump Luis, another year to leave California. The sick taste of ashes was still in his mouth. On the plane, he envisioned his mother sitting alone in the dark, smoking. She did not leave his mind until he was circling New York, staring down at the dawn rising over Queens. The song playing in his earphones would remain hovering on the edges of his memory, always associated with her absence. After collecting his baggage, he took a bus into the city. Boys were selling newspapers in the middle of highways, through the windows of stopped cars. It was seven in the morning when he reached Manhattan. He stood for ten minutes on East Thirty-fourth Street, breathed the cold air, and felt bubbles rising in his blood.

Neil got a job as a paralegal—a temporary job, he told himself. When he met Wayne a year later, the sensations of that first morning returned to him. They'd been up all night, and at six they walked across the park to Wayne's apartment with the nervous, deliberate gait of people aching to make love for the first time. Joggers ran by with their dogs. None of them knew what Wayne and he were about to do, and the secrecy excited him. His mother came to mind, and the song, and the whirling vision of Queens coming alive below him. His breath solidified into clouds, and he felt happier than he had ever felt before in his life.

The second day of Wayne's visit, he and Neil go with Mrs. Campbell to pick up the dogs at the dog parlor. The grooming establishment is decorated with pink ribbons and photographs of the owner's champion pit bulls. A fat, middle-aged woman appears from the back, leading the newly trimmed and fluffed Abigail, Lucille, and Fern by three leashes. The dogs struggle frantically when they see Neil's mother, tangling the woman up in their leashes. "Ladies, behave!" Mrs. Campbell commands, and collects the dogs. She gives Fern to Neil and Abigail to Wayne. In the car on the way back, Abigail begins pawing to get on Wayne's lap.

"Just push her off," Mrs. Campbell says. "She knows she's not supposed to do that."

"You never groomed Rasputin," Neil complains.

"Rasputin was a mutt."

"Rasputin was a beautiful dog, even if he did smell."

"Do you remember when you were a little kid, Neil, you used to make Rasputin dance with you? Once you tried to dress him up in one of my blouses."

"I don't remember that," Neil says.

"Yes. I remember," says Mrs. Campbell. "Then you tried to organize a dog beauty contest in the neighborhood. You wanted to have runners-up—everything."

"A dog beauty contest?" Wayne says.

"Mother, do we have to—"

"I think it's a mother's privilege to embarrass her son," Mrs. Campbell says, and smiles.

When they are about to pull into the driveway, Wayne starts screaming, and pushes Abigail off his lap. "Oh, my God!" he says. "The dog just pissed all over me."

Neil turns around and sees a puddle seeping into Wayne's slacks. He suppresses his laughter, and Mrs. Campbell hands him a rag.

"I'm sorry, Wayne," she says. "It goes with the territory."

"This is really disgusting," Wayne says, swatting at himself with the rag.

Neil keeps his eyes on his own reflection in the rearview mirror and smiles.

At home, while Wayne cleans himself in the bathroom, Neil watches his mother cook lunch—Japanese noodles in soup. "When you went off to college," she says, "I went to the grocery store. I was going to buy you ramen noodles, and I suddenly realized you weren't going to be around to eat them. I started crying right then, blubbering like an idiot."

Neil clenches his fists inside his pockets. She has a way of telling him little sad stories when he doesn't want to hear them—stories of dolls broken by her brothers, lunches stolen by neighborhood boys on the way to school. Now he has joined the ranks of male children who have made her cry.

"Mama, I'm sorry," he says.

She is bent over the noodles, which steam in her face. "I didn't want to say anything in front of Wayne, but I wish you had answered me last night. I was very frightened—and worried."

"I'm sorry," he says, but it's not convincing. His fingers prickle. He senses a great sorrow about to be born.

"I lead a quiet life," she says. "I don't want to be a disciplinarian. I just don't have the energy for these—shenanigans. Please don't frighten me that way again."

"If you were so upset, why didn't you say something?"

"I'd rather not discuss it. I lead a quiet life. I'm not used to getting woken up late at night. I'm not used—"

"To my having a lover?"

"No, I'm not used to having other people around, that's all. Wayne is charming. A wonderful young man."

"He likes you, too."

"I'm sure we'll get along fine."

She scoops the steaming noodles into ceramic bowls. Wayne returns, wearing shorts. His white, hairy legs are a shocking contrast to hers, which are brown and sleek.

"I'll wash those pants, Wayne," Mrs. Campbell says. "I have a special detergent that'll take out the stain."

She gives Neil a look to indicate that the subject should be dropped. He looks at Wayne, looks at his mother; his initial embarrassment gives way to a fierce pride—the arrogance of mastery. He is glad his mother knows that he is desired, glad it makes her flinch.

Later, he steps into the back yard; the gardener is back, whacking at the bushes with his shears. Neil walks by him in his bathing suit, imagining he is on parade.

That afternoon, he finds his mother's daily list on the kitchen table:

TUESDAY
7:00—breakfast
Take dogs to groomer
Groceries (?)
Campaign against Draft—4–7
Buy underwear
Trios—2:00
Spaghetti
Fruit
Asparagus if sale
Peanuts
Milk
Doctor's Appointment (make)
Write Cranston/Hayakawa
re disarmament
Handi-Wraps
Mozart
Abigail
Top Ramen
Pedro

Her desk and trash can are full of such lists; he remembers them from the earliest days of his childhood. He had learned to read from them. In his own life, too, there have been endless lists—covered with check marks and arrows, at least one item always spilling over onto the next day's agenda. From September to November, "Buy plane ticket for Christmas" floated from list to list to list.

The last item puzzles him: Pedro. Pedro must be the gardener. He observes the accretion of names, the arbitrary specifics that give a sense of his mother's life. He could make a list of his own selves: the child, the adolescent, the promiscuous faggot son, and finally the good son, settled, relatively successful. But the divisions wouldn't work; he is today and will always be the child being licked by the dog, the boy on the floor with Luis; he will still be everything he is ashamed of. The other lists—the lists of things done and undone—tell their own truth: that his life is measured more properly in objects than in stages. He knows himself as "jump rope," "book," "sunglasses," "underwear."

"Tell me about your family, Wayne," Mrs. Campbell says that night, as they drive toward town. They are going to see an Esther Williams movie at the local revival house: an underwater musical, populated by mermaids, underwater Rockettes.

"My father was a lawyer," Wayne says. "He had an office in Queens, with a neon sign. I think he's probably the only lawyer in the world who had a neon sign. Anyway, he died when I was ten. My mother never remarried. She lives in Queens. Her great claim to fame is that when she was twenty-two she went on *The $64,000 Question.* Her category was mystery novels. She made it to sixteen thousand before she got tripped up."

"When I was about ten, I wanted you to go on *Jeopardy,*" Neil says to his mother. "You really should have, you know. You would have won."

"You certainly loved *Jeopardy,*" Mrs. Campbell says. "You used to watch it during dinner. Wayne, does your mother work?"

"No," he says. "She lives off investments."

"You're both only children," Mrs. Campbell says. Neil wonders if she is ruminating on the possible connection between that coincidence and their "alternative life style."

The movie theater is nearly empty. Neil sits between Wayne and his mother. There are pillows on the floor at the front of the theater, and a cat is prowling over them. It casts a monstrous shadow every now and then on the screen, disturbing the sedative effect of water ballet. Like a teenager, Neil cautiously reaches his arm around Wayne's shoulder. Wayne takes his hand immediately. Next to them, Neil's mother breathes in, out, in, out. Neil timorously moves his other arm and lifts it behind his mother's neck. He does not look at her, but he can tell from her breathing that she senses what he is doing. Slowly, carefully, he lets his hand drop on her shoulder; it twitches spasmodically, and he jumps, as if he had received an electric shock. His mother's quiet breathing is broken by a gasp; even Wayne notices. A sudden brightness on the screen illuminates the panic in her eyes, Neil's arm frozen above her, about to fall again. Slowly, he lowers his arm until his fingertips touch her skin, the fabric of her dress. He has gone too far to go back now; they are all too far.

Wayne and Mrs. Campbell sink into their seats, but Neil remains stiff, holding up his arms, which rest on nothing. The movie ends, and they go on sitting just like that.

"I'm old," Mrs. Campbell says later, as they drive back home. "I remember when those films were new. Your father and I went to one on our first date. I loved them, because I could pretend that those women underwater were flying—they were so graceful. They really took advantage of Technicolor in those days. Color was something to appreciate. You can't know what it was like to see a color movie for the first time, after years of black-and-white. It's like trying to explain the surprise of snow to an East Coaster. Very little is new anymore, I fear."

Neil would like to tell her about his own nostalgia, but how can he explain that all of it revolves around her? The idea of her life before he was born pleases him. "Tell Wayne how you used to look like Esther Williams," he asks her.

She blushes. "I was told I looked like Esther Williams, but really more like Gene Tierney," she says. "Not beautiful, but interesting. I like to think I had a certain magnetism."

"You still do," Wayne says, and instantly recognizes the wrongness of his comment. Silence and a nervous laugh indicate that he has not yet mastered the family vocabulary.

When they get home, the night is once again full of the sound of crickets. Mrs. Campbell picks up a flashlight and calls the dogs. "Abbylucyferny, Abbylucyferny," she shouts, and the dogs amble from their various corners. She pushes them out the door to the back yard and follows them. Neil follows her. Wayne follows Neil, but hovers on the porch. Neil walks behind her as she tramps through the garden. She holds out her flashlight, and snails slide from behind bushes, from under rocks, to where she stands. When the snails become visible, she crushes them underfoot. They make a wet, cracking noise, like eggs being broken.

"Nights like this," she says, "I think of children without pants on, in hot South American countries. I have nightmares about tanks rolling down our street."

"The weather's never like this in New York," Neil says. "When it's hot, it's humid and sticky. You don't want to go outdoors."

"I could never live anywhere else but here. I think I'd die. I'm too used to the climate."

"Don't be silly."

"No, I mean it," she says. "I have adjusted too well to the weather."

The dogs bark and howl by the fence. "A cat, I suspect," she says. She aims her flashlight at a rock, and more snails emerge—uncountable numbers, too stupid to have learned not to trust light.

"I know what you were doing at the movie," she says.

"What?"

"I know what you were doing."

"What? I put my arm around you."

"I'm sorry, Neil," she says. "I can only take so much. Just so much."

"What do you mean?" he says. "I was only trying to show affection."

"Oh, affection—I know about affection."

He looks up at the porch, sees Wayne moving toward the door, trying not to listen.

"What do you mean?" Neil says to her.

She puts down the flashlight and wraps her arms around herself. "I remember when you were a little boy," she says. "I remember, and I have to stop remembering. I wanted you to grow up happy. And I'm very tolerant, very understanding. But I can only take so much."

His heart seems to have risen into his throat. "Mother," he says, "I think you know my life isn't your fault. But for God's sake, don't say that your life is my fault."

"It's not a question of fault," she says. She extracts a Kleenex from her pocket and blows her nose. "I'm sorry, Neil. I guess I'm just an old woman with too much on her mind and not enough to do." She laughs halfheartedly. "Don't worry. Don't say anything," she says. "Abbylucyferny, Abbylucyferny, time for bed!"

He watches her as she walks toward the porch, silent and regal. There is the pad of feet, the clinking of dog tags as the dogs run for the house.

He was twelve the first time she saw him march in a parade. He played the tuba, and as his elementary-school band lumbered down the streets of their then small town she stood on the sidelines and waved. Afterward, she had taken him out for ice cream. He spilled some on his red uniform, and she swiped at it with a napkin. She had been there for him that day, as well as years later, at that more memorable parade; she had been there for him every day.

Somewhere over Iowa, a week later, Neil remembers this scene, remembers other days, when he would find her sitting in the dark, crying. She had to take time out of her own private sorrow to appease his anxiety. "It was part of it," she told him later. "Part of being a mother."

"The scariest thing in the world is the thought that you could unknowingly ruin someone's life," Neil tells Wayne. "Or even change someone's life. I hate the thought of having such control. I'd make a rotten mother."

"You're crazy," Wayne says. "You have this great mother, and all you do is complain. I know people whose mothers have disowned them."

"Guilt goes with the territory," Neil says.

"Why?" Wayne asks, perfectly seriously.

Neil doesn't answer. He lies back in his seat, closes his eyes, imagines he grew up in a house in the mountains of Colorado, surrounded by snow—endless white snow on hills. No flat places, and no trees; just white hills. Every time he has flown away, she has come into his mind, usually sitting alone in the dark, smoking. Today she is outside at dusk, skimming leaves from the pool.

"I want to get a dog," Neil says.

Wayne laughs. "In the city? It'd suffocate."

The hum of the airplane is druglike, dazing. "I want to stay with you a long time," Neil says.

"I know." Imperceptibly, Wayne takes his hand.

"It's very hot there in the summer, too. You know, I'm not thinking about my mother now."

"It's O.K."

For a moment, Neil wonders what the stewardess or the old woman on the way to the bathroom will think, but then he laughs and relaxes.

Later, the plane makes a slow circle over New York City, and on it two men hold hands, eyes closed, and breathe in unison.

Counting Months

Mrs. Harrington was sitting in the oncology department waiting room and thinking about chicken when the realization came over her. It was like a fist knocking the wind out of her, making her need to gasp and whoop air. Suddenly the waiting room was sucking up and churning; the nurses, the magazine racks, the other patients turning over and over again like laundry in a washer. Faces grew huge, then shrank back away from her until they were unrecognizable. Dimly she felt the magazine she had been reading slip out of her hand and onto the floor.

Then it was over.

"Ma'am?" the woman next to her was asking. "Ma'am, are you all right?" she was asking, holding up the magazine Mrs. Harrington had dropped. It was *Family Circle*. "You dropped this," the woman said.

"Thank you," said Mrs. Harrington. She took the magazine. She walked over to the fish tank and dropped herself onto a soft bench. The fish tank was built into a wall that separated two waiting rooms and could be looked into from either side. Pregnant guppies, their egg sacs visible through translucent skin, were swimming in circles against the silhouette of a face, vastly distorted, that peered in from the other waiting room. One angelfish remained still, near the bottom, near the plastic diver in the corner.

Mrs. Harrington's breath was fogging the fish tank.

The thought had come to her the way the carrier of a plague comes to an innocent town. She was reading a Shake 'n Bake ad, thinking about the chicken waiting to be cooked in the refrigerator at home, and whether she would broil it; she was tense. She began to consider the date,

December 17th: Who was born on December 17th? Did anything historic happen on December 17th?

Then, through some untraceable process, that date—December 17th—infected her with all the horror of memory and death. For today was the day she was supposed to be dead by.

Mrs. Harrington?" she heard the head nurse call. "Yes," she said. She got up and moved toward the long hallway along which the doctors kept their secret offices, their examination rooms. She moved with a new fear of the instruments she could glimpse through slightly open doors.

It was an intern who had told her, "Six months."

Then Dr. Sanchez had stood in front of her with his greater experience and said, "That's youthful hubris. Of course, we can't date these things. We're going to do everything we can for you, Anna. We're going to do everything humanly possible. You could live a long time, a full life."

But she had marked the date on a mental calendar: six months. December 17th would be six months. And so it was. And here she was, still alive, having almost forgotten she was to die.

She undressed quickly, put on the white paper examination gown, lay down on the cold table. Everything is the same, she told herself. Broil the chicken. Chicken for dinner. The Lauranses' party tonight. Everything is the same.

Then the horror swept through her again. Six months ago she had been planning to be dead by this day. Her children on their way to a new home. But it had been a long time.

Things dragged on. Radiation therapy, soon chemotherapy, all legitimate means of postponement. She lost quite a bit of hair, but a helpful lady at the radiation therapy center directed her to a hairdresser who specialized in such cases as hers, could cut around the loss and make it imperceptible. Things dragged on. She made dinner for her children.

She went to one meeting of a therapy group, and they told her to scream out her aggression and to beat a pillow with a hammer. She didn't go back.

"Hello, Anna," Dr. Sanchez said, coming in, sitting at the opposite end of the table. He smelled of crushed cigars, leather. "How're things?"

He obviously didn't remember. December 17th.

"Fine," she said.

As if she didn't notice, he began to feel around her thighs for lumps.

"The kids?" he said.

"Fine," she said.

"You've been feeling all right, I hear," he said.

"Fine," she said.

"And you aren't finding the results of the radiation too trying?"

"No, not bad."

"Well, I've got to be honest with you, when you start the chemotherapy in January, you're not going to feel so hot. You'll probably lose quite a bit of weight, and more hair. Feel like you have a bad flu for a while."

"I could stand to lose a few pounds," Mrs. Harrington said.

"Well, what's this?" said Dr. Sanchez, his hand closing around a new lump.

"You know, they come and go," said Mrs. Harrington, turning over. "That one on my back is pretty much gone now."

"Um-hum," said Dr. Sanchez, pressing between her buttocks. "And have you had any pain from the one that was pressing on the kidney?"

"No."

"That's good, very good."

He went on in silence. Every now and then he gave grunts of approval, but Mrs. Harrington had long since realized that rather than indicating some improvement in her condition, these noises simply signified that the disease was following the course he had mapped out for it. She lay there. It no longer embarrassed her, because he knew every inch of her body. Though there were certain things she had to be sure of before she went. She always made sure she was clean everywhere.

"Well," Dr. Sanchez said, pulling off his plastic gloves and throwing them into a repository, "you seem to be doing fine, Anna."

Fine. What did that mean? That the disease was fine, or her?

"I guess I just keep on, don't I?" she said.

"Seriously, Anna, I think it's marvellous the way you're handling this thing. I've had patients who've just given up to depression. A lot of them end up in hospitals. But you keep up an active life. Still on the PTA? Still entering cooking contests? I'll never forget those terrific brownies you brought. The nurses were talking about them for a week."

"Thank you, Doctor," she said. He didn't know. No more than the woman hitting the pillow with the hammer. All these months she had been so "active," she suddenly knew for a lie. You had to lie to live through death, or else you die through what's left of your life.

As she got dressed she wondered if she'd ever be able to sleep again, or if it would be as it was at the beginning, when she would go to sleep in fear of never waking up, and wake up unsure if she were really alive.

Lying there, terrified, in her flannel nightgown, the mouthpiece firmly in place (to prevent teeth-grinding), her eyes searching the ceiling for familiar cracks, her hands pinching what flesh they could find, as if pain could prove life.

It had taken her many months to learn to fall asleep easily again.

She was one with the people in the lobby now. She had been aloof from them before. One she knew, Libby, a phone operator. She waved from across the waiting room. Then there was the man with the bandage around his head. A younger woman, probably a daughter, always had to bring him. She noticed an older man with a goiter on his neck, or something that looked like a goiter, in the corner, looking at a fish.

"Good night," she said to the nurses, tying her scarf around her head. Paper Santa Clauses were pasted to the walls; a tiny tree gleamed dully in a corner. Outside the waiting room, the hospital corridors extended dim and yellow all the way to the revolving door. Mrs. Harrington pushed at the glass, and the first gusts of wind rose up, seeping in from outside. She pushed the glass away, emerging, thankfully, outside, and the cold, heavy wind seemed to bruise her alive again, brushing away the coat of exhaustion that had gathered on her eyelids while she was inside. It was cold, very cold. Her small heels crushed frozen puddles underfoot, so that they fragmented into tiny crystal mirrors. Rain drizzled down. California winter. She smoothed her scarf under her chin and walked briskly toward her car, a tall, thick woman, a genteel yacht in a harbor.

The car was cold. She turned on the heat and the radio. The familiar voice of the local newscaster droned into the upholstered interior, permeated it like the thick, unnatural heat. Rain clicked against the roof. Slowly she was escaping the hospital, merging into regular traffic. She saw the stores lit up, late-afternoon shoppers rushing home to dinner. She wanted to be one of them, to push a cart down the aisles of a supermarket again. She pulled into the Lucky parking lot.

In the supermarket the air was cool and fresh, smelled of peat and wet sod and lettuce. Small, high voices chirped through the public address system:

Our cheeks are red and rosy,
and comfy cozy are we;
We're snuggled up together
like birds of a feather should be.

Mrs. Harrington was amazed by the variety of brightly colored foods and packages, as if she had never noticed them before. She felt among the apples until she found one hard enough to indicate freshness; she examined lettuce heads. She bought Spaghetti-Os for her youngest son, gravy mix, Sugar Pops. A young family pushed a cart past her, exuberant, the baby propped happily in the little seat at the top of the shopping cart, his bottom on red plastic and his tiny legs extending through the metal slats. She was forgetting.

An old woman stood ahead of her in the nine-items-or-less line. She was wearing a man's torn peacoat. She bought a bag of hard candy with seventy-eight cents in pennies, then moved out the electric doors. "We get some weird ones," the checkout boy told Mrs. Harrington. He had red hair and bad acne and reminded her of her oldest son.

Back in the car, she told herself, "Try to forget. Things aren't any different than they were yesterday. You were happy yesterday. You weren't thinking about it yesterday. You're not any different." But she was. The difference was growing inside her, through the lymph nodes, exploring her body.

It was all inside. At the group therapy session a woman had said, "I think of the cancer as being too alive. The body just keeps multiplying until it can't control itself. So instead of some dark interior alien growth that's killing me, it's that I'm dying of being too alive, of having lived too much. Isn't that better?" the woman had said, and everyone had nodded.

Or is it, Mrs. Harrington was thinking, the body killing itself, from within?

She was at a red light. "If the light changes by the time I count to five," she said, "I will become normal again. One. Two. Three. Four. Five."

It changed.

And maybe if I had asked for six, Mrs. Harrington was thinking, that would have meant another ten years. Ten years!

* * *

As soon as Mrs. Harrington got home, she hurried into the kitchen. Her son Roy was watching *Speed Racer* on television. He was fourteen. She heard loud music in the background: Jennifer; Blondie—"Dreaming, dreaming is free." And then the sounds of her youngest child, Ernest, imitating an airplane. She was grateful for the noise, for the chance to quiet them with her arrival.

"What's for dinner?" Roy asked.

"Nothing," Mrs. Harrington answered, "unless Jennifer cleans up like she promised. Jennifer!"

"Ma," Ernest said, flying into the kitchen, "the party's tonight, right? Timmy's gonna be there, right?"

"Right," she said. He was her youngest child. His nose was plugged with cotton because it had been bleeding.

Her daughter came in, sucking a Starburst. She had on a pink blouse Mrs. Harrington didn't much care for. "How was it?" she asked, beginning to scrub the pots.

"Fine," said Mrs. Harrington.

"What's for dinner?" Roy asked again.

"Chicken. Broiled chicken."

"Again?"

"Yes," Mrs. Harrington said, remembering the days before when chicken hadn't mattered. Those days took on a new luxury, a warmth to match Christmas, in this light—the four of them, eating, innocent.

"Can I make some noodles?" Roy asked.

"Noodles!" Ernest shouted.

"As long as *you* make them," Jennifer said.

Roy stuck out his chest in a mimicking gesture.

"I'll make them, I'll make them. In a few minutes," he said.

The boys left the room.

"Dad called," Jennifer said.

"Was he at home?"

"He and Sandy are in Missoula, Montana."

"Ha," said Mrs. Harrington. "One minute in Trinidad, the next in Missoula, Montana."

"He asked how you were."

"And what did you tell him?"

"The truth," said Jennifer.

"And what might that be?" asked Mrs. Harrington.

"Fine."

"Oh." Mrs. Harrington melted butter in a saucepan, for basting.

"Are you looking forward to the party tonight?" Mrs. Harrington asked.

"Yes," Jennifer said. "As long as there are some kids my age."

Occasional moments it came back to her, and she had to hold on to keep from fainting. Such as when she was sitting on the toilet, in her green bathrobe, among the plants, her panty hose and underpants around her knees. Suddenly the horror swept through her again, because in the last six months the simple act of defecation had been so severely obstructed by the disease—something pushing against the intestine.

She held the edges of the toilet with her hands. Pushed. She tried to imagine she was caught in ice, frozen, surrounded by glacial cold, and inside, only numb.

But then, looking at the bathroom cabinet—the rows of pills, the box with the enema, the mouthpiece to keep her from grinding her teeth (fit into her mouth like a handkerchief stuffed in there by a rapist)—it came back to her, all of it.

Roy tossed the noodles with butter and cheese; Jennifer sliced the chicken. A smell of things roasting, rich with herbs, warmed the kitchen.

"Niffer, is there more cheese?"

"Check the pantry."

"I'd get it if I could reach," Ernest said.

Their mother came in. "Looks like you've got everything under control," she said.

"I put paprika on the chicken," Jennifer said.

"I helped with dessert," Ernest said.

"It's true, he helped me operate the blender."

Mrs. Harrington set the table, laid out familiar pieces of stainless steel. One plate was chipped.

"Rat tart!" Roy was shrieking in a high imitation of a feminine voice. He was recounting something he had seen on television to his sister. She was laughing as she tossed salad. Ernest rolled on the floor, gasping, as if he were being tickled. Mrs. Harrington smiled.

They sat down to dinner.

Food made its way around the table—the bowl of noodles, the

chicken, the salad. Everyone ate silently for a few minutes, in huge mouthfuls. "Eat more slowly," Mrs. Harrington said.

She wondered where they'd be today if, indeed, she had died. After all, in those frantic first weeks, she had planned for that possibility. Jennifer and Roy, she knew, were old enough to take care of themselves. But her heart went out to Ernest, who had stayed at her breast the longest, born late in life, born after the divorce had come through. Little Ernest—he had lots of colds, and few friends; crybaby, tattletale, once, a teacher told her, even a thief. He sat there across from her, innocent, a noodle hanging from his mouth.

"I wonder if Greg Laurans will be at the party," Jennifer said.

"Why, do you like him?" asked Roy, leering.

"Screw you. He's very involved." Jennifer reached to put a chicken liver she had accidentally taken back on the platter. "He runs a singing group at the state hospital through Young Life."

"Watch out for him, Jennifer," Mrs. Harrington said. "This is just another phase for him. Last year he was stealing cars."

"But he's been born again!" Ernest said loudly. He said everything loudly.

"Talk softer."

"He's reformed," Jennifer said. "But anyway, he won't be there. His parents aren't speaking to him, Gail told me."

Mrs. Harrington didn't blame the Lauranses. They were good Jews—gave a sizeable chunk of their income to the UJA. Jennifer played loud music and got low grades; Roy had bad acne, didn't wash enough, smoked a lot of marijuana; but compared to Greg Laurans, they were solid, loving kids, who knew what they wanted and weren't caught up in the craziness of the world.

Jennifer and Roy both knew about the illness—though of course she couldn't tell them "six months," and they never talked about time. She guessed, however, that they guessed what she guessed. Dr. Sanchez had told her, "If you're alive in two years, it won't be a miracle, but if you're not, we can't say it would be unexpected."

Ernest, however, knew nothing. He wasn't old enough. He wouldn't be able to understand. It would be hard enough for him, she had reasoned, after she was gone; at least let him live while he could under the pleasant delusion that she would be there for him forever.

But now, Mrs. Harrington stared across the table at her son, and the reasoning that had kept her going for six months seemed warped, perverse. The way it stood, she would die, for him, as a complete surprise. It might ruin him. He might turn into Greg Laurans. And already she saw signs that worried her.

She knew she would have to tell him soon. In a way that his seven-year-old mind could understand, she would have to explain to him the facts of death.

For in light of new knowledge, she was questioning everything. In those dim months when the doctors themselves, as well as Mrs. Harrington, had stopped thinking about the fact that she was to die, she had become too complacent, she had not made enough plans for what would be left after her. Die. The word struck, and bounced off her skull. Soon, she knew, when the chemotherapy began, she would start to get thinner, and her hair would fall out in greater quantities. She envisioned herself, then, months, or perhaps only weeks from now, so different—bones jutting out of skin, hair in clumps like patches of weeds on a desert. She anticipated great weariness, for she would be lucid, fiercely lucid, and though she would look like death, she would live for the day when once again she would feel well. Her friends would come to see her, frightened, needing reassurance. "You look so tired, Anna," they'd say. Then she would have to explain, It's the radiation, the drugs, it's all to make me better. And when they assailed her, begging her to complete that tantalizing hint of hopefulness so that they could leave without worry or fear for themselves, she would have to temper their desire for anything in only the middle ranges of despair; though she was getting better, she would probably be dead by next Christmas.

Dead by Christmas; she wondered if her children suspected that this would be her last Christmas. Then Jennifer would go to college, Roy and Ernest to her sister in Washington (though her ex-husband would probably fight for a custody she had made sure he would never get; she had at least covered that base).

Now she looked at her children. They ate, they gossiped between bites. Dear God, she thought, how will they get along without me? For if she had died today, they would probably be eating in a friend's kitchen—the Lauranses' or the Lewistons'—in shock, as yet not really believing she was gone. There would be the unfamiliar smell of someone else's cooking, someone else's dinner, another way of making spaghetti sauce. And at home, the unmade bed, her clothes, her *smell* still in the closet, in the bed, lingering a few days, then disappearing from the world forever. Soon Ernest would start to cry for her, and alien arms would take him up. There would be nothing she could do. She would be gone.

They didn't notice anything different. Happily eating, arguing, in the cramped kitchen full of steam and the smell of butter.

"Pass the noodles," Mrs. Harrington said.

"Mom, you never eat noodles."

She dressed in a big, dark gown with an Indian design stitched into it—a birthday present from Jennifer. A life of objects spread out before her—the bed, the television, so many cans of Spaghetti-Os for Ernest. New products in the grocery store. The ads for reducer-suits in *TV Guide.*

"Mom, let's go, we're gonna be late!" Ernest shouted.

"Ern, let's watch *The Flintstones,*" Jennifer said. To help her mother. She tried to help.

"Is Ernie dressed?" Mrs. Harrington asked.

"Yes, he is."

But when she emerged, perfumed, soft, Ernest didn't want to leave. "Dino's run away," he said.

"We have to go, Ern," Jennifer said. "Don't you want to go to the Lauranses'? Don't you want to see Timmy?"

Ernest started to cry. "I want to watch," he said in a tiny voice.

"All your friends will be at the party," Mrs. Harrington consoled.

"Oh, shit," said Roy, "why do you treat him like such a baby when he mopes like this? You're a baby," he said to his brother.

"I am not a baby," Ernest said.

"Babies cry 'cause they can't watch TV 'cause they're going to a party instead. You're a baby."

Ernest's crying got suddenly louder.

"You've done it," Jennifer said.

Thirty minutes later, Dino was safely home, and the Harringtons were on their way. Dry-eyed. "Happy now?" Mrs. Harrington asked.

Jennifer and Ernest climbed into the back. "I hope Timmy's there," Ernest said.

"Can I drive?" Roy asked.

"Not tonight, I'd be scared," Mrs. Harrington said.

"Then can we at least listen to KFRC?" Roy asked.

"Yeah! Maybe they'll have the Police!" Ernest shouted gleefully.

"O.K., sure," said Mrs. Harrington.

"You're in a good mood," said Roy, switching one of the preset buttons to the station he wanted.

They pulled out of the driveway. The dark, warm car filled up with a loud, sad song:

Why did you have to be a heartbreaker,
When I was be-ing what you want me to be . . .

Roy beat his hand against the dashboard. He looked funny in his orange shirt and green tie—long hair spilling over corduroy jacket—as if he had never been meant to dress that way and had adjusted the standard male uniform to his particular way of life.

Oh, Mrs. Harrington relished that moment: her children all around her. What amazed her was that she had made them—they wouldn't be who they were, they wouldn't be at all, if it hadn't been for her. Aside from a few sweaters and a large macramé wall hanging, they were her life's artwork. She was proud of them, and fearful.

They turned onto a dark road that twisted up into the hills. From the Lauranses' high window, Mrs. Harrington's house was one of a thousand staggered lights spreading like a sequined dress to the spill of the bay.

The Lauranses had introduced her to a woman who was involved with holistic healing. "Meditate on your cancer," the woman had said. "Imagine it. Visualize it inside of you. Then, imagine it's getting very cold. Imagine the tumors freezing, dying from freezing. Then a wind chips at them until they disappear."

"Oh," Mrs. Harrington said, overcome again. "Oh."

"Mom, what's wrong?" Roy asked her. In the dark car, concern seemed to light up his face. She could only look at him for a second because the road was curving up to meet her stare.

"Nothing," she said. "I'm sorry. Just a little pensive tonight, that's all."

But in her mind she could see Dr. Sanchez's hairy hands.

The party was already in full swing when they arrived. All over the Lauranses' carpeted living room the clink of drinks sounded, a slow, steady murmur of conversation. Ernest held Mrs. Harrington's hand.

She lost Jennifer and Roy instantly, lost them to the crowd, to their friends. Suddenly. They were on their own, moving in among the guests, who said hello, asked them what their plans were. They smiled. They were good kids, eager to find their friends.

"Hey, Harrington!" she heard a gravelly adolescent voice call, and Roy was gone. Jennifer lost as well, to the collegiate generation—a boy just back from Princeton.

Mrs. Harrington's friends the Lewistons were the first to greet her. Mr. Lewiston had taught in the law school with Mrs. Harrington's ex-husband, and they had remained friends.

"How are you feeling, Anna?"

"How're the kids?"

"You know, anything we can do to help."

She motioned toward Ernest with her eyes, don't talk about it. Ernest, who had not been listening, asked, "Where's Timmy?"

"Timmy and Kevin and Danielle are in the family room playing," Mrs. Lewiston said. "Would you like to join them?"

"Kevin!" Ernest turned to his mother, his eyes and mouth breaking. There was a red sore on his chin from drool. He started to cry.

"Ernie, baby, what's wrong?" Mrs. Harrington said, picking him up, hugging him fiercely.

"I don't like Kevin," Ernest sobbed. "He's mean to me."

Kevin was the Lewistons' son. As a baby, he had been on commercials.

And the Lewistons looked at Mrs. Harrington in vague horror.

"When was he mean to you?" Mrs. Harrington asked.

"The other day on the bus. He threw—um, he threw—he took my lunch and he threw it at me and it got broken. My thermos."

Mrs. Harrington looked at the Lewistons, for a brief moment accusingly, but she quickly changed her look to one of bewilderment.

"He did come home the other day with his thermos broken. Ernest, you told me you dropped it."

"Kevin told me not to tell. He—he said he'd beat me up."

"Look, Anna, how can you—how can you think . . ." Mrs. Lewiston couldn't complete her sentence. "I'll get Kevin," she said. "Your son's accused him of something he'd never do."

She ran off toward the family room.

"Anna, are you sure Ernest's not making all this up?" Mr. Lewiston asked.

"Are you accusing him of lying?" Mrs. Harrington said.

"Look, we're adults. Let's keep cool. I'm sure there's an explanation to all of this." Mr. Lewiston took out a handkerchief and swatted at his face.

Ernest was still crying when Mrs. Lewiston came back, dragging Kevin by the arm.

Ernest wailed. Mrs. Laurans, the hostess, came over to find out what was causing such a commotion. She ushered the families into the master bedroom to have it out.

"Kevin," Mr. Lewiston said, seating his son on top of forty or fifty coats piled on the bed, "Ernest has accused you of doing something very bad—of taking his lunch and hitting him with it. Is this true? Don't lie to me."

"Bill, how can you talk to him that way?" Mrs. Lewiston cried. "You're never that way with him."

Kevin, a handsome, well-dressed child, began to cry. The adults stood among their sobbing children.

"Oh dear," Mrs. Harrington said. Then she laughed just a little.

Mrs. Lewiston took her lead, and laughed, too. The tension broke.

But Mr. Lewiston, overcome by guilt for treating his son badly, was holding Kevin, and begging his forgiveness.

Mrs. Harrington knew what that was like. She also knew that Ernest had lied before. She led him over to the corner.

"Did you make that story up, Ernest?" she asked him.

"No."

"Tell the truth."

"I didn't," Ernest said.

"Kevin says you did," Mrs. Harrington said with infinite gentleness.

"He's lying."

"You can't pretend with me, young man." Her voice grew stern. "Look, I want the truth."

Sternly, she lifted up his chin so that his eyes met hers; she was on her knees. For a moment, he looked as if he might once again break out in full-fledged sobs. But Ernest changed his mind.

"All right," he said. "He didn't throw it at me. But he took it."

"I gave it back!" Kevin yelled. "I threw it *to* you, and you dropped it and the thermos broke!"

"Ah!" all the parents said at once.

"Two parties misinterpret the same incident. Happens all the time in the courts. I teach about it in my class," Mr. Lewiston said. Everyone laughed.

"Now, Mrs. Harrington, I think both these young men owe each other an apology, don't you? Kevin for taking Ernest's lunch, and Ernest for saying he threw it at him."

"Boys," Mrs. Harrington said, "will you shake hands and make up?"

The children eyed each other suspiciously.

"Come on," Mr. Lewiston said to Kevin. "Be a good cowboy, pardner."

Kevin, like a good cowboy, reached out a swaggering arm. Sheepishly, Ernest accepted it. They shook.

"All right, all right," Mrs. Lewiston said. "Now why don't you two go play with Timmy and Danielle?"

"O.K.," Kevin said. The two ran off.

"And we'll all get a drink," Mr. Lewiston said.

The adults emerged from the bedroom and made their way through the crowd. All of them were relieved not to have to face the possibility that one of their children had done something consciously malicious. But Mrs. Harrington had to admit that, of the two, Ernest had come off the more childish, the less spirited. Kevin Lewiston was energetic, attractive. He had spirit—took lunch boxes but gave them back, would go far in life. Ernest cried all the time, made more enemies than friends, kept grudges.

Small children, dressed in their best, darted between and among adult legs. Mrs. Harrington, separated from the Lewistons by a dashing three-year-old girl, found herself in front of a half-empty bowl of chopped liver.

A trio of women whose names she didn't remember greeted her, but they didn't remember her name either, so it was all right. They were talking about their children. One turned out to be the mother of the boy from Princeton. "Charlie spent the past summer working in a senator's office," she told the other women, who were impressed.

"What's your daughter doing next summer?" the woman asked Mrs. Harrington.

"Oh, probably doing what she did last summer, working at Kentucky Fried Chicken." Or, perhaps, living in another town.

The ladies made noises of approval. Then, looking over their heads to the crowd to see if her children were within earshot, Mrs. Harrington saw someone she had no desire to talk to.

"Excuse me," she hurriedly told the women. But it was too late.

"Anna!"

Joan Lensky had seen her; now she was done for. Her black hair tied tightly behind her head, dressed (as always) in black, Joan Lensky was coming to greet her.

"Anna, darling," she said, grasping Mrs. Harrington's hand between sharp fingers, "I'm so glad to see you could come out."

"Yes, well, I'm feeling quite well, Joan," Mrs. Harrington said.

"It's been so long. Are you really well? Let's chat. There's a room over there we can go to and talk privately."

Regretfully, Mrs. Harrington was pulled away from the crowd into an empty room. She did not enjoy talking to Joan Lensky; the details of their histories, at least on the surface, bore too much resemblance to each other. Up until his death, Joan's husband had been famous for making advances to his female graduate students—so often, and so clumsily, that his lechery had become a joke at the faculty wives' teas.

Mrs. Harrington's husband was more serious; he left her suddenly and flatly for a law student, quit his job, and moved with her to Italy. After that Mrs. Harrington stopped going to the faculty wives' teas, though most of the wives remained steadfastly loyal—none more so than Joan, who seized on the wronged Mrs. Harrington as a confidante. It made Mrs. Harrington nervous to realize how much she knew about Joan's life that Joan herself didn't know—Joan, with her black poodles, her immaculate kitchen. Nevertheless, she put up with this demanding friendship for many years, chiefly because she felt sorry for the old woman, who seemed to need so badly to feel sorry for her. When she got sick she changed her priorities. Now she only saw Joan when she had to.

Tell me, then, how are you?" Mrs. Lensky asked her gravely. They were sitting on an Ultrasuede sofa in a small sitting room, close together. Mrs. Harrington could feel Mrs. Lensky's breath blowing on her face.

"I'm all right. I feel well. The kids are doing fine."

"No, no, Anna," Mrs. Lensky said, shaking her head emphatically. "How *are* you?"

She couldn't put off the inevitable any longer.

"All right. I'm on the tail end of radiation therapy. It's about fifty percent effective."

"Oh, you poor, poor dear," Mrs. Lensky said. "Is there much pain?"

"No."

"And your hair? Is that a wig?"

"No, I have it specially cut."

Mrs. Lensky looked toward the ceiling and closed her eyes rapturously.

"You are so lucky, my dear Anna, you don't know," she said. "My sister has a friend who is going through terrible ordeals with the radiation. All her hair. She weighs seventy pounds. Terrible. Don't let them increase your dose! Or that awful chemotherapy!"

"All right," Mrs. Harrington said.

"You must avoid chemotherapy. I know a woman who died from it. They said it was the treatment that killed her, because it was worse than the disease. Another woman I know was so sick she had to stay in bed for three months. She's still so pale. Also during surgery make sure they don't leave any of their sponges inside your stomach . . ."

Mrs. Harrington counted her breaths, thought, It's all she has to live for, other people's sorrows to compare with her own.

"Have you heard from Roy? Is he still married to that child?"

"Yes," Mrs. Harrington said. "He is. She's actually very nice. They're quite happy."

Mrs. Lensky nodded. Then she moved even closer to Mrs. Harrington, to deliver some even greater confidence.

"I heard of an organization I thought you would want to know about," she said. "It arranges for . . . things . . . before you go. So that your children won't have to worry about it. I'm a member. The dues aren't heavy, and they take care of everything . . . just everything."

She handed Mrs. Harrington a small slip of paper that she had produced from her purse. "That's all you need to know," she said.

At that moment, thank heavens, the door opened.

Jennifer had come to rescue her mother. To help her out.

"Mom, I need to talk to you," she said.

"I'm sorry, Joan," Mrs. Harrington said, standing. "We'll talk."

"Thank you for rescuing me," Mrs. Harrington whispered to her daughter.

"Mom, you're not going to believe it," Jennifer said. "Greg Laurans is here. And he brought those people with him."

"You mean from Young Life?"

"Them . . . and some others."

In the dining room, the mass of guests had separated into small clumps, all engaged in *not* looking at the sunken bowl of the living room, *not* listening to the music rising up from it.

Mrs. Harrington glanced down curiously. Seated around the fireplace, by the Christmas tree, were Greg and a group of cherubic young people, all clean-cut, wearing little gold glasses and down vests. One had a guitar, and they were singing:

"And she draws dragons
And dreams become real
And she draws dragons
To show how she feels."

Mrs. Harrington looked behind her. Mrs. Laurans was dropping an olive into a martini; *this*, she thought, is cruel and unusual punishment.

Then she noticed the others. There were three of them. The boys were dressed neatly in sweaters. One had dark blond hair and round eyes. Occasionally the girl next to him had to take his chin between her thumb and forefinger and wipe it with a Kleenex. The other boy was darker, squatter, and could not seem to keep his head up. Every few minutes, the girl with the Kleenex would lift up his chin and he would look around himself curiously, like a child held before an aquarium. Near them was a dwarf girl with a deformed head, too large, the shape of an ostrich egg, and half of it forehead, so that the big eyes seemed to be set unnaturally low. Yet they were alert eyes, more focused than those of the boys. From the corner where they were gathered, the three sang along:

"An se dwaw daguhs
And de becuh ree
An se dwaw daguhs
Ta so ha se fee."

"They're from the state hospital," Jennifer told her mother. "They'll probably live there all their lives. It was really amazing that they let them go to come here. It's incredibly nice, really, even though it's pretty horrifying for us."

"And for Greg's mother," Mrs. Harrington said, distantly.

She stared down at the circle of singers. Now some of them were shoving pieces of paper and crayons into the invalids' hands.

"And she draws unicorns
And makes us all free
(An se dwaw oonicaws)."

"Come on," the pretty young people were saying. "Draw a daguh. Draw an oonicaw."

"This is the cruelest thing of all," Mrs. Harrington said to her daughter.

She turned around again, but Mrs. Laurans had disappeared. Quickly she walked toward the bedroom. She rapped on the door, opened it. Ursula Laurans lay on her bed, on top of fifty or sixty coats, crying.

Mrs. Harrington sat down next to her, rubbed her back.

"I'm sorry, Ursie. I'm sorry," she said.

"Why does he do this to me?" Mrs. Laurans asked. "He was getting so much better, he went to synagogue. For Christ's sake, he was a physics major, a goddamn physics major. Then one day he comes home and he tells me he's found Jesus. He tries to convert *us*, his parents. You don't know how it upset Ted. He tried to argue with him. He wouldn't even accept the theory of evolution. A physics major! He thinks everything in the Bible is true! And now this."

"I'm sorry, Ursie," Mrs. Harrington said.

Ted Laurans entered the room. "Oh, God," he said to his wife. "Oh, God. I'll kill him. How can he do this?"

"Shut up," Ursula said. "It's futile. You gave him all that bullshit already, about questioning. He's beyond reason."

Why were they telling her this? Mrs. Harrington tried to be comforting. "Oh, Ursie," she said.

Then, very suddenly, Ursula Laurans launched up and landed against Mrs. Harrington. She fell against her, dead weight, cold and heavy. Mrs. Harrington's arms went around her instinctively.

Ted Laurans was crying, too. Standing and crying, softly, his hands over his face, the way men usually do.

"Maybe this is his way of trying to reestablish a relationship," Mrs. Harrington offered. "It's very kind, bringing them here. No other person would have done it."

"It's all aggression," Ursula said. "We've been seeing a family therapist. It's all too clear. I wasn't enough of a mother to him, so he took the first maternal substitute he came across."

Mrs. Harrington chose not to say anything more. Soon Ted Laurans ran into the bathroom, leaving the two women alone with the coats.

Eventually, Mrs. Harrington emerged. Many of the guests were leaving; in the kitchen she bumped into the dwarf girl, who was washing a glass in the sink with remarkable expertise despite the fact that her chin barely reached the counter.

"Excuse me," she said quite clearly. "I get under people's feet a lot."

They both laughed. The dwarf girl smiled pleasantly at her, and Mrs. Harrington was glad to see that she had the capacity to smile. The dwarf girl wore a houndstooth dress specially tailored for her squat body, and fake pearls. She had large breasts, which surprised Mrs. Harrington; she wore a gold necklace and a little ring on one of her fingers. Obviously she wasn't as retarded as the two boys.

Mrs. Harrington turned around to look for her children. Then Ernest ran into the kitchen. He was crying again. He held his arms out, and she lifted him up. "Oh, Ernie, you'll get sick from so much crying," she said.

"I want to go home," Ernest said.

"What's wrong? Didn't you have fun?"

"They ditched me."

"Oh, Ernie."

Three little children, two boys and a girl, ran into the kitchen, laughing, stumbling. As if she were a red light, they screeched to a halt at Mrs. Harrington's feet. "Ernie, you don't want to play anymore?" Kevin Lewiston asked. All the children's faces stared up, vaguely disturbed.

"Go away!" Ernest screamed, turning in to his mother's shoulder.

"All right, that's enough," Mrs. Harrington said. "I think you kids better find your parents."

"Yes, ma'am," they said in unison. Then all three ran out of the room.

Mrs. Harrington was left in the kitchen, holding her child like a bag of wet laundry. He would probably want to sleep in her bed tonight, as he did all those nights he had to wear the eye patch, to deflect lazy left eye syndrome. "We'll go home, Ernie," she said to him. Then she noticed the dwarf girl. She was still standing by the sink, staring up at her.

"Roy's in the bedroom with some boys and they're smoking pot," Ernie mumbled to Mrs. Harringston's shoulder, which was now soaked through with tears and drool.

"Don't be a tattletale," Mrs. Harrington whispered.

She looked down at the dwarf girl, who looked up at her.

The dwarf girl held a glass of water in her tiny fat hand; the owl eyes in the huge head seemed gentle, almost pretty; in the bright light of the kitchen, she wore an expression that could have indicated extreme stupidity, or great knowledge.

Unmoving, the dwarf girl stared at Mrs. Harrington, as if the big woman were a curiosity, or a comrade in sorrow.

The Lost Cottage

The Dempson family had spent the last half of June in a little rented cottage called "Under the Weather," near Hyannis, every summer for twenty-six years, and this year, Lydia Dempson told her son, Mark, was to be no exception. "No matter what's happened," she insisted over two thousand miles of telephone wire, "we're a family. We've always gone, and we'll continue to go." Mark knew from her voice that the matter was closed. They would go again. He called an airline and made a plane reservation. He arranged for someone to take care of his apartment. He purged the four pages of his *Week-at-a-Glance* which covered those two weeks of all appointments and commitment.

A few days later he was there. The cottage still needed a coat of paint. His parents, Lydia and Alex, sat at the kitchen table and shucked ears of corn. Alex had on a white polo shirt and a sun visor, and talked about fishing. Lydia wore a new yellow dress, and over it a fuzzy white sweater. She picked loose hairs from the ears Alex had shucked, which were pearl-white, and would taste sweet. Tomorrow Mark's brother and sister, Douglas and Ellen, and Douglas's girlfriend, Julie, would arrive from the West Coast. It seemed like the opening scene from a play which tells the family's history by zeroing in on a few choice summer reunions, presumably culled from a long and happy series, to give the critical information. Mark had once imagined writing such a play, and casting Colleen Dewhurst as his mother, and Jason Robards as his father. The curtain rises. The lights come up to reveal a couple shucking corn. . . .

Six months before, Alex and Lydia had gathered their children around another kitchen table and announced that they were getting a divorce. "For a long time, your mother and I have been caught up in providing a stable home for you kids," Alex had said. "But since you've been out on your own, we've had to confront certain things about our relationship, certain facts. And we have just decided we'd be happier if we went on from here separately." His words were memorized, as Mark's had been when he told his parents he was gay; hearing them, Mark felt what he imagined they must have felt then: not the shock of surprise, but of the unspoken being spoken, the long-dreaded breaking of a silence. Eight words, four and a half seconds: a life changed, a marriage over, three hearts stopped cold. "I can't believe you're saying this," Ellen said, and Mark knew she was speaking literally.

"For several years now," Alex said, "I've been involved with someone else. There's no point in hiding this. It's Marian Hollister, whom you all know. Your mother has been aware of this. I'm not going to pretend that this fact has nothing to do with why she and I are divorcing, but I will say that with or without Marian, I think this would have been necessary, and I think your mother would agree with me on that."

Lydia said nothing. It was two days before Christmas, and the tree had yet to be decorated. She held in her hand a small gold bulb which she played with, slipping it up her sleeve and opening her fist to reveal an empty palm.

"Years," Ellen said. "You said years."

"We need you to be adults now," said Lydia. "I know this will be hard for you to adjust to, but I've gotten used to the idea, and as hard as it may be to believe, you will, too. Now a lot of work has to be done in a very short time. A lot has to be gone through. You can help by sorting through your closets, picking out what you want to save from what can be thrown away."

"You mean you're selling the house?" Mark said. His voice just barely cracked.

"The sale's already been made," Alex said. "Both your mother and I have decided we'd be happier starting off in new places."

"But how can you just sell it?" Ellen said. "You've lived here all our lives—I mean, all your lives."

"Ellen," Alex said, "you're here two weeks a year at best. I'm sorry, honey. We have to think of ourselves."

As a point of information, Douglas said, "Don't think we haven't seen what's been going on all along. We saw."

"I never thought so," Alex said.

Then Ellen asked, "And what about the cottage?"

* * *

Three months later, Alex was living with Marian in a condominium on Nob Hill, where they worked at twin oak desks by the picture window. Lydia had moved into a tiny house in Menlo Park, twenty miles down the peninsula, and had a tan, and was taking classes in pottery design. The house in which Douglas, Mark, and Ellen grew up was emptied and sold, everything that belonged to the children packed neatly in boxes and put in storage at a warehouse somewhere—the stuffed animals, the old school notebooks. But none of them were around for any of that. They had gone back to Los Angeles, Hawaii, New York—their own lives. Mark visited his mother only once, in the spring, and she took him on a tour of her new house, showing him the old dining room table, the familiar pots and pans in the kitchen, the same television set on which he had watched *Speed Racer* after school. But there was also a new wicker sofa, and everywhere the little jars she made in her pottery class. "It's a beautiful house," Mark said. "Harmonious." "That's because only one person lives here," Lydia said, and laughed. "No one to argue about the color of the drapes." She looked out the window at the vegetable garden and said, "I'm trying to become the kind of person who can live in a house like this." Mark imagined it, then; Alex and Lydia in their work clothes, sorting through twenty-six years of accumulated possessions, utility drawers, and packed closets. They had had no choice but to work through this final housecleaning together. And how had it felt? They had been married more years than he has lived.

"Under the Weather" is not the strangest name of a Cape Cod cottage, nor the most depressing. On Nantucket, for instance, there is a house called "Beyond Hope"; another called "Weak Moment"; another called "Seldom Inn." "Under the Weather" is small for such a large group, has lumpy beds and leaky faucets, but stands on a bluff, directly over a shoal where lobstermen pull up their traps. Alex and Lydia spent their honeymoon in the cottage one weekend twenty-six years ago, and loved it so much they vowed to return with their children, should they survive the war. A couple of years later, right after Lydia had Douglas, they persuaded the old woman who owned it to rent it to them for two weeks a year on a regular basis, and since then they have come every summer without fail. They hold on to the cottage as a principle, something which persists even when marriages fail, and other houses crumble. Perhaps for this reason, they have never bothered to ask anyone how it got its name. Such a question of origin interests only Mark, for whom the cottage has always been a tainted place. He remembers, as a child, coming upon his parents before dinner piercing live, writhing sea urchins with their forks, drawing them out and eating them raw. He remembers hearing them knocking about in the room next to his while he lay in bed, trying to guess if they were making love or fighting. And he remembers his own first sexual encounters, which took place near the cottage—assignations with a fisherman's son in a docked rowboat puddled with stagnant seawater. The way he figures it now, those assignations were the closest thing he has known to being in love, and his parents must have been fighting. No noise comes out of their bedroom now. Alex sleeps in the living room. What keeps Mark awake is the humming of his own brain, as he makes up new names for the place: "Desperate Efforts," perhaps, or simply, "The Lost Cottage." And what of "Under the Weather"? Who gave the cottage that name, and why? He has asked some of the lobstermen, and none of them seem to remember.

Since their arrival, Mark's parents have been distant and civil with each other, but Mark knows that no one is happy with the situation. A few weeks after he got back from his visit with his mother, Alex called him. He was in New York on business, with Marian, and they wanted Mark to have dinner with them. Mark met them at an Indian restaurant on the top of a building on Central Park South where there were gold urinals in the men's room. Marian looked fine, welcoming, and Mark remembered that before she was his father's lover, she had been his friend. That was the summer he worked as her research assistant. He also remembered that Alex almost never took Lydia with him on business trips.

"Well," Alex said, halfway through the meal, "I'll be on Cape Cod this June, as usual. Will you?"

"Dad," Mark said. "Of course."

"Of course. But Marian won't be coming, I'm afraid."

"Oh?"

"I wish she could, but your mother won't allow it."

"Really," Mark said, looking sideways at Marian for some hint as to how he should go on. She looked resolute, so he decided to be honest. "Are you really surprised?" he said.

"Nothing surprises me where your mother is concerned," Alex said. Mark supposed Alex had tried to test how far he could trespass the carefully guarded borders of Lydia's tolerance, how much he could get away with, and found he could not get away with that much. Apparently Lydia had panicked, overcome by thoughts of bedroom arrangements, and insisted the children wouldn't be able to bear Marian's presence. "And is that true?" he asked Mark, leaning toward him. "Would the children not be able to bear it?"

Mark felt as if he were being prosecuted. "I don't think Mom could bear it," he said at last—fudging, for the moment, the question of his siblings' feelings, and his own. Still, that remark was brutal enough. "Don't push it, Alex," Marian said, lighting a cigarette. "Anyway, I'm supposed to visit Kerry in Arizona that week. Kerry's living on a ranch." She smiled, retreating into the haven of her own children.

Once, Mark had been very intimate with Marian. He trusted her so much, in fact, that he came out to her before anyone else, and she responded kindly, coaxing him and giving him the strength to tell his parents he was gay. He admires her, and understands easily why his father has fallen in love with her. But since the divorce, he will not talk to Marian, for his mother's sake. Marian is the one obstacle Lydia cannot get around. Lydia never uses Marian's name because it sticks in her throat like a shard of glass and makes her cry out in pain. "Certain loyalties need to be respected" was all she could say to Alex when he suggested bringing Marian to the Cape. And Alex relented, because he agreed with her, and because he realized that two weeks in June was a small enough sacrifice, considering how far she'd stretched, how much she'd given. "Marian and I can survive," he told Mark at the Indian restaurant. "We've survived longer separations." That intimacy scalded him. As if for emphasis, Alex took Marian's hand on top of the table and held it there. "We'll survive this one," he said.

Marian laughed nervously. "Your father and I have been waiting ten years to be together," she said. "What's two weeks?"

Little about the cottage has changed since the Dempson children were children. Though Alex and Lydia talked every year about renovating, the same rotting porch still hangs off the front, the same door creaks on its hinges. The children sleep in the bedrooms they've always slept in, do the chores they've always done. "You may be adults out there," Lydia jokes, "but here you're my kids, and you do what I tell you." Ellen is a lawyer, unmarried. Two days before her scheduled departure she was asked to postpone her vacation in order to help out with an important case which was about to go to trial. She refused, and this (she thinks) might affect her chances to become a partner someday. "Ellen, why?" Mark asked her when she told him. "The family is more important," she said. "Mother is more important." Douglas has brought with him Julie, the woman he's lived with for the past five years. They do oceanographical research in a remote village on Kauai, and hold impressive fellowships. Only Mark has no career and no aspirations. He works at temporary jobs in New York and moves every few months from sublet to sublet, devoting most of his time to exploring the city's homosexual night life. For the last few months he's been working as a word processor at a bank. It was easy for him to get away. He simply quit.

Now, a week into the vacation, things aren't going well. Lydia is angry most of the time, and whenever anyone asks her why, she mentions some triviality: an unwashed pot, an unmade bed. Here is an exemplary afternoon: Douglas, Julie, Mark, and Ellen arrive back from the beach, where they've been swimming and riding waves. Lydia doesn't say hello to them. She sits, knitting, at the kitchen table. She is dressed in a fisherman's sweater and a kilt fastened with a safety pin—an outfit she saves and wears only these few weeks on the Cape. "Are we late?" Douglas asks, bewildered by her silence, out of breath.

"No," Lydia says.

"We had fun at the beach," Julie says, and smiles, unsure of herself, still a stranger in this family. "How was your day?"

"Fine," Lydia says.

Ellen rubs her eyes. "Well, Mom," she says, "would you like me to tell you I nearly drowned today? I wish I had. One less person to make a mess. Too bad Mark saved me."

Lydia puts down her knitting and cradles her face in her hands. "I don't deserve that," she says. "You don't know what it's like trying to keep ahead of the mess in this house. You have no right to make fun of me when all I'm trying to do is keep us from drowning in dirty dishes and dirty clothes."

"Didn't we do the dishes after lunch?" Douglas asks. "We must have done the dishes after lunch."

"If you can call that doing them," Lydia says. "They were soapy *and* greasy."

"I'm sorry, Lydia," says Julie. "We were in such a hurry—"

"It's just that if anything's going to get done right around here, I have to do it, and I'm sick of it. I'm sick of it." She reaches for a pack of sugarless chewing gum, unwraps a stick, and goes to work on it.

"This is ridiculous, Mom," Ellen says. "Dishes are nothing. Dishes are trivial."

"It's that attitude that gets me so riled up," Lydia says. "They're trivial to people like you, so people like me get stuck with them."

"I'm not people. I'm your daughter, Ellen, in case you've forgotten. Excuse me, I have to change."

She storms out of the kitchen, colliding with Alex, whose face and clothes are smeared with mud and sand.

"What are you in such a hurry for?" he asks.

"Ask *her*," Ellen says, and slams the door of her bedroom.

Lydia is rubbing her eyes. "What was that about?" Alex asks.

"Nothing, nothing," she says, in a weary singsong. "Just the usual. Did you fix that pipe yet?"

"No, almost. I need some help. I hoped Doug and Mark might crawl under there with me." All day he's been trying to fix a faulty pipe which has made the bathtub faucet leak for twenty-five years, and created a bluish tail of rust near the spigot. The angrier Lydia gets, the more Alex throws himself into repair work, into tending to the old anachronisms of the house which he has seen fit to ignore in other years. It gives him an excuse to spend most of his days alone, away from Lydia.

"So can you help me?" Alex asks.

"Well," Mark says, "I suppose so. When?"

"I was thinking right now. We have to get out and pick up the lobsters in an hour or so. Henry said we could ride out on the boat with him. I want to get this job done."

"Fine," Douglas says. "I'm game."

Mark hesitates. "Yes," he says. "I'll help you with it. Just let me change first."

He walks out of the kitchen and into his bedroom. It is the smallest in the house, with a tiny child-sized bed, because even though Mark is the tallest member of the family by three inches, he is still the youngest. The bed was fine when he was five, but now most of the springs have broken, and Mark's legs stick a full four inches over the edge. He takes off his bathing suit, dries himself with a towel, and—as he dresses—catches a glimpse of himself in the mirror. It is the same face, as always.

He heads out the door to the hallway, where Alex and Douglas are waiting for him. "All right," he says. "I'm ready."

Of course, it was not this way at first. The day they arrived at the cottage, Lydia seemed exuberant. "Just breathe the air," she said to Mark, her eyes fiery with excitement. "Air doesn't smell like this anywhere else in the world." They had spaghetti with clams for dinner—a huge, decadent, drunken meal. Halfway through Mark fell to the floor in a fit of laughter so severe it almost made him sick. They went to bed at three, slept dreamlessly late into the morning. By the time Mark woke up, Lydia was irritated, and Alex had disappeared, alone, to go fishing. That evening, Ellen and Julie baked a cake, and Lydia got furious at them for not cleaning up immediately afterward. Douglas and Julie rose to the occasion, eager to appease her, and immediately started scrubbing. Douglas was even more intent than his parents on keeping up a pretense of normality over the vacation, partially for Julie's sake, but also because he cherished these two weeks at the cottage even more than his mother did. Ellen chided him for giving in to her whim so readily. "She'll just get angrier if you take away her only outlet," she said. "Leave the dirty dishes. If this house were clean, believe me, we'd get it a lot worse from her than we are now."

"I want to keep things pleasant," Douglas said. he kowtowed to his mother, he claimed, because he pitied her, but Mark knew it was because he feared more than anything seeing her lose control. When he and Douglas were children, he remembers, Lydia had been hit on the head by a softball one afternoon in the park. She had fallen to her knees and burst into tears, and Douglas had shrunk back, terrified, and refused to go near her. Now Douglas seemed determined to make sure his mother never did that to him again, even if it meant she had to suffer in silence.

Lydia is still in the kitchen, leaning against the counter, when Mark emerges from under the cottage. She is not drinking coffee, not reading a recipe; just leaning there. "Dad and Doug told me to pack up and come inside," Mark says. "I was more trouble than help."

"Oh?" Lydia says.

"Yes," Mark says, and sits down at the table. "I have no mechanical aptitude. I can hold things and hand things to other people—sometimes. They knew my heart wasn't in it."

"You never did like that sort of thing," Lydia says.

Mark sits silent for a few seconds. "Daddy's just repairing everything this vacation, isn't he?" he says. "For next summer this place'll be tiptop."

"We won't be here next summer," Lydia says. "I'm sure of it, though it's hard to imagine this is the last time."

"I'm sorry it's such an unhappy time for you," Mark says.

Lydia smiles. "Well," she says, "it's no one's fault but my own. You know, when your father first told me he wanted a divorce, he said things could be hard, or they could be very hard. The choice was up to me. I thought I chose the former of those two. Then again, I also thought, if I go along with him and don't make trouble, at least he'll be fair."

"Mom," Mark says, "give yourself a break. What did you expect?"

"I expected people to act like adults," she says. "I expected people to play fair." She turns to look out the window, her face grim. The table is strewn with gum wrappers.

"Can I help you?" Mark asks.

She laughs. "Your father would be happy to hear you say that," she says. "He told me from the beginning, I'll let them hate me, I'll turn the kids against me. Then they'll be there for you. He was so damn sacrificial. But no. You can't help me because I still have some pride."

There is a clattering of doors in the hallway. Male voices invade the house. Alex and Douglas walk into the kitchen, their clothes even more smeared with mud, their eyes triumphant. "Looks like we fixed that pipe," Alex says. "Now we've got to wash up; Henry's expecting us to pick up those lobsters ten minutes ago."

He and Douglas stand at the kitchen sink and wash their hands and faces. From her room, Julie calls, "You fixed the pipe? That's fantastic!"

"Yes," Douglas says, "we have repaired the evil leak which has plagued this house for centuries."

"We'd better get going, Doug," Alex says. "Does Julie want to come hunt lobsters?"

"Lobsters?" Julie says, entering the room. Her smile is bright, eager. Then she looks at Lydia. "No, you men go," she says. "We womenfolk will stay here and guard the hearth."

Lydia looks at her, and raises her eyebrows.

"O.K., let's go," Alex says. "Mark, you ready?"

He looks questioningly at Lydia. But she is gathering together steel wool and Clorox, preparing to attack the stain on the bathtub.

"Yes, I'm ready," Mark says.

At first, when he was very young, Mark imagined the lobstermen to be literal lobster-men, with big pink pincers and claws. Later, as he was entering puberty, he found that all his early sexual feelings focused on them—the red-faced men and boys with their bellies encased in dirty T-shirts. Here, in a docked boat, Mark made love for the first time with a local boy who had propositioned him in the bathroom of what was then the town's only pizza parlor. "I seen you look at me," said the boy, whose name was Erroll. Mark had wanted to run away, but instead made a date to meet Erroll later that night. Outside, in the pizza parlor, his family was arguing about whether to get anchovies. Mark still feels a wave of nausea run through him when he eats with them at any pizza parlor, remembering Erroll's warm breath on his neck, and the smell of fish which seemed to cling to him for days afterward.

Alex is friends with the local lobstermen, one of whom is his landlord's cousin. Most years, he and Douglas and Mark ride out on a little boat with Henry Traylor and his son, Henry Traylor, and play at being lobstermen themselves, at hauling pots and grabbing the writhing creatures and snapping shut their jaws. The lobsters only turn pink when boiled; live, they're sometimes a bluish color which reminds Mark of the stain on the bathtub. Mark has never much liked these expeditions, nor the inflated caricature of machismo which his father and brother put on for them. He looks at them and sees plump men with pale skin, men no man would ever want. Yet they are loved, fiercely loved by women.

Today Henry Traylor is a year older than the last time they saw him, as is his son. "Graduated from high school last week," he tells Alex.

"That's terrific," Alex says. "What's next?"

"Fixing to get married, I suppose," Henry Traylor says. "Go to work, have kids." He is a round-faced, red-cheeked boy with ratty, bright blond hair. As he talks, he manipulates without effort the outboard rudder of the little boat which is carrying them out into the sound, toward the marked buoys of the planted pots. Out on the ocean, Alex seems to relax considerably. "Your mother seems unhappy," he says to Mark. "I try to talk to her, to help her, but it doesn't do any good. Well, maybe Julie and Ellen can do something." He puts his arm around Mark's shoulder—an uncomplicated, fatherly gesture which seems to say, this love is simple. The love of men is simple. Leave the women behind in the kitchen, in the steam of the cooking pot, the fog of their jealousies and compulsions. We will go hunt.

Henry Traylor has hauled up the ancient lobster trap. Lobster limbs stick out of the barnacle-encrusted woodwork, occasionally moving. "Now you just grab the little bugger like this," Henry Traylor instructs Douglas. "Then you take your rubber band and snap him closed. It's simple."

"O.K.," Douglas says. "Here goes." He stands back and cranes his arm over the trap, holding himself at a distance, then withdraws a single, flailing lobster.

"Oh, God," he says, and nearly drops it.

"Don't do that!" shouts Henry Traylor. "You got him. Now just take the rubber band and fix him tight. Shut him up like he's a woman who's sassing you. That's right. Good. See? It wasn't so hard."

"Do that to your wife," says Henry Traylor the elder, "she'll bite your head off quicker than that lobster."

Out of politeness, all three of the Dempson men laugh. Douglas looks at his handiwork—a single lobster, bound and gagged—and smiles. "I did it," he says. Mark wonders if young Henry Traylor has ever thought of making love to other boys, thinks rudely of propositioning him, having him beneath the boat. "I seen you look at me," he'd say. He thinks of it—little swirls of semen coagulating in the puddles, white as the eddies of foam which are gathering now on the sea in which they float, helpless, five men wrestling with lobsters.

They go back to shore. The Traylors have asked Alex and Douglas to walk up the hill with them and take a look at their new well, so Mark carries the bag of lobsters back to the house. But when he gets to the screen door to the kitchen, he stops in his tracks; Ellen, Lydia, and Julie are sitting at the table, talking in hushed voices, and he steps back, fearful of interrupting them. "It would be all right," Ellen is saying. "Really, it's not that outrageous these days. I met a lot of really decent guys when I did it."

"What could I say?" Lydia asks.

"Just be simple and straightforward. Attractive woman, divorced, mid-fifties, seeks whatever—handsome, mature man for companionship. Who knows? Whatever you want."

"I could never put that down!" Lydia says, her inflection rising. "Besides, it wouldn't be fair. They'd be disappointed when they met me."

"Of course they wouldn't!" Julie says. "You're very attractive."

"I'm an old woman," Lydia says. "There's no need to flatter me. I know that."

"Mom, you don't look half your age," Ellen says. "You're beautiful."

Mark knocks and walks through the door, his arms full of lobsters. "Here I am," he says, "back with the loot. I'm sorry for eavesdropping, but I agree with everything Ellen says."

"Oh, it doesn't matter, Mark," Lydia says. "Alex wouldn't care anyway if he found out."

"Mom, will you stop that?" Ellen says. "Will you just stop that? Don't worry about him anymore, for Christ's sake, he isn't worth it."

"Don't talk about your father that way," Lydia says. "You can tell me whatever you think I need to know, but you're not to speak of your father like that. He's still your father, even if he's not my husband."

"Jesus," Ellen says.

"What did you say?"

"Nothing," Ellen says, more loudly.

Lydia looks her over once, then walks over to the stove, where the water for the lobsters is boiling. "How many did you get, Mark?" she asks.

"Six. Daddy and Douglas went to look at the Traylors' well. They'll be back any minute."

"Good," Lydia says. "Let's put these things in the water." She lifts the top off the huge pot, and steam pours out of it, fogging her reading glasses.

Dinner passes quietly. Alex is in a questioning mood, and his children answer him obediently. Douglas and Julie talk about the strange sleeping habits of sharks, Ellen about her firm, Mark about a play he saw recently Off Broadway. Lydia sits at the head of the table, and occasionally makes a comment or asks a question—just enough to keep them from panicking, or staring at her all through the meal. Mark notices that her eyes keep wandering to Alex.

After dinner is finished, Julie and Lydia carry the dishes into the kitchen, and Douglas says, "O.K., are we getting ice cream tonight, or what?" Every night since their arrival, they have gone to get ice cream after dinner, primarily at the insistence of Douglas and Julie, who thrive on ice cream, but thrive more on ritual. Ellen, who has visited them in Hawaii, revealed to Mark that they feed their cat tea every morning, in bed. "They're daffy," she said, describing to him the way Douglas held the cat and Julie the saucer of tea it licked from. Over the five years they've been together, Mark has noticed, Douglas and Julie have become almost completely absorbed in one another, at the expense of most everything around them, probably as a result of the fact that they've spent so much of that time in remote places, in virtual isolation. They even share a secret language of code words and euphemisms. When Julie asked Douglas, one night, to give her a "floogie," Mark burst out laughing, and then they explained that "floogie" was their private word for backrub.

Tonight, Ellen is peculiarly agreeable. Usually she resists these ice cream expeditions, but now she says, "Oh, what a great idea. Let's go." Mark wonders what led her and Lydia to the conversation he overheard, then decides he'd prefer not to know. "Let's go, let's go," Douglas says. "Mom, are you game?"

But Lydia has her face buried in the steam rising from the sink of dishes, which she has insisted on doing herself. "No," she says. "You go ahead."

Douglas backs away from the sorrow in her voice—sorrow which might at any moment turn into irritation, if he pushes her harder. He knows not to. "How about you, Dad?" he asks Alex.

"No," Alex says, "I'm pooped. But bring me back some chocolate chip."

"Give me money?" Douglas says.

Alex hands him a twenty, and the kids barrel into the car and head off to the ice cream parlor in town. They sit down at a pink booth with high-backed, patent-leather seats which remind Mark of pink flamingos on people's lawns, and a waitress in a pink uniform brings them their menus. The waitress is a local girl with bad teeth, and Mark wonders if she's the one Henry Traylor's going to marry someday. He wouldn't be surprised. She's got a lusty look about her which even he can recognize, and which he imagines Henry Traylor would find attractive. And Douglas is watching her. Julie is watching Douglas watch, but she does not look jealous. She looks fascinated.

Ellen looks jealous.

They order several sundaes, and eat them with a kind of labored dedication. Halfway through the blueberry sundae he is sharing with Ellen, Mark realizes he stopped enjoying this sundae, and this ritual, four days before. Julie looks tired, too—tired of being cheerful and shrieking about fixed faucets. And Mark imagines a time when his brother and Julie will feed their cat tea for no other reason than that they always have, and with no pleasure. He remembers one weekend when Julie and Douglas came to visit him in New York. They had taken the train down from Boston, where they were in school, and they were flying to California the next afternoon. All that day on the train Douglas had been looking forward to eating at a Southern Indian restaurant he had read about, but the train arrived several hours late, and by the time he and Julie had gotten their baggage the restaurant was closed. Douglas fumed like a child until tears came to his eyes. "All that day on the train, looking forward to that dinner," he said on the subway ride back to Mark's apartment. Julie put her arms around him, and kissed him on the forehead, but he turned away. Mark wanted to shake her, then, ask her why she was indulging him this way, but he knew that Douglas had indulged her just as often. That was the basis of their love—mutual self-indulgence so excessive that Mark couldn't live with them for more than a few days without thinking he would go crazy. It wasn't that he wasn't welcome. His presence or absence seemed irrelevant to them; as far as they were concerned, he might as well not have existed. And this was coupledom, the revered state of marriage? For Mark, the amorous maneuverings of the heterosexual world are deserving of the same bewilderment and distrust that he hears in his sister's voice when she says, "But how can you just go to bed with someone you've hardly met? *I* could never do that." He wants to respond by saying, I would never pretend that I could pledge eternal allegiance to one person, but this isn't really true. What is true is that he's terrified of what he might turn into once he'd made such a pledge.

"So when's the summit conference taking place?" Ellen says now, dropping her blueberry-stained spoon onto the pink table. Everyone looks at her. "What do you mean?" Julie asks.

"I mean I think we should have a talk about what's happening with Mom and Dad. I mean I think we should stop pretending everything's normal when it isn't."

"I'm not pretending," Douglas says.

"Neither am I," says Julie. "We're aware of what's going on."

Mark watches Ellen's blueberry ice cream melt down the sides of her parfait glass. "What has Mama said to you?" he asks.

"Everything and nothing," Ellen says. "I hear her when she's angry and when she wants to cry she does it in my room. One day she's cheerful, the next miserable. I don't know why she decided to make me her confidante, but she did." Ellen pushes the sundae dish away. "Why don't we just face the fact that this is a failure?" she says. "Daddy doesn't want to be here, that's for sure, and I think Mom's beginning to think that she doesn't want to be here. And I, for one, am not so sure I want to be here."

"Mom believes in tradition," Douglas says softly, repeating a phrase they've heard from her a thousand times.

"Tradition can become repetition," Ellen says, "when you end up holding on to something just because you're afraid to let it go." She shakes her head. "I am ready to let it go."

"Let what go?" Douglas says. "The family?"

Ellen is silent.

"Well, I don't think that's fair," Douglas says. "Sure, things are stressful. A lot has happened. But that doesn't mean we should give up. We have to work hard at this. Just because things are different doesn't mean they necessarily have to be bad. I, for one, am determined to make the best of this vacation—for my sake, but also for Mom's. Except for this, without this—"

"She already has nothing," Ellen says.

Douglas stares at her.

"You can face it," Ellen says. "She has. She's said as much. Her whole life went down the tubes when Daddy left her, Cape Cod or no Cape Cod. This vacation doesn't matter a damn. But that's not the end. She could start a new life for herself. Mark, remember the first time Douglas didn't come home for Christmas? I'll bet you never guessed how upset everyone was, Douglas. Christmas just wasn't going to be Christmas without the whole family being there, I said, so why bother having it at all? But then Christmas came, and we did it without you. It wasn't the same. But it was still Christmas. We survived. And maybe we were a little relieved to find we weren't as dependent on your presence as we thought we'd be, relieved to be able to give up some of those old rituals, some of that nostalgia. It was like a rehearsal for other losses we probably all knew we'd have to face someday—for this, maybe."

Douglas has his arm around Julie, his fingers gripping her shoulder. "No one ever told me that," he says. "I figured no one cared."

Ellen laughs. "That's never been a problem in this family," she says. "The problem in this family is that everybody cares."

They get back to the cottage around eleven to find that the lights are still on. "I'm surprised she's still up," Ellen says to Mark as they clamber out of the car.

"It's not so surprising," Mark says. "She's probably having a snack." The gravel of the driveway crunches beneath his feet as he moves toward the screen door to the kitchen. "Hi, Mom," Mark says as he walks through the door, then stops abruptly, the other three behind him.

"What's going on?" Mark asks.

Alex is standing by the ironing board, in his coat, his face red and puffy. He is looking down at Lydia, who sits in her pink bathrobe at the kitchen table, her head resting on her forearms, weeping. In front of her is half a grapefruit on a plate, and a small spoon with serrated edges.

"What happened?" Ellen asks.

"It's nothing, kids," Alex says. "Your mother and I were just having a discussion."

"Oh, shut up," Lydia says, raising her head slightly. Her eyes are red, swollen with tears. "Why don't you just tell them if you're so big on honesty all of a sudden? Your father's girlfriend has arrived. She's at a motel in town. They planned this all along, and your father never saw fit to tell any of us about it, except I happened to see her this morning when I was doing the grocery shopping."

"Oh, God," Mark says, and leans back against the wall of the kitchen. Across from him, his father also draws back.

"All right, let's not get hysterical," Ellen says. "Let's try to talk this through. Daddy, is this true?"

"Yes," Alex says. "I'm sorry I didn't tell any of you, but I was afraid of how you'd react. Marian's just here for the weekend, she'll be gone Monday. I thought I could see her during the day, and no one would know. But now that everything's out, I can see that more deception was just a bad idea to begin with. And anyway, am I asking so much? All I'm asking is to spend some time in town with Marian. I'll be home for meals, and during the day, everything for the family. None of you ever has to see her."

"Do you think all this is fair to Marian?" Ellen asks.

"It was her idea."

"I see."

"Fair to Marian, fair to Marian," Lydia mumbles. "All of this has been fair to Marian. These two weeks you were supposed to be fair to me." She takes a Kleenex and rubs at her nose and eyes. Mark's fingers grip the moldings on the walls, while Julie buttons and unbuttons the collar of her sweater.

"Lydia, look," Alex says. "Something isn't clear here. When I agreed to come these weeks, it was as your friend and as a father. Nothing more."

"So go then!" Lydia shouts, standing up and facing him. "You've brought me lower than I ever thought you would, don't stand there and rub it in. Just go." Shaking, she walks over to the counter, picks up a coffee cup, and takes a sip out of it. Coffee splashes over the rim, falls in hot drops on the floor.

"Now I think we have to talk about this," Ellen says. "We can deal with this if we just work on it."

"There's no point," Douglas says, and sits down at the table. "There's nothing left to say." He looks at the table, and Julie reaches for his hand.

"What do you mean there's nothing left to say? There's everything to be said here. The one thing we haven't done is talk about all of this as a family."

"Oh, be quiet, both of you," Lydia says, putting down her cup. "You don't know anything about this. The whole business is so simple it's embarrassing." She puts her hand on her chest and takes a deep, shaky breath. "There is only one thing to be said here, and I'm the one who has to say it. And that is the simple fact that I love your father, and I will always love your father. And he doesn't love me. And never will."

No one answers her. She is right. None of them know anything about *this*, not even Ellen. Lydia's children are as speechless as spectators watching a woman on a high ledge: unable to do any good, they can only stare, waiting to see what she'll do next.

What she does is turn to Alex. "Did you hear me?" she says. "I love you. You can escape me, but you can never escape that."

He keeps his eyes focused on the window above her head, making sure never to look at her. The expression on his face is almost simple, almost sweet: the lips pressed together, though not tightly, the eyes averted. In his mind, he's already left.

Aliens

A year ago today I wouldn't have dreamed I'd be where I am now: in the recreation room on the third floor of the State Hospital, watching, with my daughter, ten men who sit in a circle in the center of the room. They look almost normal from a distance—khaki pants, lumberjack shirts, white socks—but I've learned to detect the tics, the nervous disorders. The men are members of a poetry writing workshop. It is my husband Alden's turn to read. He takes a few seconds to find his cane, to hoist himself out of his chair. As he stands, his posture is hunched and awkward. The surface of his crushed left eye has clouded to marble. There is a pale pink scar under his pale yellow hair.

The woman who leads the workshop, on a volunteer basis, rubs her forehead as she listens, and fingers one of her elephant-shaped earrings. Alden's voice is a hoarse roar, only recently reconstructed.

"Goddamned God," he reads. "I'm mad as hell I can't walk or talk."

It is spring, and my youngest child, my eleven-year-old, Nina, has convinced herself that she is an alien.

Mrs. Tompkins, her teacher, called me in yesterday morning to tell me. "Nina's constructed a whole history," she whispered, removing her glasses and leaning toward me across her desk, as if someone might be listening from above. "She never pays attention in class, just sits and draws. Strange landscapes, star-charts, the interiors of spaceships. I finally asked some of the other children what was going on. They told me that Nina says she's waiting to be taken away by her real parents. She says she's a surveyor, implanted here, but that soon a ship's going to come and retrieve her."

I looked around the classroom; the walls were papered with crayon drawings of cars and rabbits, the world seen by children. Nina's are remote, fine landscapes done with Magic Markers. No purple suns with faces. No abrupt, sinister self-portraits. In the course of a year Nina suffered a violent and quick puberty, sprouted breasts larger than mine, grew tufts of hair under her arms. The little girls who were her friends shunned her. Most afternoons now she stands in the corner of the playground, her hair held back by barrettes, her forehead gleaming. Recently, Mrs. Tompkins tells me, a few girls with glasses and large vocabularies have taken to clustering around Nina at recess. They sit in the broken bark beneath the slide and listen to Nina as one might listen to a prophet. Her small eyes, exaggerated by her own glasses, must seem to them expressive of martyred beauty.

"Perhaps you should send her to a psychiatrist," Mrs. Tompkins suggested. She is a good teacher, better than most of her colleagues. "This could turn into a serious problem," she said.

"I'll consider it," I answered, but I was lying. I don't have the money. And besides, I know psychiatry; it takes things away. I don't think I could bear to see what would be left of Nina once she'd been purged of this fantasy.

Today Nina sits in the corner of the recreation room. She is quiet, but I know her eyes are taking account of everything. The woman with the elephant-shaped earrings is talking to one of the patients about poetry *qua* poetry.

"You know," I say to her afterward, "it's amazing that a man like Alden can write poems. He was a computer programmer. All our married life he never read a book."

"His work has real power," the teacher says. "It reminds me of Michelangelo's Bound Slaves. Its artistry is heightened by its rawness."

She hands me a sheet of mimeographed paper—some examples of the group's work. "We all need a vehicle for self-expression," she says.

Later, sitting on the sun porch with Alden, I read through the poems. They are full of expletives and filthy remarks—the kind of remarks my brother used to make when he was hot for some girl at school. I am embarrassed. Nina, curled in an unused wheelchair, is reading *The Chronicles of Narnia* for the seventeenth time. We should go home soon, but I'm wary of the new car. I don't trust its brakes. When I bought it, I tested the seatbelts over and over again.

"Dinner?" Alden asks. Each simple word, I remember, is a labor for him. We must be patient.

"Soon," I say.

"Dinner. It's all—" He struggles to find the word; his brow is red, and the one seeing eye stares at the opposite wall.

"Crap," he says. He keeps looking at the wall. His eyes are expressionless. Once again, he breathes.

Nearby, someone's screaming, but we're used to that.

A year ago today. The day was normal. I took my son, Charles, to the dentist's. I bought a leg of lamb to freeze. There was a sale on paper towels. Early in the evening, on our way to a restaurant, Alden drove the car through a fence, and over an embankment. I remember, will always remember, the way his body fell almost gracefully through the windshield, how the glass shattered around him in a thousand glittering pieces. Earlier, during the argument, he had said that seatbelts do more harm than good, and I had buckled myself in as an act of vengeance. This is the only reason I'm around to talk about it.

I suffered a ruptured spleen in the accident, and twenty-two broken bones. Alden lost half his vision, much of his mobility, and the English language. After a week in intensive care they took him to his hospital and left me to mine. In the course of the six months, three weeks, and five days I spent there, eight women passed in and out of the bed across from me. The first was a tiny, elderly lady who spoke in hushed tones and kept the curtain drawn between us. Sometimes children were snuck in to visit her; they would stick their heads around the curtain rod and gaze at me, until a hand pulled them back and a voice loudly whispered, "Sorry!" I was heavily sedated; everything seemed to be there one minute, gone the next. After the old woman left, another took her place. Somewhere in the course of those months a Texan mother arrived who was undergoing chemotherapy, who spent her days putting on make-up, over and over again, until, by dusk, her face was the color of bruises.

My hospital. What can you say about a place to which you become addicted? That you hate it, yet at the same time, that you need it. For weeks after my release I begged to be readmitted. I would wake crying, helplessly, in the night, convinced that the world had stopped, and I had been left behind, the only survivor. I'd call the ward I had lived on. "You'll be all right, dear," the nurses told me. "You don't have to come back, and besides, we've kicked you out." I wanted cups of Jell-O. I wanted there to be a light in the hall at night. I wanted to be told that six months hadn't gone by, that it had all been, as it seemed, a single, endless moment.

To compensate, I started to spend as much time as I could at Alden's hospital. The head nurse suggested that if I was going to be there all day, I might as well do something productive. They badly needed volunteers on the sixth floor, the floor of the severely retarded, the unrecoverable ones. I agreed to go in the afternoons, imagining story corner with cute three-year-olds and seventy-year-olds. The woman I worked with most closely had been pregnant three times in the course of a year. Her partner was a pale-skinned young man who drooled constantly and could not keep his head up. Of course she had abortions. None of the administrators were willing to solicit funds for birth control because that would have meant admitting there was a need for birth control. We couldn't keep the couple from copulating. They hid in the bushes and in the broom closet. They were obsessive about their lovemaking, and went to great lengths to find each other. When we locked them in separate rooms, they pawed the doors and screamed.

The final pregnancy was the worst because the woman insisted that she wanted to keep the baby, and legally she had every right. Nora, my supervisor—a crusty, ancient nurse—had no sympathy, insisted that the woman didn't even know what being pregnant meant. In the third month, sure enough, the woman started to scream and wouldn't be calmed. Something was moving inside her, something she was afraid would try to kill her. The lover was no help. Just as easily as he'd begun with her, he'd forgotten her, and taken up with a Down's syndrome dwarf who got transferred from Sonoma.

The woman agreed to the third abortion. Because it was so late in the pregnancy, the procedure was painful and complicated. Nora shook her head and said, "What's the world coming to?" Then she returned to her work.

I admire women who shake their heads and say, "What's the world coming to?" Because of them, I hope, it will always stop just short of getting there.

Lately, in my own little ways, I, too, have been keeping the earth in orbit. Today, for instance, I take Alden out to the car and let him sit in the driver's seat, which he enjoys. The hot vinyl burns his thighs. I calm him. I sit in the passenger seat, strapped in, while he slowly turns the wheel. He stares through the windshield at the other cars in the parking lot, imagining, perhaps, an endless landscape unfolding before him as he drives.

Visiting hours end. I take Alden in from the parking lot, kiss him goodbye. He shares a room these days with a young man named Joe, a Vietnam veteran prone to motorcycle accidents. Because of skin-grafting, Joe's face is six or seven different colors—beiges and taupes, mostly—but he can speak, and has recently regained the ability to smile. "Hey, pretty lady," he says as we walk in. "It's good to see a pretty lady around here."

Nina is sitting in the chair by the window, reading. She is sulky as we say goodbye to Alden, sulky as we walk out to the car. I suppose I should expect moodiness—some response to what she's seen this last year. We go to pick up Charles, who is sixteen and spends most of his time in the Olde Computer Shoppe—a scarlet, plum-shaped building which serves as a reminder of what the fifties thought the future would look like. Charles is a computer prodigy, a certified genius, nothing special in our circuit-fed community. He has some sort of deal going with the owner of the Computer Shoppe which he doesn't like to talk about. It involves that magical stuff called software. He uses the Shoppe's terminal and in exchange gives the owner a cut of his profits, which are bounteous. Checks arrive for him every day—from Puerto Rico, from Texas, from New York. He puts the money in a private bank account. He says that in a year he will have enough saved to put himself through college—a fact I can't help but appreciate.

The other day I asked him to please explain in English what it is that he does. He was sitting in my kitchen with Stuart Beckman, a fat boy with the kind of wispy mustache that indicates a willful refusal to begin shaving. Stuart is the dungeon master in the elaborate medieval war-games Charles's friends conduct on Tuesday nights. Charles is Galadrian, a lowly elfin-warrior with minimal experience points. "Well," Charles said, "let's just say it's a step toward the great computer age when we won't need dungeon masters. A machine will create for us a whole world into which we can be transported. We'll live inside the machine—for a day, a year, our whole lives—and we'll live the adventures the machine creates for us. We're at the forefront of a major breakthrough—artificial imagination. The possibilities, needless to say, are endless."

"You've invented that?" I asked, suddenly swelling with Mother Goddess pride.

"The project is embryonic, of course," Charles said. "But we're getting there. Give it fifty years. Who knows?"

Charles is angry as we drive home. He sifts furiously through an enormous roll of green print-out paper. As it unravels, the paper flies in Nina's hair, but she is oblivious to it. Her face is pressed against the window so hard that her nose and lips have flattened out.

I consider starting up a conversation, but as we pull into the driveway I, too, feel the need for silence. Our house is dark and unwelcoming tonight, as if it is suspicious of us. As soon as we are in the door, Charles disappears into his room, and the world of his mind. Nina sits at the kitchen table with me until she has finished her book. It is the last in the Narnia series, and as she closes it, her face takes on the disappointed look of someone who was hoping something would never end. Last month she entered the local library's Read-a-Thon. Neighbors agreed to give several dollars to UNICEF for every book she read, not realizing that she would read fifty-nine.

It is hard for me to look at her. She is sullen, and she is not pretty. My mother used to say it's one thing to look ugly, another to act it. Still, it must be difficult to be betrayed by your own body. The cells divide, the hormones explode; Nina had no control over the timing, much less the effects. The first time she menstruated she cried not out of fear but because she was worried she had contracted that disease which causes children to age prematurely. We'd seen pictures of them—wizened, hoary four-year-olds, their skin loose and wrinkled, their teeth already rotten. I assured her that she had no such disease, that she was merely being precocious, as usual. In a few years, I told her, her friends would catch up.

She stands awkwardly now, as if she wants to maintain a distance even from herself. Ugliness really is a betrayal. Suddenly she can trust nothing on earth; her body is no longer a part of her, but her enemy.

"Daddy was glad to see you today, Nina," I say.

"Good."

"Can I get you anything?"

She still does not look at me. "No," she says. "Nothing."

* * *

Later in the evening, my mother calls to tell me about her new cordless electric telephone. "I can walk all around the house with it," she says. "Now, for instance, I'm in the kitchen, but I'm on my way to the bathroom." Mother believes in Christmas newsletters, and the forces of fate. Tonight she is telling me about Mr. Garvey, a local politician and neighbor who was recently arrested. No one knows the details of the scandal; Mother heard somewhere that the boys involved were young, younger than Charles. "His wife just goes on, does her gardening as if nothing happened," she tells me. "Of course, we don't say anything. What could we say? She knows we avoid mentioning it. Her house is as clean as ever. I even saw *him* the other day. He was wearing a sable sweater just like your father's. He told me he was relaxing for the first time in his life, playing golf, gardening. She looks ill, if you ask me. When I was your age I would have wondered how a woman could survive something like that, but now it doesn't surprise me to see her make do. Still, it's shocking. He always seemed like such a family man."

"She must have known," I say. "It's probably been a secret between them for years."

"I don't call secrets any basis for a marriage," Mother says. "Not in her case. Not in yours, either."

Lately she's been convinced that there's some awful secret between Alden and me. I told her that we'd had a fight the night of the accident, but I didn't tell her why. Not because the truth was too monumentally terrible. The subject of our fight was trivial. Embarrassingly trivial. We were going out to dinner. I wanted to go to a Chinese place. Alden wanted to try an Italian health food restaurant that a friend of his at work had told him about. Our family has always fought a tremendous amount about restaurants. Several times, when the four of us were piled in the car, Alden would pull off the road. "I will not drive with this chaos," he'd say. The debates over where to eat usually ended in tears, and abrupt returns home. The children ran screaming to their rooms. We ended up eating tunafish.

Mother is convinced I'm having an affair. "Alden's still a man," she says to me. "With a man's needs."

We have been talking so long that the earpiece of the phone is sticking to my ear. "Mother," I say, "please don't worry. I'm hardly in shape for it."

She doesn't laugh. "I look at Mrs. Garvey, and I'm moved," she says.

"Such strength of character. You should take it as a lesson. Before I hang up, I want to tell you about something I read, if you don't mind."

My mother loves to offer information, and has raised me in the tradition. We constantly repeat movie plots, offer authoritative statistics from television news specials. "What did you read, Mother?" I ask.

"There is a man who is studying the Holocaust," she says. "He makes a graph. One axis is fulfillment/despair, and the other is success/failure. That means that there are four groups of people—those who are fulfilled by success, whom we can understand, and those who are despairing even though they're successful, like so many people we know, and those who are despairing because they're failures. Then there's the fourth group—the people who are fulfilled by failure, who don't need hope to live. Do you know who those people are?"

"Who?" I ask.

"Those people," my mother says, "are the ones who survived."

There is a long, intentional silence.

"I thought you should know," she says, "that I am now standing outside, on the back porch. I can go as far as seven hundred feet from the house."

Recently I've been thinking often about something terrible I did when I was a child—something which neither I nor Mother has ever really gotten over. I did it when I was six years old. One day at school my older sister, Mary Elise, asked me to tell Mother that she was going to a friend's house for the afternoon to play with some new Barbie dolls. I was mad at Mother that day, and jealous of Mary Elise. When I got home, Mother was feeding the cat, and without even saying hello (she was mad at me for some reason, too) she ordered me to take out the garbage. I was filled with rage, both at her and my sister, whom I was convinced she favored. And then I came up with an awful idea. "Mother," I said, "I have something to tell you." She turned around. Her distracted face suddenly focused on me. I realized I had no choice but to finish what I'd started. "Mary Elise died today," I said. "She fell off the jungle gym and split her head open."

At first she just looked at me, her mouth open. Then her eyes—I remember this distinctly—went in two different directions. For a brief moment, the tenuousness of everything—the house, my life, the universe—became known to me, and I had a glimpse of how easily the fragile network could be exploded.

Mother started shaking me. She was making noises but she couldn't speak. The minute I said the dreaded words I started to cry; I couldn't find a voice to tell her the truth. She kept shaking me. Finally I managed to gasp, "I'm lying, I'm lying. It's not true." She stopped shaking me, and hoisted me up into the air. I closed my eyes and held my breath, imagining she might hurl me down against the floor. "You monster," she whispered. "You little bastard," she whispered between clenched teeth. Her face was twisted, her eyes glistening. She hugged me very fiercely and then she threw me onto her lap and started to spank me. "You monster, you monster," she screamed between sobs. "Never scare me like that again, never scare me like that again."

By the time Mary Elise got home, we were composed. Mother had made me swear I'd never tell her what had happened, and I never have. We had an understanding, from then on, or perhaps we had a secret. It has bound us together, so that now we are much closer to each other than either of us is to Mary Elise, who married a lawyer and moved to Hawaii.

The reason I cannot forget this episode is because I have seen, for the second time, how easily apocalypse can happen. That look in Alden's eyes, the moment before the accident, was a look I'd seen before.

"I hear you're from another planet," I say to Nina after we finish dinner.

She doesn't blink. "I assumed you'd find out sooner or later," she says. "But, Mother, can you understand that I didn't want to hurt you?"

I was expecting confessions and tears. Nina's sincerity surprises me. "Nina," I say, trying to affect maternal authority, "tell me what's going on."

Nina smiles. "In the Fourth Millennium," she says, "when it was least expected, the Brolian force attacked the city of Landruz, on the planet Abdur. Chaos broke loose all over. The star-worms escaped from the zoo. It soon became obvious that the community would not survive the attack. Izmul, the father of generations, raced to his space-cruiser. It was the only one in the city. Hordes crowded to get on board, to escape the catastrophe and the star-worms, but only a few hundred managed. Others clung to the outside of the ship as it took off and were blown across the planet by its engines. The space-cruiser broke through the atmosphere just as the bomb hit. A hundred people were cast out into space. The survivors made it to a small planet, Dandril, and settled there. These are my origins."

She speaks like an oracle, not like anything I might have given birth to. "Nina," I say, "*I* am your origin."

She shakes her head. "I am a surveyor. It was decided that I should be born in earthly form so that I could observe your planet and gather knowledge for the rebuilding of our world. I was generated in your womb while you slept. You can't remember the conception."

"I remember the exact night," I say. "Daddy and I were in San Luis Obispo for a convention."

Nina laughs. "It happened in your sleep," she says. "An invisible ray. You never felt it."

What can I say to this? I sit back and try to pierce through her with a stare. She isn't even looking at me. Her eyes are focused on a spot of green caught in the night outside the window.

"I've been receiving telepathic communications," Nina says. "My people will be coming any time to take me, finally, to where I belong. You've been good to this earthly shell, Mother. For that, I thank you. But you must understand and give me up. My people are shaping a new civilization on Dandril. I must go and help them."

"I understand," I say.

She looks at me quizzically. "It's good, Mother," Nina says. "Good that you've come around." She reaches toward me, and kisses my cheek. I am tempted to grab her the way a mother is supposed to grab a child—by the shoulders, by the scruff of the neck; tempted to bend her to my will, to spank her, to hug her.

But I do nothing. With the look of one who has just been informed of her own salvation, the earthly shell I call Nina walks out the screen door, to sit on the porch and wait for her origins.

Mother calls me again in the morning. "I'm in the garden," she says, "looking at the sweetpeas. Now I'm heading due west, toward where those azaleas are planted."

She is preparing the Christmas newsletter, wants information from my branch of the family. "Mother," I say, "it's March. Christmas is months away." She is unmoved. Lately, this business of recording has taken on tremendous importance in her life; more and more requires to be saved.

"I wonder what the Garveys will write this year," she says. "You know, I just wonder what there is to say about something like that. Oh my. There he is now, Mr. Garvey, talking to the paper boy. Yes, when I think of it, there have been signs all along. I'm waving to him now. He's waving back. Remember, don't you, what a great interest he took in the Shepards' son, getting him scholarships and all? What if they decided to put it all down in the newsletter? It would be embarrassing to read."

As we talk, I watch Nina, sitting in the dripping spring garden, rereading *The Lion, the Witch and the Wardrobe*. Every now and then she looks up at the sky, just to check, then returns to her book. She seems at peace.

"What should I say about your family this year?" Mother asks. I wish I knew what to tell her. Certainly nothing that could be typed onto purple paper, garnished with little pencil drawings of holly and wreaths. And yet, when I read them over, those old newsletters have a terrible, swift power, each so innocent of the celebrations and catastrophes which the next year's letter will record. Where will we be a year from today? What will have happened then? Perhaps Mother won't be around to record these events; perhaps I won't be around to read about them.

"You can talk about Charles," I say. "Talk about how he's inventing an artificial imagination."

"I must be at least seven hundred feet from the house now," Mother says. "Can you hear me?"

Her voice is crackly with static, but still audible.

"I'm going to keep walking," Mother says. "I'm going to keep walking until I'm out of range."

That night in San Luis Obispo, Alden—can you remember it? Charles was already so self-sufficient then, happily asleep in the little room off ours. We planned that night to have a child, and I remember feeling sure that it would happen. Perhaps it was the glistening blackness outside the hotel room window, or the light rain, or the heat. Perhaps it was the kind of night when spaceships land and aliens prowl, fascinated by all we take for granted.

There are some anniversaries which aren't so easy to commemorate. This one, for instance: one year since we almost died. If I could reach you, Alden, in the world behind your eyes, I'd ask you a question: Why did you turn off the road? Was it whim, the sudden temptation of destroying both of us for no reason? Or did you hope the car would bear wings and engines, take off into the atmosphere, and propel you—us—in a split second, out of the world?

I visit you after lunch. Joe doesn't bother to say hello, and though I kiss you on the forehead, you, too, choose not to speak. "Why so glum?" I ask. "Dehydrated egg bits for breakfast again?"

You reach into the drawer next to your bed, and hand me a key. I help you out, into your bathrobe, into the hall. We must be quiet. When no nurses are looking, I hurry us into a small room where sheets and hospital gowns are stored. I turn the key in the lock, switch on the light.

We make a bed of sheets on the floor. We undress; and then, Alden, I begin to make love to you—you, atop me, clumsy and quick as a teenager. I try to slow you down, to coach you in the subtleties of love, the way a mother teaches a child to walk. You have to relearn this language as well, after all.

Lying there, pinned under you, I think that I am grateful for gravity, grateful that a year has passed and the planet has not yet broken loose from its tottering orbit. If nothing else, we hold each other down.

You look me in the eyes and try to speak. Your lips circle the unknown word, your brow reddens and beads with sweat. "What, Alden?" I ask. "What do you want to say? Think a minute." Your lips move aimlessly. A drop of tearwater, purely of its own accord, emerges from the marbled eye, snakes along a crack in your skin.

I stare at the ruined eye. It is milky white, mottled with blue and gray streaks; there is no pupil. Like our daughter, Alden, the eye will have nothing to do with either of us. I want to tell you it looks like the planet Dandril, as I imagine it from time to time—that ugly little planet where even now, as she waits in the garden, Nina's people are coming back to life.

Danny in Transit

Danny's cousins, Greg and Jeff, are playing catch. A baseball arcs over the green lawn between them, falls into the concavity of each glove with a soft thump, and flies again. They seem to do nothing but lift their gloves into the ball's path; it moves of its own volition.

Danny is lying facedown on the diving board, his hands and feet dangling over the sides, watching the ball. Every few seconds he reaches out his hands, so that his fingers brush the surface of the pool. He is trying to imagine the world extending out from where he lies: the Paper Palace, and the place he used to live, and the Amboys, Perth and South. Then Elizabeth. Then West New York. Then New York, Long Island, Italy. He listens to the sucking noise of the wind the ball makes, as it is softly swallowed. He listens to his cousins' voices. And then he takes tight hold of the diving board and tries to will it into flight, imagining it will carry him away from this back yard. But the sounds persist. He isn't going anywhere.

The huge back yard is filled with chilly New Jersey light, elegant as if it were refracted off the surface of a pearl. Carol and Nick, his aunt and uncle, sip tomato juice under an umbrella. Nearby, but separate, Elaine, Danny's mother, stares at nothing, her lips slightly parted, her mouth asleep, her eyes taking account. All that is between them is a plate of cheese.

"We went to a new restaurant, Elaine," Carol says. She is rubbing Noxzema between her palms. "Thai food. Peanut sauce and—oh, forget it."

"Keep that pitch steady, buddy," Nick calls to his sons. "Good wrist action, remember, that's the key." Both of the boys are wearing T-shirts which say *Coca-Cola* in Arabic.

"What can I do?" Carol asks.

"She's not going to talk. I don't see why we have to force her." Nick turns once again to admire his children.

"Greg, Jeff, honey, why don't you let Danny play with you?" Carol calls to her sons. They know Danny too well to take her request seriously, and keep throwing. "Come on, Danny," Carol says. "Wouldn't you like to play?"

"No, no, no, no, no," Danny says. He is roaring, but his mouth is pressed so tightly against the diving board that his voice comes out a hoarse yowl. Such an outburst isn't hard for Danny to muster. He is used to bursting into tears, into screams, into hysterical fits at the slightest inclination.

Nick gives Carol a wearied look and says, "Now you've done it." Danny bolts up from the diving board and runs into the house.

Carol sighs, takes out a Kleenex, and swats at her eyes. Nick looks at Elaine, whose expression has not changed.

"He's your son," Nick says.

"What?" says Elaine, touching her face like a wakened dreamer.

Carol rocks her face in her hands.

Belle, Danny's grandmother, is in the kitchen, pulling burrs from the dog and cooking lunch, when Danny runs by. "Danny! What's wrong?" she shouts, but he doesn't answer, and flies through the door at the back of the kitchen into the room where he lives. Once inside, he dives into the big pink bed, with its fancy dust ruffle and lace-trimmed pillows; he breathes in the clean smell of the linen. It is Belle's room, the maid's quarters made over for her widowhood, and it is full of photographs of four generations of champion Labrador retrievers. When Danny arrived he was supposed to live with Greg and Jeff in their room, but he screamed so loudly that Belle—exhausted—said he could sleep in her room, and she would sleep with her other grandsons—at least for the time being. It has been two months, and Danny has not relented.

Belle is pulling burrs from her pants suit. "I'm coming in, Danny," she says, and he buries his face—hard—in the pillow. He has learned that he can usually make himself cry by doing this, even when he is actually feeling happy. The trick is to clench your eyes until a few drops of water squeeze out. And then it just happens.

Danny feels hot breath on his hair, and a soft body next to his on the bed. Belle crawls and eases her way around him, making the bed squeak, until her wet mouth is right at his ear. "What's wrong, sweetie pie?" she whispers, but he doesn't answer, only moans into his pillow.

Belle gets up abruptly. "Oh, Danny," she says, "things would be so much easier if you'd just be nice. What happened to the old Danny I used to know? Don't you know how much happier everyone else would be if you'd just be happy?"

"I hate baseball," Danny says.

Danny is an only child and he looks like the perfect combination of his two parents. His eyes are round and blue, like his mother's, his mouth small and pouting, like his father's, and his wavy brown hair halfway between Elaine's, which is red and packed in tight curls, and Allen's, which is black and straight and dense. Growing up, Danny rarely saw his parents together, and so he doesn't know the extent to which he resembles them. He remembers that his father would come home from work and insist that Danny not disturb him. In those days Allen believed that when a man got back to the house in the evening he deserved time alone with his wife as a reward for his labors. Every night Elaine ate two dinners—Spaghetti-Os or Tater Tots with Danny, at six, and later, after Danny had gone to bed, something elaborate and romantic, by candlelight, with Allen. She would usually talk about the later dinners with Danny during the earlier ones. "Your father's very demanding," she said once, proudly. "He has strict notions of what a wife should do. Tonight I'm making chicken cacciatore." Danny knows that both he and his mother must have been very young when she said this, because he remembers the dreamy deliberateness with which Elaine pronounced "cacciatore," as if it were a magical incantation.

Sometimes, before Elaine put Danny to bed, Allen would pick him up and twirl him around and make sounds like an airplane. Danny slept. Through the open crack in his bedroom door he could see the candles flickering.

As he grew up Danny got to know his mother better. Starting when he was six or seven she lost her enthusiasm for dinner. "I can't manage you, Danny," she'd grumble to him. "I can't manage children. I'm unfit." Danny thought of how she always wrote DANNY G. on his lunchbag (and would continue to do so, even when he entered middle school, where last names matter). He thought of the way she made his lunch each day—

peanut butter sandwich, apple, bag of cheese puffs, paper napkin. The candlelit dinners stopped, and Danny, who had never attended any of them, probably missed the ritual more than either of his parents. The three of them ate together, now, usually in silence. In those days, Elaine had a habit of staring darkly at Allen when he wasn't looking. Danny remembers Allen's anxious looks back, when he caught her face full of questions, before she shifted her eyes and changed the subject. In retrospect, Danny knows that his mother was trying to guess something, and that his father was trying to figure out how much she already knew. "I still wanted to cover my tracks," Allen recently told his son. "I knew it was futile. I knew there was no going back. I don't think I even wanted to go back. But I still covered my tracks. It becomes a habit when you do it your whole life."

One day Danny's mother did not show up to pick him up at day camp. It was getting dark, and he was the only one left. The counselor who had stayed behind began to grow impatient. Watching the sky darken, Danny felt more embarrassment than fear. He was worried that Elaine would be misconstrued as the neglectful mother she believed herself to be, and he knew her not to be.

He lied. "Oh, I forgot," he said. "She had a doctor's appointment. She said I should ask you to drive me home."

"Drive you home?" the counselor said. "Why didn't she send a note?"

"I guess she just thought you would," Danny said.

The counselor looked at him, her face full of confusion, and the beginnings of pity. Perhaps she would call child welfare. Perhaps he would be taken away. But nothing happened. She drove him home. His mother offered no explanation for what she had done, but she did not forget to pick him up again. Danny was relieved. He had feared that she would break down, sobbing, and say to the counselor, "I'm an unfit mother. Take him away."

Somehow they survived the winter. One night at dinner, a few days before spring vacation, Elaine stood up and said, "This is a sham." Then she sat down again and continued eating. Allen looked at her, looked at Danny, looked at his plate. A few nights later she picked up the top of a ceramic sugar bowl which Danny had made her for Christmas and threw it overhand at Allen. It missed him, and shattered against the refrigerator door. Danny jumped, and fought back tears.

"See what I can do?" she said. "See what you've driven me to?"

Allen did not answer her. He quietly put on his jacket, and without a word walked out the back door. He was not home for dinner the next night. When Danny asked Elaine where he'd gone, she threw down her fork and started to cry. "Danny," she said, "there have been a lot of lies in this house."

The next day was the first Monday of vacation, and when Danny came home from playing his mother was still in bed.

"It's O.K., Danny," she said. "I just decided to take the day off. Lie in bed all day, since it's something I've never done before. Don't worry about me. Go ahead and play."

Danny did as she said. That night, at dusk, when he got home, she was asleep, the lights in her room all turned out. He was frightened, and he kept the house lights on even after he'd gone to bed. In the morning he knew that his father was really gone. Only his mother was in the bed when he gently pushed open the door. "I'm not getting up again," she said. "Are you all right, honey? Can you go to the Kravitzes' for dinner?"

"Don't you want anything to eat?" Danny asked.

"I'm not hungry. Don't worry about me."

Danny had dinner with the Kravitzes. Later, returning home, he heard her crying, but he couldn't hear her after he turned on *Star Trek*.

Every afternoon for a week he stood in the threshold of her doorway and asked if she wanted to get up, or if she wanted something to eat. He bought Spaghetti-Os and Doritos with the money in the jar at the back of the pantry he was not supposed to know about. He never asked where his father was. Her room was musty from the closed windows, and even in the morning full of that five o'clock light which is darker than darkness, and in which the majority of car accidents happen. "Leave me alone," she would call out from the dark now. "I'm tired. For Christ's sake, just let me get some sleep. Go play or something."

Then he would close the door and make himself some Campbell's soup and watch forbidden TV all night—variety shows and detective shows and reruns after eleven. Elaine had always allotted him three hours of TV per day; when she came home from shopping she'd feel the TV to see if it was warm, if he'd been cheating. Now there were no rules.

The first day of school—a week after Elaine had gone to bed—Danny woke up to hear her screaming. He ran to her bedroom, and found her sitting up on the bed, streaked in light. She had ripped the curtains open, and the bared morning sun, through the shutters, bisected her face, the mat of her unwashed hair, the nightgown falling over her shoulders. She sat there and screamed, over and over again, and Danny rushed in, shouting, "What's wrong? What's wrong?"

And then she grabbed the ends of her hair and began tearing at them, and grinding her teeth together, and wailing. Finally she collapsed, in tears, onto the bed. She turned to look at Danny and she screamed, "I can't change! Don't you see, no matter how much I want to, I just can't change!"

Danny got Mrs. Kravitz. She came over and hoisted Elaine out of bed and began marching her around the hall. "One, two, three, let's go, let's go," Mrs. Kravitz said. "Danny, go look in the bathroom for empty pill bottles, sweetheart, your mommy's going to be just fine."

Danny didn't find any empty pill bottles, and when he came out of the bathroom some paramedics were coming through the kitchen with a stretcher. "I can't stand up," Elaine was telling Mrs. Kravitz. "I'll be sick."

"Just lie down now," Mrs. Kravitz said. Danny remembered that today was the first day of school, and he wondered whether he should go to his home-room class or not, but when he looked at the clock, he saw that it was already eight o'clock. School had started.

Danny spent the night at the Kravitzes' house, and the next day he went to Nick and Carol's. This was in a different school district, but nobody talked about school. That night, when his cousins wanted to watch a different television show from Danny, he threw his first fit.

A few days later, while he was eating his cereal at the kitchen table, Danny's father arrived. Danny didn't say hello. He continued to spoon the sweet milk into his mouth, though the cereal was gone. Belle, who was making pancakes, turned the burner off and quietly slunk out of the room. Allen sat down across from Danny, holding a cup of coffee. He had a new short haircut, and was growing a stubbly beard. They were alone in the room.

"I know you're angry," Allen said. "I know you wonder where I've been and why your mother got sick. I don't know where to begin, and I don't expect instant forgiveness, but I do want you to hear me out. Will you do that for me? I know you'll have a lot of questions, and I'm prepared to answer them. Just give me a chance."

Danny looked at his father and didn't say anything.

* * *

On weekends Danny went to visit his father in the city. Allen was living with a man named Gene in an apartment in Greenwich Village, and though he had quit being a stockbroker, he continued to live off his own investments. Each Friday Danny rode the train up, past the fast-food franchises thrown up around the railroad stations, the muddy Amboys, the rows of tenements in Elizabeth. Allen took him to museums, to the theater, to restaurants. On Sunday he saw his son off at Penn Station. "I used to ride this train every day," he told Danny, as they waited on the platform. "I used to play cards with Uncle Nick on this train. It seems like hundreds of years."

"That was when you and Mom had dinner by candlelight," Danny said, remembering how his father twirled him in the air, how his mother pronounced the word "cacciatore"—slowly, and with such relish.

"We were innocent," Allen said. "Your mother and I believed in something that was wrong for us. Wrong for me, I should say."

Danny looked away from his father, toward the train which was now moving into the station.

"You probably think your mother's getting sick is the result of my being gay," Allen said, putting his hand on his son's shoulder. "But that's only partially true. It goes much further, much deeper than that, Danny. You know your mother hasn't been well for a long time."

From where he's lying, his face against the pillow, Danny hears the harsh sound of tires against gravel, and bolts up in bed. Through his window he sees a taxi in the driveway, and Allen, dressed in bluejeans and a lumberjack shirt, fighting off Belle's furious barking dog. Elaine, seeing Allen, has crawled up on her haunches, and is hugging her knees. When Allen sees Elaine, he turns to rehail the taxi, but it is already out of the driveway.

"Now, Allen, don't be upset," Nick says, walking out onto the gravel, taking Allen's shoulder in one hand, the dog in the other.

"You didn't tell me she was going to be here," Allen says.

"That's because you wouldn't have come out," says Carol, joining them. "You two have to talk. We're sorry to do this, but it's the only way. Someone's got to take some responsibility."

As if he is a child about to ride a bicycle for the first time without training wheels, Allen is literally pushed by Carol toward his wife.

"What's going on? What's happening here?" shouts Belle. When she sees Allen, she stops dead in her tracks.

"You didn't tell him?" Belle asks.

Allen begins to move uncertainly toward Elaine, who is still rearing, and Carol and Nick push Belle into the kitchen. Danny jumps out of his bed and kneels next to the door.

They whisper. Nick nods and walks outdoors. "Relax, Mom," says Carol. "They've got to talk. They've got to make some decisions."

"Elaine's hospitalized." Belle announces this known fact in a low voice, and looks toward the door to her room.

"She's been hiding her whole life. She's got to face up to facts. I can't take this much longer." Carol lights a cigarette, and rubs her eyes.

Belle looks away. "He's just a child," she says.

"Their child," Carol says. "Not ours."

"Not so loudly!" Belle says, and points to the bedroom door. "Have some sympathy. She's been through a personal hell."

"I know things were hard," Carol says. "But to commit herself! I'm sorry, Mom, but as far as I'm concerned, that's just self-dramatizing. No one commits themselves these days. You see a psychiatrist on Central Park West once a week. You continue your life, and you deal with your problem."

"Her problem is worse than that," Belle says. "She needs help. All my life I never said so, but I knew she was—not strong. And now I have to admit, knowing she's taken care of, I feel relieved."

"But it's not like she's crazy!" Carol says. "It's not like she's a raving lunatic, or schizophrenic, or anything. She's basically just fine, isn't she? She just needs some help, doesn't she?"

Belle doesn't answer. Carol sits down, lays her head on the kitchen table, and starts to cry.

"Oh, my poor girl," Belle says, and strokes her daughter's hair. "I know you're worried about your sister. And she is fine. She'll be fine."

"Then why can't she just check herself out of that hospital and take her kid and start seeing a goddamned shrink once a week?" Carol says, lifting up her head and turning to face her mother. "I'll pay for it, if that's what she needs."

"Keep your voice down!" Belle whispers loudly. "Let's talk outside."

She pulls Carol out of her chair, and out the screen door. As soon as they've left the kitchen, Danny makes a run for the stairs. He sneaks into his cousins' room, which is full of baseball cards and *Star Wars* toys, closes the door, and perches on the window seat, which overlooks the swimming pool. Below him, he can see his parents arguing in one corner, while in another, Belle and Carol continue their discussion. Belle is trying to explain that Elaine cannot take care of a household, and this is her problem, and Carol is shaking her head. As for Nick, he has moved out onto the lawn, where he is playing baseball with Greg and Jeff.

Danny can just barely make out his parents' voices. "They arranged this," he hears Elaine saying. "They think Danny's a pain in the ass."

"You know I'd take him if I could," Allen answers.

"I thought you were leading such a model life!"

"There's nothing about my life which would create an unhealthy atmosphere for Danny. I'm just not ready for him yet."

"Good," Elaine says. "He can come live with me."

Danny closes the window. He knows to cover up his tracks. Then he runs back downstairs, through the kitchen, and out the screen door. He runs alongside the pool, past his parents, and toward the woods. Allen catches his eye, and waves. Danny waves back, keeps running.

When Danny first arrived at Nick and Carol's, everything was alien: the extra bed in Greg and Jeff's room which pulled out from under, the coloration of the television set, the spaghetti sauce. They were so indulgent toward him, in his unhappiness, that he wondered if perhaps he had leukemia, and they weren't telling him. And then he realized that he did not have leukemia. He was merely the passive victim of a broken home. For months he had held back his own fear and anger for the sake of his mother. Now she had betrayed him. She *was* unfit. He *had* been taken away, as had she. There was no reason to be good anymore.

What Danny didn't count on was Carol and Nick's expectation that somehow he would change, shape himself to their lives. No child with leukemia would be asked to change. Danny decided to become a child with leukemia—a sick child, a thwarted child, a child to be indulged. Nick and Carol asked him if he wouldn't maybe consider trading places with his grandmother and moving into his cousins' room, which would be fun for all three, like camp. Danny threw his biggest fit ever. They never asked him again. They gave him wearied looks, when he refused to eat, when he demanded to watch what he wanted to watch, when he wouldn't talk to company. They lost patience, and he in turn lost patience: Didn't they understand? He was a victim. And certainly he had only to mention his mother's name, and his own stomach would sink, and Carol's eyes would soften, and suddenly she would become like his grandmother—maternal and embracing. He made himself need her to be maternal and embracing.

The night his mother went to bed forever, Danny learned two things: to be silent was to be crazy, and to be loud was also to be crazy. It seemed to him that he did not have a choice. He knew no way of living that did not include morose silences and fits of fury. When Carol asked him why he wouldn't just enjoy the life he had, he felt a fierce resistance rise in his chest. He was not going to give himself up.

Now, running from his crazy parents, Danny arrives at a place in the woods—a patch of dry leaves sheltered by an old sycamore—which he has designated his own. Only a few feet away, the neighborhood children are playing Capture the Flag in the cul-de-sac, and he can hear their screams and warnings through the trees. He turns around once, circling his territory, and then he begins. Today he will invent an episode of *The Perfect Brothers Show*, the variety show on his personal network. He has several other series in the works, including *Grippo*, a detective drama, and *Pierre!*, set in the capital city of South Dakota.

He begins. He does all the voices, and makes the sound of applause by driving his tongue against the roof of his mouth. "And now," he says, "for your viewing pleasure, another episode of *The Perfect Brothers Show*!"

The orchestra plays a fanfare. In another voice, Danny sings:

"*A perfect night for comedy!*
For fun and musicality!
We'll change you!
Rearrange you!
Just you wait and see!
Welcome to The Perfect Brothers Show!"

He is in the midst of inventing a comic skit, followed by a song from this week's guest star, Loni Anderson, when Jeff—the younger and more persistently good-natured of the brothers—appears from between the trees. "Can I play?" he asks.

Danny, to his own surprise, doesn't throw a fit. "Yes," he says. "We'll do a comedy skit. You're the housewife and I'm Superman."

"I want to be Superman," Jeff says.

"All right, all right." Now Danny begins to give instructions for the skit, but halfway through Jeff interrupts and says, "This is boring. Let's play baseball."

"If you want to play something like *that*," Danny says, "go play Capture the Flag." He throws up his hands in disgust.

"There are girls playing," Jeff says. "Well, if you won't play, I'll play baseball with my dad!"

"Good," says Danny. "Leave me alone."

Jeff runs off towards the house. Part of the way there, he turns once. "You're weird," he says.

Danny ignores him. He is halfway through his skit—playing both parts—when he is interrupted again. This time it is his father. "How are you, old man?" Allen asks. "Want to go to the Paper Palace?"

For a moment Danny's eyes widen, and then he remembers how unhappy he is. "All right," he says.

They take Carol's station wagon, and drive to the Paper Palace, a huge pink cement structure in the middle of an old shopping center. The shopping center is near Danny's old house.

"You've loved the Paper Palace—how long?" Allen asks. "I think you were four the first time I brought you here. You loved it. Remember what I bought you?"

"An origami set and a Richie Rich comic book," Danny says. He rarely gets to the Paper Palace anymore; Carol shops in the more elegant mall near her house.

"When we lived here, all I wanted to do was to get into Carol and Nick's neighborhood. A year ago today. Just think. All I could think about was getting a raise and buying a house. I might have bought the house next door to Carol and Nick's. I wanted you to grow up in that area. All those trees. The fresh air. The great club."

"I am anyhow, I guess," Danny says.

"Don't let it fool you," Allen says. "It all seems so perfect. It all looks so perfect. But soon enough the paint chips, there are corners bitten by the dog, you start sweeping things under the bed. Believe me, under the beds, there's as much dust in Nick and Carol's house as there was in ours."

"Carol has a maid," Danny says.

"Just never trust cleanness. All the bad stuff—the really bad stuff—

happens in clean houses, where everything's tidy and nobody says anything more than good morning."

"Our house wasn't like that," Danny says.

Allen looks at him. But now they are in the parking lot of the shopping center, and the colorful promise of the Paper Palace takes both of them over. They rush inside. Danny browses ritualistically at stationery and comic books, reads through the plot synopses in the soap opera magazines, scrupulously notes each misspelling of a character's name. Allen lags behind him. They buy a copy of *Vogue* for Elaine. In front of them in line, a fat, balding man upsets a box of candy on the sales counter as he purchases a copy of *Playgirl.* His effort to avoid attention has backfired, and drawn the complicated looks of all around him. Danny avoids looking at Allen, but Allen's eyes shoot straight to Danny, whose face has a pained, embarrassed expression on it. They do not mention the fat man as they walk out of the store.

Years ago, when Danny was only six or seven, he found a magazine. He was playing in the basement, dressing up in some old clothes of Allen's which he had found in a cardboard box. The magazine was at the bottom of the box. When Elaine came down to check what Danny was up to, she found him sitting on a trunk, examining a series of pictures of young, dazed-looking men posed to simulate various acts of fornication. Elaine grabbed the magazine away from Danny and demanded to know where he'd gotten it. He told her that he had found it, and he pointed to the box.

Elaine looked again at the magazine, and then at the box. She thumbed through the pages, looking at the photographs. Then she put the magazine down on top of the box and wrapped her arms around herself.

"Danny," she said, "for God's sake, don't lie about this. You don't have to. You can tell me the truth. Are you sure that's where you got this thing?"

"Swear to God and hope to die, stick a needle in my eye," Danny said.

"Get upstairs," said Elaine.

"Do you want a Velamint?" Allen asks Danny in the car, as they drive back from the Paper Palace. They are riding down a wide, dark road, lined with sycamores. Danny takes the small blue wafer from his father, without saying anything. He opens the window, sticks his hand out into the breeze.

"You know, Danny, I've been thinking," Allen says. "I know this fantastic place, this school, in New Hampshire. It's great—really innovative—and it's specially for bright, motivated kids like you."

Danny doesn't answer. When Allen turns to look at him, he sees that his son is clutching the armrest so hard his knuckles have turned white, and biting his lip to hold back tears.

"Danny," Allen says. "Danny, what's wrong?"

"I know I've been a problem," Danny says. "But I've decided to change. Today. I've decided to be happy. Please. I'll make them want me to stay."

Allen is alarmed by Danny's panic. "Danny," he says, "this school isn't punishment. It's a great place. You deserve to go there."

"I played with Jeff today!" Danny says. His voice is at its highest register. He is staring at Allen, his face flushed, a look of pure pleading in his eyes.

Allen puts his hand over his mouth and winces. When they reach a stop sign, he turns to Danny and says, as emphatically as he can, "Danny, don't worry, no one's going to *make* you go anywhere. But, Danny, I don't know if I *want* you to stay with Nick and Carol. After fifteen years in that world, I don't know if I want my son to be hurt by it like I was."

"I won't become a stockbroker. I won't sweep the dust under the bed. But, please, don't send me away."

"Danny, I thought you didn't like it here," Allen says.

"I'm not unfit."

They are still at the stop sign. Behind them, a car is honking, urging them to move on. Danny's eyes are brimming with tears.

Allen shakes his head, and reaches for his son.

They go to Carvel's for ice cream. Ahead of them in line a flustered-looking woman buys cones for ten black children who stand in pairs, holding hands. Two of the girls are pulling violently at each other's arms, while a boy whose spiral of soft-serve ice cream has fallen off his cone cries loudly, and demands reparations. Allen orders two chocolate cones with brown bonnets, and he and Danny sit down in chairs with tiny desks attached to them, like the chairs in Danny's elementary school. There are red lines from tears on Danny's face, but he doesn't really cry—at least, he doesn't make any of the crying noises, the heaves and stuttering wails. He picks off the chocolate coating of the brown bonnet and eats it in pieces before even touching the actual ice cream.

"I'm glad you haven't lost your appetite," Allen says.

Danny nods weakly, and continues to eat. The woman marches the ten children out the door, and into a small pink van. "Danny," Allen says, "what can I say? What do you want me to say?"

Danny bites off the bottom of his cone. Half-melted ice cream plops onto the little desk. "Jesus Christ," Allen mutters, and rubs his eyes.

When they get back to the house, Allen joins Nick and Carol under the umbrella on the patio. Elaine is still lying on the chaise, her eyes closed. Danny gets out of the car after his father, walks a circle around the pool, biting his thumbnail, and resumes his position on the diving board. Nearby, Greg and Jeff are again playing catch. "Hey, Danny, want to throw the ball?" Allen shouts. He does not hear Carol hiss her warning, "No!" But Danny neither does nor says anything.

"Danny!" Allen shouts again. "Can you hear me?"

Very slowly Danny hoists himself up, crawls off the diving board, and walks back toward the house.

"Oh, Christ," Carol says, taking off her sunglasses. "This is more than I can take."

Now Belle appears at the kitchen door, waving a batter-caked spatula. "What happened?" she asks.

"The same story," Carol says.

"I'll see to him," Allen says. He casts a parting glance at Elaine, and walks into the kitchen. "The same thing happened this morning," Belle tells him as they walk toward Danny's room.

But this time, the door is wide open, instead of slammed shut, and Danny is lying on his back on the bed, his face blank, his eyes tearless.

At first Belle thinks he is sick. "Honey, are you all right?" she asks, feeling his head. "He's cool," she tells Allen.

Allen sits down on the bed and arcs his arms over Danny's stomach. "Danny, what's wrong?" he asks.

Danny turns to look at his father, his face full of a pain too strong for a child to mimic.

"I can't change," he says. "I can't change. I can't change."

In the kitchen, Belle is wrathful. She does not keep her voice down; she does not seem to care that Danny can hear every word she is saying. "I see red when I look at you people," she tells her children. "In my day, people didn't just abandon everything to gratify themselves. In my day, people didn't abandon their children. You're so selfish, all you think about is yourselves."

"What do you want from me?" Allen answers. "What kind of father could I have been? I was living a lie."

"See what I mean?" Belle says. "Selfish. You assume I'm talking about you. But I'm talking about all of you. And you, too, Carol."

"For Christ's sake, Mother, he's not my son!" Carol says. "And he's wrecking my sons' lives. And my life."

Elaine has been fingering her hair. But now she suddenly slams her hand against the table and lets out a little moan. "He really said that?" she says. "Oh, Christ, he really said that."

"I've had it up to here with all of you," Belle announces. "It's unspeakable. I've heard enough."

She turns from them all, as if she has seen enough as well. Allen and Elaine and Nick look down at the table, like ashamed children. But Carol gets up, and walks very deliberately to face her mother. "Now just one minute," she says, her lips twitching with anger. "Just one minute. It's easy for you to just stand there and rant and rave. But I have to live with it, day in and day out, I have to take care of him and put up with his crap. And I have to listen to my kids say, 'What's with that Danny? When's he going away?' Well, maybe I am selfish. I've worked hard to raise my kids well. And now, just because Elaine screws everything up for herself, suddenly I'm expected to bear the brunt of it, take all the punishment. And everything I've been working for is going down the tubes because she can't take care of her own kid! Well, then, I will be selfish. I am selfish. I have had enough of this."

"Now just a minute, Carol," Allen says.

"You take him," Carol says, turning around to confront him. "You take him home, or don't say a word to me. There's not one word you have a right to say to me."

"Damn it!" Allen says. "Doesn't anybody understand? I'm doing my best."

"You've had two months," Nick says.

Belle, her arms wrapped around her waist, begins to cry softly. Sitting at the table, Elaine cries as well, though more loudly, and with less decorum.

Then, with a small click, the door to Danny's bedroom opens, and he walks into the kitchen. Allen and Nick stand up, nearly knocking their chairs over in the process. "Danny!" Carol says. Her voice edges on panic. "Are you all right?"

"Yes, thank you," Danny says.

Elaine lifts her head from the table. "Danny," she says. "Danny, I—" She moves her lips, struggling to form words. But nothing comes out. Danny looks down at her, his eyes full of a frightening, adult pity. Then he turns away and walks outside.

Everyone jumps up at once to follow him. But Allen holds up his hand. "I'll go," he says. He scrambles out the door, and after Danny, who is marching past the swimming pool, toward the patch of woods where he likes to play. When he gets there, he stops and waits, his back to his father.

"Danny," Allen says, coming up behind him. "You heard everything. I don't know what to say. I wish I did."

Danny has his arms crossed tightly over his chest. "I've thought about it," he says. "I've decided."

"What?" Allen says.

"About the school," Danny says. "I've decided I'll go."

A few days later, Danny boards the train which snakes along the Jersey coast to New York. He is riding to visit his father. An old couple is sitting across the way from him, a gnarled little man and his taller, white-haired wife, her white-gloved hands clasped calmly around each other. Like Danny, the couple is not reading the paper, but looking out the green-tinted windows at yellow grass, small shops, warehouses.

"You'd better get your things together," the husband says. "We're almost there."

"No," the wife says. "We don't want South Amboy. We want Perth Amboy." The husband shakes his head no. "South Amboy. I'm sure she said South Amboy."

The wife is quiet for a few seconds, until the conductor shouts, "South Amboy, South Amboy next!" Now she cannot control herself. "I'm *sure* it's Perth Amboy," she says. The husband is buttoning his jacket, reaching for his hat. "Will you listen to me for once?" he says. "Its South Amboy." The wife shakes her head. "I'm sure," she says. "I'm sure."

Gradually, and then with a sudden grind, the train comes to a halt. The husband lumbers down the aisle, knocking past Danny, shaking his head. "I'm getting off," he says. "Are you coming?" The wife stands, hesitates, sits down. "It's not this stop," she says. He makes a violent motion with his hands, and walks out the door, onto the station platform. She stands to follow him, but the doors close suddenly. His fist appears, as if disembodied, rapping on the window. Then the train is moving again.

For a moment, she just stands there, shocked. Then the train's lurching forces her to sit down. A look comes over her face first of indignation, then of fear and confusion, then finally, of weariness—with her husband, with the train, with their lives which will go on like this. She bends over and pulls herself into the corner of her seat, as if trying to make herself as small as possible, and picks at a loose thread of her dress with one of her white-gloved hands.

Then she comes to consciousness. She realizes that she is not alone on the train. Her eyes narrow, and focus on Danny. Late afternoon, almost dark. He is singing a song about comedy and fun and musicality. He tells her it's going to be a perfect night.

Family Dancing

Although just barely—without *laudes*, without distinction, and from an academy which is third-rate at best—Suzanne Kaplan's son, Seth, has managed to graduate from prep school, and Suzanne is having a party to celebrate. The party is also a celebration of Suzanne's own "graduation into life"—her thirty pounds thinner body, her new house, and her new marriage to Bruce Kaplan, who works in real estate. Of course, Suzanne has been planning for the party to take place outdoors, since Seth's graduation coincides with the brief, fragile season of wisteria, and the pool looks gorgeous in sunlight. Unfortunately, it's been raining every day for a week now, and Suzanne's spent a lot of time by her kitchen window, reminding herself that she should still be counting her blessings.

"It's a drowning spring," Suzanne's mother, Pearl, told her the day before the party. "Don't count on outdoors. Move everything inside to the nice family room." But Suzanne was optimistic, and sure enough, this morning, the morning of the party, the sun has risen brilliantly, and the wet grass promises to be dry by noon. In her new bathrobe, she stands in the living room, and watches Bruce drive his power mower. His children, Linda and Sam, are playing a game she doesn't recognize, and she raps on the window to get their attention.

They stop jarringly when they hear her, as if they have been caught in the act of defacing something. They look at her; it is a look she calls the "wicked witch" look, because her own daughter, Lynnette, used to give it before running off to her room, screaming, "You're a witch." Suzanne isn't privy to the secrets of Linda and Sam's lives; they are polite, but keep their distance. Of course, to them, she is the new, alien thing.

She pushes open the sliding glass door and walks out onto the patio.

"What are you playing?" she asks, but even now her voice trembles. She knows they can see right through her nonchalance.

"Nothing," Linda says. "Come on, Sam."

Her brother gives Suzanne a helpless glance, and then they are off, to another part of the yard.

The yard is spacious, green. To the north is a huge meadow where cows might still graze, if there were any more cows in this part of the world. The part of the Bronx where Suzanne grew up is now a vast region of housing projects, but when she was a child, living in a two-family house, there were still wild patches of countryside, and farmhouses, and even some farmers. These days, when she drives to visit her mother, she stops sometimes. Off the highway there are occasional plots of what used to be farmland, grown over with wild grasses and gnarled trees. The farmhouses which are left are rotting, and only squatters inhabit them.

Of course, Suzanne doesn't live in the Bronx anymore. She has moved "up" in the world, as her mother might put it, though "up" has always seemed the wrong word: it's struck her as a more lateral movement. Now, in her mother's mind, she is on some sort of summit, having recovered beautifully from the horrific fall of her divorce. In her mother's mind, Suzanne is in the clouds. She herself feels more on earth than ever before, but she is happy to know (if nothing else) that she has perhaps finally arrived somewhere.

It has been just over a year since Suzanne's first husband, Herb, informed her that he was in love with a lawyer from his office. At that time they were living in Rockville Centre, in the third of what would probably have been four houses, and Suzanne was fat. Herb, she remembers, had recently gotten a substantial salary hike, Lynnette had finally moved to Manhattan, they were out of eggs, and the dishwasher was broken. When Herb said he wanted to talk to her after dinner, she hoped he was going to suggest that they now move to a posher suburb, with larger lawns, for he had been skillfully avoiding the subject of a move for months. Instead, his announcement confirmed all the suspicions Suzanne had been trying to talk herself out of since the second house. The inevitability of it was something like relief to her, but that did not make it easier to bear.

Herb said he wouldn't leave Suzanne. He said he believed in responsibility and commitment. But he would not give up his lover, either;

everything must be aboveboard. "What is it?" Suzanne asked him that night. "Is it that I'm fat and depressed and a bitch? Is that all?"

"It is simply that I'm in love with someone else," Herb said. She supposed he meant these words to be soothing, because they included no attacks, and she was amazed that he could not know how much they pierced her. Still, she wanted him to stay.

"Fine," he said. "But two nights a week—probably Tuesday and Thursday—and some weekends, I'll stay in the city with Selena."

The first Tuesday night he was gone she thought she would go mad. She was so angry at Herb that she seriously feared losing control, doing him some terrible violence, and she resolved to tell him the next evening that he must move out. She resented even more his insinuating trick of making her kick him out when it was he who wanted to leave. Up until that night, in the recesses of Suzanne's self-hatred, there had rested an incurable sense of being blessed, an assurance that there awaited her some pleasurable vengeance against all this suffering, which gave her pain an anticipatory edge. Now Herb had shaved that edge clean off. She knew there was no guardian angel to make sure he got what he deserved, or suddenly revitalize his love for her. And she wished that Herb had simply, swiftly died in his car on the Long Island Expressway, rather than do what she most dreaded, and confirm every terrible charge she had made against herself. Wednesday night, when he came home, she told him not to bother to come back.

The human body, Suzanne remembers, seemed at that time impossibly ugly; aging, mortality, its capacity to fall apart were all part of a sick joke, played by a vengeful God. She did not want to kill herself. She wanted to last forever, rotting, like Miss Havisham in *Great Expectations*, or like the farmhouses in the Bronx. She wanted to always remind the human race of its talent for shame and ruin. When she woke up each morning, however, some irritating instinct for survival and pleasure nagged at her. She wished it would go away, but it would not, and finally she got out of bed, and washed her hair, and walked into the living room to survey the damage. Lynnette was in New York, Seth at school. The thought of continuing to live in this room made her nauseous, and for a moment, the emptiness and the loneliness of her house threatened to drive her back into bed. But this was her lot, and whether she liked it or not, she must make something—perhaps the best—out of it. And so she cleaned up. And, trembling a little, went to the grocery store and bought herself some food to make for dinner. The television set pulled her through the first week. The second week she tried to curb how much she watched, knowing that *Saturday Night Live*, like an addictive drug, might lose its effectiveness if she overdosed. The third week she signed up to join a depression therapy group.

Herb and the lawyer broke up three months after he moved into her apartment, but he decided to stay in Manhattan and get his own place. At that time, Suzanne had just met Bruce, whose own wife had left him a few weeks before. Her life seemed quite suddenly enormous with possibility, and the news of Herb's breakup filled her with a kind of vengeful glee. Of course, she told herself, if he asked her, she would not take him back, not now. But he has never asked her. Instead he says he is extraordinarily happy for Suzanne, absolutely delighted that things worked out so well for her. He expresses no resentment, no jealousy, only a kind of relief, as if a burden of guilt has been lifted from him. When they had lunch together last week, to discuss Seth's graduation, Suzanne tried to enjoy the fact that she, the loser, the victim, had come out on top in the end—better than ever before. But Herb seemed to enjoy Suzanne's happiness as much as she did, and she left the restaurant feeling choked inside. She was miserable because Herb was not miserable, yet her own victor-status demanded that she not be concerned with that. Still, she raged at his uncanny talent for happiness.

Herb says that he wants to be Suzanne's friend. He speaks to her in intimate tones unheard through the long course of their marriage. "It's amazing," he told her at last week's lunch, "but I'm beginning to realize why it bugged me so much when you used to talk about getting a new house. It wasn't just that I was planning to ask you to let me out of the marriage. It was the thought that the next house was going to be the last house, the house we'd probably die in. We were rich enough that we could finally afford the best, and that meant there was nowhere left to go. I felt like my life was over. But now, I don't know about you, Suzanne, but I've had to reassess my whole value system. I'm seeing a counselor. I'm realizing all the things I did wrong as a father. Really, for both of us, things are just beginning."

Suzanne looked at him and thought, How dare he speak like this, now? It was as if he believed the old Suzanne—the woman who would have been crushed by such a statement—had simply ceased to exist. This was a new model, in whom he could confide the ugly truth about his shrewish, fat wife and their wretched life together. And though on good days, Suzanne would almost agree with Herb—she imagines that she has been reincarnated, that the old Suzanne lived in a different age, and had a life utterly distinct from her own—on bad days, it is as if almost no time has passed; as if her marriage to Bruce, her weight loss, her new house are all simply part of a dream from which she will awaken, to find herself in the old bed, the old house. Those days, she feels like an earthquake survivor who carries around the rubble of her home in a bag, refusing to let go her buried children.

Now, coming back in from the porch, Suzanne looks at the clock. It is already eleven, and Seth is still asleep; sunlight is leaking through the crack in the guest-room door. Suzanne stands before her son's room and knocks cautiously, but she gets no answer.

"Seth," she says.

There is a sound of thrashing inside the room.

"Seth, wake up," Suzanne says. "It's already eleven."

"All right, all right," he mumbles. "Give me ten minutes."

"Seth, it's your party, you've got to get up."

"Leave me alone!" he shouts. Suzanne smiles, knowing that if she gets him angry enough, he'll be too riled to sleep. It's what she calls a mother's secret.

Now she pushes the door open, and the leak of sunlight engulfs her. Seth is splayed diagonally across the double bed, in his underwear, wrapped in a tangle of sheets and blankets.

"Come on," Suzanne says in a singsong voice. "It's time to get up!"

He sits up in bed quite suddenly and stares at her, furious. "Do you know how much sleep I got during finals week?" he asks.

"How much?"

"Maybe ten minutes. Can't I make up for it now?"

"Do you still want to?" Suzanne asks. Seth looks at her with the confused expression he often had as a child, when he would come into the kitchen in the morning, bleary-eyed, and slurp down the sweet milk in which he had drowned his cereal.

"Happy party day," she says, and walks out of the room.

But when Suzanne gets downstairs, she finds that her quiet kitchen is suddenly ablaze with activity. The caterers have arrived—a crew of large, stubbornly bourgeois black women, all related to each other in obscure ways, who have recently been earning an impressive reputation in this part of Long Island. The women are dressed in various combinations of black-and-white polyester which look to Suzanne like military uniforms, and seem to indicate a complicated hierarchy. Suzanne's mother, Pearl, has also arrived; she is now talking to a particularly large woman of middle age whose black hostess dress (without a strip of white) signals supreme authority. They are going over the hors d'oeuvres.

"Curried lobster puffs, sausage rolls au gratin, sesame chicken wings, cheese-filled mini-croissants, Polynesian turkey meatballs, baked brie. Oh, and the chopped liver," the woman says.

"Yes," Pearl says, "and tell me, Mrs. Ferguson, is the chopped liver in a shape, or what?"

"It's in the shape of a heart," Mrs. Ferguson says.

"A heart!" says Pearl.

Mrs. Ferguson folds her arms. "What's wrong with a heart?" she asks.

"Oh, nothing, nothing," Pearl says. "Why, look, here comes my daughter the hostess."

"Hello," Suzanne says, grasping Mrs. Ferguson's hand. "I'm glad to see my mother's taken charge already. I hope things are going all right."

"Things are fine, but you don't have a pastry tube!" shouts a tiny old woman in a chef's hat. "What you mean not having a pastry tube?"

"No pastry tube!" Suzanne says. "Are you sure? I've just moved in and I don't know what we have."

"I'll have to send the girl back in the van," the old woman says, shaking her head with annoyance. "We'll be late because of this. Gloria!"

A teenage girl rushes over to consult with the old woman in the chef's hat. In the meantime, all around Suzanne, other girls go to work—rolling up the sausages, filling the mini-croissants, icing the cake.

Into the kitchen now strides Suzanne's daughter, Lynnette, who is twenty-three and a secretary in Manhattan. She is not a person who can slip into rooms quietly, and so everyone has turned to notice her. With Lynnette is her best friend and roommate, John, a tall, emaciated young man with caved-in cheeks. "Hello, Mother," Lynnette says. "I see we're just in time to get in the way."

Lynnette is wearing a black dress which looks like several lace slips sewn together. She has a flower in her hair, a wild pink geranium, and her face is streaked with purple and blue make-up. If she weren't so fat, Suzanne thinks, she would look half decent, but Suzanne knows that Lynnette has chosen the dress specifically because it most explicitly reveals the bulges of her abdomen and buttocks. John is also dressed outrageously, in a purple suit and flaming yellow bow tie.

"Hello, Mrs. Kaplan," he says, the way (Suzanne thinks) he always says hello to her—grudgingly, and with an undertone of hatred. Suzanne is sure resentful Lynnette has filled his head with stories about her—the wicked witch—and as recompense, she is excessively cordial whenever she sees John. "Hello," she says, taking his hand. "I'm so happy to see you again. Just wait till you taste that baked brie, it's fabulous."

Nearby two of the girls who are rolling sausage rolls have stopped their work and are staring at John and Lynnette. They keep staring until Mrs. Ferguson slaps them simultaneously on the backs of their necks and tells them to get back to work.

"Suzanne!" Pearl whispers fiercely, grabbing her daughter's hand from behind. "The chopped liver in a heart shape! Those *shvartzeh* caterers put the chopped liver in a heart shape!"

Now, puffing, Bruce enters the kitchen. He is wearing knee-length Bermuda shorts, and his skin has reddened to the shade of his hair from the ordeal of mowing. "Everything under control?" he asks, and all the women—even Suzanne—instinctively back away from his sweating male presence, as if it might contaminate the food.

Bruce looks around himself shyly, and wraps his arms around his stomach, as if he imagines he is naked in his own kitchen. "Maybe I should just get out of the way," he says.

"That might be a good idea," Suzanne says. She feels a certain tenderness toward him right now, as if he were a lost child. And yet she knows that tenderness is simply another cover for her true feeling toward him—the feeling of disappointment. They met in the depression therapy group. Bruce's wife had upped and left him and their children to go off to California with a twenty-two-year-old auto mechanic. Suzanne and Bruce fed each other's misery and self-pity for a time, and then, drunk one night, they made love on the spur of the moment. As Suzanne tells it, Bruce made her feel attractive, like a real woman, for the first time in twenty years, she all but stopped eating, and the next week they eloped to Las Vegas.

* * *

In the corner of the kitchen, Lynnette watches her mother watch Bruce, and smirks. She actually thinks, I am smirking. Everything about the house, the caterers, the party, confirms her worst suspicions. She has no doubt but that her mother is very happy with all of it, that every petit-bourgeois value she has ascribed to Suzanne is pathetically, miserably accurate.

Though she would never admit it, Lynnette has been looking forward to this party with real ferocity. She is a loudmouthed girl whom most people find unpleasant, and she would tell you in a minute how much she hates herself. Her loyalties to others, though few, are fierce. John, for instance: She likes him more than anyone she knows her own age. John is gay, and his parents, who live only a few miles from Suzanne, will hardly speak to him. She must remember that he has probably been hurt more by this world even than she has, and she looks to him sympathetically, as his friend. She hopes her look gives him strength.

Lynnette's other great loyalty is to her father. All through her childhood the two of them cultivated a relationship which almost consciously excluded Suzanne and Seth. She will always remember the trips to the park that she and Herb took after dinner, and how up until she was thirteen or so, and too big to fit, he would push her on the swing, higher and higher, until the sky seemed to tilt wildly, and she was flying. She was a heavy little girl, but that never seemed to deter him. He picked her up effortlessly as if he were a ballet dancer, and she his prima ballerina. "You're my favorite partner," he'd tell her as he pushed her on the swing. "Your favorite?" she'd say. "Better than Mommy?" "Yes, better than Mommy," he'd say. "Someday we'll dance under the stars."

Years later, he fulfilled that promise. He had just moved in with Selena, and there was so much love between them that they seemed to need Lynnette to soak up the excess. They took her to the ballet, to see Peter Martins and Suzanne Farrell, and afterward for a spontaneous ride on the Staten Island Ferry, and there, under starlight, Herb took his daughter in his arms and danced with her while Selena sat by and beamed. Their clumsy pas de deux had no musical accompaniment, but Lynnette didn't care. She felt as if Herb's new life with Selena was her new life, as if his optimism might actually prove contagious. That night the world had seemed endless in its possibilities.

Of course, soon afterward, Herb and Selena broke up. Herb's been seeing another woman recently, an architect named Miriam, but Lynnette knows the excitement isn't there. Theirs is the moderate, efficient love of older people who have led complicated lives. Though she misses Selena, she makes every effort to be cordial to Miriam, and wants to be her friend. Above all else, she is determined not to be perceived as the jealous daughter.

Lynnette looks at her mother, who is discussing something with Mrs. Ferguson. Their relationship has never been easy, but only recently has Lynnette figured out why Suzanne resents her so much. It is because Lynnette has managed to retain what Suzanne has irretrievably lost: She has managed to retain Herb's love. Across from her Bruce stands in a corner, cowed by so much activity: small, plump, meek Bruce. Suzanne is watching Bruce as well. For a brief second, mother's and daughter's stares meet. In recent conversations, Lynnette has heard Suzanne refer to Herb still as her husband, and not even catch the slip.

They are both thinking the same thing, Lynnette knows. They are both thinking what a handsome, protective, intelligent man Herb is. The only difference is that what Suzanne thinks with a pang of regret and terror, Lynnette thinks—smirkingly—with a taste of triumph.

John—his purple suit turning a strange shade of mauve in the shadows—is flirting with one of the girls who will serve lunch.

"What's Irish and sits on your porch?" he asks, and the girl giggles, shrugging her shoulders.

"Patio furniture," John says. The girl, who is not more than sixteen, now starts to laugh uncontrollably. It's clear she doesn't want to be laughing; she keeps looking over her shoulder, to see if Mrs. Ferguson is watching her. And indeed, Mrs. Ferguson occasionally throws sidelong glances at the girl, though it's obvious she doesn't intend to do anything now. She is waiting until after the party, when she can punish in private.

Now John is telling an obscene story about Michael Jackson and the baby tiger on his record cover. Suzanne listens with some distaste. She does not trust John for a second. And not because he is gay, either. That has nothing to do with it. What annoys Suzanne about John is his intolerance. She remembers the day he and Lynnette first met Bruce, and Bruce had the mistaken impression that John was Lynnette's boyfriend. He took him outside after dinner and walked him around the garden and told John that he had a future with Bruce's real estate firm, if he wanted one. It seemed like the proper thing to do. Suzanne blushes at the thought of Bruce's naïveté, but when she remembers overhearing Lynnette and John laughing uncontrollably, and mocking her husband, her embarrassment turns to anger and impatience.

Lynnette is going through the cereal drawer. "Mom?" she asks. "Does Seth eat anything but Sugar Pops these days?"

"Corn Bran," Suzanne says.

"I'm now in the room, so please don't talk about me in the third person," Seth says. He is standing in the doorway, wearing his droopy bathrobe. "Yes," he says. "It's me."

Pearl puts down the paper graduation cap she is constructing, and rushes over to hug her grandson. "Sethela," she says, "you're so big now. A real graduation boy." She kisses him.

Over the heads of Lynnette, Suzanne, and Pearl, John and Seth—the tallest people in the room by five or six inches—nod to each other.

"Seth," Suzanne says, "you got a card from Concetta." She hands him an envelope postmarked Jamaica. "Ex-maid," Lynnette whispers to John.

Seth smiles, and tears open the envelope. The card has a picture of a happy white-faced boy holding some flowers on it. He opens it, wrinkles his brow, and begins to read, silently moving his lips.

Now he looks up, smiles, and reads aloud: "God bless you on your birthday." He looks again at the card, and begins to study the second line.

The tiny woman in the chef's hat is whispering furiously to Mrs. Ferguson. After nodding a few times, Mrs. Ferguson walks out of the kitchen, beckoning Suzanne to follow her. Suzanne goes, sheepish, expecting punishment.

"She wants all of you out of the kitchen," Mrs. Ferguson says. "Now."

"O.K.," Suzanne says. She goes back into the kitchen. "Come on, kids," she says. "The caterers have work to do."

Seth is on the fourth line of the card.

All through his childhood, Seth was a problem. Suzanne and Herb chastised him—for laziness, for addiction to television, even for occasional outbursts of hyperactive violence, during which he might bounce on their bed until the bedboard broke. He was a difficult child, and to compensate for the impenetrable closeness shared by Herb and Lynnette, Suzanne contrived an affection for him which had less to do with maternal instinct than with a mournful thirst for justice. Over the years, this bond of weakness has taken on enormous strength. Suzanne loves this difficult child, for reasons she cannot, and would not, want to articulate. And up until he was fourteen, Seth loved her as much in return.

But Suzanne was a coward. When Herb almost casually called Seth stupid, she said nothing. When Herb doled out punishment after Seth got bad grades, she said nothing. Suzanne never thought to have him tested for a learning disability because above all else, she feared annoying Herb. When Seth's guidance counselor told Suzanne of his dyslexia—adding crisply that she was shocked at how long it had gone unnoticed—Suzanne burst into a fit of tears so violent that the nurse had to be called.

Herb decided that Seth should go to boarding school. He had been told of a place in Vermont that specialized in cases such as his. Before he broke the news, he told Seth he could have anything he wanted, and the boy's face immediately darkened with suspicion, for he was a child who often wanted things fiercely, and rarely got them. After a few seconds Seth muttered that he might like a television for the back of the car. When Herb told him about the boarding school, Seth's mouth opened, and water screened his eyes. Suzanne had to leave the room.

Seth went to boarding school. At first he cried all the time, and begged to go home, but after a few weeks he adjusted to his new life. Since then, he has worked consistently and diligently to overcome the learning disability. He has won the praise and affection of his teachers. And he has told Suzanne that the school has come to seem to him more of a home than any place he's ever lived.

It occurs to Suzanne, from time to time, that she has lost Seth. Not the way mothers are supposed to lose their children—by loving them too much or hurting them or both—but the way one might lose a safety pin or a set of keys. Simply by distraction, by neglect. She might find him again soon, just as accidentally. Their lives might change, and they might come to need each other again. As it stands, she doesn't worry about it because she is nearly as impressed by Seth's capacity for recovery as she is by her own.

* * *

There has been some debate within the family as to what Herb and Suzanne should give Seth as his graduation gift. Herb wanted to buy him a car, but Suzanne doesn't trust Seth's driving. She thought of a stereo system. Then Herb learned from Lynnette that what Seth really wanted was a sewing machine. He had developed an interest in fashion design, Seth had told Lynnette, and was even thinking about taking some courses at Parson's in the fall. When Herb told Suzanne, she said, "I give up." She was really surprised to find out that Seth was confiding things in Lynnette instead of her. Bruce was also surprised, but for a different reason. "Well," he said, "I suppose if that's what he really wants, it's all right." But everyone is still a little anxious about the gift. It does not seem quite the right thing for a boy graduating from prep school (even though the model Herb chose is state-of-the-art, with computerized controls). And Suzanne wonders how Seth will react. After all, he has never said a word to her about clothes design, or Parson's, or wanting a sewing machine. He has only spoken to Lynnette. How will he feel when he receives the present, and sees that his private ambitions have become part of a public gesture?

The guests begin to arrive around two. There is no sign of the morning's chaos; flowers have been placed strategically around the patio, and the youngest of the caterers' girls are standing in clean white aprons, holding trays of hot hors d'oeuvres, at the four corners. The first guests to arrive are a couple named Barlow, who live about thirty feet away, but have nonetheless driven over. They greet Suzanne and Bruce warmly, smile, comment on the beautiful day, the beautiful wisteria, the beautiful pool. Suzanne accepts their gifts from Mrs. Barlow, while Bruce sternly shakes hands with Mr. Barlow.

"He looks better in a suit," John says to Lynnette. The two of them are sitting on the diving board of the pool, far enough away from the patio that they can comment on the guests without being overheard. "Some people do, you know. Look incredibly silly until they put on a suit. Your stepfather looks quite dapper now, actually. He looks like someone to be reckoned with."

Lynnette smiles, watching her mother crumple in deference to a second couple. "He's worth a few good laughs," she says. "Bruce can tell good jokes. Mannish ones."

John has twisted his legs one around the other, as if they were pieces of pipe cleaner. "I see there's a kiddie table," he says.

"There is. For once, Seth won't have to sit there."

"When I was a kid," John says, "I hated kiddie tables. Sometimes I refused to eat at all if it means sitting with babies."

"Well, don't worry. Mom didn't have us at the kiddie table, but close enough. We were supposed to eat at the young adult table, with some of my cousins and these people from Queens. But I switched the place-cards. Now we're sitting with Daddy and Miriam and Seth."

"Does your mother know you switched the cards?" John asks.

Lynnette smiles. "She'll find out," she says.

"Seth's disappeared again," John says, looking once again toward the house. "I hope we get a chance to talk. It's so strange seeing him in this context."

"Well, he'll be in New York soon. Then we'll see a lot of him, I'm sure. Still, I'd just love to drop it casually to Mom. You know. Seth and John are friends, Mom. They go to this club on Avenue A . . . you probably haven't heard of it. She'd die."

"Don't do anything cruel, Lynnette," John says.

She looks at him, surprised. "What does that mean?" she asks.

"I'm serious. I'm sorry to have to be so blunt, but it bothers me, all of this aggression toward your mother. Switching the placecards and all. The point is not to be pointlessly cruel. The point is different."

"I'm not being pointlessly cruel," Lynnette says. "I'm talking self-preservation. There was no way in hell I was eating lunch with my cousins after all this time."

John looks at the diving board, the still pool below. "Perhaps we should go socialize," he says.

"What is your problem today?" Lynnette says. "Angry one minute, the next everything is just hunky-dory."

"Look, I said what I had to say. Let's go socialize. A lot of people are arriving."

He stands up, brushing some leaves from his lap, and offers Lynnette his hand. "Shall we?" he says.

"All right," she says. She gets up and takes his arm, and they promenade up the grassy slope of the lawn to the patio.

"Oh, Lynnette," Suzanne says once they're in hearing range, "you're just in time to see the Friedlanders. You remember Steve and Emily Friedlander, don't you?"

"Yes, of course," Lynnette says. "I babysat for you in junior high."

"I remember. I do," Mrs. Friedlander says, and shakes Lynnette's hand.

"And this is Lynnette's roommate, John Bachman," Suzanne says.

"I work in publishing," John says, in response to Mr. Friedlander's query.

"Not much money there, is there?" Mr. Friedlander says. "But I suppose someone's got to do it. Emily and I are avid readers. What's the company?"

John names it. "Steve," Emily says, "don't we own that?" She laughs.

"Champagne cocktail," announces one of the young girls with the trays. "Fish mousse," says another. "Mini egg rolls," says another.

Lynnette and John head for the champagne cocktails. They take two each. Suzanne takes one, and drinks it quickly and subtly. Only Bruce says no. He doesn't drink. Someone runs inside to get him some sparkling cider.

In the foyer, the graduation gifts pile up—silver ribbons and designer wrapping papers and huge, ornate bows which glitter in the sunlight.

Seth finally makes it outdoors around three, still looking rumpled, though he's wearing a new pressed suit. Almost immediately he is engulfed by a circle of grandmothers and aunts and great-aunts, arrived by taxi from Brooklyn, the Bronx, Yonkers. "Sethela," Pearl says proudly, "you look handsome as a man. How old are you?"

"Almost eighteen," Seth says. Over the heads of these small women he exchanges a glance and a nod with John, who motions with his eyes toward the pool house. Seth watches his friend whisper goodbye to Lynnette, and make his way down the grassy slope to the pool.

"So what are your plans?" Pearl asks. "Tell us all, tell us your plans, you great big graduation man, you."

Suzanne sees Seth talking from the kiddie table, where she is setting up paper plates and special placemats. Bruce's children, Linda and Sam, will sit at the kiddie table, along with two babies, some pubescent nieces, and the seventeen-year-old son of Concetta, the ex-maid. Suzanne can see Linda and Sam, standing glumly on the porch, surveying this party full of strangers. She thinks they are menacing children. She feels a little tipsy after two drinks, and thinks she will have more.

And there, across the porch, is Lynnette, who, in the midst of looking for John, has been swept up by a stronger urge to find her father. Discovering he hasn't arrived, she has sat down and decided to analyze her mother, who is having another drink. Her prognosis: Things are turning over on Suzanne (a turnover which will be completed when she sees the switched placecards). And then Lynnette remembers what John has said, and feels a stab of guilt. It is not her fault, she tells herself, if Suzanne is still in love with Herb, if Bruce is a weak, inferior person. Perhaps there is something wrong with her taking such pleasure in her mother's sad predicament. And yet she takes pleasure in so few things, and if she tells no one, and does nothing to make things worse for Suzanne than Suzanne has already made them for herself, who can fault her? In the long run, Lynnette decides, she is doing her mother a favor by switching the placecards, saving her from the pain of sitting with Herb and Miriam, who are genuinely in love, and would only make Suzanne envious and unhappy.

Where is John? He has disappeared somewhere. Seth is still surrounded by the circle of old women. Her mother is drinking, laughing, chatting. Bruce holds his wife's hand with a kind of tentativeness—the hold of a man who isn't sure what he's clinging to.

No one—not even Lynnette—notices when Seth slips away from his relatives, and makes his way toward the pool house.

Suzanne is standing in the kitchen, holding on to the counter so hard her knuckles are turning white as the marble. She is biting her lower lip and she is fighting back a wave of nausea. Because suddenly, inexplicably, standing with her husband, she felt as alone and bereft as the first day she got out of bed after Herb's departure and stood in the living room on her wobbly legs and cried. There is no need for this, she tells herself. She is in a new house, she is a new person, and she is surrounded by friends and relations, she is having a party. Yet none of it seems real to her. Why now, when she has no time to control it, must the pain return?

She breathes deeply, counts her breaths. Next to her on the counter is a half-empty martini. Without thinking she gulps the drink down, before noticing that someone has extinguished a cigarette butt in it. A pleasant warmth seeps through her, and seems to numb her. She wants desperately to disappear, to watch television, to go to the grocery store. But she cannot, she must not.

And strengthened—at least for the moment—by her drink, she goes back outside.

* * *

Suzanne knows Herb has arrived when she gets outside because his name hums in the background, on the lips of all the guests. He is wearing a black-striped suit and a red tie, and he is standing with a pretty blond woman in her thirties who is wearing a white dress: Miriam. Herb has spoken of her, over lunch. They may be married in the spring.

"Daddy, Daddy!" Lynnette shouts, abandoning her search for John and Seth. And she runs from where she is sitting to where he stands, nearly knocking Suzanne over in the process.

"Hi, baby doll," Herb says, sweeping heavy Lynnette up in his arms, clear into the air, as if she is weightless. Miriam stands next to him, her hands crossed over her stomach, holding a small gift. She is the kind of woman who knows how to stand and look comfortable while she is waiting to be introduced, while she is being assessed.

"Hello, Miriam," Lynnette says. "I'm glad you could come." And she whispers something to Herb which no one can catch.

"Hello, Herb," Suzanne says, walking to greet him. If she didn't know about Miriam, she could say something sultry, like, "Who's your friend?" Because she is drunk, she has no idea how she actually sounds.

"You're looking radiant as usual," Herb says. Miriam smiles.

"Oh, Miriam," Herb says, suddenly remembering his companion. "Suzanne, this is Miriam. Miriam, Suzanne."

"Hello, Suzanne," Miriam says. "Herb's told me so much about you." She reaches out her hand, graciously.

"Likewise," Suzanne says.

"Hello, Herb!" A small man suddenly appears by Suzanne's side, and shakes Herb's hand. "Good to see you, buddy," he says. Suzanne looks at the man, a little puzzled, and then she remembers that he is her husband.

"I'll leave you all to talk," Suzanne says. "A hostess's duties call." And she slips off to the kitchen. Suzanne does not usually drink much, and when she does, it's for a reason. On those rare occasions—like today—the power of alcohol impresses her tremendously, and she wants to recommend it, like a wonder drug. She wants to do commercials advertising its effectiveness. Perhaps she can tell Mrs. Ferguson. It is amazing what this stuff can do, she might say. We are all chemicals, after all. And suddenly, her body feels as if it is nothing but chemicals—entirely mechanical, a vat of interaction, immune.

The caterers are carving several legs of lamb. "We're ready to serve if you are, ma'am," shouts the old lady in the chef's hat.

"Oh, I'm ready," Suzanne says. "I'm ready for anything."

She is only surprised, in fact, when she sees her name on a placecard at a table with her cousins from Queens. She remembers arranging things differently. No matter. The Queens cousins can be fun. Anyone can be fun as long as she looks at them, listens to them the right way.

Just as the appetizer is served, Seth and John reappear, somewhat out of breath.

"Where were you?" Lynnette asks.

"We took a walk," John says, and they sit down at the table, with Herb.

"Was it fun?" Herb asks.

"Oh, yes," Seth says. "Quite fun. Hello, Miriam."

From behind them, at another table, Suzanne raises a glass of wine and says, "*Mazel tov*, everybody." Safely ensconced between Herb and John, Lynnette doesn't even smile.

"Suzanne," Bruce says, sitting down next to her. "Suzanne, are you all right? Your eyes are all red."

By dusk, the tables have been cleared.

The caterers are cleaning up the kitchen, to the hum of the dishwasher. The old lady in the chef's hat, once so irritable, is sitting in a corner, polishing a copper skillet and humming "God Bless the Child." Near the diving board, Suzanne watches purple blotches of cloud move and crash against one another. She is dimly aware that somewhere behind her people are talking, relatives mostly. (The Barlows and the Friedlanders left hours ago.) It is hard for her to identify any one voice. Yet she does not feel weak. In some perverse way, she feels strong—strong enough to bulldoze her way through dinner, to keep Myra from talking the whole time about dentistry. Once again, she has gotten past despair. She only wonders how long it will be until the next bout, and if the gulf will have widened.

A roar of laughter is rising above the patio, and a voice—John's voice—says, "Come on, please, dance with me, please." Suzanne gets up and stumbles toward the house, to see what's causing the commotion. It seems that Seth has put a dance tape on the stereo—one he made for a party at school—and a disco song with lyrics in German is blasting out the family room windows. The person John is trying to entice into dancing with him is Pearl, and she is shaking her head, no, no, and throwing back her neck, laughing as he reaches out his hands to her and implores her.

"Come on, Pearl," an uncle says. "You used to love to dance with the young men." Yes, the family roars. Dance. And quite suddenly she relents, a smile widening on her face.

Pearl dances with amazing energy. She kicks up her heels, and her sisters and cousins and grandchildren—gathered in a circle—applaud loudly, and cheer her on. Even Seth jumps and whoops with glee. Lynnette sits with Miriam and Herb outside the circle, at a small patio table. They observe this spectacle with polite smiles on their faces, like tourists who watch a native dance and wish they, too, could be primitive and join in. Lynnette gazes at Miriam, whose face is a model of perfect composure. What a contrast, she thinks, to her mother's freak show of a party; how good it feels to be in the company of kind and well-mannered Miriam. Lynnette cannot help but smile, and move her hand toward Miriam's, which lifts slightly off the table, then falls back perfectly in place.

The next song on the tape is "It's Raining Men." Pearl is imitating John's long-legged way of dancing, to the delight of everyone around her—even Suzanne, who now stands on the periphery of the patio, clapping her hands and throwing her head back in full laughter. Now she stumbles over to the table where Herb is sitting with Miriam and Lynnette and reaches out her hands. "Let's dance," she says. "Come on, Herb, come dance with your wife. For old times' sake."

Herb looks up at her, confused. "Go ahead, Herb," Miriam says. "I think it's a lovely idea." She smiles. As for Lynnette—Lynnette's eyes bulge. Her make-up has smeared in purple and black circles under her eyes; sitting there, she looks like an old cartoon illustration of Satan Suzanne saw once, arrived uninvited at some absurdly genteel dinner party. He sat at the table in all his hideousness, and no one in the picture seemed to notice. The caption read: "The Unexpected Guest."

"Suzanne, please," Herb says. "I really don't want to dance."

"But it's all right with Miriam, isn't it?" says Suzanne.

"Go ahead, don't stop on my account," Miriam says.

Suzanne grabs Herb's hands and hoists him up. "Come on," she says loudly, so that several of her relatives turn and look. "We'll show these young people what dancing really is."

Herb has no choice but to go with her. She drags him between two of her cousins into the center of the patio, where John and Pearl are still going strong.

Pearl, who has been enjoying her spotlight, gives her daughter a look of irritation and suspicion. "Come on, Mom," Suzanne says. "You can't hog all the attention all night." And she grabs Herb's hands, and swings him into a jitterbug.

But "It's Raining Men" ends. The next song on the tape, inexplicably, is "Smoke Gets in Your Eyes." John gets down on his knees and begs Pearl, who shoos him off. "No, I just can't anymore," she says. "I'm just too tired."

"Oh, you'll break my heart," John says. "My heart is breaking."

"Good to see you haven't forgotten how to flirt, Mama," Suzanne says to Pearl, and everyone laughs. She has grabbed Herb firmly around the waist, to make sure he doesn't try to run away from the slow dance. Now, alone in the circle, they writhe, Herb trying to keep his distance, Suzanne insistently holding him down so that his chest pushes against hers.

"Hey," Herb says, "I have an idea. Let's make this a family dance. Let's have the whole family. Come on, Seth!"

Everyone roars approval. Seth nods no, but it's only for show. His grandmother pushes him out into the opening arms of his parents, who take him in. The song continues, and the three of them roll haphazardly over the patio. "When an old flame dies," Suzanne sings, "you know what happens."

There is a sound of rustling, now, behind the circle. Someone is trying to persuade Lynnette to join the dance. Indeed, several of her aunts have hoisted her up, and are pushing her toward the makeshift dance floor, refusing to heed her insistent pleas that she does not want to dance.

"Come on," Pearl says. "Don't be a spoilsport. Dance with the family, darling."

But a spoilsport is exactly what Lynnette wants to be. "I don't want to," she says through gritted teeth, and elbows her way out of her aunts' grips. To no avail. A space has cleared in the circle, and John has grabbed Lynnette by the arm so firmly that tears spring to her eyes. "Come on," he says. "Dance."

"Let me go or I'll scream," Lynnette warns him.

"Shut up and don't be a baby," John says, and plummets her into the center of the circle, into the reeling inner circle of her family.

Immediately they close around her, like a mouth. It is dank inside that circle, full of the smells of alcohol and perfume. Arms around arms, heads knocking, the family stumbles, barely able to keep its balance. "I love you, sweetie," Suzanne says from somewhere, and a mouth nuzzles Lynnette's hair.

She is crying now. Besides the music, her crying is the only sound, for the crowd has suddenly been struck silent, and is watching with wide eyes. And though Herb's hand squeezes her shoulder, though he whispers in her ear, "It's all right, honey," all she feels is the terror of inertia, like the last time he ever pushed her on the swing. Higher and higher she went, as if his strength could disprove her fatness. "Daddy, stop!" she had screamed as the swing rose. "Stop, stop, I'm scared!" Her hands clutched the metal chains, her mouth opened. She wasn't scared of the height; she was scared of him, of how he kept pushing, as if the swing were magic, and by pushing he could change her forever into the pretty little girl he really wanted to be his partner.

Radiation

Two sisters and a brother were sitting at a kitchen table watching *General Hospital.*

Is Monica good now, or bad, asked the younger sister, a girl of eight.

I can't tell, said the brother, who had just returned from a summer program for college-bound youths.

Shut up, shut up, I can't hear, said the oldest sister, waving away a fly attracted to her damp skin.

First she was bad, I think, then she was good, but now she's bad again, said the cleaning lady, who had been intimate with the show since its inception.

The younger sister got up and ran across the house to her mother's room. On the way, she played a game of her own invention involving somersaults and spinning.

The mother was riding the Exercycle, and also watching *General Hospital.*

Again the girl asked, Is Monica good or bad?

I don't know, said the mother, pushing up and back against the handlebars to improve muscle tone. I can never tell.

On the screen Monica and Lesley were arguing over Rick.

An alarm went off, a commercial came on. The mother stepped off the Exercycle, sat down at the make-up vanity, and began combing her hair. She had it cut specially by a hairdresser who specialized in ladies undergoing the treatment. As the comb went through, lifting each tuft from the scalp, it revealed the concealed bald patches.

Want to go with me to the radiation therapy center? the mother asked the daughter.

Nah, I'd rather watch, the daughter said. Bear and Ivy'll go, though. They've never been yet.

No, the mother said, they haven't. She put on her lipstick, then dabbed off the excess with a Kleenex.

Kids, you ready to go? the mother asked, walking into the kitchen.

We are, said the older daughter.

Just remember to put on your shoes, will you? the mother said.

The older sister looked at her brother and grimaced, sucking in her cheeks and curling her tongue in a way that six out of every seven people can do. Then she touched the tip of her nose with the tip of her tongue, smiled, and said in falsetto, Yes, Mother dear.

In the car, the son, who was called Bear, lay down along the full length of the back seat. His sister, who was undergoing psychotherapy as part of her training to be a psychotherapist, was explaining that often children who have had abnormally close relationships with their parents are unable to break away from them when they become adults. Consequently, they deal with their aggression by "rebelling" over and over again, well into adulthood, rather than simply letting go, saying, my parents are this way, and I accept them this way. And that, she went on to explain, was why her old best friend Katie had done what she had done.

What she had done was go through the motions of a full wedding to her boyfriend when in actuality they had never even gotten a marriage license.

In addition, the ceremony had been questionable, what with each vowing to love, honor, cherish, and always be ready to fuck the other.

So you see, the daughter finished, it's a very complicated situation when viewed psychologically.

The mother didn't see it that way. Her main point was, what a rotten kid, what a rotten thing to do. Keith, Katie's father, her *father*, she reasoned, is dying and he wants to see his daughter married before he goes. Is that too much? Is it? I always knew Katie was a sneak, the mother said. Out for herself. Selfish.

The daughter twisted in the seat and again stuck her tongue out. It's more complicated, she said again. I don't see anything complicated about it, the mother said.

Look, the daughter said. You know what I mean.

While she talked she played with the electric window.

Look, she said, Corinne's in a weird way—

Don't play with the electric window, it's already been broken once this year.

Corinne, the daughter began again, is in a weird way jealous of Keith.

Corinne was Keith's wife, getting a Ph.D. late in life.

Jealous! the mother said. Jealous of a dying man. She can't wait until—

Look! Now the daughter began to play with the seatbelt. She almost wishes it was her dying because she thinks she's so much more unhappy than he is, and she wants to justify her suffering. I think she's actually glad Katie and Evan didn't get married, even though she wouldn't admit it.

I don't buy it, the mother said. Corinne's a sneak, too. Jealous! If she was jealous, why would she want to marry your father?

What?

The son, lying in back, sat up.

What? he said again.

It's nothing, Bear, said the daughter.

Come on, Ivy, he's old enough now, the mother said. All it is, Bear, is that once Corinne got drunk and told Daddy that when I died and Keith died they could get married.

The son laughed nervously, perhaps relievedly. You're kidding, he said.

And don't you dare mention this to anyone, the mother said, especially your little sister.

Of course I won't, the son said, of course not.

By this time they had reached the radiation therapy center, which was new and modern and underground. They took an elevator down and emerged in a large, plush waiting room with carpeted walls.

Wow, the sister said.

Isn't this nice? the mother said, smiling. She led them through. It was nice. All the tables had backgammon boards and chess boards built into them. There were Folons and O'Keeffes and Wyeths on the walls. There were books and magazines, toys and puzzles for kids. The colors were bright and cheerful, but not so bright and cheerful as to leer at the dying, the architect having conferred with a noted death-and-dying specialist on the design.

Isn't this nice, Bear? the mother said. See through the glass? That's where they do the treatment.

Behind a big glass pane—too big to be called a window—the son could see a flat, silver table that looked cold. It stood like an island in the center of a room behind the glass. Above it, a large machine, resembling a machine gun, pointed down from the ceiling.

They walked over to the nurses' station.

Hello, Joanne, the mother said to the nurse.

Good to see you again, Gretl, the nurse said. These your kids?

They sure are, the mother said. This is Ivy, and this is George, but we call him Bear.

Your mom talks a lot about you, honey, the nurse said to the son. How's the new lawn furniture? You get it yet?

We sure did, the mother said. It's great. But you know, furniture you leave outside, it always gets ruined. I don't count on it lasting more than a year.

Well, said the nurse, Frank and I have had the same set for almost three years now. Where'd you get yours?

The son turned from the conversation to watch an older man emerge from the row of dressing cubicles. His sister watched him watch. The older man had put on a white robe which tied around the back. He still had on his black business shoes and short black socks; his legs were skinny and white. Having taken a moment to light his pipe, he sat down in a corner and read a copy of *Time.*

Nearby a couple of little girls played Chutes and Ladders. He remembered his little sister told him, there were always kids to play with at the radiation therapy center.

Lurene was asking for you, the nurse said. Too bad you missed her.

Lurene was a character the son had heard of, part of his mother's dinnertime monologue of her life at the radiation therapy center. She was old, a phone operator, and she had the same disease the mother had, only in the earlier stages. She was frightened because the doctors gave her contradictory reports. But the mother prevailed, took her under her wing, told her what was what, offered her whole living self as evidence that it could be got through.

Now Lurene knew what was what.

The mother had gone into a little cubicle to change, so the brother and sister sat down. The brother picked up a copy of *Highlights*; the sister chewed her hair.

Bear up, Bear, the sister said.

The son put down the magazine.

It's just I don't like this place. She pretends it's so happy, why pretend she likes to come here?

People cope in different ways, the sister said, trying not to sound holier-than-thou.

I don't know, the brother said. I guess I'll feel better when Daddy gets home. Things are better when he's here.

He turned back to the magazine. He started to read the "Goofus and Gallant" column.

Bear, the sister asked, are you still upset about what Corinne said?

Yes. No. I guess I am, the brother said. I don't know. I just think, she put him through college. Three hundred sixty-five days a year, welding battleships to put him through college. It'd be nice if he didn't have to travel so much.

He returned to the magazine.

You know they have problems, Bear, the sister said, big problems. There's so much anger between them. But anger's different than hate, Bear.

It's not like she's going to die in a year, the brother said from inside the magazine. Corinne wants to make Mama sicker than she is.

Bear . . .

Don't say it, Ivy, the brother said, standing up. You think you know so much. I've lived with them. He does love her. More than you know. Maybe even more than he knows. I tell you, I've seen it. There are things none of us know, things you don't—

Bear, when are you going to face the fact—

But he had turned from her.

The mother came out again, in a white hospital gown, smiling big.

Isn't this the height of fashion, she joked, turning a pirouette. The son laughed. Through the slightly parted back of the gown, he could see small legs, her bra, her large flowered underpants—briefs, they called them in ladies' stores, as opposed to panties.

She went behind the glass and lay down on the table. The son stood to watch. He thought he saw her flinch as her skin touched the cold metal. He could see on the far side of the glass a technician operating the controls.

Once, twice, the machine went over her in a dark sweep. She had to lie perfectly still. You couldn't see it, the miraculous, burning radiation that was making the lumps go down.

I wonder how it works, the sister said. But her brother wasn't listening. He had his whole face pressed against the glass. He was remembering stories his mother had told him, he thought, to anguish him. About the boy who stole her lunch every day for a year; about the doctor they said was going to just give her a check-up, but forced her down on the dining room table and tore her tonsils out; about the dog she had when she was first married, the dog named Brownie who was poisoned for no good reason by a psychotic neighbor, and that was why they never got a dog as children. And he remembered how a year ago she had told his father, maybe I'll go to Italy with you this year, and the father, in some private hour, told her, no, he did not want her to go to Italy with him and she had said fine, fine, that's just fine, I'll stay here. I have the pool, my friends, everything I need, and when she told her son about it she warned him, don't you dare tell your father I told you, I still have some pride.

No, the son thought, he would remember the other stories. Stories she told when she was drunk or happy. Stories of the docks where she welded. I was the best in my division, she had told him. But I was a woman, so I never got a raise. If it were today, I would've complained.

Then she modeled lady welder uniforms. The unions were crooked. Italian men traded her hot eggplant sandwiches made by their wives in the ghetto for her tuna on toast. And the son knew they wanted her in her tight metal suit.

All that was long ago, she would finish.

Why don't you weld again?

I couldn't ever. I'm too old, Bear, too set in my ways.

He looked at her through the glass. The machine passed over her again. He wanted very much to touch her through the glass. But of course he could not.

She still lay perfectly still. He heard his sister gasp. He turned, and she was bent over, her hand on her mouth, her eyes red, choking back a fit of tears that had come over her like a cough. Then the normal light went on. The mother got up. She came out.

Is that all? the son asked.

That's it, that's all. Simple as one-two-three.

I have to go to the bathroom, the sister said, running.

Eventually she came out. The mother got dressed. They left.

When they got home, the younger sister and the cleaning lady were watching *The Edge of Night*. The younger sister had been indulged, and had baked cookies, so the kitchen was filled with bowls and knives and pans, all sticky with grease and dried dough.

April doesn't know Draper's alive, and she's gonna marry Logan, the younger sister said excitedly. And they're gonna kidnap Emily to get Kirk's money, but Kirk's not Kirk, he's Draper.

Oh, my God, the mother said, staring at the filthy kitchen. Goddammit, I told you never to do this unless you asked me first. You cook, and I have to clean up all your goddamned messes. It's not fair. It's just not fair.

She lifted her hands toward them all, whether to push them away or embrace them none could tell. She looked at them, and her face twisted like when she had the palsy. Then she turned from them. They could hear her sobbing as she ran down the hallway.

Her children were stunned. Though they were used to her annoyance with them, they were not used to crying. They sat there. The younger daughter began to hum.

It's funny how people on soap operas die on one show and come back on another, the girl said.

So on earth, in heaven, answered the cleaning lady.

The other two were silent. The son stood and walked to his mother's room, ignoring the sister's warnings.

Her bedroom door was closed. He stood outside it for what seemed a long time. Finally he knocked. She didn't answer. He opened the door gently. On her huge bed the mother lay curled, very small, weeping quietly. He stood back from her.

Ma, he said.

She didn't answer. The crying had stopped, replaced by heaves.

Ma, he said again.

She did not look up. It's O.K., Bear, I'm all right, she managed to say.

The son wanted to hug her then, but he knew he couldn't. Something held him back—what had always held him back. There were rules.

I hope you'll feel better, Mama, he said. Then he left the room.

She nodded. She was glad he was gone. It annoyed her to have to comfort him in her suffering.

Once I knew a sailor, she sang to herself, a sailor from the sea . . . and she thought of her own mother, with too many children and no English.

Gradually she got up. She dried her eyes, blew her nose. Standing in front of the mirror, she pulled violently at the short hairs. None came out. Well, she thought, another day. Still, perhaps she would take her hairdresser's advice and get a wig. Funny how with time one can grow accustomed to even the most frightening changes; how even the unimaginable can become manageable.

There, she would be fine. She would apologize and dinner would be fine. Why, just five years ago, the tests she now sat through routinely, without flinching, would have made her faint with pain. She would have vomited at the sight of the scars on her body. She would have wept for fear of death. No more.

But looking at herself in the mirror, she remembered the rebellious girl she had once been, and she was only sorry she could not find it in herself to be courageous.

Out Here

They line up, from eldest to youngest: Gretchen, Carola, Jill. Leonard frames them in his viewfinder. When they stand together, posed, he can see similarities—the arcs of cheekbones, almond-shaped eyes, thin lips—but if these women were strangers to him and he met them separately, he would never guess that they were sisters. Gretchen, Leonard's wife, is the tallest as well as the oldest. As she arranges herself, she shakes out her hair and laughs. Carola—hair shorter, mouth smaller than her sisters'—sighs loudly. Jill, standing barefoot next to her, jumps from one foot to the other on the hot cement.

"Hurry up, Leonard. I have to get dinner," Carola says.

"Just let me focus," Leonard says.

The sisters grumble and link arms. Through his camera, Leonard thinks, he has captured an image that has nothing to do with these women as individuals but, rather, with how they lean away from one another, how their arms strain against touching.

"It's too hot to stand like this much longer," Jill says. She unlinks her arm from Carola's to brush away a fly.

He takes the picture. The camera spews out a piece of photographic paper, fog green. Immediately the sisters disentangle and go back to what they were doing—Gretchen to the porch, Carola to the kitchen, Jill hopping from stone to stone across the lawn to where her friend Donna Lee sits leaning against a maple tree, reading. Leonard shades the picture with his left hand and, squinting, bends over to watch the image emerge.

Even though they both live in New York City, Carola and Jill hardly ever see each other, and never on social occasions. They have been meeting only to haggle about bank accounts, trust funds, their father's health-insurance policy. Carola works at a publishing company, in subsidiary rights, and lives on the East Side; Jill lives with Donna Lee in a nameless region just below Tribeca, and is doing temp work to pay for a film course at NYU. Gretchen has been living in Mill Valley, in Northern California, since college, and for the past three years she has been married to Leonard, who has a job with a software company. What has brought the sisters together again now is the death of their father. He died of emphysema, in his late sixties, and they have gathered in an old house in Connecticut that is not "the old house" but a house completely unfamiliar to them. Their father moved into it three years ago, after their mother's death and his almost immediate remarriage to a divorcée named Eleanor Manley. It is Eleanor's "old house." She died six months ago of a stroke; her children then cleaned the house of its knickknacks, scrubbed it as best they could of early memories, and left it to the widower, whom none of them knew very well. In spite of this recent cleaning, there are still hints of another family's life here that has nothing to do with Gretchen, Carola, or Jill. They have come to sort through the few things their father brought with him when he moved here.

Jill has never been to the house before. Gretchen and Carola visited once, two years ago, in the summer. Jill refused to come that time, without explanation. It is a nineteenth-century stone house, with turrets, and ivy climbing up the walls. "Stately," the Westport real estate agents would say. That summer, Eleanor's mark was everywhere: The beds were made with flowered sheets, the halls lined with her photographs of Parisian street urchins. There were saltcellars and little pepper mills at each place at dinner, chairs with paws. The house, Carola thought, was so quintessentially Eleanor's domain that she doubted whether her father could have felt very comfortable there. Even Eleanor's children seemed to have no interest, no stake in it. Of course, Eleanor is gone now, and their father is gone. Still, his children walk the halls quietly, like invaders.

"Leonard and I are going to think of this as a vacation," Gretchen said at dinner the first night they arrived, four days ago. "A healthful retreat." They would get up at six, she said, and run—five, six miles—and in the afternoon they would do exercises. She would work out a regimen for each of them. And they should eat as little sugar and salt as possible, Gretchen told Carola, who had put herself in charge of cooking. Gretchen ate hardly any salt, and was in marvelous shape—her skin bronzed, her hair golden, her body lean.

"You're not getting me up at six," Carola said, sticking out her tongue and with great deliberateness salting her meat.

"I'll run," Jill said. "And Donna Lee will run. Donna Lee used to be a track star."

Donna Lee, surprised to be mentioned, paused in the midst of putting a forkful of stuffing into her mouth, blushed, and smiled. Everyone looked at the table.

"Tomorrow morning, then," Gretchen said. "Carola can decide if she wants to join us."

Now, in the late-afternoon sunlight, Jill, her face smudged, is climbing a tree. There are twigs in her clothes and in her hair, which hangs down to her waist. Donna Lee is watching her from behind her book, while on the porch Gretchen is watching Donna Lee. The porch is far enough away so that Gretchen can say to Leonard, "What *is* the story with that girl?"

He shakes his head, and gazes absently at the line of maples bordering the lawn. He is disappointed because no one cares about his photograph. He showed it to Gretchen, and she brushed it off—glanced at it, said, "Neat," and put it down next to her iced coffee.

"I'm still puzzled," Gretchen says. "She's nice enough, I suppose, but she's so withdrawn. It's impossible to talk to her. She's on her guard every second."

"She's probably scared."

"Why?"

"Coming into a strange family is scary," Leonard says. "You feel like an intruder. Especially at a time like this."

Gretchen puts on her sunglasses and lies back in the chair. "Jill probably shouldn't have brought her," she says.

"Young love," Leonard murmurs.

"*What?*"

He turns, and Gretchen is staring straight at him.

Carola, in the kitchen, notices through the window how suddenly Gretchen has turned her head, and is pleased to see her taken off her guard, particularly by Leonard. The kitchen is hot. Carola has cooked every meal so far; she feels in control, at ease, only in the kitchen. This is why she refuses when Donna Lee and Gretchen offer to help. She knows they're only doing it to be polite, and she'd rather not have their help anyway. It has been her experience that people who try to help in the kitchen usually end up just milling around—getting in the way and nibbling at the food. Carola hates to have anyone touch the food before it's served. Her father used to infuriate her by eating spoonfuls of jam right from the jar. He and Gretchen and Jill always came into the kitchen and disrupted everything just when dinner was ready. Gretchen picked the bacon out of the salad, Jill refused to eat what their mother had prepared and made herself a grilled-cheese sandwich. And then they all disappeared when the dishes had to be done—all but Carola. She would stay and help her mother dry.

Outside the window, Gretchen and Leonard appear to have stopped talking for the moment. Jill has climbed down from the tree and is leaping about the yard, head back, flinging out her hair like a mane.

"She is a child," Carola says out loud, mostly to hear how it sounds, and breaks an egg into a bowl. As for Gretchen, she is simply selfish. Both of them all but abandoned the family these last years—especially when their mother got sick. Carola alone stuck around, stuck it out, sat day after day by the hospital bed when the cancer started to spread. She knows they resent her, out of guilt, but she also knows she did the right thing, no matter what Gretchen might say.

Tonight, as usual, they will wolf down the dinner she has made them and thank her for it only in the most cursory way, if at all. Especially Donna Lee. Carola does not like that woman. Last night, when everyone else had carefully counted out the shrimp, to make sure that each person got the same amount, Donna Lee simply reached the spoon onto the platter and took a huge heap—at least twice as much as anyone else. And then halfway through the meal, embarrassed, she tried to shovel them back onto the platter when no one was looking.

Leonard is rapping at the window, waving. Carola smiles at him. Her scalp itches from the steam, making her long to wash her hair. But she washes her hair too often, she has decided; it's getting brittle. She takes all of her hair in her left hand and pulls until it hurts, then lets it spring back.

Leonard walks into the kitchen. "What is she doing?" he asks Carola. He points out the window at Jill, who is galloping back and forth across the lawn, making wheezing noises.

"She's pretending to be a horse," Carola says.

Leonard looks at her, confused more by her nonchalance than by Jill's strange cavorting.

"She's done it forever," Carola says. "Since we were kids. She calls it playing horse."

"I see," Leonard says. "Are there rules to the game?"

"Oh, in Jill's mind there's probably a very complicated set of rules."

Leonard smiles, and returns to gazing out the window at Jill. In this strange house, Leonard is awed by the women who surround him—women who paint their fingernails, wear tiger-striped underwear, were once track stars. Women who run in circles pretending that they are horses.

Leonard has never before been to the East Coast. The world of the East is different, he has decided. Because his own family is so close-knit, he is puzzled by Gretchen's sisters, and wonders how they could have splintered and lost touch so easily. And he is puzzled by the landscape. He can cope with desert, and wild plains of brush, and yellow hills, but these green, green lawns and trees make him feel as if he were in some foreign land.

"Can I see your photograph?" Carola asks, and Leonard turns, suddenly shaken out of his reverie, to see that she is staring at him.

"Sure," he says, and fishes in his back pocket. "Here it is."

He hands her the snapshot, and immediately her face seems to break. "Oh, I look horrible," she says.

"No, you don't," Leonard says, as he takes the picture back from her. "You look great. But something's missing. When I took this picture, I saw something that didn't have to do with any one of you. It had to do with all of you, really. I'm not good at explaining things. Whatever it was, it's not in the picture."

"It's not something that's missing," Carola says. "It's what's there. It's me. I'm ugly in pictures. Also, my hair's dirty; is there time for me to wash it before dinner?"

"Look at her," Leonard says, and gazes at Jill, who is still galloping across the yard.

Jill is still running back and forth, neighing, her hair flying, when Leonard goes back out to the porch. "Perhaps she really thinks she is a horse," he says to Gretchen, but she isn't listening. Across the lawn, Donna Lee leans against the maple tree, reading, or pretending to read.

In fact she is absorbed by the gargantuan image of her own eyeball, staring back at her, reflected in the left lens of her glasses. They always stare at her, Jill's sisters. They scrutinize her, their faces full of curiosity and disapproval. The other day, Gretchen asked her what her parents did. "My mother's a librarian," Donna Lee said. "Oh, I see," Gretchen said, and then—nothing. The long, horrible pause that comes when it is too early for a conversation to end, too late to keep it from starting.

Donna Lee puts down her book and stands up, arching her back against the tree. Jill stops in the midst of a gallop and, laughing, falls against Donna Lee, her breath coming hard. Donna Lee can see Gretchen and Leonard on the porch trying not to stare. She still wakes up each morning convinced that Jill will have tired of her, be gone. The winter they met, Jill wore a green down jacket that she kept buttoned down to her knees, and Donna Lee used to tease her, telling her she looked like a giant Chiclet. She loves Jill.

"I'm tired," Jill says, pulling Donna Lee down to the ground with her. "I haven't done that in ages. When I was a kid I could play horse for hours. I used to like to spin, too. I'd just twirl, like a top. Everyone thought I was nuts. But I liked the way everything blurred and only my own body stayed in focus."

Carola, in an upstairs window, looks down at them. She is standing in her father's bedroom, the room he died in. It is a woman's room, with a pink satin comforter on the bed, a huge armoire in the corner, a mirror surrounded by light bulbs. Since she began to clean the room out, Carola has found medicines, a pile of spy novels, rubbing alcohol, and brandy. She had hoped to find some pornographic magazines, some sign of impropriety and decay. She had hoped to find something she could hold against him.

Even now, two weeks after his death, the room smells of her father's cigars and after-shave. It was different when her mother was dying. her mother left no smell. She packed up everything before she went to the hospital, and when she died she was gone without a trace. Carola never saw the body—just a stripped mattress where an hour before her mother had lain, pale and thin, and asked for a copy of *Vogue*. Carola had been living at home for three months, and visited the hospital every day. Yet when her mother died, it was not in her arms, or even in her presence. She died alone, while Carola was out of the room. When she came back,

Vogue in hand, there was the stripped mattress, the half-empty water glass. Her mother had died while Carola was sitting in the cafeteria, drinking her coffee and thumbing through *Cosmopolitan*. It had not seemed fair to Carola, and she wanted to call out to her mother to come back, if only to say a proper goodbye. She wanted to rage against this abandonment. After her mother's death, there was no home to be responsible to anymore, and her father put the house on the market. She moved to New York, found an apartment and a job, but the life she has been leading does not seem real to her, and with perverse nostalgia she thinks back on the year of her mother's dying as the happiest of her life.

Carola does not like to remember these things. She moves to her father's bureau. Every day, she has forced herself to open one drawer and sort through its contents. Today it is the bottom drawer, which contains things of Eleanor's—some silk scarves, old photographs, jewels, and perfume bottles. Perhaps they are things her father could not bear to part with when Eleanor died. They remind Carola that her father loved Eleanor—perhaps more than he loved her mother, and while he was still married.

Eleanor and Carola met only once before her father's second marriage. That was when she was seventeen, and traveling in Europe; her father arranged for her to stay with Eleanor in Paris, where she was living for the year. Eleanor was divorced by then. She courted Carola that week—took her out to dinner, and to Montmartre late at night. Every time they ate, Carola tried to pay for her share, but Eleanor wouldn't allow it. Before Carola left, Eleanor bought her an expensive orange silk scarf with streaks of brilliant blue. Back then, when she knew nothing, Carola idolized Eleanor. It was only years later that she was able to put the visit into a larger perspective.

There is no need to save these things. The photographs are of no one Carola knows, and the scarves are garish; besides, whatever meaning they once had is buried with her father. She has a hard enough time with her own nostalgia; she does not have room for his as well. But, Carola decides, she will keep the jewelry and the perfume bottles. Someone might want them, or they can be sold at a garage sale.

While Carola is going through the drawer, Gretchen and Leonard move upstairs to their room and make love. In the next room, Jill and Donna

Lee are resting. Donna Lee's arms are wrapped around Jill's waist, her face buried in Jill's stomach. She is snoring, and Jill—her eyes closed—is weaving her fingers through Donna Lee's hair.

They all sit down to dinner at eight o'clock. Gretchen is examining one of the perfume bottles Carola found, which Gretchen likes and has decided to keep. Leonard is telling everyone about some young men who hatched a plot to turn Marin County into a medieval fiefdom by setting up a laser gun on top of Mt. Tamalpais. They planned a strategic reorganization of society, re-creating a world of serfs and vassals, round tables and court ladies. When a friend got wind of the plot, the young men murdered him in his garage, and were exposed. It was all baffling, insane, yet Leonard sometimes longingly imagines what castles would look like perched on the rough, dry hills, shrouded in fog.

"What I think is so funny," Gretchen says, "is the idea of Marin County as a fiefdom. Can you imagine? I mean, you can't tell the lord he's invading your personal space when he comes around to make you his serf." She laughs, and Carola stares at her. All through her girlhood, Gretchen had boyfriends; she would never give up one until she had found another. She had that kind of control.

Carola is not eating the meal she spent most of the afternoon preparing. Instead, she has brought in from the kitchen a Styrofoam cup of tea and a bowl of tomato soup, which she now stabs at with her fork. (She has forgotten to put out spoons.) She has poured most of her tea out of the cup and into her water glass and shredded the top half of the cup, making a little pile of Styrofoam pieces on her plate.

"Everyone thinks California is so weird," Leonard is saying, rather defensively. "If you ask me, it's the other way around. People are pretty strange out here. No one's polite, everyone pushes and shoves. I think California's fairly civilized, by and large."

No one says anything to this. Carola has captured everyone's attention by making a boat from her Styrofoam cup and floating it in the soup. Now she is pushing the cup back and forth. The red soup crawls slowly up the sides.

"I have a question for everyone," Carola says. "What if you got stuck on a desert island and you only had one piece of paper and one pen? What would you do?"

Sitting across the table, Gretchen puts her hand to her forehead and wonders how Carola has survived alone for so long. And now—right here, of all places—is she going to have a breakdown? She looks at Leonard, who will be no help to her; he never is in crises. And Jill will run away, as she always does.

The Styrofoam cup has finally sunk. Carola is pathetic, Gretchen thinks. Sad. She could be pretty. Who but Carola would worry about being stuck on a desert island? If she would only take herself in hand and *do* something, half the problem would be solved right there. Gretchen wishes that she could sympathize with Carola, but instead she wants to take her by the shoulders and shake some sense into her.

"I think," Donna Lee says, "that I would only allow myself to write one sentence a week, and that in a very small hand. It would probably be a quite marvelous sentence, given that I'd have a week to think about it before writing it down." It is the first thing she has said at dinner all week that was not required of her.

Carola looks at Donna Lee and smiles. "It's good to know that I'm not the only person in the world who thinks about this kind of thing. Thank you."

Jill drops her fork and falls into a sudden convulsion of laughter. Carola, looking at her, begins to laugh, too, and then Leonard and Gretchen, not because they understand what Jill is laughing at but because the laughter itself is contagious. Only Donna Lee doesn't laugh. There is nothing left on her plate; adrift, she stares at Jill helplessly for direction.

"I'm sorry," Jill says. "I was just remembering that time when Mom was in a bad mood and Daddy put on one of her scarves and did a little imitation of her. He came up behind her and kind of growled and shook his hands. Even she started laughing, he looked so funny. I laugh every time I think of how he looked that day."

As soon as Jill starts to tell the story, everyone stops laughing. Another instance of her father's cruelty, Carola is thinking—to mimic her mother's sorrow, to make it so funny even she had to laugh. How could her mother have loved him so much? He had a lover and he made fun of his wife, yet she was devoted to him. In sickness, she insisted that he be with her, calling out for him in her sleep. He was always there, those last days. Toward the end, belief in responsibility was the only thing that he and Carola shared.

The subject has switched now. Leonard is back on California, its joys and civilities. He's a little drunk, and he waves his fist as he speaks. "Where I grew up," he says, "family meant something. Connections meant something. My brothers and sisters and I always go home for Christmas, every year, and I call my mother every week. But your family! It's terrible how split up you are, all of you so isolated from your father. There's no shared ground, no homestead. It's been lost."

"It never existed," Carola says. "It never was in the first place."

"Oh, that's not true," Gretchen says. "There was lots of family feeling when we were growing up. You've just made yourself forget it."

"And you've made yourself forget all the nights of no one saying a word at dinner," Carola says. "Of Mom and Dad fighting. You and Jill couldn't wait to get away on your own."

"No institution," Jill says, "has been more destructive to women than the nuclear family."

They all look at her, rather puzzled by this generalization.

"What!" Leonard yells. "I'll tell you, I have six sisters, and growing up the way they did they're all better for it."

Jill smiles and shakes her head. "You miss my point," she says. "It's a means of exploitation. Since the sixteenth century, the nuclear family has fit in perfectly with the capitalist system and its whole exploitative program of gender roles. And nothing has caused more psychological damage to women. Fortunately, it's breaking up now."

"How breaking up? What do you mean?" Gretchen asks.

"I mean the divorce rate, the alternatives that women are finding."

Donna Lee looks at the table. Carola grips the edges of her chair. Her eyes are getting wide. "You're one to talk," she says, nearly inaudibly.

"What?"

"I said you're one to talk," Carola says again, slightly more loudly. She looks around, alarmed at having suddenly changed the tenor of the conversation. "I'm sorry," she says. "I just don't see where *you* come off attacking the family."

"Carola, please," Gretchen says, reaching across the table, touching her arm. "Do we have to talk about this now?"

"Oh, let's talk about it," Jill says. "Let's talk about it."

Carola pushes her chair back and sits straight up. "Look," she says. "I don't mean to be confrontational. All I know is it's easy for you to sit there and talk about the demise of the nuclear family and its being a bad thing. You never gave it a chance. You ran away as soon as you could. It's in sickness that families matter, in sickness that they have to pull together, and I just want to ask where were the two of you when Mother got sick?"

"Oh, let's not open this up again," Gretchen says.

"You have no right to say that, Gretchen," Carola says. "I just think there is such a thing as family responsibility. I stuck it out with Mother, you didn't."

"It was your choice," Jill says.

"My responsibility."

"Your choice."

"You can't say I didn't visit," Gretchen says. "I visited three times."

"More than Jill can say," Carola says.

"I made a clean, healthy break and forged my own life," Jill says. "Don't blame me because you didn't."

"You ran away," Carola says.

"I didn't owe Daddy anything."

"When parents take care of you, support you, love you for years, you don't owe them anything? That doesn't work for me, I'm sorry."

"I just think you have to ask yourself something, Carola," Gretchen says. "When Mom got sick, did you stick around because she and Daddy needed you or because you needed them?"

Carola's mouth opens slightly. "Just what do you mean by that?" she asks.

"I don't think they needed you nearly as much as you needed them to need you. I think in some ways they would have been better off if you'd gone and made your own life. I'm sorry to be so blunt, Carola, but you asked for it."

Now Carola stands up, kicks her chair away. "Oh, damn you," she says. "Damn you, damn you. You were hardly even there."

"Don't blame us for leading our own lives," Jill says.

"Don't tell me I didn't have a life," Carola says. "It *was* my life. It had to be. Just because I didn't abandon my mother doesn't mean I wasn't alive."

"No one's saying that, Carola," Jill says.

"I really think we've talked about this long enough," Gretchen says. "I really don't think this is very productive."

"Well, in that case, let's all bow to Her Highness and never say another word," Carola says.

"I didn't start it."

"Yes. Of course. I start everything, don't I?"

Gretchen rubs her eyes. "Why are you doing this, Carola?" she asks wearily.

"Because you're talking about my life. You've made it easy for yourself, but you can't tell me I'm invalid. You just can't."

"No one's saying that, Carola," Jill says. "We're saying that you made a choice. We made choices, too."

"You have to accept our lives if you want us to accept yours," Gretchen says. "You have to respect what we chose."

"Excuse me," Donna Lee says, pushing her chair away and walking out of the room. Jill looks over her shoulder.

Carola sits down again, slumping in her chair. There are tears in her eyes. "That's what you can't understand," she says. "Maybe for you, but for me there never was a choice."

The first time Gretchen visited her mother in the hospital, it was in response to a call from Carola. "She may be dying," Carola said flatly—something of an exaggeration, Gretchen found out later. Her mother lay in bed, her weight dropping, her hair falling. The TV ran all day—cartoons, game shows, Mike Douglas, the news. Gretchen flew out on a Friday from California and found Carola in the room, sitting by the bed, crossing and uncrossing her legs. Her father was out getting something to eat. Earlier, Carola had managed to sneak her mother's dog into her room for a visit, and what Gretchen remembers most vividly is that the room smelled of dog—a much more pleasant smell, she thought, than the antiseptic odor she usually associated with hospital rooms. Their mother asked Carola to go to the hospital gift shop and buy her some magazines and eye make-up. Carola was immediately off, grateful to have a purpose. Then her mother beckoned Gretchen closer to her.

"I don't know what to do," she said. "Carola's driving me crazy. She's here every minute. I have to pretend I'm better, just to keep her from feeling guilty. Things are bad enough. I just want her out of here."

"Have you asked Daddy to talk to her?" Gretchen said.

"Yes, yes. He keeps putting it off. She doesn't realize that this has nothing to do with her. It's between me and your father. It's our business, not hers."

What friends of theirs would say, for years afterward, was that their mother used her sickness to keep a hold on him. Of course, it wasn't that simple. Gretchen is convinced that there was a bond—thin as a wire but incredibly tough—that held her parents together. Perhaps it was this bond that Carola had imposed upon. That night, her father finally had a talk with Carola. She stormed out of the house, red-eyed, screaming, "You're not being fair!" Her father followed her to the door, calling her name. Years earlier, he had demanded their dedication, when the number of business trips he took suddenly doubled and their mother started to cry, spontaneously, whenever she did the dishes. He had said, "I'd like you to stick around the house while I'm away, keep your mother company." Only Carola heeded his request, never went out on dates. And now, suddenly, with that generation gone, she is thrown on her own. Though Gretchen has suffered through depression and worry, real pain is something she has rarely felt. Her lack of empathy disturbs her—a sort of dull ache. She knows it is nothing compared to what Carola must feel.

There was another confrontation, two months to the day after their mother's death. Gretchen's father had called the daughters together, in his office, to inform them of his plans to remarry. They sat in chairs in front of his desk, and he stood stiffly and would not look at them. "I'm planning to be married," he said. "To Eleanor Manley. She's been a dear friend for years, and a great comfort. I know this may be hard for you to accept, but I've made my decision. We'll be married in two weeks."

"Mother died so recently," Gretchen said. "Are you sure this is wise?"

He looked at them. "I feel no need to justify this course of action to you," he said. "It's my decision, not yours."

Gretchen clutched her chair, holding herself together against his attack. Jill began to button her coat. Only Carola's eyes narrowed in anger. "How long have you been involved with her?" she asked.

He cracked his knuckles. "For quite some time," he said. "Before your mother's death, but she never knew."

"She knew," Carola said.

"This is none of your business, Carola," their father said.

Jill went back to New York that afternoon. Gretchen and Carola stayed in his house, avoiding him and each other. The house no longer seemed theirs. When Gretchen woke up the next morning, Carola was already gone.

* * *

I'd better go talk to her. Someone has to," Gretchen says now to Leonard. They are sitting in the living room, alone. She gets up; Leonard watches her in silence, unsure of what to say or do.

There is a fragrant smell of shampoo in Carola's room. She is sitting on the bed in her bathrobe, a towel wrapped around her head. Gretchen sits down next to her.

"I've decided to go back to New York before the week's over," Carola says. "I have things to do."

"Fine," Gretchen says. "We can finish up here. It's more of a vacation for us."

"Thanks."

"I wanted to apologize," Gretchen says.

"Of course, you know, you're right," Carola says. "About everything. About Mom and Dad. But I'm still angry. To move away—to move to New York, and find that apartment and that job, and keep them—you can't know how hard it was for me just to sustain my life."

"You're right," Gretchen says. "I can't know. I only wish I could."

When she was a teenager, Donna Lee liked to become the confidante of girls with boyfriends, so that after the boyfriends left, as they always did, the girls would cry on her shoulder and she could embrace them. It wasn't until years later that she realized what she was doing—contriving intimacy, setting herself up to be let down. Love is still a contrivance for Donna Lee, a yearning for Jill to trust her, to touch her unexpectedly in sleep. She fully expects Jill to forget her at any moment.

"I want to leave," Donna Lee says to Jill after the scene at dinner. "I feel lost."

"I'll leave with you, then," Jill says.

Donna Lee shakes her head, unable to keep from smiling in gratitude. "You should stay," she says.

"This happens whenever I see them. They badger me about running away until I do it. Besides, I have other priorities. I have you to think of."

"Don't worry about me," Donna Lee says, amazed that she could be someone worth thinking of.

In the morning, Jill and Donna Lee are standing on the front porch, packed and ready to go.

"Before you leave," Leonard says to Jill, "let me just ask you one thing. What does it do for you, that horse game?"

Jill smiles. "Let's call it my alternative to the nuclear-family dynamic."

"I see," Leonard says. He laughs and claps his hands. Gretchen smiles at him as if she were his mother. Soon Jill and Carola will be gone; it will be her job to finish the cleaning out. She can be devastated, or she can go about it with a healthy contempt. For what remains in this house is a history about which she can hardly be nostalgic, and memories she would like to move beyond. Perhaps now she can sort through her father's belongings with that blunt dispassion which is the essence of revenge. Perhaps she, too, can be cruel.

"Have a nice trip," Leonard says. "Come visit us in California." And Carola, leaning against the wall of the house, waves, thinking that if she were on that desert island she would not write a word on the piece of paper. She would invent an alphabet of folding—an impermanent origami language that would mean nothing to anyone but her. It's her secret answer; she's sure none of the others have thought of it.

how to hurt each other. The memory's precious, but look what it's given rise to, look at yourselves now."

They are walking again, away from the beach, back toward Nathan's parents' house. Andrew has his hands in his pockets, and keeps his eyes on the ground in front of him. "Celia," he says, "there's something you've got to understand about me and Nathan. He taught me things."

"Taught you what?"

"Growing up a fag is a strange thing. You never learn about boys' bodies because you're afraid of what you will feel and you never learn about girls' bodies because you're afraid of what you won't feel. And so the first time you sleep with someone, it's like the first time you've ever noticed a body. I watched everything. I remember I was amazed to see the way his diaphragm moved up and down when he slept because I'd never watched anyone sleep before. And for showing me that, because of that, I'll always love him, even if he acts the way he does. I'll never forget the way he looked, sleeping."

They keep walking. Celia doesn't say anything.

"It's because of that," Andrew says, after a few seconds, "that he'll always have an advantage on me. You know what I was just remembering? How that whole summer we stayed in *pensiones*, and usually there were two single beds in the rooms we were given. And in the morning, Nathan always insisted we unmake the bed we hadn't slept in. And I always assumed, and he always assumed, that the unslept-in bed was mine."

They are in the garden now. Celia looks at the tilled earth beneath her feet, raw end-of-season, everything picked. No sign of Nathan.

"Oh, Celia," Andrew says, "this is mean of me."

"What?"

"It's cruel of me. It must make you feel like you aren't a part of it. But you are. You're very dear to us both."

"You sound like I'm your adopted child," Celia says.

"I'm sorry. I don't mean to. It's just—well, I think you should know. Nathan's always thought you were in love with him on some level, and that's why you've stuck around with us."

Celia looks up at him, startled, and her eyes narrow. She tells herself that she knows what he is doing. He is trying to get her on his side. Nothing unusual. Even so, the revelation, which is no revelation at all, hits her hard, in the stomach.

Dedicated

Celia is treading the lukewarm blue water of Nathan's parents' swimming pool. It is a cloudless Sunday in late June, the sun high and warm. She is watching the shadows which the waves she makes cast on the bottom of the pool—pulses of light and darkness whose existence is frenzied and brief, so different from the calm, lapping waves they reflect. Celia is at the center. The waves radiate out from where she treads, her arms and legs moving as instinctively as those of a baby held up in the air. Near the French doors to the library, Nathan and Andrew, her best friends, are dancing to a song with a strong disco beat and lyrics in German which emanates from a pair of two-foot-high speakers at either end of the library. The speakers remind Celia of the canvas bases her mother uses for her macramé wall hangings, but she knows that in spite of their simplicity, or because of it, they are worth thousands of dollars each, and represent a state-of-the-art technology. Nathan has told her this several times in the course of the weekend; he worries that she or Andrew might knock one of the speakers over, or carelessly topple a precious vase, or spill Tab on one of the leather sofas. They are not rich, he tells them jokingly; they do not know about these things. (The expensiveness of his parents' house is, by both necessity and design, easy to overlook, but Celia's eye for what she does not have has already rooted out the precious, notices that there are fresh bowls of roses in every room and that the gray parachute-cloth sofas are actually made of silver silk.)

The song changes. "Oh, I love this," Andrew says. He is an enthusiastic and uncontrolled dancer. He twists and jolts, and lunges forward accidentally, nearly colliding with one of the speakers. "Will you be careful?" Nathan shouts, and Andrew jumps back onto the patio. "Relax," he says. "I'm not going to break anything."

Celia kicks her legs, pulls her neck back, and gracefully somersaults into the water; suddenly the music is gone, Nathan and Andrew are gone, though she can see their distorted reflections above the pool's surface. She breathes out a steady stream of bubbles, pulls herself head over heels, and emerges once again, sputtering water. The music pounds. They are still fighting. "Andrew, if you don't calm down," Nathan says, "I'm going to turn off the music. I swear."

"Go to hell," Andrew says, and Celia takes another dive, this time headfirst, pulling herself deep into the pool's brightness. She can hear nothing but the sound of the pool cleaning itself—a wet buzz. When she reaches the bottom, she turns around and looks up at the sun refracted through the prisms of the water. She is striped by bars of light. She would stay underwater a long time, but soon she's feeling that familiar pressure, that near-bursting sensation in her lungs, and she has to push off the bottom, swim back up toward the membrane of the water's surface. When she breaks through, she gulps air and opens her eyes wide. The music has been turned off, Andrew is gone, and Nathan is sitting on the chaise next to the pool, staring at his knees.

"You were sitting on the bottom of the pool," he says to Celia.

"What happened? Where's Andrew?" she asks, wiping the chlorine off her lips.

"He stormed off," Nathan says. "Nothing unusual."

"Oh," Celia says. She looks at her legs, which move like two eels under the water. "I wish I knew what to tell you," she says.

"There's nothing to tell."

Celia keeps her head bowed. Her legs seem to be rippling out of existence, swimming away with the tiny waves.

Celia has spent every free moment, this weekend, in the water. She lusts after Nathan's tiled swimming pool, and the luminous crystal liquid which inhabits it. In the water, Celia's body becomes sylphlike, a floating essence, light; she can move with ease, even with grace. On land, she lumbers, her body is heavy and ungainly and must be covered with dark swatches of fabric, with loose skirts and saris. Celia is twenty-three years old, and holds the position of assistant sales director at a publishing company which specializes in legal textbooks. Of course, Nathan and Andrew always encourage her to quit her job and apply for a more creative position somewhere, to move downtown and leave behind her tiny apartment and terrible neighborhood. But Andrew is blessed, and Nathan is rich. They don't understand that things like that don't work out so easily for other people.

Here are Andrew and Nathan, as someone who hasn't known them for very long might see them: blond boy and dark boy, WASP and Jew, easy opposites. They work for rival advertising companies, but work seems to be just about the only thing they don't fight about. Nathan has dark, pitted skin, curly hair, a face always shadowed by the beginnings of a beard, while Andrew is fine-boned and fair, with a spindly, intelligent nose, and a body which in another century might have been described as "slight." He likes to say that he belongs in another century, the nineteenth, in the tea-drinking circle of Oscar Wilde; Nathan is invincibly devoted to present-day. They live on opposite poles of Manhattan—Nathan on the Lower East Side, Andrew in an East Ninety-sixth Street tenement on the perilous border of Harlem. From his window, Andrew can see the point where the ground ruptures and the train tracks out of Grand Central emerge into open air. Three blocks down Park Avenue he can see Nathan's parents' apartment building. Sometimes he runs into Nathan's mother at D'Agostino's, and they chat about the price of tomatoes, and Nathan's mother, who knows nothing, tells Andrew that he really must come to dinner sometime. Publicly, they are ex-lovers and enemies; privately (but everyone guesses) current lovers and (occasionally) friends. As for Celia, she floats between them, suspended in the strange liquid of her love for them—a love, she likes to think, that dares not speak its name.

That is what they look like to their friends from work, to the people they eat dinner with and sleep with, to all those acquaintances who find them interesting and likeable, but have other concerns in their lives.

And what, Celia wonders now, floating in the pool, is she doing here this weekend, when she has sworn time and again never to travel alone with them anywhere, not even to a restaurant? She always ends up in the middle of their battleground, the giver of approval, the spoils which they fight over, forget, and abandon. She tells herself she is here because it is over a hundred degrees in Manhattan, because her super has confided that the old woman across the hall from her apartment hasn't opened the door for days, and he's getting worried. She tells herself she is here because Nathan's parents are in Bermuda, the maid is on vacation, there is the swimming pool and the garden with fresh basil growing in it. And it's true, they've had a good time. Friday, sticky with Penn Station grime, they walked along the beach, ran in the tide, let the dry, hot wind blow against their faces. Saturday, they went into East Hampton, and looked at all the pretty people on the beach, and Celia decided it really wasn't all that surprising that those people should be rich and happy, while she was poor and miserable. They ate salad and watched a rerun of *The Love Boat*, and then Nathan and Andrew tucked Celia into Nathan's parents' big bed and disappeared together to another part of the house. She closed her eyes and cursed herself for feeling left out, for being alone, for having come out here in the first place. She tried, and failed, to imagine what they looked like making love. She tried to hear them. Now, Sunday morning, they have begun fighting because the fact that they still sleep together is a source of shame to both of them. And why not? Even Celia is ashamed. She is not supposed to know that Nathan and Andrew still sleep together, but Andrew calls her every time it happens. "I don't even like him," he tells Celia, his voice hoarse and strained. "But he has this power over me which he has to keep reasserting for the sake of his own ego. Well, no more. I'm not going to give in to him anymore." But even as he says these words, she can hear his voice grow hesitant with doubt, desire, love.

Celia swims to the pool ladder and hoists herself onto the deck. She has been in the water so long that her hands and feet have wrinkled and whitened. She wraps a towel around herself, suddenly ashamed of how her thighs bounce out of water, lies down on an empty chaise, and picks up a magazine called *Army Slave* from the patio table between her and Nathan. Andrew bought the magazine as a belated birthday present for Nathan, but neither of them has shown much interest in it this weekend. Now Celia thumbs through the pages—a man in green fatigues sitting on a bunk bed, clutching his groin; then a few shots of the man fornicating with another man, in officer's garb. In the last pages, a third figure shows up, dressed in leather chaps, and looks on from the sidelines. "Do you like it?" Nathan asks. "Does it turn you on?"

"I don't understand what's so erotic about army bases and locker rooms," Celia says. "I mean, I suppose I understand that these are very male places. But still, they're very anti-gay places. I mean, do you find this erotic? Did you find locker rooms erotic when you were growing up? And this guy in the leather—"

Nathan thrusts out his hips and purses his lips. "Oh, don't let's talk about whips and leather. Let's talk about Joan Crawford!" He makes little kissing gestures at Celia.

"Be serious," Celia says. "I was wondering because I want to know, to understand, genuinely."

"From a sociological perspective?" Nathan asks, returning to a normal posture.

"You could call it that," Celia says.

"I'll tell you this," Nathan says. "When draft registration was reintroduced, I saw a magazine with a picture on the cover of it of this very big hairy guy in a torn-up army uniform, staring out at you very lewdly. And underneath him it said, 'The Gay Community salutes the return of the military draft.' It was really very funny."

Celia's eyes light up. "Oh, that's great!" she says. "That's reclamation!"

Nathan doesn't respond, so she returns to the magazine. She picks up a pencil from the table and starts to scribble something in the margin when Andrew appears, seemingly from nowhere, before her and Nathan. "I'm mad," he says. "But I'm not going to play your stupid game and just run away and hide out and sulk. I want to face things."

"Andrew," Nathan says, "explain to Celia why that magazine is a turn-on. Note I do not use the word 'erotic.' "

"Oh, Christ, Celia," Andrew says, "I can't talk about that with you."

"I should've figured you'd be prudish about things like this when I found out you slept in pajamas," Celia says.

"Andrew doesn't want to spoil the integrity of his double life," Nathan says. "He doesn't want you to know that though by day he is your average preppie fashion-conscious fag, by night he goes wild—leather, cowboy hats, water sports. You name it, he's into it."

"Speak for yourself," Andrew says. "You're the one with the double life." He glances significantly at the pool.

"This isn't sociology. This isn't objective curiosity," Celia says. "You should know that by now."

They both look at her, puzzled. She closes her eyes. The sun beats down, and Celia imagines that the temperature has risen ten degrees in the last ten minutes. She opens her eyes again. Andrew has sat down on the end of Nathan's chaise and is berating him.

In a single, swift lunge, Celia pulls herself up and hurls herself into the water.

Celia, Nathan, and Andrew have known each other since their freshman year in college, when they were all in the same introductory English class. For most of that year, however, Nathan and Andrew recognized each other only as "Celia's other friend"; they had no relationship themselves. She recalls the slight nausea she experienced the day when she learned Nathan was gay. Up until that point, she had never known a homosexual, and she felt ashamed for having liked him, shyly as she did, so shyly that she phrased her feelings like that: "I like him," she confided to her roommate, who played varsity hockey. Celia felt ashamed as well for not having known better, and she feared her naïve affection might seem like an insult to Nathan, and turn him against her. Nathan was something new to Celia; she idolized him because he had suffered for being different, and because his difference gave him access to whole realms of experience she knew nothing of. Celia had never had many friends in school, had never been terribly popular, and this had always seemed just to her: She was fat and shy, and she was constantly being reprimanded for being fat and shy. She never considered that she might be "different" in the intense, romantic way Nathan was. She was simply alone, and where Nathan's aloneness was something that ennobled him, hers was something to regret.

At first, Nathan accepted Celia's gestures of affection toward him because she would listen—endlessly, it seemed—and talk to him, respond, as well. She was fascinated by the stories that he told her so willingly, stories about mysterious sexual encounters in men's rooms, adolescent fumblings in changing rooms. Her curiosity grew; she read every book and article she could find on the subject of homosexuality, including explicit diaries of nights spent cruising the docks and beaches, the bars and bathhouses of New York and L.A. and Paris. She read all of Oscar Wilde, and most of Hart Crane. She started to speak up more, to interrupt in class, and found in her underused vocal cords her mother's powerful, Bronx-born timbre, capable of instantly bringing crowds to attention. At their college, it was quite common for women in certain majors—women with long hair and purple clothes and a tendency to talk loudly and quickly and a lot—to spend most of their time in the company of gay men. Celia became the prime example of this accepted social role, so much so that some people started referring to her as the "litmus paper test," and joking that one had only to introduce her to a man to determine his sexual preference. It was not a kind nickname, implying that somehow she drove them to it, but Celia bore it stoically, and worse nicknames as well. She joked that she was the forerunner of a new breed of women who emitted a strange pheromone which turned men gay, and would eventually lead to the end of the human race. All the time she believed herself to be better off for the company she kept. What Celia loved in her gay friends was their willingness to commit themselves to endless analytical talking. Over dinner, over coffee, late at night, they talked and talked, about their friends, their families, about books and movies, about "embodying sexual difference," and always being able to recognize people in the closet. This willingness to talk was something no man Celia had ever known seemed to possess, and she valued it fiercely. Indeed, she could go on forever, all night, and invariably it would be Nathan who would finally drag himself off her flabby sofa and say, "Excuse me, Celia, it's four A.M. I've got to get to bed." After he left, she would lie awake for hours, unable to cease in her own mind the conversation which had finally exhausted him.

As their friendship intensified, she wanted still to probe more deeply, to learn more about Nathan. She knew that he (and, later, Andrew) had a whole life which had nothing, could have nothing to do with her—a life she heard about only occasionally, when she was brave enough to ask (the subject embarrassed Nathan). This life took place primarily in bars—mysterious bastions of maleness which she imagined as being filled with yellow light creeping around dark corners, cigarettes with long fingers of ash always about to crumble, and behind every door, more lewdness, more sexuality, until finally, in her imagination, there was a last door, and behind it—here she drew a blank. She did not know. Of course Nathan scoffed at her when she begged him to take her to a bar. "They're boring, Celia, totally banal," he said. "You'd be disappointed the same way I was." They were just out of college, and Nathan was easily bored by most things.

A few weeks later Andrew arrived in the city. The night he got in he and Celia went to the Village for dinner, and as they walked down Greenwich Avenue she watched his eyes grow wide, and his head turn, as they passed through the cluster of leather-jacketed men sporting together in front of Uncle Charlie's. The next night he asked Celia to accompany him to another bar he was scared to go to alone (he'd never actually been to a gay bar), and she jumped at the opportunity. At the steel doors of the bar, which was located on a downtown side street, the bouncer looked her over and put out his arm to bar their entrance. "Sorry," he said, "no women allowed"—pronouncing each syllable with dental precision, as if she were a child or a foreigner, someone who barely understood English. No women: There was the lure of the unknown, the unknowable. She could catch riffs of disco music from inside, and whiffs of a strange fragrance, like dirty socks, but slightly sweet. Here she was at the threshold of the world of the men she loved, and she was not being allowed in, because that world would fall apart, its whole structure of exclusive fantasy would be disrupted if she walked into it. "No women," the bouncer said again, as if she hadn't heard him. "It's nothing personal, it's just policy."

"When all the men you love can only love each other," Celia would later tell people—a lot of people—"you can't help but begin to wonder if there's something wrong with being a woman. Even if it goes against every principle you hold, you can't help but wonder." That night she stood before those closed steel doors and shut her eyes and wished, the way a small child wishes, that she could be freed from her loose skirts, her make-up and jewels, her interfering breasts and buttocks. If she could only be stripped and pared, made sleek and svelte like Nathan and Andrew, then she might slip between those doors as easily as the men who hurried past her that night, their hands in their pockets; she might be freed of the rank and untrustworthy baggage of femininity. But all she could do was turn away. Andrew remained near the door. "Well," he said. "Well, what?" Celia asked. "Would you mind terribly much if I went in myself, anyway?" he asked. She saw in his eyes that desperate, hounded look she recognized from the times they'd walked together, and passed good-looking men in the streets; that look she realized was probably on her face tonight as well. There was something behind those doors which was stronger than his love for her, much stronger. She didn't say anything, but walked away into the street, vowing never to go downtown again. On the subway, riding home, she watched a bag lady endlessly and meticulously rearrange her few possessions, and she decided that she would become bitter and ironic, and talk about herself in witticisms, and live alone always. "For most young women," she decided she'd say, "falling in love with a gay man was a rite of passage.

For me it became a career." Then she would take a puff—no, a drag—from her cigarette (she would of course have taken up smoking). And laugh. And toss it off.

Celia has made Andrew and Nathan eggs, and garnished each plate with a sprig of watercress and a little tuft of alfalfa sprouts. Now, balancing the plates on her arm, she walks toward the library, where they've retreated from the sun for the afternoon. When she enters the library, she sees Andrew leaning against the windowsill, and Nathan lying with his legs slung over the leather sofa, his head resting on the floor.

"Lunch," Celia says.

"Sundays are always horrible," Andrew says. "No matter what. Especially Sundays in summer."

Nathan does a backflip off the sofa, and makes a loud groaning noise. "Such depression!" he says. "What to do, what to do. We could go tea dancing! That's a lovely little Sunday afternoon tradition at the River Club. Thumping disco, live erotic dancers . . ."

"I'm not going back to the city one more minute before I have to," Celia says.

"Yes," Andrew says. "I'm sure Celia would just love it if we went off tea dancing."

Celia looks at him.

"I'm surprised at you, Andrew," Nathan says. "You usually enjoy dancing tremendously. You usually seem to have a really euphoric time dancing."

"Enough, Nathan," Andrew says.

"Yes, watching Andrew dance is like—it's like—how to describe it? I think we see in Andrew's dancing the complete realization of the mind-body dualism."

He stands up, walks around the sofa, and hoists himself over its back, resuming his upside-down position. "The body in abandon," Nathan continues. "Total unself-consciousness. Nothing which has anything to do with thought."

Celia gives Nathan a glance of disapproval. It is unnecessary; Andrew is on the defensive himself today. "I find your hypocrisy laughable," he says. "One minute you're telling me, 'Why don't you just stop analyzing everything to death?' and the next you're accusing me of not thinking. Get your attacks straight, Nathan."

"Ah," Nathan says, lifting up his head and cocking it (as best he can) at Andrew, "but I'm not criticizing your dancing, Andrew! I'm just extrapolating! Can you imagine what it would be like to never, ever think, really? I think it would be wonderful! You'd just sort of trip along, not particularly enjoying yourself but never having a bad time, either! Never feeling anguish or jealousy—too complicated, too tiring. I know people who are really like that. You see, Celia, Andrew thinks I'm dishonest. He thinks I run scared from the full implications of my sexual choice. He would like my friends, the Peters. Lovers, Celia. They're both named Peter, and they live together, but they're completely promiscuous, and if one has an affair, the other isn't bothered. Peter just has to tell Peter all about it and it's as if Peter's had the affair, too. But they're happy. They've fully integrated their gayness into their lives. Isn't that what we're supposed to do, Andrew?"

He hoists himself up, and sits down again on the sofa, this time normally.

"Don't be ridiculous," Andrew says. "People like that aren't even people."

Celia, sitting cross-legged on the floor, has finished her eggs. Now she reaches for Nathan's plate and picks the watercress off it. Nathan has eaten only a few spoonfuls. At restaurants, Celia often finds herself picking food off other people's plates, completely unintentionally, as if she's lost control over her eating.

Nathan, his head right side up, is humming the tune to the Pete Seeger song "Little Boxes." Now he glances up at Celia. "Shall we sing, my dear?" he asks.

"You can," she says. "I don't ever want to sing that song again."

Nathan sings:

"Little faggots in the Village,
And they're all made out of ticky-tacky,
Yes, they're all made out of ticky-tacky,
And they all look just the same.
There's a cowboy and a soldier and a UCLA wrest-i-ler,
And they're all made out of ticky-tacky,
And they all look just the same."

Andrew bursts out laughing. "That's funny," he says. "When did you make that up?"

"*I* made it up," Celia says. "Walking down the street one night." She smiles, rather bitterly, remembering the evening they walked arm in arm, very drunk, past Uncle Charlie's Downtown and sang that song. Nathan suddenly became very self-conscious, very guilty, and pulled away from Celia. He had a sudden horror of being mistaken for half of a heterosexual couple, particularly here, in front of his favorite bar. "Just remember," he had said to Celia. "I'm not your boyfriend."

"Why do I even speak to you?" Celia had answered. It was right after Andrew had abandoned her outside that other bar. That summer Andrew and Nathan, singly and collectively, stood her up at least fourteen times; twice Nathan, who was living at his parents' place, asked to use her apartment to meet people and she let him. She didn't think she was worth more than that. She was fat, and she was a litmus test. The only men she cared about were gay, and she didn't seem to know many women. She was Typhoid Celia. But finally she got angry, one Sunday, when she was at Jones Beach with Andrew. "Answer me this," she said to him, as they settled down on that stretch of the beach which is the nearly exclusive domain of Puerto Rican families. Andrew wasn't even looking at her; he couldn't keep his head from pulling to the left, straining to catch a glimpse of the gay part of the beach, where Celia had refused to sit. "Answer me this," Celia said again, forcing him to look at her. "A nice hypothetical question along the lines of, would you rather be blind or deaf? Why is it that no matter how much you love your friends, the mere possibility of a one-night stand with someone you probably won't ever see again is enough to make you stand them up, lock them out, pretend they don't exist when you pass them in the street? Why do we always so willingly give up a beloved friend for any lover?"

Even now she could see Andrew's head drifting just slightly to the left. Then he looked at her, pointed a finger at her face, and said, "There's a tea leaf lodged between your front teeth."

Celia doesn't realize until she's doing it that she is eating the last of the alfalfa sprouts off Andrew's plate. In horror, she throws them down. She slaps her hand and swears she won't do it again.

"When are your parents getting back?" Andrew asks.

"Not until tonight," Nathan says. "They're due in at seven."

"I spoke to my parents last week. They said they'd look for me in the TV coverage of the Pride March next week. It really touched me, that they'd say that. I didn't even have to mention that there was going to be a Pride March, they already knew."

Silence from Nathan. Celia gathers her hands into fists.

"Are you going to march this year, Nathan?"

Nathan stands up and walks over to the stereo. "No," he says. He puts a recording of Ravel on the turntable.

"That's too bad," Andrew says.

Celia considers screaming, insisting that they stop right here. Andrew knows that Nathan has never marched, will never march, in the annual Gay Pride Parade, ostensibly because he considers such public displays "stupid," but really because he lives in fear of his parents discovering his homosexuality. The last time she visited him here Nathan and his father sat in the library and talked about stocks. All night he was the perfect son, the obedient little boy, but on the train ride back he bit his thumbnail and would not speak. "Do you want to talk about it?" Celia asked him, and he shook his head. He would hide from them always. The happy relationship Andrew enjoys with his liberal, accepting parents is probably his most powerful weapon against Nathan, and the one which he withholds until the last minute, for the final attack.

"I'm carrying the alumni group banner in the march this year," Andrew says.

"Good," says Nathan.

"I really wish you'd come. You'd like it. Everyone will be there, and it's a lot of fun to march."

"Drop it, Andrew," Nathan says. "You know how I feel. I think that kind of public display doesn't do any good to anyone. It's ridiculous."

"It does the marchers a lot of good. It does the world a lot of good to see people who aren't ashamed of who they are."

"That's not who *I* am," Nathan says. "Maybe it's part of *what* I am. But not who." He turns and looks at the rose garden outside the window. "Don't you see," he says, "that it's a question of privacy?"

"In any battle for freedom of identity there can be no distinction between the private and the political."

"Oh, great, quote to me from the manual," Nathan says. "That helps. You know what's wrong with your party-line political correctness? Exactly what's wrong with your march. It homogenizes gay people. It doesn't allow for personal difference. It doesn't recognize that maybe for some people what's political correct is personally impossible, emotionally impossible. And for a politics which is supposed to be in favor of difference, it certainly doesn't allow for much difference among the 'different.' " His pronunciation of this word brings to their minds the voices of elementary school teachers.

"I think you're underselling politics, Nathan," Andrew says.

"Oh, just give me a break, Andrew, give me a break," Nathan says. "You know the only reason you ever found politics was because you had a crush on what's-his-name—Joel Miller—senior year. You had a huge crush on him and you were scared little Andrew and you were afraid to use the word 'gay.' I remember distinctly all the little ways you had of talking around that word. 'I'm joining the widening circle,' was all you could say to Celia. I remember that. 'The widening circle.' Where in hell you came up with that phrase is beyond me. And then there's hunky Joel Miller who'll only sleep with you if you wear a lavender armband and talk about 'pre-Stonewall' and 'post-Stonewall' every chance you get and suddenly our little Andrew is Mr. Big Political Activist. Jesus. You're right about your politics, about there being no separation between the private and the political."

He turns away from Andrew, clearly disgusted, picks up the jacket of the Ravel record, and begins to read the liner notes furiously.

"I can't stand this anymore," Celia says, then sits down on the sofa. Neither of them seems to have heard her. Nathan looks as if he might start crying any second—he cries easily—and a slick smile is beginning to emerge on Andrew's face.

"Nathan," he says, "do I detect a note of jealousy in your voice?"

"Go to hell," Nathan says, and storms out of the room.

"That's right, that's right, run away," says Andrew, marching after him to the library door. "Just go cry on Daddy's lap, why don't you, you just go tell him all about it."

"Stop it," Celia says. He turns around, and she is in front of him, her face wrathful. "Jesus Christ," she says, "you two are children. He overreacts to you, and the minute he's vulnerable, you just go for the balls, don't you? You just hit him right where it hurts?"

"Give me a break, Celia," Andrew says. "He's been asking for it, he's been taunting me all weekend. I'm sorry, but I'm not going to be his little punching bag, not anymore. I'm the stronger one. What just happened proves it."

"All it proves is that you can be as cruel to him as he can be to you," Celia says. "Big shit."

"He knows I'm sensitive about dancing, so he goes after me about it. He treats me like a heedless fool whose only purpose in life is to break all his parents' precious possessions. Well, I'm not a fool, Celia, I'm a hell of a lot better put-together person than he is."

"All the more reason why you shouldn't hurt him," Celia says. "You know all that stuff about the march, about his parents, you know what a sore subject that is for him. Not to mention Joel Miller."

"And all that time I was seeing Joel, did he say a word to me? Did he even talk to me? No! That time, Celia, he hurt me more than I could ever possibly have hurt him."

Celia laughs, then—a hard, shrill laugh. "Let's add up points," she says. "Let's see who's been hurt the most."

Nathan and Andrew became lovers in Florence, the summer after junior year. It happened only a few days before their scheduled rendezvous with Celia in Rome. That summer, like every summer, Nathan was a wanderer, a rich boy, one of hordes of backpack-bearing students trying to make the most of their Eurail passes. Andrew was in Europe under more impressive auspices; he had won a fellowship to study the influence of Mannerism on the Baroque, using as his chief example the statuary of several late-sixteenth-century Italian gardens. Celia's journey began later and ended earlier than her friends' because she didn't have much money, and had to get back to slave at a secretarial job in order to earn funds for her next year in college. She had never been to Europe before, and when she met her friends in Rome, she was exuberant with stories to tell them about her travels in England and France. In particular she wanted to tell them about a tiny town in Wales which had a wall and a moat, and how—big and uncoordinated as she was—she had climbed to the top of the old stone wall and marched its perimeter, as guardian knights had done in the thirteenth century. From the top of the wall, she could see the town—snug houses crammed together, and ruins of a castle, and the bay where fishermen caught salmon at high tide. And there, above it all, was Celia. She felt a rare self-confidence, and for once she liked the way she imagined she looked to other people—smart and self-assured, aware of how to travel right, able to drink in the pleasures of Europe without falling prey to its pitfalls and inconveniences. Indeed, arriving in Italy, Celia was so distracted by herself that it took her a few days to figure out what was going on between Nathan and Andrew. She talked and talked, and they sat across from her, their hands in front of them, and listened politely. Then, on the third day of their week together, the two of them insisted on keeping the double room they were sharing, and keeping Celia in an expensive single, even though a cheaper triple had opened up. She wondered why, and knew. That afternoon they walked out to the Catacombs, and on the way they played a game called In My Grandmother's Trunk. "In my grandmother's trunk," Nathan began, "I found an addlepated aardvark." Now it was Andrew's turn. "In my grandmother's trunk," he declaimed, "I found an addlepated aardvark and a bellicose bovine." Celia twisted her hair around her pinky and thought about it. "In my grandmother's trunk, I found an addlepated aardvark, a bellicose bovine, and a crenellated chrysanthemum," she said at last, smiling, proud of her answer. Nathan didn't even look at her, though he had laughed at Andrew's response. She realized they were in love as well as lovers then—recognizing, she supposes now, a certain secretiveness in the way they spoke, the way they listened for each other's answers, as if they were talking in code. They offered each other enervated earwigs and truncated turnips as if they were precious gifts, until the game became something which had no place for Celia. Andrew was not out of the closet, then, and as far as she knew, he and Nathan knew each other only through her. The meeting among the three of them had been arranged spontaneously over one of the dinners the three of them had together. "Let's say, July twenty-fourth, in front of the Pantheon," said Nathan, who knew Rome (he claimed) as well as he knew New York. Andrew and Celia, neither of whom had been to Europe before, both marveled that it was even possible to plan here, in the New World, for actual rendezvous in the strange Old World of Marcus Aurelius and Isabella Sforza and Eleanora de Toledo. And Nathan, too, enjoyed his status as expert, as experienced traveler. He would show them everything, he told them. He would be a marvelous tour guide. Falling asleep that night, Celia had thought of books she had read as a child in which trios of children went on adventures together in distant lands and on other worlds. But apparently, Nathan and Andrew had made some other plans without telling her, to meet earlier, and alone; apparently they had been seeing each other without her, and without her knowing; apparently, she realized, walking away from Rome, they were no longer hers, but each other's.

Celia finally confronted them over Orzata at a café on the Piazza

Navona. "I want you to know that I'm aware of what's going on," she said, "and I think we should talk about it." In fact, Nathan did all the talking, while Andrew wriggled, embarrassed and terrified. What Celia remembers most vividly about that afternoon is the overwhelming desire to bolt and run which took her over. She thought longingly of her town in Wales, and of the old, crumbling wall, and of herself atop it, and she wished she could transport herself back there, just for an instant, and regain—now, when she needed it—that rare feeling of freedom, of having surpassed the needy world.

She congratulated them (and thought, how stupid, as if it's an achievement); said she was happy for them (and thought, why am I so unhappy for myself?); agreed willingly to stay in her single room. But should she stay at all? Wouldn't it be better if she left, and left the two of them alone? No, never! Of course they wanted her, she must stay. So she did. A few days later, they visited the garden of the Villa d'Este at Tivoli. Andrew was doing his research, taking furious notes about certain bas-reliefs of men turning into fishes. Andrew read to Nathan from his notebook:

> It is the final act of reclamation that moss is destroying their faces. What's thematized here is an endless battle between nature and art. On one level, nature subjugates the men by turning them into lower forms of life, but really art is subjugating nature. The fishes' mouths are part of the drainage system—a technical wonder in the sixteenth century—which allows the fountain water to ceaselessly recirculate, by means of a number of pumps. Only now is nature taking its revenge, by destroying these fish faces, a little at a time, year after year. Wearing them down, growing them over with moss. Moss and wind and time. How long can Tivoli last?

Triumphantly he closed the blue notebook, which was printed with the insignia of their university. "Well?" he said.

"How poetic," said Nathan.

Andrew looked at him. "What do you mean?" he asked.

"I mean," Nathan said, "it's all lovely and sensitive, but I really can't believe you're making all these claims when you have no basis in historical fact. How can you know that what you say is going on is what was intended?"

"Historical fact," Andrew said, "is the historicist's fiction. I don't pretend I can know anyone's intention. I'm doing a *reading* of the garden."

It went on from there. Andrew accused Nathan of being a pedant, and Nathan accused Andrew of evading the rigors of scholarship. Already Celia understood more about them than they did about themselves: Andrew was impulsive, Nathan cautious; Andrew had a reason to be in Europe, Nathan had none (and was jealous). She found the matter altogether tedious, so she wandered away from them and fell in with a tour group from Oklahoma. The group was standing in front of the statue of Diana of Ephesus, her twelve breasts spouting water into an ancient urn, and the guide was talking about the Goddess being a symbol of natural fertility. "Some say she is related to Vishnu," he said solemnly, "the God with the thirteen hands."

"I'll bet her husband was the guy with the thirteen hands!" a woman with a beehive hairdo bellowed, and everyone roared, and Celia—standing among them—realized suddenly that she, too, was laughing, and that she had to leave.

She went the next morning. At the train station, Nathan and Andrew pleaded with her, begged her to stay, but she was decided. She got on an all-night train to Calais, and a ferry back to England, and another train to London. And after a single night in a hostel in Knightsbridge she took all the money she had left and bought a round-trip ticket to her beloved little town in Wales. Almost as soon as she got there she checked into a bed-and-breakfast and went to look at the old stone wall. There was a group of children no more than nine or ten years old being led around it, children from some industrial town in the Midlands, with Mohawk haircuts and dirty black vinyl jackets on. They were fighting with each other over candy, pretending to push each other off the wall. Then they started yelling things at her—obscenities she could hardly understand—and she hurriedly walked away and stood on the grass of the town green and closed her eyes. The air was fresh with the smell of recent rain, as well as the smell of biscuits baking nearby. An old man sitting on a stone bench hobbled over to her, and started speaking to her, but his Welsh accent was so strong that she thought he was speaking in another language, Finnish or Dutch. "Slower, please, slower," she said, until she finally realized he was asking her why she was crying. "Crying?" she said, and put her hands to her eyes, which were moist with tears.

Across a continent, Nathan and Andrew were not even thinking about her.

Although they've knocked repeatedly on his door, Nathan has apparently resolved not to acknowledge the presence of his friends this afternoon, and so, around three o'clock, Andrew and Celia take a walk to the beach. Celia is determined to spend most of the day outdoors, with or without Nathan. He has brooded too long, and she is losing patience with him. Andrew, on the other hand, cannot stop worrying about his friend; his brief triumph has left in its wake a weighty sense of guilt. "I guess I won," he tells Celia, "and it felt so good. But now I wish I'd lost. I don't like this feeling. You know, he's won practically every argument we've ever had."

"Don't be too upset about him," Celia says. "You know how he is. He broods. Anyway, I thought you were so happy to have put him in his place."

"But that's just it," Andrew says. "I'm not supposed to put him in his place. I'm not supposed to do that."

"Andrew, that's ridiculous," Celia says. "Things change in relationships, and maybe this means you're breaking out of the old pattern."

Andrew shakes his head violently, and pushes a mosquito out of his face. "It just doesn't work that way," he says. "For years I've had this idea of who he was and who I was. I knew I was more politically aware and had a healthier attitude toward sex and toward being gay. And I knew he was politically backward and closeted and conservative and torn apart because the fact that he liked to sleep with men contradicted everything he was raised to be. But all that time, he still had this power over me because he was the first person I slept with. He'll never let go of the fact that I was a scared little boy and he knew exactly what he was doing."

"I'm not so sure that's true," Celia says.

"But he did that for me, Celia. That first night we met in Florence, we were so scared, we both knew what we were there for, why we'd come, but we couldn't even seem to talk about it. Every gesture—every mention of anything having to do with being gay—seemed very courageous, because I still believed, on some level, that he'd be horrified if he found out I wanted to sleep with him, and say something like, 'How could you think I'd want to do that?' I mean, I really didn't know about

Nathan. I was going on instinct. And then, finally, we were both in the room in the *pensione*, and we were sitting on his bed, and he wouldn't do anything. We just sat there, and five minutes went by, and not a word. I couldn't move."

"Why?"

"You see, it was understood that he was more experienced. And that he would make the first move. I can't explain why, but it just was. And then he started coughing. Oh, God, I was scared. And I patted him on the back. And I just didn't move my hand away again.

"He said, 'You're very suave,' and then I hoisted my legs up on the bed—I was sitting and he was lying—and in the middle of getting up on the bed I got this terrible charley horse and started screaming and he just laughed. He bent me over and sort of wrenched my leg into shape again. And then—well, we made love. It was very greedy. No subtlety, no technique. But it was still very definitely 'making love,' not just sex." He laughs. "I remember there were these two drunk Americans who came into the room next to ours late that night from the Red Garter singing 'Superfreak.' And then around three one of them must have had a nightmare because he ran out into the hall and started screaming, and then crying. The other one tried to shut him up, but he just wailed and wailed. I remember exactly what his friend said. He said. 'Hey, man, chill out, don't freak.' Nathan was asleep, and we were wrapped around each other in an incredibly complicated way. I could feel all the hairs on his body, and his breath, and his heartbeat. I lay awake all night."

For several minutes they have been walking by the ocean without realizing it. The beach is almost empty except for a single sunbather, and a woman swimming laterally alongside the shore.

"The next day," Andrew says, "we ran into this girl I knew from my botany class the semester before. Charlotte Mallory, you remember her? We had dinner with her. Nathan had his leg pressed against mine under the table the whole time. It was a wonderful secret, something to look forward to, what we'd try that night, everything I had to learn."

He stops, smiles, and turns to face Celia. "This isn't fair of me, is it?" he says. "Imposing this all on you."

"Oh, don't start on that," Celia says. "Andrew, I just wonder why you and Nathan feel you have to keep this thing up. I mean, sure, it was nice once, but it always turns out like it did today. You two know too well

She looks away from him. "Why I've stuck around with you?" she says. "I've stuck around with you because I love you both. I'm devoted to you both. But if Nathan thinks I've just been panting after him all these years, he's flattering himself."

Andrew laughs, and she curses the slight timbre of resentment in her voice. She does not want to satisfy him by seeming recriminating. Yet she is thinking, why, after all? And she thinks, has it finally arrived, the day when she must confront herself? It has almost arrived many times, and there has always been a reprieve.

"He's just an egotist, I guess," Andrew says. "I mean, he thinks of himself as being like those thousand-dollar speakers of his parents. You have to be so careful around him, though God knows he's willing to hurt everyone else." He smiles affectionately. "Poor Nathan," he says. "You know where he is now? He's in his parents' bedroom, all curled up like a little kid, and he's just lying there, on that huge bed. That's where he goes when he feels small; somewhere where he is small."

They are at the front door now. Andrew turns and looks down at Celia, and suddenly he seems much taller than he did an hour ago. "Would you mind terribly if I went in to him for a little while?" he asks. "Just lie there with him? You can wait in the library, or by the pool. We'll all be ready to leave on the six forty-five."

Celia wraps her arms around her chest. "Sure," she says. "Fine." She does not look at Andrew, but at the maple trees, the vines twining up the sides of the house, the fragrant bunches of wisteria.

"I'll see you soon, then," Andrew says. Then there is the sound of his footsteps, the sound of the screen door as it slaps the house.

It is, Celia realizes, a kind of reprieve to be forgotten.

One night, late in the spring of senior year when they were both drunk on big, deceptive rum-and-fruit concoctions, Nathan told Celia the story of the first time he and Andrew slept together. He told it more cheerfully, and he did not mention the unused bed, though he dwelled with loving attention on the painful conversations they had had that night at dinner. "Our feet touched once," Nathan said, "and we both sort of jumped, as if we had given each other an electric shock. The second time our feet touched we just sort of left them there. I kept thinking, If he says anything, I could just say I thought I was resting my foot against a part of the table." And of course, Nathan wasn't asleep either. He remembered the boys next door singing "Superfreak," and the exact words with which the one comforted the other: "Hey, man, chill out, don't freak."

"The thing was," Nathan said, "I had Andrew convinced that I was Mr. Suave, very experienced. And it's true, I was more experienced than he was, but I was a nervous wreck anyway. I mean, being the seducer is a very different thing from knowing how to be seduced. Anyway, when we were alone in the room, I just decided to be brave. So I walked over to Andrew—he was unbuttoning his shirt—and I said, 'Why don't you let me do that?' He just froze. And then I kissed him."

He smiled. Celia knew better than to believe his version, recognizing even then that there were situations in which Nathan had to change the truth, to fit an image of himself which was just a bit wrong, a size too small or too large. After all, Andrew's affair with Joel Miller was at its apex. Nathan was terribly jealous, and it was important to him to prove himself to Celia, since she provided the only link between them. All that year Celia had been insisting that she wanted time to herself, time to pursue her own social life, but almost from the first day Andrew and Nathan wouldn't leave her alone. They wanted her to take sides in the fight they were having. The argument she had witnessed at the Villa d'Este, it seemed, had continued and festered after she left them. They bickered and lashed out at each other until finally, in Paris, Andrew packed his backpack in a fury and, in the middle of the night, stormed out of their little room in the Latin Quarter and boarded a train for Salzburg. By the time he arrived his anger had cooled, and he got on another train back to Paris, but when he got back to their *auberge*, Nathan had checked out and left no forwarding address.

Andrew was seized with panic, for now he was alone, absolutely alone, and there was no way he could find Nathan unless they happened upon each other by chance. Their itinerary was vague, but they had more or less planned to go to Cannes, so Andrew went there, and for two days walked the town tirelessly, scanning the streets and beaches for Nathan, planning what he'd say when he saw him, how aloof and distant he'd be and how he'd draw forgiveness from him. He found it hard to sleep alone again, and he couldn't get out of his nostrils that clean smell of soap and cologne and Nathan. But he never found Nathan in Cannes, or anywhere else in Europe. He continued traveling. By the time he got back to the States, his longing had hardened into something like hatred. And

Nathan was angry, too. It was hard to say, after all, who had abandoned whom first, who was to blame for what had happened.

At school they could hardly talk to each other, and so they talked to Celia instead, each giving her his version of what happened in Paris, and trying to win her over to his side. It was the only time, Celia reflected, that two men were rivals for her affections.

She told herself that her position was difficult. At first she had to make sure that Nathan never saw her with Andrew, or vice versa; they insisted on pumping her for information about one another. Then she began to arrange accidental meetings between them; they couldn't help but talk to each other—silence would have seemed too stilted a response, and they both prided themselves on their originality. Finally Andrew called Celia at three o'clock one morning, in tears; she couldn't understand what he was saying, but she managed to get him to tell her where he was, and she put on her coat and trudged out after him. It was just beginning to feel wintry out, and the sky was fringed with blue, as if it were dawn or dusk, and not the middle of the night; and since it was Sunday morning, and just after midterms, there were a few drunk football players still out, tromping around and causing trouble. Celia found Andrew sitting on the post of an old fence, wrapped in a coat he had bought at the Salvation Army, inert. She walked him back to her room, brewed some tea, and sat down in front of him, settling her still-gloved hands comfortably on his knees.

"Now," she said, "what's wrong?"

He started crying almost immediately; she let him cry, hugging him, until his body shivered and his teeth chattered, and, stuttering, he said exactly what she expected him to say: "He doesn't want me. And I love him."

Celia tracked Nathan down the next day, in the library. As soon as she mentioned Andrew's name, he shushed her, and pointed to his roommate—a tall young man smoking a pipe a few feet away—and hurried her off to a nearby cubicle. There he explained that he had had absolutely enough of Andrew's impulsiveness and silliness. To first simply run away in the middle of the night, stranding Nathan in Paris, and now, after two months, to show up suddenly in his room—thank God his roommate hadn't been home!—and start blubbering about not wanting to keep up the charade, about wanting to talk, about feeling hurt and intimidated by Nathan's behavior toward him in Paris. All of this,

naturally, was too much, considering it was Andrew who had all but abandoned Nathan, and to cap it off, he had to be loud about it. So Nathan told him to get out, it was over, he was making a mountain out of a molehill. Of course, even then, sitting in the library cubicle, Celia knew better than to take Nathan's version of things at face value. She realized Nathan was angry, but also, that he was frightened by Andrew's willingness to make a passionate display over matters Nathan felt best left in the bedroom. Where Nathan's skill lay in small, private insults, Andrew's great tactic was, and would always be, display. Probably Nathan realized that his friend was, as Celia would put it, about to shoot out of the closet like a cannonball, and this was more than his ingrained sense of propriety would allow him to accept. Fear lay behind that sense of propriety. Little Andrew, for all his innocence, was turning out to be the one thing Nathan never could be: He was turning out to be brave. So Nathan chose not to forgive Andrew his actions in Paris, and dropped him.

Shortly thereafter, people started seeing Andrew in the company of the famous activist Joel Miller, and the rest was fairly predictable. Joel Miller had done it before, with other apparently uncorruptible young men, and they always emerged from the affairs card-carrying members of the lavender left. Ostensibly, Nathan shouldn't have cared, but Celia could see what was in his eyes when he spied Andrew and Joel eating together in a dining hall. Nathan couldn't stay silent very long about it. "What's he doing spending so much time with that Joel Miller person?" he'd say to Celia, figuring she'd leak information, but Celia made it a new policy not to talk about Andrew with Nathan, or vice versa. Soon the affair became a public phenomenon, and Nathan's discomfort increased. He slunk away whenever he saw them, and usually left the parties they attended together. ("They walk into the room like they're the football captain and the homecoming queen," he'd tell Celia.) As for Andrew, he was in bliss; Joel was a genius; he wanted to marry Joel. Celia could afford to be happy for him, because she had her hands full taking care of Nathan, who showed up at her door at all hours. She pitied Nathan; he could never admit that he was terribly intimidated by Joel Miller, or that he might have loved Andrew. Still, she had him. He was there all the time—at her door, waiting for her in the dining hall, in the library. She controlled what he and Andrew heard about one another, and she, of course, knew everything about both of them. One night she would listen to Nathan's

anxieties, his claims to misery and loneliness; the next night, to Andrew's praises of the wonders of love, the transcendence of gender roles, and the lovely, dark hair which curled over Joel Miller's shoulder blades.

It did not occur to Celia until a long time later—when she was able to gain some perspective on that year, in which things had been the most intense between them—that her happiness with Nathan and Andrew depended on Nathan and Andrew being unhappy with each other.

Around dusk, Nathan and Andrew emerge from the house. They are dressed in different clothes from the ones they were wearing earlier, and they are talking animatedly, eagerly, occasionally laughing. As soon as she sees them, Celia closes her eyes. She is lying by the pool, the copy of *Army Slave* open on her lap, and all around her fireflies are exploding with light, crickets screeching. "Come on, Celia, get ready to go," Nathan says. She opens her eyes and he is leaning over her, smiling. "My parents may be back any second, and I don't want to be here when they arrive." He pats her knee, and heads back to the patio, where Andrew is waiting. "Oh," he says, turning around, "and don't forget to bring the magazine." She lifts up her head, but in the dusk light, she can just barely make out their faces. "I guess you're feeling better," she says.

"Yes," Nathan says. "Much better."

She nods, and gets up to pack her things. It is about a ten-minute walk to the train station, and when they get there, the platform is already full of tired-looking people in shorts, all yawning and opening up their newspapers. When the train pulls in, it's already crowded; there are no sets of three seats together. Andrew sits with Celia, and Nathan sits alone, two rows behind them, but the arrangement is entirely for her benefit. Something has happened between Nathan and Andrew this afternoon: They appear to have forgiven each other. Why else would they be thinking about her?

She lies back, watches the pleasurable journey from the scum of Penn Station to the beautiful Hamptons run backward; now they are in the famous suburbs of the Guyland (as Nathan calls it), now in the nether regions of Queens. When they pass the exact border between New York City and the rest of the world, Nathan cannot resist walking up to point it out to them.

Then they are in the tunnel under the East River, and under the famous city where they spend their lives.

They get off the train. Penn Station has no air-conditioning, and is packed with people. Celia wipes the sweat off her brow, and rearranges her bags between her legs. She will take the Broadway local to the Upper West Side, while Nathan and Andrew must walk across town to catch the East Side subway, and ostensibly ride it in opposite directions. She has no doubt but that they will spend tonight, and perhaps tomorrow night, together; and she wonders if they will eat dinner out, see a movie, talk about her, and shake their heads. It will last a few days; then, she is confident, they will fight. One of them will call her, or both of them will call her. Or perhaps they will decide to move in together, and never call her again.

"I've got to catch my train," Celia says, when it becomes clear that they're not going to invite her out with them. She offers them each her cheek to kiss as if to give her blessing. They look at her a little awkwardly, a little guiltily, and she can't believe they're acting guilty now, when it's been like this for so many years between them. Besides, there really isn't anything anyone can apologize for. Celia begins to walk away, and Nathan calls out her name. She turns, and he is next to her, a big smile plastered on his face. "You know," he says, "you're wonderful. When I write my book, I'm dedicating it to you."

She smiles back, and laughs. He said the same thing the day she left them at Termini station in Rome and boarded a train for Calais. All that night the couchette car in which she slept was added on and taken off of other strings of lit cars, passed among the major trains and in this way, like a changeling infant, carried singly to the coast. She shared a cabin with two Englishwomen on their way back from holiday and a Swiss man who was going to Liverpool to buy a spare part for his car. Like college roommates, the four of them lay in their bunk beds and talked late into the night. The wheels rumbled against the tracks, the train moved on; every minute she was closer to England. Then she fell asleep, wondering to herself what kind of book Nathan could ever possibly write.

A Place I've Never Been

I had known Nathan for years—too many years, since we were in college—so when he went to Europe I wasn't sure how I'd survive it; he was my best friend, after all, my constant companion at Sunday afternoon double bills at the Thalia, my ever-present source of consolation and conversation. Still, such a turn can prove to be a blessing in disguise. It threw me off at first, his not being there—I had no one to watch *Jeopardy!* with, or talk to on the phone late at night—but then, gradually, I got over it, and I realized that maybe it was a good thing after all, that maybe now, with Nathan gone, I would be forced to go out into the world more, make new friends, maybe even find a boyfriend. And I had started: I lost weight, I went shopping. I was at Bloomingdale's one day on my lunch hour when a very skinny black woman with a French accent asked me if I'd like to have a makeover. I had always run away from such things, but this time, before I had a chance, this woman put her long hands on my cheeks and looked into my face—not my eyes, my face—and said, "You're really beautiful. You know that?" And I absolutely couldn't answer. After she was through with me I didn't even know what I looked like, but everyone at my office was amazed. "Celia," they said, "you look great. What happened?" I smiled, wondering if I'd be allowed to go back every day for a makeover, if I offered to pay.

There was even some interest from a man—a guy named Roy who works downstairs, in contracts—and I was feeling pretty good about myself again, when the phone rang, and it was Nathan. At first I thought he must have been calling me from some European capital, but he said no, he was back in New York. "Celia," he said, "I have to see you. Something awful has happened."

Hearing those words, I pitched over—I assumed the worst. (And why not? He had been assuming the worst for over a year.) But he said, "No, no, I'm fine. I'm perfectly healthy. It's my apartment. Oh, Celia, it's awful. Could you come over?"

"Were you broken into?" I asked.

"I might as well have been!"

"Okay," I said. "I'll come over after work."

"I just got back last night. This is too much."

"I'll be there by six, Nathan."

"Thank you," he said, a little breathlessly, and hung up.

I drummed my nails—newly painted by another skinny woman at Bloomingdale's—against the black Formica of my desk, mostly to try out the sound. In truth I was a little happy he was back—I had missed him—and not at all surprised that he'd cut his trip short. Rich people are like that, I've observed; because they don't have to buy bargain-basement tickets on weird charter airlines, they feel free to change their minds. Probably he just got bored tooting around Europe, missed his old life, missed *Jeopardy!*, his friends. Oh, Nathan! How could I tell him the Thalia had closed?

I had to take several buses to get from my office to his neighborhood—a route I had once traversed almost daily, but which, since Nathan's departure, I hadn't had much occasion to take. Sitting on the Madison Avenue bus, I looked out the window at the rows of unaffordable shops, some still exactly what they'd been before, others boarded up, or reopened under new auspices—such a familiar panorama, unfolding, block by block, like a Chinese scroll I'd once been shown on a museum trip in junior high school. It was raining a little, and in the warm bus the long, unvarying progress of my love for Nathan seemed to unscroll as well—all the dinners and lunches and arguments, and all the trips back alone to my apartment, feeling ugly and fat, because Nathan had once again confirmed he could never love me the way he assured me he would someday love a man. How many hundreds of times I received that confirmation! And yet, somehow, it never occurred to me to give up that love I had nurtured for him since our earliest time together, that love which belonged to those days just past the brink of childhood, before I understood about Nathan, or rather, before Nathan understood about himself. So I persisted, and Nathan, in spite of his embarrassment at my occasional outbursts, continued to depend on me. I think he hoped that my feeling for him would one day transform itself into a more maternal kind of affection, that I would one day become the sort of woman who could tend to him without expecting anything in return. And that was, perhaps, a reasonable hope on his part, given my behavior. But: "If only," he said to me once, "you didn't have to act so crazy, Celia—" And that was how I realized I had to get out.

I got off the bus and walked the block and a half to his building—its façade, I noted, like almost every façade in the neighborhood, blemished by a bit of scaffolding—and, standing in that vestibule where I'd stood so often, waited for him to buzz me up. I read for diversion the now familiar list of tenants' names. The only difference today was that there were ragged ends of Scotch tape stuck around Nathan's name; probably his subletter had put his own name over Nathan's, and Nathan, returning, had torn the piece of paper off and left the ends of the tape. This didn't seem like him, and it made me suspicious. He was a scrupulous person about such things.

In due time—though slowly, for him—he let me in, and I walked the three flights of stairs to find him standing in the doorway, unshaven, looking as if he'd just gotten out of bed. He wasn't wearing any shoes, and he'd gained some weight. Almost immediately he fell into me—that is the only way to describe it, his big body limp in my arms. "Oh, God," he murmured into my hair, "am I glad to see you."

"Nathan," I said. "Nathan." And held him there. Usually he wriggled out of physical affection; kisses from him were little nips; hugs were tight, jerky chokeholds. Now he lay absolutely still, his arms slung under mine, and I tried to keep from gasping from the weight of him. But finally—reluctantly—he let go, and putting his hand on his forehead, gestured toward the open door. "Prepare yourself," he said. "It's worse than you can imagine."

He led me into the apartment. I have to admit, I was shocked by what I saw. Nathan, unlike me, is a chronically neat person, everything in its place, all his perfect furniture glowing, polished, every state-of-the-art fountain pen and pencil tip-up in the blue glass jar on his desk. Today, however, the place was in havoc—newspapers and old Entenmann's cookie boxes spread over the floor, records piled on top of each other, inner sleeves crumpled behind the radiator, the blue glass jar over-turned. The carpet was covered with dark mottlings, and a stench of old cigarette smoke and sweat and urine inhabited the place. "It gets worse," he said. "Look at the kitchen." A thick, yellowing layer of grease encrusted the stovetop. The bathroom was beyond the pale of my descriptive capacity for filth.

"Those bastards," Nathan was saying, shaking his head.

"Hold on to the security deposit," I suggested. "Make them pay for it."

He sat down on the sofa, the arms of which appeared to have been ground with cigarette butts, and shook his head. "There *is* no security deposit," he moaned. "I didn't take one because supposedly Denny was my friend, and this other guy—Hoop, or whatever his name was—he was Denny's friend. And look at this!" From the coffee table he handed me a thick stack of utility and phone bills, all unopened. "The phone's disconnected," he said. "Two of the rent checks have bounced. The landlord's about to evict me. I'm sure my credit rating has gone to hell. Jesus, why'd I do it?" He stood, marched into the corner, then turned again to face me. "You know what? I'm going to call my father. I'm going to have him sic every one of his bastard lawyers on those assholes until they pay."

"Nathan," I reminded, "they're unemployed actors. They're poor."

"Then let them rot in jail!" Nathan screamed. His voice was loud and sharp in my ears. It had been a long time since I'd had to witness another person's misery, a long time since anyone had asked of me what Nathan was now asking of me: to take care, to resolve, to smooth. Nonetheless I rallied my energies. I stood. "Look," I said. "I'm going to go out and buy sponges, Comet, Spic and Span, Fantastik, Windex. Everything. We're going to clean this place up. We're going to wash the sheets and shampoo the rug, we're going to scrub the toilet until it shines. I promise you, by the time you go to sleep tonight, it'll be what it was."

He stood silent in the corner.

"Okay?" I said.

"Okay."

"So you wait here," I said. "I'll be right back."

"Thank you."

I picked up my purse and closed the door, thus, once again, saving him from disaster.

But there were certain things I could not save Nathan from. A year ago, his ex-lover Martin had called him up and told him he had tested positive. This was the secret fact he had to live with every day of his life, the secret fact that had brought him to Xanax and Halcion, Darvon and Valium—all crude efforts to cut the fear firing through his blood, exploding like the tiny viral time bombs he believed were lying in wait, expertly planted. It was the day after he found out that he started talking about clearing out. He had no obligations—he had quit his job a few months before and was just doing free-lance work anyway—and so, he reasoned, what was keeping him in New York? "I need to get away from all this," he said, gesturing frantically at the air. I believe he really thought back then that by running away to somewhere where it was less well known, he might be able to escape the disease. This is something I've noticed: The men act as if they think the power of infection exists in direct proportion to its publicity, that in places far from New York City it can, in effect, be outrun. And who's to say they are wrong, with all this talk about stress and the immune system? In Italy, in the countryside, Nathan seemed to feel he'd feel safer. And probably he was right; he would feel safer. Over there, away from the American cityscape with its streets full of gaunt sufferers, you're able to forget the last ten years, you can remember how old the world is and how there was a time when sex wasn't something likely to kill you.

It should be pointed out that Nathan had no symptoms; he hadn't even had the test for the virus itself. He refused to have it, saying he could think of no reason to give up at least the hope of freedom. Not that this made any difference, of course. The fear itself is a brutal enough enemy.

But he gave up sex. No sex, he said, was safe enough for him. He bought a VCR and began to hoard pornographic videotapes. And I think he was having phone sex too, because once I picked up the phone in his apartment and before I could say hello, a husky-voiced man said, "You stud," and then, when I said "Excuse me?" got flustered-sounding and hung up. Some people would probably count that as sex, but I'm not sure I would.

All the time, meanwhile, he was frenzied. I could never guess what time he'd call—six in the morning, sometimes, he'd drag me from sleep. "I figured you'd still be up," he'd say, which gave me a clue to how he was living. It got so bad that by the time he actually left I felt as if a great burden had been lifted from my shoulders. Not that I didn't miss him, but from that day on my time was, miraculously, my own. Nathan is a terrible correspondent—I don't think he's sent me one postcard or letter in all the time we've known each other—and so for months my only news of him came through the phone. Strangers would call me, Germans, Italians, nervous-sounding young men who spoke bad English, who were staying at the YMCA, who were in New York for the first time and to whom he had given my number. I don't think any of them actually wanted to see me; I think they just wanted me to tell them which bars were good and which subway lines were safe—information I happily dispensed. Of course, there was a time when I would have taken them on the subways, shown them around the bars, but I have thankfully passed out of that phase.

And of course, as sex became more and more a possibility, then a likelihood once again in my life, I began to worry myself about the very things that were torturing Nathan. What should I say, say, to Roy in contracts, when he asked me to sleep with him, which I was fairly sure he was going to do within a lunch or two? Certainly I wanted to sleep with him. But did I dare ask him to use a condom? Did I dare even broach the subject? I was frightened that he might get furious, that he might overreact, and I considered saying nothing, taking my chances. Then again, for me in particular, it was a very big chance to take; I have a pattern of falling in love with men who at some point or other have fallen in love with other men. All trivial, selfish, this line of worry, I recognize now, but at that point Nathan was gone, and I had no one around to remind me of how high the stakes were for other people. I slipped back into a kind of women's-magazine attitude toward the whole thing: for the moment, at least, *I* was safe, and I cherished that safety without even knowing it, I gloried in it. All my speculations were merely matters of prevention; that place where Nathan had been exiled was a place I'd never been. I am ashamed to admit it, but there was even a moment when I took a kind of vengeful pleasure in the whole matter—the years I had hardly slept with anyone, for which I had been taught to feel ashamed and freakish, I now wanted to rub in someone's face: I was right and you were wrong! I wanted to say. I'm not proud of having had such thoughts, and I can only say, in my defense, that they passed quickly—but a strict accounting of all feelings, at this point, seems to me necessary. We have to be rigorous with ourselves these days.

In any case, Nathan was back, and I didn't dare think about myself. I went to the grocery store, I bought every cleaner I could find. And when

I got back to the apartment he was still standing where he'd been standing, in the corner. "Nate," I said, "here's everything. Let's get to work."

"Okay," he said glumly, even though he is an ace cleaner, and we began.

As we cleaned, the truth came out. This Denny to whom he'd sublet the apartment, Nathan had had a crush on. "To the extent that a crush is a relevant thing in my life anymore," he said, "since God knows, there's nothing to be done about it. But there you are. The libido doesn't stop, the heart doesn't stop, no matter how hard you try to make them."

None of this—especially that last part—was news to me, though Nathan had managed to overlook that aspect of our relationship for years. I had understood from the beginning about the skipping-over of the security payment, the laxness of the setup, because these were the sorts of things I would have willingly done for Nathan at a different time. I think he was privately so excited at the prospect of this virile young man, Denny, sleeping, and perhaps having sex, between his sheets, that he would have taken any number of risks to assure it. Crush: what an oddly appropriate word, considering what it makes you do to yourself. His apartment was, in a sense, the most Nathan could offer, and probably the most Denny would accept. I understood: You want to get as close as you can, even if it's only at arm's length. And when you come back, maybe, you want to breathe in the smell of the person you love loving someone else.

Europe, he said, had been a failure. He had wandered, having dinner with old friends of his parents, visiting college acquaintances who were busy with exotic lives. He'd gone to bars, which was merely frustrating; there was nothing to be done. "What about safe sex?" I asked, and he said, "Celia, please. There is no such thing, as far as I'm concerned." Once again this started a panicked thumping in my chest as I thought about Roy, and Nathan said, "It's really true. Suppose something lands on you—you know what I'm saying—and there's a microscopic cut in your skin. Bingo."

"Nathan, come on," I said. "That sounds crazy to me."

"Yeah?" he said. "Just wait till some ex-lover of yours calls you up with a little piece of news. Then see how you feel."

He returned to his furious scrubbing of the bathroom sink. I returned to my furious scrubbing of the tub. Somehow, even now, I'm always stuck with the worst of it.

Finally we were done. The place looked okay—it didn't smell anymore—though it was hardly what it had been. Some long-preserved pristineness was gone from the apartment, and both of us knew without saying a word that it would never be restored. We breathed in exhausted—no, not exhausted triumph. It was more like relief. We had beaten something back, yet again.

My hands were red from detergents, my stomach and forehead sweaty. I went into the now-bearable bathroom and washed up, and then Nathan said he would take me out to dinner—my choice. And so we ended up, as we had a thousand other nights, sitting by the window at the Empire Szechuan down the block from his apartment, eating cold noodles with sesame sauce, which, when we had finished them, Nathan ordered more of. "God, how I've missed these," he said, as he scooped the brown slimy noodles into his mouth. "You don't know."

In between slurps he looked at me and said, "You look good, Celia. Have you lost weight?"

"Yes, as a matter of fact," I said.

"I thought so."

I looked back at him, trying to re-create the expression on the French woman's face, and didn't say anything, but as it turned out I didn't need to. "I know what you're thinking," he said, "and you're right. Twelve pounds since you last saw me. But I don't care. I mean, you lose weight when you're sick. At least this way, gaining weight, I know I don't have it."

He continued eating. I looked outside. Past the plate-glass window that separated us from the sidewalk, crowds of people walked, young and old, good-looking and bad-looking, healthy and sick, some of them staring in at our food and our eating. Suddenly—urgently—I wanted to be out among them, I wanted to be walking in that crowd, pushed along in it, and not sitting here, locked into this tiny two-person table with Nathan. And yet I knew that escape was probably impossible. I looked once again at Nathan, eating happily, resigned, perhaps, to the fate of his apartment, and the knowledge that everything would work out, that this had, in fact, been merely a run-of-the-mill crisis. For the moment he was appeased, his hungry anxiety sated; for the moment. But who could guess what would set him off next? I steadied my chin on my palm, drank some water, watched Nathan eat like a happy child.

* * *

The next few weeks were thorny with events. Nathan bought a new sofa, had his place recarpeted, threw several small dinners. Then it was time for Lizzie Fischman's birthday party—one of the few annual events in our lives. We had known Lizzie since college—she was a tragic, trying sort of person, the sort who carries with her a constant aura of fatedness, of doom. So many bad things happen to Lizzie you can't help but wonder, after a while, if she doesn't hold out a beacon for disaster. This year alone, she was in a taxi that got hit by a bus; then she was mugged in the subway by a man who called her an "ugly dyke bitch"; then she started feeling sick all the time, and no one could figure out what was wrong, until it was revealed that her building's heating system was leaking small quantities of carbon monoxide into her awful little apartment. The tenants sued, and in the course of the suit, Lizzie, exposed as an illegal subletter, was evicted. She now lived with her father in one half of a two-family house in Plainfield, New Jersey, because she couldn't find another apartment she could afford. (Her job, incidentally, in addition to being wretchedly low-paying, is one of the dreariest I know of: proofreading accounting textbooks in an office on Forty-second Street.)

Anyway, each year Lizzie threw a big birthday party for herself in her father's house in Plainfield, and we all went, her friends, because of course we couldn't bear to disappoint her and add ourselves to her roster of worldwide enemies. It was invariably a miserable party—everyone drunk on bourbon, and Lizzie, eager to re-create the slumber parties of her childhood, dancing around in pink pajamas with feet. We were making s'mores over the gas stove—shoving the chocolate bars and the graham crackers onto fondue forks rather than old sticks—and *Beach Blanket Bingo* was playing on the VCR and no one was having a good time, particularly Nathan, who was overdressed in a beige Giorgio Armani linen suit he'd bought in Italy, and was standing in the corner idly pressing his neck, feeling for swollen lymph nodes. Lizzie's circle dwindled each year, as her friends moved on, or found ways to get out of it. This year eight of us had made it to the party, plus a newcomer from Lizzie's office, a very fat girl with very red nails named Dorrie Friedman, who, in spite of her heaviness, was what my mother would have called dainty. She ate a lot, but unless you were observant, you'd never have noticed it. The image of the fat person stuffing food into her face is mythic: I know from experience, when fat you eat slowly, chew methodically, in order not to draw attention to your mouth. Over the course of an hour I watched Dorrie Friedman put away six of those s'mores with a tidiness worthy of Emily Post, I watched her dab her cheek with her napkin after each bite, and I understood: This was shame, but also, in some peculiar way, this was innocence. A state to envy.

There is a point in Lizzie's parties when she invariably suggests we play Deprivation, a game that had been terribly popular among our crowd in college. The way you play it is you sit in a big circle, and everyone is given ten pennies. (In this case the pennies were unceremoniously taken from a huge bowl that sat on top of Lizzie's mother's refrigerator, and that she had upended on the linoleum floor—no doubt a long-contemplated act of desecration.) You go around the circle, and each person announces something he or she has never done, or a place they've never been—"I've never been to Borneo" is a good example—and then everyone who has been to Borneo is obliged to throw you a penny. Needless to say, especially in college, the game degenerates rather quickly to matters of sex and drugs.

I remembered the first time I ever played Deprivation, my sophomore year, I had been reading Blake's *Songs of Innocence* and *Songs of Experience*. Everything in our lives seemed a question of innocence and experience back then, so this seemed appropriate. There was a tacit assumption among my friends that "experience"—by that term we meant, I think, almost exclusively sex and drugs—was something you strove to get as much of as you could, that innocence, for all the praise it received in literature, was a state so essentially tedious that those of us still stuck in it deserved the childish recompense of shiny new pennies. (None of us, of course, imagining that five years from now the "experiences" we urged on one another might spread a murderous germ, that five years from now some of our friends, still in their youth, would be lost. Youth! You were supposed to sow your wild oats, weren't you? Those of us who didn't—we were the ones who failed, weren't we?)

One problem with Deprivation is that the older you get, the less interesting it becomes; every year, it seemed, my friends had fewer gaps in their lives to confess, and as our embarrassments began to stack up on the positive side, it was what we *had* done that was titillating. Indeed, Nick Walsh, who was to Lizzie what Nathan was to me, complained as the game began, "I can't play this. There's nothing I haven't done." But Lizzie, who has a naive faith in ritual, merely smiled and said, "Oh come on, Nick. No one's done *everything*. For instance, you could say, 'I've never been to Togo,' or 'I've never been made love to simultaneously by twelve Arab boys in a back alley on Mott Street.'"

"Well, Lizzie," Nick said, "it is true that I've never been to Togo." His leering smile surveyed the circle, and of course, there *was* someone there—Gracie Wong, I think—who had, in fact, been to Togo.

The next person in the circle was Nathan. He's never liked this game, but he also plays it more cleverly than anyone. "Hmm," he said, stroking his chin as if there were a beard there, "let's see . . . Ah, I've got it. I've never had sex with anyone in this group." He smiled boldly, and everyone laughed—everyone, that is, except for me and Bill Darlington, and Lizzie herself—all three of us now, for the wretched experiments of our early youth, obliged to throw Nathan a penny.

Next was Dorrie Friedman's turn, which I had been dreading. She sat on the floor, her legs crossed under her, her very fat fingers intertwined, and said, "Hmm . . . Something I've never done. Well—I've never ridden a bicycle."

An awful silence greeted this confession, and then a tinkling sound, like wind chimes, as the pennies flew. "Gee," Dorrie Friedman said, "I won big that time." I couldn't tell if she was genuinely pleased.

And as the game went on, we settled, all of us, into more or less parallel states of innocence and experience, except for Lizzie and Nick, whose piles had rapidly dwindled, and Dorrie Friedman, who, it seemed, by virtue of lifelong fatness, had done nearly nothing. She had never been to Europe; she had never swum; she had never played tennis; she had never skied; she had never been on a boat. Even someone else's turn could be an awful moment for Dorrie, as when Nick said, "I've never had a vaginal orgasm." But fortunately, there, she did throw in her penny. I was relieved; I don't think I could have stood it if she hadn't.

After a while, in an effort not to look at Dorrie and her immense pile of pennies, we all started trying to trip up Lizzie and Nick, whose respective caches of sexual experience seemed limitless. "I've never had sex in my parents' bed," I offered. The pennies flew. "I've never had sex under a dry-docked boat." "I've never had sex with more than one other person." "Two other people." "Three other people." By then Lizzie was out of pennies, and declared the game over.

"I guess I won," Dorrie said rather softly. She had her pennies neatly piled in identically sized stacks.

I wondered if Lizzie was worried. I wondered if she was thinking about the disease, if she was frightened, the way Nathan was, or if she just assumed death was coming anyway, the final blow in her life of unendurable misfortunes. She started to gather the pennies back into their bowl, and I glanced across the room at Nathan, to see if he was ready to go. All through the game, of course, he had been looking pretty miserable—he always looks miserable at parties. Worse, he has a way of turning his misery around, making me responsible for it. Across the circle of our nearest and dearest friends he glared at me angrily, and I knew that by the time we were back in his car and on our way home to Manhattan he would have contrived a way for the evening to be my fault. And yet tonight, his occasional knowing sneers, inviting my complicity in looking down on the party, only enraged me. I was angry at him, in advance, for what I was sure he was going to do in the car, and I was also angry at him for being such a snob, for having no sympathy toward this evening, which, in spite of all its displeasures, was nevertheless an event of some interest, perhaps the very last hurrah of our youth, our own little big chill. And that was something: Up until now I had always assumed Nathan's version of things to be the correct one, and cast my own into the background. Now his perception seemed meager, insufficient: Here was an historic night, after all, and all he seemed to want to think about was his own boredom, his own unhappiness.

Finally, reluctantly, Lizzie let us go, and relinquished from her grip, we got into Nathan's car and headed onto the Garden State Parkway. "Never again," Nathan was saying, "will I allow you to convince me to attend one of Lizzie Fischman's awful parties. This is the last." I didn't even bother answering, it all seemed so predictable. Instead I just settled back into the comfortable velour of the car seat and switched on the radio. Dionne Warwick and Elton John were singing "That's What Friends Are For," and Nathan said, "You know, of course, that that's the song they wrote to raise money for AIDS."

"I'd heard," I said.

"Have you seen the video? It makes me furious. All these famous singers up there, grinning these huge grins, rocking back and forth. Why the hell are they smiling, I'd like to ask?"

For a second, I considered answering that question, then decided I'd better not. We were slipping into the Holland Tunnel, and by the time we got through to Manhattan I was ready to call it a night. I wanted to get back to my apartment and see if Roy had left a message on my answering machine. But Nathan said, "It's Saturday night, Celia, it's still early. Won't you have a drink with me or something?"

"I don't want to go to any more gay bars, Nathan, I told you that."

"So we'll go to a straight bar. I don't care. I just can't bear to go back to my apartment at eleven o'clock." We stopped for a red light, and he leaned closer to me. "The truth is, I don't think I can bear to be alone. Please."

"All right," I said. What else could I say?

"Goody," Nathan said.

We parked the car in a garage and walked to a darkish café on Greenwich Avenue, just a few doors down from the huge gay bar Nathan used to frequent, and which he jokingly referred to as "the airport." No mention was made of that bar in the café, however, where he ordered latte machiato for both of us. "Aren't you going to have some dessert?" he said. "I know I am. Baba au rhum, perhaps. Or tiramisu. You know *tirami su* means 'pick me up,' but if you want to offend an Italian waiter, you say, 'I'll have the *tiramilo su*,' which means 'pick up my dick.' "

"I'm trying to lose weight, Nathan," I said. "Please don't encourage me to eat desserts."

"Sorry." He coughed. Our latte machiatos came, and Nathan raised his cup and said, "Here's to us. Here's to Lizzie Fischman. Here's to never playing that dumb game again as long as we live." These days, I noticed, Nathan used the phrase "as long as we live" a bit too frequently for comfort.

Reluctantly I touched my glass to his. "You know," he said, "I think I've always hated that game. Even in college, when I won, it made me jealous. Everyone else had done so much more than me. Back then I figured I'd have time to explore the sexual world. Guess the joke's on me, huh?"

I shrugged. I wasn't sure.

"What's with you tonight, anyway?" he said. "You're so distant."

"I just have things on my mind, Nathan, that's all."

"You've been acting weird ever since I got back from Europe, Celia. Sometimes I think you don't even want to see me."

Clearly he was expecting reassurances to the contrary. I didn't say anything.

"Well," he said, "is that it? You don't want to see me?"

I twisted my shoulders in confusion. "Nathan—"

"Great," he said, and laughed so that I couldn't tell if he was kidding. "Your best friend for nearly ten years. Jesus."

"Look, Nathan, don't melodramatize," I said. "It's not that simple. It's just that I have to think a little about myself. My own life, my own needs. I mean, I'm going to be thirty soon. You know how long it's been since I've had a boyfriend?"

"I'm not against your having a boyfriend," Nathan said. "Have I ever tried to stop you from having a boyfriend?"

"But, Nathan," I said, "I never get to meet anyone when I'm with you all the time. I love you and I want to be your friend, but you can't expect me to just keep giving and giving and giving my time to you without anything in return. It's not fair."

I was looking away from him as I said this. From the corner of my vision I could see him glancing to the side, his mouth a small, tight line.

"You're all I have," he said quietly.

"That's not true, Nathan," I said.

"Yes, it is true, Celia."

"Nathan, you have lots of other friends."

"But none of them count. No one but you counts."

The waitress arrived with his goblet of tiramisu, put it down in front of him. "Go on with your life, you say," he was muttering. "Find a boyfriend. Don't you think I'd do the same thing if I could? But all those options are closed to me, Celia. There's nowhere for me to go, no route that isn't dangerous. I mean, getting on with my life—I just can't talk about that simply anymore, the way you can." He leaned closer, over the table. "Do you want to know something?" he said. "Every time I see someone I'm attracted to I go into a cold sweat. And I imagine that they're dead, that if I touch them, the part of them I touch will die. Don't you see? It's bad enough to be afraid you might get it. But to be afraid you might give it—and to someone you loved—" He shook his head, put his hand to his forehead.

What could I say to that? What possibly was there to say? I took his hand, suddenly, I squeezed his hand until the edges of his fingers were white. I was remembering how Nathan looked the first time I saw him, in line at a college dining hall, his hands on his hips, his head erect, staring worriedly at the old lady dishing out food, as if he feared she might run out, or not give him enough. I have always loved the boyish hungers—for food, for sex—because they are so perpetual, so faithful in their daily revival, and even though I hadn't met Nathan yet, I think, in my mind, I already understood: I wanted to feed him, to fill him up; I wanted to give him everything.

Across from us, now, two girls were smoking cigarettes and talking about what art was. A man and a woman, in love, intertwined their fingers. Nathan's hand was getting warm and damp in mine, so I let it go, and eventually he blew his nose and lit a cigarette.

"You know," he said after a while, "it's not the sex, really. That's not what I regret missing. It's just that— Do you realize, Celia, I've never been in love? Never once in my life have I actually been in love?" And he looked at me very earnestly, not knowing, not having the slightest idea, that once again he was counting me for nothing.

"Nathan," I said. "Oh, my Nathan." Still, he didn't seem satisfied, and I knew he had been hoping for something better than my limp consolation. He looked away from me, across the café, listening, I suppose, for that wind-chime peal as all the world's pennies flew his way.

Spouse Night

During the day, when Arthur is at work, the puppy listens to the radio—"Anything with voices," Mrs. Theodorus advised when Arthur went to pick up the puppy; "it calms them." And so, sitting in her pen in Arthur's decaying kitchen, while she chews on the newspaper that is meant to be her toilet, or urinates on the towel that is meant to be her bed, the puppy is surrounded by a comforting haze of half-human noise. For a while Arthur tried KQRT, the leftist station, and the puppy heard interviews with experts on Central American insurgency and radical women of color. Then he tuned in to a station that broadcast exclusively for the Polish community. "Mrs. Byziewicz, who has requested this polka, is eighty-five, the mother of three, and the grandmother of eleven," the puppy heard as she pounced on her rubber newspaper, or tried to scale the chicken-wire walls of her pen. Now Arthur's settled on KSXT, a peculiar station which claims to feature "lite" programming, and which Arthur thinks is ideally suited to the listening needs of a dog, so the puppy is hearing a ten-minute-long radio play about Edgar Allan Poe when Arthur rushes in the door with Mrs. Theodorus, both breathing hard.

"Edgar, why are your poems so strange and weird?" Mrs. Poe is asking her husband on the radio, and the puppy looks at the woman who midwifed her birth ten weeks earlier. Mrs. Theodorus's blouse is partially undone, and the drawstring on her purple sweatpants is loosened, but all the puppy notices is the faint, half-familiar smell of her mother, and smelling it, she cries, barks, and, for the first time in her short life, leaps over the edge of her pen. No one is there to congratulate her. Sniffing, the puppy makes her way into the bedroom, where Arthur and Mrs. Theodorus are in the midst of a sweaty half-naked tumble. The puppy jumps into the fray, barking, and Mrs. Theodorus screams.

"Arthur, you have got to teach her who's boss," she says, and climbs off him. "Remember—you must be in control at all times." She looks down at the puppy, who sits on the floor now, humbled before the sight of Mrs. Theodorus, naked except for her black bra, disapproval shining in her eyes. A small trickle of moisture snakes through the thick-pile carpet, darkening its yellow whorls, and quickly, quicker than Arthur can believe, Mrs. Theodorus has the puppy in hand and is carrying her back into the kitchen, shouting, "No! No!" She returns with a sponge and a bottle of urine-stain remover. "I'm a whiz at this," she says.

"Eva," Arthur says, rolling over and unbuttoning his pants, "you never fail to amaze me."

Across the house the puppy wails for her mother.

In Arthur's bathroom one medicine cabinet is full, one empty, but still, for some reason, on the soap dish, one of Claire's earrings hangs haphazardly, as if she'd just pulled it out of the tiny hole in her earlobe. Next to it lies a fake gold tooth, from the days when crowns were removable, which Claire wore most of her life and only took out during her last stay in the hospital. Arthur saved the earring because he couldn't find its partner; for hours he searched the bedroom and the bathroom, desperate to complete his inventory of Claire's jewelry so that he could finally get rid of it all, but the second earring failed to materialize. Finally he gave up. After the rest of the jewelry was distributed among the children and Claire's sisters he could not bring himself to throw the one earring away—it would have killed him, he said in group. It is a gold earring, shaped like a dolphin; its tiny jade eye glints up at him from the syrupy moat of the soap dish.

"Have you been brushing her regularly?" Mrs. Theodorus asks, examining the puppy on the kitchen table. "Her furnishings look a little matted. Remember, Arthur, this is a high-maintenance dog you've got here, and you'd better get in the habit of taking care of her now if you don't want her to scream when she goes to the groomer later on."

"I'm sorry, Eva," Arthur says.

Mrs. Theodorus smiles. "Well, I'll be happy to help you," she says, as, yelping loudly, the puppy tries to bite the comb that is pulling the fur from her skin. "But you've got to remember," Mrs. Theodorus adds, looking at Arthur sternly, "she's your puppy, and finally it's your responsibility to take care of her. You can't count on me being around all the time to do it."

"We're going to be late, Eva," Arthur says.

"I know. I'll be done in a minute."

She finishes, and the puppy is returned to the dark, private world in which she spends most of her time. "What I'm interested in, Kathy," a voice on the radio says, "is how *you* feel when your husband makes these suggestions. You have to think about your own desires, too."

"That puppy is going to be ruined, listening to Dr. Pleasure," Mrs. Theodorus says as she gets into her car. They still go in separate cars.

It is the third Thursday of the month—spouse night—and even though Arthur and Mrs. Theodorus are no longer technically spouses—both have recently lost their loved ones—they still attend with needful regularity. Claire, Arthur's wife, died two months ago of a sudden, searing chemical burn, a drug reaction, which over five days crisped and opened her skin until she lay in the burn unit, her face tomato-red, her body wrapped in mummylike bandages, and wrote to Arthur, her hand shaking, "I'm scared."

"Scared of what?" Arthur asked, and she pointed a bloody finger, as best she could, to the tubes thrust down her throat to keep her breathing; she had pneumonia. In the terrible humidity of the burn unit, surrounded by the screams of injured children, Arthur tried to reassure her. He had on three gowns, two masks, a flowered surgical cap, rubber gloves. His spectacled eyes stared out from all that fabric. A children's tape deck he had bought at Walgreen's played Hoagy Carmichael songs in the corner. Above it the nurse had written: "Hello, my name is Claire. Please turn over the tape in my tape deck. Thanx."

Meanwhile, Mr. Theodorus—jolly, warm, wonderful Mr. Theodorus, with his black suits, his little mustache, his slicked-back hair; Spiro Theodorus, brother of the maître d' at the Greek Tycoon's, mixer of the best daiquiris and joy of group night—was in a coma a few floors below. Arthur and Mrs. Theodorus met to drink coffee in the cafeteria with the tired-out residents. They shook their heads, and sometimes they wept, before returning to the ordeal, the vigil. Mrs. Theodorus told Arthur that her champion bitch Alicia was dying as well, of canine degenerative myelopathy; when she wasn't with Spiro she was at the animal hospital, stroking Alicia and feeding her small pieces of boiled chicken through the slats in her cage. She talked often, while she drank her coffee, about Alicia's coat. It was the best coat in the country, she said. Walking out of the cafeteria, Mrs. Theodorus said she honestly did not know which was going to hurt more: the death of her husband or that of her dog. They parted at the third floor. Riding back to the burn unit, Arthur rallied to face his own terrible dilemma of which-was-worse: the possibility that Claire had died without him versus the probability that she was still alive.

Arthur and Mrs. Theodorus now return to the hospital only once a month, for spouse night. Olivia, the social worker, insists that they are welcome to continue coming to group as long as they want. And Arthur does want to come. He depends on the group not only for continuity but because toward the end it constituted the very center of Claire's life; in some ways the members were more important to her than he was, or the children. Still, he is afraid of becoming like Mrs. Jaroslavsky, who attends spouse night faithfully even now, a year after Mr. Jaroslavsky's passing. Because of Mrs. Jaroslavsky, the big conference table is covered each spouse night with a pink tablecloth and platters of poppy-seed cake, chocolate cake, pudding cake, blueberry pie. Each month there is an excuse, because each month brings dark news, death and sudden spasms of hope in equal quantity. This week, Mrs. Jaroslavsky explains, the cakes are because Christa is having her six-month interim X rays, and she wants to help. "Everyone does what they can," she says to Christa.

Across the room, Christa—freckled arms, a long sandy braid, and a spigot in her arm for the chemotherapy to be poured into—looks away from the food, biting the thumbnail of one of her hands, while Chuck, her husband, holds the other. They are both professional ski instructors but have been living in this snowless climate since the illness, hand-to-mouth. Kitty Mitsui got Chuck a job busing dishes at Beefsteak Hirosha's, but that hardly scratches the surface of the bills.

"Thank you, Mrs. Jaroslavsky," Chuck says now, smiling faintly, then turning again to make sure Christa isn't going to cry.

"Well, you're welcome," Mrs. Jaroslavsky says. "You know I do what

I can. And if you need anything else—anything cooked, anything cleaned—don't hesitate to ask."

She sits back, satisfied, in her chair, and takes out her knitting. She is a large, amiable-looking woman with red cheeks and hair, and oddly, the odor that dominates the room tonight is not that of the food, but the faint, sickly-sweet, waxy perfume of her lips. Arthur and Mrs. Theodorus, taking off their coats, know, as some do not, that underneath the pink cloth is a table stained with cigarette burns, and pale, slightly swollen lesions where coffee cups have leaked, and chicken-scratched nicks in the wood where hands have idly ground pencils or scissor points or the ends of ballpoint pens. The carpet is pale yellow and worn in places, and above the table is a poster, its corners worn through with pinprickings, of a cat clinging to a chinning bar. "We all have days like this," the poster says.

It is a hard room for the healthy; it looks like death. But the members of the group don't seem to notice, much less mind it. When she came home from group those first few Thursday nights, in fact, her tires skidding on the gravel, Arthur sometimes asked Claire what the room was like, and she said, "Oh, you know. Just a room." This was before Arthur stopped repressing and started going to spouse night. After taking off her coat, Claire went straight out onto the porch and smoked a cigarette, and Arthur stood by the kitchen window, watching her as she blew rings into the night. She stared at the sky, at the stars, and that was how Arthur knew the group was changing her life. She looked exhilarated, like a girl dropped off from a date during which a boy she could not care less about has told her that he loves her.

Arthur still cannot quite believe, looking at her this spouse night, that he and Mrs. Theodorus have become lovers. It seems a most unlikely thing for them to be doing, not three months after their loved ones' deaths. Still, even now, staring at her across the room, he is filled with the panicked desire for Eva that has characterized this affair since it began. For the first time in his life Arthur feels lust, insatiable lust, and apparently Eva feels it too. They make love wildly, whispering obscene phrases in each other's ears, howling with pleasure. He has scratch marks on his back from Eva's long nails. Sometimes, in the middle of the night, they get up and sit in her kitchen and eat giant pieces of the chocolate cream pie and Black

Forest cake that Mr. Theodorus's brother sends over from his restaurant. The whipped cream dots their noses and chins. Once they spread it on each other and licked it off, which Arthur had read about people doing in *Penthouse*; it was Eva's idea, however.

She is not the sort of woman Arthur ever imagined when he imagined lust. Tall, with big breasts, high hips, a heavy behind, she has steel-gray hair which she wears piled on her head, stuck randomly with bobby pins. Her face is rubbery and slightly squashed-looking. Her clothes are uniformly stretchy; they smell of dog. And still, Arthur feels for her an attraction stronger than any he has felt for any woman in his life, even Claire. He wonders if this is grief, insatiable grief, masquerading as lust to trick him, or spare him something. Sundays he lies all day in Eva's bed, reading the copies of *Dog World* and *Dog Fancy* that cover the floor. He can identify any breed now, from Chinese crested to owczarek nizinny, from Jack Russell terrier to bichon frise. She has infected him with her expertise.

And now Mrs. Theodorus gently nudges him, points to Mrs. Jaroslavsky, who sits across the table. She knits. He sees stitches being counted and measured in the raising of eyebrows, the slight parting of lips. He once read that all human gestures, if filmed in slow motion, can be shown to be coordinated with sounds, and he is trying to see if Mrs. Jaroslavsky's eyes and lips are indeed pursing and opening to the calm voice of Olivia, the social worker. Olivia's voice is like water, and so is her bluish hair, which falls down her back in an effortless ponytail.

Christa, tears in her eyes, tells the group, "If he makes me wait three hours again tomorrow, I don't know—I'll just give up." She shakes her head. "I'm ready to give up," she says. "I stare at the stupid fish tank. I read *Highlights for Children*. Sometimes I just want to say to hell with it."

Collectively, the members of the group have spent close to three of the past ten years in doctors' waiting rooms. Cheerily, Bud Israeloff reminds everyone of this statistic, and the group responds with a low murmur of laughter. Only the spouses are silent. They sit next to their sick beloved, clutching hands, looking worriedly across the table to see whose husbands and wives are worse off than theirs.

"We all understand, Christa," Kitty Mitsui says. "You know what happened to me once? I had to wait two hours in the waiting room, and then I had to wait an hour and a half in the examining room for the doctor, and then I had to wait another hour for them to take my blood. So when I heard the B.R. finally coming I pulled the sheet up over my face and pretended I was dead. It gave him a shock, I'll tell you."

"What's a B.R.?" a new wife asks sheepishly.

"That's just group talk, honey," responds a more experienced spouse. "It means 'bastard resident.' "

Olivia does not like to encourage this particular subject. "Let's talk about what to do, practically, to allay waiting anxiety," she says. "How can we help Christa get through tomorrow?"

"One of us could go with her," Kitty Mitsui says. "Christa, do you play Scrabble?"

"I don't know," Christa says.

"I could do it," Kitty says. "I've got the day off. I'll sit with you. I'll bring my portable Scrabble set. We'll play Scrabble, and when we get bored with that, we'll make origami animals. I know it's not much, but it's better than the fish tank."

"Waiting to hear if I'm going to live or not, if I can have a baby," Christa says, "and they keep me in the waiting room. Christ, my life is on the line here and they make me wait."

Under the table, Eva's hand takes Arthur's. He folds the note she has given him into quarters, then furtively reads it.

"Have you been putting the oil in her dinner?" Eva has written. "You need to for her coat."

It is decided. Kitty will go with Christa and Chuck to Christa's doctor's office tomorrow. She'll bring her portable Scrabble set. And now, that matter concluded, Iris Pearlstein takes the floor and says, "If no one minds, I have something I'd like to address, and it's this food. It's hard enough for me to come here without it looking like I'm at a bar mitzvah."

For once Mrs. Jaroslavsky stares up from her knitting. "What?" she says.

"This food, this food," Iris says, and waves at it. "It makes me sick, having to stare at it all night."

"I just wanted to make things a little more cheerful," Mrs. Jaroslavsky says, her mouth trembling. She puts down her knitting.

"Oh, who're you kidding, Doris? You want to make it more pleasant, but I'm sorry, there's nothing nice about any of this." She looks at her husband, Joe, broken by recent radiation, dozing next to her, and puts her hand on her forehead. "Christ," she says, lighting a cigarette, "we don't want to stare at fucking cake."

Arthur wonders if Mrs. Jaroslavsky is going to cry. But she holds her own. "Now just one minute, Iris," she says. "Don't think any of this is easy for me. When Morry was in the hospital, I was up every night, I was half crazy. What was I supposed to do? So I baked. That food was the fruit of suffering for my dying husband. You know how it was. I kept thinking that maybe if I just keep baking it'll keep the clock ticking, thinking, God, for one more cake, give him six months." She frowns. "Well, God defaulted. Now Morry's gone, and my freezers are stuffed. The truth is I bake for all of you the way I baked for him. There's nothing nice about it."

She resumes her knitting. Iris Pearlstein takes out a Kleenex to blow her nose. Once again Mrs. Theodorus takes Arthur's hand under the table. Mrs. Jaroslavsky looks vibrant.

"Ask if you can take home the poppy-seed," Arthur reads when he unfolds Eva's note.

Arthur got the puppy when Mrs. Theodorus offered the group a discount on her new litter. "A pet can really cheer you up," she explained at spouse night. "The human-animal bond is so important in this stressful world."

After that, Arthur approached Mrs. Theodorus and said, "I might be interested in a puppy. Since Claire passed on—"

"I know, I know," she said. "Come tomorrow, in the afternoon."

He drove through a rainstorm. Mrs. Theodorus lived in a small, sleek, cobalt-blue house in a neighborhood where the streets flounced into cul-de-sacs and children played capture the flag with unusual viciousness. The puppies stared up at him from their kitchen enclosure, mewing and rubbing against one another, vying for his attention. "This little girl is the one for you," Mrs. Theodorus said, and he was amazed that she could tell them apart. "Look at this." She pried the puppy's mouth open, revealing young fangs.

"Looks okay," Arthur said.

"Can't you tell?" said Mrs. Theodorus. "Her bite's off. She'll never show. A pity, because her coat's really good, almost as good as Alicia's was, and she's got the best bone structure of any of them."

"We had a dog once, a Yorkie," Arthur said. "She died when my oldest daughter was twelve. Just went to sleep and never woke up."

"Oh, I can't talk about the death of dogs right now," Mrs. Theodorus said.

He took the puppy home with him that day. Claire had been gone a week, and still he was finding things he could not bear—today it was a half-finished *New York Times* acrostic puzzle. It was three weeks old. Already her handwriting was shaky. Did she have any idea then, he wondered, that the rash creeping over her skin, that unbearable itchy rash, was going to kill her? He certainly didn't. You don't die from a rash. A rash would have been embarrassing to bring up in group, where hematomas and bone loss were the norm. Claire's bane, her great guilt, in the group was that she was one of the healthier ones, but she hoped that meant she could help. "What the group does—what we mostly do—is figure out how to help each other," Arthur remembered Claire saying, as the two of them sat at the kitchen table, drinking coffee. She had just come back from her second night at group. The third night she didn't come back until four in the morning, and he went half mad with panic. "We went to the Greek Tycoon's," she explained blithely. "Mr. Theodorus bought us all drinks."

The fourth night was spouse night, and he went.

He sat down at the kitchen table with the acrostic and tried to finish it; one of the clues Claire hadn't been able to get was a river that ran through the Dolomites, and he became obsessed with figuring it out, but as soon as he saw how thick and strong his own handwriting looked in comparison with the jagged, frail letters of Claire's decline, he laid his head down on the newsprint and wept. The puppy watched him from the corner. When he got up, he used Claire's last puzzle to line her pen.

Just before spouse night ends, Kitty Mitsui announces that she and Mike Watkins and Ronni Holtzman will be going to Poncho's for margaritas and nachos. "It'll be a good time," she says halfheartedly. But everyone knows she is fighting a losing battle. Since Mr. Theodorus died the after-group outings have lost their momentum.

Then, in the group's golden age, its giddy second childhood, in the reign of Mr. Theodorus, there was wild revelry, screaming laughter in the hospital parking lot, until finally Mrs. Leon, a Mormon, brought up her moral objections at group.

The next week Mr. Theodorus arrived with a rubber dog's snout tied over his nose. That was the end of Mrs. Leon, Claire reported afterwards to Arthur, her eyes gleaming. He smiled. It seemed that Claire's greatest ambition was to be fully accepted into that subgroup of the group which played charades until four in the morning, drank, and drove all night, one Thursday, to watch the sun rise over Echo Lake, where Kitty Mitsui had a cabin. Claire reported it all—the wind on her cheeks, the crispness of the air, the glory of the mountain sunrise. They built a fire and lay bundled together in sleeping bags, five of them, like Campfire Girls, she said.

Claire believed until the end that she was peripheral, barely accepted. She believed that Spiro and Kitty and the others were going out together without her, excluding her from the best, the most intimate gatherings. This was ironic, for as Arthur learned after her death, Claire was, if anything, the group's spiritual center; without her it fragmented. Mournful couples went home alone on spouse night, the healthy clinging testily to the sick. Then Mr. Theodorus died, and the group entered a period of adolescent turmoil. Furious explosions occurred; well-buried animosities were laid bare. For the first time the group included enemies, who sat as far across the table from each other as possible, avoiding each other's glances.

Arthur can't help but wonder sometimes if any of it was sexual; if Claire might have slept with one of the men. It's hard for him to imagine. Usually, when he tries to envision those post-group revels, or when he dreams about them, he sees only five bodies huddled in sleeping bags by a lake as dawn breaks. Sometimes he wakes up with itchy hands, and bursts into tears because he wasn't there.

When spouse night ends, Mrs. Theodorus says to Mrs. Jaroslavsky, "Doris, if you don't need it—well, I could sure use that spice cake. I have this important show judge coming over tomorrow."

"Don't do me any favors," Mrs. Jaroslavsky says. She is grim-faced, puffy. Then, cautiously: "You really want it?"

"If you don't mind. This judge is very powerful, and God knows, I could never bake anything like that. All I have around are these horrible Black Forest things Spiro's brother sends over, with ten pounds of synthetic whipped cream."

"Terrible, the things they call a cake," Mrs. Jaroslavsky says, as, smiling, she hands Mrs. Theodorus an aluminum-wrapped package.

They walk out to the parking lot together. "I know when I've outstayed my welcome," Mrs. Jaroslavsky explains to Mrs. Theodorus and Arthur. "I know it's been too long. I feel I can talk about that with you two, since we're all in the same position. The rest of them, they're fickle. When Morry died, they couldn't have been nicer, they kept saying, 'Doris, anything you want, anything you want.' Now they'd like to slap my face. And that Olivia. She gets my goat. Every day it's, 'Stay as long as you need, Doris, anything you need, Doris,' but I know the score. She'd like to get rid of me too." She blows out breath, resigned. "So this is it, Mrs. Jaroslavsky," she says. "No more spouse night. The rest of the way you have to go it alone."

"I know how you feel, Doris," Arthur says. "The group's my last link to Claire. How can I leave them? Toward the end, sometimes I think, they knew her better than I did."

"Oh, but they don't, don't you see?" Mrs. Jaroslavsky says. "That's just their illusion. They have each other for a year, maybe a little more. But what I have to remember, what I must remember, is I had Morry a lifetime." She smiles, breathes deeply. "The wind feels wonderful, doesn't it?" she says, and turning from Arthur, opens her face to the sky, as if to absorb the starlight.

Across the parking lot Kitty Mitsui calls, "Hey, you guys want to come for a nightcap? Come on! It'll be fun!" She smiles too widely at them, as if she imagines that by sheer force of will she can muster the energy to bring the dead back to life.

Arthur smiles back. "No thanks," he says. "You go ahead."

"Suit yourself," Kitty Mitsui says, "but you're missing a big blowout." She has four with her, including Christa and Chuck. Clearly she is destined to become the group's perpetual cheerleader, unflagging in her determination to bring back the glory of the past with a few loudly-called-out cries. Poor Kitty Mitsui. The rest of them had lives, but she's thirty-two and unmarried. The group is her life, and it will be her doomed nostalgia.

Mrs. Jaroslavsky winces as Kitty's car roars off. "That smell," she says. "That particular smell of burnt rubber. I remember it from Morry's room when he was dying. It must have been something in one of the machines. Now I smell it—and I can hardly keep myself standing up." She looks at the ground, clearly cried out for an entire lifetime, and Arthur is suddenly grateful to have Mrs. Theodorus, grateful for the nights they may spend together in her dog-hair-covered bed. He will lie awake, listening for occasional yelps from the kennel.

"What you need," Mrs. Theodorus says, "is a puppy," and Mrs. Jaroslavsky's mouth opens into a wide smile. "My dear girl," she says, "I'm allergic." Her face, against the dark sky, expands into a comic vision of the moon, eager-eyed and white-faced.

When Claire died, Arthur arranged for her ashes to be scattered at sea. It was what she had wanted. Everyone in the group had decided what they wanted, "B vs. C," or burial versus cremation, being one of the most popular discussion topics at the post-group gatherings. He and the children took the plastic vial of ashes out on a boat, which they had to share with another family—a staunch couple named MacGiver who had lost their son, and who resembled the protagonists of *American Gothic*. Arthur felt faintly embarrassed as the two families engaged in nervous small talk. The wind was too strong to go out to sea that day, the young captain informed them: the scattering would have to take place in the bay. Arthur, as he figures it now, went crazy. "She said the ocean," he kept repeating to the captain, who in turn kept explaining, calmly and compassionately, that the wind situation simply made it impossible for them to go to the ocean. "It's okay, Dad," Arthur's daughters told him. "The bay's almost the ocean anyway." But he was adamant. "I told her the ocean," he kept saying. "I told her she'd be scattered over the ocean." He clutched the vial to his chest, while the MacGivers discreetly did their own dumping, shaking the little plastic bag over the water as if it were a sand-filled towel. "Mister," the captain said, "we're going to have to turn back soon." It was getting to be dusk. Finally, miserably, Arthur said, "Oh, the hell with it," and without even warning his children (Jane was in the bathroom at the time) dumped the vial over the side of the boat in a rage. The ashes swirled into the water like foam; the big chunks plopped and sank instantly. Nothing was left but a fine powder of ash, coating the inside of the bag, and in a moment of turmoil and indecision Arthur bent over and touched his tongue to the white crust, lapped it up. He was crying wildly. Dismayed, the MacGivers pretended to look the other way, pointing out to one another the Golden Gate Bridge, Angel Island, Alcatraz.

* * *

At Mrs. Theodorus's house, the puppy writhes on the floor, urinates, rolls onto her back. Her mother ignores her. "It's the hormonal change," Mrs. Theodorus explains blithely. "After a few months, the mothers don't recognize their offspring anymore."

"I think that's sad," Arthur says, even though he doesn't quite believe it, and Mrs. Theodorus shrugs and pours out coffee. "In a sense, it's better," she says. "They're spared the sensation of loss."

She looks out at the grooming table, empty now, but still festooned with Alicia's ribbons and silver cups and photographs of Mrs. Theodorus posed with her prize bitch. Across the room the remaining puppies lie with their mother in various states of repose. Only Arthur's puppy wags her tail, and stretches her legs behind herself, barely holding herself back from her uninterested mother.

"I think they slept together," Mrs. Theodorus says.

For a moment Arthur thinks she is talking about the dogs. "All of them," Eva goes on, and her voice is low. "That night they went to Echo Lake."

"Eva," he says, "why are you saying this?"

"Oh, I think it's pretty obvious," she says. "You see, there were things I overheard—on the phone."

Arthur is surprised at how panicked he feels, and tries to hide it. "What did you hear?" he asks finally—not wanting to sound too curious, though he is.

"I heard Spiro talking to a woman. A woman he was clearly . . . intimate with. I think it was Kitty. But then again, now that I think about it, it might just as well have been Claire." She is quiet a moment. "It wasn't just the two of them, if you know what I mean. So I thought I would ask you if you knew anything—"

"I don't know anything," Arthur says. He stares up at the ceiling. "And I don't want to know anything. I don't want to know another bloody thing about that group."

"Don't sound so holier-than-thou, Arthur. The two of us aren't exactly being saintly in our loyalty to the memory of our lost loved ones. So what if Claire was sleeping with Spiro? So what if they were all sleeping together? Look at us."

"Claire is in the water," Arthur says. "Spiro is buried."

"He wouldn't have had it any other way," Mrs. Theodorus says.

They are again quiet. In the bright light of the kennel Arthur can see the portrait of Alicia that hangs over the table. Mouth open, red tongue hanging, the dog stares. Does anyone know how long it takes? Did Claire guess, that morning she woke up and said, "My hands are itching, Arthur. Were we near any poison oak last night?" All it took was three short weeks, and she was fighting to live. What did the group matter then? He was an egotist, a child, to think that his losing Claire to the group was anything even close to tragedy, to think his suffering came anywhere close to hers.

"Oh, Arthur," Mrs. Theodorus says. "I shouldn't impose my weird ideas on you. Since Spiro died, I just don't know what I'm saying or thinking, or where I'm going. I could have read a lot into that conversation, I realize now. It was hard to make it all out. I just think that if I knew . . . maybe I wouldn't feel so lost."

"Neither of us exactly feels found," Arthur says. "Remember how that first night at group after Claire died, I almost hit Ronni Holtzman when she said she was sorry? What was I supposed to say to that? It's okay? Claire's not really dead? It wasn't your fault?"

"Oh, Arthur," Mrs. Theodorus says. "I know how you feel." But Arthur doesn't answer. To know how *Claire* felt—that is the knowledge he longs for: lying in that bed, skin cracked and bleeding, tubes in his kidneys, his lungs, his arms. That is what he wants, craves, lusts to know—that harsh condition by which Claire was taken from him. Isn't it the great lie of the living, after all, that grieving is worse, is anything near death?

Distantly he feels hands, lips on him. It is Eva, wanting, he supposes, to make love, and he obeys, allowing her to walk him into her bedroom. But in his mind he is still on that boat, clinging to the vial of Claire's ashes. "All right, already," is what he thinks he shouted, when the captain said they would have to leave, and in fury he threw to the water those ashes he had cradled in his arms, those ashes he had loved and lived with. His daughters, he is sure, still murmur together about "Dad's awful moment," "Dad's terrible behavior," but in truth he is still angry at how grief carped around on that boat, pretending to dignity. "Why did you have to embarrass us like that?" his daughter Jane said to him in the car—it was she who had been in the bathroom—and yet he knows he would do it again; he would throw those ashes over in graceless fury, again and again.

"Kiss me," Eva says nervously. He takes her in his arms. Through the window, the moon illuminates Mr. Theodorus's supply of after-shave lotion, hair tonic, shoe polish—a row of dark bottles lined up carefully, like sentries, guarding the way in.

My Marriage to Vengeance

When I got the invitation to Diana's wedding—elegantly embossed, archaically formal (the ceremony, it stated, would take place at "twelve-thirty o'clock")—the first thing I did was the *TV Guide* crossword puzzle. I was not so much surprised by Diana getting married as I was by her inviting me. What, I wondered, would motivate a person like Diana to ask her former lover, a woman she had lived with for a year and a month and whose heart she had suddenly and callously broken, to a celebration of her union with a man? It seems to me that that is asking for trouble.

I decided to call Leonore, who had been a close friend of Diana's and mine during the days when we were together, and who always seemed to have answers. "Leonore, Diana's getting married," I said when she picked up the phone.

"If you ask me," Leonore said, "she's wanted a man since day one. Remember that gay guy she tried to make it with? He said he wanted to change, have kids and all?" She paused ominously. "It's not him, is it?"

I looked at the invitation. "Mark Charles Cadwallader," I said.

"Well, for his sake," Leonore said, "I only hope he knows what he's getting into. As for Miss Diana, her doings are of no interest to me."

"But, Leonore," I said, "the question is: Should I go to the wedding?" imagining myself, suddenly, in my red T-shirt that said BABY BUTCH (a present from Diana), reintroducing myself to her thin, severe, long-necked mother, Marjorie Winters.

"I think that would depend on the food," Leonore said.

After I hung up, I poured myself some coffee and propped the invitation in front of me to look at. For the first few seconds it hadn't even clicked who was getting married. I had read: "Mr. and Mrs.

Humphrey Winters cordially invite you to celebrate the wedding of their daughter, Diana Helaine," and thought: Who is Diana Helaine? Then it hit me, because for the whole year and a month, Diana had refused to tell me what her middle initial stood for—positively refused, she said, out of embarrassment, while I tried to imagine what horrors could lie behind that "H"—Hildegarde? Hester? Hulga? She was coyly, irritatingly insistent about not letting the secret out, like certain girls who would have nothing to do with me in eighth grade. Now she was making public to the world what she insisted on hiding from me, and it made perfect sense. Diana Helaine, not a different person, is getting married, I thought, and it was true, the fact in and of itself didn't surprise me. During the year and a month, combing the ghost of her once knee-length hair, I couldn't count how many times she'd said, very off-the-cuff, "You know, Ellen, sometimes I think this lesbian life is for the birds. Maybe I should just give it up, get married, and have two point four babies." I'd smile and say, "If you do that, Diana, you can count on my coming to the wedding with a shotgun and shooting myself there in front of everybody." To which, still strumming her hair like a guitar and staring into the mirror, she would respond only with a faint smile, as if she could think of nothing in the world she would enjoy more.

First things first: We were lovers, and I don't mean schoolgirls touching each other in exploratory ways in dormitories after dark. I mean, we lived together, shared tampons and toothpaste, had one bed to sleep in, and for all the world (and ourselves) to see. Diana was in law school in San Francisco, and I had a job at Milpitas State Hospital (I still do). Each day I'd drive an hour and a half there and an hour and a half back, and when I got home Diana would be waiting for me in bed, a fat textbook propped on her lap. We had couple friends, Leonore and Callie, for instance, and were always invited to things together, and when she left me, we were even thinking about getting power of attorney over each other. I was Diana's first woman lover, though she had had plenty of boyfriends. I had never slept with a boy, but had been making love with girls since early in high school. Which meant that for me, being a lesbian was just how things were. But for Diana—well, from day one it was adventure, event, and episode. For a while we just had long blushing talks over pizza, during which she confessed she was "curious." It's ridiculous how many supposedly straight girls come on to you that way—plopping themselves down on your lap and fully expecting you to go through all the hard work of initiating them into Sapphic love out of sheer lust for recruitment. No way, I said. The last thing I need is to play guinea pig, testing ground, only to be left when the fun's over and a new boyfriend shows up on the horizon. But no, Diana said. I mean, yes. I think I *do*. I mean, I think I *am*. At which point she would always have just missed the last bus home and have to spend the night in my bed, where it was only a matter of time before I had no more defenses.

After we became lovers, Diana cut her hair off, and bought me the BABY BUTCH T-shirt. She joined all sorts of groups and organizations, dragged me to unsavory bars, insisted, fiercely, on telling her parents everything. (They did not respond well.) Only in private did she muse over her other options. I think she thought she was rich enough not to have to take any vow or promise all that seriously. Rich people are like that, I have noticed. They think a love affair is like a shared real estate venture they can just buy out of when they get tired of it.

Diana had always said the one reason she definitely wanted to get married was for the presents, so the day before the wedding I took my credit card and went to Nordstrom's, where I found her name in the bridal registry and was handed a computer printout with her china pattern, silver, stainless, and other assorted requirements. I was already over my spending limit, so I bought her the ultimate—a Cuisinart—which I had wrapped to carry in white crêpe paper with a huge yellow bow. Next came the equally important matter of buying myself a dress for the wedding. It had been maybe five, six years since I'd owned a dress. But buying clothes is like riding a bicycle—it comes back—and soon, remembering age-old advice from my mother on hems and necklines, I had picked out a pretty yellow sundress with a spattering of daisies, and a big, wide-brimmed hat.

The invitation had been addressed to Miss Ellen Britchkey and guest, and afterwards, in the parking lot, that made me think about my life—how there was no one in it. And then, as I was driving home from Nordstrom's, for the first time in years I had a seizure of accident panic. I couldn't believe I was traveling sixty miles an hour, part of a herd of speeding cars which passed and raced each other, coming within five or six inches of collision and death every ten seconds. It astonished me to realize that I drove every day of my life, that every day of my life I risked ending my life, that all I had to do was swerve the wrong way, or look only in the front and not the side mirror, and I might hit another car, or hit a child on the way to a wedding, and have to live for the rest of my life with the guilt, or die. Horrified, I headed right, into the slow lane. The slow lane was full of scared women, crawling home alone. It was no surprise to me. I was one with the scared women crawling home alone. After Diana left me, I moved down the peninsula to a miniature house—that is the only way to describe it—two rooms with a roof, and shingles, and big pretty windows. It was my solitude house, my self-indulgence house, my remorse-and-secret-pleasure house. There I ate take-out Chinese food, read and reread *Little House on the Prairie*, stayed up late watching reruns of *Star Trek* and *The Honeymooners*. I lived by my wits, by survival measures. The television was one of those tiny ones, the screen smaller than a human face.

Diana—I only have one picture of her, and it is not a good likeness. In it she wears glasses and has long, long hair, sweeping below the white fringe of the picture, to her behind. She cut all her hair off as an offering to me the day after the first night we made love, and presented it that evening in a box—two neat braids, clipped easily as toenail parings, offered like a dozen roses. I stared at them, the hair still braided, still fresh with the smell of shampoo, and joked that I had bought her a comb, like in "The Gift of the Magi." "Don't you see?" she said. "I did it for you—I changed myself for you, as an act of love." I looked at her, her new boyish bangs, her face suddenly so thin-seeming without its frame of yellow hair. She was used to big gestures, to gifts that made an impact.

"Diana," I lied (for I had loved her long hair), "it's the most generous thing anyone's ever done for me." To say she'd done it for me—well, it was a little bit like a mean trick my sister pulled on me one Christmas when we were kids. She had this thing about getting a little tiny tree to put on top of the piano. And I, of course, wanted a great big one, like the Wagner family down the block. And then, about ten days before Christmas, she said, "Ellen, I have an early Christmas present for you," and she handed me a box, inside which were about a hundred miniature Christmas-tree ornaments.

I can recognize a present with its own motive.

If I've learned one thing from Diana, it's that there's more to a gift than just giving.

The next day was the day of the wedding, and somehow, without hitting any children, I drove to the hotel in Hillsborough where the ceremony and reception were taking place. A doorman escorted me to a private drawing room where, nervous about being recognized, I kept the Cuisinart in front of my face as long as I could, until finally an older woman with a carnation over her breast, apparently an aunt or something, said, "May I take that, dear?" and I had to surrender the Cuisinart to a table full of presents, some of which were hugely and awkwardly wrapped and looked like human heads. I thanked her, suddenly naked in my shame, and sturdied myself to brave the drawing room, where the guests milled. I recognized two or three faces from college, all part of Diana's set—rich, straight, preppy, not the sort I had hung around with at all. And in the distance I saw her very prepared parents, her mother thin and severe-looking as ever in a sleeveless black dress, her streaked hair cut short, like Diana's, her neck and throat nakedly displaying a brilliant jade necklace, while her father, in his tuxedo, talked with some other men and puffed at a cigar. Turning to avoid them, I almost walked right into Walter Bevins, who was Diana's gay best friend, or "hag fag," in college, and we were so relieved to see each other we grabbed a couple of whiskey sours and headed to as secluded a corner as we could find. "Boy, am I glad to see a familiar face," Walter said. "Can you believe this? Though I must say, I never doubted Diana would get married in anything less than splendor."

"Me neither," I admitted. "I was just a little surprised that Diana was getting married at all."

"Weren't we all!" Walter said. "But he seems like a nice guy. A lawyer, of course. *Very* cute, a real shame that he's heterosexual, if you ask me. But apparently she loves him and he loves her, and that's just fine. Look, there he is."

Walter pointed to a tall, dark man with a mustache and beard who stood in the middle of a circle of elderly women. To my horror, his eye caught ours, and he disentangled himself from the old women and walked over to where we were sitting. "Walter," he said. Then he looked at me and said, "Ellen?"

I nodded and smiled.

"Ellen, Ellen," he said, and reached out a hand which, when I took it, lifted me from the safety of my sofa onto my feet. "It is such a pleasure to meet you," he said. "Come with me for a second. I've wanted a chance to talk with you for so long, and once the wedding takes place—who knows?"

I smiled nervously at Walter, who raised a hand in comradeship, and was led by the groom through a door to an antechamber, empty except for a card table piled high with bridesmaids' bouquets. "I just want you to know," he said, "how happy Diana and I are that you could make it. She speaks so warmly of you. And I also want you to know, just so there's no tension, Diana's told me everything, and I'm fully accepting of her past."

"Thank you, Mark," I said, horrified that at my age I could already be part of someone's "past." It sounded fake to me, as if lesbianism was just a stage Diana had passed through, and I was some sort of perpetual adolescent, never seeing the adult light of heterosexuality.

"Charlie," Mark said. "I'm called Charlie."

He opened the door, and as we were heading back out into the drawing room, he said, "Oh, by the way, we've seated you next to the schizophrenic girl. Your being a social worker and all, we figured you wouldn't mind."

"Me?" I said. "Mind? Not at all."

"Thanks. Boy, is Diana going to be thrilled to see you."

Then he was gone into the crowd.

Once back in the drawing room I searched for Walter, but couldn't seem to find him. I was surrounded on all sides by elderly women with elaborate, peroxided hairdos. Their purses fascinated me. Some were hard as shell and shaped like kidneys, others made out of punctured leather that reminded me of birth control pill dispensers. Suddenly I found myself face to nose with Marjorie Winters, whose eyes visibly bulged upon recognizing me. We had met once, when Diana had brought me home for a weekend, but that was before she had told her mother the nature of our relationship. After Diana came out—well, I believe the exact words were, "I never want that woman in my house again."

"Ellen," Marjorie said now, just as I had imagined she might. "What a surprise." She smiled, whether with contempt or triumph I couldn't tell.

"Well, you know I wouldn't miss Diana's wedding, Mrs. Winters," I said, smiling. "And this certainly is a lovely hotel."

She smiled. "Yes, isn't it? Red, look who's here," she said, and motioned over her husband, who for no particular reason except that his name was Humphrey was called Red. He was an amiable, absent-minded man, and he stared at me in earnest, trying to figure out who I was.

"You remember Diana's friend Ellen, from college, don't you?"

"Oh yes," he said. "Of course." Clearly he knew nothing. I believe his wife liked to keep him in a perpetual dark like that, so that he wouldn't be distracted from earning money.

"Ellen's a social worker," Marjorie said, "at the state hospital at Milpitas. So Diana and I thought it would be a good idea to seat her next to the schizophrenic girl, don't you think?"

"Oh yes," Red said. "Definitely. I imagine they'll have a lot of things to talk about."

A little tinkling bell rang, and Marjorie said, "Oh goodness, that's my cue. Be a dear, and do take care of Natalie." Squeezing my hand, she was gone. She had won, and she was glorying in her victory. And not for the first time that day, I wondered: Why is it that the people who always win always win?

The guests were beginning to move outdoors, to the garden, where the ceremony was taking place. Lost in the crowd, I spied Walter and maneuvered my way next to him. "How's it going, little one?" he said.

"I feel like a piece of shit," I said. I wasn't in the mood to make small talk.

"That's what weddings are for," he said cheerfully. We headed through a pair of French doors into a small, beautiful garden, full of blooming roses and wreaths and huge baskets of wisteria and lilies. Handsome, uniformed men—mostly brothers of the groom, I presumed—were helping everyone to their seats. Thinking we were a couple, one of them escorted Walter and me to one of the back rows, along with several other young couples, who had brought their babies and might have to run out to change a diaper or something in the middle of the ceremony.

As soon as everyone was seated the string quartet in the corner began to play something sweet and Chopin-like, and then the procession started—first Diana's sister, who was matron of honor; then the bridesmaids, each arm in arm with an usher, each dressed in a different pastel dress which was coordinated perfectly with her bouquet; and then, finally, Diana herself, looking resplendent in her white dress. Everyone gave out little oohs and aahs as she entered, locked tight between her parents. It had been two years since we'd seen each other, and looking at her, I thought I'd cry. I felt like such a piece of nothing, such a worthless piece of garbage without her—she was really that beautiful. Her hair was growing back, which was the worst thing. She had it braided and piled on her head and woven with wildflowers. Her skin was flawless, smooth—skin I'd touched hundreds, thousands of times—and there was an astonishing brightness about her eyes, as if she could see right through everything to its very heart. From the altar, the groom looked on, grinning like an idiot, a proud possessor who seemed to be saying, with his teary grin, see, look what I've got, look what chose me. And Diana too, approaching him at the altar, was all bright smiles, no doubt, no regret or hesitation registering in her face, and I wondered what she was thinking now: if she was thinking about her other life, her long committed days and nights as a lesbian.

The music stopped. They stood, backs to us, the audience, before the reverent reverend. He began to lecture them solemnly. And then I saw it. I saw myself stand up, run to the front of the garden, and before anyone could say anything, do anything, pull out the gun and consummate, all over the grass, my own splendid marriage to vengeance.

But of course I didn't do anything like that. Instead I just sat there with Walter and listened as Diana, love of my life, my lover, my life, repeated the marriage vows, her voice a little trembly, as if to suggest she was just barely holding in her tears. They said their "I do"s. They exchanged rings. They kissed, and everyone cheered.

At my table in the dining room were seated Walter; the Winterses' maid, Juanita; her son; the schizophrenic girl; and the schizophrenic girl's mother. It was in the darkest, most invisible corner of the room, and I could see it was no accident that Marjorie Winters had gathered us all here—all the misfits and minorities, the kooks and oddities of the wedding. For a minute, sitting down and gazing out at the other tables, which were full of beautiful women and men in tuxedos, I was so mad at Diana I wanted to run back to the presents table and reclaim my Cuisinart, which I really couldn't afford to be giving her anyway, and which she certainly didn't deserve. But then I realized that people would probably think I was a thief and call the hotel detective or the police, and I decided not to.

The food, Leonore would have been pleased to know, was mediocre. Next to me, the schizophrenic girl stabbed with her knife at a pathetic-looking little bowl of melon balls and greenish strawberries, while her mother looked out exhaustedly, impatiently, at the expanse of the hotel dining room. Seeing that the schizophrenic girl had started, Juanita's son, who must have been seven feet tall, began eating as well, but she slapped his hand. Not wanting to embarrass him by staring, I looked at the schizophrenic girl. I knew she was the schizophrenic girl by her glasses—big, ugly, red ones from the seventies, the kind where the temples start at the bottom of the frames—and the way she slumped over her fruit salad, as if she was afraid someone might steal it.

"Hello," I said to her.

She didn't say anything. Her mother, dragged back into focus, looked down at her and said, "Oh now, Natalie."

"Hello," Natalie said.

The mother smiled. "Are you with the bride or the groom?" she asked.

"The bride."

"Relation?"

"Friend from college."

"How nice," the mother said. "We're with the groom. Old neighbors. Natalie and Charlie were born the same day in the same hospital, isn't that right, Nat?"

"Yes," Natalie said.

"She's very shy," the mother said to me, and winked.

Across the table Walter was asking Juanita's son if he played basketball. Shyly, in a Jamaican accent, he admitted that he did. His face was as arch and stern as that of his mother, a fat brown woman with the eyes of a prison guard. She smelled very clean, almost antiseptic.

"Natalie, are you in school?" I asked.

She continued to stab at her fruit salad, not really eating it as much as trying to decimate the pieces of melon.

"Tell the lady, Natalie," said her mother.

"Yes."

"Natalie's in a very special school," the mother said.

"I'm a social worker," I said. "I understand about Natalie."

"Oh really, you are?" the mother said, and relief flushed her face. "I'm so glad. It's so painful, having to explain—you know—"

Walter was trying to get Juanita to reveal the secret location of the honeymoon. "I'm not saying," Juanita said. "Not one word."

"Come on," said Walter. "I won't tell a soul, I swear."

"I'm on TV," Natalie said.

"Oh now," said her mother.

"I am. I'm on *The Facts of Life*. I'm Tuti."

"Now, Natalie, you know you're not."

"And I'm also on *All My Children* during the day. It's a tough life, but I manage."

"Natalie, you know you're not to tell these stories."

"Did someone mention *All My Children*?" asked Juanita's son. Walter, too, looked interested.

"My lips are forever sealed," Juanita said to no one in particular. "There's no chance no way no one's going to get me to say one word."

Diana and Ellen. Ellen and Diana. When we were together, everything about us seethed. We lived from seizure to seizure. Our fights were glorious, manic, our need to fight like an allergy, something that reddens and irritates the edges of everything and demands release. Once Diana broke the air conditioner and I wouldn't forgive her. "Leave me alone," I screamed.

"No," she said. "I want to talk about it. Now."

"Well, I don't."

"Why are you punishing me?" Diana said. "It's not my fault."

"I'm not punishing you."

"You are. You're shutting me up when I have something I want to say."

"Damn it, won't you just leave me alone? Can't you leave anything alone?"

"Let me say what I have to say, damn it!"

"What?"

"I didn't break it on purpose! I broke it by accident!"

"Damn it, Diana, leave me the fuck alone! Why don't you just go away?"

"You are so hard!" Diana said, tears in her eyes, and slammed out the door into the bedroom.

After we fought, consumed, crazed, we made love like animals, then crawled about the house for days, cats in a cage, lost in a torpor of lazy carnality. It helped that the air conditioner was broken. It kept us slick. There was always, between us, heat and itch.

Once, in those most desperate, most remorse-filled days after Diana left, before I moved down the peninsula to my escape-hatch dream house, I made a list which was titled "Reasons I love her."

1. Her hair.
2. Her eyes.
3. Her skin. (Actually, most of her body except maybe her elbows.)
4. The way she does voices for the plants when she waters them, saying things like "Boy was I thirsty, thanks for the drink." [This one was a lie. That habit actually infuriated me.]
5. Her advantages: smart and nice.
6. Her devotion to me, to us as a couple.
7. How much she loved me.
8. Her love for me.
9. How she loves me.

There was less to that list than met the eye. When Diana left me—and it must be stated, here and now, she did so cruelly, callously, and suddenly—she said that the one thing she wanted me to know was that she still considered herself a lesbian. It was only me she was leaving. "Don't think I'm just another straight girl who used you," she insisted, as she gathered all her things into monogrammed suitcases. "I just don't feel we're right for each other. You're a social worker. I'm not good enough for you. Our lives, our ideas about the world—they're just never going to mesh."

Outside, I knew, her mother's station wagon waited in ambush. Still I pleaded. "Diana," I said, "you got me into this thing. You lured me in, pulled me in against my will. You can't leave just like that."

But she was already at the door. "I want you to know," she said, "because of you, I'll be able to say, loud and clear, for the rest of my life, I am a lesbian," and kissed me on the cheek.

In tears I stared at her, astonished that this late in the game she still thought my misery at her departure might be quelled by abstract gestures to sisterhood. Also that she could think me that stupid. I saw through her quaking, frightened face, her little-boy locks.

"You're a liar," I said, and, grateful for the anger, she crumpled up her face, screamed, "Damn you, Ellen," and ran out the door.

As I said, our fights were glorious.
All she left behind were her braids.

Across the dining room, Diana stood with Charlie, holding a big knife over the wedding cake. Everyone was cheering. The knife sank into the soft white flesh of the cake, came out again clung with silken frosting and crumbs. Diana cut two pieces. Their arms intertwined, she and Charlie fed each other.

Then they danced. A high-hipped young woman in sequins got up on the bandstand and sang, "Graduation's almost here, my love, teach me tonight."

After the bride and groom had been given their five minutes of single glory on the dance floor, and the parents and grandparents had joined them, I felt a tap on my shoulder. "Care to tango *avec moi*, my dear?" Walter said.

"Walter," I said, "I'd be delighted."

We got up from the table and moved out onto the floor. I was extremely nervous, sweating through my dress. I hadn't actually spoken to Diana yet, doubted she'd even seen me. Now, not three feet away, she stood, dancing and laughing, Mrs. Mark Charles Cadwallader.

I kept my eyes on Walter's lapel. The song ended. The couples broke up. And then, there she was, approaching me, all smiles, all bright eyes. "Ellen," she said, embracing me, and her mother shot us a wrathful glance. "Ellen. Let me look at you."

She looked at me. I looked at her. Close up, she looked slightly unraveled, her make-up smeared, her eyes red and a little tense. "Come with me to the ladies' room," she said. "My contacts are killing me."

She took my hand and swept me out of the ballroom into the main hotel lobby. Everyone in the lobby stared at us frankly, presuming, I suppose, that she was a runaway bride, and I her maid. But we were only running away to the ladies' room.

"These contacts!" she said once we got there, and opening one eye wide peeled off a small sheath of plastic. "I'm glad you came," she said, placing the lens on the end of her tongue and licking it. "I was worried that you wouldn't. I've felt so bad about you, Ellen, worried about you so much, since—well, since things ended between us. I was hoping this wedding could be a reconciliation for us. That now we could start again. As friends."

She turned away from the lamplit mirror and flashed me a big smile. I just looked up at her.

"Yes," I said. "I'd like that."

Diana removed the other lens and licked it. It seemed to me a highly unorthodox method of cleaning. Then, nervously, she replaced the lens and looked at herself in the mirror. She had let down her guard. Her face looked haggard, and red blush was streaming off her cheeks.

"I didn't invite Leonore for a reason," she said. "I knew she'd do something to embarrass me, come all dyked out or something. I'm not trying to deny my past, you know. Charlie knows everything. Have you met him?"

"Yes," I said.

"And isn't he a wonderful guy?"

"Yes."

"I have nothing against Leonore. I just believe in subtlety these days. You, I knew I could count on you for some subtlety, some class. Leonore definitely lacks class."

It astonished me, all that wasn't being said. I wanted to mention it all—her promise on the doorstep, the gun, the schizophrenic girl. But there was so much. Too much. Nowhere to begin.

When she'd finished with her ablutions, we sat down in parallel toilets. "It is nearly impossible to pee in this damned dress," she said to me through the divider. "I can't wait to get out of it."

"I can imagine," I said.

Then there was a loud spilling noise, and Diana gave out a little sigh of relief. "I've got a terrible bladder infection," she said. "Remember in college how it was such a big status symbol to have a bladder infection because it meant you were having sex? Girls used to come into the dining hall clutching big jars of cranberry juice and moaning, and the rest of us would look at them a little jealously." She faltered. "Or some of us did," she added. "I guess not you, huh, Ellen?"

"No, I was a lesbian," I said, "and still am, and will be until the day I die." I don't know why I said that, but it shut her up.

For about thirty seconds there was not a sound from the other side of the divider, and then I heard Diana sniffling. I didn't know what to say.

"Christ," Diana said, after a few seconds, and blew her nose. "Christ. Why'd I get married?"

I hesitated. "I'm not sure I'm the person to ask," I said. "Did your mother have anything to do with it?"

"Oh, Ellen," Diana said, "please!" I heard her spinning the toilet paper roll. "Look," she said, "you probably resent me incredibly. You probably think I'm a sellout and a fool and that I was a royal bitch to you. You probably think when Charlie does it to me I lie there and pretend I'm feeling something when I'm not. Well, it's not true. Not in the least." She paused. "I was just not prepared to go through my life as a social freak, Ellen. I want a normal life, just like everybody. I want to go to parties and not have to die inside trying to explain who it is I'm with. Charlie's very good for me in that way, he's very understanding and generous." She blew her nose again. "I'm not denying you were part of my life, that our relationship was a big thing for me. I'm just saying it's finished. That part's finished."

Defiantly she flushed.

We stood up, pulled up our underpants, and stepped out of the toilet booths to face each other. I looked Diana right in the eye, and I noticed her weaken. I saw it. I could have kissed her or something, I knew, and made her even more unhappy. But I didn't really see the point.

Afterwards, we walked together out of the ladies' room, back into the ballroom, where we were accosted by huge crowds of elderly women with purses that looked to me like the shellacked sushi in certain Japanese restaurant windows.

"Was it okay?" Walter asked me, taking my arm and leading me back to our table for cake.

"Yes," I said. "Okay." But he could see from my face how utterly miserable I was.

"Don't even try," Juanita said, giggling hysterically to herself as we got back to the table. "You're not getting a word out of me, so don't even begin to ask me questions."

Once I knew a schizophrenic girl. Her name was Holly Reardon and she was my best friend from age five to eight. We played house a lot, and sometimes we played spaceship, crawling together into a cubbyhole behind my parents' sofa bed, then turning off the lights and pretending the living room was some fantastic planet. We did well with our limited resources. But then money started disappearing, and my mother sat me down one day and asked me if I had noticed the money always disappeared when Holly came to visit. I shook my head vigorously no, refusing to believe her. And then one day my favorite stuffed animal, a dog called Rufus, disappeared, and I didn't tell my mother, and didn't tell my mother, until one day she said to me, "Ellen, what happened to Rufus?" and I started to cry. We never found Rufus. Holly had done something with him. And it wasn't because of me that she went away, my parents assured me, it wasn't because of me that her parents closed up the house and had to move into an apartment. Holly was not well. Years later, when I went to work at the state hospital, I think somewhere, secretly, I hoped Holly might be there, a patient there, that we might play house and spaceship in the linen closets. But of course she wasn't. Who knows where she is now?

After the wedding I felt so depressed I had ice cream for dinner. I did several acrostic puzzles. I watched *The Honeymooners* and I watched *Star Trek.* I watched Sally Jessy Raphael. I watched *The Twilight Zone.* Fortunately, it was not one of the boring Western ones, but an episode I like particularly, about a little girl with a doll that says things like, "My name is Talking Tina and I'm going to kill you." I wished I'd had a doll like that when I was growing up. Next was *Night Gallery.* I almost never watch *Night Gallery*, but when I do, it seems I always see the same episode, the one about two people who meet on a road and are filled with a mysterious sense of déjà vu, of having met before. It turns out they live in the mind of a writer who has been rewriting the same scene a thousand times. Near the end they rail at their creator to stop tormenting them by summoning them into existence over and over, to suffer over and over. At the risk of mysticism, it seems to me significant that every time I have tuned into *Night Gallery* in my life it is this episode I have seen.

Then there was nothing more good to watch.

I got up, paced around the house, tried not to think about any of it: Holly Reardon, or Natalie, or Diana, or those poor people living in the mind of a writer and getting rewritten over and over again. I tried not to think about all the Chinese dinners I wasn't going to be able to have because I'd spent so much money on that Cuisinart for Diana, who probably could afford to buy herself a hundred Cuisinarts if she wanted. I tried not to think about their honeymoon, about what secret, glorious place they were bound for. It was too late for it to still make me mad that the whole world, fired up to stop me and Diana, was in a conspiracy to protect the privacy of the angelic married couple she had leapt into to save herself, to make sure their perfect honeymoon wasn't invaded by crazy lesbian ex-lovers with shotguns and a whole lot of unfinished business on their minds. Unfortunately, any anger I felt, which might have saved me, was counteracted by how incredibly sorry I felt for Diana, how sad she had seemed, weeping in the ladies' room on her wedding day.

I went to the closet and took out Diana's braids. God knows I hadn't opened the box for ages. There they were, the braids, only a little faded, a little tangled, and of course, no longer smelling of shampoo. I lifted one up. I was surprised at how silky the hair felt, even this old. Carefully, to protect myself, I rubbed just a little of it against my face. I shuddered. It could have been her.

I went to the bed, carrying the braids with me. I laid them along my chest. I have never had long hair. Now I tried to imagine what it felt like, tried to imagine I was Diana imagining me, a woman she had loved, a woman she had given her hair, a woman who now lay on a bed somewhere, crying, using all the strength she could muster just to not force the braids down her throat. But I knew Diana was on a plane somewhere in the sky, or in a car, or more likely than that, lying in a heart-shaped bed while a man hovered over her, his hands running through her new hair, and that probably all she was thinking was how much better off she was than me, how much richer, and how lucky to have escaped before she was sucked so far in, like me, that it would be too late to ever get out. Was I so pathetic? Possibly. And possibly Diana was going to be happier for the choice she had made. But I think, more likely, lying on that mysterious bed, she was contemplating a whole life of mistakes spinning out from one act of compromise, and realizing she preferred a life of easy mistakes to one that was harder but better. Who was I to criticize? Diana had her tricks, and so did Juanita, and so, for that matter, did that schizophrenic girl stabbing at her melon balls. We all had our little tricks.

I took the braids off myself. I stood up. A few hairs broke loose from the gathered ropes, fell lightly to the floor. They didn't even look like anything; they might have been pieces of straw.

Ayor

The summer I turned nineteen I took a short, sad, circular trip to the Great Smoky Mountains National Park, in Tennessee, with a friend I was in love with, or would have been in love with, had I known more about him or about myself. His name was Craig Rosen, and he lived down the hall from me freshman year in college. When he suggested taking the trip as a way of passing the interval between the end of school and the beginning of our summer jobs, I said yes in a second. Craig was good-looking, dark-haired and dark-eyed, and I desperately wanted to see him naked. I didn't know much about him except that he was an economics major, and sang in the glee club, and spent most of his time with a fellow glee-clubber, a thin-mouthed Japanese girl named Barbara Love. Nevertheless I had certain suspicions, not to mention a rabid eagerness to be seduced, which, in the end, was never satisfied. For five nights Craig and I shared a bed in that curry-smelling motel in Gatlinburg, and for five nights we never touched each other—a fact which, in all the years since, we have not talked about once. There is a code which applies here, I think, having to do with friendship and sex and their exclusivity, a code at least as mysterious and hermetic as the code of the *Spartacus Guide* which led us through Europe a few summers later. But that is jumping ahead of things.

We were, then, nineteen, East Coast college boys, Jews, homosexuals (though this we hadn't admitted). Gatlinburg, Tennessee, on the fringe of the park, with its sticky candy shops, its born-again bookstores and hillbilly hayrides, may seem an unlikely place for us to have confronted (as we never did, it turned out) our shared secret sexuality. But I had grown up in amusement parks, glorying in the smell of diesel fuel and cotton candy, in roller coasters, in the wildness of rides that whirled at high speeds, round and round. I had had my first inkling of erotic feeling on those rides, when I was eleven, when the heavy artificial wind of a machine called a Lobster pushed my best friend Eric's body into mine, so that I couldn't breathe. Gatlinburg, with Craig, was full of that same erotic heat, that camaraderie of boys which seems always on the verge of dissolving into lust. Like children released from the better advice of our parents, we ate only the junk food that was on sale everywhere in the town—candied apples, wheels of fried dough swirling in vats of grease, gargantuan hamburgers and cheeseburgers. Craig shaved in his underwear, like a man in a television commercial, something I imagined to be a gesture of sexual display. Soon, I hoped, his eyes would meet mine; he would turn away from the mirror in the bathroom, his face still half covered with shaving cream, and begin walking toward me. But it never happened. Why? I wondered each night, curled into my half of the bedsheets, far away from Craig. It would have been so easy for him to have done me that favor, I thought, and liberated me from my crabbed, frightened little body. And though I have come up, over the years, with many elaborate psychological explanations for why Craig and I didn't sleep together in Gatlinburg, only recently have I been able to admit the simple truth: we didn't sleep together because Craig didn't want to; to put it flatly, he wasn't in the least attracted to my body. I did not know it yet, but even at nineteen he had already had hundreds of men, including a famous porn star. Sex—for me a quaking, romantic, nearly unimaginable dream—was for him an athletic exercise in alleviating boredom. It was—and this, I think, is the key—a way of determining self-worth; he wanted only the most beautiful, most perfect men, not in order to possess them, but because their interest in him, their lust for him, confirmed that he was part of their elite. It was a matter of class, pure and simple; like his father before him, he wanted into a country club. And though it probably gratified him, on some mean level, to see his preening self reflected in my burning eyes in the bathroom mirror, sleeping with me not only wouldn't have gained him any points, it probably would have lost him some.

So why did Craig want me to come to Tennessee in the first place? It occurs to me now that my very lack of sexual appeal might have made me appealing to Craig in other ways, that week we spent together. I think I offered him a kind of escape, a safety hatch through which he could flee a life that, as I would later learn, was beginning to consist of little other than showers at the gym, circle jerks in Central Park, afternoons at the glory holes near Times Square. Perhaps he craved my innocence; perhaps he envisioned a wholesome, rejuvenating week in the wilderness; perhaps he was recovering from some casually transmitted disease. I don't know because, as I said, Craig and I have never discussed that week in Gatlinburg, and I doubt we ever will.

When we arrived at the Great Smoky Mountains National Park, the first thing we did was go to the ranger station to plan our trip. We were going to do a six-day circle of the park, long planned by Craig, hiking seventy-five miles of forested mountain, much of it along the famous Appalachian Trail. The ranger girl chewed gum as she drew us a map. When she explained that we would probably be four days without human contact, four days in the depths of the park, more than a day's hike away from civilization, we looked at each other. Perhaps, in all this organizing, we simply hadn't thought enough about the realities of camping out for so long. What if something went wrong? What if a bear attacked us? Six days, alone, sleeping outdoors, the weather unpredictable—the prospect was terrifying to us.

So instead of risking the dangers of the forest, we "camped out" in a motel in Gatlinburg that was operated by a family of Sikhs. The proprietress painted a dot on her forehead each morning which by nighttime, when we saw her drift by in her mass of sari, was beginning to stream out like a black-rayed sun. She and her family lived in a group of rooms behind the desk from which a strong odor of cumin emanated, wafting down the linoleum hallways, inhabiting our room like an incense. There was only one bed. We lay far apart, on either side of it, Craig in his skimpy underpants, me in pajamas. I tried to engage him in the closest thing I could muster to sexy talk: I asked him why he preferred jockeys to boxers. He said he liked the "tighter feel," whatever that means. Then he fell asleep.

For lunch, out of guilt, we sat at a picnic site and ate the dehydrated spaghetti and meatballs and chicken à la king I had been so eager to taste ever since we had bought them in that camping store on Park Row. Afterwards—having made our perfunctory stab at the park—we headed back into town, to wander the shopping malls of Gatlinburg, ride the funicular, play at the hillbilly miniature-golf courses. Craig had never said anything explicit to me about his sexual life, though he was always mentioning his ex-girlfriend in Connecticut. Eager for signs, evidence, some sort of recognition, I tried to give off feeble signals of my own—that is, I glanced at him needfully, and sat with him, smiling like an indulgent mother, while he ate the fried dough he so loved. None of these techniques worked. As I have witnessed a hundred times over the years we've known each other, Craig is not in the least impressed by romantic mooning; in fact, it rather disgusts him. If he spared me his contempt, that week in Gatlinburg, it was probably only because he didn't recognize how far gone I was into fantasy.

The fourth day, having done everything else, we went to the Ripley's Believe-It-or-Not Museum. It didn't seem like much of a place at first. In the window a mock witch's den was set up, with a wax witch, a little cauldron, many elaborate rugs, a crystal ball. I was looking in the window rather uninterestedly when I heard a voice say, "Hey, you!" I looked around, behind me, but there was no one. "You," the voice said, "in the green shirt. I'm in here." I looked in the window, and saw the face of a pale girl reflected in the crystal ball. "I'm the Genie of the Crystal," she said, with a strong Southern accent, "and I want to tell you what a great time you'll have here in the Gatlinburg Ripley's Believe-It-or-Not Museum."

"What the hell is that?" Craig said.

"And you too, in the red shirt, with the dark hair and pretty eyes," said the Genie of the Crystal. "Y'all can have a wonderful time here in the Gatlinburg Ripley's Believe-It-or-Not Museum, so why not come on in?"

Craig and I looked at each other. "Can she see us?" I asked.

"Sure I can," said the Genie of the Crystal, "just like you can see me. So why don't you come on in? A couple of cute guys like you could have lots of fun."

She was flirting with us—or rather, flirting with Craig. I imagined her in her little room in the back, looking at us on a television screen like the ones in the corners in drugstores, noticing Craig. Even through two layers of glass and several TVs, it was obvious where her eyes were focused.

"What happens inside?" I asked.

The Genie of the Crystal laughed. "You get to see all the attractions," she said and, smiling some more at Craig, added, "like me."

Craig smiled thinly.

"Do you want to go in?" I said. "I think it might be fun."

He tried for anger. "Look," he said, "I didn't come camping for a week to spend all my time in stupid museums like this." But I persisted. "Come on, Craig," I said. "When are we ever going to have the chance again?" The Genie's flirtation titillated me, as if she and I were conspirators in Craig's seduction.

"Listen to your friend, Craig," she said. "Don't you want to see the inside of my lamp?"

Craig looked for a moment through the window, at the crystal ball. He sighed loudly. "All right," he said finally, making it clear he was doing me a big favor.

"Good," I said.

We paid our three seventy-five each and slipped through the turnstile, where a comforting sign which could only have existed in Tennessee assured us, "This is not a scary museum." For an hour we wandered among stuffed six-toed cats and immense toothpick mansions. We looked at pictures of a family of giants, listened to a tape recording of twins who had invented their own language. But the Genie of the Crystal really had been only doing her job; she was nowhere to be found.

"Did y'all have a good time?" she asked us afterwards, all mock-innocence, and we glared at her. Then a family—grandparents, parents, a blur of children—was crowding around the window, pushing us out of the Genie's view and mind. "What's that?" a little girl asked.

"I'm the Genie of the Crystal, honey," said the Genie of the Crystal.

The little girl started to cry.

"Don't be scared," the Genie said. "I'm your friend. And y'all can have a wonderful time here at the Gatlinburg Ripley's Believe-It-or-Not Museum."

Now—as Craig would say—"time warp." Five years passed. I was still a sexual innocent, compared to Craig, but I believed genuinely that I was making up for lack of experience with density of experience. Not Craig. Fear of AIDS had not compelled him to limit his activities, only to reduce their scope. He had as much sex as ever, but it was "safe sex," the rules outlined clearly from the beginning: no kissing, no fluid exchange, no collision of mucous-membrane areas. I don't think it was really much of a sacrifice for him; he claimed to have always liked it best that way anyway, watching someone watch him make love to himself.

We were both living in New York that summer just out of college. I had a stupid job at a bookstore, and Craig had an impressive job at a law firm which allowed him to make his own hours. Since I didn't have that many other friends in the city, I found myself becoming quite dependent on Craig—as a teacher, a tour guide, a mentor. We would go out to coffee shops together, in the afternoons, and he would tell me about having sex with soap in the West Side Y showers, and then about how he had developed bad sores between his legs from having sex with soap in the West Side Y showers. He described to me in detail the bizarre sexual practice of "felching," and what Kwell was. I memorized these words, imagining they would be as important in my life as they appeared to be in his. At night, when we went to bars together, vain Craig refused to wear his glasses, and insisted I act as his Seeing Eye dog. "That guy over there," he'd say. "Is he cute? Is he looking at me?" I'd tell him faithfully, though often our opinions differed. Always the tourist; I went home from these nocturnal expeditions alone, and woke up to Craig's phone call the next morning, describing the night's experience, usually bad. He was living with his parents, and had an immense collection of pornography stashed right under their noses, which he liked to trade from and bargain with, like a child with baseball cards. He claimed he could always tell how much hair a man had on his ass by looking at his wrists. And once, when we were in the park, he led me on a circuitous route through bushes where men stood leaning against trees, caressing the prominent erections outlined in their pockets, and I burst out laughing. "Shut up," he whispered, grabbing my arm and dragging me away, back onto one of the park's main avenues. "How could you do that? How could you embarrass me like that?"—as if I'd told a dirty joke to his grandmother. I kept laughing. I don't know why I was laughing—what I'd seen in the bushes hadn't struck me as particularly funny—but somehow I couldn't get hold of myself. The laughter controlled me, like hiccups, and would not abate, the same way a sly smile sometimes crept across my face just after I'd heard a piece of terrible news. It was as if a demon were shifting circuits inside my brain to turn Craig against me.

In the end, when I finally stopped laughing, I apologized to Craig. I did not, after all, want to offend him. I needed Craig a lot that summer because I felt safe doing things with him that I would never dare do by myself. When I entered the bars and pornographic bookstores alone, they were full of threats, and the biggest threat was that I might become, like Craig, their denizen. I could feel that urge in myself—it would be so easy to slip through the turnstile into the Adonis Theatre, as Craig often did, and once there, do what was beckoned of you, in the dark. With Craig I was protected. I could live vicariously. I was never tempted, because no man, seeing me and Craig together, would even notice me. He was dazzling in his dark, Semitic handsomeness, the perfect Jewish lawyer every mother wants her girl to marry. Neat tufts of hair poked out of his shirt collar. He was everyone's freshman-year roommate, the president of the debate society, your sister's sexy boyfriend. I used his attractiveness as a shield; in its shadow I was invisible, and could watch, fascinated, as men approached him, as he absorbed all the damage that might be inflicted in those late-night places. It was Craig who got crabs, amoebas, warts. I always ended up at home—alone, but unscathed. Safe.

Craig's appeal, in truth, is limited. What boyfriends he has managed to keep more than a week have emerged from extended relationships with him itchy and unsatisfied, for no matter how irresistible the prospect of a night with Craig, there is not much to warm up to in the thought of a life with him. This is, perhaps, his greatest tragedy, for when he does fall in love, it is with an intensity and fervor unlike any I've ever seen. So used is he to sexual control that, robbed of it, he becomes a madman, furious in his jealousy, pathetic in his adoration. If Craig loves a man, the man must be a god. It is a condition of his ego. I remember Sam, the blond architect he saw for a month, and finally scared out of New York with his loud worship; and Willie, the downtown artist, whose ripe body odor Craig found ambrosial, and spoke about with everyone, until Willie found out and got so embarrassed he refused even to speak to Craig. After his lovers broke up with him, Craig was bitter, churlish, stingy. His contempt was loud and cruel, and usually directed toward those men who made the mistake of trying to court him in conventional ways—that is, with phone calls, letters, (God forbid) love poems. I remember one poor man who approached him on a Friday night at Boy Bar, an elementary-school teacher who wanted to make him dinner. "I'm a competent cook," he kept saying, pleadingly. I think he only really meant that—that he wanted to cook him dinner. He just kept talking, telling everything to Craig, who never said a word, never even looked at him. And I thought, as I often thought when I was with him, how glad I was to be Craig's friend, because it meant I was spared the indignity of being his suitor.

At the end of the summer I quit my job at the bookstore and started business school—a mistake, I realize now, calculated primarily to please my father. It did not go well, but I passed most of my courses, and my parents, for my birthday, gave me what I'd been begging them for—a round-trip ticket to Paris, where I'd spent the spring semester of my junior year in college, and where I'd felt happier, I believed, than anywhere else I'd ever lived. When the ticket arrived, it was sealed in a red gift envelope bearing the airline's name, and there was wrapped around it a wildflower-patterned note from my mother on which she'd written a poem to me: "You've worked hard all year / To make your career / But now the term's done / So go have some fun! XXX, Mom." She fully believed, of course, that I was going to be coming back from Paris, that I was going to return to business school, and I wasn't about to tell her otherwise. Not that I had alternative plans. I had simply decided, in my own mind, that I wasn't going to come back. My life in New York was starting to repulse me, and I had to get away from it, from the endless repetition of my nights with Craig, or rather, the endless repetition of Craig's nights, the ragged edges of which I clung to. Perhaps I was also beginning to want things Craig would never have been able to get for himself, much less for me: a lover, nights watching television in bed instead of in bars. And I knew I wouldn't be able to free myself from my dependency on Craig unless I got far, far away from him.

In Paris, I lived in a beautiful apartment that belonged to an Italian woman, a friend of my parents'—a sleek, modern studio in a crumbling fifteenth-century building near the Pompidou Center, in the Marais. *Marais* means swamp, and riding to the airport on the JFK Express, I looked out the window at the bayoulike hinterlands of Queens: a muddy delta of broken-down houses, their little jetties thrust out into the sludge. It was a depressing view, and it didn't bode well for the summer. But the Marais turned out to be no swamp; it was an ancient neighborhood of tiny cobblestoned streets, too narrow for most cars, in which art galleries and fancy bookstores, like newly planted exotic flowers, were just beginning to bloom. There were chickens and urinating children in the courtyard, sawdust on the uneven steps. Most of my neighbors were stooped old women who eyed me suspiciously, muttering *"L'Italienne"* to one another under their breath. Their rooms were as squalid as the courtyard; they shared squat toilets in the hall. I suspect they resented *L'Italienne* not because she was young and chic and was part of a growing movement to gentrify their neighborhood, but because she had her own fancy bathroom and water heater. I myself had never met *L'Italienne*, my patroness, so kindly allowing me to live rent-free in her pied-à-terre, though she made her presence and personality known to me in the form of little notes stuck all over the apartment, instructing me how to turn on the water, which drawers to use, how to light the stove, not to mention the many notes which said "Privé," or "Personal Drawer—Do Not Touch." I never did.

June afternoons in Paris are melancholic. Craig, who was himself going to be spending the summer Eurailing his way through Spain and Italy and Greece, had encouraged me to buy the *Spartacus Guide for Gay Men* before I left, and according to its instructions, I walked up and down the Tuileries each night at dusk, astonished at how many men there were there, some shirtless, others dressed head to toe in leather, lounging on benches, or leaning against the Orangerie, or staring dissolutely at the Seine. The *Spartacus Guide* really was, as it claimed, a world unto itself. Its entire middle was composed of advertisements from various pedophiliac presses for novels, short-story collections, diatribes, and defenses of the "boy-loving man" and "man-loving boy." When you looked up a bar, or a bathhouse, or an "outdoor cruising area" in the *Spartacus Guide*, you would get an entry something like this: B D LX M OG AYOR. You would then look in the key at the front of the book for a translation. B meant bar, D dancing, LX lesbians excluded, all the way down to AYOR—"At Your Own Risk." This last abbreviation appealed to me especially because I read it as a word—"ayor." "Ayor," I'd say to myself, walking up and down the length of the dusky Tuileries. I loved the sound of it, the way it rolled off my tongue into definitiveness. It was like a signal, a code of unwelcome, the opposite of "ahoy." "Ayor." Stay away. There are dangers here.

Because I was a good boy, I avoided the places that were labeled AYOR. I only went to Le Broad, the big disco that the guide gave four stars and described as "certainly the classiest and best-run gay establishment in Paris." It was a giant, cavernous place, with elaborate catacombs, dark links of rooms where who knows what happened, where I might have ventured with Craig, but never alone. Instead, I stayed on the dance floor, where, as it was perfectly acceptable to do so in Paris, I often danced by myself, for hours, caught up in the frenzy of music and movement, swept to my feet by the moment. The biggest song that summer was a ridiculous, campy concoction by Eartha Kitt, called "I Love Men," though she sang it "I Love-ah Men-ah."

In the end, they always resist-ah
And pretend you didn't exist-ah
But, my friend, somehow they persist-ah
And remain at the top of my list-ah . . .

I remember how the French men—so exotic-looking to me, with their thick syrupy smell of *parfum* and cigarettes, their shirts open to the waist, their dark skin, thin lips, huge black eyes—tried so hard to sing along with Eartha Kitt, though they didn't understand anything she was saying. Drunk and in love with themselves, they howled animalistically some rough approximation of the song. They made out in pairs and trios on the fringes of the dance floor. They were joyous in their collectivity. And why not? *"Le SIDA"* hadn't caught up with them yet. It was the first time in my life and the only place in the world where I have ever been able to imagine sex with a man without feeling fear or guilt. Instead, I imagined the prospect of adventure, celebration. I could taste it on my lips.

I met Laurent the second night I went to that disco. A fight had broken out somewhere across the dance floor, and the ripples of movement threw us literally into each other's arms. Laughing, we just stayed there. It was a glorious, easy meeting. Laurent was twenty, a literature student at Nanterre, son of an Italian mother and a French father, and the birthdate carved on the gold chain around his neck was a lie. "Why?" I asked him that night, while we lay naked and sweating in my big bed, in the heat of the night, and I, at least, in the heat of love. He explained that his mother was already two months pregnant when she married his father, and that they had had to lie to the Italian relatives about the birthday to avoid a *scandale.* He didn't mind because it meant he had two birthdays a year—one in France and another, two months later, in Italy. Except that he rarely saw the Italian relatives. His father, whom he hated, who drove a silver "Bay-Em-Double-vay," had left his mother for her cousin. His mother had not been the same since; he had had to move home with her, to take care of her. He also had to babysit his own *petite cousine*, Marianne, every morning at nine, and therefore couldn't spend the night. (This seemed to be the ultimate, consequential point of the saga.) I said that was fine. I was ready to agree to just about anything.

From the moment I let Laurent out the door, in the early hours of the morning, I was jubilant with love for him—for his long, dark eyelashes, his slightly contemptuous mouth, his odd insistence on wearing only white socks. ("*Non, ce n'est pas les Français,*" he explained when I asked him, "*c'est seulement moi.*") Like most Europeans, he was uncircumcised—the only uncircumcised lover I have ever had. That small flap of skin, long removed from me in some deeply historical *bris*, was the embodiment of our difference. It fascinated me, and my fascination chafed poor Laurent, who couldn't understand what the big deal was—I, the American, was the one who was altered, *pas normal*, after all. I pulled at it, played with it, curious and delighted, until he made me stop. "*Tu me fais mal,*" he protested. Craig's eyes would have lit up.

But Craig was nowhere near, and I was in a limited way happy. My love affair with Laurent was simple and regular, a series of afternoons, one blending into the other. Around eleven-thirty in the morning, after finishing with *la petite Marianne*, he would arrive at my apartment, and I would feed him lunch. Then we would make love, perfunctorily, for an hour or so. Then we would take a walk to his car, and he would drive me for a while through the suburbs of Paris—Choisy-le-Roi, Vincennes, Clamart, Pantin. He classified these suburbs as either *pas beau*, *beau*, or *joli*, adjectives which seemed to have more to do with class than aesthetics. I was inept at understanding the distinctions. "*Neuilly est joli, n'est-ce pas?*" I'd ask him, as we drove down tree-lined avenues, past big, imposing houses. "*Non, c'est beau.*" "*Clamart, c'est aussi beau, n'est-ce pas?*" "*Non, c'est joli.*" Eventually I'd give up, and Laurent, frustrated by my intransigence, would drop me off at my apartment before going off to his job. All night he sold Walkmans in a Parisian "drugstore," a giant, futuristic shopping mall of red Formica and chrome that featured at its heart a seventy-foot wall on which sixty-four televisions played rock videos simultaneously. This huge and garish place is the sentimental center of my memories of that summer, for I used to go there often in the evenings to visit Laurent, unable to resist his company, though I feared he might grow tired of me. Then I'd stand under the light of the videos, pretending not to know him, while he explained to someone the advantages of Aiwa over Sony. When he wasn't with a customer, we'd talk, or (more aptly) he'd play with one of the little credit-card-sized calculators he had in his display case, and I'd stare at him. But I couldn't stay at the drugstore forever. After twenty minutes or so, fearful of rousing the suspicions of the ash-blond woman who was in charge of Laurent, I'd bid him adieu, and he'd wink at me before returning to his work. That wink meant everything to me. It meant my life. Powered by it, I might walk for miles afterwards down the Rue de Rivoli, along the Seine, across the brilliant bridges to the Latin Quarter, filled in summer with joyous young Americans singing in the streets, eating take-out couscous, smiling and laughing just to be there. Often friends from college were among their number. We'd wave across the street as casually as if we were seeing each other in New York. It astonishes me to think how many miles I must have charted that summer, zigzagging aimlessly across the Parisian night for love of Laurent. It was almost enough, walking like that, wanting him. That wink was almost enough.

Laurent had been to America only once, when he was fourteen. His parents had sent him to New York, where he was to meet an aunt who lived in Washington, but the aunt's son was in a car accident and she couldn't come. For a week he had stayed alone at the Waldorf-Astoria, a little French boy who didn't speak English, instructed by his mother to avoid at all costs the subways, the streets, the world. These days, when the meanderings of my life take me to the giant, glittering lobby of the Waldorf-Astoria, I sometimes think I see him, in his French schoolboy's suit, hiding behind a giant ficus, or cautiously fingering magazines in the gift shop. I imagine him running down the halls, or pacing the confines of his four-walled room, or sitting on the big bed, entranced by the babbling cartoon creatures inhabiting his television.

Craig is by nature a suburbanite. He grew up in Westport, Connecticut, where his father is a prominent dermatologist and the first Jew ever admitted to the country club. One evening in college he embarrassed me by getting into a long argument with a girl from Mount Kisco on the ridiculous subject of which was a better suburb—Mount Kisco or Westport. On the way back to our dorm, I berated him. "Jesus, Craig," I said, "I can't believe you'd stoop so low as to argue about a subject as ridiculous as who grew up in a better suburb." But he didn't care. "She's crazy," he insisted. "Mount Kisco doesn't compare to Westport. I'm not arguing about it because I have a stake in it, only because it's true. Westport is much nicer—the houses are much farther apart, and the people, they're just classier, better-looking and with higher-up positions. Mount Kisco's where you go on the way to Westport."

Suburbs mattered to Craig. He apparently saw no implicit contradiction in their mattering to him at the same moment that he was, say, being given a blowjob by a law student in one of the infamous library men's rooms, or offering me a list of call numbers that would point to the library's hidden stashes of pornography. But Craig has never been given much to introspection. He is blessed by a remarkable clarity of vision, which allows him to see through the levels, the aboves and belows, that plague the rest of us. There are no contradictions in his world; nothing is profane, but then again, nothing is sacred.

He was in Europe, that same summer as me, on his parents' money, on a last big bash before law school. In Paris I'd get postcards from Ibiza, from Barcelona, where he'd had his passport stolen, from Florence (this one showing a close-up of the *David*'s genitalia), and he would talk about Nils, Rutger, and especially Nino, whom he'd met in the men's room at the train station. I enjoyed his postcards. They provided a much-needed connection with my old life, my pre-Paris self. Things were not going well with Laurent, who, it had taken me only a few days to learn, lived in a state of continuous and deep depression. He would arrive afternoons in my apartment, silent, and land in the armchair, where for hours, his eyes lowered, he would read the Tintin books I kept around to improve my French, and sometimes watch *Les Quatres Fantastiques* on television. The candy-colored cartoon adventures of Tintin, androgynous boy reporter, kept him busy until it was nearly time for him to go to work, at which point I would nudge my way into his lap and say, "*Qu'est-ce que c'est?* I want to help you." But all he would tell me was that he was depressed because he was losing his car. His aunt, who owned it, was taking it back, and now he would have to ride the train in to work every day, and take a cab back late at night. I suggested he might stay with me, and he shook his head. "*La petite Marianne,*" he reminded me. Of course. *La petite Marianne.*

I think now that in continually begging Laurent to tell me what was worrying him, it was I who pushed him away. My assumption that "talking about it" or "opening up" was the only way for him to feel better was very American, and probably misguided. And of course, my motives were not, as I imagined, entirely unselfish, for at the heart of all that badgering was a deep fear that he did not love me, and that that was why he held back from me, refused to tell me what was wrong. Now I look back on Laurent's life in those days, and I see he probably wasn't hiding things from me. He probably really was depressed because he was losing his car, though that was only the tip of the iceberg. His fragile mother depended on him totally, his father was nowhere to be seen, his future, as a literature student at a second-rate university, was not rosy. It is quite possible, I see now, that in his sadness it was comforting for him simply to be in my presence, my warm apartment on a late afternoon, reading Tintin books, drinking tea. But I wasn't content to offer him just that. I wanted him to notice me. I wanted to be his cure. I wish I'd known that then; I might not have driven him off.

In any case, I was very happy when Craig finally came to visit, that summer, because it meant I would have something to occupy my time other than my worrisome thoughts about Laurent. It was late July by then, and the prospect of August, when Paris empties itself of its native population and becomes a desiccated land of closed shops, wandered by aimless foreigners, was almost sufficiently unappealing to send me back to business school. In ten days Laurent would quit his job and take off to the seaside with his mother. There was no mention of my possibly going with him, though I would have gladly done so, and could imagine with relish staying by myself in a little pension near the big, elegant hotel where Laurent and his mother went every year, going for tea and sitting near them on the outdoor promenade, watching them, waiting for Laurent's wink. There would be secret rendezvous, long walks on beaches—but it was all a dream. Laurent would have been furious if I'd shown up.

And so I was happily looking forward to Craig, to the stories I knew he'd tell, the sexual exploits he'd so willingly narrate, and in such great detail. I met his train at the Gare de Lyon. There he was, on schedule, in alpine shorts and Harvard T-shirt, the big ubiquitous backpack stooping him over. We embraced, and took the métro back to my apartment. He looked tired, thin. He had lost his traveler's checks in Milan, he explained, had had his wallet stolen in Venice. He had also wasted a lot of money renting double rooms at exorbitant prices just for himself, and was worried that his parents wouldn't agree to wire him more. I tried to sympathize, but it seemed somehow fitting that he should now be suffering the consequences of his irresponsibility. Stingy with anyone else, he was rapacious in spending his parents' money on himself—a trait I have observed often in firstborn sons of Jewish families. (I myself was the second-born son, and live frugally to this day.)

We went out, that night, for dinner, to a Vietnamese restaurant I liked and ate in often, and Craig started to tell me about his trip—the beaches at Ibiza, the bars in Amsterdam. "It's been fun," he concluded. "Everything's been pretty good, except this one bad thing happened."

"What was that?" I asked.

"Well, I was raped in Madrid."

Delicately he wrapped a spring roll in a sprig of mint and popped it in his mouth.

"What?" I said.

"Just what I told you. I was raped in Madrid."

I put down my fork. "Craig," I said. "Come on. What do you mean, 'raped'?"

"Forcibly taken. Fucked against my will. What better definition do you want?"

He took a swig of water.

I sat back in my chair. As often happens to me when I'm struck speechless, a lewd, involuntary smile pulled apart my lips. I tried to suppress it.

"How did it happen?" I asked, as casually as I could.

"The usual way," he said, and laughed. "I was walking down the street, cruising a little bit, and this guy said *'Hola'* to me. He was cute, young. I said *'Hola'* back. Well, to make a long story short, we ended up back at his apartment. He spoke a little English, and he explained to me that he was in a big hurry. Then there was a knock on the door and this other guy walked in. They talked very quickly in Spanish, and he told me to get undressed. I didn't much want to do it anymore, but I took off my clothes—"

"Why?" I interrupted.

He shrugged. "Once you've gone that far it's hard not to," he said. "Anyway, as far as I could gather, he and his friend were arguing over whether the friend would have sex with us or just watch. After a while I stopped trying to understand and just sat down on the bed. It didn't take me too long to figure out the guy was married and that was why he was in such a hurry. I could tell from all the woman's things around the apartment.

"Anyway, they finally decided the friend would just watch. The first guy—the one who said *'Hola'*—saw I was naked and he took off his clothes and then—Well, I tried to explain I only did certain things, 'safe sex' and all, but he didn't listen to me. He just jumped me. He was very strong, and the worst thing was, he really smelled. He hadn't washed for a long time, he was really disgusting." Craig leaned closer to me. "You know," he said, "that I don't get fucked. I don't like it and I won't do it. And I kept trying to tell him this, but he just wouldn't listen to me. I don't think he meant to force me. I think he just thought I was playing games and that I was really enjoying it. I mean, he didn't hit me or anything, though he held my wrists behind my back for a while. But then he stopped."

He ate another spring roll, and called the waiter over to ask for chopsticks. There were no tears in his eyes; no change was visible in his face. A deep horror welled in me, stronger than anything I'd ever felt with Craig, so strong I just wanted to laugh, the same way I'd laughed that afternoon in Central Park when he showed me the secret places where men meet other men.

"Are you O.K.?" I asked instead, mustering a sudden, surprising self-control. "Do you need to see a doctor?"

He shrugged. "I'm just mad because he came in my ass even though I asked him not to. Who knows what he might have been carrying? Also, it hurt. But I didn't bleed or anything. I didn't come, of course, and he couldn't have cared less, which really pissed me off. He finished, told me to get dressed fast. I guess he was worried his wife would come home."

I looked at the table, and Craig served himself more food.

"I think if that happened to me I'd have to kill myself," I said quietly.

"I don't see why you're making such a big deal out of it," Craig said. "I mean, it didn't hurt *that* much or anything. Anyway, it was just once."

I pushed back my chair, stretched out my legs. I had no idea what to say next. "Aren't you going to eat any more?" Craig asked, and I nodded no, I had lost my appetite.

"Well, I'm going to finish these noodles," he said, and scooped some onto his plate. I watched him eat. I wanted to know if he was really feeling nothing, as he claimed. But his face was impassive, unreadable. Clearly he was not going to let me know.

Afterwards, we walked along the mossy sidewalks of the Seine—

"good cruising," the *Spartacus Guide* had advised us, but "very AYOR"—and Craig told me about Nils, Rutger, Nino, etc. I, in turn, told him about Laurent. He was mostly interested in the matter of his foreskin. When I started discussing our problems—Laurent's depression, my fear that he was pulling away from me—Craig grew distant, hardly seemed to be listening to me. "Uh-huh," he'd say, in response to every phrase I'd offer, and look away, or over his shoulder, until finally I gave up.

We crossed the Île de la Cité, and Craig asked about going to a bar, but I told him I was too tired, and he admitted he probably was as well. He hadn't gotten a *couchette* on the train up here, and the passport-control people had woken him up six or seven times during the night.

Back at my apartment, we undressed together. (Since Laurent, I had lost my modesty.) I watched as Craig, like any good first son, carefully folded his shirt and balled his socks before climbing into the makeshift bed I had created for him on my floor. These old habits, taught long ago by his mother, were second nature to him, which I found touching. I looked at him in the bed. He had lost weight, and a spray of fine red pimples covered his back.

Raped, I can hardly say that word. Besides Craig, the only person I know who was raped was a friend in my dorm in college named Sandra. After it happened, I avoided her for weeks. I imagined, stupidly, that simply because I was male, I'd remind her of what she'd gone through, make her break down, melt, weep. But finally she cornered me one afternoon in the library. "Stop avoiding me," she said. "Just because I was raped doesn't mean I'm made out of glass." And it was true. It was always Sandra who brought up the fact of the rape—often in front of strangers. "I was raped," she'd say, as if to get the facts out of the way, as if saying it like that—casually, without preparation—helped to alleviate the terror, gave her strength. Craig had told me with a similar studied casualness. And yet I suspect his motive was not so much to console himself as to do some sort of penance; I suspect he genuinely believed that he had been asking for it, and that he deserved it, deserved whatever he got.

Perhaps I am wrong to use the word "underside" when I describe the world Craig led me through that first summer in New York, perhaps wrong in assuming that for Craig, it has been a matter of surfaces and depths, hells and heavens. For me, yes. But for him, I think, there really wasn't much of a distance to travel between the Westport of his childhood and the dark places he seemed to end up in, guide or no guide, in whatever city he visited. Wallets, traveler's checks, your life: these were just the risks you took. I lived in two worlds; I went in and out of the underside as I pleased, with Craig to protect me. I could not say it was my fault that he was raped. But I realized, that night, that on some level I had been encouraging him to live in the world's danger zones, its ayor zones, for years now, to satisfy my own curiosity, my own lust. And I wondered: How much had I contributed to Craig's apparent downfall? To what extent had I, in living through him, made him, molded him into some person I secretly, fearfully longed to be?

He lay on my floor, gently snoring. He always slept gently. But I had no desire to embrace him or to try to save him. He seemed, somehow, ruined to me, beyond hope. He had lost all allure. It is cruel to record now, but the truth was, I hoped he'd be gone by morning.

The next afternoon, we had lunch with Laurent. Because Craig spoke no French and Laurent spoke no English, there was not much conversation. I translated, remedially, between them. Craig did not seem very impressed by Laurent, which disappointed me, and Laurent did not seem very impressed by Craig, which pleased me.

Afterwards, Laurent and I drove Craig to the Gare du Nord, where he was catching a train to Munich. He had relatives there who he hoped would give him money to spend at least a few weeks in Germany. For a couple of minutes, through me, he and Laurent discussed whether or not he should go to see Dachau. Laurent had found it very moving, he said. But Craig's only response was, "Uh-huh."

Then we were saying goodbye, and then he was gone, lost in the depths of the *gare*.

On the way back to my apartment I told Laurent about Craig's rape. His eyes bulged in surprise. "*Ton ami,*" he said, when I had finished the story, "*sa vie est tragique.*" I was glad, somehow, that the rape meant something to Laurent, and for a moment, in spite of all our problems, I wanted to embrace him, to celebrate the fact of all we had escaped, all we hadn't suffered. But my French wasn't good enough to convey what I wanted to convey. And Laurent was depressed.

He dropped me off at my apartment, continued on to work. I couldn't bear the thought of sitting alone indoors, so I took a walk over to the Rue

St. Denis and Les Halles. The shops had just reopened for the afternoon, and the streets were full of people—giggly Americans and Germans, trios of teenaged boys.

I sat down in a café and tried to stare at the men in the streets. I wondered what it must have been like, that "*Hola,*" whispered on a busy Madrid sidewalk, that face turning toward him. Was the face clear, vivid in its intent? I think not. I think it was probably as vague and convex as the face of the Genie of the Crystal in Gatlinburg. Then, too, it was the surprise of recognition, the surprise of being noticed; it will do it every time. The Genie of the Crystal, she, too, had wanted Craig, and even then I had urged him on, thinking myself safe in his shadow.

I drank a cup of coffee, then another. I stared unceasingly at men in the street, men in the café, sometimes getting cracked smiles in response. But in truth, as Craig has endlessly told me, I simply do not have the patience for cruising. Finally I paid my bill, and then I heard the church bells of Notre Dame strike seven. Only five days left in July. Soon it would be time to head up to Montmartre, to the drugstore, where Laurent, like it or not, was going to get my company.

Gravity

Theo had a choice between a drug that would save his sight and a drug that would keep him alive, so he chose not to go blind. He stopped the pills and started the injections—these required the implantation of an unpleasant and painful catheter just above his heart—and within a few days the clouds in his eyes started to clear up; he could see again. He remembered going into New York City to a show with his mother, when he was twelve and didn't want to admit he needed glasses. "Can you read that?" she'd shouted, pointing to a Broadway marquee, and when he'd squinted, making out only one or two letters, she'd taken off her own glasses—harlequins with tiny rhinestones in the corners—and shoved them onto his face. The world came into focus, and he gasped, astonished at the precision around the edges of things, the legibility, the hard, sharp, colorful landscape. Sylvia had to squint through *Fiddler on the Roof* that day, but for Theo, his face masked by his mother's huge glasses, everything was as bright and vivid as a comic book. Even though people stared at him, and muttered things, Sylvia didn't care; he could *see.*

Because he was dying again, Theo moved back to his mother's house in New Jersey. The DHPG injections she took in stride—she'd seen her own mother through *her* dying, after all. Four times a day, with the equanimity of a nurse, she cleaned out the plastic tube implanted in his chest, inserted a sterilized hypodermic, and slowly dripped the bag of sight-giving liquid into his veins. They endured this procedure silently, Sylvia sitting on the side of the hospital bed she'd rented for the duration of Theo's stay—his life, he sometimes thought—watching reruns of *I Love Lucy* or the news, while he tried not to think about the hard piece of pipe stuck into him, even though it was a constant reminder of how wide and unswimmable the gulf was becoming between him and the ever-receding shoreline of the well. And Sylvia was intricately cheerful. Each day she urged him to go out with her somewhere—to the library, or the little museum with the dinosaur replicas he'd been fond of as a child—and when his thinness and the cane drew stares, she'd maneuver him around the people who were staring, determined to shield him from whatever they might say or do. It had been the same that afternoon so many years ago, when she'd pushed him through a lobbyful of curious and laughing faces, determined that nothing should interfere with the spectacle of his seeing. What a pair they must have made, a boy in ugly glasses and a mother daring the world to say a word about it!

This warm, breezy afternoon in May they were shopping for revenge. "Your cousin Howard's engagement party is next month," Sylvia explained in the car. "A very nice girl from Livingston. I met her a few weeks ago, and really, she's a superior person."

"I'm glad," Theo said. "Congratulate Howie for me."

"Do you think you'll be up to going to the party?"

"I'm not sure. Would it be O.K. for me just to give him a gift?"

"You already have. A lovely silver tray, if I say so myself. The thank-you note's in the living room."

"Mom," Theo said, "why do you always have to—"

Sylvia honked her horn at a truck making an illegal left turn.

"Better they should get something than no present at all, is what I say," she said. "But now, the problem is, *I* have to give Howie something, to be from me, and it better be good. It better be very, very good."

"Why?"

"Don't you remember that cheap little nothing Bibi gave you for your graduation? It was disgusting."

"I can't remember what she gave me."

"Of course you can't. It was a tacky pen-and-pencil set. Not even a real leather box. So naturally, it stands to reason that I have to get something truly spectacular for Howard's engagement. Something that will make Bibi blanch. Anyway, I think I've found just the thing, but I need your advice."

"Advice? Well, when my old roommate Nick got married, I gave him a garlic press. It cost five dollars and reflected exactly how much I felt, at that moment, our friendship was worth."

Sylvia laughed. "Clever. But my idea is much more brilliant, because it makes it possible for me to get back at Bibi *and* give Howard the nice gift he and his girl deserve." She smiled, clearly pleased with herself. "Ah, you live and learn."

"You live," Theo said.

Sylvia blinked. "Well, look, here we are." She pulled the car into a handicapped-parking place on Morris Avenue and got out to help Theo, but he was already hoisting himself up out of his seat, using the door handle for leverage. "I can manage myself," he said with some irritation. Sylvia stepped back.

"Clearly one advantage to all this for you," Theo said, balancing on his cane, "is that it's suddenly so much easier to get a parking place."

"Oh Theo, please," Sylvia said. "Look, here's where we're going."

She leaned him into a gift shop filled with porcelain statuettes of Snow White and all seven of the dwarves, music boxes which, when you opened them, played "The Shadow of Your Smile," complicated-smelling potpourris in purple wallpapered boxes, and stuffed snakes you were supposed to push up against drafty windows and doors.

"Mrs. Greenman," said an expansive, gray-haired man in a cream-colored cardigan sweater. "Look who's here, Archie, it's Mrs. Greenman."

Another man, this one thinner and balding, but dressed in an identical cardigan, peered out from the back of the shop. "Hello there!" he said, smiling. He looked at Theo, and his expression changed.

"Mr. Sherman, Mr. Baker. This is my son, Theo."

"Hello," Mr. Sherman and Mr. Baker said. They didn't offer to shake hands.

"Are you here for that item we discussed last week?" Mr. Sherman asked.

"Yes," Sylvia said. "I want advice from my son here." She walked over to a large ridged crystal bowl, a very fifties sort of bowl, stalwart and square-jawed. "What do you think? Beautiful, isn't it?"

"Mom, to tell the truth, I think it's kind of ugly."

"Four hundred and twenty-five dollars," Sylvia said admiringly. "You have to feel it."

Then she picked up the big bowl and tossed it to Theo, like a football.

The gentlemen in the cardigan sweaters gasped and did not exhale. When Theo caught it, it sank his hands. His cane rattled as it hit the floor.

"That's heavy," Sylvia said, observing with satisfaction how the bowl had weighted Theo's arms down. "And where crystal is concerned, heavy is impressive."

She took the bowl back from him and carried it to the counter. Mr. Sherman was mopping his brow. Theo looked at the floor, still surprised not to see shards of glass around his feet.

Since no one else seemed to be volunteering, he bent over and picked up the cane.

"Four hundred and fifty-nine, with tax," Mr. Sherman said, his voice still a bit shaky, and a look of relish came over Sylvia's face as she pulled out her checkbook to pay. Behind the counter, Theo could see Mr. Baker put his hand on his forehead and cast his eyes to the ceiling.

It seemed Sylvia had been looking a long time for something like this, something heavy enough to leave an impression, yet so fragile it could make you sorry.

They headed back out to the car.

"Where can we go now?" Sylvia asked, as she got in. "There must be someplace else to go."

"Home," Theo said. "It's almost time for my medicine."

"Really? Oh. All right." She pulled on her seat belt, inserted the car key in the ignition, and sat there.

For just a moment, but perceptibly, her face broke. She squeezed her eyes shut so tight the blue shadow on the lids cracked.

Almost as quickly she was back to normal again, and they were driving. "It's getting hotter," Sylvia said. "Shall I put on the air?"

"Sure," Theo said. He was thinking about the bowl, or more specifically, about how surprising its weight had been, pulling his hands down. For a while now he'd been worried about his mother, worried about what damage his illness might secretly be doing to her that of course she would never admit. On the surface things seemed all right. She still broiled herself a skinned chicken breast for dinner every night, still swam a mile and a half a day, still kept used teabags wrapped in foil in the refrigerator. Yet she had also, at about three o'clock one morning, woken him up to tell him she was going to the twenty-four-hour supermarket, and was there anything he wanted. Then there was the gift shop: She had literally pitched that bowl toward him, pitched it like a ball, and as that great gleam of flight and potential regret came sailing his direction, it had occurred to him that she was trusting his two feeble hands, out of the whole world, to keep it from shattering. What was she trying to test? Was it his newly regained vision? Was it the assurance that he was there, alive, that he hadn't yet slipped past all her caring, a little lost boy in rhinestone-studded glasses? There are certain things you've already done before you even think how to do them—a child pulled from in front of a car, for instance, or the bowl, which Theo was holding before he could even begin to calculate its brief trajectory. It had pulled his arms down, and from that apish posture he'd looked at his mother, who smiled broadly, as if, in the war between heaviness and shattering, he'd just helped her win some small but sustaining victory.

Houses

When I arrived at my office that morning—the morning after Susan took me back—an old man and woman wearing wide-brimmed hats and sweatpants were peering at the little snapshots of houses pinned up in the window, discussing their prices in loud voices. There was nothing surprising in this, except that it was still spring, and the costume and demeanor of the couple emphatically suggested summer vacations. It was very early in the day as well as the season—not yet eight and not yet April. They had the look of people who never slept, people who propelled themselves through life on sheer adrenaline, and they also had the look of kindness and good intention gone awry which so often seems to motivate people like that.

I lingered for a few moments outside the office door before going in, so that I could hear their conversation. I had taken a lot of the snapshots myself, and written the descriptive tags underneath them, and I was curious which houses would pique their interest. At first, of course, they looked at the mansions—one of them, oceanfront with ten bathrooms and two pools, was listed for $10.5 million. "Can you imagine?" the wife said. "Mostly it's corporations that buy those," the husband answered. Then their attentions shifted to some more moderately priced, but still expensive, contemporaries. "I don't know, it's like living on the starship *Enterprise*, if you ask me," the wife said. "Personally, I never would get used to a house like that." The husband chuckled. Then the wife's mouth opened and she said, "Will you look at this, Ed? Just look!" and pointed to a snapshot of a small, cedar-shingled house which I happened to know stood not five hundred feet from the office—$165,000, price negotiable. "It's adorable!" the wife said. "It's just like the house in my dream!"

I wanted to tell her it was my dream house too, my dream house first, to beg her not to buy it. But I held back. I reminded myself I already had a house. I reminded myself I had a wife, a dog.

Ed took off his glasses and peered skeptically at the picture. "It doesn't look too bad," he said. "Still, something must be wrong with it. The price is just too low."

"It's the house in my dream, Ed! The one I dreamed about! I swear it is!"

"I told you, Grace-Anne, the last thing I need is a handyman's special. These are my retirement years."

"But how can you know it needs work? We haven't even seen it! Can't we just look at it? Please?"

"Let's have breakfast and talk it over."

"O.K., O.K. No point in getting overeager, right?" They headed toward the coffee shop across the street, and I leaned back against the window.

It was just an ordinary house, the plainest of houses. And yet, as I unlocked the office door to let myself in, I found myself swearing I'd burn it down before I'd let that couple take possession of it. Love can push you to all sorts of unlikely threats.

What had happened was this: The night before, I had gone back to my wife after three months of living with a man. I was thirty-two years old, and more than anything in the world, I wanted things to slow, slow down.

It was a quiet morning. We live year-round in a resort town, and except for the summer months, not a whole lot goes on here. Next week things would start gearing up for the Memorial Day closings—my wife Susan's law firm was already frantic with work—but for the moment I was in a lull. It was still early—not even the receptionist had come in yet—so I sat at my desk, and looked at the one picture I kept there, of Susan running on the beach with our golden retriever, Charlotte. Susan held out a tennis ball in the picture, toward which Charlotte, barely out of puppyhood, was inclining her head. And of course I remembered that even now Susan didn't know the extent to which Charlotte was wound up in all of it.

Around nine forty-five I called Ted at the Elegant Canine. I was halfway through dialing before I realized that it was probably improper for me to be doing this, now that I'd officially gone back to Susan, that Susan, if she knew I was calling him, would more than likely have sent me packing—our reconciliation was that fragile. One of her conditions for taking me back was that I not see, not even speak to, Ted, and in my shame I'd agreed. Nonetheless, here I was, listening as the phone rang. His boss, Patricia, answered. In the background was the usual cacophony of yelps and barks.

"I don't have much time," Ted said, when he picked up a few seconds later. "I have Mrs. Morrison's poodle to blow-dry."

"I didn't mean to bother you," I said. "I just wondered how you were doing."

"Fine," Ted said. "How are you doing?"

"Oh, O.K."

"How did things go with Susan last night?"

"O.K."

"Just O.K.?"

"Well—it felt so good to be home again—in my own bed, with Susan and Charlotte—" I closed my eyes and pressed the bridge of my nose with my fingers. "Anyway," I said, "it's not fair of me to impose all of this on you. Not fair at all. I mean, here I am, back with Susan, leaving you—"

"Don't worry about it."

"I do worry about it. I do."

There was a barely muffled canine scream in the background, and then I could hear Patricia calling for Ted.

"I have to go, Paul—"

"I guess I just wanted to say I miss you. There, I've said it. There's nothing to do about it, but I wanted to say it, because it's what I feel."

"I miss you too, Paul, but listen, I have to go—"

"Wait, wait. There's something I have to tell you."

"What?"

"There was a couple today. Outside the office. They were looking at our house."

"Paul—"

"I don't know what I'd do if they bought it."

"Paul," Ted said, "it's not our house. It never was."

"No, I guess it wasn't." Again I squeezed the bridge of my nose. I could hear the barking in the background grow louder, but this time Ted didn't tell me he had to go.

"Ted?"

"What?"

"Would you mind if I called you tomorrow?"

"You can call me whenever you want."

"Thanks," I said, and then he said a quick good-bye, and all the dogs were gone.

Three months before, things had been simpler. There was Susan, and me, and Charlotte. Charlotte was starting to smell, and the monthly ordeal of bathing her was getting to be too much for both of us, and anyway, Susan reasoned, now that she'd finally paid off the last of her law school loans, we really did have the right to hire someone to bathe our dog. (We were both raised in penny-pinching families; even in relative affluence, we had no cleaning woman, no gardener. I mowed our lawn.) And so, on a drab Wednesday morning before work, I bundled Charlotte into the car and drove her over to the Elegant Canine. There, among the fake emerald collars, the squeaky toys in the shape of mice and hamburgers, the rawhide bones and shoes and pizzas, was Ted. He had wheat-colored hair and green eyes, and he smiled at me in a frank and unwavering way I found difficult to turn away from. I smiled back, left Charlotte in his capable-seeming hands and headed off to work. The morning proceeded lazily. At noon I drove back to fetch Charlotte, and found her looking golden and glorious, leashed to a small post in a waiting area just to the side of the main desk. Through the door behind the desk I saw a very wet Pekingese being shampooed in a tub and a West Highland white terrier sitting alertly on a metal table, a chain around its neck. I rang a bell, and Ted emerged, waving to me with an arm around which a large bloody bandage had been carefully wrapped.

"My God," I said. "Was it—"

"I'm afraid so," Ted said. "You say she's never been to a groomer's?"

"I assure you, never in her entire life—we've left her alone with small children—our friends joke that she could be a babysitter—" I turned to Charlotte, who looked up at me, panting in that retriever way. "What got into you?" I said, rather hesitantly. And even more hesitantly: "Bad, bad dog—"

"Don't worry about it," Ted said, laughing. "It's happened before and it'll happen again."

"I am so sorry. I am just so—sorry. I had no idea, really."

"Look, it's an occupational hazard. Anyway we're great at first aid around here." He smiled again, and, calmed for the moment, I smiled back. "I just can't imagine what got into her. She's supposed to go to the vet next week, so I'll ask him what he thinks."

"Well, Charlotte's a sweetheart," Ted said. "After our initial hostilities, we got to be great friends, right, Charlotte?" He ruffled the top of her head, and she looked up at him adoringly. We were both looking at Charlotte. Then we were looking at each other. Ted raised his eyebrows. I flushed. The look went on just a beat too long, before I turned away, and he was totaling the bill.

Afterwards, at home, I told Susan about it, and she got into a state. "What if he sues?" she said, running her left hand nervously through her hair. She had taken her shoes off; the heels of her panty hose were black with the dye from her shoes.

"Susan, he's not going to sue. He's a very nice kid, very friendly."

I put my arms around her, but she pushed me away. "Was he the boss?" she said. "You said someone else was the boss."

"Yes, a woman."

"Oh, great. Women are much more vicious than men, Paul, believe me. Especially professional women. He's perfectly friendly and wants to forget it, but for all we know she's been dreaming about going on *People's Court* her whole life." She hit the palm of her hand against her forehead.

"Susan," I said, "I really don't think—"

"Did you give him anything?"

"Give him anything?"

"You know, a tip. Something."

"No."

"Jesus, hasn't being married to a lawyer all these years taught you anything?" She sat down and stood up again. "All right, all right, here's what we're going to do. I want you to have a bottle of champagne sent over to the guy. With an apology, a note. Marcia Grossman did that after she hit that tree, and it worked wonders." She blew out breath. "I don't see what else we *can* do at this point, except wait, and hope—"

"Susan, I really think you're making too much of all this. This isn't New York City, after all, and really, he didn't seem to mind at all—"

"Paul, honey, please trust me. You've always been very naive about these things. Just send the champagne, all right?"

Her voice had reached an unendurable pitch of annoyance. I stood up. She looked at me guardedly. It was the beginning of a familiar fight between us—in her anxiety, she'd say something to imply, not so subtly, how much more she understood about the world than I did, and in response I would stalk off, insulted and pouty. But this time I did not stalk off—I just stood there—and Susan, closing her eyes in a manner which suggested profound regret at having acted rashly, said in a very soft voice, "I don't mean to yell. It's just that you know how insecure I get about things like this, and really, it'll make me feel so much better to know we've done something. So send the champagne for my sake, okay?" Suddenly she was small and vulnerable, a little girl victimized by her own anxieties. It was a transformation she made easily, and often used to explain her entire life.

"O.K.," I said, as I always said, and that was the end of it.

The next day I sent the champagne. The note read (according to Susan's instructions): "Dear Ted: Please accept this little gift as a token of thanks for your professionalism and good humor. Sincerely, Paul Hoover and Charlotte." I should add that at this point I believed I was leaving Susan's name off only because she hadn't been there.

The phone at my office rang the next morning at nine-thirty. "Listen," Ted said, "thanks for the champagne! That was so thoughtful of you."

"Oh, it was nothing."

"No, but it means a lot that you cared enough to send it." He was quiet for a moment. "So few clients do, you know. Care."

"Oh, well," I said. "My pleasure."

Then Ted asked me if I wanted to have dinner with him sometime during the week.

"Dinner? Um—well—"

"I know, you're probably thinking this is sudden and rash of me, but— Well, you seemed like such a nice guy, and—I don't know—I don't meet many people I can really even stand to be around—men, that is—so what's the point of pussyfooting around?"

"No, no, I understand," I said. "That sounds great. Dinner, that is—sounds great."

Ted made noises of relief. "Terrific, terrific. What night would be good for you?"

"Oh, I don't know. Thursday?" Thursday Susan was going to New York to sell her mother's apartment.

"Thursday's terrific," Ted said. "Do you like Dunes?"

"Sure." Dunes was a gay bar and restaurant I'd never been to.

"So I'll make a reservation. Eight o'clock? We'll meet there?"

"That's fine."

"I'm so glad," Ted said. "I'm really looking forward to it."

It may be hard to believe, but even then I still told myself I was doing it to make sure he didn't sue us.

Now, I should point out that not *all* of this was a new experience for me. It's true I'd never been to Dunes, but in my town, late at night, there is a beach, and not too far down the highway, a parking area. Those nights Susan and I fought, it was usually at one of these places that I ended up.

Still, nothing I'd done in the dark prepared me for Dunes, when I got there Thursday night. Not that it was so different from any other restaurant I'd gone to—it was your basic scrubbed-oak, piano-bar sort of place. Only everyone was a man. The maître d', white-bearded and red-cheeked, a displaced Santa Claus, smiled at me and said, "Meeting someone?"

"Yes, in fact." I scanned the row of young and youngish men sitting at the bar, looking for Ted. "He doesn't seem to be here yet."

"Ted Potter, right?"

I didn't know Ted's last name. "Yes, I think so."

"The dog groomer?"

"Right."

The maître d', I thought, smirked. "Well, I can seat you now, or you can wait at the bar."

"Oh, I think I'll just wait here, thanks, if that's O.K."

"Whatever you want," the maître d' said. He drifted off toward a large, familial-looking group of young men who'd just walked in the door. Guardedly I surveyed the restaurant for a familiar face which, thankfully, never materialized. I had two or three co-workers who I suspected ate here regularly.

I had to go to the bathroom, which was across the room. As far as I could tell there was no ladies' room at all. As for the men's room, it was small and cramped, with a long trough reminiscent of junior high school summer camp instead of urinals. Above the trough a mirror had been strategically tilted at a downward angle.

By the time I'd finished, and emerged once again into the restaurant,

Ted had arrived. He looked breathless and a little worried and was consulting busily with the maître d'. I waved; he waved back with his bandaged hand, said a few more words to the maître d', and strode up briskly to greet me. "Hello," he said, clasping my hand with his unbandaged one. It was a large hand, cool and powdery. "Gosh, I'm sorry I'm late. I have to say, when I got here, and didn't see you, I was worried you might have left. Joey—that's the owner—said you'd been standing there one minute and the next you were gone."

"I was just in the bathroom."

"I'm glad you didn't leave." He exhaled what seemed an enormous quantity of breath. "Wow, it's great to see you! You look great!"

"Thanks," I said. "So do you." He did. He was wearing a white oxford shirt with the first couple of buttons unbuttoned, and a blazer the color of the beach.

"There you are," said Joey—the maître d'. "We were wondering where you'd run off to. Well, your table's ready." He escorted us to the middle of the hubbub. "Let's order some wine," Ted said as we sat down. "What kind do you like?"

I wasn't a big wine expert—Susan had always done the ordering for us—so I deferred to Ted, who, after conferring for a few moments with Joey, mentioned something that sounded Italian. Then he leaned back and cracked his knuckles, bewildered, apparently, to be suddenly without tasks.

"So," he said.

"So," I said.

"I'm glad to see you."

"I'm glad to see you too."

We both blushed. "You're a real estate broker, right? At least, that's what I figured from your business card."

"That's right."

"How long have you been doing that?"

I dug back. "Oh, eight years or so."

"That's great. Have you been out here the whole time?"

"No, no, we moved out here six years ago."

"We?"

"Uh—Charlotte and I."

"Oh." Again Ted smiled. "So do you like it, living year-round in a resort town?"

"Sure. How about you?"

"I ended up out here by accident and just sort of stayed. A lot of people I've met have the same story. They'd like to leave, but you know—the climate is nice, life's not too difficult. It's hard to pull yourself away."

I nodded nervously.

"Is that your story too?"

"Oh—well, sort of," I said. "I was born in Queens, and then—I was living in Manhattan for a while—and then we decided to move out here—Charlotte and I—because I'd always loved the beach, and wanted to have a house, and here you could sell real estate and live all year round." I looked at Ted: Had I caught myself up in a lie or a contradiction? What I was telling him, essentially, was my history, but without Susan—and that was ridiculous, since my history was bound up with Susan's every step of the way. We'd started dating in high school, gone to the same college. The truth was I'd lived in Manhattan only while she was in law school, and had started selling real estate to help pay her tuition. No wonder the story sounded so strangely motiveless as I told it. I'd left out the reasons for everything. Susan was the reason for everything.

A waiter—a youngish blond man with a mustache so pale you could barely see it—gave us menus. He was wearing a white T-shirt and had a corkscrew outlined in the pocket of his jeans.

"Hello, Teddy," he said to Ted. Then he looked at me and said very fast, as if it were one sentence, "I'm Bobby and I'll be your waiter for the evening would you like something from the bar?"

"We've already ordered some wine," Ted said. "You want anything else, Paul?"

"I'm fine."

"O.K., would you like to hear the specials now?"

We both nodded, and Bobby rattled off a list of complex-sounding dishes. It was hard for me to separate one from the other. I had no appetite. He handed us our menus and moved on to another table.

I opened the menu. Everything I read sounded like it would make me sick.

"So do you like selling houses?" Ted asked.

"Oh yes, I love it—I love houses." I looked up, suddenly nervous that I was talking too much about myself. Shouldn't I ask him something about himself? I hadn't been on a date for fifteen years, after all, and even then the only girl I dated was Susan, whom I'd known forever. What was the etiquette in a situation like this? Probably I should ask Ted something about his life, but what kind of question would be appropriate?

Another waiter arrived with our bottle of wine, which Ted poured.

"How long have you been a dog groomer?" I asked rather tentatively.

"A couple of years. Of course I never intended to be a professional dog groomer. It was just something I did to make money. What I really wanted to be, just like about a million and a half other people, was an actor. Then I took a job out here for the summer, and like I said, I just stayed. I actually love the work. I love animals. When I was growing up my mom kept saying I should have been a veterinarian. She still says that to me sometimes, tells me it's not too late. I don't know. Frankly, I don't think I have what it takes to be a vet, and anyway, I don't want to be one. It's important work, but let's face it, I'm not for it and it's not for me. So I'm content to be a dog groomer." He picked up his wineglass and shook it, so that the wine lapped the rim in little waves.

"I know what you mean," I said, and I did. For years Susan had been complaining that I should have been an architect, insisting that I would have been happier, when the truth was she was just the tiniest bit ashamed of being married to a real estate broker. In her fantasies, "My husband is an architect" sounded so much better.

"My mother always wanted me to be an architect," I said now. "But it was just so she could tell her friends. For some reason people think real estate is a slightly shameful profession, like prostitution or something. They just assume on some level you make your living ripping people off. There's no way around it. An occupational hazard, I guess."

"Like dog bites," said Ted. He poured more wine.

"Oh, about that—" But Bobby was back to take our orders. He was pulling a green pad from the pocket on the back of his apron when another waiter came up to him from behind and whispered something in his ear. Suddenly they were both giggling wildly.

"You going to fill us in?" Ted asked, after the second waiter had left.

"I'm really sorry about this," Bobby said, still giggling. "It's just—" He bent down close to us, and in a confiding voice said, "Jill over at the bar brought in some like really good Vanna, just before work, and like, everything seems really hysterical to me? You know, like it's five years ago and I'm this boy from Emporia, Kansas?" He cast his eyes to the ceiling. "God, I'm like a complete retard tonight. Anyway, what did you say you wanted?"

Ted ordered grilled paillard of chicken with shiitake mushrooms in a papaya vinaigrette; I ordered a cheeseburger.

"Who's Jill?" I asked after Bobby had left.

"Everyone's Jill," Ted said. "They're all Jill."

"And Vanna?"

"Vanna White. It's what they call cocaine here." He leaned closer. "I'll bet you're thinking this place is really ridiculous, and you're right. The truth is, I kind of hate it. Only can you name me someplace else where two men can go on a date? I like the fact that you can act datish here, if you know what I mean." He smiled. Under the table our hands interlocked. We were acting very datish indeed.

It was all very unreal. I thought of Susan, in Queens, with her mother. She'd probably called the house two or three times already, was worrying where I was. It occurred to me, dimly and distantly, like something in another life, that Ted knew nothing about Susan. I wondered if I should tell him.

But I did not tell him. We finished dinner, and went to Ted's apartment. He lived in the attic of a rambling old house near the center of town.

We never drank more than a sip or two each of the cups of tea he made for us.

It was funny—when we began making love that first time, Ted and I, what I was thinking was that, like most sex between men, this was really a matter of exorcism, the expulsion of bedeviling lusts. Or exercise, if you will. Or horniness—a word that always makes me think of demons. So why was it, when we finished, there were tears in my eyes, and I was turning, putting my mouth against his hair, preparing to whisper something—who knows what?

Ted looked upset. "What's wrong?" he asked. "Did I hurt you?"

"No," I said. "No. You didn't hurt me."

"Then what is it?"

"I guess I'm just not used to—I didn't expect— I never expected—" Again I was crying.

"It's O.K.," he said. "I feel it too."

"I have a wife," I said.

At first he didn't answer.

I've always loved houses. Most people I know in real estate don't love houses; they love making money, or making deals, or making sales pitches. But Susan and I, from when we first knew each other, from when we were very young, we loved houses better than anything else. Perhaps this was because we'd both been raised by divorced parents in stuffy apartments in Queens—I can't be sure. All I know is that as early as senior year in high school we shared a desire to get as far out of that city we'd grown up in as we could; we wanted a green lawn, and a mailbox, and a garage. And that passion, as it turned out, was so strong in us that it determined everything. I needn't say more about myself, and as for Susan—well, name me one other first-in-her-class in law school who's chosen—*chosen*—basically to do house closings for a living.

Susan wishes I were an architect. It is her not-so-secret dream to be married to an architect. Truthfully, she wanted me to have a profession she wouldn't have to think was below her own. But the fact is, I never could have been a decent architect because I have no patience for the engineering, the inner workings, the slow layering of concrete slab and wood and Sheetrock. Real estate is a business of surfaces, of first impressions; you have to brush past the water stain in the bathroom, put a Kleenex box over the gouge in the Formica, stretch the life expectancy of the heater from three to six years. Tear off the tile and the paint, the crumbly wallboard and the crackly blanket of insulation, and you'll see what flimsy scarecrows our houses really are, stripped down to their bare beams. I hate the sight of houses in the midst of renovation, naked and exposed like that. But give me a finished house, a polished floor, a sunny day; then I will show you what I'm made of.

The house I loved best, however, the house where, in those mad months, I imagined I might actually live with Ted, was the sort that most brokers shrink from—pretty enough, but drab, undistinguished. No dishwasher, no cathedral ceilings. It would sell, if it sold at all, to a young couple short on cash, or a retiring widow. So don't ask me why I loved this house. My passion for it was inexplicable, yet intense. Somehow I was utterly convinced that this, much more than the sleek suburban one-story Susan and I shared, with its Garland stove and Sub-Zero fridge—this was the house of love.

The day I told Susan I was leaving her, she threw the Cuisinart at me. It bounced against the wall with a thud, and that vicious little blade, dislodged, rolled along the floor like a revolving saw, until it gouged the wall. I stared at it, held fast and suspended above the ground. "How can you just come home from work and tell me this?" Susan screamed. "No preparation, no warning—"

"I thought you'd be relieved," I said.

"Relieved!"

She threw the blender next. It hit me in the chest, then fell on my foot. Instantly I dove to the floor, buried my head in my knees, and was weeping as hoarsely and furiously as a child.

"Stop throwing things!" I shouted weakly.

"I can't believe you," Susan said. "You tell me you're leaving me for a man and then you want me to mother you, take care of you? Is that all I've ever been to you? Fuck that! You're not a baby!"

I heard footsteps next, a car starting, Charlotte barking. I opened my eyes. Broken glass, destroyed machinery all over the tiles.

I got in my car and followed her. All the way to the beach. "Leave me alone!" she shouted, pulling off her shoes and running out onto the sand. "Leave me the fuck alone!" Charlotte romped after her, barking.

"Susan!" I screamed. "Susan!" I chased her. She picked up a big piece of driftwood and hit me with it. I stopped, dropped once again to my knees. Susan kept running. Eventually she stopped. I saw her a few hundred feet up the beach, staring at the waves.

Charlotte kept running between us, licking our faces, in a panic of barks and wails.

Susan started walking back toward me. I saw her getting larger and larger as she strode down the beach. She strode right past me.

"Charlotte!" Susan called from the parking lot. "Charlotte!" But Charlotte stayed.

Susan got back in her car and drove away.

At first I stayed at Ted's house. But Susan—we were seeing each other again, taking walks on the beach, negotiating—said that was too much, so I moved into the Dutch Boy Motel. Still, every day, I went to see the house, either to eat my lunch or just stand in the yard, feeling the sun come down through the branches of the trees there. I was learning a lot about the house. It had been built in 1934 by Josiah Applegate, a local contractor, as a wedding present for his daughter, Julia, and her husband, Spencer Bledsoe. The Bledsoes occupied the house for six years before the birth of their fourth child forced them to move, at which point it was sold to another couple, Mr. and Mrs. Hubert White. They, in turn, sold the house to Mr. and Mrs. Salvatore Rinaldi, who sold it to Mrs. Barbara Adams, a widow, who died. The estate of Mrs. Adams then sold the house to Arthur and Penelope Hilliard, who lived in it until their deaths just last year at the ages of eighty-six and eighty-two. Mrs. Hilliard was the first to go, in her sleep; according to her niece, Mr. Hilliard then wasted away, eventually having to be transferred to Shady Manor Nursing Home, where a few months later a heart attack took him. They had no children. Mr. Hilliard was a retired postman. Mrs. Hilliard did not work, but was an active member of the Ladies' Village Improvement Society. She was famous for her apple cakes, which she sold every year at bake sales. Apparently she went through periods when she would write letters to the local paper every week, long diatribes about the insensitivity of the new houses and new people. I never met her. She had a reputation for being crotchety, but maternal. Her husband was regarded as docile and wicked at poker.

The house had three bedrooms—one pitifully small—and two and a half baths. The kitchen cabinets were made of knotty, dark wood which had grown sticky from fifty years of grease, and the ancient yellow Formica countertops were scarred with burns and knife scratches. The wallpaper was red roses in the kitchen, leafy green leaves in the living room, and was yellowing and peeling at the edges. The yard contained a dogwood, a cherry tree, and a clump of gladiolas. Overgrown privet hedges fenced the front door, which was white with a beaten brass knocker. In the living room was a dusty pair of sofas, and dark wood shelves lined with Reader's Digest Condensed Books, and a big television from the early seventies. The shag carpeting—coffee brown—appeared to be a recent addition.

The quilts on the beds, the Hilliards' niece told me, were handmade, and might be for sale. They were old-fashioned patchwork quilts, no doubt stitched together over several winters in front of the television. "Of course," the niece said, "if the price was right, we might throw the quilts in—you know, as an extra."

I was a man with the keys to fifty houses in my pockets. Just that morning I had toured the ten bathrooms of the $10.5 million oceanfront. And I was smiling. I was smiling like someone in love.

I took Ted to see the house about a week after I left Susan. It was a strange time for both of us. I was promising him my undying love, but I was also waking up in the middle of every night crying for Susan and Charlotte. We walked from room to room, just as I'd imagined, and just as I'd planned, in the doorway to the master bedroom, I turned him around to face me, bent his head down (he was considerably taller than me), and kissed him. It was meant to be a moment of sealing, of confirmation, a moment that would make radiantly, abundantly clear the extent to which this house was meant for us, and we for it. But instead the kiss felt rehearsed, dispassionate. And Ted looked nervous. "It's a cute house, Paul," he said. "But God knows I don't have any money. And you already own a house. How can we just *buy* it?"

"As soon as the divorce is settled, I'll get my equity."

"You haven't even filed for divorce yet. And once you do, it could take years."

"Probably not *years*."

"So when *are* you filing for divorce?"

He had his hands in his pockets. He was leaning against a window draped with white flounces of cotton and powderpuffs.

"I need to take things slow," I said. "This is all new for me."

"It seems to me," Ted said, "that you need to take things slow and take things fast at the same time."

"Oh, Ted!" I said. "Why do you have to complicate everything? I just love this house, that's all. I feel like this is where I—where we—where we're meant to live. Our dream house, Ted. Our love nest. Our cottage."

Ted was looking at his feet. "Do you really think you'll be able to leave Susan? For good?"

"Well, of course, I— Of course."

"I don't believe you. Soon enough she's going to make an ultimatum. Come back, give up Ted, or that's it. And you know what you're going to do? You're going to go back to her."

"I'm not," I said. "I wouldn't."

"Mark my words," Ted said.

I lunged toward him, trying to pull him down on the sofa, but he pushed me away.

"I love you," I said.

"And Susan?"

I faltered. "Of course, I love Susan too."

"You can't love two people, Paul. It doesn't work that way."

"Susan said the same thing, last week."

"She's right."

"Why?"

"Because it isn't fair."

I considered this. I considered Ted, considered Susan. I had known Susan since Mrs. Polanski's homeroom in fourth grade. We played *Star Trek* on the playground together, and roamed the back streets of Bayside. We were children in love, and we sought out every movie or book we could find about children in love.

Ted I'd known only a few months, but we'd made love with a passion I'd never imagined possible, and the sight of him unbuttoning his shirt made my heart race.

It was at that moment that I realized that while it is possible to love two people at the same time, in different ways, in the heart, it is not possible to do so in the world.

I had to choose, so of course, I chose Susan.

That day—the day of Ed and Grace-Anne, the day that threatened to end with the loss of my beloved house—Susan did not call me at work. The morning progressed slowly. I was waiting for Ed and Grace-Anne to reappear at the window and walk in the office doors, and sure enough, around eleven-thirty, they did. The receptionist led them to my desk.

"I'm Ed Cavallaro," Ed said across my desk, as I stood to shake his hand. "This is my wife."

"How do you do?" Grace-Anne said. She smelled of some sort of fruity perfume or lipstick, the kind teenaged girls wear. We sat down.

"Well, I'll tell you, Mr. Hoover," Ed said, "we've been summering around here for years, and I've just retired—I worked over at Grumman, upisland?"

"Congratulations," I said.

"Ed was there thirty-seven years," Grace-Anne said. "They gave him a party like you wouldn't believe."

"So, you enjoying retired life?"

"Just between you and me, I'm climbing the walls."

"We're active people," Grace-Anne said.

"Anyway, we've always dreamed about having a house near the beach."

"Ed, let *me* tell about the dream."

"I didn't mean *that* dream."

"I had a dream," Grace-Anne said. "I saw the house we were meant to retire in, clear as day. And then, just this morning, walking down the street, we look in your window, and what do we see? The very same house! The house from my dream!"

"How amazing," I said. "Which house was it?"

"That cute little one for one sixty-five," Grace-Anne said. "You know, with the cedar shingles?"

"I'm not sure."

"Oh, I'll show you."

We stood up and walked outside, to the window. "Oh, that house!" I said. "Sure, sure. Been on the market almost a year now. Not much interest in it, I'm afraid."

"Now why is that?" Ed asked, and I shrugged.

"It's a pleasant enough house. But it does have some problems. It'll require a lot of TLC."

"TLC we've got plenty of," Grace-Anne said.

"Grace-Anne, I told you," Ed said, "the last thing I want to do is waste my retirement fixing up."

"But it's my dream house!" Grace-Anne fingered the buttons of her blouse. "Anyway, what harm can it do to look at it?"

"I have a number of other houses in roughly the same price range which you might want to look at—"

"Fine, fine, but first, couldn't we look at that house? I'd be so grateful if you could arrange it."

I shrugged my shoulders. "It's not occupied. Why not?"

And Grace-Anne smiled.

Even though the house was only a few hundred feet away, we drove. One of the rules of real estate is; Drive the clients everywhere. This means your car has to be both commodious and spotlessly clean. I spent a lot—too much—of my life cleaning my car—especially difficult, considering Charlotte.

And so we piled in—Grace-Anne and I in front, Ed in back—and drove the block or so to Maple Street. I hadn't been by the house for a few weeks, and I was happy to see that the spring seemed to have treated it well. The rich greens of the grass and the big maple trees framed it, I thought, rather lushly.

I unlocked the door, and we headed into that musty interior odor which, I think, may well be the very essence of stagnation, cryogenics, and bliss.

"Just like I dreamed," Grace-Anne said, and I could understand why. Probably the Hilliards had been very much like the Cavallaros.

"The kitchen's in bad shape," Ed said. "How's the boiler?"

"Old, but functional." We headed down into the spidery basement. Ed kicked things.

Grace-Anne was rapturously fingering the quilts. "Ed, I love this house," she said. "I love it."

Ed sighed laboriously.

"Now, there are several other nice homes you might want to see—"

"None of them was in my dream."

But Ed sounded hopeful. "Grace-Anne, it can't hurt to look. You said it yourself."

"But what if someone else snatches it from under us?" Grace-Anne asked, suddenly horrified.

"I tend to doubt that's going to happen," I said in as comforting a tone as I could muster. "As I mentioned earlier, the house has been on the market for over a year."

"All right," Grace-Anne said reluctantly, "I suppose we could look—*look*—at a few others."

"I'm sure you won't regret it."

"Yes, well."

I turned from them, breathing evenly.

Of course she had no idea I would sooner make sure the house burned down than see a contract for its purchase signed with her husband's name.

I fingered some matches in my pocket. I felt terrified. Terrified and powerful.

When I got home from work that afternoon, Susan's car was in the driveway and Charlotte, from her usual position of territorial inspection on the front stoop, was smiling up at me in her doggy way. I patted her head and went inside, but when I got there, there was a palpable silence which was far from ordinary, and soon enough I saw that its source was Susan, leaning over the kitchen counter in her sleek lawyer's suit, one leg tucked under, like a flamingo.

"Hi," I said.

I tried to kiss her, and she turned away.

"This isn't going to work, Paul," she said.

I was quiet a moment. "Why?" I asked.

"You sound relieved, grateful. You do. I knew you would."

"I'm neither of those things. Just tell me why you've changed your mind since last night."

"You tell me you're in love with a man, you up and leave for three months, then out of the blue you come back. I just don't know what you expect—do you want me to jump for joy and welcome you back like nothing's happened?"

"Susan, yesterday you said—"

"Yesterday," Susan said, "I hadn't thought about it enough. Yesterday I was confused, and grateful, and— God, I was so relieved. But now—now I just don't know. I mean, what the hell has this been for you, anyway?"

"Susan, honey," I said, "I love you. I've loved you my whole life. Remember what your mother used to say, when we were kids, and we'd come back from playing on Saturdays? 'You two are joined at the hip,' she'd say. And we still are."

"Have you ever loved me sexually?" Susan asked, suddenly turning to face me.

"Susan," I said.

"Have you?"

"Of course."

"I don't believe you. I think it's all been cuddling and hugging. Kid stuff. I think the sex only mattered to me. How do I know you weren't thinking about men all those times?"

"Susan, of course not—"

"What a mistake," Susan said. "If only I'd known back then, when I was a kid—"

"Doesn't it matter to you that I'm back?"

"It's not like you never left, for Christ's sake!" She put her hands on my cheeks. "You *left*," she said quietly. "For three months you *left*. And I don't know, maybe love *can* be killed."

She let go. I didn't say anything.

"I think you should leave for a while," Susan said. "I think I need some time alone—some time alone knowing you're alone too."

I looked at the floor. "Okay," I said. And I suppose I said it too eagerly, because Susan said, "If you go back to Ted, that's it. We're finished for good."

"I won't go back to Ted," I said.

We were both quiet for a few seconds.

"Should I go now?"

Susan nodded.

"Well, then, good-bye," I said. And I went.

This brings me to where I am now, which is, precisely, nowhere. I waited three hours in front of Ted's house that night, but when, at twelve-thirty, his car finally pulled into the driveway, someone else got out with him. It has been two weeks since that night. Each day I sit at my desk, and wait for one of them, or a lawyer, to call. I suppose I am homeless, although I think it is probably inaccurate to say that a man with fifty keys in his pocket is ever homeless. Say, then, that I am a man with no home, but many houses.

Of course I am careful. I never spend the night in the same house twice. I bring my own sheets, and in the morning I always remake the bed I've slept in as impeccably as I can. The fact that I'm an early riser helps as well—that way, if another broker arrives, or a cleaning woman, I can say I'm just checking the place out. And if the owners are coming back, I'm always the first one to be notified.

The other night I slept at the $10.5 million oceanfront. I used all the bathrooms; I swam in both the pools.

As for the Hilliards' house—well, so far I've allowed myself to stay there only once a week. Not because it's inconvenient—God knows, no one ever shows the place—but because to sleep there more frequently would bring me closer to a dream of unbearable pleasure than I feel I can safely go.

The Cavallaros, by the way, ended up buying a contemporary in the woods for a hundred and seventy-five, the superb kitchen of which turned out to be more persuasive than Grace-Anne's dream. The Hilliards' house remains empty, unsold. Their niece just lowered the price to one fifty—quilts included.

Funny: Even with all my other luxurious possibilities, I look forward to those nights I spend at the Hilliards' with greater anticipation than anything else in my life. When the key clicks, and the door opens onto that living room with its rows of Reader's Digest Condensed Books, a rare sense of relief runs through me. I feel as if I've come home.

One thing about the Hilliards' house is that the lighting is terrible. It seems there isn't a bulb in the house over twenty-five watts. And perhaps this isn't surprising—they were old people, after all, by no means readers. They spent their lives in front of the television. So when I arrive at night, I have to go around the house, turning on light after light, like ancient oil lamps. Not much to read by, but dim light, I've noticed, has a kind of warmth which bright light lacks. It casts a glow against the woodwork which is exactly, just exactly, like the reflection of raging fire.

When You Grow to Adultery

Andrew was in love with Jack Selden, so all Jack's little habits, his particular ways of doing things, seemed marvelous to him: the way Jack put his face under the shower, after shampooing his hair, and shook his head like a big dog escaped from a bath; the way he slept on his back, his arms crossed in the shape of a butterfly over his face, fists on his eyes; his fondness for muffins and Danish and sweet rolls—what he called, at first just out of habit and then *because* it made Andrew laugh, "baked goods." Jack made love with efficient fervor, his face serious, almost businesslike. Not that he was without affection, but everything about him had an edge; his very touch had an edge, there was the possibility of pain lurking behind every caress. It seemed to Andrew that Jack's touches, more than any he'd known before, were full of meaning—they sought to express, not just to please or explore—and this gesturing made him want to gesture back, to enter into a kind of tactile dialogue. They'd known each other only a month, but already it felt to Andrew as if their fingers had told each other novels.

Andrew had gone through most of his life not being touched by anyone, never being touched at all. These days, his body under the almost constant scrutiny of two distinct pairs of hands, seemed to him perverse punishment, as if he had had a wish granted and was now suffering the consequences of having stated the wish too vaguely. He actually envisioned, sometimes, the fairy godmother shrugging her shoulders and saying, "You get what you ask for." Whereas most of his life he had been alone, unloved, now he had two lovers—Jack for just over a month, and Allen for close to three years. There was no cause and effect, he insisted, but had to admit things with Allen had been getting ragged around the edges for some time. Jack and Allen knew about each other and had agreed to endure, for the sake of the undecided Andrew, a tenuous and open-ended period of transition, during which Andrew himself spent so much of his time on the subway, riding between the two apartments of his two lovers, that it began to seem to him as if rapid transit were the true and final home of the desired. Sometimes he wanted nothing more than to crawl into the narrow bed of his childhood and revel in the glorious, sad solitude of no one—not even his mother—needing or loving him. Hadn't the hope of future great loves been enough to curl up against? It seemed so now. His skin felt soft, toneless, like the skin of a plum poked by too many housewifely hands, feeling for the proper ripeness; he was covered with fingerprints.

This morning he had woken up with Jack—a relief. One of the many small tensions of the situation was that each morning, when he woke up, there was a split second of panic as he sought to reorient himself and figure out where he was, who he was with. It was better with Jack, because Jack was new love and demanded little of him; with Allen, lately, there'd been thrashing, heavy breathing, a voice whispering in his ear, "Tell me one thing. Did you promise Jack we wouldn't have sex? I have to know."

"No, I didn't."

"Thank God, thank God. Maybe now I can go back to sleep."

There was a smell of coffee. Already showered and dressed for work (he was an architect at a spiffy firm), Jack walked over to the bed, smiling, and kissed Andrew, who felt rumpled and sour and unhappy. Jack's mouth carried the sweet taste of coffee, his face was smooth and newly shaven and still slightly wet. "Good morning," he said.

"Good morning."

"I love you," Jack Selden said.

Immediately Allen appeared, in a posture of crucifixion against the bedroom wall. "My God," he said, "you're killing me, you know that? You're killing me."

It was Rosh Hashanah, and Allen had taken the train out the night before to his parents' house in New Jersey. Andrew was supposed to join him that afternoon. He looked up now at Jack, smiled, then closed his eyes. His brow broke into wrinkles. "Oh God," he said to Jack, putting his arms around his neck, pulling him closer, so that Jack almost spilled his coffee. "Now I have to face Allen's family."

Jack kissed Andrew on the forehead before pulling gingerly from his embrace. "I still can't believe Allen told them," he said, sipping more coffee from a mug that said WORLD'S GREATEST ARCHITECT. Jack had a mostly perfunctory relationship with his own family—hence the mug, a gift from his mother.

"Yes," Andrew said. "But Sophie's hard to keep secrets from. She sees him, and she knows something's wrong, and she doesn't give in until he's told her."

"Listen, I'm sure if he told you she's not going to say anything, she's not going to say anything. Anyway, it'll be fun, Andrew. You've told me a million times how much you enjoy big family gatherings."

"Easy for you to say. You get to go to your nice clean office and work all day and sleep late tomorrow and go out for brunch." Suddenly Andrew sat up in bed. "I don't think I can take this anymore, this running back and forth between you and him." He looked up at Jack shyly. "Can't I stay with you? In your pocket?"

Jack smiled. Whenever he and his last boyfriend, Ralph, had had something difficult to face—the licensing exam, or a doctor's appointment—they would say to each other, "Don't worry, I'll be there with you. I'll be in your pocket." Jack had told Andrew, who had in turn appropriated the metaphor, but Jack didn't seem to mind. He smiled down at Andrew—he was sitting on the edge of the bed now, smelling very clean, like hair tonic—and brushed his hand over Andrew's forehead. Then he reached down to the breast pocket of his own shirt, undid the little button there, pulled it open, made a plucking gesture over Andrew's face, as if he were pulling off a loose eyelash, and, bringing his hand back, rubbed his fingers together over the open pocket, dropping something in.

"You're there," he said. "You're in my pocket."

"All day?" Andrew asked.

"All day." Jack smiled again. And Andrew, looking up at him, said, "I love you," astonished even as he said the words at how dangerously he was teetering on the brink of villainy.

Unlike Jack, who had a job, Andrew was floating through a strange, shapeless period in his life. After several years at Berkeley, doing art history, he had transferred to Columbia, and was now confronting the last third of a dissertation on Tiepolo's ceilings. There was always for him a period before starting some enormous and absorbing project during which the avoidance of that project became his life's goal. He had a good grant and nowhere to go during the day except around the cluttered West Side apartment he shared with Allen, so he spent most of his time sweeping dust and paper scraps into little piles—anything to avoid the computer. Allen, whom he had met at Berkeley, had gotten an assistant professorship at Columbia the year before—hence Andrew's transfer, to be with him. He was taking this, his third semester, off to write a book. Andrew had stupidly imagined such a semester of shared writing would be a gift, a time they could enjoy together, but instead their quiet afternoons were turning out one after the other to be cramped and full of annoyance, and fights too ugly and trivial for either of them to believe they'd happened afterwards—shoes left on the floor, phone messages forgotten, introductions not tendered at parties: these were the usual crimes. Allen told Andrew he was typing too fast, it was keeping him from writing; Andrew stormed out. Somewhere in the course of that hazy afternoon when he was never going back he met Jack, who was spending the day having a reunion with his old college roommate, another art-history graduate student named Tony Melendez. The three of them chatted on the steps of Butler, then went to Tom's Diner for coffee. A dirty booth, Andrew across from Jack, Tony next to Jack, doing most of the talking. Jack talking too, sometimes; he smiled a lot at Andrew.

When one person's body touches another person's body, chemicals under the skin break down and recombine, setting off an electric spark which leaps, neuron to neuron, to the brain. It was all a question of potassium and calcium when, that afternoon at Tom's, Jack's foot ended right up against Andrew's. Soon the accidental pressure became a matter of will, of choice. Chemistry, his mother had said, in a rare moment of advisory nostalgia. Oh, your father, that first date we didn't have a thing to talk about, but the chemistry!

At home that evening, puttering around while Allen agonized over his book, Andrew felt claustrophobic. He wanted to call Jack. Everything that had seemed wonderful about his relationship with Allen—shared knowledge, shared ideologies, shared loves—fell away to nothing, desiccated by the forceful reactions of the afternoon. How could he have imagined this relationship would work for all his life? he wondered. Somehow they had forgotten, or pushed aside, the possibilities (the likelihoods) of competitiveness, disagreement, embarrassment, disapproval, not to mention just plain boredom. He called Jack; he told Allen he was going to the library. The affair caught, and as it got going Andrew's temper flared, he had at his fingertips numberless wrongs Allen had perpetrated which made his fucking Jack all right. He snapped at Allen, walked out of rooms at the slightest provocation, made several indiscreet phone calls, until Allen finally asked what was going on. Then came the long weekend of hair-tearing and threats and pleas, followed by the period of indecision they were now enduring, a period during which they didn't fight at all, because whenever Andrew felt a fight coming on he threatened to leave, and whenever Allen felt a fight coming on he backed off, became soothing and loving, to make sure Andrew wouldn't leave. Andrew didn't want to leave Allen, he said, but he also didn't want to give up Jack. Such a period of transition suited him shamefully; finally, after all those years, he was drowning in it.

In skeptical or self-critical moments, Andrew perceived his life as a series of abandonments. This is what he was thinking about as he rode the train from Hoboken out toward Allen's parents' house that afternoon: how he had abandoned his family, fleeing California for the East Coast, willfully severing his ties to his parents; then, one after another, how he had had best friends, and either fought with them or became disgusted with them, or they with him, or else just drifted off without writing or calling until the gap was too big to dare crossing. There were many people he had said he could spend his life with, yet he hadn't spent his life with any of them, he saw now. Nathan and Celia, for instance, who it had seemed to him in college would be his best friends for all time—when was the last time he'd seen them? Five, six months now? Berkeley had severed Andrew from that ineradicable threesome of his youth, and now that he was in New York again it seemed too much had happened for them to fill each other in on, and in the course of it all happening their perceptions and opinions had changed, they were no longer in perfect synch, they weren't able to understand each other as gloriously as they once had because, of course, their lives had diverged, they did not have endless common experience to chew over, and on which to hone shared attitudes. After those first few disastrous dinners, in which arguments had punctuated the dull yawn of nothing to be said, he had given up calling them, except once he had seen Nathan at the museum, where they stood in front of a Tiepolo and Nathan challenged Andrew to explain why it was any good—a familiar, annoying, Nathanish challenge, a good try, but by then it was too late. All of this was guilt-inspiring enough, but what made Andrew feel even guiltier was that Nathan and Celia still saw each other, went to parties together, lived in the clutch of the same old dynamic, and presumably the same glorious synchronicity of opinion. They were going on ten years with each other even without him, and Andrew felt humbled, immature. Why couldn't he keep relationships up that long? As for leaving Allen for Jack—wouldn't it amount to the same thing? In three years, would he leave Jack as well?

Perhaps it was just his nature. After all, he had lived for the entire first twenty-two and most of the next six years of his life virtually alone, surviving by instinct, internal resources. This was not uncommon among gay men he knew; some reach out into the sexual world at the brink of puberty, like those babies who, tossed in a swimming pool, gracefully stay afloat; but others—himself among them—become so transfixed by the preposterousness of their own bodies, and particularly the idea of their coming together with other bodies, that they end up trapped in a contemplation of sex that, as it grows more tortured and analytic, rules out action altogether. Such men must be coaxed by others into action, like the rusty Tin Man in Oz, but as Andrew knew, willing and desirable coaxers were few and far between. For him sexual awakening had come too late, too long after adolescence, when the habits of the adult body were no longer new but had become settled and hard to break out of. Chronically alone, Andrew had cultivated, in those years, a degree of self-containment which kept him alive, but was nonetheless not self-reliance, for it was based on weakness, and had at its heart the need and longing for another to take him in. He remembered, at sixteen, lying in his room, his hands exploring his own body, settling on his hip, just above the pelvis, and thinking, No other hand has touched me here, not since infancy, not since my mother. Not one hand. And this memory had gone on for six more years. Had that been the ruin of him? he wondered now. Doomed by necessity to become self-contained, was he also doomed never to be able to love someone else, always to retreat from intimacy into the cozy, familiar playroom of his old, lonely self?

Outside the train window, the mysterious transformations of late afternoon were beginning. It was as if the sun were backing off in horror at what it had seen, or given light to. The train Andrew was on had bench seats that reversed direction at a push, and remembering how impressed by that he had been the first time Allen had taken him on this train, he grew nervous: suddenly he remembered Allen, remembered he was on his way to a man who considered his life to be in Andrew's hands. Already he recognized the litany of town names as the conductor announced them: one after another, and then they were there. By the crossing gate Allen sat in his father's BMW, waiting.

He smiled and waved as he stepped off the train. Allen didn't move. He waved again as he ran toward the car, waved through the window. "Hi," he said cheerily, getting in and kissing Allen lightly on the mouth. Allen pulled the car out of the parking lot and onto the road.

"What's wrong?" (A foolish question, yet somehow the moment demanded it.)

"This is the very worst for me," he said. "Your coming back. It's worse than your leaving."

"Why?"

"Because you always look so happy. Then you fall into a stupor, you fall asleep, or you want to go to the movies and sleep there. Jack gets all the best of you, I get you lying next to me snoring." He was on the verge, as he had been so many times in these last weeks, of saying inevitable things, and Andrew could sense him biting back, like someone fighting the impulse to vomit. Andrew cleared his throat. A familiar, dull ache somewhere in his bowels was starting up again, as if a well-trusted anesthesia were wearing off. It felt to him these days, being with Allen, as if a two-bladed knife lay gouged deep into both of them, welding them together, and reminded anew of its presence, Andrew turned futilely to the car window, the way you might turn from the obituary page to the comics upon recognizing an unexpected and familiar face among the portraits of the dead. Of course, soon enough, you have to turn back.

Andrew closed his eyes. Allen breathed. "Let's not have a fight," Andrew said quietly, surprised to be on the verge of tears. But Allen was stony, and said nothing more.

As they pulled into the driveway the garage doors slowly opened, like primeval jaws or welcoming arms; Sophie, Allen's mother, must have heard the car pulling up, and pushed the little button in the kitchen. A chilly dusk light was descending on the driveway, calling up in Andrew some primeval nostalgia for suburban twilight, and all the thousands of days which had come to an end here, children surprised by the swift descent of night, their mothers' voices calling them home, the prickly coolness of their arms as they dropped their balls and ran back into the warm lights of houses. It had been that sort of childhood Allen had lived here, after all, a childhood of street games, Kickball and Capture the Flag, though Allen was always the one the others laughed at, picked last, kicked. A dog barked distantly, and in the bright kitchen window above the garage Andrew saw Sophie rubbing her hands with a white dish towel. She was not smiling, and seemed to be struggling to compose herself into whatever kind of studied normalness the imminent arrival of friends and relatives demanded. Clearly she did not know anyone could see her, for in a moment she turned slightly toward the window, and seeing the car idle in the driveway, its lights still on, started, then smiled and waved.

A festive, potent smell of roasting meats came out the porch door. "Hello, Andrew," Sophie said as they walked into the kitchen, her voice somehow hearty yet tentative, and she kissed him jauntily on the cheek, bringing close for one unbearable second a smell of face powder, perfume, and chicken stock he almost could not resist falling into. For Jack's sake he held his own. Of all the things he feared losing along with Allen, this family was the one he thought about most. How he longed to steep forever in this brisket smell, this warmth of carpeting and mahogany and voices chattering in the hall! But Allen, glumly, said, "Let's go upstairs," and gestured to the room they always shared, his room. Even that a miracle, Andrew reflected, as they trundled up the stairs: that first time Andrew had visited and was worrying where he'd sleep, Sophie had declared, "I never ask what goes on upstairs. Everyone sleeps where they want; as far as I'm concerned, it's a mystery." It seemed a different moral code applied where her homosexual son was concerned than the one that had been used routinely with Allen's brothers and sister; in their cases, the sleeping arrangements for visiting boyfriends or girlfriends had to be carefully orchestrated, the girls doubling up with Allen's sister, the boys with Allen himself—a situation Allen had always found both sexy and intolerable, he had told Andrew, the beautiful college boys lying next to him in his double bed for the requisite hour or so, then sneaking off to have sex with his sister, Barrie. Well, all that was long past—Barrie was now married and had two children of her own—and what both Allen and Andrew felt grateful for here was family: it was a rare thing for a gay man to have it, much less to be able to share it with his lover. Their parents had not yet met each other, but a visit was planned for May, and remembering this, Andrew gasped slightly as the prospect arose before him—yet another lazily arranged inevitability to be dealt with, and with it the little residual parcel of guilt and nostalgia and dread, packed up like the giblets of a supermarket chicken. His half of the knife twisted a little, causing Allen's to respond in kind, and Allen looked at Andrew suspiciously. "What is it?" he asked. Andrew shook his head. "Nothing, really." He didn't want to talk about it. Allen shrugged regretfully; clearly he sensed that whatever was on Andrew's mind was bad enough not to be messed with.

"Well," Allen said, as they walked into his room, "here we are," and threw himself onto the bed. Andrew followed more cautiously. The room had changed hands and functions many times over the years—first it had been Allen's sister's room, then his brother's, then his, then a guest room, then a computer room, then a room for visiting grandchildren. It had a peculiar, muddled feel to it, the accretions of each half-vain effort at redecoration only partially covering over the leavings of the last occupant. There was archaeology, a sense of layers upon layers. On the walnut dresser, which had belonged to Allen's grandmother, a baseball trophy shared space with a Strawberry Shortcake doll whose hair had been cut off, a two-headed troll, and a box of floppy disks. Odd-sized clothes suggesting the worst of several generations of children's fashions filled the drawers and the closets, and the walls were covered with portraits of distant aunts, framed awards Allen had won in high school and college, pictures of Barrie with her horse. The bed, retired here from the master bedroom downstairs, had been Sophie's and her husband Lou's for twenty years. The springs were shot; Allen lay in it more than on it, and after a few seconds of observation Andrew joined him. Immediately their hands found each other, they were embracing, kissing, Andrew was crying. "I love you," he said quietly.

"Then come back to me," Allen said.

"It's not that simple."

"Why?"

Andrew pulled away. "You know all the reasons."

"Tell me."

The door opened with a tentative squeak. Some old instinctual fear made both of them jump to opposite sides of the bed. Melissa, Allen's five-year-old niece, stood in the doorway, her hand in her mouth, her knees twisted one around the other. She was wearing a plaid party dress, white tights, and black patent-leather Mary Janes.

"Hello," she said quietly.

"Melly! Hello, honey!" Allen said, bounding up from the bed and taking her in his arms. "What a pretty girl you are! Are you all dressed up for Rosh Hashanah?" He kissed her, and she nodded, opening her tiny mouth into a wide smile clearly not offered easily, a smile which seemed somehow precious, it was so carefully given. "Look at my earrings," she said. "They're hearts."

"They're beautiful," Allen said. "Remember who bought them for you?"

"Uncle Andrew," Melissa said, and looked at him, and Andrew remembered the earrings he had given her just six months before, for her birthday, as if she were his own niece.

"Look who's here, honey," he said, putting Melissa down. "Uncle Andrew's here now!"

"I know," Melissa said. "Grandma told me."

"Hi, Melissa," Andrew said, sitting up on the bed. "I'm so happy to see you! What a big girl you are! Come give me a hug!"

Immediately she landed on him, her arms circling as much of him as they could, her smiling mouth open over his face. This surprised Andrew; on previous visits Melissa had viewed him with a combination of disdain and the sort of amusement one feels at watching a trained animal perform; only the last time he'd been to the house, in August, for Sophie's birthday, had she shown him anything like affection. And it was true that she'd asked to speak to him on the phone every time she was visiting and Allen called. Still, nothing prepared Andrew for what he saw in her eyes just now, as she gazed down at him with a loyalty so pure it was impossible to misinterpret.

"I love you," she said, and instantly he knew it was true, and possibly true for the first time in her life.

"I love you too, honey," he said. "I love you very much."

She sighed, and her head sank into his chest, and she breathed softly, protected. What was love for a child, after all, if not protection? A quiet descended on the room as Andrew lay there, the little girl heavy in his arms, while Allen stood above them in the shrinking light, watching, it seemed, for any inkling of change in Andrew's face. Downstairs were dinner smells and dinner sounds, and Sophie's voice beckoning them to come, but somehow none of them could bring themselves to break the eggshell membrane that had formed over the moment. Then Melissa pulled herself up, and Andrew realized his leg was asleep, and Allen, shaken by whatever he had or hadn't seen, switched on the light. The new, artificial brightness was surprisingly unbearable to Andrew; he had to squint against it.

"We really ought to be going down now," Allen said, holding his hand out to Andrew, who took it gratefully, surprised only by the force with which Allen hoisted him from the bed.

Chairs and plastic glasses and Hugga Bunch plates had to be rearranged so Melissa could sit next to Andrew at dinner. This position, as it turned out, was not without its disadvantages; he was consistently occupied with cutting up carrots and meat. The conversation was familiar and soothing; someone had lost a lot of money in the stock market, someone else was building a garish house. Allen's sister sang the praises of a new health club, and Allen's father defended a cousin's decision to open a crematorium for pets. All through dinner Melissa stared up at Andrew, her face lit from within with love, and Allen stared across at Andrew, his face twisted and furrowed with love, and somewhere miles away, presumably, Jack sat at his drafting table, breaking into a smile for the sake of love. So much love! It had to be a joke, a fraud! Someone—his mother—must have been paying them! Wait a minute, he wanted to say to all three of them, this is me, Andrew, this is me who has never been loved, who has always been too nervous and panicked and eager for love for anyone to want actually to love him! You are making a mistake! You are mixing me up with someone else! And if they did love him—well, wouldn't they all wake up soon, and recognize that they were under an enchantment? Knowledge kills infatuation, he knew, the same way the sudden, perplexing recognition that you are dreaming can wake you from a dream. He almost wanted that to happen. But sadly—or happily, or perhaps just frustratingly—there appeared to be no enchantment here, no bribery. These three loves were real and entrenched. His disappearance from any one of them was liable to cause pain.

Even with Melissa! Just an hour later—screaming as her mother carried her to the bathtub, screaming as her mother put her in her bed—no one could ignore who she was calling for, though the various aunts and cousins were clearly surprised. Finally Barrie emerged from the room Melissa shared with her on visits, shaking her head and lighting a cigarette. "She says she won't go to sleep unless you tuck her in," Barrie told Andrew. "So would you mind? I'm sorry, but I've had a long day, I can't hack this crying shit anymore."

"You don't have to, Andrew," Sophie said. "She has to learn to go to sleep."

"But I don't mind," Andrew said. "Really, I don't."

"Well, thanks then."

Sophie led him into the darkened room where Melissa lay, rumpled-looking, in Cabbage Patch pajamas and sheets, her face puffy and her eyes red from crying, then backed out on tiptoe, closing the door three quarters. Immediately upon seeing him Melissa offered another of her rare and costly smiles.

"Hi," Andrew said.

"Hi."

"Are you all right?"

"Uh-huh."

"You want me to sing you a bedtime song?"

"Uh-huh."

"Okay." He brushed her hair away from her forehead, and began singing a version of a song his own father had sung to him:

Oh go to sleep my Melly-o
And you will grow and grow and grow
And grow and grow right up to be
A great big ugly man like me . . .

Melissa laughed. "But I'm a girl," she said.

"I told you, honey, this is a song my daddy sang to me."

"Go on."

And you will go to Timbuktu
And you'll see elephants in the zoo.
And you will go to outer space
And you will go to many a place.
Oh think of all the things you'll see
When you grow to adultery.

This last line, of course, caught him. It had always been a family joke, a mock pun. Had his father known something he hadn't?

"That's a funny song," said Melissa, who was, of course, too young to know what adultery meant anyway.

"I'm glad you liked it, but since I've sung it now, you have to go to sleep. Deal?"

She smiled again. Her hand, stretched out to her side, rested lightly now at that very point on his hip he had once imagined no one would ever touch. Now her tiny handprints joined the larger ones which seemed to him tonight to be permanently stamped there, like tattoos.

Though he'd left the light on, Allen was already tightly encased between the sheets by the time Andrew came to bed. He lay facing rigidly outward, and Andrew, climbing in next to him, observed the spray of nervous pimples fanning out over his shoulders. He brushed his fingers over the bumpy, reddened terrain, and Allen jumped spasmodically. Andrew took his hand away.

"Don't," Allen said.

"All right, I won't, I'm sorry."

"No, no. Don't *stop*, don't stop touching me. Please, I need you to touch me. You never touch me anymore."

Andrew put his hand back. "Don't," he said. "Stop. Don't. Stop. Don't stop, don't stop, don't stop."

"Thank you," Allen said. "Thank you."

"Switch off the light."

"You don't know," Allen said, "how much I've missed your hands."

"Allen, I've been touching you plenty," Andrew said.

"No, you haven't. You really haven't."

"This really is a stupid topic for an argument," Andrew said, not wanting to let on the sensation he was just now feeling, of a spear run through him, the whole length of his body. He reached over Allen's head and switched off the light. "Just relax," he said, and settled himself into a more comfortable position against the pillow. "I won't stop touching you."

"Thank you," Allen whispered.

In the dark things broke apart, becoming more bearable. His hand traveled the mysterious widths of Allen's back, and as it did so its movements slowly began to seem as if they were being controlled by some force outside Andrew's body, like the pointer on a ouija board. He had the curious sensation of his hand detaching from his arm, first the whole hand, at the wrist, and then the fingers, which, as they started to run up and down Allen's back in a scratch, sparked a small moan; this too seemed disembodied, as if it were being issued not from Allen's mouth but from some impossible corner or depth of the room's darkened atmosphere. Allen's back relaxed somewhat, his breathing slowed, and Andrew, with his index finger, scratched out the initials "J.S." My God, what was he doing? For a moment he lifted his hand, then thrust it back, ordering his fingers into a frenzy of randomness, like someone covering up an incriminating word with a mass of scribbling. But Allen didn't seem to notice, and breathed even more slowly. Andrew held his breath. What was possessing him he couldn't name, but cautiously he wrote "Jack" on Allen's back, elongating the letters for the sake of disguise, and Allen sighed and shifted. "Jack Selden," Andrew wrote next. "I love Jack Selden." His heart was racing. What if those messages, like invisible ink, suddenly erupted in full daylight for Allen to read? Well, of course that wouldn't happen, and closing his eyes, Andrew gave himself up to this wild and villainous writing, the messages becoming longer and more incriminating even as Allen moved closer to sleep, letting out, in his stupor, only occasional noises of pleasure and gratitude.

I See London,
I See France

I

Here is Celia, not so many years later, sitting on a bench in a park in a village in Chianti, staring at her hands. Beyond the trio of little girls playing jacks, beyond the edge of the park and the crumbling cobbled houses, beyond the *fattorie* and the villas and the half-collapsed town wall, a glorious vista of hills rises, hills Celia can still not quite believe she is sitting in the midst of, hills which belong in the backgrounds of fifteenth-century paintings—dry yet supple, their greenness occasionally broken by rock, just beginning to burn under the late-spring sun. Christ might be kneeling for baptism in those hills, his waist wrapped in a sodden cloth; or the Virgin, in an open stone house, might be poised over her spinning wheel, awaiting the angel's visitation.

Celia is looking at her hands. They are city hands, more used to typing or sealing envelopes than they are to pulling tiny clams from their shells, or picking sprigs of wild thyme from fields at the sides of roads, or raking the uneven landscape of Seth's chest—Seth, the man who has brought her here, the man who, she is tempted to say (though she resists saying it), has saved her from all that. What intrigues her is that her hands *look* the same, the fingers a little puffy, the meat of the palms pale and blotched with red. Only when her hands change, she believes, will she have changed, only then will this new life become something she can believe is going to last. But so far the signs are minimal. Her nails are no longer chewed to the quick; the hairs on her wrists are bleaching from the sun. And her lifeline—so mysterious, Seth had said the first night they spent together, as he opened her palm and traced it—it's broken in the middle. Two distinct halves, and in the center a void, a gap. "They'll have grown together before I'm through with you," he concluded, wrapping her hand back up into a fist, and she'd flinched at the notion that he'd *ever* be through with her, even though she knew it was just a figure of speech. Now she looks carefully and wonders if the two halves really have grown a fraction of an inch closer to one another, or if she's just imagining it.

Across the street from the park sits the rented Fiat Panda that has brought them here; next to it, Seth waits for a farmer in a wobbling *Ape* to pass by on the road. Seth's arms are full of sandwiches and pastries he's bought at a little bar across the street, but before he crosses, he stops to chat with the driver of the *Ape*, a three-wheeled vehicle which is halfway between a truck and a motorcycle. Seth is a translator and interpreter, and since they're on their way to an important literary conference—his first Italian interpreting job in two years—he's talking to everyone he can, determined to oil the rusty wheels of what is, unbelievably, his fifth language.

Celia watches him nod as the farmer, with great, sweeping gesticulations, tells a story. She is thinking that even though it has been only three weeks since they arrived in Italy, the job she quit in New York, the apartment she sublet, seem as mysterious to her now as winter coats happened upon when cleaning a closet in August. And just as for years after graduating from college she dreamed that she'd missed an exam and had to go back to retake it, each night this week the plane that carried her to Rome has pulled up outside of whatever *pensione* they were sleeping in, and the stewardess has come through the door to tell her it's time to go back—back to her black Formica desk on 55th Street, her bumpy-floored apartment on 107th Street, the overstuffed trio of rooms on Kissena Boulevard in Queens where she was raised and where her mother still lives. Sometimes the New York dreams get mixed up with the college dreams—she sits down at the desk on 55th Street and instead of being handed a manuscript by her boss, Ruth Feldschmidt, she's handed a list of exam questions by her Italian Renaissance art professor, Lucy Cumberland, and then the paintings start flashing on the screen, and she has to identify them: artist, title, date, museum. It's a relief to wake up, after that, and see Seth's freckled back, and remember that yesterday she saw those paintings not flashed on a screen, but hanging in the museums the names of which Lucy Cumberland had made her memorize in the first place.

For Celia, Italy has always been a place recognized in the background of paintings. Behind the head of La Gioconda, or Isabella Sforza, or her husband, the Duca di Montefeltro, was a landscape of hills somersaulting down to dry, clay-colored valleys; overviews of cities burnished by the sun; and always, those strange, wonderful Italian trees: mysterious, noble cypresses lined along empty avenues like sentries; umbrella pines, with their green clouds of leaf; olives aligned in perfect orchard geometry. On her first trip to Florence, a college girl trying to make her way on almost no money, she stood in the big stone halls of the Uffizi, staring at those portraits, and hearing even there the din of the hot, crowded piazzas below. How she longed to carry herself through the frame, to enter, like the children in *The Voyage of the "Dawn Treader,"* the world of the picture, the better world behind the glass. But of course she could not.

She looks. Below the park where she sits a slope of yellowing grass rolls toward a tiny village where a waterwheel is turning. And of course, there are those mysterious trees, those very un-American trees. A flash, suddenly, of her childhood—the straight, heat-baked blocks of Kissena Boulevard in Queens, oak and elm and ash. Not a pleasant flash—she pushes it aside. And straining to absorb every detail of the view, swears she can see, when she looks toward Florence, the gargantuan, braided back of a Tuscan lady's head as she poses for her portrait, glorying in the countryside of her domain.

"Celia?" Seth says, and she turns. He has finished his conversation with the man in the *Ape* and is sitting down next to her. "Are you all right?"

"Yes," she says. "Fine."

"Good. I had a funny conversation with that man. He was telling me a story about a knight who fought a battle here in the fourteenth century. And he was speaking real Tuscan dialect, the old kind that no one speaks anymore. It was fascinating." He unwraps sandwiches. "*Bel Paese, prosciutto, salsiccia, tonno*—take your pick." She does so silently, reverently. It is eleven o'clock in the morning, and they are on their way to lunch at the villa of some friends of Seth's from when he lived in Rome, ten years earlier.

"But you can't drive on an empty stomach," Seth says. "And anyway, what's the point of Italy if you don't eat in every town you stop in? Who knows what you might miss?"

It's been only a few months since Celia found Seth, since he swept her off her feet and out of her life. Now, when people ask how they met, they say it was at a party—a lie mutually agreed upon, since both are too embarrassed to admit the truth: that they were introduced into each other's lives through one of those phone lines that randomly connect women and men, men and men—in this case, a number, 970-RMNC, geared especially toward those seeking "romance." Celia is convinced that her description of herself over the phone that evening—not false, exactly, but elusive, embellished—implanted in Seth's mind an image of an object of desire which somehow, miraculously, the truth of her has failed to obliterate. When he looks at her, the urgency in his eyes can only mean that he still sees the fantasy she presented to him on the telephone, not who she really is. She wonders how long this can last.

A mutual love of travel—in Italy especially—was something they started talking about even during that first conversation. Seth had lived in Rome for five years; Celia had gone three times, once for a month in college, twice for two weeks each during her working years—vacations long planned, long saved for, and terribly lonely, spent mostly in museums, or sitting in cafés, always waiting for love to spring out from behind a painting or across a piazza and claim her. It never did. She and Seth had their first date in an Italian restaurant on Bleecker Street—an extraordinary, expensive restaurant, Seth's choice, where they ate imported tiny salad leaves with olive oil and lemon, roasted artichokes, whole garlic cloves baked to the point of sweetness. A week later Celia quit her job; they bought tickets.

Now, only two months since they first happened upon each other over the telephone, they are driving together along a back road near Siena, on their way to the reconstructed *fattoria* of Alexander and Sylvie Foster, and Seth is filling Celia in. "They've had an amazing life," he is saying, as he opens the window to let out his cigarette ash. "Both of them have very famous fathers—Alexander's was Julian Foster, the painter, and Sylvie's was Louis Roth, the conductor. And they've been married since they were sixteen. Sixteen! Can you imagine? They met on the southern coast of France, in Sanary, where their parents both had summer houses. A boy and a girl, just kids, with an enormous amount of wealth between them. They'd grown up in unreal places—Sylvie in East Hampton, Alex on the French coast. And they didn't want to live in the world. So they bought this farm. They bought it twenty years ago, when they were maybe eighteen. And they've lived there ever since, raised their daughters there. When they need money, Alex sells one of his father's paintings and that keeps them going maybe five, six years. And their house! You'll be astonished. It's the closest thing I've seen to paradise."

"How amazing," Celia says. But what she means is, How amazing that other people can have had such extraordinary lives, when my life has been so—what is the word? So *un*extraordinary. And suddenly she envisions these people she has never met, sixteen years old, strolling along a French beach, in love. Whereas she, at sixteen . . . There are tears in her eyes, she is bottomed out with grief, scooped hollow, suddenly so light, so tightly filled with air, that like a balloon, she might lift from the seat of the car, float out the window and over the hills. Travel, she knows, heightens the emotions; tears and laughter and rage come upon her as easily as a blush.

"It's an odd part of Italy around here," Seth says. "People call it 'Chiantishire,' because it's so filled with English and Australians. And they're all very tight with each other, they gossip all the time. For some reason there's particularly a lot of gossip about Sylvie, maybe because her father's so famous. For instance, once I met a Spanish woman who said, 'Oh, Sylvie Foster, Louis Roth's daughter. I heard she had a glass shower built in the middle of her living room and likes to shower in front of her guests.' Such a strange idea, that one! But people imagine all sorts of outrageous things about each other which really say much more about themselves, don't they? And Sylvie *is* brash. She'll probably be checking you out, seeing if you fit her standards, if you're good enough for me. But don't be intimidated."

"I'll try," Celia says, even though Seth's description has made her pale. These are not the sort of people she's used to. (Well, for that matter, most of her life she's been around people she wasn't used to. Her mother used to call her "my scholarship girl" when she was in college, and even though it's been ten years, and most of her student loans have finally been paid off, she still thinks of herself as a scholarship girl—fraudulent, somehow, not quite belonging, brought into the houses of these rich, sophisticated people more as a gesture of charity than a reflection of the value of her company. She has stayed in huge Southampton mansions, eaten dinner at the apartments of famous film stars, and still, each time, she quakes with fear, convinced that this once they'll see through to who she really is.)

Soon they're pulling up to the Fosters' farmhouse. Three cars are parked in front. "The house is called 'Il Mestolo,' " Seth says, getting out and stretching his legs. "That means 'the ladle.' Because of the way the hills slope down to this sort of plateau, and the house and barn and outbuildings are leveled on the plateau, like bits of vegetable and pasta in a soup being ladled into the bowl." He smiles with appreciation. "It's an old name. It predates the Fosters."

"*Carino!*" calls a rugged-looking woman with streaked gray hair, dressed in overalls, who is striding out of the farmhouse. She is clutching one breast rather oddly, and continues clutching it as she and Seth embrace, kiss each other on both cheeks, exchange a torrent of fast Italian which seems to Celia unnecessary, given that they're both Americans. Awkwardly Celia stands, looks at the sky, waits for them to include her, prays Seth will save her before she has to introduce *herself* to the reedy, windblown-looking man, also in overalls, who is now coming out of the kitchen, reaching out a hand.

"I'm Alex Foster," he says.

"Hello," Celia says. "I'm Celia." She doesn't think to mention her last name. And like a man awakened from a trance, Seth jolts, midsentence, back into English, and slides out of Sylvie's embrace.

"I'm sorry," he says. "I was so happy to see Sylvie I forgot to introduce Celia." He clears his throat. "So: Alex, Sylvie, this is Celia Hoberman, my fiancée."

It almost makes Celia not want to get married, she likes the sound of "fiancée" so much.

"A pleasure, Celia, a pleasure," says Sylvie, in a clipped British accent with just the slightest Tuscan undertone. "Come in, come in. Ginevra and Fabio and Ginevra's mother have just arrived."

She leads them into a large farmhouse kitchen where wooden rocking chairs circle an enormous stone fireplace. Each of the chairs has a ladle painted on the back. A huge pot of water is boiling on an ornate antique stove with polished brass fixtures, above which hang maybe a dozen bronze and stainless-steel ladles. Two women and a man are sitting in the rocking chairs. The older woman has feathery blond hair and is waving a fan over her face. Although she is scrupulously powdered, her forehead shines in the heat. She is wearing a cream-colored silk blouse and skirt, stockings, and pointy-toed alligator shoes. Next to her, the younger woman and the man argue in muted, deep voices. The younger woman is boxy, with short-cropped brown hair, the man handsome and Nordic; both are wearing cotton turtlenecks and blue jeans.

Sylvie, Celia notices, is still clutching her breast in that odd way. She notices Celia staring, laughs, says in a mock-Cockney accent, "I'm such a peasant I've got a chick on me tit!"

"What do you mean, a chick, on your tit?" Seth says.

"Just what I said." And reaching into her blouse, she presents to them a small, yellow-feathered chick, which wobbles on her palm. The old woman by the fireplace fans her face even more furiously.

"The mother abandoned it, left it to die. So I'm keeping it warm. Such a farm woman I've become, after all these years!"

"Let me introduce you," Alex says to Celia. "Ginevra, Fabio, this is Celia."

The younger man and woman, abandoning their argument, stand up. Ginevra says "Ciao," and shakes Celia's hand briskly. Fabio's handshake is like a glove being pulled off. "Scylla?" he says. "Like the monster?"

"No, Celia. Ce-li-a."

"Ah, Celia! *Certo.*" He pronounces it "Chaylia."

"And this is Signora Dorati, Ginevra's mother," Alex says.

The older lady stands and reaches out a hand gloved in lace and jewels.

"Ciao," Celia says.

Signora Dorati looks alarmed at this overly familiar greeting, and withdraws her hand. "*Piacere*," she murmurs, her voice faint, and returns to her chair.

"And where are the girls?" Seth asks, breaking the silence of Celia's mortification. "I must say hello to them!"

"Out at the pool, swimming," Sylvie calls, her head buried in a high cabinet from which she is pulling boxes of pasta. "You know Francesca leaves for school in England in a month. Can you believe it? She's almost sixteen."

"Where's she going?"

"Cheltenham, of course," says Alex.

"Francesca! Sixteen! It's hard to imagine!"

"And Adriana's almost thirteen, and looks twenty," Sylvie says. "Boys come around all the time asking for her."

"It's hard for her," says Alex. "Francesca can't wait to grow up, but Adriana clings to childhood. The last thing she wants to be is the woman her body makes her resemble. She'd like to stay a child forever." He looks wistful, as if he sympathizes with that desire.

"I must see them," Seth says now. "Come on, Celia." And grabbing her hand, he leads her out the back kitchen door, past an arbor covered with grapevines, a table set for lunch, the barn where Alex makes his sculptures, a chicken coop, an herb garden. Around a hedgerowed bend, the swimming pool sits on a ledge, littered with floating toys, the ladleful of soup itself.

A girl is swimming in the pool, her red hair floating out around her head. Another girl, slightly older and also red-haired, stands over her on a diving board, positioning herself for the dive.

"Adriana! Francesca!" Seth calls.

"Seth? Seth, is that you?" the older girl says. And abandoning her dive, she runs across the grass, catching Seth in an embrace from which he lifts her, effortlessly, into the air.

"My God, you've grown up!" he says.

"You look the same," Francesca says, laughing.

"Seth!" calls Adriana, hoisting herself from the pool and running up to join her sister. She pulls on Seth's hand, dances around him in a frenzy of appreciation. Sylvie was right: she does look twenty. She is tall, with olive-colored skin, a flat waist, large pretty breasts. The sort of body Celia's always envied. A woman's body. Yet there is an old doll lying on the grass, and the bathing suit Adriana wears—much too small and patterned with bears—is clearly that of a child.

"Adriana, Francesca, this is Celia," Seth says. "My fiancée."

"Hello," they say, and shake her hand, but it's only out of politeness. Celia is invisible to them. She listens, fascinated, as they barrage Seth with information about their lives—the dress Francesca wants to buy to take to England, but her mother won't let her, the Nintendo video game their uncle Martin sent Adriana for her birthday from the States, the Bon Jovi concert next week in Florence. "You must play Nintendo with me!" Adriana cries. "You will, won't you? Promise?"

"Promise."

"And you'll convince Mummy to let me go to the concert?" asks Francesca.

"Of course."

What odd accents they have! Part British, part Italian. But unlike Sylvie's accent, not acquired, not chosen—no, this is the voice of being raised at once in two worlds, the voice of placelessness.

"You must swim with us, Seth!" Francesca says.

"Yes, you must!"

"But I don't have my bathing suit!"

"Then swim in your underwear!"

"Well—" He looks pleadingly at Celia.

"Go ahead," she says. "I'll play lifeguard."

"All right, then. Why not?"

Instantly the girls are tearing at his clothes, one pulling a shoe off, the other unbuttoning his shirt, until he's down to his underpants, at which point, of course, lunging and grasping, they drag him into the water with them. Celia steps back from the splash, watches, still as a statue, a thin smile frozen on her mouth, filled with—what can she call it? Well, it's obvious. Grief.

What is here—what the people here have—is beauty. Whereas what she has—what she's always had, what is irrefutably hers in the world—is nothing anyone would ever call beautiful. Books: *Nancy Drew and the Mystery of the Ivory Charm.* Good Humor ice cream bars. Dry sidewalks, the gridded streets and avenues, playing jacks when it was cool enough at sunset.

Suddenly she feels a cold, wet tentacle grasp her ankle. She jumps back, nearly screams. But it's only Seth, reaching his arm from the swimming pool.

"Let me guess what you're thinking," Seth says.

"All right."

"You're thinking that this is the most beautiful place in the world. So beautiful it makes you sad, it breaks your heart, because you can never have it. But you can have it. I'll give it to you, Celia."

She turns away from him, toward the view of the walled city. "Only . . . It's not that I want to live here *now*, it's that I want to *have* lived here. To have grown up here. Or rather, to be the sort of person who grew up in this sort of place with that sort of parents, and feel the things that sort of person could feel which a different sort of person—the sort of person I am, for instance—could never feel. And not feel the sort of things the sort of person I am has to feel—does this make sense?"

"You don't have to be trapped anymore," Seth says. "I've saved you from feeling trapped. I've taken you away from your dreary apartment and your dreary job. Look where we are now and be happy. You don't have to go back."

It seems important to Seth that Celia understand that he has saved her, and for a moment she wonders how much this "saving" really was for her benefit, and how much for his, and if it really matters.

"Well, of course," she says finally, laughing, and mostly to please him. "It's just that I can't quite believe it."

"Believe it," Seth says. And letting go of her leg he returns, splashing, to pool games.

II

Celia grew up in a few rooms on the fourth floor of a brick apartment building fringed with fire escapes. One of hundreds, thousands of identical buildings all over Queens, yet she never got lost, never mistook one for another, never had any trouble distinguishing where her friends lived. You noticed the differences when you actually *lived* among so much sameness: Her building, for instance, had the drugstore across the street. And another building, where her friend Janet Cohen lived, was covered with climbing vines. And Great-Aunt Leonie's building had the lady who filled her balcony each year with expensive lawn furniture, and could be seen sunning herself in harlequin-shaped sunglasses and a white one-piece bathing suit as late as November and as early as March.

Across the street, on the stoop next to the drugstore, Hasidic boys traded "Torah Personalities" the way most boys trade baseball cards. "I'll give you a Rev Mordechai Hager for a Yehuda Zev Segal!" "You've really got Menachem Mendel Taub?" There was at dusk the thwack of the jump rope against the sidewalk, the elaborate reverberating chants of double-dutch.

"I see London, I see France,
I see Celia's underpants!"

Street games: Capture the Flag, Spud.

> "*Eeny meeny miny mo,*
> *Catch a tiger by the toe,*
> *If he hollers let him go,*
> *My mother says that you are not It.*"

The Good Humor man, twice a day, ringing his bell. Chip Candy. Red, White and Blue. Nutty Buddy.

Upstairs lived Celia's mother, Rose, and her grandmother, Lena. There was no father; he had died before Celia ever had a chance to meet him, in a bus accident. Celia had rich uncles and aunts: in Westchester, in Great Neck, one in California. On holidays she'd visit them, watch her cousins as they played effortlessly in great pools, sleep in pull-out trundle beds in rooms that were impossibly big, impossibly good-smelling and filled with toys. Then she and Rose and Lena would head back to Queens, to the stuffy apartment house in the old neighborhood where the three of them had been left behind, presumably because her father, who was expected to get rich, died instead.

What they did, Celia's mother and grandmother, was watch television. Especially when Celia was a teenager and in college, when her mother had gotten so fat it was hard for her to move outside the apartment, and her grandmother was more or less bedridden. In that overheated, shag-carpeted room with its plastic-covered flowery sofas, and shelves full of tchotchkes, and old dinner dishes piled on breakfast trays, they'd eat Pepperidge Farm cookies and fight over the remote control. Rose got up from her armchair now and then to do a little dusting or clean a plate. Lena stayed mostly in bed. All over the room were elephants: glass elephants, china elephants, stuffed elephants. They were what Rose collected, what everyone gave her. Every birthday, every Mother's Day, another elephant. The TV, in Celia's memory, never goes off. It is on at dawn when she gets out of bed and goes into the kitchen for milk (later coffee): morning talk shows, exercise shows her mother observes with detached bemusement while eating crullers. It is on at midday when she comes home for lunch: soap operas. It is on all night: the evening news, and then situation comedies and cop shows, and more news. Celia usually fell asleep to the sound of *Honeymooners* reruns, old episodes of *The Twilight Zone* she knew by heart.

The soap operas, however, were most important, in particular *The Light of Day*, which was Lena's favorite. It seemed to make her genuinely suffer, this show; if on Friday the heroine was left dangling from a small plane while a villain crushed her fingers with his shoes, there would be no living with Lena that weekend. What had drawn them to the show in the first place was a story line that occurred in the mid-seventies, concerning a sweet girl nun who found herself torn between her faith and the pleas of a handsome, severely smitten Jewish boy determined to woo her away from the convent. Anxiety bled with a little bit of love was the formula of this soap opera. If love for the nun started Rose and Lena watching, anxiety for her fate compelled them to keep watching—especially after the nun went off to a war-torn Central American country to do good works, and wound up being kidnapped by guerrillas. The cycle was eternal, and designed to addict: an adored heroine had to be in trouble if you were going to care about her at all. Soon Lena and Rose became experts, they predicted things long before they happened: too much happiness meant something terrible, a psychopath, a car accident. Vague tiredness boded terminal illness or unwanted pregnancy.

For years, day after day, *The Light of Day* evolved. Hairdos changed, as did clothes. Occasionally new actors would replace old ones, the transformation explained by a quick car accident and facial reconstruction. The show seemed never to have begun (though Celia knew it had, once, before her birth). Apparently it would never end. And there was no assurance that the characters' suffering would end, either. Whereas in a movie you could pretty much assume a hostage taken at the beginning was a hostage saved at the end, here torture, detainment, misunderstanding might drag on for months.

The year Celia was applying to colleges, Lena became preoccupied with the fate of a couple on the show, a girl named Brandy and a boy named Brad. They were in love, but a series of miscommunications mostly engineered by an evil older woman named Mallory had led each to believe the other was cheating. Finally Brandy called Brad and left a message on his answering machine: "If I hear from you tonight, I'll know you love me; otherwise, I'll assume you don't." Then Mallory stole the tape. Brandy assumed Brad didn't love her, but of course, Brad had never heard the message. Mallory continued to stir up trouble until finally Brad, despairing, sure that Brandy didn't love him, allowed himself to be seduced by and then to become engaged to Mallory. Brandy, in the meantime, kept almost finding the incriminating tape, which Mallory had saved and hidden inside a jade statue in the museum where Brandy worked. This jade statue seemed to have mysterious powers. Then Mallory started putting drugs in Brandy's coffee, slowly addicting her, making it look like she was going mad.

All through this Lena roiled in bed, shuffling and moaning: "Oy, oy!" She said it was killing her; she said it was giving her an ulcer. "If I have to die soon," Lena said, "let me at least die knowing that Brandy and Brad got back together." So Rose wrote a letter to the show, and showed it to Celia first, to make sure the grammar was perfect.

Dear Sirs and Mesdames [it read]:
For many years my mother, Mrs. Lena Lieberman, aged eighty-nine, and myself have been loyal viewers of your show, *The Light of Day*. We have seen the characters through thick and thin, good and bad. Lately, however, my mother has been very disturbed by the extended troubles being suffered by Brandy and Brad. Surely seven and a half months is long enough for such a sweet and loving pair of young people to have to endure the evil doings of Mallory, not to mention painful and unnecessary separation! Life is short, as we all know. I myself lost my husband in 1959, and watching the travails suffered by Brandy and Brad, I can only think what a shame it is that they are wasting their youthful years apart when very likely anything can and will happen to them in the near future. Youth is golden, and should be enjoyed. If you don't mind my quoting the name of a rival (and in my opinion much inferior) program, each of us has only one life to live.

Sirs and mesdames, let me come to my point. My mother is an old woman not long for this world. She is sick, and her anxiety for Brandy and Brad is making her sicker. I doubt I am exaggerating when I say it could be the straw that breaks the camel's back. A life is at stake here, and that is why I am writing to ask you, with all speed, to bring Brad and Brandy back together, marry them to each other, punish the wicked Mallory. Only knowing they are reunited in matrimony will my elderly mother breathe easy, and die peacefully.

Yours sincerely,
Rose (Mrs. Leonard) Hoberman

Celia didn't think much about the letter except to wonder whether her mother really was as far gone as she sounded, or whether this was some joke going on between Rose and herself. She was busy with her college applications, and filling out scholarship forms, and entering competitions (the Optimists' Club Speech Competition, theme: Together we will . . .; the Ladies' Auxiliary of B'nai B'rith; Young Women of Merit Awards), doing everything she could to scrounge up all the money she'd need for school. When she got the letter informing her of her acceptance, she couldn't wait for the elevator; instead she raced up the stairs, shouting, "Ma! Ma!" But her mother didn't hear her. She had a letter of her own. "Celia!" she said breathlessly as Celia ran into the living room. "Listen, listen! It's from the show!"

"Ma, I've got great news!"

"Listen to this letter, you won't believe it!"

Dear Mrs. Hoberman:

I received your letter, and was sure to share it with our writers and cast, all of whom join me in wishing your mother a speedy recovery. While it is our policy never to reveal what's going to happen on *The Light of Day* in advance—even the actors only see the scripts a few days before shooting—I believe I can assure you that all is going to work out for Brandy and Brad, and that Mallory will receive her comeuppance.

In conclusion, let me say that viewers such as you and your mother mean everything to us here at *The Light of Day*; we hope you'll accept the enclosed autographed photo of Mark Metzger (Brad Hollister) and Alexandra Fisher (Brandy Teague) as a token of that appreciation.

Very sincerely yours,
Donna Ann Finkle
Public Relations Associate

"It's amazing," Rose cried. "They listened to us! They answered!" And Celia, all at once, fell silent in her rapture, for she understood, as if for the first time, how rarely her mother had been listened to, and how even more rarely answered.

"Now, I'm sorry, honey, sit down and tell me your news." But Celia was quiet.

"Celia. I'm waiting."

Celia sat next to her mother on the sofa, indifferent to the crunch of plastic underneath her. For a year now she'd anticipated the moment she'd receive this letter, she'd imagined herself tearing open the envelope, reading the words "We are happy to inform you," then throwing her arms up to the sky, because they signaled the end of one life—a life of stuffy entrapment, washed-out colors, dirty air—and the beginning of another, a glamorous life, a glorious life, a life of books and green grass and ivy-covered walkways. But now, sitting with her mother while Rose clutched her own letter, Celia saw that it wouldn't matter; she saw that though she might walk through those halls, she'd do so as a ghost, a guest, a stranger, the same way she walked the commodious halls of her Westchester and Long Island relatives. How could college make a difference when her mother was still here, trapped in where and who she was? No matter what, Celia knew, she too would always end up back in this apartment, on this sofa. Never listened to. Never answered.

"I got in," she said hopelessly. Her mother turned. "You did what?"

"I got in."

Then Rose screamed in a way that reminded Celia of the noises Great-Aunt Leonie's parrot made. "You got in! She got in!" And jumping to her feet, Rose called toward the bedroom: "She got in! Mama, Celia got in!" She opened the window, leaned out, screamed so all the neighbors could hear, and the Hasidic boys across the street: "My Celia, Celia Hoberman, is a scholarship girl! She got in!"

Three months later, in August, Brandy married Brad. Mallory, exposed and humiliated, left town, swearing she'd be back to get even. Rose took Celia up to New Haven. Everything according to clockwork, except for Lena, who didn't die until two years later, and by then Brad was an alcoholic failure, and Brandy a famous TV talk-show host, played by a different actress and carrying the child of a mysterious stranger named Señor Reyes.

Celia came down from New Haven when her grandmother died, even though it was the middle of exam week. Her Westchester aunts and uncles were sitting in the living room, looking uncomfortable and crowded. Rose was serving them cups of tea. Without even saying hello, Rose instructed Celia to bring a plate of cookies in from the kitchen. Celia took off her coat and got the cookies. "You remember these cookies, Belle?" Rose was saying to her sister. "Seidman's Bake Shop?

It's still around. The neighborhood hasn't changed that much, in the end."

"They're delish, honey," Belle said.

"You know, Celia's in the middle of exams at Yale. Tell Aunt Sadie your major, honey."

"Art history."

"Not too many career options there!" Uncle Louis said.

"My Marc's majoring in economics *and* political science at Brown," Aunt Belle said. "He's planning on law school."

"Now that's a sensible major."

"Bring some more tea, Celia. The funeral's in half an hour."

Celia went back into the kitchen. Her mother followed her, closed the door, and dropped herself onto a chair, looking defeated and collapsed.

"I feel so ashamed," she said. "I feel like such a failure."

"Don't feel that way, Mama," said Celia.

"I do. They pity me."

Suddenly Rose fell to the floor, weeping. "Mama," she cried, clutching Celia's knees. "Mama."

"Mama, no," Celia said. "I'm Celia."

"Mama, come back," Rose called into Celia's scabby knees. "Come back, Mama. Mama."

III

Lunch is still ten minutes off when Celia and Seth get back from the pool, so Alex takes them on a tour of Il Mestolo. "It was a wreck when we bought it," he explains as he leads them down stony corridors to the room where Sylvie has set up her spinning wheel. "Then slowly, over the years, we worked on it, picking up furniture here and there at estate sales. It wasn't until Francesca was born that we put in electricity and got a phone."

There is a huge bathroom, the size of a bedroom, with a toilet built into a marble bench, and a tub on claws, big enough to hold a family. Much of the furniture Alex made himself, in his shop in the barn—fanciful sofas and beds with elaborate animal carvings in the moldings, down-stuffed cushions wrapped in brightly colored cotton fabric. But it is the girls' rooms that take Celia's breath away. In each is a handcarved sleigh bed of dark cherry, above which Alex has painted a mural. The background of the mural in Adriana's room is sky blue, the letters of her name, spread out against it, festooned with birds—every imaginable bird, each species distinct and colorful and exact. "Francesca," by contrast, floats in an undersea green, surrounded by fish. "Like the Grotto of the Animals," Alex says, as Celia stares admiringly. "Outside Florence, in a place called Castello. A little leftover of the Mannerist period. You go into this grotto, and what you see is a stone-carved catalogue of the birds of the air, the beasts of the land, the fish of the sea. This is my slightly less ambitious version."

There are differences between the rooms. Whereas Adriana's is neat and filled with toys—as many handmade by Alex, Celia notices, as bought at town shops—Francesca's is a mess, the covers thrown off the bed, underwear tangled on the floor, Bon Jovi and Guns 'n Roses posters thumbtacked into the great sea wall. The posters make Celia flinch with pain—a defacement—but Alex is blasé. "The worst thing in the world," he says, "is to tell children how to lead their lives. Their rooms belong to them. The murals are my gift, to make of what they wish. I've always thought it a mistake to expect appreciation from your children. You'll never get it that way."

From the kitchen, Sylvie calls out, "Al-ex! Lunch!" so they head outside to the table under the grape arbor. Seth has told Celia that at formal Italian meals, the eldest guest is always seated at the host's right, so she is surprised when Sylvie—who clearly knows better—seats Signora Dorati at Alex's left. The old woman once again flutters her fan frantically, her face tight with distress. Celia is seated between Ginevra and Fabio. Ginevra, she knows from Seth, is a famous poet, although not a very productive one: two slim white volumes over twenty years, published by the best literary house.

While Alex fills glasses with wine, Adriana and Francesca, freshly dressed, their hair still wet from the pool, emerge from the kitchen, bearing huge, steaming bowls of pasta. Ah, pasta! Celia has always loved it, and now, as she spoons *penne* into a bowl handpainted by Alex with purple garlic bulbs, she sees that Sylvie is an expert. The tubed *maccheroni* are luminous with bits of sausage, basil, tomato, glints of yellow garlic. What a far cry from the spaghetti and meatballs of her childhood, the overcooked, mushy noodles swimming in a bright red bath of watery, sweet tomato sauce, the whole plate periodically dented by boulders of ground beef and bread crumbs! Her mother used to sing a song as she cooked it, to the tune of "On Top of Old Smoky," her voice loud in the cramped, steamy kitchen:

On top of spaghetti, all covered with cheese,
I lost my poor meatball, when somebody sneezed.
It rolled off the table, and onto the floor
And then my poor meatball rolled out of the door . . .

Celia puts down her fork. Oh, her poor foolish, sad mother! She is overwhelmed, suddenly, by the poverty of her childhood, by all she didn't know, all she didn't even know to ask. Here, of all places, in Chiantishire, sitting at this perfect table with these beautiful people under a grape arbor on a gloriously sunny spring day, she is haunted.

"The weather will be bad tomorrow," Ginevra says. "I can feel it."

"How?" asks Seth. "Today is beautiful."

"Today beautiful, tomorrow hot, humid, uncomfortable. My mood always tells me. I'm getting depressed."

"Ginevra can recognize the bad weather coming," Fabio says. "And she's right much more than the newspaper."

"Well, I'm not going to haul in the garden furniture yet!" Sylvie says, still stroking the small bulge in her breast. "Anyway, Ginevra, why should we listen to you? You've been in a bad mood since you lost your manuscript. I don't trust your senses so much."

This last remark is greeted by a tense silence. Ginevra puts down her fork and rubs her forehead.

"Really, Sylvie," Alex says.

"Well, it's not like a death," says Sylvie, her back tensing defensively. "I'm tired of avoiding the subject."

"I just don't think one should refer to tragedies . . . quite so casually—"

"No, Alex, never mind," Ginevra says. "It's all right. I don't know if Seth told you, but I'm sometimes a poet. Sometimes, because I don't write very often—I have great blocks. And last year I was working on a poem, a long poem, which I loved like a person. I loved it so much I carried it with me everywhere. And I lost it. So for a year I've been in grief, and everyone is silent about my poem as if it were my lover who is gone."

Again, a tense silence stretches out. "That must have been terrible," Celia says at last.

"Terrible, yes," Ginevra says. "I suppose. Yes."

"Ginevra is a wonderful cook," Seth says now, brightly, to change the subject. "You know, Ginevra, Celia's very interested in Italian food. Maybe you could give her lessons."

Ginevra looks at Celia and smiles. "Are you ready to be an obedient pupil?" she says. "Because the Italian kitchen, it is only about obedience. Obedience to the old ways."

"Ginevra is a perfectionist," Fabio says. "Last week in Rome, she made a duck. And she drove miles and miles to a little village in Lazio to buy the duck, because it had to be just so. And then she spent an hour picking through the vegetables at Campo dei Fiori because they had to be just so. And then she spent three hundred fifty thousand lire for caviar and *tartufi* even though she cannot pay her house. And then—"

"*Basta*, Fabio, *basta*—" Ginevra covers her mouth, laughing.

"No," Sylvie says. "Not *basta*. Go on."

"And then she made the duck, and we ate, and it was the most delicious duck we ever taste, and we tell her, 'Ginevra, it is marvelous,' but she takes one taste and says, 'No, no, it's awful, throw it away, throw it away,' and starts taking our plates from us. She is mad!"

Ginevra is still laughing. "I told you, the fourth taste wasn't right!"

"The fourth taste?" Seth asks.

"There were supposed to be five tastes, and the fourth—"

"*Che cosa?*" asks Signora Dorati, bewildered, and Alex offers her a quick summation in Italian, at the end of which she laughs halfheartedly. She has not touched her pasta. He pours more wine for himself and her.

A barrage of heavy-metal music stuns the atmosphere; apparently Francesca has put on one of her Bon Jovi records.

Sylvie puts down her glass, closes her eyes, and rubs her temples. Francesca, nonchalant and challenging, comes out of the kitchen, picks up some empty bowls, goes back in.

"Alex," Sylvie says, "can't you do something?"

"Do what? You do something for once."

"You're useless," Sylvie says. Then she turns and shouts, "Will you please shut that dreadful noise down?"

"All right, all right!"

The music is turned off, not down, the needle pulled from the record with a violent scratch meant to be heard.

There is a quiet which feels dangerous, like the moment after the screams of someone dying have finally stopped.

"So, Celia," Sylvie says, with a smile that seems to cost, "tell us about yourself. Where did you grow up?"

"New York."

"Really! Me too. Though mostly in East Hampton. Did you ever go to East Hampton?"

"Not until I was grown up."

"And where did you go to school?"

"Bronx Science."

"I was at Spence. I dated a boy from Bronx Science once. Gerald Ashenauer. Did you know him?"

"No, I didn't."

"Well, of course not, you're probably just decades younger than me, aren't you?"

"Not *decades*."

"And what kind of work do you do?"

"For God's sake, Sylvie, don't interrogate the poor girl," Alex says, pouring more wine. "After all, she's only come to lunch."

"I don't mind answering," Celia says. "Only it's not very glamorous. I was a proofreader and copy editor."

"Any kind of work sounds glamorous to me," Alex says, "never having done any myself."

"Why do you say 'was'?" Sylvie asks.

"Celia's quit her job," Seth says. "We're not going back. We're going to stay here in Italy."

"Oh, jolly good for you!" Alex says, lifting his wineglass. "Wonderful. A new wave of expatriation, that's what we need over here. A shot in the arm, since all the British around here are so bloody boring."

Francesca and Adriana come out from the kitchen again.

"We've washed the bowls, Mummy," Adriana says.

"Thank you, sweetie."

"Mummy," Francesca says, "can't I please go to the Bon Jovi concert next week?"

Sylvie's hand once again cradles her breast. "We'll talk about it another time, Francesca."

"But Seth says it's all right, he says nothing will happen and he likes Bon Jovi, don't you, Seth?"

"Uh—yes," Seth says. "Absolutely."

No one laughs.

"Please, Mummy."

"Just say yes," Alex says.

"I said we'd talk about it later," Sylvie says.

"Oh, I'm so sick of you!" Then Francesca picks up an empty bowl from the table and smashes it against the bricks, where it shatters loudly; her father's beautiful, hand-painted bowl.

Signora Dorati gives the only audible gasp.

Sylvie is standing in an instant. "Get in the house," she says, but though Adriana runs indoors, Francesca doesn't move. "You're fakes, you and Daddy," she says, "you haven't worked a day in your lives, you just sit out here on your asses. I'd rather be dead than grow up like you." Then her eyes bulge, and she brings her hand tentatively to her teeth, as if to stuff the words back in.

"Mummy, I—"

"Get in the house," Sylvie says again, with dental precision, her voice dangerous. Francesca turns, and is gone.

"Excuse us just a moment," Sylvie says. "Just your run-of-the-mill family catastrophe."

She follows her daughter into the house. Signora Dorati, fluttering her fan, whispers something furiously to Ginevra, who whispers something back. Signora Dorati wipes her brow with a handkerchief.

"I think," Alex says, "that a toast is in order, don't you, Seth?"

"Ah, sure," says Seth. "What shall we toast? Mothers and daughters?"

"I was thinking, not working a day in one's life. Sitting on one's bum." He is pouring himself yet another glass of wine.

"Here's to bum-sitting, then," Seth says.

"Cin-cin," Ginevra says. The glasses clang.

The chick on Sylvie's tit, in spite of her best efforts, has died. With a sort of sentimentalist's imitation of peasant hardness—her face stoic, her lower lip not quivering one bit—she buries the small, feathered corpse in the garden. Francesca and Adriana, their eyes red but dry, watch her, don't say a word. Then the three of them disappear into the kitchen together, the girls clinging to their mother's arms, tied to her by some blood bond not even broken pottery can threaten, and from which Celia is naturally, painfully excluded.

On the patio, Seth practices his Italian on a bored-looking Signora Dorati. "*Che meraviglia,*" she responds tiredly to everything he says. "*Che bravo. Che stupendo.*" Ginevra and Fabio play a foolish game of Ping-Pong at a green table. Once the ball goes rolling under Signora Dorati's chair, but she has apparently been so defeated by the events of the afternoon that she hardly notices when her daughter reaches under her legs to get it.

Then Alex—drunk, but pleasantly so—invites Celia for a tour of his studio, and together the two of them head off down the hill toward the old barn. "Now you'll get to see my 'work,'" he says, making little quotation marks around the word with his fingers.

"I can't wait," Celia says, as he pulls open the wide, scarred doors. Inside the barn the air is dark and moist, and all around them are animals—willowy, spindly, brass tigers and antelopes, gazelles, stone cats, their eyes painted black.

"So you see," he says, "I have my own grotto of the animals."

Looking at all these animals, the first thing Celia thinks of is her mother's shelves and shelves of elephants.

"They're fantastic," she says.

"My daughter's right," Alex says. "There's no reason for Francesca to take me and Sylvie seriously, to listen to us. We're anachronisms. Useless, really. Look at what I do all day! A toy man!" He laughs. "When they were young, that was fabulous, there was nothing better a father could be than a toy man. But now—well, you only have to look at what happened. I don't understand these young people. They're so—practical. They have no romance in them. Francesca, especially. She says her ambition is either to be a rock star or go to work on the stock exchange and make her first million pounds by the time she's thirty. Sixteen years old, and talking like that. Whereas when I was sixteen—well, a lot has changed."

Celia cautiously strokes the neck of a ceramic giraffe painted with blue spots.

"Do you sell them?" she asks.

"Now and then, through friends. I don't have much of a mind for business. Once Sylvie and I went to New York to talk to some gallery people, people who'd known my father—very intimidating, those people were, not encouraging and not very kind. We fled back here as fast as we could. We really aren't made for the world, you see. Francesca is. She'll go to England, get a job, be a Sloane Ranger in London, just like she says. And maybe on the way she'll join a punk band, she'll live in a tenement in Brixton. The world. Adriana's more like us. I'm not so sure about Adriana."

He has led Celia over to the working space of his studio. Here the animals are smaller—the size of hands and fingers. She notices a brass elephant, like many of the other animals, so spindly she's afraid it will break in half when she picks it up. But it doesn't.

"My mother collects elephants," she says.

"Then why don't you give her this one?"

"What?" Celia puts the elephant down. "No, no, I didn't mean that, really. Oh, you probably think I mentioned my mother just because I hoped you'd offer, when really—"

"Just give it to her," Alex says, pressing the elephant into her palm. "After all, there's nothing else for me to do with them. If you don't take it, it'll just sit here getting dusty."

Celia is flustered from too much speech. "Well, then, all right. Thank you." She looks again at the tiny elephant.

"We were beastly this afternoon," Alex is saying. "I hope you'll forgive us. My family has a tendency to behave rather animalistically, to just express ourselves all over the place, and sometimes that can be a bit of a strain for visitors. Signora Dorati, for instance. Somehow I don't suspect we're going to be receiving an invitation to lunch at *her* villa anytime soon." He laughs halfheartedly. "Supposed to be quite a splendid villa, too. I would've liked to have seen it."

"Well, *I* didn't mind," Celia says. "It made me feel like one of the family."

"You're kind," Alex says.

The tiny elephant in Celia's palm looks up at her, its face inscrutable but knowing, as if it has a secret to tell but no mouth.

"You can't imagine how much my mother will appreciate this," Celia says. "Why, she'll probably clear a whole shelf for it, a special shelf, and when her friends come in, Mrs. Segal or Mrs. Greenhut or the ladies from the block association, she'll gather them round and say, 'Now look at this, Elaine, this elephant was made by a real artist in Italy. My daughter

Celia got it for me. Isn't it gorgeous?' 'Oh, gorgeous!' 'Now don't touch, it's fragile!' "

Alex laughs mildly. "I wish everyone I gave a sculpture to was so enthusiastic," he says. "Most often they just sort of shrug. If I'm visiting the person, and I'm lucky, it'll turn up in the bathroom, and I'll look under the sink and see the bowl of flowers it's been brought out to replace for the afternoon."

"Oh, I doubt that," Celia says.

But Alex once again doesn't seem to have heard her. And once again, this strange afternoon, it seems to Celia as if a piece of fragile thread, spun like spider's web, has been cast out across the ocean, from this ancient Tuscan barn to her mother's apartment in Queens, pulling these two disparate places into a nearness so intimate she feels as if she could reach across the darkness and brush Rose's arm. She has known for some time now that Seth cannot save her, at least the way he says he wants to, that he can never "take her away from all that"; no one can ever take anyone else away from all that. There are always those threads, billions of them, crisscrossing and crossing again, wrapping the world in their soft, suffocating gauze.

The futility, the falseness of her romance with Seth—each of them playacting for the other the role of something long sought, long needed—she sees clearly now, but at a remove: the sort of truth you can gaze at for years; ponder; affirm; ignore.

Yes, she sees it all now; sees that she will stay in Italy, no matter how ardently her better judgment tells her not to; sees that, to the extent that it's possible, she'll become a different person from the person she used to be. And then one day she'll be walking down the cobbled street of her own Tuscan village, thinking about something properly Italian—olive trees, maybe, or art—when suddenly that mysterious thread will start to tighten, and Queens and Tuscany will be pulled to somewhere in the middle of the ocean, and briefly, magically merged. She'll turn and see, sitting on a bench in her own piazza near where the old men smoke cigars and play dominos, two Hasidic boys trading rabbi cards. And two little girls playing jump rope. And hearing the thwack of the jump rope against the pavement, she'll feel her feet start to dance, and want to jump herself, jump until the rope slipping under her is no longer anything real, is just a blur of speed. "I see London, I see France . . ." (But of course they didn't see any of those places, didn't even imagine they'd ever see any of those places.) Who, after all, is speaking? And in what language? And how can those boys be here, and her mother's voice calling to her down this ancient cobbled street? "Celia, come home, dinner's ready! It's spaghetti and meatballs! Your favorite!"

Chips Is Here

Here is why I decided to kill my neighbor:

On a rainy morning in midsummer, after several failed efforts, my cat finally managed to scale the fence that separated my yard from Willoughby Wayne's. The cat landed on all four feet in the narrow space behind a privet hedge. At first he sat there for a moment, licking his paws and acquainting himself with his new situation. Then, quite cautiously, he began making his way through the brushy underside of the hedge toward Willoughby's lawn. Unfortunately for him, the five Kerry blue terriers with whom Willoughby lives were aware of the cat's presence well before he actually stepped out onto the grass, and like a posse, they were there to greet him. The cat reared, hissed, and batted a paw in the face of the largest of the Kerry blues, who in turn swiftly and noisily descended with the efficient engine of his teeth. "Johnny! Johnny!" I heard Willoughby call. "Bad dog, Johnny! Bad dog!" There was some barking, then things got quiet again.

A few hours later, after I'd searched the house and checked most of the cat's outdoor hiding places, I called Willoughby. "Oh, a young cat?" he said. "Orange and white? Yes, he was here. Needless to say I did my best to introduce him to my pack, but inexperience has resulted in their maintaining a very puppylike attitude toward cats; the introductions—shall we say—did not go well. I interceded delicately, breaking up the mêlée, then, for his own good, lifted the feline fellow over the fence and deposited him in the field adjacent to my property. I believe he was quite frightened by Johnny, and suspect he's probably hiding in the field even as we speak."

I thanked Willoughby, hung up, and headed out into the field that adjoins both our yards. It was a fairly wild field, unkempt, thick with waist-high weeds and snarls of roots in which my dog, accompanying me, kept getting trapped. I'd be thrashing along, breaking the weeds down with a stick and calling, "Kitty! Here, kitty!" when suddenly the dog would start barking, and turning around I'd see her tangled in an outrageous position, immobilized by the vines in much the same way she often became immobilized by her own leash. Each time I'd free her, and we'd continue combing the field, but the cat apparently chose not to answer my repeated calls. I went back three times that afternoon, and twice that night. In the morning I canvassed the neighbors, without success, before returning to comb the field a sixth time. "Still looking for your young feline?" Willoughby called to me over the fence. He was clipping his privet hedge. "I'm really terribly sorry. If I'd had any idea he was *your* cat I most certainly would have hand-delivered him to you on the spot."

"Yes, well," I said.

"For whatever it's worth, it was right here, right here where I'm standing, that I lifted him over."

"Well, I've been meaning to ask you. He *was* all right when you handed him over, wasn't he? He wasn't hurt."

"Oh, he was perfectly fine," Willoughby said. "Why, I would never put an injured cat over a fence, never."

"No, I'm sure he's just hiding somewhere. I'll let you know when I find him."

"Do," Willoughby said, and returned to his clipping. The thwack of the clippers as they came down on the hedge followed me through the field and out of the field.

I'm not sure what it was, but the next day something compelled me to search Willoughby's yard. I waited until he wasn't home, then, like my cat before me, crept stealthily through a side gate. From their outdoor pen the Kerry blues growled at me. I circled the lawn, until I was standing at the place where Willoughby was standing when he claimed to have put the cat over the fence. On the other side of the fence a thorny bush blocked my view of the field, and just to the left of it lay my cat, quite dead. I didn't make a sound. I went around the other way, into the field, and dug behind the bush, in the process cutting myself quite severely on the brambles. There was a gash running from the cat's chest to near his tail.

I picked up the carcass of my cat. His orange-and-white markings were still the same, but he was now just that—a carcass. I went to the house and got a garbage bag and shovel, and then I buried my cat in the overgrown field.

On the way home, climbing over my own fence, I decided to kill my neighbor.

At home I took a shower. The soap eased me. I considered methods. I felt no urge to confront Willoughby, to argue with him, to back him up against a wall and force him to confess his lie. I did not want to watch him writhe, or try to wriggle away from the forceful truth inhabiting my gaze. I simply wanted to kill him—cleanly, painlessly, with a minimum of fuss and absolutely no discussion. It was not a question of vengeance; it was a question of extermination.

Of course a shotgun would have been best. Then I could simply ring his doorbell, aim, and, when he answered, pull the trigger.

Unfortunately, I did not own a shotgun, and had no idea where to get one. Knives seemed messy. With strangulation and plastic bags, there was almost invariably a struggle.

Then, drying myself after the shower, I noticed the andirons. They were Willoughby's andirons; nineteenth-century, in the shape of pug dogs. He had loaned them to me one night in the winter. I'd lived next door to him for three years by then, but for the first two years I was living with someone else, and he hadn't seemed very interested in us. We'd exchanged the merest pleasantries over the fence. All I knew of Willoughby at that point was that he was exceedingly red-cheeked, apparently wealthy, and a breeder of Kerry blue terriers. It was only when the person I was living with decided to live somewhere else, in fact, that suddenly—at the sight of moving vans, it seemed—Willoughby showed up at the fence. "Neigh-bor," he called in a singsong. "Oh, neigh-bor." I walked up to the fence and he told me that one of his dogs had escaped and asked if I'd seen it, and when I said no he asked me over for a drink. I didn't take him up on the offer. One day my dog managed to dig under the fence to play with his Kerry blues, and when she returned there was a small red Christmas-tree ornament in the shape of a heart fastened to her collar. It hadn't been there before.

A few nights later a smoldering log rolled out of my fireplace, setting off the smoke alarm but bringing no one but Willoughby to the rescue.

He was wearing a red sweatsuit and a Vietnam jacket with his name printed over his heart. I thought, Rambo the Elf.

"I must loan you a pair of andirons," he said happily as he looked down at the charred spot on my rug. "Firedogs, you know. I'll be right back."

"Ah—no need. I'll buy a pair."

"No, no, you must accept my gesture. It's only neighborly."

"Thanks very much, then. I'll come by and pick them up in the morning."

Willoughby beamed. "Oh, too eager, I am always too eager when smitten. Well, yes, then. Fine." But in the morning, when I woke up, the andirons were waiting on my doorstep, along with a piece of notepaper illustrated with a picture of a Kerry blue terrier. On it, in red pen, was drawn a question mark.

From the fireplace, now, I picked one of the andirons up. It was cold and slightly sooty, yet it felt heavy enough to kill. "Blunt instrument," I said aloud to myself, savoring the words.

My dog was sitting in the backseat of the car. Since the cat's disappearance, this had become her favorite resting place, as if she feared above all else being left behind, and was determined to make sure I didn't set foot out of the house without her being aware of it. Now, however, I was traveling on foot, and figuring that anywhere I could walk was close enough not to pose a threat to her, she remained ensconced. It was a bright, sunny day, not the sort of day on which you would think you would think of killing someone. As I passed each house and turned the bend toward Willoughby's, I wondered when my resolve was going to lessen, when, with a rocket crash, I'd suddenly come to my senses. The thing was, it was the decision to kill Willoughby that felt like coming to my senses to me.

Halfway to his house, a Jeep Wagoneer pulled up to the side of the road ahead of me. On the bumper was a sticker that read, THE BETTER I GET TO KNOW PEOPLE, THE MORE I LOVE MY DOGS, and leaning out the driver's window was Tina Milkowski, the proprietress of a small, makeshift, and highly successful canine-sitting service. She was a huge woman, three hundred pounds at least.

"How you doing, Jeffrey?" she called.

"Not bad," I said. "How are you, Tina?"

"Can't complain." She seemed, for a moment, to sniff the air. "Where's the Princess today?"

"Home. She's spending the afternoon in my car."

"Hope you left the windows open. Say, what you got there? Firedogs?"

"They're Willoughby's."

Tina shook her head and reached for something in her glove compartment. "He's a strange one, Willoughby. Never been very friendly. The dogs are nice, though. He give those firedogs to you?"

She pulled a stick of gum out of a pack and began chewing it ruthlessly. I nodded.

"I didn't know you two were friends," Tina said in what seemed to me a suggestive manner.

"We're not friends. In fact, I'm on my way to kill him."

Tina stopped chewing. Then she laughed—a surprisingly high, girlish laugh, given her hoarse, bellowslike voice.

"Now why do you want to kill Willoughby?"

"One of his dogs murdered my cat. Then he threw the corpse over the fence into the field. But he told me the cat was alive, that he'd thrown the cat alive into the field because he didn't know it was my cat, and for three days now I've been searching that field for my cat when the whole time he was dead. At least I hope he was dead. It's possible he threw the cat over injured and let him bleed to death, though I can't believe, I honestly can't believe . . ."

I believed Tina had seen her fair share of the crimes human beings commit against one another; for this reason, perhaps, it was the crimes human beings commit against animals toward which she brought her harshest judgment.

She narrowed her eyes. "Listen, honey, don't do anything you'll regret. Think of it this way. His dog kills the cat, he throws it over, he isn't even thinking, probably. He figures it was a wild cat, pretends it'll just disappear. Then you ask him, he never knew it was your cat, and he just makes something up. On the spur of the moment. Probably he's over in that church right now saying a hundred Hail Marys and praying to Jesus to forgive him."

"It was worse than that." I cleared my throat. "Look, there's no point in going into details."

"The doggy probably didn't know what he was doing. Sometimes they just act instinctually."

"I don't blame the dog. I blame Willoughby."

Tina chewed her gum even more ferociously. For a few moments we were silent, her Wagoneer idling, until I realized what it was she was waiting for me to say.

It was easy enough. I laughed. "Don't worry," I said, "I'm not *really* going to kill him. I'm just going to bring back his andirons and have it out with him."

"You sure you're all right? You want to come by for a cup of coffee and talk it over?"

"Really, it's okay. Anyway, Tina, do I look like a murderer?"

She smiled, and I saw how tiny her mouth was, lost in her huge face. "You don't look to me," she said, "like you could kill a deer tick if it was biting you on the face."

I was learning something about murder. Before—that is, before the cat—I had always assumed that when the thought of killing someone enters the mind, a sudden knowledge of its consequences rears up almost automatically in response, saving the would-be killer from himself by reminding him, in glorious Technicolor, of all the cherished things he stands to lose. Today, however, no vision of jail cells or courtrooms or electric chairs entered my head. Nothing compelled me to replace the gun gratefully in its holster, the knife happily in its drawer, the firedog cheerily in its fireplace. The urge to kill had fogged every other feeling; walking down the street in its grip, I could see nothing but the immediate goal, and that goal was so clear, so obvious, it seemed so justly demanded, that the rest of the world, the world after the murder, the world of repercussions and punishments, receded and became dimly unreal. Indeed, as I approached Willoughby's house and rang his doorbell, I felt as if I were no longer a person; I felt as if I were merely a function waiting to be performed.

"Good afternoon," Willoughby said automatically as he pulled open the door; then, faced by mine, his face sank.

He looked down quickly. "I see you're returning my andirons."

"Yes," I said.

"Please come in." Willoughby led me into his living room. He was wearing a bright purple polo shirt and green shorts. I had one andiron in each hand, and what I hadn't counted on was having to put one down in order to kill him with the other one.

"I'll just take those from you," he said.

I allowed him to remove the andirons from my hands and replace them in his fireplace, along with several other sets.

"Have you found your little cat?"

"Yes. He was dead. Just where you threw him over."

Willoughby seemed to do some quick thinking, then said, "Oh dear, how terrible. I suspect one of those roaming dogs must have gotten to him. You know, with no leash law, this town is full of roaming, wild dogs. Most irresponsible of their owners, but I've always felt the folk here were a cretinous brood." He shook his head, turned from me, sat down on the edge of a settee.

"The corpse was at the exact spot where you told me you set him over the fence—alive."

"It is possible the dog—the wild dog—brought the corpse back after killing him, or—or did it right then—right after I—put him over." Willoughby coughed. "I am truly most terribly sorry about your cat. You know, Johnny really is very frightened of cats. He killed another—killed a cat once, another cat, that is. It was wandering in that field, and it attacked him. The cat attacked him. Viciously. He reacted in self-defense. With that cat, of course, the other cat, not with yours. In your case I interceded in the nick of time and removed the cat unharmed." He looked up at me. "Are you sure I can't induce you to take *some* libation?" he said.

"I'm going to kill you," I said.

Willoughby stood. "I'll call the police," he said. "I'll scream. My neighbor can be here in thirty seconds. My dogs are trained to kill. Believe me, I've dealt with thugs like you before and I know what to do. Many people have tried to take advantage of me, and not one has ever succeeded. There's a gun in that drawer. There's a knife in the kitchen. I was in Vietnam. I'm trained to kill. I know karate. I'm warning you. Stand back! Johnny! Johnny!"

His eyes were bulging. He stood pressed against a sliding glass door, as if pinned back, as if he were waiting for knives to land in a pattern around his body. Then he pulled the door open and ran out into the backyard. The dogs came leaping to him. He ran past them, toward the side gate which opened into the field, and then he ran out the gate, not bothering to close it. The dogs huddled around the open gate, but hesitated to follow their master through it.

I turned around and left Willoughby's living room. I closed his door behind me. I did not kill him, and I went home.

I did not know my cat well when he died. I had had him just over a month. But I liked him, and I was beginning to look forward to our life together. Not much distinguished him from other young cats. He was orange and white, and looking at him always made me hungry for those orange Popsicles with vanilla ice cream inside. He liked to romp around the house, to play with balls of string, to climb trees, and to hide. For hours he and Johnny sat across the fence from each other, staring, not making a move. He climbed tablecloths, and the smell of tuna fish made him yowl with an urgent desire which I could not seem to talk him out of. At first he had been wary of my dog, but then they grew loving toward each other. He used to nip at her legs for hours, trying to get her to play with him, while she sat there, unreacting, an enduring, world-weary matron. Sometimes he'd bat her face with his paw, and his claws would stick in her wiry fur.

When I got home from Willoughby's that afternoon my dog was still in the car. The paint on the driver's door, I noticed, was scratched from her nails. I got in and pulled out of the driveway. From where she was lying behind the backseat she lifted her head like the stuffed dog with the bobbing head my aunt kept in the back of her car in my childhood. She jumped onto the seat. I opened the back window a little, and she nudged her nose through the crack, sniffing the wind. We passed the empty field next to Willoughby's house, and I saw Willoughby on the side of the road, barefoot, red-faced, and panting. I honked, and his mouth opened, and he ran across the street. In my rearview mirror I watched him grow smaller and smaller until I turned a corner and he disappeared. Soon we were in open country—long fields where corn had been planted in narrow even rows.

Once, on a snow-blind winter night, I had heard Willoughby whistling. I stood up and went to the back door. There he was, just on the other side of the fence. "Jeffrey," he said, "are you really my friend?"

"Excuse me?" I said.

"I'm asking if you're really my friend," he said. "I must know, you see, because the Lord has seen fit to lock me out of my house, and I must rely upon the kindness of strangers."

"Wait a minute. You're locked out?"

"Afraid so."

"Have you lost your key?"

"No, I haven't lost my key."

"Is the lock broken, or frozen?"

"There's nothing wrong with the lock."

"Well, I don't understand then—"

"The *Lord* has seen fit to lock me out of my house. It is a test. I must throw myself upon the mercy of strangers, the kindness of strangers. I must be humble."

"Call a locksmith," I said, and went back inside.

A few hours later the phone rang. I let the answering machine pick it up. "Jeffrey, among the many things you may not ever forgive me for is calling you at this indecent hour," Willoughby said. "It's ten—or rather, two o'clock." For a long while he was silent. Then he said, "Whenever you're ready, I'll be waiting. And my house is all alit by the Christmas tree."

When I got back from my drive that afternoon, the phone was ringing. "Excuse me," said a voice I didn't recognize. "Is this Mr. Jeffrey Bloom?"

"It is."

"Oh, hello. You don't know me, I'm your neighbor, Mrs. Bob Todd?"

"Hello," I said. I knew the house: a standard poodle, a children's pool, and a sign in front which read, THE BOB TODDS.

"I'm sorry to bother you in the evening, Mr. Bloom, but Tina Milkowski told me what happened to your little kitty and I wanted to extend my sympathies. It's just monstrous what that Willoughby Wayne did."

"Thank you, Mrs. Todd."

"Willoughby has been a nuisance ever since he moved into the Crampton place. Piles of money from his grandfather, and nothing to do with it. Now that was a man. Norton Wayne, he had character. But you know what they say, every family spawns one bad seed, and Willoughby Wayne is it. Always yammering on about his family tree. One poor couple, they were new at the club? They thought they had to be polite. I was at the next table, and I heard. Willoughby told them his family tree from 1612. Forty-five minutes, and he didn't even pause to take a breath. And those dogs. They bark like crazy, annoying the whole neighborhood. Then one day a few years ago he was leaving the club, and he hit a woman. He was drunk."

"My goodness," I said.

"And he's never married. I don't have to tell you *why*." Mrs. Bob Todd hiccuped. "Everyone says it's the Jews that are wrecking the neighborhood, but if you ask me, it's the old good-for-nothings like Willoughby. Nothing but trouble. Now I'm not rich, but I've lived in this town my whole life, and I can tell you honestly, I think you Jewish people are just fine."

"Thank you," I said.

"Anyway, dear, the reason I'm calling is Tina and I have decided to take some action. This has just gone far enough, with Willoughby and those dogs, and we're going to do something about it. I've already complained to the dog warden, and now I'm going to start a petition to have Willoughby thrown off the board of the Animal Protection Society. He has no business being on that board, given what he did, no business whatsoever."

"Mrs. Todd," I said, "really, this isn't necessary—"

"Oh, don't you worry. You won't have to lift a little finger. Your kitty's murder will be avenged!"

I was quiet. "Thank you," I said again.

"You're very welcome," she said. "Good-bye." She hung up.

I looked outside the window. My dog was flat on her back, being licked by an elderly Labrador named Max, neither of them deterred from this flirtation by the fact that one was spayed and the other neutered. And suddenly I remembered that I had an appointment for my own cat's neutering just the next week. I'd have to cancel it in order to avoid being charged.

I put the phone down. I was sorry I'd mentioned the whole thing to Tina Milkowski, and thus inadvertently begun the machine of vengeance rolling. Revenge anticipated is usually better than revenge experienced. (Then again, when I had wanted to kill Willoughby, it hadn't felt like revenge, what I'd wanted—or had it?)

I decided to clip a leash onto my dog and take her for a walk. It was the dog-walking hour. The Winnebago of our local mobile dog groomer was parked in Libby LaMotta's driveway, Libby pacing nervously alongside while within that mobile chamber her cocker spaniel puppy, Duffy, was given a bath. We waved. Across the street Susan Carlson had Nutmeg, her Manx cat, on a leash. We waved. Further down the street Mrs. Friedrich was watering her plants. She often spoke wistfully about the "big, velvety balls" of which *her* cat, Fred, had finally to be deprived, once he'd sprayed too many sofas. We waved. Then I passed Mrs. Carnofsky, quite literally dragging her resistant Dandie Dinmont terrier behind her, unmoved by the scraping sounds the dog's paws were making against the pavement, the wheezing and choking as he gasped against the tug of his collar, determined to pull her back to a pile of shit a few feet down the sidewalk. "He won't budge," she said. Her blue-gray hair was exactly the same tint as her dog's. We did not wave.

As for Willoughby—just past midnight that night there was whistling at the fence. There he stood, in his elf suit, having somehow climbed through or over the privet hedge.

"Jeffrey," he said.

"What is it, Willoughby?"

"Why do you hate me so?"

"I don't hate you," I said honestly.

"If you don't hate me, then why are you persecuting me?"

I crossed my arms, and turned away from him. "Look, I'm sorry I said I wanted to kill you. I was just angry. I'm not going to kill you. I apologize."

"Nadine Todd called me this evening and she said the most horrid things. She called me a monster and a drunk and worse. She's going to have me thrown off the board of the Animal Protection Society."

"I really didn't have anything to do with that, Willoughby—"

"The Animal Protection Society is one of my great loves. Disregarding the humiliation for the moment, you'll be taking away one of the few ways in the world in which I'm able to feel truly useful."

"I'm sorry," I said. "Really, I have nothing to do with it. Mrs. Todd is acting on her own."

He looked away. "I am lost and forlorn. I have nowhere to turn. I throw myself upon your mercy."

"Good night, Willoughby," I said, and went inside.

A few minutes later there was a knock on the door.

"Do with me what you will," Willoughby said, and threw his arms out at his sides, like Christ.

"Willoughby, it's past midnight."

"The Lord has directed me to you, Jeffrey. He has told me to throw myself upon your mercy. I must learn to be humble, to act humbly."

"Is it humble to barge uninvited into someone's house in the middle of the night? Is that humble?"

"I am a pathetic and desperate man," Willoughby said. He hung his head in shame.

"All right," I said. "Come in."

He smiled, then, came through the door gratefully, and sat down on the sofa. My dog ran up to him from where she was sleeping, barked, sniffed at his haunches. He reached down and stroked her neck. There was something incalculably gentle and expert about the way he stroked her neck, and I wondered, for a moment, if he suffered from a kind of autism; if, in lieu of his clumsy and imperfect relations with humans, he had developed an intricate knowledge of the languages and intimacies of dogs. There were people who, for all the affection they felt, hadn't the foggiest idea how to stroke a dog. They pushed the fur the wrong way, their hands came down rough and ungentle. I suspected Willoughby was like this with people, and always had been.

I brought him a cup of tea, which he thanked me for. The dog had crawled into his lap and gone to sleep. "This is not, of course, the first time that I've been the object of persecution and derision," Willoughby was saying. "Even when I was a little boy it happened. My parents for some reason insisted I attend public school. Another child circulated a petition which read, 'We, the undersigned, hate Willoughby Wayne.' I didn't understand why. I had tried to ingratiate myself with those children, in spite of the enormous gulf which separated us." Tears welled in his eyes. "The ancient Hebrews were cursed with the vice of avarice, and often I have felt the modern Hebrews have inherited that vice, yet in spite of this I feel deeply for the persecution they suffered at the hands of the Nazis, for I too have suffered such persecution." And like a litany, he incanted: "I am a pathetic and desperate man."

I sat down next to him. "You don't have to be that way," I said.

"I am very set in my ways." His hand, I noticed, was on my thigh, following, even at this dark moment, its sly and particular agenda. I moved it away. The dog lifted her head, sniffed, and jumped barking onto the floor.

"I'll call Mrs. Todd," I said. "I'll try to persuade her not to throw you off the board. But I can't guarantee anything. Now I have to go to bed."

Willoughby stood up. I handed him a Kleenex and he blew his nose. "I assure you," he said at the door, "that when I threw your cat over the fence, he was unharmed," and I realized that whether or not this was true, he believed it.

"Good night, Willoughby," I said.

"Good night, Jeffrey." And I watched him go out the door and head down the street. I was remembering how when I was digging the grave that afternoon, I'd kept repeating to myself over and over, "It's just a cat, just an animal, with a small brain, a tail, fur." Then I started thinking about the night my dog—spooked by thunder—bolted out the front door and ran. For three hours I'd driven through the neighborhood, calling her name, knocking on doors. Various sightings were reported in a direct line from Mrs. Friedrich's house, to the Italian deli by the train station, to the laundromat; then the trail disappeared. Finally I went to bed, making sure her dog door was open for her, while outside the storm railed on, and my dog, lost somewhere in it, struggled to make her way home. And what a miracle it was when at four in the morning she jumped up onto my bed—filthy, shivering, covered with leaves and brambles. Like the dogs of legends, she had found her way back.

I thought I'd *had* my brush with death then. I thought from then on I might be spared.

It must have been at that moment—when I was digging the grave, remembering how nearly I'd lost my dog—that the thought of murder came to me, growing more vivid with each thwack of the shovel against the stony earth. Really, I was no better than Willoughby; I just hadn't been alone so long.

"I am a pathetic and desperate man," I said to myself—trying the words on for fit—and standing in the doorway, watched Willoughby stumble home, bereft in the starlight. All along the street, houses were dark, and inside each of those houses were people with cats and dogs, and stories to tell: the time Flossie fell four stories and broke a tooth; the time Rex disappeared for weeks, then showed up one afternoon on the back porch, licking his paw; the time Bubbles was mangled under the wheels of a car. They would tell you, if you asked them, how they had to put Darling to sleep; how Fifi went blind, then deaf, then one day just didn't wake up; how Bosco could jump through a hoop; how Kelly swam under water; how Jimbo begged, how Millie spoke, how Sophie ate nothing but tuna fish. The night was brisk, and somewhere distantly a dog barked. My dog growled, then barked in response. The distant dog barked back. Their conversation, like mine and Willoughby's, might, I knew, go on all night.

Here is my story: When I was young, my family lived in Cleveland, and we had a dog named Troubles. Next door was a dog named Chips, and sometimes in the afternoon, when Chips wandered into our yard, my sister would yell, "Troubles, Chips is here! Chips is here!" and Troubles would leap up from wherever she was sleeping and bound into the yard to see her friend. Then we moved away to California, and Troubles got old and cranky and seemed no longer to like other dogs. Chips was still in Cleveland, or dead; we didn't know.

One day my sister had a friend over. They were going through the old photo albums from Cleveland, and my sister was telling stories. "All we had to do," I heard her saying to her friend, "was yell, 'Troubles, Chips is here! Chips is here!' and then—" And before she could even finish the story Troubles had leapt into the room once more, barking and jumping and sniffing the air. Something had lasted, in spite of all the time that had passed and the changes she had weathered, the trip cross-country, and the kennel, and the cats. My sister put her hand to her mouth, and tears sprang in her eyes, and like the young enchantress desperate to reverse the powerful incantation she has just naively uttered, she cried out, "Troubles, stop! Stop! Stop!" but it did no good. Nothing would calm Troubles, and nothing would dissuade her, as she barked and jumped and whined and nosed for that miraculous dog who had crossed the years and miles to find her.

Roads to Rome

Fulvia's house: old, swollen bricks, a buckling terra-cotta floor. A child could stand inside the fireplace. In the middle of the kitchen is an oval oak table, big enough to seat twenty, which Fulvia bought at an auction of retired theater-set furniture. For many years she'd noticed it on the stage of the Rome Opera, where perhaps the grandeur of the gestures put its massiveness in perspective; more than one of the guests has joked today that Fulvia's house may not be such a far cry from all of that. "Anyway, I feel like a minor character in Puccini," Giuliana told Marco, laughing, out on the patio. Below them lush hills spread out, and in the distance, in the plain, they could see the spa—Terme di Saturnia—where until recently Fulvia spent most of her days, lazing in the hot sulfurous waters.

It is a lukewarm, drizzly afternoon, late in spring. Outside Fulvia's house rain beats at the metal roofs and hoods of the twenty or so cars parked in the moss-covered courtyard. "My family," Fulvia jokes to the American from where she's lying, half covered in a blanket, on the worn velvet sofa by the fireplace. "Look around you, try to figure it all out." The American turns. Giuliana, Fulvia's daughter, has just come in from the patio with Marco. He was her best friend when they were teenagers, and then when he was sixteen he and Fulvia became lovers and she swept him off to Paris. For possibly unrelated reasons Giuliana ran away to India, became a junkie, then settled in Singapore, where she is now married, the mother of three children Fulvia has never seen. Across the room is Rosa, Fulvia's closest friend and Marco's mother, and his sister, Alba. Grazia, Marco's wife, sits at the huge oval table with Alberto, the man she lives with. The man Marco lives with is the American. His name is Nicholas. Laura has just emerged from the bathroom; she is the mother of a little boy, Daniele, whom Marco has raised as his own, even though, biologically, technically, he is not his son. Daniele is outside, playing with Alba's little girl, whose name is also Rosa.

"I think I've got it clear who everyone is," Nicholas says.

"Not for long," jokes Fulvia, and coughs violently. "More are coming. More come every day. Everyone wants to say good-bye because I am the queen and I'm dying. The queen! It's funny. It's amazing, really. Look at all these people, they are rich, well-educated, they are the best Italy has to offer. And they are ruined, every single one of them. You can't guess. If you knew the drugs they've put into their veins, the things they've seen and done—corrupt, utterly." She smiles, as if this pleases her.

"What are you saying about me now, *cara*?" Marco asks, in English. "You think you can tell Nicky anything, no one will understand, but you forget that some of us have been living in New York a long time now."

"Nothing you haven't already heard from me," Fulvia says, laughing, then breaks into a rasping, huge, dangerous smoker's cough.

Fulvia seems determined to die the way she has lived all these years: with drama and pronouncements. Just this morning a famous movie star whose villa is down the road came to pay a visit. Much was made over the movie star, pasta with truffles was prepared for her, as well as a rabbit and a salad of wild greens. Afterwards, from her place on the couch, Fulvia told the movie star she ought really to take more care choosing her films.

"And wasn't that just like Fulvia," Rosa says, after the movie star has left. She is drying dishes and speaking—ostensibly—to her daughter Alba, though Fulvia is within full hearing range. "Does it matter that poor Marina couldn't get a part in a decent film if her life depended on it? Does it matter that she is about to be divorced and must take pills to sleep?" She shakes her head. "The creature deserves our pity, not Fulvia's meanness."

"You're too sentimental, Rosa!" Fulvia calls from the living room. "The woman is richer than the pope. As for those American films she's been in lately, she'd be wiser to make nothing than that kind of *trippa*."

"Fulvia, you haven't even seen Marina's latest films," Rosa says. "Not that that ever stopped you from passing judgment." (Fulvia, for most of her life, has been a kind of all-purpose cultural critic for a famous Communist newspaper.)

"*I* saw one of Marina's films," says Giuliana. "She was a mafiosa whose daughter decided to leave the family. It was dubbed in Chinese, so it was hard for me to understand."

"Probably better than the original. And you're telling me to waste my money on garbage like that?" Fulvia laughs hoarsely. "Bring me a cigarette, *carissimo*," she calls to Nicholas, who waits for someone to object, then, when no one does, fetches the ever-present box of Rothmans from the table.

"You're jealous, that's all," Rosa is saying. "You would have liked to be a movie star too."

"Oh, Rosa, shut up! You're the one who's jealous. You always have been, since we were girls."

"And why's that?"

"Because I'm prettier," Fulvia says.

"Ah, I see."

"Because people care about me so, and want to visit me, and no one likes you."

"Yes, it's true," Rosa says. "I'm an ugly duckling. What is her name, Cinderella? Every summer Fulvia invites half of Rome to this house, and who washes all the dishes? Who cooks the pasta?"

"You've always been the housewifely type," Fulvia says. "Unlike you, I'm glamorous. Like that American soldier from the waterfall called me, during the war. La Glamorosa."

"Marina told me something about that English lord down the road," Giuliana says, coming into the room. "She says he likes to make love to women while wearing rubber boots inside of which he's put live canaries. He bounces on the balls of his feet and feels the crunch—"

"Giuliana, that is the most ridiculous thing I've ever heard," Rosa says.

"No, it's true," Giuliana says. "Marina went there for lunch last week, and there'd been a party the night before. When she walked in, there were ten pairs of boots lined up and the floor was covered with feathers."

"Bah!" Rosa says. "*Ridicolo.*"

"I don't know why you can't believe it," says Grazia. "Stranger things have happened, and within the walls of this house."

"The only people more twisted than the rich Italians around here," Fulvia says, "are the rich English."

"Marina is a sick woman," Rosa says.

"I wonder if that's where Dario got it from," says Laura.

"What?" Grazia asks.

" 'La Glamorosa.' "

Fulvia waves her cigarette in annoyance. "It was my mistake to tell Dario too many stories when he was young."

Laura, looking distressed, says, "I'm sorry, Fulvia, I didn't mean to mention all that."

"You think just because I'm dying I've become sentimental? I'm not sentimental." She blows out smoke dramatically. "No, 'bored' is a better word to describe my feelings about Dario these days. Bored with his *myth.* He was a naughty boy, and I loved him, but I am as bored with him as I am with Marina's movies."

"I saw Dario do Marina once," Alba pipes in. "It was marvelous, he looked just like her."

"Fulvia," says Rosa, "you are not really so callous."

Fulvia extinguishes her cigarette in an empty bottle of cough syrup. "I at least have no delusions. I say the truth. If people don't like it, they can leave my house."

"Excuse me," Marco says, and walks out of the room, onto the balcony. Everyone watches him.

"Well, well, well," Grazia says, after a few seconds.

"Who is Dario?" Nicholas asks.

Rosa, who is drying her hands on a dish towel, stops suddenly.

"I have to use the toilet," Fulvia announces, rather grandly.

"Speaking of Dario?" Laura asks. Grazia suppresses a laugh.

"Very funny," Fulvia says. "Rosa, can you get over here and help me? There's not much time."

"Yes, yes," Rosa says wearily. "Giuliana?"

"I'm coming."

Even though she can barely walk, Fulvia refuses a wheelchair. She says she prefers being carried around, "like a queen." "Careful! Careful!" she scolds Giuliana as the two women pick Fulvia up from the sofa. "Don't be a clumsy girl."

"A mother of three, and she still calls me a clumsy girl."

"When you start supporting yourself, then I'll call you a clumsy woman," Fulvia says as Rosa closes the bathroom door behind them.

"La Glamorosa," Alba is saying. "That must have been part of his act too. Like when he did Marina Albieri."

"La Glamorosa!" says Alberto, Grazia's boyfriend, who up until this point has been busily engaged in cleaning his pipe. He grabs a tablecloth from a pile on the cabinet, drapes it over his shoulder, and starts singing.

"That's a Patty Pravo song," Laura says. "Did Dario do it? My Brazilian husband was so in love with her in 1968."

"You have a Brazilian husband?" Nicholas asks.

"Perhaps, *caro*. Unless he's dead. I haven't heard a word from him since 1972, nor do I care to."

Though Nicholas has been living with Marco in New York for just under a year now—Marco is employed by a large international drug company; Nicholas works at a bookstore—this is the first time they've traveled to Italy together. Of course, Nicholas was nervous about meeting Marco's large, strangely shaped, and strange-sounding family—fearful that they wouldn't like him, that they'd find him boring, bourgeois, or parochial. Fulvia especially. Everything Marco told Nicholas about Fulvia scared him. Marco had grown up with Fulvia and her children, and when he was sixteen and she was fifty, she'd taken him as her lover. It didn't matter that Marco was the son of her best friend, Rosa, or that she'd changed his diapers; what she wanted, he said, Fulvia took. They lived together in Fulvia's apartment in Paris for just over a year—the only year in their lives that Fulvia and Rosa didn't speak, and don't speak, about still. (That was considered the major calamity, the split between Fulvia and Rosa.) In those days Fulvia liked Marco to make love to her while holding her wrists together behind her back, and once he did this so tightly her wrists turned blue and started to bleed. Being a boy, he began, almost immediately, to weep, but Fulvia managed to calm him, wrap her wrists in gauze, and get by herself to the hospital, where she had to do quite a bit of talking to convince the doctor that what he was treating was not, as it appeared, a suicide attempt. Of course, the truth sounded so improbable that finally the doctor believed her.

It was Fulvia who told Marco he was gay. Announced it to him, in fact, quite casually, at a restaurant.

"And how do you know that?" a flustered Marco had asked her. (He was just sixteen, and easily unnerved.)

"A woman knows these things about a man," Fulvia said. "Anyway, am I right?"

"I'm not sure."

"I'm right," Fulvia said. And she was. "But don't worry over it, *amore*. It's your nature. It's good. Just start sleeping with other boys and don't feel guilty."

Marco was nothing if not obedient. He went off to find a boy, and found many. Eventually, for reasons mysterious to everyone except the two of them, he married Grazia, who was not thirty but twenty years older than he was. They lived together for a few years. Then Marco moved to New York with Laura, whose son he'd adopted, and Grazia moved to Milan with Alberto. Fulvia took as a new lover the doctor who'd treated her wounds and was eager to try out that sexual position her fondness for which had brought her to his hospital in the first place. His name was Caino, and he spent his summers in Capri, with his wife.

Almost instantly after Marco went off to find boys, Rosa and Fulvia became friends again, which was lucky, since summer was coming, and everyone was in an uproar about what would happen with the house if Rosa and Fulvia were fighting. Later, Grazia insisted Fulvia had timed it that way. An affair was an affair, but the summer house—that was a different matter.

Technically, it's Fulvia's house. She inherited it from her parents, who died in the war—they were both Resistance fighters—and since their youth, she and Rosa and all their husbands and children have shared it. When Fulvia dies, it will become Rosa's property—"the least I deserve," Rosa joked, after the pronouncement was made. "After all, Fulvia, have you once planted a seed or painted a wall or boiled a pot of water? I was the *casalinga*, summer after summer. It should have been mine years ago."

"Don't forget who found the furniture."

"Don't forget who dusted it."

"*Puttana.*"

"Don't call me a *puttana*," Rosa said. "*I've* only had *two* husbands." And Fulvia laughed. "Come here," she called to Nicholas. She cleared a space on the sofa in the living room, the sofa from which she conducted the business of the house, then slapped the space like a baby's bottom, shouting, "Sit! Sit!" Nicholas sat. "Now tell me, are you having a good time here? Are you enjoying your new Italian relatives?"

"I'm loving it," Nicholas said. "I can't tell you how much I wish I'd grown up in a household like this. I think about Marco's childhood and I get envious—mine was so boring by comparison."

"Don't say that!" Fulvia clucked her tongue. "I know what it looks like to you. You think it was all warmth and singing, *la mamma* and *il papà* and pots of pasta and wine pouring out of the bottle onto the floor. But there was more to it than that, *caro*. Corruption. Cruelty. Not to mention the drugs. You know all our children used heroin—even Marco."

"I know."

She beckoned him closer. "I'll tell you a secret. Every one of these people in this house, every single one, I'd just as soon they would leave today and never come back. Except for Rosa. Without Rosa I'd be dead. Rosa walks out that door, I die."

"Ridiculous," Rosa muttered from the other sofa, where she was reading the newspaper.

"Rosa is the only person I love," Fulvia went on. "If God had had any sense at all, he would have made us lesbians. But, unfortunately, we're both too fond of *cazzo* for that. A pity. We would have treated each other better than any of our husbands. No, don't think the men had anything to do with it. *We* built this family, Rosa and me. We raised all the children together, didn't we, Rosa?"

Absorbed in her paper, Rosa only murmured a concurrence.

"Ah, I'm getting boring," Fulvia said. "Now, *caro*, tell me about you. Your dull family."

"Well," Nicholas said, "my mother's a schoolteacher, and my father's—"

"A schoolteacher! I was supposed to be a schoolteacher when I was a girl! Can you imagine? Me? I can't. Anyway, I lost the chance for that glamorous career when I married Carlo. I had to settle for being a famous journalist and cultural arbiter. Sad, when I could have been a schoolteacher."

"*Cagna*," Rosa said, under her breath.

"*Porca*," Fulvia muttered. They both giggled.

On the balcony, Marco stands, his back to the house, the household, Fulvia. In the distance, at the bottom of the hills, are the famous hot springs: a spa with pools, and down the road from it, a waterfall where you can swim without paying. At Nicholas's insistence, they went at midnight the night they arrived, even though Marco was jet-lagged and would have preferred to wait until the morning. But Nicholas was emphatic. He'd been hearing about the waterfall for too long. Now he saw: Naked men with big muscles and bulging stomachs stood under the dark heavings of water, their eyes cast up to a sky thick with stars. Women and babies. Grandmothers, their breasts distended. There was a strong, ugly smell of rotten eggs. "The sulfur," Marco explained, pulling his shirt off. "Smells like farts, doesn't it? But you'll grow to love it soon."

And Nicholas has. Since their arrival a week ago he's gone every afternoon to the spa, lying limp in the hot pool, or allowing the pounding weight of an artificial waterfall to beat his back. In the evenings he goes back to the natural waterfall, sometimes for hours. There are a big pool and a small pool at the spa. Near the big pool is a little fountain, a perpetual trickle, with plastic cups and a sign extolling the water's health-giving properties. At first the thought of drinking the stuff repelled Nicholas, but by the second day he was ready, and lined up behind a family of fat Germans for his first taste of the acrid, sulfurous water. He could barely get it down, but once he had, felt purified.

"There's not a wrinkle on my body," Fulvia boasted, the one afternoon she felt well enough to go down to the spa. "And I'm ninety-seven years old."

"Fulvia, don't be absurd," Rosa said. "Everyone here knows you're just ninety-six."

Even so, when Fulvia pulled off her bathrobe, people gasped or turned away. She laughed. "You think I've been making it up, the dying part?" she asked, pulling loose the gathered leg-holes of her bathing suit. "Skinny, yes. But even at the hospital the doctors couldn't keep their hands off me. Such *skin*. And you know why? This water. Help me, will you?" And Marco and Nicholas eased her in. Instantly she fell silent, and dropped her head back into the water, so that her hair floated out like strands of seaweed, her mouth open.

"Stay with me," she said. "I'm so skinny I might go down the drain."

On the porch, the rain has stopped. Small puddles reflect the peeling stucco that covers the old house. From where Marco stands, there is a good view of the spa, the brightly suited bathers standing out like colored beads against the green water. Nicholas touches Marco's shoulder, and Marco flinches before turning.

"Oh, hi."

"Are you all right?"

Marco stretches. "Yes, all right."

"Why did you leave the room?"

"I just didn't feel like listening to Fulvia and my mother chatter." He puts his hands on Nicholas's shoulders. "So how are you enjoying my—shall we say—family?"

"I'm a bit perplexed," Nicholas admits. "Everyone seems to be married to someone who's dead, or in South America, or living with someone else, and they don't care."

"Marriage Italian style," Marco says, laughing. "Haven't you read about it in books? But there's an explanation. In a country where divorce has only been legal for fifteen years, people just get used to finding—shall we say—alternatives. For centuries we couldn't divorce, and now that we can, nobody sees the point in taking the trouble when probably if you get remarried you'll just end up divorcing again anyway. Why, look at Fulvia. I can't even remember who she's married to. The men she married, the men she lived with, they all blend together."

"It's just different than what I'm used to," Nicholas says. "I mean, my sister's divorced. A lot of my friends too. But in America, even if you get a divorce, at least it's a big deal. You don't just leave a marriage behind like a shirt that doesn't fit you anymore."

"Why?"

"Because it has emotional ramifications."

"A marriage is a legal document. A legal document does not have, as you say, emotional ramifications unless you give them to it."

Both of them lean over the railing, staring down at the plain.

"Who's Dario?" Nicholas asks.

"Ah, the Dario question," Marco says. "Dario was Fulvia's son."

"But why isn't—"

"He's dead. He killed himself seven years ago."

Nicholas catches his breath. "I didn't know," he says.

"Of course not. I didn't tell you."

"Why?"

"Because," Marco says. "Why don't you ask Fulvia? Fulvia will be more than glad to give you the whole story. All the gory details, including the shit."

"Shit?"

"Ask her." Then Marco turns and goes back into the house. Nicholas follows. From the front door he watches as Marco gets into Grazia's little Fiat and drives off.

"Coprophagy," Alberto is saying to Alba. "That's the technical term for it."

"I've never heard that word before."

"So you've learned something new for the day, haven't you? And what a thing to learn."

"Sit down," Fulvia says, making room for Nicholas on the sofa. "Sit down and Fulvia will tell you the whole story."

Nicholas sits down. Fulvia is flanked on one side by Rosa, who is knitting, and on the other by Grazia, who is running her fingers through her pale blond hair. Giuliana and Laura mill about, pretending not to listen.

"My son," Fulvia begins, "was a strange young man. He liked to wear dresses and eat shit."

Nicholas blinks.

"A coprophagist," Grazia says. "He had a whole philosophy about it."

"Why, look at him!" Rosa says. "The poor boy is shocked. Oh dear, Fulvia, it's like you're the worldly *principessa* in some Henry James novel, corrupting the innocent American. But there it is. He asked."

"Well, if he's shocked, he shouldn't be," Fulvia says. "Worse things go on in New York. And every day."

"I've just never heard of someone eating—"

"It's not an ordinary practice," Fulvia says. "Then again, Dario was not an ordinary young man. He had theories."

"For him, it was the ultimate transgression," Grazia says. "The ultimate sin, the ultimate, unspeakable, unforgivable sin. And once you'd done it, well—you pierced through—what was it he called it?—the membrane of ordinary morality. You entered a kind of ecstasy, a freedom. You committed the final transgression, and it felt wonderful."

"My son was full of shit—if you'll excuse the expression. He just wanted to shock."

"He'd read a lot of the Marquis de Sade. There was a scene where the nobleman who is the hero, after doing every imaginable thing, every vile thing, announces that he is going to take the village idiot into a room and once there do something with him so unspeakably obscene the other people in the book won't ever in their dreams be able to imagine what it is. Then he leads the village idiot into the room and closes the door. The others wait. After about ten minutes, he comes out and announces he's done it. He's done the unspeakable thing with the village idiot. Then they all sit down and he gives them a thirty-page lecture on hedonism."

"Really, Grazia, you were rather too taken in by Dario—"

"Dario was fascinated by de Sade. He wanted to know what it was the nobleman and the village idiot had done. He wanted to do it. You see, he was determined to show all of us what a joke our bourgeois lives were. He wasn't ashamed of being homosexual. He was a beautiful boy, Dario, and he looked beautiful in dresses. Sometimes he sang."

"La Glamorosa," Rosa says.

"Dario," Fulvia says, "liked attention, and never felt he got enough from me. That was all there was to it. He wanted to impress me. But I never attended one of his evenings."

"He said the taste of shit was ambrosial," Grazia continues, rather dreamily. "He wanted me to try it, but I thought I'd throw up. I never did, that I knew of. But once he gave a party and baked a big *torta di cioccolata*. And he put it in it—the shit. And everyone at that party kept saying, 'But *Madonna*, this is the best *torta* I've ever tasted! So delicious! Dario, what is your recipe?' "

"Really, Grazia," Rosa says, "must you remind us?"

"Well, anyway," Fulvia says, "to make a long story short, Marco became Dario's lover. Don't ask me why; Marco was very impressed by him. He even went on stage once and made love. That was when Dario was performing."

"Performing?"

"Yes, it was the early seventies, when even intelligent people were behaving like fools. Dario would get on a stage, recite some of his ludicrous texts, lift up his dress, and squat—"

"But Fulvia, you're too hard on him!" Grazia says. "You were never there, you never saw. It's true, seen from today, it was a bit strange. But what he read was—brilliant. And when you watched him—what he did—it seemed beautiful."

"Grazia, you're a stupid *vacca*. You'll fall for anything, even today when most people have gotten their brains back in order. I never understood what Marco saw in you, except you allowed him to get away with his own stupidity, which I never did."

"Fulvia, please," Rosa says.

"Oh, shut up, Rosa, I'm dying. I'll say the truth, for once."

Grazia stands. "You really think you're the queen, Fulvia. And like a queen, you assume that just because you're cruel, you're right. But you're not always right."

She turns and marches out of the room.

"Che sensibilità!" Fulvia says. "Hand me a cigarette." Nicholas obliges. "So, to get on with the story: As time went on, the fashions changed. Fewer and fewer people came to Dario's performances. He was—how would you say it in English—'a flash in the bedpan'?"

Nicholas doesn't laugh. He is looking at the door through which Grazia has just passed.

"Of course," Fulvia says, "there were drugs. And even though nobody was listening to him anymore except stupid Grazia, he was still having his delusions of grandeur. He thought he was the Savior, the Messiah. Naturally Marco became sick of this soon enough, and left him. Dario was alone. The drugs were getting bad. Finally he took an overdose. They found him in the morning. He wasn't trying to get attention, for once. He just wanted it over." She blows smoke.

"Fulvia acts cold," Rosa says. "But that's just her way of hiding her pain."

"Oh shut up, Rosa. Don't speak for me. I act cold because I *am* cold."

"Marco never told me any of this," Nicholas says.

"Marco made a big exit, going to New York. He said he never wanted to have anything to do with any of us ever again. It doesn't surprise me one bit that he never mentioned Dario to you."

"Dario was a disturbed boy, but he had something," Rosa says. "He had charm and a certain real genius. A kind of genius. It was just that everyone mistook it for another kind of genius. He acted like a messiah, and everyone was looking for a messiah, so that's what they turned him into."

"You're too kind to him, Rosa."

"You're too cruel."

"Perhaps. But I made him." Fulvia takes a drag from her cigarette. "Now, for God's sake, will someone empty this ashtray? And close the window! I feel a wind coming up."

Years before, during the war, when they were girls, Fulvia and Rosa lived alone in the house near Saturnia with an old crone and her cretinous son. They were being hidden, protected. Fulvia's parents, they thought, were still alive; Rosa's were fighting it out in Rome. One night the two girls sneaked out of the house to take a swim at the waterfall. It was winter and there wasn't any heat; the hot water warmed them up. A pair of soldiers surprised them, where they were splashing, and the dread they felt, those first few moments, looking into the soldiers' faces and wondering if they were Nazis, was worse than anything either of them had ever imagined they might have to feel. They covered their breasts with their hands and waited to see what would happen next. "You think they speak English?" one of the soldiers said. He was tall, blond, with fair skin. He seemed to be making a noble effort not to look at their bodies. The other soldier, who was shorter and more muscular, couldn't keep his eyes from Fulvia's breasts. "I'm not sure," he answered. Then he stepped forward, and clearing his throat, said, "We are Americans. *Americani.* We've come to liberate you. From the Nazis." The soldier spoke slowly and very loudly, as if he imagined an increase in volume might help to bridge the gap between languages. *"Liberazione,"* he tried. "The war is over."

"We understand English," Fulvia said. "But is it true? We cannot believe it. The war is over?"

"Maybe you could bring us our towels," Rosa said.

"Oh yes," said the shorter soldier, and taking the towels from the tree, threw them out to where the girls were standing, knee deep, in the water. Rosa and Fulvia covered themselves. They were both laughing, yelling, really, with joy and disbelief. Could it be true? The war over?

"Come in the water!" Fulvia said. "You must come in the water! The war is over!" She flung aside her towel and traipsed onto the shore toward the two soldiers, who stepped back. "Oh no," the taller soldier said. "We can't." But the shorter was already taking off his shirt. "Hell, Wayne, why not?" he asked. "Shit, the war's over." Soon he was naked, splashing in the hot water with Rosa and Fulvia, while Wayne stood staring on the shore.

"Come on, Wayne!" called the shorter soldier. "Get your clothes off!"

"Yes, come on, Wayne!" Rosa called. She jumped out of the water and started tearing at the soldier's uniform with wet hands. "Well, why not?" Wayne said finally. From the village on the hill, a sound of screaming was starting up. The girls climbed onto the soldiers' shoulders and battled each other for a while, and then the four of them broke into pairs and moved together to opposing shadowy regions. In one corner of dry grass and moonlight, the shorter soldier, whose name was Nelson Perkins, Jr., called Fulvia "La Glamorosa" and after they made love gave her chewing gum. In another, Wayne Smith asked Rosa to come back to America and marry him.

Fulvia thought Rosa was crazy, and told her so. "You're nineteen, the war is over, you have everything ahead of you! How can you waste it all on a silly American? You'll go mad with boredom wherever it is he lives—what is the place called, Canvas?"

"I love him," Rosa said stoically.

"Love him! You hardly know him! Trust me, Rosa, very soon you'll find another man to love—an Italian, preferably with some power and intellect. If you'll pardon my saying so, your Wayne has eaten too much *granoturco*; they say it makes them feebleminded."

"Shut up, Fulvia. Why must you always know what's best for other people? You're envious of me, that's all."

"Envious!"

"Because my soldier loves me, and yours couldn't care less. Wayne told me, Nelson said he thought you were—what was his word—'uppity.' He said you were uppity."

"Rosa, you are a fool."

"Fine, if that's what you think. I'll go. Then we'll see." And she went. They got married in a Presbyterian church in Kansas City. Then, for almost a year, Rosa lived—irony of ironies—in Rome, Kansas, the wife of an auto mechanic, while Fulvia—fueled, some said, by rage over her parents' death—worked her way through a number of powerful men and eventually got a job interviewing people for a newspaper. She later wrote a column in which she expressed her resentment at the assumption that she'd only gotten where she was because of who she'd slept with; at the time she'd done it, she pointed out, sleeping with them was the only way for an intelligent woman to get powerful men to listen to her in the first place. Then she named the men. The article, like much of what Fulvia wrote, caused a stir, and had people arguing for a month. All this while Rosa—just nineteen—tried to make a go of it in Rome, Kansas, got pregnant, had a miscarriage. Her arrival had been greeted by an article in the local newspaper, a clipped copy of which she still keeps stowed in a kitchen drawer in Saturnia:

Wartime Romance

Rome Boy Marries Rome Girl

Private Wayne Arthur Smith, 20, son of Mr. and Mrs. Ludlow J. Smith of Ellsworth Street, Rome, Kansas, was married yesterday to Rosa Signorelli, 19, of Rome, Italy. The bride and bridegroom met in Italy, where Private Smith was stationed.

Private Smith, who is employed at Sam's Service Station on Mott Avenue, is a graduate of Rome Regional High School. He and his bride plan to make their home in the new development on Warren Drive.

The bride's parents, Mr. and Mrs. Luigi Signorelli of the Appian Way, Rome, Italy, did not attend the nuptials.

So Rosa ended up living in a blue asbestos-shingled house near a wheat field. Every day Wayne got up near dawn and drove his pickup truck to the garage. Rosa played bridge with his mother and sisters, made elaborate *torte* for the church bake sales, which, because they were not frosted pink, no one wanted, and searched futilely for foods that would at least approximate the tastes she'd grown up with—good, green olive oil, fresh pecorino cheese, ripe tomatoes. But the oil was like soap scum, the tomatoes pale orange and mealy, the cheese the consistency of pencil erasers. Rome, Kansas, the late 1940s: It might seem a strange place for a sophisticated Roman girl, the child of intellectual leftists, to end up. And yet, how many more couples like them did the war produce? Differences become detectable much more slowly when there's a language barrier; also, in the flummox of the aftermath, the joyous, wrecked catharsis that marked the end of the war, such differences might have seemed romantic, exciting, there might have appeared something deeply challenging about the prospect of crossing such barriers and thereby—in a small, private way—healing the broken world. They went off to America, in love, got married, in love; it took Rosa nearly a year to realize what a mistake she'd made.

Fortunately, she was not the kind of girl who digs her grave and lies in it. The first time Wayne blackened her eye she was gone. It wasn't hard; she didn't feel settled; the whole marriage had seemed like a dream, a sojourn, some sort of penance for the war. She was young, she healed easily; as soon as she got back to Rome—the real Rome—she would just start afresh, it would all seem distant and quick and nothing to be regretted. These days, she remembers with visceral clarity that windy afternoon she stood at the bus depot in Rome, Kansas, make-up covering her blackened eye. Wayne was at the garage; he didn't even know she was leaving. She had just enough money to get her to New York; once there, she planned to wire Fulvia, who'd just married a rich industrialist from Milan and would certainly provide fare for the boat. There is an illusory calm about this memory; a sensation of peace and clarity, of having finally come to her senses, which cannot be accurate, since, looking back forty years on the incident, Rosa realizes she must have been panicked and terrified that somehow he'd find her and drag her home. The bus glides down the long, straight road, its headlights seeming to warble and shimmer in the gasoline fumes. It pulls up to the depot, enveloping her in dust and the smell of diesel fuel. She lifts her little suitcase to the driver, steps up. Light, free, young. On the bus there is only one other passenger, an old woman with a back stiffened by church chairs. The woman is wearing a high, elaborate hat covered with flowers in candy tones of yellow and red. Rosa looks at the hat and she finds she can't help but laugh. She laughs and laughs. The woman looks at her, surprised, then enraged. Rosa can't stop laughing.

By six o'clock, they're in another state; she can see Wayne stepping into the house in Rome, Kansas, calling for her. Of course she's left no note.

Three weeks later she was back in Italy.

Fulvia had a party for her, with champagne. At the party were a number of men Rosa decided she would like to go to bed with. She forgot about Wayne Smith, forgot about him completely, until the letter came to her parents' house, inquiring as to her whereabouts. She tore it up. There were no communications, then, for a long time, and Rosa, who was in love again, decided to pretend the marriage hadn't really happened—after all, it was an American marriage, it had never been officially registered in Italy, therefore it didn't really count. She married her second husband, Paolo, without even mentioning the first to him, without a thought as to the consequences, and they stayed married for almost twenty years without hearing a word from Wayne Smith. Then one day in the early seventies—they were living in Rome, Marco was fifteen and Alba ten—Rosa received an official communication from a lawyer in Salina, Kansas. She remembers standing by her mailbox, staring at the unfamiliar, foreign-looking envelope, pulled back, suddenly, over decades, as if a bill she'd once neglected to pay, and assumed she had evaded, had just found her, hugely multiplied by interest into an astronomical fee. She opened the letter. After considerable effort—several years', it seemed—Wayne Smith had finally tracked her down. And suddenly in her mind she was dragged back to Rome, Kansas, strung up while Wayne's mother and sisters laughed and applauded, whipped by the woman in the high flowered hat, before being taken back to Wayne's blue-shingled house. What was the dream and what the reality? Perhaps all of this—her marriage to Paolo, her children—was the dream. Perhaps she was about to wake up and find herself back there, in Rome, Kansas, scrubbing potatoes, while Wayne, in the living room, drank beer and polished his fist.

But in fact, all Wayne wanted was a legal divorce. He was now the president of a company that manufactured spare parts for tractors, the lawyer wrote, lived in Dallas, and was eager to remarry. Naturally this put Rosa in a rather sticky situation: Which husband, she wondered, would take priority?

Fortunately, Fulvia knew people in the right offices who owed her favors. A number of bribes were paid; certain documents were rewritten so that the marriage between Rosa and Paolo had never happened, and thus the marriage between Rosa and Wayne could be discreetly dissolved. Rosa assumed that she and Paolo would then remarry, but it turned out Paolo had a girlfriend he'd been planning to move in with for a while now and just hadn't known how to tell Rosa about. So that was that. Rosa, vowing she'd never marry again, started spending more and more time at Fulvia's house near Saturnia, less and less in Rome. She visited the waterfall sometimes, and thought about Wayne Smith, and felt guilty for having just abandoned him like that. Finally she wrote to him in care of the lawyer in Salina, Kansas; it was a long letter, one she spent days on. In it she tried to explain to him why she'd left him; they were both so young, after all, and so traumatized by the war, she said, and then it had just seemed like a dream—hadn't it seemed like a dream to him? Anyway, she wrote, she was sorry she hadn't bothered to formalize the divorce. She hoped it hadn't caused him too much inconvenience. She hoped he and his new wife were very happy. She told him about her life in Italy, included snapshots of her children and Fulvia's children. She told him how famous Fulvia was, how they went to the waterfall frequently, these days, and reminisced. Did he have any news of Nelson Perkins, who'd called Fulvia "La Glamorosa" and given her chewing gum?

But Wayne Smith never wrote back.

Fulvia, who had just divorced her third husband, felt little sympathy. "You were stupid to marry him," she said. "I told you then."

"I wish," Rosa said, "you had more gentleness, Fulvia. Yes, it was a mistake, yes, I shouldn't have done it. But even so, when I think back now to the girl I was then, the thrill I felt, getting on that boat with Wayne, or the thrill I felt coming back to Rome, for that matter—I don't know if I'll ever feel anything like that again. It was my adventure, my madness of youth, and I'm glad I had it."

"If you want to call spending a dreary year in the middle of nowhere your madness of youth, that's your choice," Fulvia said. "To me it was madness plain and simple." Then she went out to meet a politician for an illicit rendezvous. Rosa, as often happened in those days, was left to take care of the children.

Later that afternoon, after she got back from the market, Rosa found Dario in her bedroom. He was wearing a pink chenille evening gown which she herself hadn't been able to fit into for years, and was admiring himself in the mirror. He was just sixteen. He looked good. "La Glamorosa," he said, and smiled.

She stayed in the doorway, didn't let him know she'd seen him. She thought, So Fulvia isn't as all-knowing as she thinks she is, then tiptoed away, storing the discovery for rumination and future use.

What she didn't know was that the "politician" Fulvia had gone off to have an illicit rendezvous with was Marco.

This afternoon, Grazia takes Nicholas on a walk along a decaying cobblestone path which begins at the crumbling village wall in Saturnia, on top of the hill, and passes by Fulvia's house. It's an ancient Roman road, dating from the time of Nero. The bumpy, herniated path narrows and widens and occasionally disappears altogether under the weeds and grasses which are choking it, but Grazia seems to know it well, and they never lose the trail. "But does it really go all the way to Rome?" Nicholas asks, and Grazia nods. "If you kept walking and walking through these hills, eventually you'd end up at Fulvia's apartment." She laughs, shielding her eyes with her hand. The sun is huge now, the same red-orange as the yolks of the eggs Rosa picks up every morning from a chicken farm outside the village. It gives the dry grasses which cover the hills the golden cast of wheat ready to be threshed.

"It's beautiful here, no?" Grazia says. "Fulvia and Rosa talk about Saturnia like it's their place, but they're Romans, they don't really know. I grew up near Grossetto, on a farm. We had olive groves. My father used to drive me when he took the olive oil to Rome. I know everything of this countryside."

"Yes?"

"Maremma, it's called. The swamp. It used to be a swamp, in the fourteenth century. Now it is a wild land, full of *cinghiali*. Our dogs, the *Maremmani*, are the fiercest in Italy, and white as snow."

They continue their downward trek. Nicholas has to make a conscious effort to slow himself down in order to avoid getting too far ahead of Grazia, who takes tiny steps, and studies the misshapen cobblestones cautiously, as if in fear of tripping over pebbles.

"I wanted to talk to you more about Dario," she says after a few minutes. "Fulvia paints such an ugly picture. And I thought you should know more."

"She must suffer a lot, otherwise she wouldn't have to act so callous."

"But you make a mistake. You assume Fulvia has a heart. Fulvia has no heart. In the old days, she always acted hard, but underneath she was soft. Now she's hard even underneath. Marco will tell you it's jealousy, that she went mad because he chose Dario instead of her. But the truth is, Fulvia didn't care about Marco after he married me. No, the only reason Fulvia is jealous is because Dario's genius was something she couldn't take credit for. Imagine! Fulvia Bellini, the great cultural critic, the maker and breaker of reputations, has a son who is suddenly famous all over Italy, and she's had nothing to do with it! In fact, she's discouraged him! She couldn't stand that. Even now, she wants to punish Dario's memory." They stop for a moment, and Grazia turns to face Nicholas. "I'll tell you a secret. Dario's writings, the things he read during the performances? I've saved them all. I keep them in a safety-deposit box in Milano. They are works of brilliance, as the world will someday know. Well, just after Dario died—he'd entrusted his papers to me—I tried to get them published. I approached every publisher in Italy, and one by one, they refused me. And you know why? Because of her. Because they were afraid of her. Believe Fulvia when she tells you how much power she has. It's all true. She kept those writings from being published because she couldn't stand the idea that someday her son would be more famous than she was. But he will. In a few years' time, no one in the world will remember who Fulvia Bellini was. But Dario—he will be one of the great ones." Grazia smiles. "Have you seen a picture of him?"

"No."

She opens her purse and pulls from it a snapshot of a young man with dark-blond hair, freckles, bright green eyes. "Such eyes!" she says. "He used to recite in the performance a poem Fulvia said to him when he was small, something she made up:

Verdi come le acque di Saturnia, gli occhi del mio bambino.
Caldo come le acque di Saturnia, il cuore del mio bambino.
Fragrante come le acque di Saturnia, la cacca del mio bambino.

"What that means is: 'As green as the waters of Saturnia, my little son's eyes. As hot'—hot? No, 'As warm as the waters of Saturnia, my little son's heart. As fragrant as the waters of Saturnia, my little son's shit.' "

Grazia is, for a moment, triumphantly silent.

"He couldn't resist that. He found that so funny. If she had any idea of the future, singing that little poem, can you imagine? But now you see the truth. Fulvia loved him best of all. It's true, she couldn't say anything loving to him without making it a joke in the end, even when he was just a *bimbo*. But she loved him anyway. And Dario was the only man who broke with her instead of the other way around. I'll tell you something else." Again Grazia stops, leans close. "The night Dario killed himself, Marco was with him. Marco had been trying to leave him for months. And Dario said to him, 'If you leave me tonight, Marco, I'll kill myself.' And Marco walked right out the door."

Nicholas looks down into Grazia's face as she tells him this. Her face is pale and fat and looks like the face of one of those very innocent Madonnas, as chubby and unknowing as the babies they hold in their arms.

"I'm telling you this for your own good," she says. "I'm telling you this so you'll understand. Marco was my husband. I know him better than Fulvia, better than Dario."

"Thank you," Nicholas says uneasily.

There is, in the distance, the sound of engines. The ancient road has met up with the new road, the road for cars.

"It's why Marco left, you see. He couldn't stand the guilt."

A car rounds the bend, slows. It is Alberto, with one arm around Alba. Grazia seems hardly to notice.

"Did someone call a taxi?" Alberto calls to them in English, across the little field. And Alba laughs.

In the late afternoon, Fulvia naps. The house shuts up, quiets down, in deference to her. Most everyone is down at the spa, lounging in the waters, or having mud baths, or themselves napping. Only in the kitchen is there activity, where Rosa, assisted by a girl from the village, has started preparations for the evening supper. The wine bottles are yet to be uncorked, the tablecloth is yet to be spread, a heady odor of garlic and olive oil wafts from the stove, where Rosa is making a *soffrito*.

"Understand, Nicholas," she is saying, "we're all fools. But none of us so much as Grazia."

Then it's time for the dinner, which, like every meal in this household, is a messy, complicated affair, starting at ten and lasting until one, with a crowd of people whose names Nicholas can't keep straight gathered around the huge operatic table, and big bowls of pasta and risotto making the rounds, and prosciutto and cheeses and *bollito misto*, and of course, gallons of wine—expensive bottles from Montalcino and Montepulciano as well as casks of the locally produced, pale yellow *vino dei contadini*. By the end of the evening the table is strewn with walnut shells, and the peels of clementines, and wineglasses in which cigarette butts have been snuffed out. "*Dio*," Rosa mutters, surveying the huge pile of dishes to be done. "*Mai più*. Never again."

"But Mamma, Simonetta's coming in the morning," Alba reminds her. "She'll take care of it. Go to bed, Mamma."

Rosa shakes her head. "You know that Simonetta's been threatening to quit. She says there's just too much work to be done here, when she could get the same money washing a plate and a glass for Signora Favetta down the road. No, I must start now. I must get some of this cleared away."

In the end, only Nicholas volunteers to help her—Nicholas, the American, raised to believe you can never do too much for people who are putting you up for free.

They are just starting the ritual business of plunging plates into steaming water when Fulvia calls from the sofa, "I want to go to the waterfall!"

"Absolutely not," Rosa says. "You're a sick woman, Fulvia, you can't just go out swimming at one in the morning."

"Don't treat me like an old lady," Fulvia says. "I do what I want. Marco! Take me to the waterfall!"

"But you've got to think of your health!"

"I've got to think of my sanity! Really, Rosa, every night this week, I've sat through dinner, then watched as everyone went off to the *cascata* except for you and me, the two *vecchie*. Enough of that!"

"Do what you want then," says Rosa, turning from the sink to face her. "Kill yourself. I have dishes to wash."

"You always have dishes to wash! Leave the dishes! I forbid you to do the dishes!"

"Simonetta—"

"Forget Simonetta, you're as much a fool as she! Now get my swimming suit."

Rosa turns again from the sink, marches into the living room, stands over her friend. It seems, for a moment, as if she's going to say something terrible, unforgivable; indeed, even Fulvia looks as if she wonders if this time she's gone too far. But whatever it is Rosa is about to say she apparently chooses to keep to herself. Her shoulders sink. "Marco, help Fulvia into her bedroom," she says. Then she leaves the room.

"I think we'll go down now and you can join us later," Alberto says. "Alba and I. Anyone else want to come?"

"Go ahead," says Grazia. She doesn't look at them.

"Fine. Ciao, then," Alberto says, and before anyone else has a chance to ask for a ride, he and Alba are out the door. Laura goes to put the children to bed, and then only Nicholas and Grazia are left at the table. He watches while with small and vicious fingers she tears the peel of a clementine into tiny pieces.

At the falls, lowering Fulvia into the water proves to be an even more complicated business than it was at the pool. "Careful, you *caproni*!" she chastises, as they ease her in. "Slowly! Ah, yes, that feels wonderful." Immersed, she leans her head back, her body wraithlike in the dark water. "Stay with me, Nicholas," she says.

"Of course."

"Fulvia, it's too cold," Rosa says. She herself is still dressed, and standing at the edge of the water. "You shouldn't be here."

"Oh get lost, Rosa. You and Marco. Let me talk to the *ragazzo*."

"Don't tell me what to do," Rosa says, and Nicholas notices a surprising, new inflection of hurt in her voice.

"Come on, Mamma," Marco says. And he leads his mother around to the other side of the little pond under the waterfall, where Alberto and Alba are cavorting.

"You know, I only feel good when I'm in the water these days," Fulvia says. "Too bad I'm so weak, otherwise I'd be here all day. I've been swimming in these springs for sixty years, since I was a very little child. Even before the hotel existed, Rosa and I used to come and swim here. And once, at the end of the war, we met an American soldier. He looked a bit like you: same freckles."

"And he called you 'La Glamorosa,'" Nicholas says.

"Yes," Fulvia says, wrapping her arms around her chest. "His Italian was bad, but creative. He was at least trying to speak the language, which is more than I can say for most of those soldiers. And what a lover he was. My God!" She laughs, then stops laughing. "Dario was shameless about using my life in his so-called performances. For that I forgive him."

"But not for much else, I gather."

"Oh, I don't blame Dario. Dario was merely disturbed. No, I'll tell you who I blame. Them." And she points across the water, at her swimming friends. "They'll deny it now—all except stupid Grazia—but every one of them was there, at Dario's performances. They all sat in the audience, in those cafés and clubs, their hands on their laps, watching my son make an idiot of himself. Now they speak skeptically, like it was some craziness of other people. But you can mark my words, when Dario ate his shit on stage, the people in the audience cheering him on were these people: serious intellectuals, bourgeois, from good families. The way Grazia talks about him—that was how they all spoke of him, in those days. That's what makes me so angry: If they hadn't been so taken in, they could have stopped him. They could have saved him."

For a moment, she almost looks sad.

"But if you wanted to stop him, why didn't you talk to him?"

"Would he listen to me? I'm his mother." She laughs and shakes her head. "No, I couldn't do it. These people, my friends, they could have just stopped paying attention to him. That would have been all it took. Unfortunately, they liked watching him think he was a messiah too much. And soon enough he really believed what he started out pretending to believe. That's all it takes, you know. You convince one person, you've convinced yourself."

The contrast between the cool air and the hot water makes Nicholas's teeth start to chatter, but Fulvia doesn't seem to notice.

"People will drool at anything. They'll drool over a boy in a dress eating shit until something else comes along to grab their attention, which is exactly what I predicted, and exactly what happened. Soon Dario was threatening to kill himself ten times a day. Every time I came over, every time Marco came over, when we left, he'd threaten to kill himself. Of course, by that time, no one else was bothering to visit him. Dario was alone in the end. For that I can never forgive them."

"Even Rosa?"

"Even Rosa."

Little wavelets of water are splashing around Fulvia. She leans back, regal, silent. The wavelets get bigger. It's Rosa, who's put on her swimming suit and is walking in the shallows toward them.

"Have you had enough yet?" she says. "Because I, for one, am ready to go to bed."

"Rosa, why must you always spoil my fun? I never hired you to be my nursemaid. Now go away."

"Oh fine!" Rosa says. "In that case, why don't we settle the bill now for thirty years of cooking, cleaning, taking care of your children—"

"Rosa, I said go away!"

"—wiping their asses, wiping *your* ass, I don't even have to mention Dario's ass—"

"Shut up, Rosa!"

"What do you think the total ought to come to, Fulvia? Well, I'll have my lawyers call you to settle, because I've had enough of it, I'm sick and tired of being your dishrag and listening while you rave on as if anyone cares anymore, and treating me like a worthless piece of garbage. And now, saying I didn't try to help Dario. I might as well have been his mother, since you never lifted a finger for the boy."

Fulvia, still immersed in the water, puts her hands over her ears and screams—a single, sharp, hoarse tone, ascending in pitch and volume.

"What's going on here? Are you two at it again?" It's Marco, who's come over from the other side of the falls.

"And you!" Rosa says, turning on him. "Why should I listen to you?

You, who let her take you into her bed when you were a boy? The shame I felt, the betrayal."

"I will not listen to this!" Fulvia shouts, hands over her ears.

"All jealousy, of course," Rosa says. "Jealousy because I at least had two normal, healthy children, while Fulvia was blessed with a junkie daughter and a son who, if there's anything worse than a child who's a junkie—well, he was determined to find out what it was and become just that."

Suddenly Fulvia thrusts out an arm, grabbing Rosa by the leg, pulling her down. Rosa screams and tumbles. Obscenities fly back and forth in the air, until finally the two women lie in a heap, wet and muddy, weeping. "Don't talk that way about my children!" Fulvia is saying. "Don't you dare say such things about my children!"

"Why not? You do."

"I loved Dario. I did everything for Dario."

"And now you speak of him like you wish he had never been born!"

"That's my right!"

"How?"

Fulvia sits up, rubs her eyes. "I'm a dying woman, Rosa, it's not fair to interrogate me like this." And Rosa falls silent.

"Are you two finished?" Marco asks, sounding annoyed, and they look up at him. Rosa starts to laugh.

"Imagine," Rosa says, "being chastised by your children."

"I suppose the day had to come," Fulvia says. "They couldn't be more foolish than we are, so I guess that means they have to be wiser." She coughs and presses her fingers against her temples. "I'm tired," she says. "Rub my shoulders, Rosa. Oh, Rosa, I'm tired of hurting."

"You see, she *does* need me," Rosa says. "And I'll take care of her. She knows I'll take care of her." And turning from where she's sitting, in the wet sand, Rosa begins to massage Fulvia's shoulders.

Fulvia closes her eyes, giving herself over to the strength of Rosa's hands. Across the pond, Alberto has Alba on his shoulders; he is singing, and strutting, and she is screaming for him to put her down. The waterfall pounds gracelessly around them.

When Rosa's massage is finished, she and Fulvia share a cigarette. "I tell you," Fulvia says, "he looks just like him."

"Fulvia, your memory's playing tricks on you."

"Looks just like who?" asks Nicholas.

"The American soldier. The one I met here at the end of the war."

"Fulvia's feeling romantic tonight," Rosa says, handing the cigarette to Fulvia.

"He had freckles, and he came from Ames, Iowa," Fulvia says. "His name was Nelson Perkins, and he gave me chewing gum."

"Fulvia looked him up once, when we were in New York. She called information in Ames, Iowa. She actually found him."

"I said I was the little Italian girl he met at the springs of Saturnia and made love with and gave chewing gum. And now, I said, I was a cultural critic, and I was in New York City to write about the ballet. I don't think he remembered me. He sold cars, he said. Oldsmobiles. He was married and had some children. He sounded nervous, like he was afraid I'd had a child and was going to ask him for money."

"Fulvia was sad, though she pretended she wasn't."

"No, I wasn't." And suddenly she turns and takes Nicholas's face in her hands.

"You look just like him," she says, smiling. "Really, you could be him."

"One American looks like another to Fulvia."

"And here, in this pond, we swam, and he told me I was a glamorous Italian girl and he had saved me from the Nazis. Maybe you can too, *caro*. Save me."

Her face is suddenly radiant, her hands warm against Nicholas's cold cheeks.

"But I don't know how," Nicholas says.

"Yes you do," says Fulvia. "It's simple. Just pick me up on your shoulders and carry me away."

Crossing St. Gotthard

It was the tunnel—its imminence—that all of them were contemplating that afternoon on the train, each in a different way; the tunnel, at nine miles the longest in the world, slicing under the gelid landscape of the St. Gotthard Pass. To Irene it was an object of dread. She feared enclosure in small spaces, had heard from Maisie Withers that during the crossing the carriage heated up to a boiling pitch. "I was as black as a nigger from the soot," Maisie Withers said. "People have died." "Never again," Maisie Withers concluded, pouring lemonade in her sitting room in Hartford, and meaning never again the tunnel but also (Irene knew) never again Italy, never again Europe; for Maisie was a gullible woman, and during her tour had had her pocketbook stolen.

And it was not only Maisie Withers, Irene reflected now (watching, across the way, her son Grady, his nose flat against the glass), but also her own ancient terror of windowless rooms, of corners, that since their docking in Liverpool had brought the prospect of the tunnel looming before her, black as death itself (a being which, as she approached fifty, she was trying to muster the courage to meet eye to eye), until she found herself counting first the weeks, then the days, then the hours leading up to the inevitable reckoning: the train slipping into the dark, into the mountain. (It was half a mile deep, Grady kept reminding her, half a mile of solid rock separating earth from sky.) Irene remembered a ghost story she'd read as a girl—a man believed to be dead wakes in his coffin. Was it too late to hire a carriage, then, to go *over* the pass, as Toby had? But no. Winter had already started up there. Oh, if she'd had her way, they'd have taken a different route; only Grady would have been disappointed, and since his brother's death she dared not disappoint Grady. He longed for the tunnel as ardently as his mother dreaded it.

"Mama, is it coming soon?"

"Yes, dear."

"But you said half an hour."

"Hush, Grady! I'm not a clock."

"But you said—"

"Read your book, Grady," Harold interrupted.

"I finished it."

"Then do your puzzle."

"I finished that, too."

"Then look out the window."

"Or just shut up," added Stephen, his eyes sliding open.

"Stephen, you're not to talk to your brother that way."

"He's a pest. Can't a fellow get some sleep?"

Stephen's eyes slid shut, and Grady turned to examine the view. Though nearly fourteen, he was still a child. His leg shook. With his breath he fogged shapes onto the glass.

"Did I tell you it's the longest in the world? Did I tell you—"

"Yes, Grady. Now please hush."

They didn't understand. They were always telling him to hush. Well, all right, he would hush. He would never again utter a single word, and show them all.

Irene sneezed.

"Excuse me," she said to the red-nosed lady sitting next to her.

"Heavens! You needn't apologize to *me*."

"It's getting cold rather early this year," Irene ventured, relieved beyond measure to discover that her neighbor spoke English.

"Indeed it is. It gets cold earlier every year, I find. Judgment Day must be nigh!"

Irene laughed. They started chatting. She was elegantly got up, this red-nosed lady. She knitted with her gloves on. From her hat extended a fanciful aigrette that danced and bobbed. Grady watched it, watched the moving mountains outside the window. (Some were already capped with snow.) Then the train turned, the sun came blazing into the compartment so sharply that the red-nosed lady murmured, "Goodness me," shielded her eyes, pulled the curtain shut against it.

Well, that did it for Grady. After all, hadn't they just told him to look at the view? No one cared. He had finished his book. He had finished his puzzle. The tunnel would never arrive.

Snorting, he thrust his head behind the curtain.

"Grady, don't be rude."

He didn't answer. And really, behind the curtain it was a different world. He could feel warmth on his face. He could revel in the delicious sensation of apartness that the gold-lit curtain bestowed, and that only the chatter of women interrupted. But it was rude.

"Oh, I know, I know!" (Whose voice was that? The red-nosed lady's?) "Oh yes, I know!" (Women always said that. They always knew.)

Harold had his face in a book. Stephen was a bully.

"Oh dear, yes!"

Whoever was talking, her voice was loud. His mother's voice he could not make out. His mother's voice was high but not loud, unless she shouted, which she tended to do lately. Outside the window an Alpine landscape spread out: fir groves, steep-roofed wooden houses, fields of dead sunflowers to which the stuffy compartment with its scratched mahogany paneling bore no discernible relation. This first-class compartment belonged to the gaslit ambience of stations and station hotels. It was a bubble of metropolitan, semipublic space sent out into the wide world, and from the confines of which its inmates could regard the uncouth spectacle of nature as a kind of *tableau vivant*. Still, the trappings of luxury did little to mask its fundamental discomforts: seats that pained the back, fetid air, dirty carpets.

They were on their way to Italy, Irene told Mrs. Warshaw (for this was the red-nosed lady's name). They were on their way to Italy for a tour—Milan, Venice, Verona, Florence, Rome (Irene counted off on her fingers), then a villa in Naples for the winter months—because her sons ought to see the world, she felt; American boys knew so little; they had studied French but could hardly speak a word. (Mrs. Warshaw, nodding fervently, agreed it was a shame.)

"And this will be your first trip to Italy?"

"The first time I've been abroad, actually, although my brother, Toby, came twenty years ago. He wrote some lovely letters for the *Hartford Evening Post*."

"Marvelous! And how lucky you are to have three handsome sons as escorts. I myself have only a daughter."

"Oh, but Harold's not my son! Harold's my cousin Millie's boy. He's the tutor."

"How nice." Mrs. Warshaw smiled assessingly at Harold. Yes, she thought, tutor he is, and tutor he will always be. He looked the part of the poor relation, no doubt expected to play the same role in the lady's life abroad that his mother played in her life at home: the companion to whom she could turn when she needed consolation, or someone to torture. (Mrs. Warshaw knew the ways of the world.)

As for the boys, the brothers: the older one looked different. Darker. Different fathers, perhaps?

But Irene thought: She's right. I do—*did*—have three sons.

And Harold tried to hide inside his book. Only he thought: They ought to treat me with more respect. The boys ought to call me Mr. Prescott, not Cousin Hal, for they hardly know me. Also, he smarted at the dismissive tone with which Aunt Irene enunciated the word *tutor*, as if he were something just one step above the level of a servant. He deserved better than that, deserved better than to be at the beck and call of boys in whom art, music, the classical world, inspired boredom at best, outright contempt at worst. For though Uncle George, God rest his soul, had financed his education, it was not Uncle George who had gotten the highest scores in the history of the Classics Department. It was not Uncle George whose translations of Cicero had won a prize. Harold had done all that himself.

On the other hand, goodness knew he could never have afforded Europe on his own. To his charges he owed the blessed image of his mother's backyard in St. Louis, his mother in her gardening gloves and hat, holding her shears over the roses while on the porch the old chair in which he habitually spent his summers reading, or sleeping, or cursing—my God, he wasn't in it! It was empty! To them he owed this miracle.

"And will your husband be joining you in Naples?"

"I'm afraid my husband passed away last winter."

"Ah."

Mrs. Warshaw dropped a stitch.

The overdecorated compartment in which these five people were sitting was small—four feet by six feet. Really, it had the look of a theater stall,

Harold decided, with its maroon velvet seats, its window like a stage, its curtain—well, like a curtain. Above the stained headrests wrapped in slipcovers embellished with the crest of the railway hung six prints in reedy frames: three yellowed views of Rome—Trajan's Column (the glass cracked), the Pantheon, the Colosseum (over which Mrs. Warshaw's aigrette danced); and opposite, as if to echo the perpetual contempt with which the Christian world regards the pagan, three views of Florence—Santa Croce, the Duomo, the Palazzo Vecchio guarded by Michelangelo's immense nude David—none of which Harold, who reverenced the classical, could see. Instead, when he glanced up from his book, it was the interior of the Pantheon that met his gaze, the orifice at the center of the dome throwing against its coffered ceiling a coin of light.

He put down his book. (It was Ovid's *Metamorphoses*, in Latin.) Across from him, under the Pantheon, Stephen sprawled, his long legs in their loose flannel trousers spread wide but bent at the knees, because finally they were too long, those legs, for a compartment in which three people were expected to sit facing three people for hours at a time. He was asleep, or pretending to be asleep, so that Harold could drink in his beauty for once with impunity, while Mrs. Warshaw knitted, and Grady's head bobbed behind the curtain, and Aunt Irene said she knew, she knew. Stephen was motionless. Stephen was inscrutable. Still, Harold could tell that he too was alert to the tunnel's imminence; he could tell because every few minutes his eyes slotted open, the way the eyes of a doll do when you tilt back its head: green and gold, those eyes, like the sun-mottled grass beneath a tree.

He rarely spoke, Stephen. His body had the elongated musculature of a harp. His face was elusive in its beauty, like those white masks the Venetians wear at Carnival. Only sometimes he shifted his legs, in those flannel trousers that were a chaos of folds, a mountain landscape, valleys, passes, peaks. Most, Harold knew, if you punched them down, would flatten; but one would grow heavy and warm at his touch.

And now Harold had to put his book on his lap. He had to. He was twenty-two years old, scrawny, with a constitution his doctor described as "delicate"; yet when he closed his eyes, he and Stephen wore togas and stood together in a square filled with rational light. Or Harold was a great warrior, and Stephen the beloved *eremenos* over whose gore-drenched body he scattered kisses at battle's end. Or they were training together, naked, in the gymnasium.

Shameful thoughts! He must cast them out of his mind. He must find a worthier object for his adoration than this stupid, vulgar boy, this boy who, for all his facile handsomeness, would have hardly raised an eyebrow in the age of Socrates.

"Not Captain Warshaw, though! The Captain had a stomach of iron."

What were they talking about? The Channel crossing, no doubt. Aunt Irene never tired of describing her travel woes. She detested boats, detested hotel beds, hated tunnels. Whereas Harold, if anyone had asked him, would have said that he looked forward to the tunnel not as an end in itself, the way Grady did, but because the tunnel meant the south, meant Italy. For though it did not literally link Switzerland with Italy, on one side the towns had German names—Göschenen, Andermatt, Hospenthal—while on the other they had Italian names—Airolo, Ambri, Lurengo—and this fact in itself was enough to intoxicate him.

Now Stephen stretched; the landscape of his trousers surged, earthquakes leveled the peaks, the rivers were rerouted, and the crust of the earth churned up. It was as if a capricious god, unsatisfied with his handiwork, had decided to forge the world anew.

"Ah, how I envy any traveler his first visit to Italy!" Mrs. Warshaw said. "Because for you it will be new—what is for me already faded. Beginning with Airolo, the campanile, as the train comes out the other end of the tunnel . . ."

Harold's book twitched. He knew all about the campanile.

"Is it splendid?" Irene asked.

"Oh, no." Mrs. Warshaw shook her head decisively. "Not splendid at all. Quite plain, in fact, especially when you compare it to all those other wonderful Italian towers—in Pisa, in Bologna. I mustn't forget San Gimignano! Yes, compared to the towers of San Gimignano, the campanile of Airolo is utterly without distinction or merit. Still, you will never forget it, because it is the first."

"Well, we shall look forward to it. Grady, be sure to look out for the tower of . . . just after the tunnel."

The curtain didn't budge.

Irene's smile said: "Sons."

"And where are you traveling, if I might be so bold?"

"To Florence. It's my habit to spend the winter there. You see, when I lost the Captain, I went abroad intending to make a six-months tour of Europe. But then six months turned into a year, and a year into five years, and now it will be eight years in January since I last walked on native soil. Oh, I think of returning to Toronto sometimes, settling in some little nook. And yet there is still so much to see! I have the travel bug, I fear. I wonder if I shall ever go home." Mrs. Warshaw gazed toward the curtained window. "Ah, beloved Florence!" she exhaled. "How I long once again to take in the view from Bellosguardo."

"How lovely it must be," echoed Irene, though in truth she had no idea where Bellosguardo was, and feared repeating the name lest she should mispronounce it.

"Florence is full of treasures," Mrs. Warshaw continued. "For instance, you must go to the Palazzo della Signoria and look at the Perseus."

Harold's book twitched again. He knew all about the Perseus.

"Of course we shall go and see them straightaway," Irene said. "When do they bloom?"

When do they bloom!

It sometimes seemed to Harold that it was Aunt Irene, and not her sons, who needed the tutor. She was ignorant of everything, and yet she never seemed to care when she made an idiot of herself. In Harold's estimation, this was typical of the Pratt branch of the family. With the exception of dear departed Toby (both of them), no one in that branch of the family possessed the slightest receptivity to what Pater called (and Harold never forgot it) "the poetic passion, the desire of beauty, the love of art for its own sake." Pratts were anti-Paterian. Not for them Pater's "failure is forming habits." To them the formation of habits—healthy habits—was the very essence of success. (It was a subject on which Uncle George, God rest his soul, had taken no end of pleasure in lecturing Harold.)

Still, Harold could not hate them. After all, they had made his education possible. At Thanksgiving and Christmas they always had a place for him at their table (albeit crammed in at a corner in a kitchen chair). "Our little scholarship boy," Aunt Irene called him. "Our little genius, Harold."

Later, after Uncle George had died, and Toby had died, and Toby the Second as well, Irene had come to him. "Harold, would you like to see Europe?" she'd asked, fixing his collar.

"More than anything, Aunt Irene."

"Because I'm planning a little tour this fall with the boys—following my brother's itinerary, you know—and I thought, Wouldn't it be marvelous for them to have a tutor, a scholar like yourself, to tell them what was what. What do you think, Harold? Would your mother mind?"

"I think it's a capital idea."

"Good."

So here he was.

So far, things hadn't gone well at all.

In Paris, Harold had decided to test the boys' receptivity to art by taking them to the Louvre. But Grady wanted only to ride the métro, and got infuriated when Harold explained that there was no need to take the métro: the museum was only a block from their hotel. Then they were standing in front of the Mona Lisa, Harold lecturing, Grady quivering with rage at having been deprived of the métro, Stephen leaning, inscrutable as ever, against a white wall. Harold spoke eloquently about the painting and, as he spoke, he felt the silent pressure of their boredom. They had their long bodies arranged in attitudes of sculptural indifference, as if to say, we have no truck with any of this. Curse our mother for pulling us out of our lives, and curse our father for dying, and our brother for dying, and curse you. To which Harold wanted to answer: Well, do you think I like it any more than you do? Do you think I enjoy babbling like an idiot, and being ignored? For the truth was, the scrim of their apathy diffused his own sense of wonder. After all, he was seeing this for the first time, too: not a cheap reproduction, but *La Gioconda.* The real thing. How dare they not notice, not care?

Yes, Harold decided that morning, they were normal, these boys. They would never warm to art. (As if to prove his point, they now gravitated away from his lecturing, and toward an old man who had set up an easel and paints to copy a minor annunciation—their curiosity piqued by some low circus element in the proceedings: "Gosh, it looks exactly like the original!" an American man standing nearby said to his wife.) Why Aunt Irene had insisted on bringing them to Europe in the first place Harold still couldn't fathom; what did she think was going to happen, anyway? Did she imagine that upon contact with the sack of

Rome, the riches of Venice, some dormant love of beauty would awaken in them, and they would suddenly be transformed into cultured, intellectual boys, the sort upon whom she could rely for flashes of wit at dinner parties, crossword solutions on rainy afternoons? Boys, in other words, like their brother Toby, or their uncle Toby, for that matter, who had kept a portrait of Byron on his desk. Grady, on the other hand, couldn't have cared less about Byron, while Stephen, so far as Harold could tell, liked only to lean against white walls in his flannel trousers, challenging the marble for beauty. Really, he was too much, Stephen: self-absorbed, smug, arrogant. Harold adored him.

There was a rapping on the compartment door.

"Entrez," announced Mrs. Warshaw.

The conductor stepped in. Immediately Grady pulled back the curtain, splaying the light. Stephen's eyes slotted open again.

"Permit me to excuse myself," the conductor said in tormented French, "but we are approaching the St. Gotthard tunnel. I shall now light the lamps and make certain that the windows and ventilators are properly closed."

"Bien sûr."

The conductor was Italian, a handsome, sturdy fellow with a thick black mustache, blue eyes, fine lips. Dark hairs curled under his cuffs, rode down the length of his hands to the ends of his thick fingers.

Bowing, he stepped to the front of the compartment, where he got down on his knees and fiddled with the ventilator panel. As he knelt he winked manfully at Grady.

"Oh, I don't like tunnels," Irene said. "I get claustrophobic."

"I hope you don't get seasick!" Mrs. Warshaw laughed. "But never mind. When you've been through the St. Gotthard as often as I have, you shall sleep right through, as I intend to do."

"How long is it again?"

"Nine miles!" Grady shouted. "The longest in the—" He winced. He had broken his vow.

"Nine miles! Dear Lord! And it will take half an hour?"

"More or less."

"Half an hour in the dark!"

"The gas jets will be lit. You needn't worry."

The conductor, having finished with the ventilators, stood to examine the window latches. In securing the one on the right he pressed a wool-covered leg against Harold's knees.

"Va bene," he said next, yanking at the latch for good measure. (It did not give.) Then he turned to face Harold, over whose head the oil lamp protruded; raised his arms into the air to light it, so that his shirt pulled up almost but not quite enough to reveal a glimpse of what was underneath (what *was* underneath?); parted his legs around Harold's knees. Harold had no choice but to stare into the white of that shirt, breathe in its odor of eau de cologne and cigar.

Then the lamp was lit. Glancing down, the conductor smiled.

"Merci, mesdames," he concluded merrily. And to Harold: *"Grazie, signore."*

Harold muttered, *"Prego,"* kept his eyes out the window.

The door shut firmly.

"I shall be so happy to have my first glimpse of Milan," Irene said.

Why French for the women and Italian for him?

They had been traveling forever. They had been traveling for years: Paris, the gaslit platform at the Gare de Lyon, a distant dream; then miles of dull French farmland, flat and blurred; and then the clattery dollhouse architecture of Switzerland, all that grass and those little clusters of chalets with their tilted roofs and knotty shuttered windows, like the window the bird would have flown out on the cuckoo clock . . . if it had ever worked, if Uncle George had ever bothered to fix it. But he had not.

Really, there was nothing to do but read, so Harold read.

Orpheus: having led Eurydice up from the Underworld, he turned to make sure she hadn't tired behind him. He turned even though he had been warned in no uncertain terms not to turn; that turning was the one forbidden thing. And what happened? Exactly what Orpheus should have expected to happen. As if his eyes themselves shot out rays of plague, Eurydice shrank back into the vapors and died a second death, fell back down the dark well. This story of Orpheus and Eurydice Harold had read a hundred times, maybe even five hundred times, and still it frustrated him; still he hoped each time that Orpheus would catch on for once, and not look back. Yet he always looked back. And why? Had love turned Orpheus's head? Harold doubted it. Perhaps the exigencies of story, then: for really, if the episode had ended with the happy couple emerging safely into the dewy morning light, something in every reader would have been left slavering for the expected payoff.

Of course there were other possible explanations. For instance: perhaps Orpheus had found it impossible not to give in to a certain self-destructive impulse; that inability, upon being told "Don't cross that line," not to cross it.

Only God has the power to turn back time.

Or perhaps Orpheus, at the last minute, had changed his mind; decided he didn't want Eurydice back after all. This was a radical interpretation, albeit one to which later events in Orpheus's life lent credence.

Harold remembered something—*Huck Finn*, he thought—you must never look over your shoulder at the moon.

Something made him put his book down. Stephen had woken up. He was rubbing his left eye with the ball of his fist. No, he did not look like his brother, did not look like any Pratt, for that matter. (Mrs. Warshaw was correct about this, though little else.) According to Harold's mother, this was because Aunt Irene, after years of not being able to conceive, had taken him in as a foundling, only wouldn't you know it? The very day the baby arrived she found out she was pregnant. "It's always like that," his mother had said. "Women who take in foundlings always get pregnant the day the foundling arrives."

Nine months later Toby was born—Toby the Second—that marvelous boy who rivaled his adopted brother for athletic skills, outstripped him in book smarts, but was handsome, too, Pratt handsome, with pale skin and small ears. Toby had been a star pupil, whereas Irene had had to plead with the headmaster to keep Stephen from being held back a grade. Not that the boys disliked each other: instead, so far as Harold could tell, they simply made a point of ignoring each other. (And how was this possible? How was it possible for anyone to ignore either of them?)

"Be kind to your aunt Irene," his mother had told him at the station in St. Louis. "She's known too much death."

And now she sat opposite him, here on the train, and he could see from her eyes that it was true: she had known too much death.

Harold flipped ahead a few pages.

> Throughout this time Orpheus had shrunk from loving any woman, either because of his unhappy experience, or because he had pledged himself not to do so. In spite of this there were many who were fired with a desire to marry the poet, many were indignant to find themselves repulsed. However, Orpheus preferred to center his affection on boys of tender years, and to enjoy the brief spring and early flowering of their youth: he was the first to introduce this custom among the people of Thrace.

Boys of tender years, like Stephen, who, as Harold glanced up, shifted again, opened his eyes, and stared at his cousin malevolently.

And the train rumbled, and Mrs. Warshaw's aigrette fluttered before the Colosseum, and the cracked glass that covered Trajan's Column rattled.

They were starting to climb at a steeper gradient. They were nearing the tunnel at last.

From the *Hartford Evening Post*, November 4, 1878: Letter Six, "Crossing from the Tyrol into Ticino," by Tobias R. Pratt:

> As we began the climb over the great mountain of San Gottardo our *mulattiere*, a most affable and friendly fellow within whose Germanic accent one could detect echoes of the imminent South, explained that even as we made our way through the pass, at that very moment men were laboring under our feet to dig a vast railway tunnel that upon completion will be the longest in the world. This tunnel will make Italy an easier destination for those of us who wish always to be idling in her beneficent breezes . . . and yet how far the Palazzo della Signoria seemed to us that morning, as we rose higher and higher into snowy regions! It was difficult to believe that on the other side the lovely music of the Italian voice and the taste of a rich red wine awaited us; still this faith gave us the strength to persevere through what we knew would be three days of hard travel.
>
> To pass the time, we asked our guide his opinion of the new tunnel. His response was ambivalent. Yes, he admitted, the tunnel would bring tourism (and hence money) to his corner of the world. And yet the cost! Had we heard, for instance, that already one hundred men had lost their lives underground? A hint of superstitious worry entered his voice, as if he feared lest the mountain—outraged by such invasions—should one

> day decide that it had had enough and with one great heave of its breast smash the tunnel and all its occupants to smithereens. . . .

And Irene thought: He never saw it. He had been dead two years already by the time it was finished.

And Grady thought: Finally.

And Mrs. Warshaw thought: I hope the *signora* saved me Room 5, as she promised.

And Harold watched Stephen's trousers hungrily, hungrily. Glimpses, guesses. All he had ever known were glimpses, guesses. Never, God forbid, a touch; never, never the sort of fraternal bond, unsullied by carnal need, to which epic poetry paid homage; never anything—except this ceaseless worrying of a bone from which every scrap of meat had long been chewed, this ceaseless searching for an outline amid the folds of a pair of flannel trousers.

Yes, he thought, leaning back, I should have been born in classical times. For he genuinely believed himself to be the victim of some heavenly imbroglio, the result of which was his being delivered not (as he should have been) into an Athenian boudoir (his mother someone wise and severe, like Plotina), but rather into a bassinet in a back bedroom in St. Louis where the air was wrong, the light was wrong, the milk did not nourish him. No wonder he grew up ugly, ill, ill-tempered! He belonged to a different age. And now he wanted to cry out, so that all of Switzerland could hear him: I belong to a different age!

The train slowed. Behind the curtain Grady watched the signs giving way one to the next, one to the next: GÖ-SCHE-NEN, GÖ-SCHE-NEN. GÖ-SCHE-NEN.

> By such songs as these the Thracian poet was drawing the woods and rocks to follow him, charming the creatures of the wild, when suddenly the Ciconian women caught sight of him. Looking down from the crest of a hill, these maddened creatures, with animal skins slung across their breasts, saw Orpheus as he was singing and accompanying himself on the lyre. One of them, tossing her hair till it streamed in the light breeze, cried out: "See! Look here! Here is the man who scorns us!" and flung her spear—

Darkness. Harold shut his book.

* * *

As soon as the train entered the tunnel the temperature began to rise. Despite the careful labors of the conductor, smoke was slipping into the compartment: not enough to be discernible at first by anything other than its dry, sharp smell; but then Harold noticed that no sooner had he wiped his spectacles clean, than they were already filmed again with dust; and then a gray fog, almost a mist, occupied the compartment, obscuring his vision; he could no longer distinguish, for instance, which of the three little prints across the way from him represented the Pantheon, which Trajan's Column, which the Colosseum.

Mrs. Warshaw's head slumped. She snored.

And Grady pressed his face up against the glass, even though there was nothing to see outside the window but a bluish black void, which he likened to the sinuous fabric of space itself.

And Irene, a handkerchief balled in her fist, wondered: Do the dead age? Would her little Toby, in heaven, remain forever the child he had been when he had died? Or would he grow, marry, have angel children?

And Toby her brother? Had *he* had angel children?

If Toby was in heaven—and not the other place. She sometimes feared he might be in the other place—every sermon she'd ever heard suggested it—in which case she would probably never get closer to him than she was right now, right here, in this infernal tunnel.

She glanced at Stephen, awake now. God forgive her for thinking it, but it should have been him, repairing the well with George. Only Stephen had been in bed with influenza, so Toby went.

Punishment? But if so, for what? Thoughts?

Could you be punished for thoughts?

Suddenly she could hardly breathe the searing air—as if a hundred men were smoking cigars all at once.

Midway—or what Harold assumed was midway—he thought he heard the wheels scrape. So the train would stall, and then what would they do? There wouldn't be enough oxygen to get out on foot without suffocating. The tunnel was too long. Half a mile of rock separated train from sky; half a mile of rock, atop which trees grew, a woman milked her cow, a baker made bread.

The heat abashed; seemed to eat the air. Harold felt the weight of mountains on his lungs.

Think of other things, he told himself, and in his mind undid the glissando of buttons on Stephen's trousers. Yet the smell in his nostrils—that smell of cigars—was the conductor's.

Light scratched the window. The train shuddered to a stop. Someone flung open a door.

They were outside. Dozens of soot-smeared passengers stumbled among the tracks, the visible clouds of smoke, the sloping planes of alpine grass. For they were there now. Through.

The train throbbed. Conductors, stripped to their waistcoats, took buckets and mops and swabbed the filthy windows until cataracts of black water pooled outside the tracks.

People had died. Her brother in Greece, her child and her husband in the backyard.

There was no heaven, no hell. The dead did not age because the dead *were not.* (Still, Irene fingered the yellowed newspaper clippings in her purse; looked around for Stephen, who had disappeared.)

And meanwhile Harold had run up the hill from the train, and now stood on a low promontory, wiping ash from his spectacles with a handkerchief.

Where was Stephen? Suddenly she was terrified, convinced that something had happened to Stephen on the train, in the tunnel. "Harold!" she called. "Harold, have you seen Stephen?"

But he chose not to hear her. He was gazing at the campanile of Airolo, vivid in the fading light.

In Airolo, Harold looked for signs that the world was becoming Italy. And while it was true that most of the men in the station bar drank beer, one or two were drinking wine; and when he asked for wine in Italian, he was answered in Italian, and given a glass.

"Grady, do you want anything?"

Silence.

"Grady!"

He still wasn't talking to them.

Aunt Irene had gone into the washroom. She was not there to forbid Harold from drinking, so he drank. Around him, at tables, local workers—perhaps the same ones who had dug the tunnel—smoked and played cards. Most of them had pallid, dark blond faces, Germanic faces; but one was reading a newspaper called *Corriere della Sera*, and one boy's skin seemed to have been touched, even in this northernmost outpost, by a finger of Mediterranean sun.

Italy, he thought, and gazing across the room, noticed that Stephen, darker by far than any man in the bar, had come inside. One hand in his pocket, he was leaning against a white wall, drinking beer from a tall glass.

Apart.

He is from here, Harold realized suddenly. But does he even know it?

Then the conductor came into the bar. Harold turned, blushing, to contemplate his wine, wondering when the necessary boldness would come: to look another man straight in the eye, as men do.

Aunt Irene had at last emerged, with Mrs. Warshaw, from the washroom. "Harold, I'm worried about Stephen," she said. "The last time I saw him was when we came out of the—"

"He's over there."

"Oh, Stephen!" his mother cried, and to Harold's surprise she ran to him, embraced him tightly, pressed her face into his chest. "My darling, I've been worried sick about you! Where have you been?"

"Can't a man take a walk?" Stephen asked irritably.

"Yes, of course. Of course he can." Letting him go, she dabbed at her eyes. "You've grown so tall! You're almost a man! No wonder you don't like Mother huging you anymore. Oh, Stephen, you're such a wonderful son, I hope you know, I hope you'll always know, how much we treasure you."

Stephen grimaced; sipped at his beer.

"Well, we're through it," Mrs. Warshaw said. "Now tell me the truth, it wasn't so bad as all that, was it?"

"How I long for a bed!" Irene said. "Is Milan much further?"

"Just a few hours, dear," Mrs. Warshaw said, patting her hand. "And only short tunnels from now on, I promise you."

The Infection Scene

Tremendous Friends

Late in his childhood, Lord Alfred (Bosie) Douglas became best friends with a nephew of one of his mother's neighbors, Lady Downshire: a boy with the extraordinary name (at least to our ears) of Wellington Stapleton-Cotton. This was in 1885. The boys went to different schools but spent their holidays together, so when Bosie was sent to Zermatt, in Switzerland, one summer, he made sure to cut his vacation short by a week in order to share the last part of it with Wellington. Though Bosie's mother's house was palatial, Lord Downshire, from whom she let it, had christened it "The Hut," for much the same reason that wealthy Long Island families call their oceanside mansions "cottages." Nearby stood Easthampstead, the *really* big house, where Lord and Lady Downshire held sway, and where Wellington, a frequent visitor, awaited Bosie's arrival. But no sooner had Bosie returned than he came down with the mumps and was quarantined. Illness thus separated the "tremendous friends."

From his sickroom Bosie smuggled a note to Wellington through the agency of the footman, Harold, suggesting a plan. If Wellington were to contract mumps as well, they could share more than a week; they could share the entirety of their convalescence, in a common bed, and not even go to school.

I don't know what Wellington looked like. I do know what Bosie looked like. Bosie was a sickeningly angelic boy. In a drawing made of him when he was twenty-four, he still has soft blond hair, huge eyes with long lashes, a small, wet mouth that asks to be kissed but might bite. Indeed, so famous would this face become over the years that you might say it established a paradigm: beatific loveliness dissembling a corrupted heart.

As for Wellington, I see him as being both stronger and bigger than Bosie, with dark skin, thin lips, a worried brow. Already he has small tufts of hair under his arms and on his chest. Bosie's body, on the other hand, is covered in a downy fuzz. He is in the last flowering of childhood, whereas Wellington is in the first flush of adolescence, and thus subject, for the first time in his life, to lust. Yet lust is a mystery to him. He has no language for it. He is at the mercy of impulses that his Victorian education insists do not exist. In this regard he differs from Bosie, who possesses an innate familiarity with lust, even though he remains innocent of ejaculation. In other words, what Wellington feels but does not yet understand Bosie understands but does not yet feel. Therefore he can manipulate Wellington, using his girlishness as bait. He wonders: To what lengths can I drive Wellington? Could I persuade him to risk illness, infection, even death, just to be with me?

Yes, apparently, for Wellington readily agrees to the plan.

The next morning a feverish Bosie climbs from his bed and peers out the window. Behind a yew hedge, Wellington is waiting for him. Already Harold has brought the ladder, leaving it, according to Bosie's instructions, propped against the wall. Now he opens the window—the sash screeches loudly—and his friend clambers up and through. Dawn: a late summer breeze freshens the fetid atmosphere with the scent of grass. Wellington hasn't combed his hair. He smells tired. Small clots of what is euphemistically called "sleep" harden in the corners of his eyes. "Hello," Bosie says, then, taking his friend by the hand, leads him toward the bed, which is still warm and slightly moist, as beds tend to become when the ill sleep in them. He sits down before Wellington, guides Wellington's fingers to his swollen salivary glands. He anticipates by a hundred years an age when swollen glands will spell terror for men of his kind. But at that time, in that place, most men who desired each other didn't even think of themselves as a "kind." Not yet. It would take a poem written by Bosie before their love would learn the name it dared not speak.

"Come on," Bosie says. "Let's get in bed."

Wellington hardly has time to pull off his shoes.

"We have to make sure the infection takes," Bosie goes on, pulling the sheets over them.

"How?"

"Like this." And holding Wellington's face between his hot palms, Bosie kisses him. Wellington, who has never been kissed before, is at first surprised, resistant. But he likes the sensation, the silkiness of the sensation, and, giving in to it, allows Bosie's tongue to open his lips. It is all for the purpose of being together, after all, of being boys together, *tremendous friends*. Bosie licks Wellington's teeth, licks his tongue, the rough surface of his lips. Wellington returns, repeats each gesture. So much early sexuality is mimicry. *Do to me what I do to you*, we think the other's tongue is telling us. Yet there are some things he would like to do to Bosie that he hopes Bosie wouldn't like to do to him.

"Do you think it's taken yet?"

"Perhaps. Still, we can't be sure."

"Anything else we might try?"

"Yes." And sitting up, Bosie runs his small hot tongue down Wellington's neck, onto his chest; he opens Wellington's shirt and licks the halos of hair around his nipples. Lower down, an erection pokes Wellington's trousers: no surprise. As for Bosie, his nightshirt has ridden up. He turns around, grinds his pinkish behind into Wellington's groin. The heat shocks. Wellington can't help but grind back. Sensation floods him, and he ejaculates, soaking the front of his pants.

Church bells chime. It's six-thirty in the morning. Shadows creep toward the bed. In the hallway, the housekeeper is upbraiding a chambermaid for the way she has folded some towels. Hearing them argue, Wellington and Bosie laugh.

"She'll be coming for us soon."

"Yes."

"Do you feel any swelling?"

Wellington presses his fingers against his neck.

"I think so. I think I do."

Under the bedclothes, he takes Bosie in his arms. They doze. Soon there's a knock on the door, and the housekeeper steps briskly through. "Good morning," she says, then stops in her tracks. "But what's this?"

The boys laugh, pull the sheet over their heads.

"Oh dear," the housekeeper says. "I'll have to fetch Lady Queensberry." And does.

"Wellington!" Lady Queensberry cries, rushing in a few minutes later. "What on earth are you doing here?"

"He's come to get sick so we can spend our holiday together."

"Wellington, get out of that bed right now. What kind of nonsense is this?"

"But, madame," the housekeeper interjects, "if he's already been infected . . ."

Lady Queensberry rubs her temples. Of her four children, she loves Bosie best. She is also starting to have inklings that he will bring her the greatest torment.

"I must consult with Lady Downshire," she concludes, and, leaving the boys to play in the feverish sheets, goes to her dressing room to write that eminence a wearied, apologetic letter.

But the infection doesn't "take," and Wellington returns to Easthampstead. Bosie recovers; the boys head off to their separate schools. Wellington, who should have become the third Viscount Combermere, dies in the Boer Wars. Bosie makes a career of ruin and infection.

Wellington didn't live to learn how narrowly he'd made it out alive.

I base this account on Bosie's own, in *My Friendship with Oscar Wilde*—one of several autobiographies he published later in his life in the hope that he might "set the record straight" concerning his disastrous love affair with Wilde. Here the incident takes up the better part of a paragraph. Bosie explains that he "adored" Wellington, and that he thought Wellington "adored" him. He says that when he came down with the mumps, Wellington climbed through the window, undressed, and got in bed with him. They stayed together half an hour. Then Wellington departed " 'as he had come, an undiscerned road,' by the window."

The rest (in particular the arrival of the housekeeper) is speculation, invention, perhaps even impudence on my part, since what I want to show up is the irony that lies behind Bosie's inclusion of this episode in a work intended specifically to *repudiate* charges that he was more than a coincidental homosexual. Indeed, Bosie seems to see the episode with Wellington as yet one more example of the ordinary, virile boyhood he enjoyed before he met Wilde, who corrupted him. No, he says, I am not the rapacious brat whose greed and rage brought down the genius giant. On the contrary, *he* was the devil, *he* seduced *my* greatness. At heart I was just a normal boy.

Of Wellington, he remarks in conclusion, "I look forward to being a boy again with him in Paradise one day not very far off. (When you go to heaven you can be what you like, and I intend to be a child.)"

The Infection Scene

Precedent: in *Philosophy in the Bedroom*, the Marquis de Sade's usual assortment of libertines are having a fine old time buggering and encunting and whipping one another, when Madame de Mistival barges into their playroom. She has come to demand restitution of her daughter Eugénie. The sudden arrival of this righteous interloper cannot, of course, be tolerated, and as punishment Madame de Mistival is raped, both anally and vaginally, the service rendered by a syphilitic valet.

Sequel: San Francisco, the mid-1990s. Two young men—their names are Christopher and Anthony; one is twenty-two, the other nineteen—move in together. They are powerfully in love, each convinced that he has found, in the other, the great, the only true friend he will ever know, the friend without whom his life can have no purpose. They cherish the reading (Dennis Cooper at A Different Light) that brought them together, worship the author under whose dark influence their story began. This was three months ago. In the meantime, because their friends might disapprove of their moving in together after such a brief courtship, they've taken to saying they've been "partners" for more than a year. And why not? They *feel* as if they've known each other for decades. Three months seems too brief a term to contain such abundant happiness. Theirs is the rare, the distinguished thing.

Oh, how they delight in each other! Before they met, neither had much hope for anything. But now a future in which peace and passion go hand in hand seems to be opening out in front of them. In the normal course of events their relations would become fractious, their passion would grow stale, they would cheat on each other, part, not speak for years, meet again, and wonder at their rancor and folly. But the normal course of events is not to be followed. Not in this case. There is an interloper present. Both of these boys come from difficult homes; Anthony, the younger of the two, from a disastrous one. When he was sixteen he ran away. An older man took him in, offering shelter and drugs in exchange for sex. The older man begged Anthony to let him fuck him without a condom. On several occasions Anthony, blitzed out on ecstasy, relented. Now he is seropositive. Christopher is not. One will live, the other will die. To Christopher, this condition is intolerable. He will not let his friend die alone. Anthony has no symptoms, nor has Christopher ever witnessed the ravages of the disease. Like many of his age, Christopher is so scorched by despair that for him the prospect of "dying together" takes on romantic connotations, seems pleasant and cozy, like sharing mumps. Anyway, his life so far has given him few other reasons to want to keep living. His abstracted mother, when she isn't working, has her alcoholic boyfriend to deal with, while his father is too busy with a batch of new children to spare time for this unhappy child of an unhappy, unwise, early marriage. All Christopher has is Anthony, and for Anthony, he decides, he is willing to make any sacrifice.

One evening they go out to dinner. A Mexican place. Chicken mole, enchiladas, greasy tortillas. Christopher makes a proposition to Anthony, who is horrified. "I couldn't," he cries, and Christopher takes his hand.

"Calm down," he says. "Hear me out." And he states his case. He speaks gently, persuasively. He says that he would kill himself if Anthony died, so what does it matter? We all have to go sometime.

Anthony is moved. "You love me that much?" he asks.

"More," Christopher answers. At which point Anthony smiles. This love is the only good thing he's ever known. A flower creeps through the cement of a blasted city, a blasted, postnuclear city: that is how it feels to him.

They fix a date. Next Saturday, they decide, they will have sex. They will not use a condom. Discussing the details, Christopher finds himself becoming surprisingly aroused. Never in his life has anyone fucked him without a condom. In sex, as in all things, he has followed the rules to the letter. But now he suspects the rules to be a lie perpetrated by Dead White Males in order to suppress the freedom of gay people, who threaten patriarchy. Doesn't he too deserve a taste of real abandon, release without restraint? He speaks nostalgically of "Stonewall," even though he wasn't yet born when it happened, even though "Stonewall" exists for him merely as grainy porn flicks, the actors mostly dead. Oh, how young he is! He sees the dead as a glorious fraternity into which he longs to be initiated. But he knows nothing of disease, much less of death.

For the rest of that week Anthony and Christopher lead their lives as always. During the day they go to their jobs (one works at a video store, the other at a coffee bar), at night they walk together up and down Castro Street, or chat with their friends at the Midnight Sun, or watch MTV. By agreement, they do not have sex. They are saving up.

Saturday arrives. Anthony is visibly panicked. "Are you sure you want to go through with this?" he asks Christopher over lunch—sprouts and avocado sandwiches at Café Flore on Market Street.

"Sure as I've ever been about anything," his friend answers, kissing him on the nose.

That evening they cook a good dinner together: spaghetti with a sauce made from a recipe handed down by Anthony's grandmother, who comes from Naples, and whose own mother was rumored to have been a witch. (Inspired by this heritage, he has dabbled in worship of "the Goddess.") Then they have chocolate ice cream. Then they smoke some hash. Neither wants to lose his nerve.

In the bedroom Anthony strips the spread off the futon, lights candles. Christopher has put Enya on the stereo; the songs bleed one into the other with a numbing sameness, like Gregorian chants. Altogether the atmosphere is early or even pre-Christian. The bedroom is a temple, the bed an altar. What is about to take place is ritual sacrifice, to which the pious victim offers himself up willingly. They watch each other undress. Because he knows it excites Christopher, Anthony has put on a jockstrap, letting his penis and balls out the right side. He is dark-haired, beefy, endomorphic. Whereas Christopher is taller, leaner. To be taken by a boy both smaller and stronger than himself excites Christopher inordinately. And now Anthony spreads him open on the bed, lifts his legs in the air. He takes the bottle of lubricant from the bedside table—but Christopher stops his hand.

"Use spit," he whispers.

"Okay." Anthony spits into his palm. *Another rule broken.*

They are doing it now. Anthony is amazed at how much better it feels this way. Without the latex barrier, flesh slides against flesh. For the first time he understands what it was that the older man who infected him had been after: this sensation. This.

As for Christopher, in his stoned state he imagines that his friend is a god hovering over him. Anthony is Apollo laboring in the sky. His voice is distant thunder. Steadily Anthony fucks him, then without warning grits his teeth; deep inside Christopher feels warm wet pulses. He imagines low tide on the Pacific. Waves receding. In the remnant tide pools, hermit crabs with their cargo of dead shells, anemones suctioned to the rocks, spiny mouths that close around his touch.

It's done. Okay, he thinks. This is what I wanted. And he reaches to embrace Anthony.

But Anthony pulls away. He pulls away, stumbles to the window, opens it. Leans out, not speaking.

Christopher sits up in the bed. *What's wrong?* he wants to ask—and doesn't dare. He knows the answer.

For some reason a strange memory assails Anthony. When he was a child, on the last day of every school year all the kids in his class wrote their names and addresses on cards that they attached to helium balloons. Their teacher then led them outside in a kind of procession, the balloons trailing behind, above her, a leashed bouquet, and when they were all assembled on the playground, she cut the strings. The balloons rose up, masses that separated, as the children, cheering the onslaught of summer, rushed out the open gates to parents, school buses. Only Anthony hesitated. He wanted to wait until he could no longer distinguish his own balloon from the others. He wanted to wait until every last one had disappeared into a dot on the horizon, and the sky was empty again, like a blank page.

Few of the balloons ever made it more than a couple of miles. Instead, for weeks afterward, he'd keep finding shreds of them twisted around the branches of neighborhood trees when he went on bike rides.

Outside the window tonight the moon is bright, not quite full. Rounder than a balloon. Pearl gray. Behind him Christopher puts his hand on Anthony's shoulders.

"Don't worry," he says. "It's what I wanted. More than anything." Kissing his neck.

But Anthony, at the window, is too busy calculating to listen. Six weeks for seroconversion, then the blood test, then a few more days for the results. Oh, the wait! They will wait the way girls wait to see if they are pregnant.

"Of course, it might not take."

Don't let it take, Anthony prays to his great-grandmother's Goddess.

"So just to play it safe, we'll do it every night."

Silence.

"O.K.?"
"O.K."
"To play it safe."
"Yes."
Anthony closes the window on the moon.

A Hotel Flirtation

1889. A big hotel on the Côte d'Azur. String quartets, a promenade, parasols. Also a busy network of back hallways in which servants and staff played out their own dramas. No bathrooms, though. In 1889 plumbing was rare, even in the most elegant French hotels. The rich, like the poor, used chamber pots.

When the tutor arrived that afternoon—dragged hither at the behest of his difficult yet enchanting charge—he gave his room a minute and thorough once-over. First he stripped the sheets off the bed and examined the mattress, in the center of which was a largish pink stain. Then he noticed a perfect circle of carpet near the plant stand which, unlike the rest, had not been leached of color by the sun. He should leave well enough alone, he told himself, it was always better to leave well enough alone—yet even as he spoke these words to himself, he was lifting the plant stand to reveal the expected discolorations, stiff to the touch. What had produced them? Various unsavory possibilities sprang to his mind, so that he became nauseated and, putting the plant stand down again, opened both windows and loosened his collar. He was bony, in his early twenties, with thin yellow hair and the sort of constitution doctors of that epoch described as "delicate." From an early age the tutor's mother had warned him not to exert himself too much. He worried excessively (and probably needlessly) about germs. He thought he could smell an evil smell.

The tutor loathes hotels. The hotel is neither public nor private space but some uneasy blending of the two. To live comfortably in a hotel you have to maintain the delusion that the room you occupy is actually your own. And yet this privacy is fictive. The walls are thin. Yes, you carry a key in your pocket, but you also know that somewhere in every hotel, someone else carries a master key.

Hundreds of people sleep on the hotel mattress before it is retired—

sleep, or do worse than sleep. The John Bull sweats; the bride spots the sheets with blood; the French doctor does not wipe himself. Some guests have actually had the audacity to die in their beds. Though the tutor doesn't know it, an old Belgian woman died in his bed last March. For six hours her body remained in the fetal lock of sleep, until a maid came in with morning coffee. Screams brought the concierge running. Yet once the corpse had been removed, the hotel manager didn't bother to change the mattress. After all, who would have been the wiser?

At that time, in that place, people settled longer at hotels than they do now. Stays of several weeks or even months were not uncommon. It was never very much time before guests were forging alliances, staking out territories, waging wars. The tutor, having spent a large chunk of his childhood living in hotels, finds the mere prospect of all this wearying. He remembers vividly the hours he had to endure sitting next to his mother in tearooms, longing to run outside, which she forbade. (To some extent he still longs to run outside.) Medieval architecture is his passion. He does not relish intrigues, rumors, cold-shoulderings—the daily bread of hotel life. His charge, on the other hand, thrives in such an atmosphere. With his stalklike body, his pale, delectable features, Bosie might have been one of those white asparagus shoots that grow only in the absence of sun. Natural light did not favor him. His skin burned easily. He required interiority to blossom, the rays of a chandelier.

He was nineteen now, and at the peak of his seraphic beauty.

The tutor checks his watch: it is almost one, the hour at which he and Bosie have agreed to meet. And so, abandoning the mattress, which he would have liked to turn over (but what worse horrors might he have found on the other side?), he leaves his room and heads out to the covered terrace that overlooks the beach. Dressed in a striped jacket, mauve trousers, and broad-brimmed hat, Bosie leans dreamily against the rail, gazing at the promenade, where some old women are strolling. Really, the spectacle of him takes the tutor's breath away. Bosie is narrow-shouldered, with light, wavy hair. His eyes, green and gold, recall the sun-mottled ground beneath a tree. Only his lips are less than classical. Narrow and bloodless, they close into a crooked line. Somehow this imperfection makes him more, not less, desirable to the tutor. Bosie's face might be a girl's face; it is certainly one that girls envy. Yet there is nothing girlish about his carriage—and that is the miraculous thing (and the thing about which everyone comments). Bosie is every inch a boy—albeit one who has to shave only twice in a week. This odd dressing up of essential masculinity in the trappings of feminine loveliness intoxicates the tutor. For the first time in his life, he is in love—a state to which, like most states, he feels unequal. With Bosie he never knows what to do or say. So he stands his ground, peering at Bosie's back, waiting for Bosie to speak, to act, to tell him what to do.

"Oh, Gerald, isn't it beautiful, the sea?" Bosie asks. "I'm so happy we came here. If we'd looked at one more flying buttress, I would have gone mad."

Gerald, who reverences the flying buttress, only nods, and curses his weakness. After all, hasn't he promised Lady Queensberry to divert Bosie's attention from the very temptations the hotel incarnates—the temptations of "society," to which Bosie is already so dangerously susceptible? Yet to this task, alas, he has also proven unequal. Instead of waking Bosie to the uplifting glory of medieval church architecture, he has allowed Bosie to sway his attentions from that holy pursuit. Instead of teaching him to love what he loves, he has let himself be dragged back into an atmosphere he detests, pettish and airless and reeking of eau de cologne.

Gerald is a few years older than Bosie, at present without fixed employment but in future to serve as assistant master at a number of schools, then as a war correspondent. He is also a nephew of one of Bosie's great-aunts. Their pairing up for this journey was the brainchild of Lady Queensberry, who had been worried lest her impatient son should have nothing to occupy him during the interval between Winchester (where he had finished in the spring) and Oxford (to which he would go down in the fall). A continental ramble under Gerald's edifying and stolid management was quickly settled upon as the ideal solution. The trip would have an educative purpose—that is to say, Gerald would ensure that Bosie direct his energies toward the pursuit of cultural enrichment—but at some point the boy got the better of his tutor. Thus the abandonment of cathedrals in favor of esplanades, this hotel, "luncheon."

What the ladies hadn't counted on was Gerald's incipient homosexuality—and Bosie's skills as a seducer.

Most likely it started long before they reached the Côte d'Azur. Indeed, very possibly it was the reason their journey veered from its cultural itinerary in the first place. As I imagine it, early in the trip Bosie picked up on his tutor's sexual anxiety—Gerald's unspoken (and largely subconscious) *looking*. A challenge presented itself. By the end of his Winchester years Bosie had honed the skills he'd practiced so awkwardly on Wellington into an efficient set of strategies for which he might even have written down the rules, much as his hyperactive father wrote (or helped to write) the rules for boxing. To lure his randy schoolmates into bed, however, was by this time becoming old hat; to seduce a relation older than himself, and charged with the responsibility of keeping him out of trouble—now that would be proof of his power!

Here is how I see him working. Though usually they secure two rooms at each hotel in which they stay, occasionally they have to share a double room. Imagine poor Gerald, then, coming in from his washing up, only to find Bosie naked before the looking glass, his very white behind thrust just slightly outward. Gerald stops in his tracks, stares a few seconds, before coughing to announce his embarrassed presence, at which point Bosie turns, laughs, pulls on his dressing gown.

That night Gerald can't keep the image of Bosie's nakedness out of his mind. His curiosity is heightened in stages. The Douglas rules: after a first flash of exposure (ideally of the backside), take care never to show more than a delectable portion of yourself; only glimpses. One night Bosie's shirt might flop open, exposing a nipple as red as a pomegranate seed. Or pulling off his socks, he might caress his own pale ankles. In his mind, meanwhile, the object of his campaign struggled to put the pieces together—a struggle made all the more anxious by the fact that the flash of entire nakedness with which Bosie had first enticed was even now fading from memory.

Oh, Bosie is merciless! He is tunneling under, undermining the foundations of Gerald's already weakened defenses. Each night poor Gerald suffers agonies of erotic dreamscape from which he wakes sweating, erection aching, on the brink of an ecstasy he cannot quite allow. In his dreams he pulses out phantom orgasms, and feels a consequent phantom relief. But coming in a dream is like eating or drinking or urinating in a dream: you wake, and the need is all the greater. Indeed, the more he suppresses it, the more the urge to uncover Bosie's sweetly sleeping body intensifies in him, fevers him—which is just as Bosie intended.

Finally there comes the night when Bosie goes in for the kill, lets Gerald walk in on him a second time, absolutely naked, but this time lying on his back. There passes a moment of invitation in which no words are spoken—Can you resist me? Bosie seems to be asking—and then Gerald, forsaking decorum, jumps on Bosie, pretends to wrestle him, inhales greedily his jasminelike scent. Squealing, Bosie rubs hot parts of himself against his tutor. Gerald thinks: just wrestling; perfectly acceptable. Only he can't keep from letting his lips brush against Bosie's cheek, he can't keep his erection (mercilessly insistent, restrained only by layers of underlinen) from pushing into Bosie's leg. Boys, boys together! *Tremendous friends.* And then they are looking at each other; the pretense of wrestling falls away; Gerald reaches down, kisses Bosie, wills Bosie's mouth to open to its own devouring.

They grope. Gerald screws his eyes shut, and suddenly sits up. Bosie looks puzzled. Prostitutes are wise to ask for payment before the act. For men sex means a lessening. Disgrace always lurks in afterglow.

Bosie doesn't understand what's happened. He doesn't understand that beneath all those layers, Gerald has just experienced a humiliating, even a defeating orgasm. He doesn't know that among poor Gerald's many woes in life is a predisposition to premature ejaculation, or as it was more often called at that time, "sexual incontinence"—not until Gerald rolls away, and sits on the edge of the bed, and blows his nose. Fear and shame arrest him in equal measure. He cannot say which fact is more painful: that he has committed a criminal offense, or that he has done it so ineptly.

He lifts his head; looks at Bosie. He's braced for the worst: protestations, threats of exposure. His overheated imagination is already thinking blackmail, jail cells, suicide. But Bosie neither teases nor reproaches him. Instead he squeezes Gerald's hand, smiles, and winks, before dashing over to the washbasin.

Bosie's nakedness is different now. It encodes no allure as he slips on his dressing gown, climbs into the bed.

"Good night," he says cheerfully.

"Good night," Gerald answers, shivering as he peels sticky cotton from his thigh.

The woman, according to Bosie's brief account of the incident, was a cousin of Gerald's; in her early thirties, divorced from her husband, and on the run from a lover. In other words, a *mondaine;* an adventuress. That she happened to be staying at the same hotel as Bosie and Gerald was probably a coincidence. Or perhaps it was a coincidence that had been arranged between the cousins. I can't know. I'm making most of this up. For now I'm going to say it was a coincidence, since it would not have been remotely in Gerald's interest to meet up with that particular cousin at that particular moment. Quite the opposite. It seemed to him a case of extremely bad timing.

Bosie gives her no name, and little by way of a description. I shall call her Laura. According to him she was simply "a lady of celebrated beauty, at least twelve years older than myself, the divorced wife of an earl." To me she is elegant, if not exactly beautiful, with small raisin-colored eyes. Her black hair has a sharp, radiant sheen: think of Susan Sontag, Martha Argerich, Tess Gallagher. (Is it cheap of me to offer such comparisons? Probably. And yet this *is* what I am thinking.)

The three of them meet in the hotel lobby. Exclamations of amazement. But what a surprise! Of all the places in the world! Bosie and Laura beam at each other, while Gerald hangs back, pretending enthusiasm even as he struggles to swallow his dread. Of course they must dine together, Laura says; of course Bosie agrees. And quickly, quickly the concierge is flagged down, tables are rearranged; Gerald, upon whose shoulders such masculine business matters seem always to fall, curses both his cousin and himself.

He's never liked her. He's always thought her a tart. Flirting with his brother the way she did. It was positively obscene.

At dinner they drink champagne. Laura and Bosie talk about society people in whom Gerald hasn't the slightest interest. They talk about royalty. They gossip about Prince Eddy. Laura's heard that Prince Eddy was Jack the Ripper.

"No!" Bosie cries.

"Yes!" Laura says. "They say he's not quite right in the head, and that after the last murder, after he killed that poor girl in her room, the police found him in the vicinity and now he's being secretly held in the palace under the care of doctors. Apparently her majesty is beside herself—absolutely beside herself."

"But that's ridiculous!" Gerald interjects. "Tabloid lies. You shouldn't believe such nonsense."

"Oh, silly," says Laura. "What do you know?"

"I think the murders were really ghastly," Bosie says.

"Ghastly," Laura repeats. "You know, they say he took things—from the bodies. I wouldn't like to say what. You might lose your appetite."

Bosie bursts into laughter. Gerald checks his watch.

"I was chilled when I heard," Laura goes on. "I felt as if it were me he'd gone after. Not that I had anything to worry about, since he only chose—well, you know: *low women.* Still, I had a dream one night. I woke up and there he was, bent over me with his knife. Breathing. I couldn't see his face. I knew I had to switch on the electric light, that if I could switch on the electric light, then he wouldn't kill me. And I reached over for the switch . . . and it wasn't there."

"How awful!" Bosie says.

"Awful!" Gerald repeats, a little mockingly.

He calls for more champagne.

The affair, in Bosie's words, advances along "classic lines." I take this to mean that it becomes a French farce in which Bosie plays the virginal initiate, Laura the sophisticated *châtelaine.* At night there are secret rendezvous; during the day delicious pretenses of innocence.

The second afternoon, neither of them shows up for luncheon. Hot with jealousy, Gerald suffers alone the tedious gaps between the courses, then forgoes coffee to search out the pair, whom he finds soon enough in the hotel gardens, sitting in a sort of bower, under a cascade of roses, holding hands and laughing over what he presumes to be some inanity, while Laura's unpleasant little Bedlington terrier—sculpted to resemble a lamb—growls at their feet. They don't see Gerald. He lurks undetected among the trees. They kiss, and he cannot move. A debased yearning to see Bosie made love to by his cousin roots him to the spot. Cautiously Bosie slips his hand into Laura's dress, cups her pear-shaped breast. Gerald thinks: I'm no match for her. Then he thinks: What am I, to put myself in competition with a woman?

Disgusted, he flees his hiding place and returns to the hotel. In the brocade and velvet sitting room, some outraged old ladies are deploring the scandalous behavior of a "certain woman" who has come to the hotel and seduced a boy nearly young enough to be her son. Gerald, his eyes in a book, listens avidly.

Eventually the old women get up to take a walk along the promenade. He doesn't notice. By now he's lost himself in the book—Winckelmann—soothing prose about Greek things. What he tries not to think about, what he knows from his own tutors, is that Winckelmann was murdered in a Trieste hotel room by a Tuscan cook. A bad end, but he was a sodomite.

At around three Bosie strolls into the sitting room. "Hello, Gerald," he says.

Gerald doesn't answer. Bosie takes the armchair opposite his. "Oh, Gerald, Gerald," he says—and still Gerald doesn't answer. So Bosie picks up a magazine from the table between the chairs and starts flipping through it. "*The Women's World,*" he reads aloud, "edited by Oscar Wilde. Oh, look at this, an article by Mrs. Wilde! About *muffs*. Well, I doubt she ever would have got that published if she hadn't been married to the editor, do you think?"

"If you wouldn't mind, I'm trying to read."

"What are you reading?"

"Winckelmann."

"Ah, Winckelmann. But I suppose Pater isn't quite your thing, is he?"

"Too subjective," Gerald says.

"Subjective!" Bosie puts down his magazine. "The trouble with you, Gerald, is that you're so . . ."

He quiets. Then: "She's very nice, your cousin."

A deeper silence. Confidingly, Bosie leans across the little table that separates him from his tutor. "Gerald, may I tell you something?"

"What?"

"I think I'm in love."

Gerald puts down his book. "Do you mean with my cousin?"

"Yes. With Laura."

"That's nonsense. She's a grown woman. You're a boy."

"Ah, but does age really matter, to the heart?"

"Your mother would not approve," Gerald says. "I was supposed to take you on a tour so that you might learn something, not lounge around some boring hotel all day flirting with my damned cousin." He sneezes. "No, this settles it. Tomorrow we leave."

"We shall not leave," says Bosie.

"I say we leave, and we shall leave."

"And I say we shall not. Or you may. You may do what you like."

"I would suggest your mother—"

"I would suggest there are some things I might tell my mother."

Gerald stands. His face has gone pale. "What are you saying?" he asks stiffly.

Then Bosie laughs. He laughs and laughs. "Oh, come now, Gerald!" he says, stands himself, and pats his tutor manfully on the back. "Must you worry so? You always worry! Don't! If you'd let yourself, you could have a perfectly good time here. Why not let yourself?"

"This is not what your mother had in mind."

"So what? Must she know?"

Gerald shakes his head. Excusing himself, he returns to his room. The bed assaults him: the knowledge of that stain. He must come up with a plan, he decides, and comes up with one. It is not a bad plan. Certainly it doesn't lack for courage.

A Piece of Bad News

"The doom room," the counselor called his office; or "the fate gate"; or "the torture chamber." Never to the faces of his clients, of course. To his clients it was "the consulting room," and nothing else. Perhaps all of us use a different language in our heads than in the world; and certainly among his colleagues the counselor would never have admitted to amusing himself with such cynical word games. Still, so long as the brain's private monologue cannot be wiretapped, he will not be fired for his thoughts; he will not be fired for thinking of his office as "the torture chamber," or for dividing his clients into the doomed (positive) and the saved (negative): terrible, archaic locutions that go against every principle of his training, which is in large part why he takes such malicious pleasure in their use.

At the moment the counselor is standing outside his office, by the water cooler. In his right hand he holds a fragile cone filled with purified water, in his left a piece of paper on which the future of a young man he has never met is spelled out. About five feet from him stands a door, behind which the young man sits, waiting, having no idea that the counselor, who is not in the least thirsty, has decided to drink another coneful of water instead of going in and ending the agony of his suspense. And why? Because he can. Nor will anyone (his colleagues, for instance) ever know that this little cruelty is intentional. That's the pleasure of the thing. He is palpating, caressing his own power. For a few minutes, the young man is his slave, and as in certain sadomasochistic sex rituals in which the counselor has also taken part, he's not going to be allowed relief until his master is good and ready.

After he finishes his third cup of water, the counselor checks his watch. Five minutes. Yes, he decides, probably he's kept the kid sweating long enough—to do so any longer would be to cross the border into detectable sadism—and dashing his paper cone into a recycling bin, he opens the door and strolls casually inside. The young man, in his seat opposite the empty desk, flinches. No surprise. His terror is so visceral it can be smelled.

"Hello," the counselor says, offering his hand, all smiles and affability and cool skin. "Christopher, right?"

"Right."

"Good to meet you."

The counselor sits down. How odd! He recognizes the boy. But where from? Christopher is brown-haired, handsome in a rough way, and according to the report the counselor spreads out before him, just twenty-two. But why does he look so familiar? Something about the eyes . . .

Then, quite suddenly and horribly, the counselor remembers: he and Christopher have had sex. Not slept together, just had sex, standing up, at a club a few blocks down Market Street. Maybe six months earlier. If he recalls correctly, he gave Christopher a blowjob.

The counselor coughs. Suddenly he is as sweaty as Christopher. Punishment, he thinks, punishment for having taken pleasure in making the boy wait . . . meanwhile he dreads actually looking at the report. (Oh, what cavalier arrogance, not to have checked, before entering, whether the news he has to dispatch was bad or good!) And now, he asks himself, what if the boy turns out to be positive? The result, for him personally, will be several very hairy days, as he awaits his own test results. Did he swallow? He can't remember if he swallowed. Probably not. Was there a lot of pre-cum? The counselor has bad gums, and therefore ought not to be in the business of giving blowjobs in the first place. Still, it's a habit of which, despite logic and remonstrance, he has failed, over the years, to break himself. For though he would never suck off a man he knew to be HIV-positive, he feels no compunction in sucking off men (witness Christopher) whose names he hasn't even learned. Ignorance, in the end, really may be bliss, or at least a prerequisite for bliss, just as safety may be less a condition than a boundary, the exact location of which we can only guess at, measuring a little with science, a little with hunches. Why listen to statistics when common sense—which tells him what he wants to hear—is so much more congenial a guide?

"Well," he says now, "let's cut to the chase, shall we?" And glancing down at the piece of paper in front of him, he prays very quickly. Blinks. "You've tested negative," he says, before he himself can even absorb the fact of it.

"Sorry?" Christopher says.

"You've tested negative."

"But that can't be."

"Why not?"

"Because . . ." The boy leans closer. "Listen, are you sure you haven't mixed up my results with someone else's?"

"We triple-screen to avoid that."

"But can't the results be wrong?"

"There are occasional false positives. Never false negatives."

"But they have to be wrong."

"Why?"

Christopher doesn't answer. Nor is the counselor—his own heartbeat decelerating with relief—in any mood to probe the matter further. Instead he goes into his negative drill, hands a rather shell-shocked Christopher a copy of *The Gay Men's Guide to Safer Sex*, and shoos him out of the office.

Through the waiting room, Christopher stumbles. Like the counselor's office itself, the waiting room has been designed by a local architect who, after his lover's death, decided to devote himself to the science of creating spaces that "minimize panic, maximize tranquility." This architect is now rich from a practice dedicated exclusively to clinics, testing centers, hospices—rooms in which bad news is given, painful treatments administered. Yet to all that yellow and blue carefulness, Christopher is oblivious, immune. How can he be negative? Before he left, Anthony fucked him six times without a condom. He shouldn't be negative. The news strikes him as a kind of curse.

Out on Market Street, in brisker air, he goes into a phone booth, drops in coins, punches buttons.

Two rings. "Hello?" Anthony says.

"Hi."

A short silence. "Christopher, I told you not to call me. I don't want to talk to you."

"I got the results."

"And?"

"Come meet me and I'll tell you."

"No. I just told you, I don't want—"

"Then I won't tell you."

"Oh, man! You're crazy, you know that? I can't believe I ever got caught up in this shit . . ."

"Anthony, please."

"How could I have been such an idiot—"

"You know what? The counselor was someone I tricked with."

"I don't care. I don't give a fuck."

"Anthony, if you'll just listen to me—all I want is to see you. Like old times. You owe me that."

"Why? You scare me, you know that? You're dangerous."

Christopher laughs. "For Christ's sake, man, I'd never hurt you. I love you."

"You love me like a suicide loves pills."

"But it's not about dying, it's about solidarity! That's the point, to prove—"

"It doesn't prove anything."

"Why don't you understand? You understood before."

"Before I was crazy too, a little bit." On the other end of the line, Anthony beats his fingers against the phone. "Now I'm going to ask you just one more time. What happened?"

"If you'll meet me, I'll tell you."

"That's blackmail."

"But if it's the only way I'll get to see you, what choice do I have? I mean, Anthony, you're all that matters."

"Is that supposed to make me feel better?"

"Yes. Why not?"

"You're the one who doesn't understand."

"I understand more than you think. If you'd just agree to see me, to sit down with me, you'd realize that."

Another silence. Then, "All right. Café Flore in fifteen minutes. But just to get the results, you hear me? Nothing else."

"Thank you, Anthony. I can't wait—"

Anthony hangs up.

"Well, goodbye," Christopher says to the dial tone. And hangs up himself.

Gerald Takes Matters in Hand

That evening, with an assurance the brazenness of which will later stun him, Gerald puts his plan into action. To begin with, he decides to enlist the aid of the old women in the lounge who have been gossiping about Laura's misbehavior. To lure two or three of them into conversation after dinner, to express to them, "in strictest confidence," his anxiety over his charge—not to mention his serious doubts as to the moral fiber of his cousin—turns out to be easy; after all, Gerald has spent most of his life in the company of old women. Unctuous and meek, he knows how to earn their allegiance. In many ways he is an old woman himself. A little confiding, a few whispered words of anxiety, and the entire female population of the hotel is set against Laura.

At around ten o'clock, he returns to his room, where he spends a gratifying half-hour with Winckelmann. Then he steps into the corridor, walks to Bosie's room, knocks at the door. As expected, no answer. Bracing himself, he heads down the hall, to the room his cousin occupies. Once again, with great deliberateness, he knocks at a door.

Loud barks from that ersatz lamb, the Bedlington terrier.

"Laura, this is Gerald," he announces manfully. "I ask you to open the door."

Again, only barks.

"I know that Bosie's there with you. Now please answer the door, else I shall have to fetch the management."

A sound of rustling. Then the door cracks, Laura's scowling face greets his. "What are you talking about? Are you mad? He's not here."

"He is there, and I demand that you open the door."

"You're mad! I'm alone, in bed."

"Laura, for the last time . . . I do not wish this scene to become public. Need I remind you that Bosie is a minor? Send him out to me at once."

The door closes in his face. The dog barks. A few seconds later, it opens again, and a teary-eyed Bosie emerges. Worse than that, a transvestite Bosie, dressed in one of Laura's gallooned nightdresses.

Some of Gerald's ladies, coming down the hall, stop in their tracks, stare in horror at the gauzy apparition.

"You shall come with me," Gerald says. And yanking Bosie roughly by the arm, he drags the boy back to his own room; shuts the door behind them. "Now get out of those ridiculous clothes."

Obediently Bosie pulls the nightdress over his head.

"You should not have done this, Gerald," he says. "I call it most unfair."

"Put this on," Gerald says, thrusting a dressing gown at Bosie, trying not to notice his nakedness. For once, Bosie does as he is told.

"Tomorrow we leave," Gerald goes on. "I expect to see you packed and ready in the lobby at seven. Nor would I like to hear that you have visited my cousin in the night."

Bosie, subdued, watches with surprise and pleasure as Gerald moves toward the door.

Perhaps the scariest thing about Bosie, particularly in his middle years: his malignant, even obsessive litigiousness. And not merely where Wilde was concerned. For though the degree to which he singularly compelled Wilde to take legal action against his father is debatable, what is a matter of public record is that after Wilde's death, Bosie himself was involved in no less than ten libel actions. He himself brought libel actions against: the Reverend R. F. Horton, who had called a newspaper Bosie was editing, *The Academy*, "an organ of Catholic propaganda"; Wilde's first biographer, Arthur Ransome, after he described Bosie as a man "to whom Wilde felt that he owed some, at least, of the circumstances of his public disgrace"; the *Morning Post*, after it accused Bosie of anti-Semitism; and the *Evening News*, which in 1921 falsely reported his death and described the Douglas bloodline as showing "many marked signs of degeneracy." (In rebuttal, Bosie argued that even though in his youth he might have exhibited "symptoms of wickedness," he was by no means a degenerate: "I am a horseman," he declared proudly, "a good shot, a manly man, able to hold my own with other people.")

In addition, Bosie was himself sued for libel on three occasions: once by Wilde's friend Robert Ross, once by his father-in-law, Colonel Custance, and once—amazingly enough—by Winston Churchill, whom

Bosie had accused publicly and repeatedly of entering into a Jewish-led conspiracy to lower the value of government stock. Churchill had no choice but to bring an action against Bosie, who lost, and was jailed for six months at Wormwood Scrubs. (While in prison, as Wilde had written *De Profundis*, he wrote *In Excelsis*, a sonnet sequence containing anti-Semitic slurs of a more than usually repellent aspect.)

The case against the *Evening News* Bosie actually won, which is probably why he crows about it in his autobiography—yet what is curious is the moment when he chooses to crow about it. The reference comes just after Bosie's seduction by Gerald Armstrong's cousin. Like his rendering of the episode with Wellington, the account he gives here is brief—only a few paragraphs—and seems to be offered in order to challenge "the accusation which has been made against me of being what is called abnormal and degenerate from a sexual point of view. (By the way, the last time this accusation of being 'degenerate' was made against me was by *The Evening News* in 1921, and it cost that enterprising journal £1000 in damages to me and a good many more thousands in costs.)"

Now that is an alarming parenthetical—alarming because its import seems to be, in essence, "Don't fuck with me": a warning even to the reader himself, who has presumably put down money to purchase Bosie's book, that he would do well to avoid offending its author.

It is the only instance I can think of, either in literature or that species of writing that purports to be literature, in which a writer has overtly threatened his reader.

As for the details: what is striking to me about Bosie's account is the degree to which it undercuts his putative intention, which is to establish once and for all his heterosexual vitality. Thus when Gerald decides he has had enough and knocks at his cousin's bedroom door "demanding restitution of his ravished ewe-lamb," the "ewe-lamb, reduced to tears and dressed in one of the lady's much-beribboned nightgowns," is delivered to his keeper "to the accompaniment of loud barks from the lady's pet dog." Hardly the paragon of boyish swagger, that description. Also, no explanation is given of why Gerald has come to think of Bosie in the first place as *his* "ravished ewe-lamb."

No, the transvestite frills in which the episode is dressed make it difficult to take seriously Bosie's pouting claim that had well enough been left alone, "my lady love would at any rate have kept me away from baser promiscuities"—presumably those committed in the company of Wilde. Indeed, one has to ask why, if Bosie's intention here is to prove his manliness, he chose to include the episode in his autobiography in the first place.

The only surprise was that in the end, Gerald did find it in himself to challenge Bosie; to wrest him from his cousin; to drag him from that hotel on the Côte d'Azur.

Courage. Perhaps it is not so surprising after all that timid Gerald grew up to be a war correspondent.

On the Edge of the Abyss

Where does it come from, this story? I'm still not certain. Probably it began with a newspaper article, something glimpsed three or four years back on the West Coast. According to this article, a San Francisco psychiatrist was noticing a dangerous trend among very young gay men: in essence, they were starting to abandon those very rules of "safer sex" that their elders had struggled so hard to instill and publicize. And this just at a moment when those rules were finally becoming second nature (and when as a consequence the rate of HIV infection was going down).

What had happened? No one seemed sure. Certainly that generalized anomie of which so many young people complained in the early 1990s could not be ignored as a contributing factor: ours is an age of suicide, and what is unprotected sex anyway but—to borrow a phrase from Wilde—"a long, lovely suicide"?

As for the gay teenagers themselves, the ones interviewed spoke not only of despair, but of exclusion; solitude; loneliness. Think about it: when everyone you know is HIV-positive, when everywhere you look HIV-positive men and women are banding together to form not merely families but a society—to serve the needs of which whole industries have cropped up—how can you not feel that you have been left behind? Bear in mind that this condition was unique to a few urban centers, San Francisco chief among them: cities in which the HIV-positive had their own magazines, rites, habits and philosophies and language; to weary further an already wearied word, their own culture. More potently, with one another (or so felt several of the boys interviewed) the HIV-positive could flout the totemic restraints of "safer sex." Infection threw them free from caution, and so they could throw caution to the wind, and with one another do what they wanted, as much as they wanted, while on the outskirts the seronegative watched meekly, enviously, nursing their fear.

It is hard for me—a child of a different (and perhaps more life-loving) age—to imagine a world where early death is the norm, and where therefore life itself may begin to seem like a death sentence.

I thought about this article for months after I read it. Then I read a biography of Bosie, and the present and past did their alchemy. Out of the flames Anthony and Christopher stepped forth, naked, almost fully formed.

As for the counselor, he is a character about whom, in my mind, an aureole of profound uncertainty hangs, perhaps because his private cowardices and hypocrisies reflect my own.

I leave him now, to follow Christopher down Market Street to the Café Flore, where at a sunny table Anthony awaits him. Passing these boys, and being told that one was HIV-negative and the other HIV-positive, you might very well confuse which was which, since Anthony looks flushed and vigorous, while Christopher is haggard, thin, his chin pimpled, his elbows scaly with psoriasis. Across from Anthony, who drinks an iced cappuccino, he sits down shyly. "You look great," he says. "Did you get your hair cut?"

"Christopher, don't waste my time. Tell me."

"How long has it been since you moved out?"

"I don't know—two weeks."

"Two weeks and three days." Christopher smiles. "So I hear you have a new lover."

"Man, do we have to talk about this now? Can't you see I'm sweating this out? I have to know. I deserve to know."

"Why?"

"Because if you're positive, I did it to you. And that's something, if I'm going to have to live with, I need to start coping with."

"If I'm positive would you stay with me? Take care of me?"

"No."

"That's blunt."

"I have to be blunt. Like I said, you scare me."

"Or I could sue you . . . like what's-his-name with Rock Hudson. Say you lied and told me you were negative."

"As if I have any money for you to get."

"Oh, I wouldn't do it for money."

Anthony stands. "I don't have to listen to this," he says. "I want to know, but not that much."

"I'm sorry. Sit down. Please sit down. I'm speaking from grief, can't you see? I'm angry because I love you, because I grieve losing you, can't you see that?"

Anthony is silent. He sits down. Then he says, "If you loved me, you wouldn't have asked me to do it. You wouldn't have burdened me with—as if I don't have trouble enough already."

"But you didn't have to agree."

"You have more power than you realize. That's why you're dangerous. You act like you're this innocent little thing, why me, why me, when all the time—"

Christopher buries his face in his hands. "How did it come to this?" he asks. "We loved each other. Three weeks ago, a month ago, we would have sworn we were together forever."

"Not anymore."

"So you're saying you don't love me?"

"No, I don't, if that's what you have to hear." Anthony scratches the back of his head. "You know what? I feel like you're trying to rope me back into a relationship with you. That this whole meeting, it's all been a pretense. I wouldn't be surprised to learn you hadn't even had the fucking test."

"Oh, no, I had it. And this morning I got the results."

"The results you won't tell me."

For a few hopeless seconds Christopher looks at the table. Then he lies. Why he lies, he'll never, for the life of him (and it will be a long one), be sure.

He says, "I'm positive."

All at once Anthony is on his feet, the table is toppling, cold mud-colored coffee streaming onto Christopher's lap. He leaps away from it. "Goddamn you!" Anthony cries, and pushes at Christopher, who pushes back. Around them strangers stand and gawk and whisper. "Odors from the abyss," one man says to another, while at the next table a woman gives her lover a look that is supposed to say, *Thank God for our more peaceable relations*. The lover, however, thinks, *We are closer than we believe. We are all closer to the edge than we believe.*

The seizure has passed. Self-consciousness revives, and with it vanity, which causes Christopher to mop halfheartedly at his ruined shirt. In the interval fighting appears to have taken place—hitting too—for blood now drips from Anthony's mouth.

"Are you O.K.?" a waiter asks, handing him a wad of paper towels.

"I'm O.K. Thanks. I'm O.K."

"Anthony, I'm sorry."

"Stay away from me."

"If you'd just let me—"

"Stay away from me. Don't follow me," says Anthony, hurrying out of the café. Of course Christopher follows. At that dangerous asterisk where Market Street intersects Noe and Twenty-third, the light is red. "Wait!" he calls. But Anthony doesn't wait. Instead he hurls himself onto Market Street, threads his way through six lanes of traffic, alights on the other side. He will die and Christopher will live. He will die and Christopher will die . . . At last the light turns green. And Christopher, who loves life more than he is willing to admit, crosses cautiously, as his mother taught him; looks both ways, as his mother taught him. Then he steps up onto the curb. Glances down Noe. (No Anthony.) Glances down Market. (No Anthony.) Where has he gone?

Only the pavement knows, and the pavement isn't talking.

The Ruins of Another's Fame

In the spring of 1901, a few months after Oscar Wilde's death in Paris, Bosie received a fan letter from a twenty-seven-year-old poetess named Olive Custance. Olive's first book of verse, *Opals*, had been published the previous year by John Lane; she loved opals; her friends called her Opal. Bosie, on the other hand—perhaps because opals were thought to bring bad luck to those not born in October—insisted on calling her Olive.

They entered almost immediately into a love affair. Olive, though lacking Bosie's pedigree, was considered a great beauty, and came from money. As a poet she was dismal—worse even than Bosie, which was perhaps why they admired each other's work. That spring, in Paris with her mother, she had flirted with the famous lesbian Natalie Barney, going so far as to write Natalie a poem about how "Love walks with delicate feet afraid / 'Twixt maid and maid." Besotted, Natalie proposed that she (Natalie) ought to marry Bosie, after which the three of them could live together in a ménage à trois. Olive demurred. Later, in a letter, Natalie made the same proposal to Bosie, who also demurred.

Like his love affair with Laura, Bosie's romance with Olive seems to have involved a certain amount of transvestitism, albeit in this case on Olive's part rather than his own. For instance, in a note to Olive written shortly before he embarked on a trip for America—where, he joked, he hoped to find a rich heiress to marry—Bosie suggests that she dress as a boy and accompany him. In letters, Olive refers to herself as Bosie's "little Page": "Write to me soon and tell me that you love your little Page, and that one day you will come back to 'him,' my Prince, my Prince." His princess Olive is not: "*She* will be very beautiful. But meanwhile love me a little please . . ."

On March 4, 1902, they marry; their son, Raymond, is born on November 17. The marriage does not go well, however, according to Bosie, because Olive loves only "the feminine part" of him: the "more manly" he became, the less attractive he was to his wife. To make matters worse, Bosie and his father-in-law, Colonel Custance, took an instant dislike to each other. An upright Christian gentleman, the Colonel—eager for an heir, and unhappy with the way that his daughter and son-in-law (flighty and irresponsible poets both) were raising his grandson—decided that it was his duty to wrest custody of Raymond from them, toward which end he duped Olive into signing away her inheritance so that she would fall into a position of financial dependence upon her parents. Enraged, Bosie barraged the Colonel with vituperative letters, and when the Colonel stopped opening them, with postcards and telegrams—the e-mail of his age. He called the Colonel "a despicable scoundrel and a thoroughly dishonest and dishonorable man," and promised to send accusatory letters to his clubs, his bank, and the tenants of his estate. Later, after the Colonel threatened to cut her off without a penny if she did not hand Raymond over, Olive left Bosie for a time, and he added his wife's name to his list of enemies. "My father is angry all the time because I love Bosie still," she wrote to Lady Queensberry. "But would it do Bosie any good if I am turned out to starve? I am helpless since I made those settlements . . . I only wish I had the courage to kill myself!"

Custance was not the only person Bosie hated at this stage of his life.

He also hated Mr. Asquith, the prime minister. He hated Asquith's wife, Margot, and Winston Churchill. He hated Robert Ross, Wilde's younger friend and literary executor, and he hated Ross's solicitor, Sir George Lewis, son of the same Sir George Lewis who had been Wilde's great advocate, and who in 1892, at Wilde's behest, had extricated Bosie (then an Oxford undergraduate) from the intimidations of a blackmailer. The second Sir George (no coincidence, in Bosie's view) numbered *both* Colonel Custance and Robbie Ross among his clients.

Where did all this hate come from? Wilde seemed to think it was linked to Bosie's "terrible lack of imagination, the one really fatal defect of your character." Hate, in Wilde's words to Bosie, "gnawed at your nature, as the lichen bites at the root of some sallow plant."

Hate, then, as disease; infection.

Wilde's gravest error—some might say his fatal error—was that he chose Bosie instead of Robbie Ross to be his lover. In making such a decision, he allied himself decisively with risk, volatility, and passion (Bosie) instead of prudence, circumspection, and restraint (Robbie). For Robbie, unlike Bosie, was reliable. When he met Wilde, he was a young man of slight build and no great beauty, with a delicate mouth set rather low on his face, a weak chin, wide, wet eyes. Scholars generally concur that he was "the first boy Oscar ever had." But then Bosie came along, and Robbie was demoted to the capacity of advisor and confidant, the friend into whose ears Oscar poured his passion when the affair was going well and his misery when it was going badly; none of which stopped him from supporting Oscar steadfastly throughout the years, even when it was both unpopular and unprofitable to do so. It was Robbie who took care of him after he got out of prison; Robbie who tried to dissuade him from reconciling with Bosie; Robbie who, in the decade following Wilde's death, managed more or less single-handedly to bring his estate out of bankruptcy and get his work back into print.

How Bosie despised him! Years before, they had quarreled over a boy called Alfred, whom Robbie had seduced, and whom Bosie had then seduced away from him. Now the prey over which they fought was Wilde's corpse and, more specifically, the manuscript of Wilde's prison letter *De Profundis*, which Robbie had given to the British Museum and which Bosie would have liked to see burned. Increasingly he was becoming aware that Wilde's resurrection (of which Robbie was the chief architect) was going to necessitate his own depiction as the instigator of the great writer's downfall. This he could not bear, and so sometime around December 1, 1909, he begins to rail in print against the cult of Wilde, whom he calls a "filthy swine . . . the greatest force for evil that has appeared in Europe during the last 350 years." Robbie, along the same lines, is "a filthy bugger and blackmailer . . . an unspeakable skunk." As for Bosie himself, he is merely a "normal" husband and father who only wants the world to know that despite youthful wickedness, he has reformed: toward this end, he transforms *The Academy* into an organ of right-wing propaganda.

There is a touch of the Victorian spinster in Robbie, a disquieting mixture of quaintness, cowardice, and spite. On the surface he is the classic nineties aesthete, quietly flouting even the creed of nationalism that ushered in the Great War by painting the walls of his rooms on Half Moon Street a tone of weary gold: an evocation of France, of "abroad." Nor does he lack for pugnacity: indeed, in his role as Wilde's literary executor he sued so many bookstores and publishers that in *Who's Who* he lists litigation as one of his hobbies. Like Bosie, he enjoys winning battles. By the teens he has grown into a small, tidy, mustached man of middle age who wears a turquoise blue scarab ring and carries a jade cigarette holder. When he entertains friends at his flat—its decor "half Italian and half Oriental," according to Siegfried Sassoon, and featuring a devotional panel of Saint Sebastian and Saint Fabian over the mantelpiece—he does a black silk skullcap, serves Turkish delight, hands out boxes of Egyptian cigarettes. Yet *quietly*. This is the key to Robbie, the factor that distinguishes him from Bosie: the open warfare Wilde invited he makes certain always to avoid. When he takes the poet Wilfred Owen to dinner (and then home after dinner) he introduces him into a world of well-bred, refined homosexuals for whom Wilde's flamboyance is a quality at once to be admired and regretted, for though Wilde is their hero, nonetheless his breaking of the rules—it cannot be denied—has made life more difficult for them. Much better to have one's say slyly, even anonymously, and without pointing any fingers.

Robbie's diligence, the earnestness with which he undertakes his labors on Wilde's behalf, suggests the degree to which he embodies that very work ethic against which Wilde, in his witty defenses of idleness, strove to rebel. For Wilde was bad: he fouled the sheets of decent hotels, went into debt, drank. Robbie, on the other hand, conducted all his affairs—even his amorous ones—with tact. Had Wilde chosen him instead of Bosie, he might have grown into an honored old man of letters, with his sons at his knee, his wife at his side, his "companion" quiet in the background. Instead of which Wilde chose Bosie—pouting, spendthrift, malicious Bosie—and died a bankrupt.

On December 1, 1908, the eighth anniversary of Wilde's death, a dinner was held in Robert Ross's honor at the Ritz Hotel in London. The purpose of this dinner was twofold: first, to announce the publication of the final two volumes of Wilde's collected works (which Robbie had midwifed); second, to celebrate the emergence of the Wilde estate into solvency (which Robbie had negotiated). One hundred sixty people—among them Somerset Maugham, the Duchess of Sutherland, and Wilde's two sons, Cyril and Vyvyan—attended. Not Bosie, however. He declined his invitation, writing that in his view the dinner was "absurd."

After Frank Harris and H. G. Wells, among others, had toasted Robbie, he himself stepped up to the dais, where he described all that he had had to undergo while resurrecting Wilde's reputation. Then—in ironic reference to himself—he quoted a fragment from an eighteenth-century poem:

I hate the man who builds his name
On the ruins of another's fame.

He could just as easily have been talking about Bosie. Though probably he would have sued anyone who dared link this couplet with his career, nonetheless Bosie must have recognized the degree to which his fate was becoming yoked to that of his dead lover. For Wilde's resurgence threatened not merely his campaign against vice, but his very identity, his new idea of himself as a reformed libertine. More and more it must have been evident to him that his success would actually require Robbie's failure, and with it the preservation of Wilde's image as an unregenerate sodomite.

They are now more intimate, Bosie and Oscar, even than in the days when they scandalized London society by taking rent boys out to dinner at the Savoy. The object of the game is Robbie's ruin, which Bosie begins to seek aggressively. In letters, he threatens to horsewhip Robbie: "You have corrupted hundreds of boys and young men in your life, and have gone on doing it right up to the present time." His intention seems to be to goad Robbie into initiating an action against him, as once his own father, goaded by Bosie, goaded Wilde. Yet Robbie refuses to answer, even when Bosie writes to the prime minister demanding that Robbie be fired from his post as assessor of picture valuations to the Board of Trade (and promising to let off a stink if Mr. Asquith continues to receive "this horrible man" in his house). Later he sends another letter, "nailing" Robbie, to two judges, the recorder of London, the prime minister, the public prosecutor, Mr. Basil Thompson of Scotland Yard, the publisher John Lane, Sir George Lewis, and the master of St. Paul's School (as once he promised to mail his defense of homosexuality to every judge, lawyer, and legislator in England), and makes sure that Robbie is informed of the fact. Already T.W.H. Crosland, his coeditor at *The Academy*, has labeled Robbie's efforts to resuscitate "the maligned and greatly suffering Wilde" merely "one dirty Sodomite bestowing white-wash upon another." Now he makes his point plain: "If these letters do not contain the truth about you, there can be little question that you would have taken a certain and obvious legal remedy."

Matters come to a head for Bosie in the spring of 1913, with a spate of lawsuits. On April 18 he initiates a libel action against Arthur Ransome before the High Court. Then on April 24 Colonel Custance initiates a libel action against Bosie before a Magistrate's Court. (At that time, in that place, libel was a criminal, not a civil, offense.) Then in early May, Bosie has to go to the Chancery Court to argue with his father-in-law over the matter of Raymond's custody.

Colonel Custance's was the only lawsuit Bosie ever backed off from; it was also the only lawsuit in which his outrage can be construed as being even remotely justified. After all, Custance really had written to Olive, "The moment he (Bosie) takes the boy away all payments to you cease."

At the Chancery Court, Bosie was granted custody of his son for two fifths—and Colonel Custance for three fifths—of Raymond's vacation time; Bosie was told to pay the boy's tuition.

The Dark Grey Man

One evening a few weeks after his last conversation with Anthony, Christopher is standing near the magazine rack at A Different Light, thumbing through a copy of *The Advocate.* Every evening, now, he comes here, to this place where his great love was born, and waits patiently. For if he keeps faith, he believes, and if he shows his faith by returning here, piously, every night, then soon enough Anthony will feel its radiance, and come through the door. Perhaps he won't realize why he's coming through the door, perhaps he'll think he's here just to look at magazines, or buy a book, or hear a lecture. But Christopher will know.

If you saw Christopher today, you might not recognize him as the boy who was waiting at Café Flore a few weeks earlier. This is mostly because of his hair: last week he got a buzzcut. Tonight he's wearing a black T-shirt, combat boots, and a fatigue jacket, an outfit that worries some members of the bookstore staff, who fear he might be packing artillery in the bulging pockets of his pants. Not that they need be concerned: in fact, Christopher poses no danger to anyone but himself. If you looked inside the sleeve of his T-shirt you would find, on his right biceps, a healing tattoo (his first), an old-fashioned heart of the sort that sailors used to favor, except that instead of saying "Mother," the ribbon that bisects it says "Anthony."

Anthony. No one else is allowed to see the tattoo. Even the men Christopher sometimes permits to pick him up and take him home are not permitted to take off his T-shirt, for if they did, then they would see it, and the spell would be broken; Anthony would never come to his senses; he would never come home. Yet if the tattoo remains secret—somehow Christopher knows this—then he *will* come, drawn as if by a talisman, if not tonight then tomorrow, if not tomorrow then next week. Nor will Christopher ever have to admit that he lied at Café Flore, for by then, if he plays his cards right, the lie will have come true. More and more, people are doing it, he's heard. *Bareback*, they call it. *No glove. Skin to skin.*

At the moment, next to where Christopher is browsing, there stands a bearded man with a beer gut, alternately glancing at the pictures in the latest issue of *Bound & Gagged*, giving Christopher the eye, and attending to the back of the store, where a lecture has started—nothing as exciting as that mobbed reading at which Christopher met Anthony (Dennis Cooper, the dark lord of American gay literature); no, this is just another Dead White Male, or nearly. At least eighty. At present he's standing before the lectern and two dozen folding chairs, of which two thirds are empty. On and on he drones, his coughy voice no match for the claque of strong-lunged young lesbians who have just started a conversation about Jodie Foster near the cash register. Their oblivious disregard offends one of the listeners, who turns, glowers, says, "Will you please be quiet, girls?" Christopher starts. It's the counselor! For a nanosecond their eyes meet; the counselor's lips contort. Then he returns his attention to the lecturer.

By now the bearded man has taken his copy of *Bound & Gagged* to the cash register and is paying for it. Should he follow him? Christopher wonders. After all, older guys are more likely to have it; if he does enough of them, it'll be a sure thing . . . only this one looks like he might be psycho. He offers a last glance of entreaty, then leaves. Putting down *The Advocate*, Christopher listens for a moment to the speaker. He explains that he is here to eulogize a friend of his, a poet who died of AIDS sometime back in the dark ages. "The vivid influence of Cavafy," the old man says about the poet, and points to a poster set up on an easel behind the lectern: two skinny boys with golden hair, posed before a severe arrangement of cactuses. "As Roger used to put it, if only for the sake of the forty-seven people in the world who still read poetry," he goes on, and suddenly Christopher recognizes—the idea rather floors him—that *he*, the old man, is one of the boys in the poster. (The other must be the poet.) And what a mind-blowing idea that is! To grow, to grow old . . . (*Not if I can help it!*)

The audience, what little there is of it, is becoming restless. The old man's voice is monotonous and harsh. He is a bore. A fat, weary-looking youth gets up to leave. The bag lady who comes to all these readings, to sit alone in a corner chair amid her shreds of blanket, ceaselessly opening and closing the top of a plastic water bottle, starts humming to herself. Again the counselor turns, levels a glance at Christopher that makes him smile.

Gravy train, Christopher thinks.

"What Henry James called 'the air-blown grain' . . . Byron in Thessalonica . . . The muse of history." History! Well, Christopher has *really* had it now. For he hates history, which for him means his high school teacher, Mrs. Helfgott, chattering nasally about the War Between the States. Earlier, when the lesbians were being so rude, he felt sorry for the old man. But now, by invoking history's muse, he has proven himself merely to be another dumbass fart. Part of the status quo. What good will history do us in nuclear winter? Christopher thinks as the lecture ends, and a thin runnel of applause rises from the folding chairs, out of which most of the few listeners immediately bolt. As for the bag lady, she opens her water bottle and closes it, opens her water bottle and closes it. Hums.

"Does anyone have any questions?"

Silence. The counselor raises his hand.

"Yes, John?"

"Professor McMaster, forgive me if this sounds gossipy—"

"The best kind of question. Go on."

"Thank you. Well, when I was a graduate student at Berkeley I remember a rumor went around that Roger Hinton—"

"Many rumors have circulated about Roger, most of them true."

"Very likely. Anyway, according to this rumor, when he was on leave from the Marine Corps near the end of the Second World War, he went to Brighton to seduce Lord Alfred Douglas, so that he could say he'd slept with someone who'd slept with Oscar Wilde."

A low murmur of surprise now rises from the hinterlands of the bookstore. Indeed, such is the magnetism of Wilde's name that even the lesbians cease talking and turn toward the lectern.

"Ah yes," the old man says. "Unfortunately, that one I've never been able to corroborate. There is evidence that Roger was in England in 1944, the year before Douglas died. There's even evidence that he went to Brighton. Beyond that, though, I haven't been able to prove anything except—you see, Roger learned early on that the best way to keep people interested in him was to keep them guessing. So whenever anyone asked him about that particular rumor—or any rumor—he'd make a point of sort of dancing around the question without actually answering it, just the sort of maneuver our political leaders have become so adept at lately. Still, if one is, as I am, a literary critic—which amounts, in essence, to being a snoop—then it's hard to resist the impulse to dig around in the poetry for clues, even though, as we all know, the purpose of poetry is never merely to render up autobiographical ore. Perhaps, John, you will recall an odd little ballad of Roger's called 'The Dark Grey Man.'"

The counselor (John) smiles at the name, recites: " 'I remember him treading dark water, / The dark-souled, dark grey man.' "

"Very good, very good. Yes, it's a puzzle, that one. For years I couldn't work it out, which surprised me, because as we all know, Roger's poetry is usually fairly *un*opaque—at least by design. He used to say that he was a novelist manqué. And yet that poem always struck me as being, in certain ways—well, very *unlike* the rest of his work. Intentionally obscurist. I always thought of it as a puzzle or riddle for which you had to find the key . . . and then one day, while I was researching my biography, I happened upon an extraordinary fact." From the lectern he picks up his book. "According to Rupert Hart-Davis in his biography of Bosie, the name Douglas derives from the Gaelic *dubh glas*, and means 'dark water' . . . which Walter Scott rendered in *The Abbot* as 'dark grey.' In that novel an eighteenth-century Douglas, a warrior, is 'the Dark-Grey man.' "

The old man clears his throat; quotes: " 'As if fishing for Neptune's daughter / In the dark grey, roiling water, / Or perhaps he'd already caught her, / That dark-souled, dark grey man.'

"Well, and what, after all, is the most obvious synonym for 'roiling'?"

John raises his hand. "You," the old man says—suddenly a professor again, as John is suddenly a student.

"Wild," John says.

"Wild. Exactly. Exactly."

He smiles. The bag lady hums.

Campden Hill, or the Abyss

Now we enter into what is perhaps the most difficult period in Bosie's life to make out. The problem is not lack of information. On the contrary, documents abound, too many of them: police reports, trial transcripts, lurid coverage in the tabloid press. (Excessive paper is a side effect of the litigious life.) These documents ensnare and obfuscate, they are a jungle of innuendo and error. Under their canopy details meld: one forgets at which trial Freddie Smith, Robbie Ross's erstwhile thespian lover, admitted to wearing powder and paint not only on stage, but in church. (And is Freddie Smith in any way related to F. E. Smith? No, *he* was Robbie's counsel . . . though only in the first of the trials.)

The sheer quantity of actions in which Bosie was involved means that even *he* has difficulty keeping them in order, with the result that when he is arrested upon his arrival at Folkestone in 1914 (for the last few months he had been hiding out in France) he has no idea on which warrant he is being charged: is it Colonel Custance's bench warrant, revived after Bosie wrote a letter to King George V complaining of the "foul way" he was being treated by his father-in-law? No, that one appears to have escaped the officer's attention. Is it a warrant left over from Robbie's earlier action against Crosland, then, the one in which he asserted that Crosland, "being concerned with Lord Alfred Douglas, did, on September 17, 1913, and on diverse other dates between September 17 and February 14 last, unlawfully and wickedly conspire, combine, confederate, and agree together, and with diverse other persons unknown, unlawfully, falsely, and corruptly to charge Robert Baldwin Ross with having committed certain acts with one Charles Garratt?" No, that case Robbie has already lost.

Instead the warrant turns out to be new, issued by Robbie, and accusing Bosie of "falsely and maliciously publishing a defamatory libel" about him. Bosie only finds this out when he gets to London, though; already his cousin Sholto Douglas, along with an Anglican parson called Mills, is standing in the courtroom, waiting to bail him out. But hold on! At the last minute, Sir George Lewis stalks in dramatically from the wings, declaring that as long as a warrant still exists for Bosie's arrest regarding "certain other charges of which he has been convicted"—charges involving a gentleman who just happens to be another client of his, Colonel Frederic Hambledon Custance—bail cannot be granted! So Bosie is shipped off to jail for five days, an experience no doubt intended to provoke second thoughts in him but from which he emerges more rather than less determined to ruin Robbie.

Provocation is seduction. In the atmosphere of panic that took hold just before the Great War, even Bosie's most ludicrous delusions take on the heft of reality. Reviewing the coverage, one begins to believe that there actually was a sodomitical conspiracy afoot, the intention of which was to depose the king of England and put Robert Ross—as heir to dear dead Oscar—onto the throne. Nor do Bosie's ravings about Robbie—whom he calls "the High Priest of all the sodomites of London"—lack their equivalent in public life. More and more, the language of infection (and disinfection) seeps into the national discourse. Thus it is reported that German agents provocateurs have begun circulating among the healthy ranks of the military, handing out venereal diseases like candy. (According to the article, these Germans are sexual kamikazes, motivated by duty instead of lust—which elides the trickier question of why Albion's sons are so susceptible to their charms.) Foreigners are "parasites who live on the blood of fighting men." War is "the sovereign disinfectant," Robbie's friend Edmund Gosse writes, "its red stream of blood . . . the Condy's fluid that cleans out the stagnant pools and clotted channels of the intellect." A few years later, in Wormwood Scrubs prison for libeling Churchill, Bosie himself declares in verse:

The leprous spawn of scattered Israel
Spreads its contagion in your English blood . . .

Of course, he was playing to the gallery here, to that philistine majority from whose ranks jurymen were selected, and for whom homosexuality, artistic talent, and pacifism necessarily went hand in hand with pro-Hun and pro-Jewish sentiment (and possibly espionage). For the downside of Bosie's anti-Oscar stance is that it puts him in the awkward position of having to rely for support upon a "public" toward which, as a snob and an aristocrat, he feels only contempt. This was where Crosland became invaluable. Crosland—it cannot be denied—had a certain prescient genius; he could smell the xenophobic terror of the middle classes, to which war had not yet given a voice. He also understood that above all else, a prophet must be a good public speaker, someone who can transform inchoate rage into eloquent diatribe. And who better to play the part of prophet than Bosie? Because he is not *of* them, then maybe he can win them, convince them that far from Oscar Wilde's boy, he is their savior, sent from heaven to crusade against sin, sodomy, socialism, Judaism, and all foreigners who have chosen to make their home in England.

By now Bosie is forty-three years old. He is no longer beautiful. The fate of men who resemble Renaissance seraphim in their twenties is that as they age their handsomeness does not mature. Thus Bosie, in a photograph taken of him in 1919, looks exactly the same as Bosie in a photograph taken in the 1890s—same glossy dark blond hair, same high cheekbones and wide eyes, same slim torso—except that (how else to put it?) he is no longer young. Instead of weathering his features, time has let

Bosie rot, leaving us with this circus spectacle, the prematurely elderly child.

Whenever he writes, odors rise from the page. His hatred—his "lack of imagination"—is boundless. For example, one day in 1913 he reads in the *Reynolds* newspaper that a male prostitute called Charles Garratt has been arrested upon leaving the flat of one Christopher Millard. Millard, as Bosie well knows, is Robbie Ross's secretary, and Wilde's bibliographer; might the boy, then, count Robbie among his clients too? (Very likely; from experience Bosie knows the sodomite's habit of trading boys like recipes.) There is no time to lose, and promptly he sends a solicitor to speak to Garratt, who admits that he knows of Robbie but refuses to say more until he is let free. Next Crosland visits Garratt's mother, a charwoman in Lincolnshire, stands her a drink at a pub, and says that if she speaks up, the men who corrupted her son will be punished. She is alarmed, and takes him to meet her daughter, a Mrs. Flude, to whom he explains that recently two men named Millard and Ross got her brother so drunk that he passed out, only to awaken the next morning dressed as a woman and smelling of perfume. All of this is invention—as Garratt will later testify, he's never even met Ross—which does nothing to stop the fantasy from taking a fierce hold on the national imagination. For such a scenario—the boy seduced, drugged, and quite literally emasculated—speaks to the very fear that Crosland wants to exploit: the fear of foreignness, contamination, contagion. No doubt the Germans are behind it all . . . and haven't we heard plenty already about the sorts of things that go on in Berlin?

Provocation is seduction. When Robbie Ross, in 1914, finally sued Bosie for criminal libel, he seemed at last to be taking some action; in fact he was merely submitting to a prostitute's wiles. "Come on," Bosie had beckoned—for years—"climb into this warm, close bed." So at last Robbie climbed into that warm, close bed, as Oscar had; as Gerald and Wellington had. And Bosie pounced.

As soon as he's released from jail, he sets about seeking evidence with which to condemn Robbie. The stakes in the game are high. Given his record, if Bosie loses, he will probably go to prison. On the other hand, if he wins, then Robbie will probably be tried on charges of "gross indecency," found guilty, and sentenced, as Wilde was, to hard labor. A lurid spectacle, this: one spiteful queen attempting to use an unjust law to "out" (and thereby destroy) another. Nor are Robbie's own belligerent tendencies to be overlooked in the matter. For if he had simply ignored Bosie's threats, then very probably by his silence he would have done his enemy far greater damage than he did by providing him with the soapbox of a trial. After all, Bosie's diatribes in the gutter press posed no danger so far as Robbie's high-ranking friends were concerned. On the contrary, so greatly did his treatment by the police incense Margot Asquith, the prime minister's (lesbian) wife, that she went to Scotland Yard to have it out herself with the director of public prosecutions. Later, Edmund Gosse persuaded more than three hundred people, including Sir James Barrie, Thomas Hardy, H. G. Wells, and Bernard Shaw, to sign a testimonial to Robbie, which was presented to him along with a "purse" that he used to endow a scholarship "for *male* students only" at the Slade School of Art. None of this, needless to say, went down particularly well with Bosie, but then again it wasn't intended to.

Bosie's campaign to ruin Robbie begins deep in the past. He brings out the old scandal of the schoolboy called Alfred whom Robbie was supposed to have seduced in 1893; the problem here is that later Bosie had lured Alfred away from Robbie (and written him love letters). Then he tries to persuade Garratt (again) to testify that Robbie was one of his clients. Garratt refuses. Then he tries to dig up evidence to substantiate a rumor that three years earlier Robbie attended a New Year's Eve party at which men danced with other men. He fails. Finally he goes after Freddie Smith, Robbie's former boyfriend and putative secretary. Here he has more success. A fellow member of Freddie's dramatic society, Emma Rooker, agrees to state in court that she once saw Robbie embrace Freddie and call him "my darling," while the Reverend Andrew Bowring—the same pastor who had dismissed Freddie in his capacity as an acolyte after he was found to be wearing make-up and powder to church—expresses his grave doubts as to Freddie's qualifications for the position of secretary to "a man of literature." And that would have been it, the entirety of Bosie's plea of justification, had not, in his own words, a "miracle" occurred.

Having just returned from a fruitless trip to Guernsey and several other places where Robbie was supposed to have got up to no good, Bosie received a tip that during the years just after Wilde's death, while he was living in Campden Hill, Robbie had "victimized" sixteen-year-old

William Edwards, who subsequently went off to South Africa and died. *Go to Campden Hill*, a tipster told him, *go to a certain address and ask for Mr. Edwards. He will tell you what you need to know.* So Bosie went. His hope was to persuade the boy's father to testify against Robbie at his trial. But when he knocked at the door of the address given, he was told not only that no Mr. Edwards lived there, but that no Mr. Edwards had ever lived there.

At an utter loss, looking up and down a street lined by "at least 150 houses"—this was probably Campden Hill Road, near Holland Park, now one of London's most notorious cruising grounds—Bosie sent up a prayer to Saint Anthony of Padua (the patron saint of lost objects) and waited. It was then that a little boy strode up to him and asked him if he needed help. Bosie stated his dilemma; the little boy smiled and explained that all the numbers in the street had recently been changed. Then he took Bosie by the hand and led him to the right house.

"I firmly believe," Bosie wrote later, "that the child was an angel . . . He was a most beautiful little boy, and he had an angelic face and smile." Just as Bosie did.

When you go to heaven you can be what you like, and I intend to be a child.

At the trial Mr. Edwards testified that in 1908 his son William had come home wearing a shirt with the name "Ross" printed on its collar. His older son, a soldier, testified that after William's disappearance he had gone to a bar on Copthall Avenue in search of Robbie, who had tried to buy his silence and then, when he refused the bribe, threatened to accuse him of blackmail. (I am sorry to say that such a tactic sounds just like Robbie.) Emma Rooker testified, as did the Reverend Andrew Bowring, and Vyvyan Holland (his mother had changed their name), and Bosie. Robbie himself testified—not very well, apparently, for in his summing up the judge complained that his performance had been inadequate. "I waited and waited, but I waited in vain for any moral expression of horror at the practice of sodomitical vices . . . It was certainly not so emphatic a denial as you would expect from a man with no leprosy on him."

After three hours the foreman of the jury announced that it had failed to reach a verdict. The judge sent them back. The foreman returned with the same news. Later it was revealed that they were split eleven to one in favor of acquittal—yet the holdout refused to budge. In future ravings, Bosie would insist that this gentleman—who robbed him of complete victory—was a plant, a vassal of the nefarious Sir George Lewis.

Not long after, Robbie died. He did not live to be old. Bosie lived to be old.

A Link in a Chain

"You've got more books than the bookstore," Christopher says, slinging his backpack off his shoulder and sitting down on John's (the counselor's) sofa.

From across the room, where he's opening a bottle of wine, John looks at him cautiously. Is there reproach in Christopher's voice? he wonders, the reproach of youth, of a generation that disdains history? Or is *he* too much of a skeptic? Perhaps, he thinks, Christopher is expressing simple wonder. This is closer to the truth. The fact of the matter is that John's apartment—in which there are only books, buckling shelves full of books, books piled on either side of the sofa—somewhat intimidates Christopher. From near where he's sitting he picks one up, turns to the title page. *Real Presences*, he reads, *Is There Anything in What We Say?* He puts the book down as if it's bitten him, picks up another. *Roger Hinton: A Life*, by Jack McMaster. "Oh, the old guy who was lecturing," he says, glancing neutrally at the photograph on the back of the jacket. (It is the same photograph that was on the lectern.)

"Do you read much?" John asks, sitting down next to him, handing him a glass of red wine.

"I like to read."

"Who do you like?"

Who, not *what*. What embarrasses Christopher now is that he can't remember the names of any authors. It's as if the question itself has expunged them from his brain.

"Dennis Cooper," he says after a moment, grateful at least to have successfully grasped at something. "I heard him at A Different Light, too."

"Anyone else?"

"Those vampire books."

"Oh, Anne Rice? Yes, I like the early ones."

Slyly John throws an arm around the back of the sofa, behind Christopher's neck. It may be the very immorality of what he's doing—the fact that by inviting a client home he's breached both the written and unwritten ethics of his profession—that excites him tonight, even more than the simple miracle of having convinced Christopher to come to his apartment. For he's not used—has never been used—to attracting. Unlike Jack McMaster, for instance (and Roger, for that matter; and *Bosie*, for that matter), John was not good-looking as a boy. *They* had that ironic loveliness of the ephebe, that delicate beauty to which the imminence of manhood lends an erotic flush. For such a beauty there has always been, will always be, a market. John, on the other hand, was at twenty both geeky and spotty; all limbs; none of the parts seemed to fit.

The irony (he sees it clearly tonight) is that while Roger aged wretchedly—Jack too—he has, as it were, grown into his body. At thirty-seven, he is a handsome man.

Now, on the sofa, he puts down his wineglass; scoots closer to Christopher, who's gazing rather vacantly at the disarranged books, the groaning shelves. "As you may have surmised," he says, "I haven't always been a social worker."

"No?"

John shakes his head. "I used to be an English professor. Well, an *assistant* English professor. Jack—the fellow who gave the lecture—was my mentor. My teacher."

"Yeah?"

"I wrote my dissertation on Oscar Wilde."

"Oh, I know about him," says Christopher. "He was, like, the first faggot, right?"

"More or less."

"And that guy Jack—that teacher of yours—when you were his student, did he fuck you?"

The question rather takes John aback; it also arouses him.

"Well, yes, actually," he admits after a moment.

"So that means that if he fucked you, and that poet he was talking about fucked him, and what's his name—Oscar Wilde's boyfriend—fucked the poet, then if you fuck me tonight it'll be like I got fucked by the first faggot."

"I guess so," John says, laughing.

"Cool."

"You like the idea?"

"I like the idea of your fucking me," Christopher says, and looks John steadily in the eye. "Will you? I really need it."

John blushes. Suddenly Christopher is lunging at him, kissing him, kneading his erection.

"But I haven't got any condoms! I meant to buy some, only—"

"It's okay," Christopher whispers urgently, "it's O.K.—"

"I could run out and—"

"Feel in my back pocket."

John does. Slipping his hand inside, he paws Christopher's buttock for a moment, then withdraws a single condom in its tidy plastic wrapper.

"You think of everything."

"There's lube in my backpack."

"That I've got in the bathroom."

"So where do you want to do it? Here? In the bedroom?"

"Bedroom's more comfortable." And standing—how terrible and thrilling is this boy's eagerness—Christopher takes John's hand and yanks him to his feet.

A Stroll on the Beach

In his later years, Bosie makes it his habit, on sunny days, to take a morning walk along the sea. Bypassing all the rubbish in Brighton, the promenade and the tearooms and holiday camps, he heads south, to where the rocky beach is emptier. Taking off his shoes, he lets the cold water run over his feet, which churn up tiny whirlpools around them before collapsing into the dense, wet life of the rocks.

It is 1944. Springtime. Though he doesn't know it, in a little less than a year he will be dead. Yet he is not a dying man. Instead he is simply an old man, one of hundreds who stroll each morning along the promenade and the beach of this seaside town, this town of pensioners. Most of his neighbors know perfectly well who he is. "The one who ruined Wilde," they say; or else, "The one Wilde ruined." Such whispering and staring, even when overtly hostile, he accepts more placidly today than he might have in the past, letting it roll over his ego as gently as the water now rolling over his feet. For time has diminished the rage that once coruscated his eyes and corroded his hours. It's not that anything has changed in the world; the change was in his soul. This is why he can regard this war—the second one—with so much more composure than he did its predecessor. Cynicism is an old man's prerogative. *You should have listened to me*, he can say; *the Hun must be squelched utterly, else he will re-emerge, time and again, with greater awfulness.* Indeed, as of today only a single blemish clouds Bosie's conscience, and that is the fact that the modern German's loathing of the Jews has rendered the anti-Semitism of Bosie's earlier poetry not only unfashionable but faintly scandalous. Without disclaiming the greatness of *In Excelsis*, Bosie cannot help but regret such lines as

Your Few-kept politicians buy and sell
In markets redolent of Jewish mud . . .

Yet he was never one to shrink from unpopular positions.

A few weeks earlier Olive, who had been ill for several years, finally died. This was both a sorrow and a relief for Bosie. True, they had not lived together for decades; still, with the coming of war their once acrimonious relations had at least resolved themselves into a state of cease-fire that did not disallow the possibility of friendship. Often they dined or took tea together—sometimes in Bosie's modest ground-floor flat at St. Ann's Court, more often at Olive's much grander digs at Viceroy Lodge, which looked onto the sea. For Colonel Custance's death had left Olive a rich woman—a fact that she sometimes lorded over her estranged husband, as for years he had lorded over her his self-proclaimed spiritual and poetic superiority. (No one admired Bosie's poetry more than he did; by the same token, he admired no one else's poetry—with the possible exception of Shakespeare's—more than his own.)

In Brighton, though, the tables were turned. Now it was Bosie who, as a consequence of his poverty, had to apply to Olive for money. She made him an allowance that she was not above occasionally threatening to suspend. No doubt the disparity in their circumstances—which, by keeping Bosie's income low, she could be certain to maintain—pleased his wife. In her will she left to her husband an opal necklace (rather ironic, considering his dislike of opals), all the money in her bank account, and an allowance of £500 per annum. (All this, however, went into receivership, as Bosie had never discharged an earlier bankruptcy.) To their son, Raymond, she left her flat at Viceroy Lodge, which did not prevent Bosie from moving in almost instantly upon her death. For a few months he lived there quite happily, until Raymond, who had for many years been an inmate at St. Andrew's Hospital, decided that he wanted to give "life outside" a try, and evicted his father. At the time Raymond was in his early forties—the same age that Bosie was when he took on Robbie Ross in court. In 1926 Raymond had been diagnosed as schizophrenic and admitted to an asylum for "electroconvulsive therapy and narcosis." (Not incidentally, that same year he had fallen in love with a grocer's daughter named Gladys Lacey, but his parents and grandparents had disapproved of the match, and kept him from marrying her.)

Let us now say that the morning of which I am writing—the morning when Bosie takes a walk along the beach—is the same morning on which Raymond is scheduled to arrive in Hove and displace his father. It is still early; Raymond's train won't pull in for hours. As Bosie strolls up and down the beach, I imagine that he is trying to suppress the rather petulant displeasure that Raymond's decision to come to Hove has provoked in him. After all, as he well knows, his son's release from the hospital where he has been living, on and off, for twenty years is—has to be looked at as—a good thing. It means that Raymond is getting well, with which Bosie has no argument. And yet must his getting well require turning his father onto the street? On the surface, at least, Raymond has been nothing but cordial to Bosie, has even vowed to give him an extra £300 per year as soon as Olive's will has gone through probate. Even so, it *does* seem hard. (All right. Let's just say it.) Bosie's weeks at Viceroy Lodge, under the capable management of Olive's maid Eileen, have been happy ones. There he has entertained, among others, his old friend Lord Tredegar and his wife, Olga, the former Princess Dolgorouki, as well as several members of the younger literary generation (by younger I mean those in their fifties), invited for elaborate teas featuring toast, scones, cream cakes, jam puffs, tarts, and other schoolboyish treats with which their middle-aged stomachs proved unable to cope. The juvenile character of these gatherings, though bewildering to Bosie's guests (after all, he was now in his seventies), delighted the host, who still looks upon his childhood years as the best of his life. His old friend Wellington, for instance, he often thinks about these nights, as he thinks about Alfred, the schoolboy he seduced away from Robbie Ross, and the boy at Oxford who blackmailed him, and the rent boys with whom, sometimes in Oscar's company and sometimes out of it, he was able to revive, for a moment, a lost dream of laddish camaraderie: *tremendous friends*. This is something he's realized only lately: when he was a wicked young man, what he was really after wasn't sex; it was those innocent attachments of boyhood to which sex—alas—only sometimes took him back. For though the route from childhood to manhood is a clear, straight path, to return, he has learned, one has to take back roads, stumble up rocky paths, try to make sense of deceptive and illegible signs. You rarely get where you want to be, and when you do, the magic place is never as you remembered.

Of course, Raymond is the worst wrong turn of all. Where his son is concerned Bosie cannot, no matter how hard he tries, shirk off the unpleasant suspicion that if the boy has grown into an ill and fragile man, it is largely Bosie's own fault. For Raymond was, in many ways, the most beloved of the many boys with whom he tried to recapture his lost adolescence. Even more than Wellington, *he* was Bosie's tremendous friend, especially during the summer when Raymond was thirteen, and Bosie—enraged by what he saw as the iniquity of a court determined to favor the claims of his vindictive father-in-law—picked him up at his school and without telling anyone spirited him to Scotland, which was outside the Chancery Court's jurisdiction. There he rented a house near the southern end of Loch Ness, and enrolled Raymond at the Benedictine Monastery and College of Fort Augustus. Every afternoon they went swimming, or fishing, or took exploratory gambols through forests in which generations of Douglases had roamed and hunted. For Bosie was Scottish, he was a Scottish laird, and Raymond—though half Custance—needed to be reminded that in his veins there ran also the blood of the dark grey man.

His point may have been to persuade Raymond that the trip amounted to a Boys' Adventure, something out of Robert Louis Stevenson, and not a traumatic kidnapping from which Raymond would never recover. Nor, apparently, did Bosie fail in this objective. Indeed, Raymond's credulous acceptance of his father's fantasy was the very thing that would do them both in.

One day, after barely a term at his new school, Raymond went fishing in Loch Ness and never came back. Fearing that he had drowned, for almost a week, day and night, his father and the monks trawled the lake's waters. Then, rather out of the blue, Bosie received a telegram from Olive informing him that Raymond was safely back at Weston, his grandfather's estate. It seems that Colonel Custance, perhaps in collusion with George Lewis, had set up a secret means of communication with the boy, whom he had then enticed to embark on an even grander adventure than the one on which his father had taken him. It would work like this: Raymond, on the pretense of wanting to fish, would take a boat and row to the opposite side of Loch Ness. There a private detective would be waiting to carry him away in a car. All very thrilling, especially the car, which in 1915 must really have seemed, to an impressionable boy, the pièce de résistance, with its promise of speed and stealth and spy novel glamour. The detective drove Raymond across the border into England, where his mother and grandfather met him. Only once he was safely ensconced again did Olive inform Bosie of what had happened. Bosie, who had had to endure almost a week of tormented uncertainty, could not forgive her for what she had put him through. Nor could he forgive Raymond, of whom he washed his hands; he would never again have anything to do with his treacherous son, he vowed—forgetting, perhaps, that the treacherous son was at the time only thirteen years old.

The tide is running out. Turning around, again like a child, Bosie walks backward, as if fitting his feet into his own footsteps, so as not to leave a trace of having made a return journey, so as to suggest that this morning he walked, and walked, and then simply disappeared.

An instant later he notices that he's not alone.

He raises his eyebrows. Not far off, shoes in his hand, stands a soldier. An unfamiliar uniform . . . Canadian, perhaps? American? From where he hovers at the water's edge, the soldier gazes out at the sea in a way that seems to Bosie both provocative and touchingly naive. For though he is old now, he was once beautiful, and so has some experience of the tactics to which nervous admirers resort in order to avoid being caught out in their curiosity.

Stopping, for the moment, Bosie watches the soldier. What does he want? Is he here by chance? Very unlikely. The soldier's presence amuses him, if for no other reason than that it is exemplary of something that has become, in recent years, so commonplace. He never expected to grow into a monument, a human equivalent of Trafalgar Square, or the Tomb of the Unknown Soldier. Yet this, as a consequence of Wilde's ever increasing fame (Robbie did a good job, in the end), has turned out to be his fate. More and more young men come to Hove for one reason only: to seek him out; to gaze at him. On those rare occasions when they muster the courage to approach him, he is never less than perfectly polite. Instead he listens quietly, smiling, as they make their elegant speeches.

If they're good-looking, he invites them home for tea, and sometimes to bed.

Now the soldier turns; approaches. Bosie straightens his back. He is, he knows, no longer attractive. Not that it isn't possible for an old man to be beautiful. Toscanini, for instance, is a beautiful old man. In his case, age preserved the thick hair, the athletic arms and limbs. In Bosie's, only the worst features seem to have emerged unscathed from the holocaust of time—the crooked mouth, the eyes with their startled rabbit's look.

Not that it matters. He has something else. In the end, Wilde gave Bosie more than he bargained for.

I hate the man who builds his name
On the ruins of another's fame.

"Mr. Douglas?"

Yes, he *is* American. Otherwise he'd have called him Lord Alfred.

"Yes?"

"I hope I'm not bothering you. I—" Sheepishly the soldier puts down his shoes, takes off his hat. His beauty startles Bosie in that it is exactly the same sort of beauty he himself possessed once.

"Yes?"

"My name is Roger Hinton. Private Roger Hinton, of the United States Marine Corps. And I just wanted to say . . . I'm a poet, and a great admirer of your work. I'm here on leave. Especially *In Excelsis* . . . Such a marvelous poem!"

Bosie allows his lips to turn up in a slight smile. What rot! he thinks. Later, when they're at Olive's flat, he'll tease the boy, try to taunt him into admitting that he's never even read *In Excelsis*. Not that it matters. Once it would have. Once he would have hoped that when young men stared at him in admiration, they'd be thinking, "Douglas at Wormswood Scrubs," not "Wilde at Reading Gaol."

"So you're a poet. How interesting. Do you write sonnets?"

"I've written a few."

"Shakespearean, or—"

"No, Petrarchan, like yours."

"What a charming coincidence, to meet a young sonneteer on the beach. And tell me, Mr. Hinson, will you be sojourning long in Hove?"

"Hinton. Only forty-eight hours. As I said, I'm on leave."

"You must take tea with me. I'm afraid it will have to be today. This evening my son arrives. If that's possible for you . . . I imagine your schedule—"

"No, I'm utterly free." (The *utterly* takes Bosie aback. Perhaps the soldier really *is* a poet.) "I don't know anyone in Hove, or Brighton, for that matter. I've only come here to see you."

"How charming. And which way are you heading, if I might ask?"

"Whichever way you are, Mr. Douglas."

"Please call me Bosie."

The young man blushes. "Bosie. And you must call me Roger."

"Very well, then. Roger."

Together they begin walking back, toward the promenade.

Sabotage

Middle of the night. While John snores in bed, Christopher, in his black T-shirt, switches on the light; fumbles in the bathroom with his backpack. So far only once, but if he plays his cards right he'll be able to get at least two more out of him before they part . . . After all, even though the guy's old, he's horny; has no trouble keeping it up, unlike some of those other sorry bastards. Opening the backpack (the fact that he is stoned—John gave him some good pot—makes the operation all the harder to perform), he extracts a fresh box of condoms, still sealed in plastic, which he tries (and fails) to tear open with his thumbnail. Finally he bites into the box; the plastic gives; little tooth marks puncture the cardboard. Tearing it open, he extracts the condoms, strung together like Christmas lights, divided by little lines of perforation. He rips until one comes loose. Dropping the others to the ground, he picks up the condom, holds it to the light. How innocent it looks, all rolled and thickened like his grandmother's aproned stomach, not the sort of thing you would expect to be capable (if you didn't already know) of smothering or saving a life! Yet there it is. The condom, his friend, his enemy . . . Anthony will die and Christopher will live. (*Not if I can help it.*) Anthony will die and Christopher will die. And now, from his backpack, he extracts a box of pins; takes one out; stabs the condom fleetly through its heart. Metal emerges out the other side. Withdrawing the pin, he holds the condom a second time to the light. Yes, there it is (though too tiny for any but a trained eye to recognize). That's the beauty of it. He will slip it into the pocket of his T-shirt now, wake John, and compel him to further acts of lust; John will not resist. Then without even being aware of it he'll do his duty to Christopher, the ironic duty of his profession, and never guess that the powdered sheath on which he is staking all the future bears beside its guarantee the harrowed and minute signature of the saboteur.

Bosie to Olive, from Loch Ness (1915): "Raymond is well and happy. He loves Scotland . . . He has given me the mumps and I have had it for the last 5 days."

Sources Consulted

Maureen Borland, *Wilde's Devoted Friend: A Life of Robert Ross*, Oxford, 1990.

Lord Alfred Douglas, *Oscar Wilde and Myself*, London, 1914. *The Complete Poems of Lord Alfred Douglas*, London, 1928. *The Autobiography of Lord Alfred Douglas*, London, 1929. *My Friendship with Oscar Wilde*, London, 1932.

Without Apology, 1938.

Oscar Wilde, A Summing-Up, 1938.

Richard Ellmann, *Oscar Wilde*, London, 1987.

Rupert Croft-Cooke, *Bosie: Lord Alfred Douglas, His Friends and Enemies*, New York, 1963.

Philip Hoare, *Wilde's Last Stand*, London, 1997.

H. Montgomery Hyde, *Lord Alfred Douglas*, London, 1984.

Douglas Murray, *Bosie: A Biography of Lord Alfred Douglas*, London, 2000.

The Marquess of Queensberry and Percy Colson, *Oscar Wilde and the Black Douglas*, London, 1949.

Timothy d'Arch Smith, *Love in Earnest*, London, 1970.

Route 80

B Movie

Josh and I are leaving each other. These last few weeks we've spent together, at "our" house, trying to see what, if anything, we could salvage from five sometimes good years. At first things went badly; then we started gardening. Josh has always been an avid gardener, while I couldn't tell a lily from a rose. How roughly my vacant acknowledgments of his work rubbed up against all the effort he put in, all those springs and summers of labor and delicacy! And did my not caring about the garden mean that I didn't care about him? After he left, naturally, the flowers turned to weeds.

The therapists in our heads told us that this was something we could do together, a way beyond talking (which meant, for us, fighting), like the trip my mother and father took to watch the sea elephants mate. Kneeling in the dirt, holding the querulous little buds in their nursery six-packs, there was another language for us to speak with each other, as virgin as the leafy basil plants we patted into the soil. Our old, gnarled, tortuous relations were rude and hideous weeds we ripped out by the roots.

I made up dramas as I planted, horticultural B movies in which I was the hero defending the valiant rose from the villainous weed. Or I was the valiant rose, and Josh the villainous weed, and the hero was someone I was hoping to meet someday. Or I was the villainous weed.

Digging, I came upon little plastic stakes from past seasons, buried deep, unbiodegraded, bearing photographs and descriptions of annuals Josh had planted in more innocent, if not happier, times, and which had long since passed into compost.

* * *

There is the top of a wedding cake in our freezer. It is frosted white, and covered with white, orange, and peach-colored frosting roses. It was left there by the young newlyweds who sublet the house when Josh and I, unable to decide who should stay and who should go, both went. Jenny and Brian are saving this wedding cake to eat on their first anniversary, which is apparently a tradition for good luck. When I came back, they moved into an apartment where the freezer was too small; the cake stayed behind.

There is a road, too. I don't like roads, the way they run through everywhere on the way to somewhere else. The road is where we lose dogs and children, the way we take when we leave each other.

This road, in my mind at least, is Route 80. Josh and I used to say that our lives and destinies were strung out along Route 80, which runs from New York, where we lived for years, through New Jersey, where he grew up, through the town where he went to school, and on to San Francisco, where I grew up. Even though our house is nowhere near Route 80—and perhaps this was the first mistake—it is Route 80 I imagine when I imagine the wedding cake, like a pie in the face, being thrown.

I was driving down the highway, this long and painfully lovely July day, when I saw the orange lilies bursting from their green sheaths. Until two weeks ago, when I finally asked and Josh told me, I wouldn't have noticed them, and I certainly wouldn't have known they were lilies. Now I know not only lily, but fuchsia, alyssum, nicotiana, dahlia, marigold. Basil needs sun, impatiens loves shade. At night I read tulip catalogues, color by color, easing gradually toward the blackest of them all, Queen of the Night.

All of this I have finally let Josh teach me—but (of course, of course) too late.

The lilies shut their petals, at dusk, over the road. And don't they become frosting flowers, freezer annuals, with their sly, false promise of good luck? I can feel them smearing under the wheels, sugar and butter, a white streak like guano where a bridegroom is racing away from his bride.

With my parents, going to watch the sea elephants became a tradition. Josh and I joined them once. The huge males shimmied along the rocks toward their waiting harems, and the hands of my parents, in spite of all that had passed between them, reached toward each other like flowers reaching toward the sun. My parents' hands were brown; there was dirt under their nails.

Who can claim that our love does not endure, less like flowers than like the little stakes with the photographs of flowers, stubborn beneath the soil?

Perennial.

Full Disclosure (*A Decade Later*)

Mark told me this story:

Years ago, he loved a cellist whom we shall call Gary. Gary loved Mark a lot, but his cello more. This was because Gary's mother had sold her own mother's wedding ring to buy him the cello. Not that she had to; she and her husband were affluent, and could easily have afforded it. No, she wanted the gift to connote sacrifice. She wanted Gary, every time he touched his bow to the strings, to know that for his sake his mother had given up something that she loved.

I understand this woman.

"Fostering dependency," the therapists call what she did, and according to them it is a real no-no. Yet it is exactly what I, too, have done. And at the heart of the matter is the fear of being alone, which makes Gary's mother the scariest person I know. So, a reasonable voice inquires, why shouldn't a child want to get away from someone so scary?

I remember another story, about my ex-boyfriend, whose name really was Gary. The ingredients in this story were: a wedding cake in the middle of the road (required by National Public Radio, which had asked a lot of writers to write stories on this theme); some elephant seals; and the little stakes with photographs of flowers on them that turn up each spring when, with shovel or spade, one reopens the soil. In that story, I called Gary Josh.

Here is the coincidence: the real Gary, the cellist, is named Josh.

So this is not a story at all, but a *tableau vivant:* a garden party, a cocktail party, at which the guests are me, Mark, Gary, Josh, the mother, and all of our fictive equivalents. Oh, and the cellist hired to provide the entertainment. Her face is shrouded. We shall call her Need. And the little air she plays, the little phrase, if we could translate music into words, would enter our ears as "Never leave me, never leave me, never leave me."

Black Box

In the late 1980s, in New York, if a homosexual man died of anything other than AIDS, people generally reacted with skepticism. Especially if the officially listed cause of death was a disease with which AIDS might have been complicit—cancer, pneumonia, some mysterious infection of the heart—it would be taken for granted that the deceased's loved ones were trying to protect his reputation, or their own.

More troubling still were those occasions when the cause of death was one to which AIDS, even in the most extreme scenario, could not be linked. This was considered bad plotting—as if in a novel a character at whose head a specific piece of ammunition, for pages, had been steadily aimed, were to be killed not by his expected assassin, but by a stray bullet, fired from a direction in which no one would have thought of looking.

Such was the case with Ralph Davenport, the noted interior designer, who had the misfortune of being one of the passengers on that London-bound plane that blew up off the coast of Newfoundland one balmy summer evening in 1988. No one felt the irony of his death more acutely than Bob Bookman, with whom he had lived for the past fifteen years. This was because the afternoon before Ralph had boarded the ill-fated Flight 20, he and Bob had had a fight over his refusal to get an HIV test. Generally speaking, in those years, men like Bob, who could count their sexual partners on two hands, were eager to get tested; Bob had been tested four times. Men like Ralph, on the other hand, whose sexual histories had been more volatile, avoided the test, arguing that it would do them no good whatsoever. As Ralph saw it, to learn that he was definitely HIV-positive (as opposed to merely *probably* HIV-positive) would be to let go the one slender reed of hope on which his sanity depended. Better to live in a cloud of unknowing, he believed, than submit to the dread of certainty. To which Bob replied, "But what if you're negative? I am."

"It wouldn't change my life."

"You could breathe a sigh of relief."

Ralph shook his head. "The waiting would kill me faster than any virus," he said, then zipped up his Travelpro, kissed Bob on the cheek, and went off to die. For days, weeks after that, fishing boats trawled the coastline over which his plane—a cursor blinking across the screen of night—had blossomed into a fireball, a parrot tulip, before raining down in pieces. They were looking for bodies. They were looking for the black box.

Bob was a literary man. With his name, what choice did he have? Small-boned and bespectacled, he looked good in the sort of interiors that were Ralph's specialty: cluttered, English-y spaces, enlivened by mad fabric mixes, chintz with checks, brocade with hot pink Indian sari silk. Not to mention, of course, the books. Books—in corners, on the staircase, piled next to sofas as an alternative to side tables (sometimes he even put lamps on them)—were Ralph's decorative calling card. He used to joke that he had chosen Bob only because Bob, with his argyle sweaters and bow ties, left just the right authenticating imprint on the pair of leather library chairs in their living room. No one accessorized these interiors more perfectly than Bob.

It was a look to which Ralph's clients, few of whom were readers, took avidly. Under his aegis, they bought old books from a dealer who sold them by the yard, and told their maids to leave the chair cushions attractively rumpled: the idea was to create the illusion of a space where people *thought*. Ralph, who read only design magazines, profited from his vision, which had gotten him twice onto the cover of *Architectural Digest*. Toward the end he was just starting to win the corporate commissions that are the bread and butter of any serious design firm; the night he died he was on his way to England to buy furniture for a downtown advertising agency that wanted to "soften its image." Then the plane went down. That was how Ralph's sister, Kitty, put it when she called. "A plane went down near Newfoundland," she said. "I'm only a little worried because I know Ralphie was planning a trip to London sometime soon. Make me feel better and tell me he didn't go today."

But of course he had. "I wouldn't be too concerned," Bob said.

"Dozens of flights leave every day for London. What's the chance he was on that one?"

Still, to play it safe, he called Ralph's assistant, Brenda, to find out which airline he'd taken: Ralph traveled so much that Bob no longer bothered to keep track of the arrangements. She was crying when she picked up the phone. "The thing is, he usually flew American," she said, "because that's where he had his frequent flyer miles. But then the last time they wouldn't give him an upgrade to business class, and he got furious. He swore he'd never fly American again, and you know how Ralph is. Once he makes up his mind, he'll never change it."

Bob hung up immediately. He lowered himself into one of the library chairs and switched on the television, which was hidden inside an eighteenth-century Tuscan bread chest. News of the crash filled every channel. On CNN, a pale boy stood in front of his mother, who was stroking his hair. "We were having a clambake," the boy said, "and I was watching the stars, when suddenly there was this explosion. The plane broke up and fell into the water."

On another channel, a second witness—a woman with sunken cheeks, her glasses taped at the right temple—insisted that before the plane had blown up, something was heading for it. "I can't be sure," she told the reporter, "but I'd swear it was a missile."

"Do you think it's likely there were survivors?" the reporter asked.

"An explosion like that? Let's put it this way, if there were survivors, I'd feel more sorry for them than the ones that died."

At that moment, just as Bob expected, the telephone rang.

The next morning Kitty, who had a therapeutic personality, flew with her husband to Newfoundland. Because Ralph's parents were both dead, she qualified as next of kin. "You should come, Bob," she told him over the phone. "At first I was dreading it, but now that we're here, with all the other families . . . I don't know, it helps, somehow."

"I'd really rather not," said Bob, who could not, in any case, envision quite how he'd explain his relationship with Ralph to the airline. After all, it had no official designation. It did not matter that they had shared an apartment for fifteen years, or that Ralph had put up the money with which Bob opened his bookstore. That was business. He wasn't in any legal sense "kin."

"But it's healing!" Kitty said. "For instance, just this morning, when

I woke up, I looked out at the water—our rooms all overlook the water, the counselors insisted on that—and it seemed so placid. Such a lovely, soothing scene."

"How long are you planning to stay?"

"Until they find Ralph. Or the black box."

"Ah, the black box," Bob repeated. For once that was pulled up from the bottom of the ocean, the television assured him, all speculation about the cause of the crash—bomb, missile, pilot error—could be put to rest. Much hung in the balance, including lawsuits. In that black box, Kitty told him, were stored the voices of the pilots in the moments just before the plane blew up. "Although it's not really black," she added. "It's orange."

"How long will it take to find it?"

"We hope only a few more days, depending on the weather. It's supposed to give off a signal. Please come," she concluded, her voice almost seductive in its entreaty. "We need you here."

But he didn't go. Instead he stayed at the bookstore. He liked the bookstore—which Ralph had also designed—far more than the apartment. Here, at least, Ralph's signature made sense, since books were the place's raison d'être, as opposed to merely a decorative device. During the day Bob sat at the cash register, ringing up purchases and giving advice to customers, much to the bewilderment of his employees, two girls from NYU, and to the chagrin of Ralph's friends, who kept dropping by to offer their condolences.

"Are you sure you want to be here?" asked Brenda.

"Why don't you come over for dinner?" suggested Gwyneth, Ralph's lawyer. "You look pale, like you need a home-cooked meal."

"I'd really rather not," Bob answered, as he had answered Kitty's pleas that he fly up to Newfoundland. In the end, he even took to sleeping in the bookstore, on a foam rubber pad dragged up from the basement. Soon the dismay of Ralph's friends ripened into a kind of scandalized horror, as if in choosing this particular method of grief Bob was throwing in their faces certain conventions on which their own ability to cope, even to be distracted from death, somehow depended.

Strange people—acquaintances of Ralph's he'd met only briefly, or never at all—started coming into the store. Four days after the crash a woman with gray hair and owlish glasses approached Bob and asked him if he was himself. When he affirmed that he was, she peered at him almost clinically, as if she were a zoologist and he the only surviving specimen of some rare genus: the disaster widow, a piece of human wreckage.

"Oh, I'm sorry, I imagined you looking quite different," the woman said, pulling a shapeless, nubbly sweater down over her hips. "I'm Veronica Feinbaum. I'm sure Ralph told you about me."

Ralph had. Of his regular clients, she was the one he had found the most trying. As Bob recalled from dinner talk, Veronica lived in a vast Park Avenue apartment, and was married to an entertainment lawyer whose wealth had bought her seats on the boards of several charitable organizations. Yet her lot in life did not satisfy her, and so she had recently gone back to school, to Columbia, where she was studying Classics.

"It's a pleasure to meet you," Bob said.

She clasped his hand in hers. "I'm so sorry," she said, then, lowering her voice, added: "Still, it must have come as a relief."

He frowned. Her face, arcaded by columns of ill-brushed hair, was fleshy with health. A curious mixture of solicitude and challenge enlivened her unctuous smile.

"A relief?" he repeated.

"Of course. Otherwise, think of all the suffering you both would have had to endure. Wasting, dementia. At least this way it was quick."

Bob let go of her hand. "Thank you for your concern," he said.

"Ralph would have told you, I'm not one to mince words. My husband always says to me, 'Ronnie, shut your yap, it'll get you into trouble.' But I say, why beat around the bush when everyone knows it's nonsense? Much better to be frank and open. Fellows like Ralph, they're basically under a death sentence, just because they lived where they did and when they did. I don't know if he mentioned it, but I sit on the board of the Gay Men's Health Crisis. It's taught me to hold with the Greek view of death—you know, that it's better for a man to be taken at his peak."

"No, he didn't."

"Well, I'm glad we've had this talk," she said, and pressed a card into Bob's palm. "I doubt there are many people you can be this open with, so please, if you need to vent, call me *any* time."

She left, floating out the door in a hazy effulgence of perfume. Bob looked at the card. GEORGE AXELROD, DDS, it read. And on the back: TUESDAY, 3/7, 2:30 P.M.

* * *

That afternoon a small man with pale blond hair came into the bookstore. "So I've found you at last," he said when Lizzie, the taller and shyer of Bob's employees, led him to the front desk. "It's so important that we talk. Could we go somewhere?"

Bob was ruffled, bemused. He almost laughed. When the man spoke, his voice was oddly honeyed, as if he were making an inept attempt at a come-on. He was in his mid-thirties, Bob guessed, with watery blue eyes and the kind of boyish good looks that have a way of cracking as a person gets older. Close up, Bob could see minute lines around his eyes. His hair was thinning. He wore a beige trench coat over his suit, which was black, a white shirt, a red-and-blue-striped tie. In his right hand he carried a briefcase.

"Excuse me?" Bob asked.

The man laughed. "Oh, I haven't said who I am yet. Sorry. My name is Ezra Hartley. I'm . . ."

He glanced furtively over his shoulder, as if to make sure that no one else in the shop—neither of Bob's employees, nor the lone customer browsing in the alternative medicine section—was listening. Then he leaned across the counter, so that Bob caught a whiff of his milky breath.

"I met Kitty in Newfoundland. She told me about you."

Bob's lips tightened. What was this? Some perverse effort of Kitty's to fix him up with the only other homo among the crash relations? He wouldn't have put it past her.

"So Kitty sent you?" he asked.

"Oh, no. I'm here completely on my own initiative. She just . . . told me about you. We got to be rather close, Kitty and I. Everyone did, in Newfoundland."

"Yes, I'm sorry I wasn't there. It just didn't quite—well, feel right."

"I understand. I tell you, it took a lot of courage for me to call up the airline, and say, 'Look, I have a right to—you know—be there.' But I did, and I'm glad I did."

"So I assume you . . . lost someone?"

"I'm connected, if that's the right word, to the children. The ones from upstate, who were going to Edinburgh. You know, the school trip."

Of course Bob knew. For days, both on television and in the newspapers, he'd been hearing about the children—about how they had raised the money for the trip themselves, by holding bake sales and car washes; about how, in this enterprise, they had been encouraged both by their parents, several of whom had also died in the crash, and their teacher, whom Peter Jennings had just named "Person of the Week"; about the eagerness with which they had anticipated the flight, which for many of them was both their first and last journey on an airplane.

Exactly what Ezra's "connection" to the children was, however, he appeared reluctant, at least in the bookstore, to divulge. "It's curious how hungry, almost lustful, people get for details," he whispered over the cash register. "Especially if there's some horrible irony, like the person had just missed another plane. Or if he was famous in some way. Your Ralph, for instance—forgive me for using his first name, but I feel as if I know him—he was probably the most famous person on board. Or that woman who won the lottery. Imagine." Ezra scratched his upper lip, on which there was a mustache so pale as to be almost invisible. "You win a hundred thousand dollars in the lottery, and then . . . But I'd really rather not keep on talkng here. Couldn't we go somewhere?"

"Yes, of course. Debbie!"

His second employee, a languid girl with a nose ring and a rose tattoo on her left wrist, now separated herself from the stack of books she was shelving and drifted over to the register.

"Could you take over? I have to go out for a while."

"Sure, whatever," Debbie said, and replaced him on his little stool. He and Ezra stepped out onto the sidewalk. A wind had come up. Across the street a bulky man with a crewcut was walking into a bar that happened to be the oldest gay bar in the Village. "We could go there, if you want," Bob said, pointing.

"Oh, I'd really rather not. I'd really rather go to your apartment."

"My apartment? Why?"

"Well, it's just . . . I mean, we're bound to end up there anyway, aren't we?" Ezra smiled.

"But why are we bound to end up there?"

"Because of what I have to show you." He indicated his briefcase. "It's not something I can show you in public."

Bob stalled. Behind Ezra's guileless lack of discretion, he was sure he could detect Kitty's interfering hand. It all seemed a bit demented to him, this propositioning, no doubt an offshoot of the enforced intimacy that had been the apparent leitmotif of Newfoundland. Or perhaps he was wrong to assume that Ezra was propositioning him; perhaps, on the contrary, he was reading into this brusque request an impulse that could not have been further from Ezra's intentions. For it went without saying that Ezra, as he stood there staring at Bob, appeared not only guileless, but childlike. Normally Bob was not, by his own admission, a libidinous man; in that department Ralph had always been the more high-octane of the two, which explained at least in part his habitual infidelities, to which he rarely owned up, but which Bob always learned about anyway, through Ralph's habit of leaving little clues everywhere: condom wrappers in the bathroom, scraps of paper with strangers' phone numbers on the kitchen counter. Men called late at night, then, learning that Ralph was out of town, hung up without leaving their names. And through it all, Bob had never gone looking for someone else, as Ralph regularly did. It had become a source of pride to him, his ability to resist the very impulses to which Ralph, time and again, proved so susceptible; only now, poised in this standoff with Ezra, something about the very oddness of the situation, their shared and mysterious link to the plane crash, skewed his perspective, made him suspicious . . . and curious.

A moment of silence passed, during which Ezra looked up the block toward Seventh Avenue, across the street at the bar—anywhere but into Bob's eyes. Finally he coughed, stuffed his left hand into his coat pocket. "Well?" he asked.

"All right, we'll go to my apartment," Bob said. "Why not?" And he started off—walking fast, as was his habit.

"I appreciate this. Listen, shall we take a taxi? My treat."

"It's not far enough for a taxi."

The wind had picked up. Ezra buttoned the collar of his coat tight around his throat. "I should tell you, I've seen your apartment already," he shouted after Bob, with whom he was having trouble keeping up. "I'm not ashamed to admit that I'm an avid reader of design magazines. So I'd heard of Ralph Davenport long before the crash. He was very talented, wasn't he?"

"They say he had a way with books." They had arrived at Bob's stolid brownstone, up the stairs of which Ezra now trotted after him, to the second-floor landing. The apartment, when they stepped inside, was stuffy, overwarm. All the curtains were drawn. "I haven't been here for a few days," Bob said, pulling up a blind.

Dust flew. "Wow," said Ezra, gazing at an English Arts and Crafts card table that Ralph had bought in London the year before. "This is beautiful. May I?" He took off his coat, sat down on one of the library chairs. "You know, there was one woman on the plane—this isn't generally known, because the family doesn't want the publicity—and she was on her way to Switzerland, where her brother—I'm not making this up—had just been killed in a plane crash. A private plane." He settled his briefcase in his lap. "Pretty extraordinary, that. In Newfoundland it became a kind of game, thinking up parallels. You know, a surgeon is performing open-heart surgery . . . when he has a heart attack. Or an ambulance is on the way back from a car accident . . . when a car rear-ends it."

"I get the drift. Oh, would you like anything to drink?"

"Just water, thanks."

Bob fetched a glass from the kitchen, then sat down across from Ezra, in the second library chair. Ezra was smiling at him. He had his legs spread in what might have been a lewd way.

"So," Bob said.

"So," Ezra said.

There was a moment of silence, almost of helplessness, during which Ezra's fingers worked the combination lock on the briefcase.

"You said you were connected to the children?" Bob prodded.

"Yes, well, to their teacher, actually. The heroic history teacher, who taught them all semester about Scotland, and was taking them to Edinburgh."

At last he opened the briefcase, producing a newspaper clipping, which he handed to Bob. A heavyset man with a gray beard—the sort of man who always wears a cap with a brim, and was wearing one—smiled out broadly from a landscape of snow and trees.

"Of course living as we did in rural New York State," Ezra went on, "we couldn't be as open as you and Ralph were. We couldn't, for instance, have lived together. You see, Larry was divorced. He might have lost visitation rights with his kids, if anyone found out." Ezra reclaimed the clipping. "I teach at the high school too, incidentally. Journalism. So that just made things more complicated."

He closed, but did not relock, the briefcase.

"Well, I'm sorry," Bob said after a moment. "I mean, about Larry."

"I appreciate that, although as I've said about a million times this week, there's really not much point to 'Sorry,' when we're all in the same boat."

"True."

"I mean, Larry and I were together seven years. I moved to an apartment near his place just so I could walk over there. We couldn't risk anyone seeing my car parked in his driveway at night. And then in the mornings, I'd sneak out early. We'd drive to school separately, always make sure to arrive at least ten minutes apart. When we took vacations, we lied about where we were going, we flew on separate planes and met at the other end. Seven years like that."

"It must have been difficult."

"It was. But let's skip all that, because I didn't just come here to get sympathy. What I came about—it's the footage. I need some help deciding what to do with the footage."

"Footage?"

Ezra nodded. As at the bookstore, he looked over his shoulder, perhaps to make sure that no unexpected stranger, no friend or domestic, was about to step into the room. Then he reopened the briefcase and took out a videotape. "To be honest, I haven't looked at it myself," he said, handing it to Bob. "I couldn't at first, and now . . . I don't know, I'd just rather not. Would you mind if I wait in another room while you watch it?"

"But what is it?"

"You'll see. Where's the bathroom?"

"On the left."

"I'll wait there." He got up. "Call me when you're finished. It shouldn't take more than ten minutes or so."

Patting Bob on the shoulder, Ezra walked to the bathroom and closed himself in. The lock clicked. Through the crack at the bottom of the door, Bob saw a light switch on; he heard the fan starting to whir.

He glanced at what he held in his hands: an ordinary videotape, it seemed. Maxell. Sixty minutes. Although an adhesive tag had been affixed to its front, nothing was written on it. Did that mean that it contained what Bob, at that moment, suspected it might contain, that is to say, pornography, probably homemade, perhaps images of Ezra's friend, the dead history teacher? No, not likely. Really, he thought, he was sinking further and further into salaciousness—had been, ever since Ezra had walked into the store.

Finally he switched on the television, and loaded the tape into the VCR. Colors appeared—a Mondrian rainbow—and then a voice (Ezra's) said, "Testing, one-two-three, testing, one-two-three." A blur of motion filled the screen, before clarifying into a corridor. Whoever held the camera was walking in the midst of a crowd, everyone wearing red. "Here we are boarding the bus," the voice declaimed, "on our way to watch Mr. Dowd's history club embark on its historic voyage to bonny Scotland. This is Ezra Hartley reporting for PVTV: Porter Valley Regional High School Television."

Then grass. A parking lot. A school bus, teenagers posed in pairs and clusters, some drinking Cokes. Inside the bus, more children mugged before the camera. "Hey, I hear those guys don't wear anything under their kilts!"

"Now, kids, no more of that—"

A huge face filled the screen. "Tigers rule!"

"Approaching the airport, you can see the excitement building on these kids' faces. Let's see, who shall we interview first? Nadine Kazanjian, class of 1988 valedictorian, how are you doing today?"

A dark-eyed girl smiled. "Fine."

"Is this your first trip to Europe?"

"Yeah."

"And you're excited?"

"Yeah."

"What are you most excited about seeing?"

She looked pensive. "Well, I guess probably it would have to be the Tower of London, when we stop in London. Or Edinburgh Castle."

"And what are your future plans, after you get back from Scotland?"

"Well, in the fall, I'll be enrolling as a freshman at SUNY New Paltz."

"Tigers rule!"

"Shut up, please, Peter, I'm conducting an interview. Have you decided on your major yet?"

"I was thinking history."

"Is that thanks to Mr. Dowd?"

"Yeah, I guess."

"You like Mr. Dowd?"

"Uh-huh, he's a great teacher."

"Tigers rule!"

"Peter, I told you—"

A sudden break, then, almost a rupture. In the next scene the kids were at the airport, checking their bags. Ezra's camera panned back, and suddenly all the red made sense: the children were wearing identical sweatshirts, red sweatshirts, that said PORTER VALLEY REGIONAL HIGH SCHOOL CLASS TRIP, 1988. Underneath was a drawing of a tiger wearing a kilt.

On to the gate. "Everybody together, I want a group shot!" Ezra shouted, and the man with the cap (Mr. Dowd; Larry) gathered them in, along with three pairs of parents. Thirty people, more or less. One girl was very beautiful, red-haired, with intense green eyes. Behind her the boy who had shouted "Tigers rule!" once again shouted "Tigers rule!" He had pimples on his cheeks. To the left, nearer Mr. Dowd, Nadine Kazanjian (already, on the news, Bob had heard about Nadine Kazanjian) put an arm around the shoulders of a short black boy whom Bob also recognized, for there had been a feature about him on CBS: he had suffered from a congenital heart defect.

Bob did not close his eyes. He did not flinch. He was horror-stricken, yes—it went without saying—yet he could not have turned away even if . . . even if at that moment Ralph had come storming through the door, dripping wet, as he had in one of Bob's dreams a few nights earlier. For these faces—he felt as if he needed to study them, if for no other reason than to see if there was anything besides innocence in them, some knowledge, some foreshadowing of their fate. It occurred to him dimly that when he had wondered if Ezra were peddling pornography, he hadn't been so far off the mark; only this was pornography of a scarier and more insidious kind; this was closer to a snuff film.

It was then that he saw Ralph. At first he wasn't sure—just a figure passing in the background. Immediately he aimed the remote control, rewound, moved forward again, this time in slow motion. Behind the mob of children and parents a figure moved, wearing a jacket Bob would have recognized anywhere, for it was Ralph's favorite jacket, a brown leather jacket he'd bought years ago, when he was still a student, and that was now patched on both elbows. With the hypnotic grace of a dancer, Ralph crossed behind the students, glanced briefly at them, then sat down. He carried two bottles of water.

Two.

Someone was sitting next to him.

Again, Bob rewound. The figure to Ralph's left was blurry. Bob couldn't even tell if it was male or female; only that Ralph—very distinctly—took one of the water bottles and handed it to . . . whom? This friend. This unsuspected companion.

Again, a break in the footage. The children were now handing in their boarding passes, waving wild goodbyes as they headed toward the gate. One by one they disappeared, as into a pair of jaws. "Well, that about wraps it up," Ezra said. "In two weeks' time, we'll be back to record the great homecoming. In the meantime, for PVTV, I'm Ezra Hartley. Goodbye, kids, and good luck."

The footage broke off. Hissing confetti filled the screen. Like a wakened dreamer, Bob started; stood; turned off the VCR. In the bathroom the fan still whirred, though the light had been switched off.

He knocked on the door. "Are you finished?" Ezra called from inside.

"Yes, I'm finished."

The lock clicked open, and he stepped out. "Well?"

"Well . . . yes."

Bob returned to his chair. Ezra followed him. "So what did you think?"

"To tell you the truth, I'm not exactly sure what I think."

"But did you find it disturbing?"

"What kind of question is that? Of course I did."

Ezra sat down. "I'm sorry, I didn't mean to put it that way . . . I'm incredibly nervous just now, as you can imagine. My heart's racing, I'm sweating like a pig—"

"Well, I suppose at the very least I ought to be grateful to you . . . you know, for giving me a last glimpse of the loved one and all."

"That's why I can't look at it myself. A last glimpse of the loved one would be more than I could bear."

"But how can you not have looked at it? Someone must have—Kitty, for instance—otherwise—"

"No, you're the only one."

Bob looked up. "But then how did you know about Ralph?"

"What about him?"

"His being on the tape."

"Ralph is on the tape?" Ezra's hands flew to his face. "Oh, I'm so sorry! If I'd . . . Ralph is on the tape? But you must think I'm monstrous! To spring something like that on you without any warning . . . Believe me, if I'd known, I'd never—"

"Hold on. Then why were you so keen for me to watch it?"

"I told you, because I need your advice about what to do with it. Where to sell it."

"Sell it!"

"That's the whole point of my coming to New York. I want to sell it to one of those scandal programs—you know, *Hard Copy*, or something. Hadn't you guessed?"

"But why?"

"For the money, of course! I thought I'd begin by asking fifty thousand. Do you think that's reasonable? Too much? Too little?"

"Wait a second, are you actually saying you think people will pay money for this?"

"Of course—but only if I act fast. I know how journalism works. People eat this stuff up. My hope is that if I can get a bidding war going, get them foaming at the mouth, the price will really climb. Only I don't have the right contacts, and if I did it myself, I might end up being sold short."

"But you'll hurt people. The parents of those kids—"

"Oh, I know people will be hurt. Only when you think about, when you consider the sort of indescribable hell they're already going through, honestly, what difference will ten minutes of footage make? It might even be a comfort, seeing their children one last time."

"You'll be cashing in on their suffering."

"Correction. My suffering, too. After all, who's front and center in that video? Larry. 'Person of the Week.' And anyway, everyone else is going to make money, a lot of money, off this thing. I mean, confidentially—it's not public yet—they're pretty sure now that the crash was due to an electrical failure—not a missile, not a bomb. There was an engine part the airline hadn't got around to replacing even though they were supposed to. And if that's the case, there are going to be lawsuits—big lawsuits—and big settlements. Everyone who's next of kin will be compensated, all the parents of all those kids, and Larry's kids, and Kitty. Has she talked to you about it, by the way? About money?"

"No."

"She'll probably give you some. Kitty's a decent sort. And yet when you think about it, why should Kitty be getting anything? I mean, is she *really* next of kin? Only legally. In every real sense, you are . . . just as I am."

Bob said nothing. Almost triumphantly, Ezra crossed his arms. "You see? Now the whole picture looks different. What's fifty thousand, after all, compared to what *they're* going to get? And of course I'll give you a percentage for your help. Twenty-five percent, I was thinking."

"But what on earth makes you think I can help you?"

"You can get me contacts. Living here in New York, you must know people in television."

"I don't know anyone in television."

"Well, then you must know someone who knows someone. Or someone who can represent me . . . us. Someone who can sell the tape for us."

The "us" stung. "I feel very strange about this. I'm not sure I want to get involved in something so . . . frankly, so questionable."

"But all you have to do is give me an introduction! I'll do the rest. And anyway"—here Ezra touched Bob's arm, which made him flinch—"it's as much for your sake as mine. You're obviously a decent guy, Bob. Still, a bookstore can't rake in a fortune, and Ralph had a big career ahead of him, didn't he? If he hadn't been killed, you would have had things to look forward to, money to look forward to, which now you'll never see. And so if everyone else is going to be compensated, why should you get left out in the cold?" He smiled. "Yes, I can see it now. His being on the tape, Ralph's being on the tape . . . that's really the icing on the cake. For that I think we can jump to seventy-five K, don't you?"

Bob moved away from Ezra's touch. "Look, I can't think right now. You'll have to give me some time."

"But there isn't any time! Every minute we waste, we lose money."

"Just until tomorrow morning?" He checked his watch. "It's nearly five now. Nothing's going to happen between now and tomorrow."

"I wish I could be sure. Still, I suppose I don't really have much choice, do I, other than to pick a lawyer at random from the phone book." He stood up. "All right. Tomorrow. Early, though."

"I'll call you by eight."

With a gesture of impatience, Ezra put on his coat, relocked his briefcase. Bob followed him to the door.

"Ezra," he said, when they got there, "you wouldn't by any chance be willing to leave the videotape with me, would you? Just for tonight. I give you my word, I won't show it to anyone."

Ezra grinned. "I never doubted for a minute that I could trust you," he said, then opened the briefcase, took the tape out, and handed it to Bob.

"Thank you."

"Besides, this isn't the only copy."

"Somehow I suspected that."

"Like I said, I know how journalism works. Well, good night. Think carefully about what I've told you. Oh, and if you need to reach me—even if you just want to talk—I'm at the Sheraton on Broadway. Room 2223."

"O.K."

"Call any time. Even the middle of the night. Or just come over . . ."

Again, he smiled—this time a bit tartishly, Bob thought. They shook hands, and Ezra left.

Almost as soon as Ezra was out the door, Bob locked it. He went into the bathroom. An unfamiliar smell of lemons hung in the air—Ezra's cologne, perhaps, or his shampoo. Bob switched the fan back on, shut the door behind him. Then he carried the tape over to the bread chest and loaded it, once again, into the VCR.

He fast-forwarded through the first scenes—the bus, the interview with the doomed valedictorian, the checking of the bags—and let the button go only once the young travelers were at the gate, gathering for their farewell. Nothing had changed in fifteen minutes. "Tigers rule!" Peter with the pimples shouted, as Ralph, still in his leather jacket, glided past with his two water bottles. How his hair was thinning! He had a birthday coming up, his thirty-ninth. Rather dispassionately, he regarded the children—was he worrying that they might make noise during the flight?—then sat down, as before, next to his shadowy companion, to whom he passed a bottle. Here Bob pressed the pause button; stepped closer to the television, so that the tip of his nose brushed the screen. Yet he was no more able to identify Ralph's blurry friend now than he had been twenty minutes earlier.

He stopped the tape. A dim idea seized him, and he stumbled to the bedroom, to Ralph's closet, which he hadn't opened since the crash. Was it possible the leather jacket might still be there? . . . but it was gone. Where it had hung, only an empty hanger dangled. Other clothes pressed in on the vacancy, like flesh crowding to close a wound: pants and belts, a hank of ties, a new wool blazer Ralph had bought the winter before but not yet worn. And how faint—yet how distinct—his smell was! It lingered in his shoes, rose up from the hamper. Still, nothing about the closet provoked the slightest nostalgia in Bob. He didn't want to bury his face in the shirts. He wanted to haul them away, have the place aired and fumigated. As swiftly as he had opened it, he shut the closet door.

The next step was to search Ralph's desk, an early-twentieth-century rolltop, positioned at the far end of the bedroom. In the past, it had never occurred to him to rifle through the trove of documents Ralph kept there, if for no other reason than because he had always felt so secure in their companionable coupledom that even when he knew Ralph was having sex with other men, the matter hadn't seemed important enough to warrant prowling; the stability of their bond, not to mention the zeal with which Ralph loved him, were givens, and if over the years sex had ceased to be a crucial part of their relationship—well, what of it? The truth was, Bob didn't care all that much about sex. To him there was nothing wrong with a man going elsewhere to seek out those gratifications with which his home—a place of safety and retreat—had never been meant to provide him in the first place. So why was it that today, in the wake of a death that rendered jealousy moot, nonetheless jealousy, for the first time in years, was rearing in him? Was it Ezra's presence that had induced this unlikely response? Or was jealousy merely one of the many cloaks in which grief costumed itself?

With a weirdly furtive anxiety, as if he feared Ralph might come striding through the door at any moment and catch him in the act, he opened all the drawers of the desk and emptied their contents onto the floor. Key rings, bookmarks, computer disks, an extra knob from the kitchen cabinets, fabric swatches, pages torn from design magazines, sketches of sofas and coffee tables and naked boys, earplugs, snapshots from a Halloween party, some old Corgi cars, a monogrammed leather passport holder that had been a Christmas gift from Kitty, extra Filofax pages, packets of tissue and gum, scissors, paper clips, a stapler, pens and pencils and pads stolen from various hotels: all this detritus, this flotsam of a life being lived at full throttle, fell in heaps on the Tabriz carpet. It made Bob think of the things Ralph had taken with him, and that had gone down with the plane: his datebook, his briefcase, the toothbrush now so conspicuously absent from the bathroom sink. A few days earlier, Kitty said, a dog's collar had washed up on the beach near her hotel. Nothing, however, of Ralph's; nor Ralph himself.

For a few moments, Bob sifted through this heap of valueless objects. Then, as nothing in it illuminated the identity of Ralph's companion, he moved on to the files. "Letters and Postcards"—from clients, from Kitty, from Brenda on her honeymoon—proved unrevealing, as did "Apartment," "Taxes," and "Insurance." The contents of the next file, "Credit Card Bills," he scanned with greater avidity, in the hope that there, at least, he might happen upon some clue, some shred of evidence pointing to an affair. Yet aside from an order for flowers, which Ralph would have normally charged through his office, nothing in the file shed light upon or even verified the stranger's existence. No extra plane tickets had been purchased in Ralph's name. Nor had he used the card to pay for any of the typical expenses of an affair: motel rooms, sex toys. Did this mean that he was being careful, taking the sort of precautions that in the past he hadn't deemed necessary? And if so, why? Because for once he had gotten caught up in something serious enough to merit deception? Yet if this was the case, nothing in his behavior, in the weeks before he'd boarded the plane, had given him away.

Kicking aside the papers, Bob lay down on the bed. What he was feeling was a maddened curiosity, a rage directed not at Ralph himself but at whatever forces were conspiring to make available only this clue, this fleeting image of a water bottle being passed into a stranger's hand. Nothing at all would have been better, he decided, or short of that, something he could work with, from which he could at least derive a lead or two. Perhaps if he scanned the lists of the dead, called the airline, and demanded to know next to whom Ralph was sitting, then he might find something out . . . only wouldn't making such calls be to presuppose a prior "arrangement" of which he had no evidence? What if, on the other hand, the friend was someone Ralph had picked up in the men's room? Or better yet, just a fellow passenger he'd started chatting with, and for whom he'd offered to fetch some water? An old lady, even. Someone who couldn't walk very well.

He closed his eyes. The mistrust in which he had been wallowing since Ezra's visit horrified him. It did not fit the profile of a man who wore argyle sweaters, and owned a bookstore, and prided himself on the civility of his domestic arrangements. For his life with Ralph had always been the very model of civility. There was no surprise here: a craving for the refinements in which their childhoods—Bob's in a Dallas suburb, Ralph's on a series of military bases in California, Korea, and Germany—had been so singularly lacking was what had attracted them to each other in the first place. Thus their courtship had taken place in antiques shops. The first purchase they had made together was a set of Sèvres porcelain dessert plates. Even when they were young and poor, and lived in an East Village walk-up, they always had good furniture, Persian rugs, old hotel silver. For these things, above all others, mattered to Ralph, and if, on occasion, an urge came upon him to go out searching for sex of the seamier variety—an urge utterly out of keeping with his otherwise scrupulous habits—well, what did it matter? Squabbling was tawdry, like paper napkins. Much better to show a bit of tolerance, to laugh the matter off, to remain, at all costs, *civilized.*

Only once before had jealousy gotten the better of Bob. This was in the early eighties, when for a few months Ralph had entered into a sort of carnal tailspin. Every night he'd gone out at around eleven (they were still living in the East Village then), only to return at dawn, reeking of cigarette fumes and sweat and poppers. Then he would shower, while Bob lay quiet in their bed with its upholstered headboard, its four-hundred-thread-count sheets, its canopy of English glazed chintz (Roses and Pansies), pretending to be asleep but really listening for the water to shut off. Eventually Ralph, moist in his cotton pajamas, would climb in next to him, lie still for a few moments, then, with great caution, wrap his arms around Bob's chest and nuzzle his neck.

One morning during this period, as they were fixing breakfast in their tiny kitchen, Ralph started washing an orange. Where cleanliness was concerned, he could be excessively fastidious—when he ate french fries, he would leave the tips on the plate, like cigarette butts, rather than put anything his fingers had touched into his mouth—and now, watching him wash his orange, which he was going to peel anyway, Bob giggled. "What is it?" Ralph asked.

"It's just . . . you'll lick some stranger's asshole through a hole in the wall, but you won't eat an orange without washing it."

Ralph put the orange down. Almost angrily he glared at Bob; he swallowed, as if swallowing back an impulse to lash out. And then he, too, laughed. He laughed and laughed.

Bob opened his eyes again, sat up. Had he fallen asleep? Behind the pillows in their beige cases, the headboard, made from a pair of Venetian gilt and painted gesso doors, creaked in reaction to his weight. Although he was alone, he was lying on the left side of the bed; he had always slept on the left, just as Ralph had always slept on the right. Each had his own table, his own drawer, Bob's containing disorder (earplugs and magazine clippings and buttons and handkerchiefs and cufflinks), Ralph's only a first-aid kit, a flashlight, matches, and a few candles. On top of each table sat a red tole lamp hand-stenciled with fritillaries. To the left was the window draped in the beige linen *toile de Jouy* it had taken Ralph so many months to settle upon, and next to the window was the dresser, and across from the dresser was the desk, its drawers pulled open, its contents spread all over the carpet, as if a thief had been searching fruitlessly for jewels . . . Getting up, Bob quickly put everything back.

Streetlamps came on; instinctively he shut the curtains against them. In the morning, he knew, he would have to answer Ezra's scandalous proposition. And what would he say? From a financial perspective, it was true, Ralph's death had left him in a precarious position. The import of his will was no secret; it was identical to Bob's, both of them stating that if one should predecease the other, the survivor would inherit the apartment, whatever money was in the dead partner's bank account, and the cash value of his business. Yet so far—just as Ezra had guessed—Ralph's business hadn't earned much in the way of profit; the big money was supposed to come next year, when he completed the first of his corporate commissions. Nor was the bookstore alone likely to generate the kind of income necessary to keep up the mortgage payments on a large Manhattan co-op, purchased at the height of an economic boom. Their whole life, when you thought about it, had been provisional, based on the assumption that Ralph wasn't going to die—and this was odd, for in recent years his health had become for both of them a chronic, if largely private, worry. Ralph, for instance, was always feeling his glands. Whenever he got a cold, an expression of grim stoicism claimed his face, only to give way, once he had recovered, to a kind of euphoria, as if getting over the cold meant that he was utterly safe: exactly the sort of reassurance the HIV test was supposed to provide.

No, Bob reflected, the problem with Veronica Feinbaum's ill-mannered remarks wasn't that they had been so off the mark; the problem was that in her contempt for the niceties, her devotion to the unvarnished truth, she had given voice to the very cynicism that the rest of their friends, out of respect for the dead, had left unspoken. Not an if, but a when: all of them—Bob too—took it for granted that one day soon Ralph would get sick. For the orange had its price. And though in recent years Ralph had made it his habit, when engaging in what he called his "extracurricular activities," always to practice the safe sex that Veronica's beloved GMHC propounded, even so, the residue of those early debauches could not so easily be leached from the blood. Every morning when they woke up, Bob wondered, Will this be the day? He'd never admitted it before, but he had. He had kept his eyes averted from the future, grateful only for what didn't happen, for every blessed deferral.

Not far away church bells rang: six o'clock. This was the hour when flights to Europe made their departures, when taxis mobbed the terminals at JFK, and travelers in whom the mere prospect of the abbreviated transatlantic night had already incited a state of proleptic weariness and disorientation dragged their luggage through the snaky line to the check-in. Then would come the journey itself—he knew it well—the mask and the earplugs, labored sleep, a too early dawn. Under the closed eyelid of the window, light would creep, heralding jet lag and the stumbling weirdness of arrival. Many times Bob and Ralph had made that trip together. He recalled with a certain tenderness early mornings in Paris, dropping off their bags at the hotel and then, because the room wasn't ready, wandering red-eyed and unwashed through the half-asleep city, stopping at a bar for coffee and a warm croissant and gazing at the brisk, freshly shaven Frenchmen as if they were members of another species . . . And had Ralph, in the same way, been looking forward to his first morning in London? Was he envisioning, just before the plane blew up, the monuments and museums through which he would lead his wide-eyed companion, or the restaurants he would take him to? The sushi bar at Harrod's? Or that Thai place on Frith Street he liked so much?

It didn't matter. His hotel room—long reserved—had gone unclaimed. Oh, no doubt the flight had begun as flights always do, with a stewardess standing at the front of the cabin and explaining the use of the life jacket and the oxygen masks. More inured to flying than his companion, Ralph would have ignored her implorations to consult the little plastic card mapping the emergency exits. But the companion—for some reason Bob was certain of this—would have studied it assiduously. "In the event of a water landing," he would have heard her intone, all the while attending to the cartoonish plane, conveniently submerged just to the level of its doors; the passengers, resembling figures from a first-grade primer, making their orderly progress onto the slides; the slides themselves detaching, floating tranquilly out onto tranquil water, as if not only people, but fate could be trusted to behave, to follow the playground rules . . . yet when you thought about it, who had ever heard of a "water landing"? When in the entire history of commercial aviation had one taken place? In the world, planes blew up. People died. Their bodies were incinerated, or eaten by sharks. And though, for the first few days after the crash, newscasters would persist in avowing that divers were still "hopeful of locating survivors," well, everyone knew that this was just a gesture, made in deference to some outmoded protocol. You knew better than to believe that someone might actually be out there, clinging to a piece of wreckage, held aloft by a life jacket when in truth there hadn't been time even to put on a life jacket.

The apartment was now so dark that Bob could hardly see the furniture. Switching on the lights, he reached for his jacket, then hurried out onto the street and hailed a taxi. Past warehouses and department stores he rode, white brick apartment blocks and condemned tenements, until the taxi dropped him off amid the headachy neon of Broadway at night. The lobby of the Sheraton, when he stepped into it, was filled with airline pilots and cocktail music, overtired children, a chaos of perfumes and accents through which he pushed his way to the elevator. Up to the twenty-second floor he rode, then walked down a long corridor to a door marked 2223, on which he knocked.

Within seconds, Ezra answered. He had taken off his jacket and tie. His cheeks glowed, as if he had just been washing his face.

Seeing Bob, he smiled without surprise. "I'm glad you came," he said.

"I wanted to return the tape," Bob said, "only I seem to have forgotten it . . ."

"Never mind about the tape," Ezra said, and, leading him through the door, closed it behind them.

After that Bob gave in to strangeness. He accepted that the terms of his life had been altered radically, perhaps irrevocably, that from now on he was going to be a citizen not of the familiar world, but of an off-kilter landscape rather resembling the villains' hideouts in the old *Batman* series, shot with the camera atilt so that children would believe the Catwoman and the Joker and the Riddler actually lived in lopsided buildings, urban Towers of Pisa, where the floors slanted up or down or swayed like a seesaw. At least the past, for all its coarseness and sorrow, had been part of a fluid traffic, enviably unremarkable and thus passed over by television's greedy eye. Here, on the other hand, dog collars washed up on Newfoundland beaches. He lived not in his own apartment, but with Ezra, on the twenty-second floor of the Sheraton. They had their dinner naked, room service club sandwiches the crumbs of which got between the sheets, all the while observing with a certain detached wonderment a battle to purchase the videotape every bit as fevered as Ezra had predicted, with Bruce Feinbaum, Veronica's husband, acting as referee.

Only forty-eight hours had passed since they had taken the tape to Veronica. While Ezra hid, once again, in the bathroom, Bob watched it through with her, the two of them perched on leather library chairs exactly like the ones in his own living room, although here the television was hidden in a Shaker cupboard instead of a Tuscan bread chest. This go-round, the children's death march did not appall him as it had before; even Ralph's brief apparition did not appall him. Instead he watched, fascinated, as an apprehension of the tape's import gradually stole over Veronica's face, opening her mouth and pulling her eyebrows taut and painting her skin first scarlet and then a dyspeptic gray. If she noticed Ralph at all, she chose not to mention it. Instead, as the tape broke off, she seemed to be struggling to compose a response in keeping with her self-appointed role as a woman immune to sentimentality.

Later, at her husband's office, she told Bob and Ezra about a legend she had recently encountered in her Greek class, in the hope that sharing it would allay any feelings of guilt they might be suffering. "Cleobis and Biton," she began, "were the sons of Hera's priestess at Argos. And one day when she was supposed to perform the rites of the goddess, the oxen that usually took her to the temple didn't show, so her sons harnessed themselves to the chariot and dragged her there themselves. Five miles. Into the mountains. When they got to the temple, the priestess was so grateful to the boys that she prayed to Hera to grant them the best gift possible. And what did Hera do? Knocked them off. Killed them, in the prime of life. That's the Greek view of death."

"Funny," her husband said. "When you got to the end, I thought you were going to say that Hera killed the mother so the boys wouldn't have to drag her all the way back. Which is, I guess, the Jewish view of death." And he picked up the phone.

Afterward Bob and Ezra went back to the Sheraton, where they spent most of the day having sex. Intermittently they would take breaks to eat, or watch television, or answer Bruce's phone calls. Progress reports came about once an hour. "We've got an offer of sixty K," Bob said at five, "but I can tell from her voice, they're prepared to go higher."

By six they had gone higher. Ezra ordered champagne with the club sandwiches. Because the windows did not open, their room had begun to stink. When the bellhop brought the food, his nose twitched. Ezra only laughed. Gratification made him giddy. He could not seem to get fucked enough. As for Bob, never in his life had he felt so horny; it was as if Ezra had tapped into some cache of libido he hadn't ever suspected himself of harboring. He was a tiny man, Ezra. He had tiny feet, a tiny penis. He was in no way Bob's type. Still, when Bob fucked him, he felt as if he were breaking through the shell of the known universe. Somewhere near the ceiling there floated an undiluted pleasure, toward which the vessel of his body flew unpiloted.

When they weren't having sex, they talked about the future. It went without saying that Ezra would never return to Porter Valley. Instead, he said, his plan was to settle in Manhattan, using the money from the sale of the tape to buy himself an apartment. Once he was fixed up, he would look for a job teaching at a private school. Then he would live quietly, his phone number unlisted, in case anyone from Porter Valley should ever decide to hunt him down and shoot him.

"And in the meantime?" Bob asked.

"In the meantime I'll stay at your place."

His place! Not a question, a declaration. "Come to think of it, what are we doing here?" Ezra went on. "This room costs a fortune. And your apartment would be so much more comfortable."

"I can't go back there yet," Bob replied, for he was thinking of the bed: he had never slept in it with anyone except Ralph.

"Why not?"

"I'm having the place exterminated."

"Exterminated!"

"I mean, I'm having the exterminators in."

Ezra frowned. They stayed on at the Sheraton. In the mornings, when the maid came to clean the crumbs out of the bed and spray room freshener, they put on their jackets and took a walk through the theater district. Generally speaking, the half hour the maid needed to clean the room was the only time they got out. "I'd love to see *Cats*," Ezra said, gazing up at a marquee. "Let's go see *Cats*. I've never been to a Broadway musical."

"We'll get tickets this afternoon," Bob promised. And yet, by the time the afternoon rolled around, they were already in bed, the club sandwiches had been ordered, the television was on.

Now the phone rang every half an hour. "We're up to a hundred twenty-five K," Bruce told them at four. Then, at four-thirty: "*Hard Copy*'s come in ten thousand higher." After hanging up, Bob aimed the remote control at the screen, unmuting whatever was on. As a rule they watched only the programs that were at war to win the rights to the tape. If two were on at the same time, they'd switch back and forth between channels. All these programs had thrusting names, and alternated the gruesome (kidnap victims buried alive) with the heartwarming (a two-year-old dialing 911 to save his grandmother). On one, a dachshund kept an alligator at bay just long enough for its master, whose arm had been bitten off, to crawl out onto the street and scream for help. In this instance, the report was accompanied by a "dramatic reenactment" of everything that had occurred, including the arm's reattachment.

At Bruce's office, negotiations continued well into the night. Already the price had climbed far beyond what Ezra had hoped for. "This thing is smoldering," Bruce said over the phone. "It's hotter than I ever could have guessed." By morning, only two contenders remained. By three that afternoon a show called *The Real Story* had finally won, with a bid of $150,000. This meant that once Bruce had deducted his percentage, Bob would clear $30,000 and Ezra $90,000.

To celebrate, they went out to dinner at a sushi bar on Park Avenue that had just gotten three stars from the *New York Times*. It was posh and quiet. The chefs were tall for Japanese, with faces and hands as gleaming as the slabs of salmon and halibut they sliced so expertly. One of them, Bob noticed after a few minutes, was missing his right thumb.

"If they're really planning to air the tape tomorrow, we'll have to get out of the hotel in the morning," Ezra said. "The last thing I want right now is to be chased down by reporters."

Bob glanced up at him. "Do you honestly think they'd find you?"

"They might."

"But there are hundreds of hotels in New York. Anyway, you told me you registered under an assumed name."

"Still, I'd rather not risk it. At your place I'll feel safer."

"All right," Bob said, gulping sake, "but you'll have to sleep on the sofa. Just until I get a new mattress."

"What's wrong with the old one? Don't tell me bedbugs, because you said you just had the exterminators in."

"No, not that . . . It's just that it was Ralph's mattress. Ralph's and mine."

Ezra's mouth narrowed; he was quiet. "Really, Bob," he said after a moment, "considering all we've been through, don't you think that attitude's a little—well—sentimental?"

"But you must understand. No one else besides Ralph and me has ever been in that bed."

"Are you sure?"

"Of course."

"But you must have gone out of town sometimes by yourself. How can you know what Ralph got up to while you were away?"

"He might have gotten up to all sorts of things. Just not in the bed."

Ezra raised his eyebrows.

"What? You're doubting me?"

"I just think that maybe you're being a tad bit naive."

"It doesn't matter," Bob said finally. "What Ralph did doesn't matter. The point is, *I* never slept with anyone else in that bed."

"Is that really what this is about? Or is the truth that you just don't want to share that bed with—you know—some scoundrel, the kind of person who'd sell a tape of innocent children to a scandal show?"

"I never said anything to suggest that."

"Still, I can read between the lines. In the anonymity of a hotel room, that's one thing . . . but to have the horrible Ezra in your precious marriage bed, oh no!"

"The tape has nothing to do with it."

The bill arrived. Ezra paid—he insisted—after which they walked back to the hotel. Most of the way they didn't speak; Ezra had his fists buried in the pockets of his trench coat, kept his head bent, seemed at once ruminative and cross. Every few minutes Bob would try to introduce a neutral topic of conversation, only to have it shooed away like an insect. Finally he gave up. They arrived at the hotel, went up to the room, where Ezra threw off his coat, sat down at the little desk across from the bed, and frowned at the window. It took Bob a few seconds to realize that he was frowning at his own reflection.

Finally he turned to Bob, and said, "I haven't been straight with you.

There are things I haven't told you—and other things I have told you that, well . . . aren't true."

"Oh?"

"Yes." He gazed at his own hands. Then he said, "Larry Dowd was never my lover. He wasn't even queer."

"What do you mean, wasn't queer?"

"We were colleagues, that's all—who sometimes ate lunch together. Oh, I admit, I had the hots for him, a little. But I never said anything. I wouldn't have dared. So far as I know, he had no idea that *I* was queer."

"You mean you made up the whole story?"

Ezra nodded.

"But what about the tape?"

"That was for the kids. You're years out of high school, you think that journalism class means a newspaper. Remember, we're living in the age of video! The kids wanted video, so I just . . . invented this idea of PVTV. And then the plane went down, and suddenly it seemed like I was being offered an opportunity."

"To make money?"

"Not only that! Also to commemorate—what might have been, what would have been, if conditions had been different, if Larry had been different . . . And then when I got to Newfoundland, and heard about Ralph, and met Kitty—well, things just fell into place. It seemed predestined that I should come to New York. That I should find you. That we should—"

"But you said it was a question of justice. *You* don't deserve justice."

"I deserve this chance. How else was I ever going to get to New York? Stuck out in Hicksville, a closet case teaching high school journalism."

"So you decided to pay for your freedom with the corpses of dead children."

"No! It was for you, too . . . for us."

Bob turned away. "If I'd known what you were up to, I'd never have helped you."

"That was why it was imperative you not know what I was up to."

"Then why are you telling me now?"

"Because you wouldn't let me sleep in Ralph's bed. Because you made me feel like shit, like my very presence was defiling. And then I thought about it, and you know what I decided? You're right."

Bob moved toward the door. "I'm sorry," he said, "I have to digest all of this. I have to figure out what I feel."

"Of course." Suddenly Ezra turned. "Only please remember, no matter how much you hate me, you'll still get the money. Thirty thousand dollars. For that, at the very least, you ought to be—"

Bob ran. At the elevator, he pressed the call button twice, focused his eyes on striped wallpaper, listened for the ringing of a bell.

"Grateful," Ezra murmured in the distance.

The elevator doors opened, admitting Bob—irony of ironies—into a throng of uniformed stewardesses.

The day after the tape aired, Kitty called to deplore Ezra's "disloyalty." Veronica called to reassure Bob that he had no reason to feel guilty. Only Ezra did not call. Every day, at the bookstore, Bob watched for him, at first with fear, then with worry. At home he waited for a message on his answering machine. None came. Perhaps Ezra had gone back to Porter Valley. Perhaps, in a fit of guilt, he had done himself in. As for whatever little storm the screening of his tape had drummed up, it took place too far outside the arena of Bob's daily life for him ever to hear about it. He was Bob Bookman, owner of Bookman's Books. What happened on programs like *The Real Story* had nothing to do with him.

One afternoon a few weeks after the airing, Kitty called to say that an umbrella monogrammed with Ralph's initials had washed up on a Maine beach. "They're bringing it to me for identification," she added, "and I wondered . . . well, if you wanted to come. If you wanted to be here when it arrived."

Bob wasn't sure how to answer. Was he sorry? Relieved? Sorry—and relieved—that it hadn't been Ralph's body that had washed up?

"I think I can trust you to handle this," he said after a moment.

"Well, I just wanted to be up front about everything," Kitty asserted, in a voice suggesting that up until now she hadn't been.

"By the way, any word on the black box?"

"Not yet. My suspicion is that if they were going to find it, they'd have found it."

"But they're still looking."

"They're still looking."

They hung up. Bob sat down in one of the library chairs. Once more, that odd feeling of dislocation had claimed him, the world suddenly tilting so acutely he feared Ralph's piles of books might come tumbling to the floor. Then the sensation passed. Opening the Tuscan bread chest, he took out Ezra's videotape—the copy he had never given back—and loaded it into the VCR. He hadn't watched it in weeks, not since the afternoon he and Ezra had taken it to Veronica. Now, however, he was on that bus again, the dressing habits of Scotsmen were being debated, Nadine Kazanjian was expressing her wish to see the Tower of London. "Tigers rule!" Peter with the pimples cried, as the members of Mr. Dowd's history club gathered for their farewell. To Bob they looked wearier than on previous viewings, as if the effort of repeating the scene so many times had exhausted them. Nadine put her arm around the black boy who had a heart condition, the beautiful girl with the green eyes brushed back her hair . . . and then Mr. Dowd (Larry) smiled, and Peter yelled "Tigers rule!" again, and a bearish man wearing an Atlanta Braves T-shirt stumbled past, carrying two bottles of water. One of them he handed to a woman who was dividing up the sections of *USA Today*. She wore her long hair piled on top of her head, like Marjorie Main in the old Ma and Pa Kettle movies. Next to her was a dachshund, asleep in its carrier.

Bob stopped the tape. He rewound it. He watched it again. Not that he expected anything to have changed: the change had already happened. Ralph was gone—if he had ever been there in the first place, ever been more than a hope, or a hallucination. Need alone had kept him there those few extra days, kept him as vivid as his companion was murky; but that was all. A sleight of hand, a trick of the imagination, or nature, the way a chicken's body will flail even after its head has been cut off. Motion without life.

"Oh, those poor children," Bob said, putting his head on his knees. And in a softer voice: "Oh, my poor Ralph." Let Veronica rejoice in the death of the young! He would never join her, just as he would never take comfort in the knowledge that if Ralph had survived, it might have been only to suffer a worse fate later on. For though the loss of those we love might cure our fear of losing them, loss, as he now knew, was worse than fear. No matter what Ezra claimed, there would be no "compensation." Yes, he would come and go from the bookstore, he would once again be Bob, and lead Bob's life, but with this difference: from now on that life would contain an element of punishment.

He took the tape out of the VCR; held it for a moment; then, with his fingers and wrists, broke it in half. How delicately the celluloid unspooled, gray-black ribbon stretching to the floor! Without its precious contents it was nothing, just another black box lost in seaweed-stained waters, in depths no human voice could hope to penetrate.

Speonk

I've never been to Speonk. To me it is just a stop on the train, a dot on a map. For all I know, it might be "Llanview," or "Pine Valley," or "Genoa City"—one of those imaginary towns that come to life an hour a day on soap operas. Probably, however, Speonk isn't like any of those places. Probably it is a town full of satellite dishes.

This begins in traffic, on a summer Sunday evening on Long Island. After a comatose weekend spent in crowded houses on the wrong side of the Montauk Highway, three people are making their sleepy way back to New York. I am in the car, along with Naomi and her friend Jonathan, an actor who for the past two years has played Evan Malloy (dubbed "Evil Evan") on *The Light of Day*. Recently Jonathan decided he'd had enough of rape, blackmail, drug peddling, larceny, and the like, and gave the producers of the show six weeks' notice: just enough time for Evan to commit a murder, frame his good-as-gold brother, Julian, and at the eleventh hour get found out. Evan went to prison, and Jonathan, on the heels of his final taping, went to Penn Station, where he caught a train to Bridgehampton, relieved that their paths had finally diverged. He spent the weekend sleeping on the beach, and now, two days later, is sitting languid in the back seat of Naomi's car, still looking a bit like the tough he's become famous for playing, in a baseball cap and dirty white T-shirt.

"Even with this traffic, I think we should be back in the city by ten," Naomi says.

He laughs. "That'll still be less time than it took me to get out here."

"You came by train, didn't you?" I ask.

"Jonathan had a little trouble getting to Bridgehampton," Naomi says. "It took him—how long was it, Jonathan? Six, seven hours?"

"Seven and a half."

"What happened?"

He stretches his arms over his head, so that when I look over my shoulder, I catch a glimpse of the hair in his armpits. "Well, you know how in Jamaica you have to change trains," he says. "I got on the train across the platform, and asked the conductor if it was going to Bridgehampton, and he said it was. So then I settled back and fell asleep, and when I woke up, a different conductor was shaking my shoulder, and saying, 'Last stop, last stop.' Only we weren't in Montauk. We were in Speonk."

"Speonk?"

"The lousy conductor in Jamaica lied to me. He put me on the wrong train."

"I think," Naomi interjects, "the conductor must have recognized you from the show and decided this was a perfect opportunity to get back at you for all the rotten things you did. Or rather, the rotten things Evan did. A woman spat at him once."

"No."

"Yes. She walked right up to him in the middle of Lincoln Center and spat in his face. Isn't that right, Jonathan?"

He shrugs. "God knows why. The show is crap. God knows why people take it seriously."

"But go on with your story," I say. "So you were in Speonk. What did you do?"

"Well, I found a pay phone and called Ben Brandt, who I was supposed to be staying with. I had no idea where I was, and I wanted to ask how far Speonk was from Bridgehampton."

"You should have called me, Jonathan," Naomi says. "I would have picked you up."

"I know, but I didn't think to. So anyway, Ben answers the phone, and he goes, 'Speonk! Where's that?' And I go, 'Nowhere.' "

"Can you believe Ben didn't offer to go get him? Some friend."

"It was, like, one-thirty in the morning, and there weren't any trains. But I read in the schedule that there was a train I could catch at four from Hampton Bays. Hampton Bays isn't that far from Speonk. So I called Ben back, and said, 'What should I do?' and he goes, 'Hitchhike.' So I hitchhiked."

"And someone picked you up."

"A truck picked me up. Finally. This great big hulk of a guy, with tattoos, and this smaller guy. They were cousins. They recognized me from the show. They said they'd take me to Hampton Bays, provided I came home with them first so the big guy could show me to his wife."

"Get out."

"Can you believe it?"

Jonathan shrugs. "It was just stupid. It was the middle of the fucking night. The guy called his wife on his cell phone, he must have gotten her out of bed. She was in her bathrobe when we got there."

"So what happened then? What did she say?"

"The usual. She wanted to know what it was like behind the scenes, if any of the couples on the show were couples in real life. She seemed sort of confused. I don't think she quite understood that we were just actors, that this was just a lousy job. So I told her what I could, and she made me some coffee, and then her husband and his cousin drove me to Hampton Bays and I caught the train."

"It was five by the time he pulled into Bridgehampton," Naomi adds. "At least Ben had the decency to pick him up *then*."

In the back seat, Jonathan yawns, stretches his legs. "It was just stupid," he says. "A stupid waste of time."

The traffic grinds to a halt.

I don't know where we were then. We might have been anywhere. We might have been in Speonk.

For a while, when I was in high school, I used to watch *The Light of Day*. This was years before Jonathan played Evil Evan. In those days, I was much preoccupied with the fate of Sister Mary, a sweet young nun torn between Faith (in the person of Jesus Christ) and Passion (in the person of a severely smitten Jewish boy who was determined to lure her from the convent). What kept me watching was anxiety bled with a little bit of love: love for Sister Mary drew me in, while anxiety over her fate brought me back, day after day, especially after she went off to war-torn "San Carlos" to do good works and ended up being kidnapped by the sadistic guerrilla leader Pedro Santos. For weeks, I lived in suspense wondering whether Jeremy, her adoring suitor, would succeed in rescuing Mary before the malevolent Santos, with his Castro-like beard and cigar, gave in to lust and raped her. Every afternoon Santos's tobacco-scented breath puffed out over Mary's face; every afternoon, at the crucial instant, Chance stopped his hand on her breast. And then Chance took a day off: Jeremy saved Mary, but only after Santos had ravished her and vanished. Returning to "Montclair Heights," Mary left the convent and married Jeremy, whose child everyone took it for granted that she was carrying. Later, though, Santos turned up in "Montclair Heights." Despite everything that had happened, the former nun found herself powerfully attracted to the ex-guerrilla—at which point I left for college. Years passed. By the time I tuned in again, Jeremy was dead, Santos was out of the picture, Mary was blowsy, much divorced, and played by a different actress. For Evil Evan had ushered in a new era: *he* was Mary's son by Pedro Santos.

Of course, if I'd been tuning in all along—as, presumably, the woman in Speonk had—then perhaps this chain of events wouldn't have surprised me so much. After all, a soap opera is something you live with every day. What keeps you watching isn't, as with movies or novels, the assurance that a hostage taken at the beginning will be a hostage freed at the end. Instead, stories verge into one another. New plots rise from the ashes of old ones. Suffering is a principle: too much happiness foretells imminent catastrophe, just as minor fatigue bodes terminal illness. Time is elastic. Generally speaking, it conforms to time in the world—that is to say, Christmas comes for them when it comes for us, their springs and summers are shaped like ours. Only sometimes time compresses, too, and a single afternoon will take weeks to unfold. And sometimes time accelerates perversely so that a boy (Evan) graduates from high school eight years after his birth. And sometimes time seems not to exist at all.

The Light of Day, of course, goes on without Jonathan. It has been going on for forty-six years. I think of it the way I think of my life, as a narration without beginning or end. Oh, I know it began once, just as I know that someday it will have to end—all things do—yet this assurance is, finally, a haze for me, less a knowledge than a vagueness. The specificity of ending, that's what's so hard to get your mind around, the fact that one day, at some specific hour and in some specific place, this thing is going to happen. And it could happen anytime, anywhere. It could be tomorrow. It could be in Speonk.

Evil Evan took some people hostage, as I recall, in the last days of Jonathan's tenure. He took his lawyer and his lawyer's pregnant wife hostage. He paraded the wife around the courtroom, holding a gun to her abdomen.

This was just the sort of thing Evil Evan did, and that Jonathan claimed he could no longer tolerate. It drove him crazy, he said, having to point a gun at a pregnant woman's abdomen, even if he knew she wasn't really pregnant, that the gun was a prop, that the softness into which he was pressing its barrel was only a foam-rubber mold affixed to the inside of her dress.

"But isn't that just part of being an actor?" Naomi asked in the car, fishing in her purse for tollbooth tokens.

To which he replied: "It was a principle of my training that you have to become the character you play. And when you have to become Evil Evan five days a week, well, after a while it starts to make you nuts, you know what I'm saying? I mean, I would wake up in the morning, and think, 'Good, today I get to rape a fourteen-year-old. Cool.' Maybe some people can go, you know, 'This is just my job,' but not me."

We reached the city, and Naomi dropped Jonathan off at Second Avenue and Fifty-eighth Street; then we headed downtown together.

"Of course, there's more to that story than meets the eye," she said, once we were alone.

"Oh?"

She nodded. "One of those wasp-waisted space cadets he's always going for. Works for Revlon or something. For the first six months they were together, she never watched *The Light of Day*, she was always working. Then one week she was home sick and decided to tune in. Wouldn't you know it? *That* was the week Evil Evan raped the fourteen-year-old."

"And his girlfriend didn't like it?"

"Are you kidding? She practically had a seizure. She kept saying that when she looked into his eyes she saw the eyes of a rapist, or some nonsense like that. I told him I thought it was idiotic, that he shouldn't take her seriously, but has Jonathan ever once listened to me where women are concerned? No. So he up and quits a perfectly decent job, gives up a great salary, just to prove to some bimbo that he's willing to make a sacrifice for her love."

"I had no idea being an actor could be so complicated," I said.

"It's not being an actor that's complicated," Naomi corrected. "It's Jonathan who makes things complicated—especially where his girlfriends are concerned."

We arrived at my building. I kissed Naomi on the cheek and stepped out of the car onto the curb. She drove off in what seemed to me an irritated fashion. Not that I cared: the truth is, I hardly know Naomi—she was just a friend of one of the girls I was sharing a beach house with that summer—and Jonathan—well, I only met him that once, that time in the car. They were just acquaintances, people who offered me a ride one weekend. Beyond what I picked up on the Long Island Expressway, I couldn't tell you much about Jonathan's life. I don't know where he grew up or went to school. (Naomi works for an Internet start-up, I believe.)

And yet, as the summer progressed, the story stayed with me. Perhaps it was the trucker with the tattoos who kept it alive, or my own memories of coffee before dawn in college, or else just the very idea of Speonk at two in the morning—an invented Speonk, the streets so silent that you could hear the thunk of the traffic light as it changed from yellow to red. Sometimes, when I tried to imagine what really happened to Jonathan, I wondered if he'd been in some kind of danger. This is the soap opera watcher in me. The soap opera watcher in me envisions the house into which the trucker led him as painted in the most ominous colors—arterial purples, the pale blues of suffocation—and filled with padlocked doors, rolls of rusty wire, rags soaking in gasoline. In this scenario, the trucker and his wife cannot even begin to distinguish Jonathan from Evil Evan. When he walks into their kitchen, she cries, "How could you do it? And to a woman in her condition!"

"It wasn't me," Jonathan answers meekly. "I swear to you, *I* didn't do it." All in vain. His fate is sealed: his mouth will be stuffed with rags, his wrists bound with rusty wire. And then, in that basement to which the padlocked door leads, he will be imprisoned, tortured, punished for deeds not his own . . .

Admittedly, the soap opera watcher in me is inclined to exaggeration.

A more realistic scenario, then: zoom in on a small, tidy, rural kitchen, the floor a blue-and-white linoleum checkerboard, the countertops corn-yellow Formica. Dishes dry on a rubber rack. Tin canisters marked FLOUR, SUGAR, and TEA are lined up next to the electric stove. There's a smell of pot roast and stale coffee. When the truck driver and his cousin bring Evan—Jonathan—inside, the wife stands from where she's been waiting at the breakfast table. Although she's still in her bathrobe, she's put on rouge, lipstick. She's wearing earrings. A Sara Lee pound cake defrosts on top of the refrigerator, where the cat can't get to it.

Jonathan sits down. He looks tired and tough and lost in his dirty white T-shirt. She stares at him, perhaps touches him, remarks at how much smaller he appears offscreen (I noticed this, too): not a villain, just a boy, a tough boy, tired and lost. He rests his head on his palm, and his head is next to the television set, the very television set on which, every weekday for two years, she's watched him, as if he really has stepped through the screen and come to life. Yet the truth is, he's been here all along: in her kitchen, in her house. In Speonk.

She asks him what it's like playing Evil Evan. He tells her that as of today, he's quit.

"But how can that be?" she asks. "The murder trial's not over yet."

"We always tape a few weeks ahead."

Her eyes widen. "So you mean that in a few weeks, Evan will be gone?"

"An inside tip—don't tell your friends, I'm sworn to secrecy on this—he's going to the slammer. The hoosegow."

The trucker's cousin laughs—probably at the word "hoosegow."

"So now you're a little bit ahead of the game," Jonathan says.

The wife blushes. "Well, don't worry, your secret's safe with me. I won't tell a soul."

Jonathan would like to say that for all he cares, she can print the news in the *Speonk Gazette*, but he controls himself. Much better to give her the gratification of a secret.

She offers him a slice of pound cake; he says no, thank you. She offers him coffee; he accepts. It is late, the middle of the night; her husband and his cousin are shifting restlessly near the refrigerator, and Evil Evan is drinking coffee in her kitchen out of a mug that says, LIFE'S A BEACH. He drinks it in three gulps, puts down the mug. The truck driver suggests they'd better scoot if they want to get to Hampton Bays in time for his train. Jonathan has fulfilled his part of the bargain, and now the truck driver intends to do the same.

Jonathan stands; the wife stands. They look at each other for a moment. Then they say goodbye. The three men leave her, as men always do, alone with the television and the kitchen. Outside, she hears the truck's engine turn over as it pulls away, toward Hampton Bays and sunlight and the train that will take Evan away from Speonk, and out of her life for good.

* * *

Well, that's one way things could have turned out. But though this might be an end to Jonathan's story, it isn't the end to mine.

One Saturday, a few weeks after Naomi drove us to New York, I ran into her on the beach in Bridgehampton.

"Guess what?" she said, leaping up from the sand. "The other day, I looked up Speonk on a map, and it's only an hour from here—less in the middle of the night, when there wouldn't be traffic."

"So?"

"Well, doesn't that make it seem a little improbable?"

"What?"

"That Ben wouldn't pick him up."

"Pick up Jonathan? Maybe Ben was busy."

She rolled her eyes. "Are you kidding? He's one of Jonathan's best friends. But even if he did say no—which I find hard to believe—then why didn't Jonathan just call a taxi to take him to Hampton Bays?"

"Well, maybe taxis don't run that late in Speonk." I sat down on the edge of her towel.

"Fine. So why didn't he call me? He *knows* I would have picked him up."

I didn't want to get into the thorny question of why he might not have wanted to call Naomi.

"What are you saying?" I asked. "That he made up the whole story?"

"Not the *whole* story, necessarily. It's just, when you think about it, it's full of holes. For instance, this idea that he had no other choice but to hitchhike. Of course he had other choices! I've just listed them. And then the larger inconsistency, which is, how likely is it that some truck driver, some guy who spends all his time on the road, is going to recognize an actor from a soap opera?"

"Don't they usually drive at night?"

"Sure. But would *The Light of Day* really be up the alley of your average trucker?"

"Who says he was your average trucker?"

Naomi threw sand at me then. "Oh, be quiet, you're just playing devil's advocate," she said. "I can hear it in your voice, you're as dubious as I am. You're wondering, was Jonathan just making the whole thing up for the sake of giving a performance? You know, poor Jonathan, he couldn't bear playing the villain anymore, so he quits, and on his last day of work, look what happens. No matter where he travels, Evil Evan follows him. It's like something out of Stephen King."

"Or a soap opera."

"Exactly."

Making an excuse, I got up, and walked farther down the beach. Somehow I couldn't stomach any more of Naomi's suspiciousness—not at that moment. And yet I have to say this for her: with the tenacity that distinguishes certain very relentless and untrusting natures, she had managed to root out from Jonathan's story every questionable detail, every immoderate coincidence, laying those trophies before me the way a cat will lay out the remnants of its prey. And faced with such evidence, how could I not revise my own imagined version of what took place?

So: third variation.

Let's agree, at the very least, that Jonathan did end up in Speonk that night. Let's also agree that, either from necessity or by choice, he decided to hitchhike to Hampton Bays. A truck picks him up, only this time the driver is alone. No cousin tags along for the ride. The driver is beer-bellied, hairy-shouldered, wears a New York Knicks baseball cap. He grips the wheel so tightly his knuckles whiten, and the contemplation of those knuckles—the knowledge that this man could crush Jonathan's neck with his bare hands if he wanted—provokes a weird commingling of panic and arousal in Jonathan. His mouth waters. From the little green cardboard tree that dangles from the rearview mirror, there emanates a smell of men's rooms; of urinal cakes.

If the driver recognizes Jonathan, though, he doesn't let on. Instead he says, "Jerry," and holds his hand out sideways as he slows for a red light.

"Jonathan."

They shake. With an audible thunk, the light changes to green. The truck accelerates. "You know, if I take you straight to Hampton Bays, you'll just have to wait at the station," Jerry says. "Tell you what, why don't we go to my place? My wife will make us some coffee."

"Won't she be asleep?"

"Norma?" He laughs. "She never sleeps. Never goes to bed before three, and then she reads."

"Well, if you're sure—"

Without signaling, Jerry maneuvers the truck off the main drag and onto a narrow street lined with shingled houses. In most of them, the lights are off. A few more turns—left, right, left, Jonathan notes, in case he has to escape—and they pull into a graveled driveway bordered with lawn and geraniums. "Home, sweet home," Jerry says, switching off the ignition.

They climb out of the cab. The house is dark except for a yellowish light glimmering in one window. Taking a ring of keys from his belt, Jerry opens the door and shouts, "Norma!"

"In here."

They step through the front hall, where Jerry hangs his cap on a peg. A smell of pot roast and stale coffee lingers in the air. Pushing open a swing door, Jerry leads Jonathan into the kitchen, where a woman with long, badly dyed hair is sitting at the breakfast table, smoking and doing the *New York Times* crossword puzzle. Behind her is a padlocked door. In front of her sits a half-empty glass of orange juice and an ashtray in which a cigarette is smoldering. She is holding a pencil.

Lifting her eyes from the puzzle, she looks Jonathan over—not with surprise, exactly, though not with complacency, either; instead, her expression might best be described as one of slight botheration, enough to tell Jonathan that, though her husband may not be in the habit of bringing strangers home at two in the morning, neither is it unheard of for him to do so.

"Norma, this is Jonathan," Jerry says, and hoists himself up to sit on the corn-yellow countertop. "Jonathan, Norma."

"Hey."

"He was hitching near the station. Got the wrong train out of Jamaica. Has to get to Hampton Bays, but the next train don't leave for a couple of hours."

"Bummer."

"Make some coffee, will you?"

Obediently—but with evident impatience—Norma puts down her pencil, gets up out of her chair, and walks to the stove. She has a big behind. She's wearing an old-fashioned lacy pink bathrobe, buttoned to the neck. Her age is difficult to read. Forty? Forty-five? Although she has the long hair of a girl, and she's painted her nails with glittery pink polish, nonetheless the skin around her throat is pliant and loose. There are tiny, colorless hairs on her cheeks. She reminds Jonathan of an over-the-hill Grateful Dead groupie he once saw interviewed on television—"rode hard and put up wet" was how Ben Brandt described her—and for that very reason, he finds her powerfully attractive, much more attractive, say, than Betsy, the pretty girlfriend for whose sake (at least in part) he quit his job. It's that slight air of tawdriness—the dyed hair, the glittery nails, and then the odd touch of the grandmotherly bathrobe: it all contributes to a fantasy he's working up, has been working up ever since Jerry invited him home. After all, he's no innocent, he's seen the ads in the back of the *Village Voice*, on Internet bulletin boards: COUPLE SEEKS SINGLE . . . INSATIABLE MOM CAN'T GET ENOUGH . . . GIVE IT TO MY WIFE WHILE I WATCH. Is this the real story, then, the real reason Jerry brought him here? And if so, will she go along with it? (Probably; to avoid trouble with her husband, he suspects, she's probably gone along with far worse things. Even so, her lack of interest is vivid, and, curiously enough, the knowledge that she would submit, if at all, reluctantly, only heightens his curiosity.)

And no one, not Betsy nor Naomi nor Ben, will ever know. For he goes unrecognized. That's the icing on the cake. Evil Evan is so far from here he might as well be dead.

Unless, of course, they *do* recognize him and are just pretending not to, so that they can spring something on him at a compromised moment.

The coffee is ready. Norma pours it into mugs and hands one to Jerry, the other to Jonathan. "Thanks," he says. "Oh, 'Life's a Beach.' You know, I never got that joke before."

Norma says nothing. She sits down, grinds out her cigarette, and takes up her pencil.

"Any milk?" Jerry asks.

"Went sour."

A sound of gulping from behind Jonathan.

"Is that today's puzzle you're doing?"

Norma nods.

"I finished it on the train, so if you get stuck on anything, just let me know."

For the first time since his arrival, something akin to a smile passes over Norma's lips. "O.K., smarty-pants, so long as you're offering. Twenty-six across: Monster's home."

He grins. "*Loch,*" he says.

"Shit. Like Loch Ness." She erases. "I had *lair*. So that means twenty-six down is—Musical Lynn. *Loretta*!"

"I was born a coal miner's daughter," Jerry sings.

"Any others?"

She scans. "Thirty-seven down: Bygone queen."

"All right. How many letters have you got?"

"T-blank-blank-blank-I-N-A. At first I thought it might be *Titania*, but that doesn't fit."

"Tsarina."

"Tsarina." She writes in the word. "Which means that fifty-two across—Bleep—is . . . *Edit out*!"

"Why do you waste your time with these stupid puzzles?" Jerry asks. "Up all night, and doing what? Working on your novel? Nope. Puzzles."

"You're writing a novel?"

"I don't like to talk about it," Norma says. "He knows that. He knows I don't like to talk about it."

She returns to the crossword. Behind where she and Jonathan are sitting, her husband chuckles a little. And how curious! Now the Grateful Dead groupie is, of all things, a novelist. She sits up at night doing crossword puzzles. Out of the lips of her jokey husband emerge the words "Butcher Holler . . ."

Soon it will be time to go. Jerry will drive him to Hampton Bays, where he will catch a train to Bridgehampton, where Ben Brandt will pick him up: his own life. And then, in that crowded summer rental on the wrong side of the Montauk Highway, maybe he will tell his friends the story of Jerry and Norma, or some variation on it, adding a twist to make it more interesting and less incriminating. Months will go by, and Betsy will or will not agree to marry him. Evil Evan will recede, and the best part is, he will recede far faster than Jerry and Norma. Far faster than Speonk.

Somewhere a bird starts singing. Only the song isn't coming from outside: it's the clock above the kitchen sink. Instead of numbers, each hour is marked by a different singing bird: great horned owl for twelve, northern mockingbird for one, black-capped chickadee . . .

Who's singing now? Northern cardinal. Three in the morning.

"We'd better scoot if you're going to make your train," Jerry says, alighting from the countertop.

"Fine, just one more clue," Norma says. "Thirty-one across: Arizona attraction."

"*Petrified forest,*" Jonathan says.

"*Petrified forest,* of course." Feverishly she erases. "Good, now I can finish the damn thing. Now, finally, I can finish the damn thing and go to bed."

The Scruff of the Neck

Lily's girl, Audrey, called Rose and asked if she could interview her; she was getting her master's degree in epidemiology, she said, and for her thesis she wanted to prepare a medical history of the entire family. "From soup to nuts" was how she put it. "And since you and Minna are the only ones of the brothers and sisters who are still alive, obviously it's worth the trip to Florida to talk to you."

"You'll want to see Minna, too, then?" Rose asked.

"Let me interview you first," Audrey said, and proposed that she come to tea at Rose's house the following Tuesday.

"Wonderful, dear. And you'll spend the night, won't you? Or a few nights."

But no, Audrey said, she was going to stay with her boyfriend's parents in Fort Lauderdale. "Oh, and if you could have your birth certificate and passport handy, plus any medical records—really, whatever you think might be relevant—that would be great. Also anything on your children. And grandchildren."

"I'll see what I can find."

Audrey hung up. This was on Friday; over the course of the weekend Rose sifted through the boxes in the basement and the files at the back of the kitchen desk, trying to dig up material that Audrey might consider useful. Yet how could she know what Audrey might consider useful? She found vaccination certificates for two of the three children, some old passports, the insurance papers from when Burt had died. (Why had she saved all this stuff?) Also her marriage license. But would that be "relevant"? Rose had no idea, so she stuffed it along with everything else into a big manila folder.

It embarrassed her that she had no pictures of Audrey, or any memories by which to gauge what the girl looked like. The truth was, where her great-nieces and -nephews were concerned, Rose always felt a little at sea. When you are the youngest of eleven, nieces and nephews have a way not only of proliferating, but of sharing the same names, so that it becomes harder and harder to keep track of which David is which, or whether it was Ernie's Sarah or Laura's who had just graduated from law school. Some of them Rose had never met; Audrey she had met only once, when she was three years old. This was only in part circumstantial. Of all her sisters, Harriet, Audrey's grandmother, was the only one to whom Rose had never had much to say. To put it mildly, Harriet had always been eccentric, sitting on the porch on summer evenings and brushing out her long, dark hair to scandalize the neighbors. Later, for reasons that remained murky, she was thrown out of nursing school, then married a rabbi and gave birth to Lily, also a bit of a weirdo. Lily had been divorced more times than Rose cared to remember, had gone to India and changed her name to Anuradha, and stayed at the Betty Ford Center. She had only the one child; was it fair to say, then, based on her phone manner, that the girl took after her mother and grandmother in many ways?

Audrey arrived, as promised, on Tuesday. That morning, Rose woke up worried about tea. Generally speaking, tea wasn't part of her vocabulary; like Minna, she preferred coffee. Although Minna was about to turn ninety-six, she still had lunch every day at Ravelstein's, where she drank black coffee with her corned beef sandwich. She even drank coffee at supper. She had no patience for the cappuccinos and espressos and whatnot that you found at the new Starbucks, which she called Starburst, or sometimes Starbust; no, she preferred good old American coffee, she said, made in a stainless-steel pot. As for Rose, what little she knew of tea she had learned from *Masterpiece Theatre*, programs like *Upstairs, Downstairs*, on which much always seemed to be made over who poured. The details she tried to excavate from memory. At Publix she bought Peek Frean biscuits and cucumbers and Pepperidge Farm thin-sliced bread, as well as several varieties of tea: Queen Mary, Earl Grey, Prince of Wales. But then when she got home she realized that she didn't have any butter. Could you make cucumber sandwiches without butter? Would it be all right to add mayonnaise instead?

She cut the crusts off the bread, spread them with Hellmann's Light Mayonnaise. From outside, barking sounded. She looked out the kitchen window and saw that Dinah, her puppy, was trying to kill the pool sweep again. Round and round Dinah went, chasing the little mechanical monster as it circled the pool, lunging at the water whenever it neared the periphery.

Rose rapped on the windowpane. "Dinah, no!" she scolded. But Dinah didn't stop. Catching the pool sweep between her teeth, she yanked it out of the water. "Dinah, no!" Rose repeated, hurrying out on the deck. "Bad girl! No!"

Dinah looked at her. From the pool sweep's underside, water jets sprayed the deck, the lawn chair, the silk dress Rose had put on for the occasion. "Oh, Dinah!" she said, extracting it from the dog's mouth. "Look what you've done. And now I'll have to change."

Then she picked Dinah up—as the dog lady on television had instructed—by the scruff of the neck. When they misbehave, this dog lady had said, just grab them by the scruff of the neck, the way their mothers did; that way they'll know you mean business.

Hem dripping, Rose carried Dinah inside. Dinah's belly was brindled, the fur on her vulva turned upward in a wet-kiss curl. With adoring eyes, eyes full of lamentation and contrition, she gazed up at Rose, who gazed back. "Oh, Dinah, why can't you learn?" she asked. "And to think that this dress cost more than you did!"

She was just undoing the buttons when the doorbell rang.

Audrey turned out to be a wisp of a thing, with short black hair and squinty eyes. A slender gold ring pierced her left nostril. She wore Groucho Marx glasses, a black turtleneck, black jeans, and carried a black backpack.

"Well, look at you," Rose said, kissing her on the cheek. "Little Audrey, all grown up."

Audrey flinched. Her shoulder blades, when Rose touched them, were bony; static electricity clung to her turtleneck. They stepped into the living room, and Rose sat her down on one of the recliners. From the kitchen she brought the tea things on a tray: the Peek Freans, the sandwiches, the cups and the sugar bowl and the milk pitcher. "You'll have to excuse my appearance," she said, "I've been having a little trouble with the puppy."

"You have a puppy?"

"A Wheaten terrier. Dinah. She's out in the yard now. You see,

George—that's my oldest boy—gave her to me last autumn when your uncle Burt passed on. And she has this thing about the pool sweep. She loves to chase the pool sweep."

"What's a pool sweep?"

"Well, it's—how do you describe it? It's that little thing that circles round the pool and cleans it."

"I've never seen one of those."

"Newer pools don't have them. Ours is almost thirty years old, if you can believe it . . . oh, but I've forgotten to give you tea. And what kind would you like? As you can see, I've got 'em all. Earl Grey, Queen Mary, the whole royal family."

"Actually, I don't drink tea. Could I have a Diet Coke?"

"Of course. If I have any. I'll check. Otherwise it may have to be normal Coke."

"That's fine." Audrey was opening her backpack, arranging notebooks and binders and spreadsheets on the coffee table.

"Georgie's a stockbroker," Rose called from the kitchen. "He lives in New York. Oh good, here's some Coke. Anyway, he worries about me—too much, if you want my opinion. That's why he got me Dinah. At first I wasn't too happy about it, let me tell you. I mean, I've raised three boys, the last thing I needed was something else to take care of. But since then, Dinah and I, we've gotten to be good friends. And I must say, it's nice having something to shout at again!"

"My mother has a Rottweiler," Audrey said.

"Does she now?"

"For protection. I always say to her, Mom, with all those alarms and window grates, you've got nothing to worry about, you could be living in Fort Knox. Still, she says she can't sleep at night. So she bought this, like, killer dog."

Rose, popping open the Coke can, nodded gravely; sat across from her niece. "Cucumber sandwich?"

"No thanks."

"Cookie?"

Audrey was studying a spreadsheet. "Maybe later." She looked her aunt in the eye. "Well, Rose—do you mind if I just call you Rose?"

"You have to ask? We're family."

"Okay. So, Rose, like I told you, for my master's thesis I'm doing a medical history of the whole family, looking at which illnesses crop up most commonly, environmental factors, genetic predispositions—that sort of thing."

"What a wonderful idea. Your mother must be very proud of you."

"She's too out of it to be proud of anything I do . . . but never mind." Audrey opened her pen. "To begin with, I'd like to get the basic data on your branch of the family—you know, dates of birth, places of birth, that sort of thing."

"I got it all ready for you." Rose pushed the manila folder in Audrey's direction.

"And the full names of your children—let me make sure I have these right. George Robert, born July 7, 1954—"

"He's my oldest. Not married yet, but we're still hoping."

"Then Daniel Jeremy, born October 20, 1957."

"He's back in New Jersey. Tenafly. Teaches high school English. Got divorced last year, I'm still sorry about it, she was a lovely girl—"

"And finally Kevin Leon, born February 14, 1960."

"The baby of the family. They just moved to Singapore. The company sends him all over the place. First Germany, then France, and now—"

"And he's got kids, right?"

"That's right. His wife is Denyse—with a Y, not an I. The little ones are adorable. David Bernard and Sarah Rose. Would you like to see pictures? I've got pictures."

"That's O.K. And all the documents are in here?" Audrey pointed to the manila folder.

"All there."

"May I take these with me and make photocopies? I'll bring them back, of course."

"Of course."

She scribbled. "So when did you move down to Florida?"

"It must have been . . . 1970? Could it have been 1970? Hard to believe, the time's gone by so fast. It's funny, most people assume that just because I'm an old lady, I must have retired here, but the fact is, we raised our kids in this house. Our boys all went to high school in West Palm."

"And Minna?"

"Oh, Minna was already here. Minna retired . . . it must have been sixty-five, sixty-six. She's been retired longer than you've been alive! But if you don't mind my asking, what have you found out so far? Anything about migraines? All my boys get terrible migraines."

"My data is really too preliminary to share. But I have prepared a survey"—she pushed some more sheets across the table—"which I wonder if you might fill out. Also your sons."

"And Minna?"

"Well, if she's—you know—clearheaded enough."

"Minna?" Rose laughed. "She's sharper than any of us. Oh, maybe she can't get around as easily as she used to, but she still drives, and she's got a mind like a steel trap. We should all be in such good shape at her age!"

"Good, then maybe you could give her a copy."

"But why don't you go see her yourself while you're here? She's just a little ways down the coast. And I'll tell you, it would make her day. She loves all the nieces and nephews, keeps up to date on all of you, I suppose because she never had children of her own."

Audrey coughed. Over her folder, she gave Rose a look of—what to call it? Curiosity? Pity? Some hybrid of the two?

"Yes, well, that was something else I wanted to talk to you about. I meant to wait until later, but since you've brought it up—"

"What, dear?"

"According to your birth certificate, you were born August 11, 1920, is that right?"

"That's right. A Leo."

"In Cape May, New Jersey."

Rose nodded. "You see, Momma wasn't feeling well that summer, and it was so hot that Poppa decided to send her away from Newark, so she went to stay at a hotel in Cape May. Minna went too—to take care of her."

"And when was Minna born?"

"When would that have been? 1902, 1903? 1902, I guess. Funny, isn't it, that of all eleven kids, only the two of us are left? Oldest and youngest. Like bookends."

Audrey pulled a stack of photocopies out of her briefcase. "Last year, I went to the hall of records in Newark," she said, "to see when all of you were born. And then, when I couldn't find your birth certificate, I asked my mother, and she told me about your being born in Cape May. So I went down to Cape May. It took me a while, but I tracked down the information."

"But, darling, you didn't have to go all the way to Cape May! You could have just called me!"

"Yes, I know. But I had another reason." She pointed at the photocopies.

"And what was that?"

"I'd better explain. As I'm sure you know, my grandmother was a major pack rat."

"Boy, do I. Harriet never threw anything away."

"Well, after the house was sold—your parents' house—she was the one who took charge of packing it up, on account of being the closest to home, and what was in the attic she just basically moved to her own attic. All those trunks and boxes, which no one ever opened. For years. My grandfather used to gripe about it, every now and then he'd threaten to burn it all, or have a sale, but Grandma wouldn't hear of it. And I suppose she had her reasons, because what Grandpa saw as just a fire hazard turned out to be a treasure trove for me, for my study. I mean, when I started going through those trunks last summer, I found everything: every doctor's bill, every dentist's bill, every medical record. Your high school grades. Your mother even made notes of all your illnesses, in a big black ledger. One for every year from when Minna was born until Grandma died."

"Momma was very meticulous."

"But here's the thing—that summer, the summer of 1920, there's just nothing."

"Well, as I said, she was in Cape May. And it was a hard pregnancy. She had to be in bed for most of it."

"And Minna went with her?"

"To take care of her. Poppa could only get away from the shop on weekends. You can ask her yourself when you see her, she remembers everything—the name of the hotel, what their room number was."

Audrey picked up the photocopies and started shuffling through them. "Have you ever seen these?" she asked, handing them to Rose.

"What are they?" Rose put on her reading glasses, which hung from a rope around her neck. "Let me see . . . Oh, doctor's bills."

"Dr. Homer M. Hayes, Cape May, New Jersey. An obstetrician."

"Oh, so this must have been the doctor that Momma saw when she was pregnant with me."

"But look at the top. Under patient's name, it doesn't say Effie Miller. It says Minna Miller. And not only on one—on all of them."

"Oh, it does, doesn't it?" Rose's hands fluttered, so that the papers made a slight noise, like birds passing overhead.

"There are bills here for ten different visits. All related to a pregnancy. And on every one of them the name is Minna Miller." Audrey leaned in closer, across the undrunk Coke and the Peek Freans. "Do you see?" she asked. "Do you understand why I had to talk to you?"

Rose played with her wedding ring. Glancing at one of the cucumber sandwiches, she observed that a little mayonnaise was dripping over the edges of the thin-sliced bread. She picked up the tea tray and carried it toward the kitchen.

"What's the matter?" Audrey asked, almost hungrily.

"It's nothing, dear," Rose said. "I think I hear Dinah, that's all. I think Dinah is crying to come in."

Once, in her youth, Rose had been thought a wild driver. Oh, how her mother had wailed whenever she'd gone off in her little roadster, in those years when it was considered shocking for a girl even to have a license! To Rose's mother driving was, quite simply, unladylike, the sort of thing you would have expected of Harriet. "But you let Minna drive!" Rose had countered.

"It's different in Minna's case," her mother had said. "Minna needs to drive to go to work." For Minna was an elementary school teacher, and the school at which she taught was out in the country, near New Vernon.

Fifty-some years later, Rose still drove—slowly. It was not that she was any less bold; rather, it seemed that the velocity of the world had increased while her own pace stayed the same, leaving her the object of impatient tailgating on the part of young women in station wagons: young women with children in the back seat, as she had had children in the back seat, not so long ago.

With Minna the problem was worse. She was always losing her car in the parking lot at Publix. That afternoon, just after Audrey left, she called Rose, and said, "I can't think where I've left it. I've been up and down every row. I can't think—"

"But, darling," Rose had said, "didn't you tie something to the antenna, like I told you the last time?"

"Yes I did. Only isn't that the joke? For the life of me I can't remember what."

"Dinah, no! Bad girl!" Rose hit the window, which shuddered.

"Listen, Minna, don't worry. Just sit yourself down in the air-conditioning, and I'll be there in a jiff."

"As soon as you can. Otherwise the ice cream will melt. Oh, and Rose"—here Minna's voice grew soft, even coy—"I promise it will never happen again."

They hung up. Rose went into the garage. Really, Minna was getting to be a bit of a trial these days. When Rose was a girl, and Harriet had said something cruel to her, Minna always sat her in front of the mirror, brushed out her hair, and counseled, "This too shall pass." And usually Minna was right: the wrong did pass, though Rose never came to understand why Harriet hated her so much. Now she wondered if that hatred had passed through the generations, like the hook of the nose or of the lip, to Audrey. Audrey, like her grandmother, was clearly not the kind ever to let go of a grudge. Instead she would build a citadel from the wrongs that had been done her, and gain what sustenance she could from leeching other people's woes.

Who was the father, anyway? "My father," Rose said to herself, climbing into the Cadillac and lighting a cigarette. For she couldn't remember Minna ever having had even a single boyfriend. She was the schoolteacher, the caregiver. And yet there must have been someone. Somewhere along the line, someone whose name was never mentioned, yet who had a name, a family with its own *meshugaas*, its own medical history to be charted by some enterprising niece. And where was that family? Was it big, with even more nieces and nephews for Rose to confuse? (Remembering that you could get a ticket for not wearing one, she put on her seat belt.) God, it was hot . . . Stupid to have stuck it out in south Florida for the summer, when in the old days she and Burt had always gotten away in August, gone north to the Cape. But Burt was dead, and she had Minna to attend to. Minna, quite simply, could not be left on her own.

Oh, what a foolish thing to do! And why had they done it? For it must have been a conspiracy. Not that anyone would have ever thought to question them, since as it stood Effie was pregnant all the time anyway, it made sense that she should be pregnant. And Minna . . . who would have ever guessed it of her? Never married. Up until today, Rose had wondered if she had ever even loved.

She pressed a button. With a creak, the garage door opened, admitting a light so harsh Rose had to squint against it. Where were her sunglasses?

In her bag? She rummaged for a moment, found them at last, put them on (the world became pink), then, turning the key, felt the first gusts of hot breeze that presaged the air-conditioning hit her wrists. Lastly she switched on the cassette player—on the highway, Mozart calmed her—and looking over her shoulder, lurched backward, with a great shudder, onto Ixora Avenue.

Cautiously, even timidly, Rose made her way to the highway. Near a red light, a station wagon bore down on her, its driver, a young woman with children in the back seat, flashing her brights, making a face Rose could see quite plainly in the rearview mirror. Seconds pulsed by, the light changed, and she rose up onto the interstate; her tormentor passed her, disappearing into a haze of motion. Ten miles of blind panic now separated Rose from Minna, ten miles of off-ramps and merging lanes and terrifying low-slung vehicles with oversized tires, windows tinted black, chain metal frames for the license tags. As if edges meant safety, she kept to the slow lane the whole way, sandwiched between a pair of trucks that let off plumes of exhaust but also offered, in their immensity, a measure of protection. Yet she was nothing as compared to Minna, who drove so slowly that she'd actually gotten a ticket for it. Yes, there was a speed limit on the other side too; you could get a ticket for going under it. Really, she had no business being behind a wheel, George said; she was a menace, and not only to herself. Only, who had the heart to stop her, when she valued her independence more than her life? For that was the thing everyone said about Minna: "She loves her independence!" Never asking anything of anybody, until lately.

Was that the reason, then? Would a child—would Rose—have compromised her beloved independence?

At last the turnoff neared. Where Minna lived was a world of old people. All the businesses catered to them. Clever entrepreneurs traded in urban nostalgia, peddling bagels with a schmear, take-out Chinese food spiced down to suit elderly stomachs. It always made Rose a little uneasy, coming here. After all, unlike her sister, she had moved to Florida as a vital woman of middle age. She had raised her boys in a nice neighborhood with frangipani and banyan trees, street games after school, and on Halloween so many trick-or-treaters they ended up having to give away the hard candy moldering on the piano.

Minna, on the other hand, had arrived already old. For three decades she'd been living in her one-bedroom apartment with its view of the Intracoastal, in a squat, modest building which had once shared the waterfront with no one, but over which, every year, more gleaming towers crouched, throwing shadows onto the patio, stealing the sun.

It was George's sensible opinion that Minna couldn't go on like this much longer. She could barely get herself dressed anymore. A nice old folks' home, he counseled, or one of those places where they *think* they're on their own, but there are nurses. And yet why was it that whenever George talked about putting Minna away, within seconds he invariably brought the conversation around to what he called Rose's own "situation"? "Why not sell the house?" he'd ask. "Now that you're on your own, it must be an awful lot to keep up with. Buy yourself a little condo instead."

The exit snuck up on her, as it always did. Alarmed by its sudden appearance, she cut across three lanes of traffic, enraging a truck, which honked and startled her. Off the highway a red light gave her a moment to collect her thoughts. Back when she and Burt had first moved here, farmland had shouldered the interstate on both sides. But now everywhere she looked there were warehouses, and warehousey strip malls, and supermarkets, including the Publix where Minna had lost the car. From where she waited, Rose surveyed its parking lot, stretching all the way to the cyclone fence that blocked off the highway.

Finally the light changed. She turned right, pulled up to the curb in front of the market, and, leaving the engine running, hurried through the doors to find Minna. There she sat, slumped on a bench by the telephone. Her white hair fell over her forehead in a wave. She was wearing a striped jersey and stretch blue jeans. Even though she was asleep, one of her hands lolled protectively over the handle of a cart brimming with groceries. And what on earth made her think she needed all that stuff? It would only go to waste.

"Darling, I'm here," Rose said, patting Minna's shoulder, at which point Minna's eyes opened.

"Oh, Rose! I must have dropped off." She hoisted herself to her feet; made to take hold of the grocery cart.

"No, I'll get it," Rose said, and pushed her away with a gesture so violent that Minna's hands flew instinctively to her face.

* * *

"Darling, what a relief it is to see you," Minna said, once they were safe in Rose's car. "You can't imagine how vulnerable I felt, sitting there by myself, with all that food. People stared."

"It's all right, I'm here now."

"A man stared . . . a long time. I was afraid."

"Only I do think that in the future you might consider asking Mrs. Lopez—"

"And then I thought, what would I have done if you hadn't been home? Sat here until the market closed, or you came back?"

"Nonsense, you would have called Mrs. Lopez and she would have fetched you."

"But her car's in the shop. She takes the bus."

"Well then, I'm sure the police would have helped." (In fact, if George had had his way, she wouldn't have rescued Minna at all. Instead she would have left her to stew in her own juices, learn her lesson the hard way.) "Anyway, now we need to concentrate on finding your car. Where do you think you left it?"

"I'm sure it was on the left. And not too far back."

"You didn't happen to write down the row number, did you?"

"I didn't think I needed to. Because I'd tied the whatchamacallit to the antenna. The whosiwhatsit. And I thought . . . Oh, look! Yes, I remember now, it was a dog toy. A little rubber blowfish, with spikes all over—look, there's one!"

"But, Minna, that's a Toyota. You drive a Ford."

They turned right. To Rose's surprise, practically every car in the parking lot had something tied to its antenna: stuffed dolls, balloons, brightly tinted clothespins. It was inevitable that there should be repetition, which was why so many anxious-looking old men and women were now pushing their carts through the heat, eyes open for signs of home, trying to stave off the terror of being lost. None of them was as lucky as Minna, with Rose at the ready to rescue her.

"Honey, forgive me for asking, but you do have your keys, don't you?"

"Yes, of course. That's the first thing I checked."

"Good. And you did lock up—"

"Of course I locked up! What do you take me for?"

"Nothing, darling, I just thought it was worth making sure—" Suddenly Rose braked. "There," she said. "There it is."

"Oh, thank God!" Tears welled in Minna's old eyes. "I didn't want to say anything, but the truth was, I was scared."

"I know," said Rose. For Minna's car had been stolen before. It had been stolen because she had left the keys in the ignition and forgotten to lock the door. Another time she *had* locked the door, but left the engine running. Both times Rose was summoned.

With a great effort, Minna climbed out of her sister's car and got into her own.

Minna's progress was glacial. It took them nearly twenty minutes to get back to her apartment building, which was three quarters of a mile from the Publix. "Thanks, honey," she said when they finally pulled into the parking lot. "Say, you want to come in for a minute? Have a cup of coffee?"

"Of course I'll come in." Rose popped the trunk. She got out of the car, picked up a bag of groceries.

"Be careful. Don't hurt yourself."

"What choice do I have? I can't leave this stuff to rot."

The apartment was on the ground floor. "Sit down," Minna said once they were inside, and she was easing herself into the lounger in front of the television. "Take a load off. You want some ice cream?"

"No thanks." Rose unpacked.

"I got chocolate marshmallow. Your favorite."

"No, I wouldn't care—Minna, what on earth do you need with three gallons of ice cream?"

"Someone might drop by."

"But no one ever drops by! When was the last time in twenty years that anyone dropped by? And look—you've got three in the freezer already. That's six gallons."

"But Georgie loves ice cream."

"Georgie lives in New York now. He only comes down twice a year." She put the ice cream away. "Honey, you've really got to start using your head, otherwise—"

"Or that Audrey. Lily's girl. What if she drops by? You said she was coming this week."

Rose closed the freezer. "Yes, Audrey might. It's interesting, she's doing a medical history of the family. For her thesis. She seems very bright."

"Lily's always been a strange one, hasn't she?"

"Takes after Harriet."

"Momma was very hard on Harriet. Especially after she got thrown out of nursing school."

"Momma always seemed to resent all of us girls for being girls."

"You can say that again."

Rose sat down across from Minna. "You know, Audrey's dug up the most incredible stuff for her study," she said. "For instance, in Harriet's attic, she found some old ledgers where Momma wrote down every time one of us got sick. Plus all the medical reports, the doctors' bills . . ."

"Momma was very organized. It's a pity women couldn't go to work in those days. She would have made a great CEO. She was much smarter than Poppa. Poor Poppa. Without her, he would have run the store into the ground."

"Yes, Minna, but as I was saying, Audrey found all the old medical bills, even from Cape May."

"You mean when you were born?"

"I've always wanted to know more about that summer."

"Well, Momma was sick. She had terrible morning sickness to start with, plus she had bleeding, so the doctor said she needed to stay in bed until it was time. And with all the kids, and the heat—it was murderous that summer—there was no use in her staying home. So we went to Cape May."

"To a hotel."

"Not much fun for me, I can tell you! Just a girl, and cooped up in that room all day with Momma."

"And was Poppa there?"

"He came when he could. But basically it was just the two of us. Momma and me. I tell you, we sure got on each other's nerves! Talk about cabin fever. And of course she was nervous, knowing that Poppa was running the store by himself. He couldn't keep books very well, not to mention the women coming in all the time. Momma was never easy in the head when she couldn't keep an eye on him."

"And then she had me?"

"We stayed on a few days more so she could recuperate. Then we went home."

"But, Minna, honey"—Rose leaned closer—"those bills that Audrey dug up, there's something funny about them. The name on them isn't Momma's, it's yours."

"Mine?"

"I mean, you're listed as the patient."

"Oh, then they must be bills from a different doctor. I remember I had a terrible flu—"

"No, they're from the obstetrician. Dr. Homer Hayes."

"Then he must have gotten our names mixed up."

Rose blinked. Minna's eyes were focused on the switched-off television, the gray amplitude of which reflected only her own face. She stared at herself as if she were a program.

Rose got up. She walked to the kitchen, where she pulled some bowls out of the cupboard.

"If you don't mind, I think I will have that ice cream now," she said.

"Have all you want. There's loads."

"And you?"

"Sure I will. Chocolate marshmallow."

The ice cream hadn't been in the freezer long enough to harden up after the wait at the supermarket. With a wet plopping noise it fell from the spoon into the dishes, which were chipped at the edges, patterned with butterflies. Rose carried them back into the living room.

"Minna—" She handed her the ice cream. "What Audrey said, it doesn't make any difference. Once, maybe. Not now."

"I did have the worst flu that summer. I could hardly get out of bed."

"We're none the worse for it," Rose said. "None the better, but none the worse." Then she sat down with her ice cream, and they ate. The sun was warm, until a cloud blocked it, throwing shadows against the television. And how curious—in that darkened moment, Minna looked to Rose like no one so much as Dinah, when she had picked her up by the scruff of the neck. Eyes wide, she gazed at Rose, helpless and inscrutable and oddly tranquil. Then the cloud passed. Light returned, revealing a greasy fingerprint on the edge of the screen, a fissure of thread where one of the curtains had been mended.

"Oh, honey, your hair's a mess. Let me brush it."

"It's all right."

"No, let me brush it," Rose insisted. And she picked up a brush from the tray table by the television; pulled her chair alongside Minna's lounger. "You used to do this for me, when I was little."

"Ow!"

"Sorry, did I pull too hard?"

"It's O.K. I did, didn't I? Whenever Harriet made you cry."

White hairs, long and fine, collected on the bristles. "You know, I always wanted to have a little girl," Rose said. "Just my luck I should end up with three boys."

"Momma was hoping for a boy," Minna said. "She was always hoping for a boy. But I wanted a little girl, too."

The List

SUBJ: **The List**
DATE: Monday, July 17, 2000, 2:43:51 PM
FROM: ivorystuds@entropy.net
TO: jkwitt@wellspring.edu

Dear Jeff,

I thought you might get a kick out of the attached list of gay/lesbian pianists from the past two centuries, which Willard Pearson and I have been putting together in our spare time. Do you know Willard, by the way? Since 1995 he's directed the piano program at St. Blaise College in New Hampshire; he's also the former president of the Paderewski Society, and editor of the society's journal. The list began as a simple exchange of gossip but gradually grew to epic proportions as each of us added names and solicited information from friends. You'll notice at the bottom there's a section called "On the Fence," featuring pianists about whom we've heard rumors but received no corroborating evidence. Any additions you might like to make would be most welcome.

Re your biography of Bulthaup: although I continue to read and enjoy the ms., I feel I must warn you that by emphasizing the sexual side of his relationship with his manager, you risk an upheaval of negative response. Many orthodox admirers will accuse you of "outing" B. just to sell copies, claiming that his sexuality was irrelevant to his playing etc. My feeling so far (I'm on Chapter 11) is that in Chapter 9 you tread on particularly shaky ground by suggesting that B.'s sexual confusion influenced his performance style. Are you trying to appease the "queer studies" crowd here? Or has your publisher been pressuring you to give the book a "gay" angle, in order to guarantee review attention?

While I know that you need my collection of photos, programs, etc., for research purposes and to reproduce, I'm sure you'll understand that I could not possibly permit you to use this precious archival material if I did not feel that the project was one with which I was in unwavering accord—i.e., one that presents B. in the proper light. We'll have to wait until I've seen your revisions before I make a decision. Please remember that I have a responsibility to B.'s heirs as well as to history.

Hugs,
Tim

P.S. Am I ever going to get to hear your voice? Or see your face? Do you ever come up to San Francisco? :)

SUBJ: **Re: The List**
DATE: Monday, July 17, 2000, 4:41:32 PM
FROM: jkwitt@wellspring.edu
TO: ivorystuds@entropy.net

Dear Tim,

Thanks very much for your e-mail of earlier this afternoon, as well as for "the list," which (not surprisingly) I've spent the last several minutes perusing. You and Pearson (whom I don't know personally but who once published a letter of mine in the *Paderewski Journal*) have certainly done your homework! Let's get Bulthaup out of the way before I proceed, however.

First of all, I want to say that I really appreciate your warnings about the risks implicit in my frank discussion of B.'s homosexuality. As I'm sure you know, one of the great difficulties inherent in any biographical project is that of balancing the short view with the long view. It's all too easy to lose perspective, until you can no longer tell what you might have overstated. And, as I'm not one of those writers who balks at the possibility that his ideas might ever be less than perfectly worked out, might I ask you a favor? As you read, could you note in the margins those passages where you feel I overdo the gay thing? I can then use your suggestions as a guideline in editing the book.

Let me state from the outset, however, that if I lay stress here to the "gay angle," as you call it, it is for none of the reasons you propose. Indeed, I bristle at the implication that I would ever write to appease anyone, queer studies professors or publishers or even you. On the contrary, I'm simply doing the biographer's job, which is to portray the subject's life as it was lived, and not as other people (including Bulthaup himself) might want it to be portrayed. Bear in mind that if Fabia Bulthaup were still alive, she'd have lawyers breathing down my neck to stop me from even mentioning his affair with Cesare, though this was common knowledge not only in New York and Paris, but in the Bulthaup household.

Now, an important question: I know you well enough to know that you would never advocate the suppression of material that would be crucial to an accurate rendering of the man's life and career. And yet you express worry lest my book should fail to show B. in the "proper light." Well, what is the proper light? If what bothers you is my referring to the possibility of a homosexual aesthetic of performance, as epitomized by Bulthaup's playing, please remember that it was Bulthaup himself who first suggested that idea, in a letter to Cesare (now published). If I take my cue from anyone, it's from him. Believe me, I've labored for many hours over this point, and have really come to believe in my argument: not only Bulthaup's interpretations, but his choice of music, program organization, obsession with lighting, etc., reveal what he himself called (I did not invent this) an "invert's preoccupations." If this part of the book provokes controversy, well, what interesting argument doesn't provoke controversy? And I would rather be attacked for saying something challenging than cosseted for having been a good boy.

As for the photos, programs, etc.—obviously I realize that you own this material, and that it is yours to do with it as you see fit. I also understand that to a great degree, your livelihood depends on the material maintaining its value on the antiquarian market. And yet I hope you will bear in mind as you make your decision that in asking you to let me reproduce some of this stuff, my motive is neither to reduce its commercial value nor to misrepresent Bulthaup; instead it is simply to make B. the human being more accessible—more "real," if you will—to an audience of admirers that has rarely seen his private side. (In this regard the photos are of far greater value than the programs.) What I'm saying is that I want to use the photos *in order* to show Bulthaup in the proper light, and that, though I hope and trust we can come to an agreement, I'm not prepared to betray my instincts in order to obtain them.

On to the list: what a curious document! Although many of the names came as no surprise to me, some, in particular [omission], quite took me aback. I mean, so far as [omission] is concerned, all you ever hear is that she's always been something of a femme fatale, with many (male) lovers. What I find hard to believe, in other words, is not that she had a taste for lesbianism, but that she had time for it.

For your "On the Fence" section, let me add two names. Years ago the horrible Crispin Fishwick told me that [omission] made eyes at him backstage during the Levintritt competition. He is hardly reliable, however. (Did I mention that he has the lowest body temperature of any human being with whom I've ever had the misfortune to share a bed? Literally a "cold Fishwick." Ha-ha.) The second name I would suggest is that of [omission]—this based on nothing except an intuition I felt when I heard him play Szymanowski last year.

All best,
Jeff

SUBJ: **Re: Re: The List**
DATE: Wednesday, July 19, 2000, 7:12:02 AM
FROM: ivorystuds@entropy.net
TO: jkwitt@wellspring.edu

Dear Jeff,

Thanks for your thorough reply to my earlier e-mail. You've given me a lot of food for thought, and it will take me several days to digest it all! For the moment, though, rest assured that of course I will note in the margins of the ms. those moments where you overdo "the gay thing," as you call it.

Re [omission]: back in the late seventies when I was living with Andy Mangold in New York City, and she was married to [omission], they were part of that swinging Studio 54 crowd. Andy and I were sort of on the fringe of all that. In those days both she and [omission] were pretty AC/DC (you'll see that he's on the list too), and I know for a fact that she had an affair with [omission], who was just starting her film career then. After that ended she took up with [omission], had a child, etc. But for a while there she was a card-carrying glamour-dyke.

I can't write much as I'm just back from a music memorabilia swap meet in Montreal, where I picked up a nice autographed Bulthaup program from 1932. On the way back I stopped off at St. Blaise to have lunch with Willard Pearson. I'm afraid that when I told him I'd shared the list with you he went into an absolute tizzy, as apparently he's just finished reading the manuscript of your book, which he got from Greg Samuels when he was visiting the Meerschaum Institute last week, and has concluded that you are a relentless gossip, not to be trusted, etc. Now his demented worry is that out of some zealous desire to "out" everyone on the list, you'll not only distribute it far and wide but make sure everyone you show it to knows that he was responsible for it, resulting in the ruin of his career, blah-blah-blah. I wouldn't worry about this too much. Willard is an hysterical queen of the old school, which means it doesn't take much to get his panties into a wad. And as he gets older, he just gets worse. In any event, by the end of lunch I'd managed to calm him down, reassure him that you would never send the list to anyone, and restore at least a little of his trust in me.

Better run—I have to take the dog for a walk.

Hugs,
Tim

SUBJ: **Re: Re: Re: The List**
DATE: Wednesday, July 19, 2000, 9:43:22 AM
FROM: jkwitt@wellspring.edu
TO: ivorystuds@entropy.net

Dear Tim,

I can't pretend it doesn't disturb me that Willard Pearson has formed such a low opinion of me. Please reassure him that I have no intention—indeed, have never had any intention—of sharing his list with anyone. In fact I've already erased it from my hard disk.

I must also confess that his attitude toward the list itself perplexes me almost as much as his attitude toward my book. I mean, why is this such a big deal to him? Does he really imagine that if the list got out, it would provoke anything more than a yawn? Things like this circulate all the time. Nor is the world of the piano one in which news of this sort would "ruin" a career—not anymore. Maybe it's generational, but I simply fail to see why the matter has assumed, in his mind, such epic proportions, or why, if he's so worried about his professional colleagues finding out that he's queer, he put the list together in the first place.

I wish Greg Samuels hadn't shown my book to him. I sent him the ms. in confidence. Indeed, aside from a few friends here at Wellspring, you and Samuels are the only people who've seen the thing so far (and a rough thing it is at this stage, too). Nor is this the sort of behavior I would have expected from Samuels, who has always struck me as upright almost to a fault—if anything, too straight an arrow.

Fondly,
Jeff

SUBJ: **Greg Samuels**
DATE: Wednesday, July 19, 2000, 10:36:12 AM
FROM: ivorystuds@entropy.net
TO: jkwitt@wellspring.edu

Dear Jeff,

Greg is a very intelligent man, and a talented musician in his own right. I wouldn't worry too much about the fact that he gave your book to Willard: they are old friends, and I'm sure Greg felt he could trust Willard with it. I've known Greg for years, ever since he was an aspirant in his own right and used to come sometimes to parties at Lenny's apartment. He was very good-looking as a youth, and I remember that once when some old pouf made a pass at him, he nearly had a stroke—he was so naive, he didn't know what homosexuality was.

Fortunately he's loosened up a lot over the years, and though his home life's pretty starchy—you know, perfect wife, 3.5 kids, suburban house—he no longer bats an eyelash when the rest of us act outlandishly. At first, when he was hired to direct the Meerschaum, I was dubious—I didn't think he had the scholarly qualifications—but since then he's surprised me by doing a superb job.

Hugs,
Tim

SUBJ: **Re: Greg Samuels**
DATE: Wednesday, July 19, 2000, 10:52:00 AM
FROM: jkwitt@wellspring.edu
TO: ivorystuds@entropy.net

Dear Tim,

While I appreciate the testimonial to Greg Samuels's good heart, I'm still very upset and angry that he would share the manuscript with *anyone* without first asking my permission. That kind of behavior, in my view, is inexcusable in a professional.

Fondly,
J.

SUBJ: **No Subject**
DATE: Wednesday, July 19, 2000, 11:45:31 AM
FROM: jkwitt@wellspring.edu
TO: gregory_samuels@meerschaum.org

Dear Mr. Samuels,

This morning I received an e-mail from Tim Kruger, who tells me that last week you gave a copy of the manuscript of my Otto Bulthaup biography to Willard Pearson. Needless to say, this came as something of a shock. When I asked you to read the manuscript, and you kindly agreed to do so, I thought it went without saying that the draft in question was meant for your eyes only. Instead it appears that you have been casually making photocopies and distributing them to all and sundry, which in my view amounts not only to a breach of civility, but of professional ethics. After all, this is only a working draft, and hence not intended for public consumption.

I believe you owe me, at the very least, an explanation.

Yours sincerely,
Jeffrey K. Witt
Assistant Professor of the Humanities
Wellspring University

SUBJ: **Re: No Subject**
DATE: Wednesday, July 19, 2000, 12:32:12 PM
FROM: gregory_samuels@meerschaum.org
TO: jkwitt@wellspring.edu

Dear Mr. Witt,

Thank you for your e-mail of earlier this morning. Despite whatever Mr. Kruger may have told you concerning Mr. Pearson, I can assure you that the charges you have made against me are completely unfounded. While Mr. Pearson did visit my office last Tuesday for the purposes of research, and while he did ask about your manuscript, which was sitting on my desk, aside from verifying that you had sent it to me for comment, I never discussed the matter with him, nor offered him the opportunity to look at anything more than the title page. At a certain point during our conversation, it is true, I was obliged to leave my office for approximately three to three and one half minutes, during which time Mr. Pearson might possibly have thumbed through the pages in question. Unless he is a devotee of Evelyn Wood, however, I cannot see how he would have been able to read the entire book in that brief span of time; nor did the pages appear to have been disturbed in any way during the period I was away from my desk.

I am not, nor have I ever been, in the habit of distributing photocopies of manuscripts sent to me in confidence to "all and sundry." Indeed, I have shared your manuscript with no one, not even my wife.

Let me suggest that in future you apprise yourself of the facts before sending e-mails of this sort, or at the very least make inquiries before making accusations.

Sincerely, Gregory C. Samuels, Director,
The Hilma Meerschaum Institute for Research on the Piano

SUBJ: **Re: Re: No Subject**
DATE: Wednesday, July 19, 2000, 12:57:01 PM
FROM: jkwitt@wellspring.edu
TO: gregory_samuels@meerschaum.org

Dear Mr. Samuels,

Thank you very much for your prompt reply to my e-mail, and please accept my apologies if in it I seemed to cast aspersions on your character. Unfortunately, I took it for granted that what Mr. Kruger reported to me regarding Mr. Pearson was true. Obviously I was mistaken. Either Mr. Kruger was misinformed by Mr. Pearson, or he misunderstood what Mr. Pearson said. I am very sorry that I jumped to conclusions, and trust that this unfortunate misunderstanding will not affect our future relationship.

Yours sincerely,
Jeffrey K. Witt
Assistant Professor of the Humanities
Wellspring University

SUBJ: **Fwd: Re: No Subject**
DATE: Wednesday, July 19, 2000, 3:44:12 PM
FROM: jkwitt@wellspring.edu
TO: ivorystuds@entropy.net

Dear Tim,

Please find enclosed a copy of a letter I just received from Greg Samuels, to whom I wrote after you told me that he had shared my ms. with Willard Pearson. If Samuels is to be believed, then Willard Pearson must have gotten the ms. from another source—Might he have read your copy? Or perhaps he only pretended to have read the manuscript. Yet if that were the case, what would have led him to assume that I was such a gossip?

Any illumination you could provide would be much appreciated.

Jeff

SUBJ: **No Subject**
DATE: Thursday, July 20, 2000, 6:49:31 AM
FROM: ivorystuds@entropy.net
TO: jkwitt@wellspring.edu

Dear Jeff,

You should not have written to Greg Samuels. Now, as a result of your interference, my friendship with Willard—a friendship of twenty years' standing—is over. Greg wrote to Willard, who wrote to me. The fragile peace we had brokered was destroyed as he accused me of betraying his confidence not once but twice—the second time by telling you that he had read Greg's copy of your book. Now he fears that Greg will never trust him again. He also considers your hotheadedness with Greg further evidence that you are a dangerous person so far as the list is concerned. Which is to say nothing of Greg's annoyance with me!

Under the circumstances, you will understand that I can no longer possibly allow you to use my Bulthaup material, no matter what revisions you make. I shall be sending the ms. back to you shortly.

Tim

SUBJ: **Tim Kruger**
DATE: Friday, July 21, 2000, 2:14:03 PM
FROM: jkwitt@wellspring.edu
TO: willard.e.pearson@music.stblaise.edu

Dear Professor Pearson,

We have not met. I am the Bulthaup biographer with whom Tim Kruger recently elected to share a certain list that you and he had compiled—a decision that has provoked all sorts of ill will, and led, at least from what I gather, to the dissolution of your long friendship. Now I find myself in the unenviable position of suddenly being persona non grata with three colleagues none of whom I have ever met. Tim blames me for wrecking his friendship with you, Greg Samuels is affronted that I accused him of behaving irresponsibly, and you consider me an untrustworthy gossip—and all this thanks to a list I never asked to see, read with only the mildest interest, and erased from my hard drive no more than half an hour after receiving it.

What has happened? Initially I approached Tim Kruger only because mutual friends had told me he owned interesting photos of Bulthaup that I could find nowhere else. But now, because of the list, Tim has virtually prohibited me from ever seeing, much less using, any of his material. In addition, I appear to have offended Greg Samuels by complaining that he had shown you my manuscript. But if Greg did not give you a copy, then who did?

I hope that in writing to you this way I am not simply deepening the hole in which I find myself. My goals are simple: I want to get along with people, and I want my book to be described accurately.

Yours sincerely,
Jeff Witt

SUBJ: **Re: Tim Kruger**
DATE: Saturday, July 22, 2000, 8:59:47 AM
FROM: willard.e.pearson@music.stblaise.edu
TO: jkwitt@wellspring.edu

Dear Mr. Witt,

Your letter saddened me. Obviously much about this case has been misrepresented to you, most notably the part I play. I shall try to clarify things as best I can.

To begin at the beginning, it is true that about sixteen years ago Tim Kruger and I began compiling a list, mostly for our own amusement, of gay and lesbian pianists. This game had its origins in an age considerably less lenient in these matters than our own, and during which homosexual pianists assumed that exposure would lead to the decimation of their careers. In his capacity as a premier antiquarian in the field of the piano, and in mine as President of the Paderewski Society, Tim and I were privy to certain information few other people possessed, and we began to exchange knowledge. Soon the list had grown into a document of considerable size, and when e-mail came along, the labor of its tracking and honing was greatly eased.

I must emphasize, however, that from the moment of its inception, the list was a private document. Rarely would Tim and I share it with anyone, and if one of us did, he would always ask the other's permission first. This is why his decision to send you the list took me aback: he had neglected to ask me first whether I approved.

On Tuesday, July 11, it is true, I did go to visit Greg Samuels at the Meerschaum Institute. We spent twenty minutes or so talking in his office, and in the course of our conversation I did notice the manuscript of a Bulthaup biography on his desk. As I am quite interested in Bulthaup, I inquired of Greg as to its provenance. In reply he told me who you were, and that you had sent him the book because you wanted his advice on the project. *At no time, however, did he offer to give me a copy of the manuscript, nor did I at any point ask for one, or even thumb through his.*

On to the following week: on his way back from a swap meet in Camden, Tim Kruger stopped by St. Blaise, where we had lunch at the faculty club. As we were beginning our first course, I mentioned my recent visit to the Meerschaum Institute, at which point we discussed Greg Samuels for some minutes, our conversation inevitably leading to your Bulthaup project, about which I inquired as to his familiarity. Immediately Tim became flustered and said (I am sorry to have to repeat this) that indeed he did know of the book, that you and he had of late established what he called an "e-mail intimacy," and that he considered you to be the worst kind of gossip, a "gay radical" whose only real interest was in outing Bulthaup. In his view, you were absolutely the wrong person to write such a book, which ought to have been penned by another friend of his, a psychiatrist, since only a psychiatrist could possibly understand Bulthaup's "childlike" nature. I listened carefully, expressing amazement and consternation at the appropriate intervals, until our entrees arrived. At this point Tim "broke down," and announced that he had a confession to make: driven to recklessness by what he called the "romantic intensity" of your e-mail rapport, he had sent you the list. Naturally I was surprised, and after questioning the wisdom of sharing the list with someone he himself had just described as a gossip, asked him to explain his actions. In response he blurted out apologies, insisted that he would never forgive himself, and asked me if I could find it in my heart to forgive him. I told him that I could, but that I would appreciate it if he would write to you, urging you not to show the list to anyone. He agreed.

That was the last I heard of the case until this past Wednesday, when to my amazement I received an outraged e-mail from Greg Samuels, accusing me of lying and threatening to take legal action if I did not immediately retract the charge that he had given me a copy of your book. He also sent me your original e-mail to him. Deeply consternated, I wrote immediately to Tim, who telephoned by way of reply, insisting pitifully that he had never told you that I had got the manuscript from Greg, that you had invented the connection in order to destroy our friendship, etc. I did not believe him, and told him so in no uncertain terms. As you may have guessed by now, this is by no means the first time that I have found myself in this kind of muddle thanks to Tim. By nature he is a machinator—he cannot help himself—and as I have learned over the course of many years on this planet, a machinator's most dangerous skill is his capacity to seduce others into doing his dirty work for him. Once Tim has one ensnared, in other words, one will often find oneself behaving in much the same way that he does, without even realizing that one is doing it. Sincerity and honesty become well nigh impossible. He had led me down this ugly path too often, and this time I resolved no longer to tolerate such behavior, and to end our friendship.

That, then, is what happened. I'm very sorry that Tim decided to involve you in such an unpleasant, if trivial, episode, and even more, sorry that you suffered over the case as you so obviously did: it is clear that you are a man of conscience, and to the sort of tactics Tim employs, unfortunately, those of conscience are particularly susceptible. It was not until I received your e-mail, however, that his motives in enacting such a petty drama became clear to me. As you know, Tim is both by profession and character an antiquarian: that is to say, he sees his own value mostly in terms of the things he possesses. By expressing a desire to use his material, you flattered him, yet you also set off an old fear that no one was interested in him for himself, only for what he owned, etc. This was why he set up so many hoops for you to jump through in order to win his trust. And yet I'm fairly certain that in the end he had no intention of giving you the photos, for fear that once you had them, you would lose all interest in him.

Well, that is the whole sorry story. Try not to let it bother you too much. So far as the photos themselves go, I have never seen them. No doubt they exist, no doubt they are fascinating, and yet with Tim it's often hard to distinguish between truth and bluff. He could have a trove, he could have a single snapshot.

All best,
Willard Pearson

SUBJ: **Re: Re: Tim Kruger**
DATE: Saturday, July 22, 2000, 4:03:42 PM
FROM: jkwitt@wellspring.edu
TO: willard.e.pearson@music.stblaise.edu

Dear Willard (if I may),

Your letter came as a great surprise to me. Yes, I am comforted to know that all of this was less my fault than I thought at first. Still, the whole affair has left such a bitter aftertaste in my mouth that I can't help but wonder if, in interpreting Bulthaup's life as I have, I might simply be displaying the same will to misapprehend that you ascribe to Tim. Perhaps the book really is just souped-up gossip, as he claimed.

It hadn't previously occurred to me that Tim might have any emotional investment in our relationship—after all, he has no idea what I look like, has never heard my voice, etc.—yet going over his e-mails in light of your observations, I see that I might have been missing the key element all along.

I will continue to trudge along with the biography, albeit sorrowfully, the wiser for having suffered.

Yours,
Jeff

SUBJ: **Bulthaup**
DATE: Monday, October 23, 2000, 4:01:27 AM
FROM: ivorystuds@entropy.net
TO: jkwitt@wellspring.edu

Dear Jeff,

How long it's been since I've heard from you! Are you well? I've been thinking about you since last week, when I happened to be at the Meerschaum Institute, sitting with Greg Samuels in his office. There on the desk was the ms. of that new collection of essays on Schumann and the "queer musicology." When I asked Greg about it, he pushed it my way and said I could have it, that it was "garbage," etc. Which set me to wondering whether he and Willard might have been lying all along about what they did with *your* ms.

And speaking of your book, the other day I saw an announcement of its forthcoming publication. Congratulations! I see that it's now scheduled to come out in April—plenty of time to include some of my material, if you're still interested. Looking back, I realize I may have been a bit liverish about the list business . . .

Will you be up in these parts any time soon? If so, perhaps we could meet for lunch and discuss the issues involved. It would be a great pleasure finally to meet you. And your book will only be the poorer if it does not include the pictures in my files.

Hugs,
Tim

Heaped Earth

To celebrate her husband's latest movie, a biography of Franz Liszt starring the much-admired John Ray, Jr., Lilia Wardwell decided to throw a party. The studio had high hopes that the film might win the Oscar that year; *Ben-Hur* had won the year before, and the word was that this time something more intimate might take the prize, so a party was just the thing. The theme would be Romanticism. A pianist, done up in Liszt's soutane, would play wonderful music, while waiters in nineteenth-century livery circulated with trays of hors d'oeuvres. Also, in addition to the usual Hollywood crowd, she would invite Stravinsky and his wife, Vera.

She called her husband at the studio, and said, "Frank, I need a pianist for the party. Any ideas?"

"I'll see what I can do," he answered. As it happened, there *was* a pianist around the studio, an immigrant called Kusnezov who, people said, could play any song without the music, just by hearing it hummed. Whenever a piano scene was required, it was Kusnezov's hands that were filmed; in the Liszt movie his hands were substituted for those of John Ray, Jr.

From the associate producer, Wardwell got Kusnezov's number. He expected he would have to do some prodding, as in his experience artist types tended to be sensitive. Instead Kusnezov proved to be extremely cordial and, having first inquired with delicacy as to his fee, agreed instantly to the job—providing, if it was no inconvenience, that he be paid in advance, and in cash. From this Wardwell deduced that he either gambled, drank, or had an ex-wife pressing him for alimony.

At seven o'clock on the evening of the party Kusnezov arrived at the Wardwells' house and knocked, as instructed, at the service entrance. In the kitchen a dozen or so waiters were fighting their way into tight suits from the studio's costume bank, while the cook and her assistants spooned caviar onto toast points, and cut sandwiches into the shapes of playing card suits, and emptied canned hearts of palms onto silver platters. Having first explained who he was to a man in butler's livery, Kusnezov waited quietly by the refrigerator until Mrs. Wardwell appeared. She was a woman of heft, with a shelflike bosom and béchamel-colored hair. Her perfume commingled perversely with the cooking smells. "Mr. Kusnezov, so glad to meet you," she said, offering a moisturized hand, and gave him the once-over. His appearance worried her. After all, though he was wearing the requisite soutane, Kusnezov—it could not be denied—was old. When he leaned forward to kiss her hand, his breath smelled of liquor. Also Liszt (and John Ray, Jr.) had those wonderful, Samson-like locks, whereas Kusnezov was mostly bald, with just a few watery hairs brushed forward over his pate; hardly what she'd envisioned when she'd planned the party.

Still, she was determined to be game and, clasping his hand in hers, took him into the living room, which was harp-shaped, sweeping, with ribbed walls. "I'm told the acoustics here are sublime," she said, leading him across the polished floor to the piano. Most of the furniture—Scandinavian, of light wood and leather—had been pushed up against the walls. As for the glossy white piano, it stood on a platform before a row of louvered floor-to-ceiling windows, through the glass of which Kusnezov could see a blue swimming pool refracting the sunset, a barbecue pit, an array of houses in crisp shades of pink and green spilling down the hills toward an ocean you could still make out in those days before smog.

They stepped up onto the platform. "I trust our humble instrument will be to your liking," Mrs. Wardwell said, positioning herself beside the piano like a soprano. "Do sit. It's a Steinway, of course. My husband wanted a cheaper brand, but I said, 'Frank, Steinway is the instrument of the immortals.' "

"And do you play yourself?" Kusnezov asked, adjusting, with a finicky backward motion of the hands, the height of the white leather stool.

"Not seriously, I'm afraid. Still, I do enjoy tinkling out a bit of Chopin now and then . . . Oh, I had the tuner up this morning."

Having first wiped his hands, which were slippery with her moisturizer, onto his handkerchief, Kusnezov sat down and played a scale.

"A lovely tone," he said. "Not too bright."

"Fine. As for the music, as I'm sure my husband explained, it should be romantic, in keeping with the film. Still, this is a party, so we don't want everyone getting down in the dumps, do we?"

"No, madame."

"So nothing dreary. I would be most grateful."

He bowed his head.

"Oh, haven't you brought any music?"

"There is no need, madame."

"Of course you're welcome to use any of *our* scores. My daughter Elise can turn pages."

"There is no need, madame."

"Fine." She rubbed her hands together. "Well, the guests should be arriving in a half an hour or so. Oh, would you like a drink? Burt"—she signaled the bartender—"get Mr. Kusnezov a drink. What will you have?"

"A whiskey and soda. Straight up."

"A whiskey and soda, Burt. And now if you'll excuse me, I must check on things in the kitchen."

He nodded. She left. Burt brought Kusnezov his drink, which he guzzled fast. Smiling, Burt mixed him a second one.

The doorbell rang. The man in butler's livery admitted a group of five into the foyer—all dear friends of Mrs. Wardwell whom she had asked to come early, to "break the ice." Sitting at the piano, Kusnezov played some Chopin waltzes. The next guest to arrive was Lee Remick. And then Mrs. Wardwell strode in, and Mr. Wardwell, who had been drinking alone in his study, and their daughter Elise, who scowled through thick glasses. Everyone except Elise chatted amiably as Mrs. Wardwell allowed her gaze occasionally to rest with approval upon the figure of Kusnezov, who had moved from the waltzes to Liszt's late evocation of the fountains at the Villa d'Este.

After forty minutes, he took a break. Burt mixed him a third whiskey and soda. In the meantime John Ray, Jr., had arrived, an event which had provoked the assembled to burst into a round of applause. Square-jawed, from Texas, the young actor had large hands and thick, blond hair that to his regret, he had recently been forced to cut in preparation for his next role, a navy lieutenant. Although his official escort for the evening was a lesbian starlet named Lorna Baskin, he had made a secret arrangement to rendezvous at the party with his lover of the moment, the young professor of musicology at UCLA who had served as musical advisor for the Liszt movie. As instructed, the professor came alone, and late. Kusnezov was by now taking his second break. Most of the guests—Hollywood socialites and actors, though alas no Stravinskys—were out on the patio. In the living room a group of studio executives took advantage of the lull to share Cuban cigars and cut deals. As for Kusnezov, he was leaning against the bar, talking with Burt about the dog races.

The professor asked Burt for a screwdriver. He was a Bostonian of thirty-five, new in Southern California, having taken his position at UCLA only the year before. In the weirdly artificial atmosphere of the party he appeared himself to be in costume, with his bow tie and eastern tweeds. His face melancholic (for he did not see his lover), he peered out the door at the humming crowd, before strolling over to examine the piano. After a few minutes Kusnezov stepped past him and took his place again. They nodded at each other.

Kusnezov started to play—a Chopin nocturne in C minor that, as it happened, was one of the professor's favorites. He sat down to listen. All at once, and quickly, the music carried him away from that ample California living room with its ribbed walls, and into a small house, a winter house, where a coal fire was burning. There was grief in the air, not fresh, but a few years old, its presence vague as the smell of cooking. No one dared address it. No one dared acknowledge the sprite of memory that danced in the heavy, soot-thickened air. Then the professor smiled, for now he felt sure of something he had long suspected: that Chopin had written this nocturne for a sister who had died in childhood. In Kusnezov's hands, the supposition became a certainty.

Burt was silent. Even the executives fell silent. As for the professor, he was remembering a poem by Oscar Wilde, written also in memory of a sister dead in childhood, a sister buried:

Tread lightly, she is near
Under the snow,
Speak gently, she can hear
The daisies grow.

From the patio John Ray, Jr., entered the room. He was talking to John Wayne. Their loud conversation dimmed only once they recognized that people were listening to the music, at which point they stopped and stood by the door, smiling respectfully.

The professor looked at John Ray, Jr. John Ray, Jr., looked over the professor.

Peace, peace, she cannot hear
Lyre or sonnet,
All my life's buried here,
Heap earth upon it.

The prelude ended. No one applauded. Once again, Kusnezov got up and got a drink, as did John Ray, Jr., John Wayne, and the professor. The lovers did not acknowledge each other.

Only once the two actors had returned to the patio did the professor dare approach Kusnezov. His eyes revealed his knowledge—that he had heard; that he had recognized.

"That was magnificent," he said.

"Yes, it was," Kusnezov answered simply.

"May I ask you a question?" The professor stepped closer. "Who *are* you?"

"Who *was* I? you mean. That is the apposite point."

"You mean before the war . . ."

Kusnezov shook his head. "The war is not to blame. I came to live in this country thirty years ago."

"Then what happened?"

"What happened? What happened?" The pianist laughed. And meanwhile Jane Russell had come into the room, Mrs. Wardwell had come into the room, bringing with her a loud, invasive odor of perfume. She shot Kusnezov a glance, the meaning of which was obvious: *Get back to work, and no more of the depressing stuff.*

"I must go," he said to the professor. And putting down his empty glass, he returned to the piano.

The Marble Quilt

Via in Selci

"Do you know of anyplace the professor might have gone to eat beans?"

I look down at the *maresciallo*'s hands, spread languidly across the gunmetal surface of the desk. His nails are neatly pared. He wears a gold wedding ring; a brilliant gold chain-link bracelet is draped loosely over the bones of his wrist. To his left, on the edge of the desk, sits one of his deputies. To his right, another of his deputies takes down my statement on an old computer, the letters pulsing green against a black background. Other *carabinieri* come and go, listen for a few minutes, light cigarettes, or snap the tops of Coke cans. All of them are Roman, in their early thirties or younger, with glossy dark hair and thick wrists. This is the homicide division, and I am here to give testimony.

"Beans?" I repeat.

"Yes, beans."

"Well, I know Tom was very fond of the Obitorio—the 'morgue'—that pizzeria down on Viale Trastevere, next to McDonald's. Of course, *obitorio* is just the nickname he gave it, because of the tables. They're made of marble, so . . ."

"Oh, of course. The pizzas are very good there."

"They also serve beans. It's one of their specialties."

The *maresciallo*'s deputy types; reads aloud, "The professor often ate at a pizzeria on Viale Trastevere that he called the 'morgue,' because of the marble tables. It was known for its beans."

"Is that all right with you?" the *maresciallo* says.

"Yes, that's fine," I say.

* * *

More than once, during this interview, I've asked questions about Tom's murder, and been told, ever so politely, that I am here to provide information, not solicit it. Nonetheless, some of the *maresciallo*'s questions reveal things. For instance: Did Tom make a habit of drinking red wine? Had he ever mentioned a trip to Tunisia? Where might he have gone to eat beans?

Not necessarily things I need, or want, to know.

Other questions merely perplex me, add to the air of confusion and hopelessness that surrounds the investigation.

"When you visited him in his apartment, did he ever ask you to take off your shoes?"

"Did he ever make reference to someone called Ludovico?"

"Do you know if he had friends on Borgo Sant'Angelo?"

"No," I answer. Repeatedly, no.

They've assured me, from the very start, that I'm not a suspect. After all, I have my alibi. When Tom was murdered, I was nowhere near his apartment; I was with some American businessmen, giving them a tour of the Vatican museum.

Still, alibis can be fabricated. Friends will lie.

"Did he ever mention an article he was writing about the floors at San Clemente?"

Actually, the article about the floors at San Clemente he did mention. It was part of his new life, his Italian life, in which I played, at best, a marginal role. In this life Tom taught English, and wrote the occasional travel piece, and devoted much of his time to exploring some of the more arcane corners of Roman history; thus his fascination with church floors, in which hand-cut pieces of marble—hexagons and triangles, circles and diamonds and teardrops—were arranged into precise geometries. Speckled deep red porphyry, green *serpentino*, butterscotch-colored *giallo antico*: "like the squares of a quilt," he once told me. "Only instead of cloth, the quilt is made of marble. A marble quilt."

"Not only San Clemente," I tell the *maresciallo*. "Also Santa Maria in Cosmedin, and San Giovanni in Laterano, and Santa Maria Maggiore."

His deputy types; reads. "The professor spoke to me of an article he was writing about the floors of Roman churches."

"He had been living in Rome for three years, is that correct?"

"Yes."

"Obviously your Italian is fluent."

"It's my job. I'm an interpreter."

"Of course. My compliments. In your view—that is, speaking as an authority on language—did the professor speak a good Italian?"

"Not bad," I say, "considering that he only started studying once he arrived here."

"Yet his mother was from Italy."

"She was born in Naples."

"Actually in Caserta. But that is very close to Naples. In your view, was the professor's Italian sufficiently fluent that he would never have misunderstood what another person was telling him?"

"Misunderstood?"

"That is to say, might he have misunderstood what another person said to him, if the other person were speaking Italian?"

"He might have."

The *maresciallo* cracks his knuckles. Then he removes his ring and polishes it with his shirtsleeve. Then he takes a cigarette from a pack lying open on the desk. "Do you smoke?"

"No, thank you."

He lights the cigarette.

"How often do you come to Rome?"

"Two or three times a year."

"For work?"

"Usually. But sometimes just for pleasure."

"Did you ever come specifically to visit the professor?"

"A few times."

"And the last time?"

"I was working."

"Where were you working?"

"PepsiCo was hosting a conference for its European executives."

"Why didn't you stay with the professor? You did on other occasions."

"There was no need. A hotel room was provided for me."

"And if a hotel room hadn't been provided for you?"

"I might have stayed with Tom. But probably not."

"Why not?"

"Well, his apartment was very far out from where I was working. Also, when you used to live with someone—when for years you shared a bed with someone—it can feel awkward, sleeping on the living room sofa. It can feel . . . wrong."

His deputy—the one sitting on the edge of the desk—smiles in sympathy. Clearly he knows of what I speak.

"How long did you live with the professor?"

"We lived together for ten years, five years ago."

"In San Francisco?"

"Yes."

"And now you live in Düsseldorf."

"Yes."

He opens a folder; examines what appears to be a list of questions; writes a note to himself.

"When you did stay with the professor—on the sofa—did he ever make advances toward you?"

"Good heavens, no! We were well beyond that."

"Did he ever bring someone home to share his bed?"

"Of course not! Tom didn't do that sort of thing."

The *maresciallo* raises his eyebrows. I wince.

"What I mean," I correct, "is that he never *admitted* to doing that sort of thing. Certainly he would never have brought anyone home when he had a friend staying. He claimed to live like a monk."

The deputy at the computer types; reads, "When I came to Rome, it was usually for work, in which case I stayed at a hotel. When I came for pleasure, I sometimes stayed with the professor, which made me uncomfortable as a consequence of our having once lived together, in San Francisco. The professor never made advances toward me, however, nor was I concerned that he might bring someone home to share his bed, because he never admitted to doing that sort of thing, and in my opinion, would never have done that sort of thing when he had a friend visiting. He told me he lived like a monk."

"Change the last line," the *maresciallo* says. "I don't like 'He told me.' Change it to 'He claimed.' "

"He claimed to live like a monk," the deputy repeats.

I wonder if in America cops would ever be so fastidious about their prose style.

Oh, what a nasty business an autopsy must be! Not that there was ever a worry about preserving "the integrity of the body," or any of that New

Agey nonsense we used to hear in San Francisco—not in this case, since by the time the police broke down the door and found it, Tom's body had very little in the way of integrity left. He was tied to the kitchen table. His skull had been smashed in. He had been rotting for seven days.

By then, of course, I was back in Düsseldorf. During the last forty-eight hours before my flight, I must have called him a dozen times. And a dozen more times from Düsseldorf. Always his answering machine picked up. The *carabinieri* listened to the messages, then got my number out of his Filofax. They were very nice. They never said I *had* to come back to Rome—only that if I were willing to, it would be a great help to their investigation. Otherwise the German police could interview me by proxy.

Naturally I agreed to come back.

Tom's San Francisco friends, those couples whose children he had baby-sat and whose dinner parties he had catered, started calling me. Over the phone they spoke cautiously of the need to "protect Tom's reputation." Obviously they'd seen the newspaper articles, the ones in which his Rome friends, the correspondents, made pretty obvious what everyone took for granted anyway: that he had been done in by a hustler, some Romanian or Albanian he'd picked up at the station and brought home. Sex, then a beating, or perhaps sex that included a beating, followed by a blunt object smashed against his skull. (Was it perhaps the obelisk of *semesanto*, the red brecciated with chunks of white, like pieces of fat in a salami?)

And then, somewhere in those hours, the red wine. And the shoes. And the beans.

Did I mention that his nose had been broken—*before* he was killed?

With his San Francisco friends, it wasn't a question of what they themselves believed; it was a question of what they wanted other people to believe: a matter, it seemed, less of protecting Tom's reputation than their own. After all, they had trusted him with their children. To have it revealed that Tom had been conning them the whole time, that in truth he was no different from any other faggot—this would have been too embarrassing. So they decided to take the line that the police and the journalists were wrong; worse, that they were homophobic, to assume that just because Tom had been beaten and bludgeoned to death, his killer had to be some lowlife he'd dragged in off the street. "Maybe those others," his friend Gina told me over the phone, referring to the twenty-two homosexual men who have been murdered in Rome over the last decade, "but not Tom." To Gina, the important thing seemed to be that his name never be added to that statistic; that the number remain twenty-two.

"It had to be something else. What if he surprised a burglar?"

"But nothing was taken."

"Or maybe it was someone he was having an affair with. A lover."

So was it better to have been murdered by a lover, I wondered, by someone you trusted, than by an immigrant you had picked up in the men's room at the train station?

That mysterious men's room, where the urinals were divided by glass partitions—glass, of all things.

Tom told me that. Not that he'd ever been there himself, he added: it was only from his friend Pepe, who frequented such places, that he garnered this intelligence. Pepe, according to Tom, spent much of his time in the park on the Monte Caprino. That kind of park. Only once had Tom accompanied him there, under duress, after a boring lunch party. He noticed the plants, not the loiterers. "Oh, that's spleenwort—*asplenium filicinophyta*!" he told Pepe. "Wait here while I go home and get my Japanese pruning shears." And Pepe waited, and Tom went home, and came back with his Japanese pruning shears. For a cutting.

Soon a rumor began to circulate in San Francisco that he had been having an affair with a fellow English teacher, and that very likely it was this teacher who had murdered him. A lover's quarrel.

If this was true, I could well understand the teacher's motives. Back when I lived with Tom, I too found myself tempted, on more than one occasion, to pick up a blunt object; to smash in his skull; to break his nose.

Oh, he could be such a hypocrite! And he met a hypocrite's just end. Like the hypochondriac who finally gets something fatal. In the angry weeks right after I heard the news, when Gina and her husband, Tony, and all sorts of other people were calling every night to talk about "damage control" (they actually used that phrase), a few times—just to horrify them—I said, "Come on, folks. What do you really think? Don't you really think he got what he deserved?"

Wool Street

A few months before he died, I went back to San Francisco. I went to look at the house we used to own together. High on a San Francisco hilltop, the fog woolly, rolling across the sky in grand, sluggish banks. And this was appropriate, because the street on which we had lived was called Wool Street.

Back then, the house was yellow. Now it was white. Pristine. There were Jaguars and Acuras and Jeeps parked along the curb: not the battered pickup trucks and Volkswagen Beetles of our day. For when we lived there, Bernal Heights was a run-down neighborhood, even a bad neighborhood. At that point, of course, I couldn't have afforded in a million years to buy back our old home. Now that San Francisco was the dot-com capital of the world, even a funny, creaky little house like ours, with no backyard and a crumbling foundation, went for $700,000 or $800,000. Or more.

A strange sensation, to be priced out of a place you once thought of as yours. But then again, one of the lessons of marble—one of the lessons Tom taught me—is that ownership of any kind is a dream.

Were any of them still around, our old neighbors? Walking across the street, I peered at a letterbox: LOPEZ, it said. But it should have said, COOPER.

Where was Dominic Cooper, whom I barely knew, but who sometimes waved to me, walking past with his dog? An Old English sheepdog, the fur on her head pulled back into a topknot so that it wouldn't get into her eyes.

Dead, I supposed. Most of them were, our neighbors, either because, a dozen years ago, they were already old, or because they were faggots.

Bad faggots.

Tom and I were not bad faggots, so we remained alive. For the moment.

Tom was the good faggot. He wrote children's books that never got published. (Not getting them published—this was an essential part of being the good faggot.) He rolled his own pasta, and volunteered at an AIDS hospice, and never went to any of the bars or sex clubs for which San Francisco was infamous—oh no! Instead he lived with me. We had matching gold rings. We told people we'd met at a party in New York, when really I'd seen his dick before I ever saw his face, emerging inquisitively from under the partition between two stalls in the men's room at Bloomingdale's.

Most of Tom's friends were young marrieds. They trusted their children with him. Not only that, they made a fuss over how much they trusted their children with him. "Tom's so good with kids!" they'd say. "He's Justin/Samuel/Max's favorite babysitter. When we go away, Justin/Samuel/Max *loves* spending the weekend with Tom."

In other words, not a child molester. To leave their little boys with Tom was to make a sally into that favorite West Coast game of More Liberal Than Thou. It was to flaunt their tolerance in the same way that a few years later, when they got rich, they would flaunt their immunity to greed. Not BMWs, not Manolo Blahnik pumps. Instead Birkenstocks, SUVs, and several million in stock options.

It goes without saying that they never asked Tom to babysit their *daughters*. What would have been the point of that?

He was godfather to something like eleven little boys, at least three of whom were named after him.

And now all those Justins and Samuels and Maxes—yes, and Toms—they must be teenagers. I wonder if they remember the June mornings when he would take them to watch the Gay Pride Parade. Hoist them onto his shoulders. Their parents alongside, smiling at the drag queens done up as Carol Burnett or Debbie Reynolds.

And of course, when the coalition from the North American Man/Boy Love Association marched by, all those clerkish men in suits and ties, what did his friends think? They never said a word. Instead they kept their eyes averted, until the NAMBLA guys had filed past, and there were safe, funny drag queens again.

Our house on Wool Street could not have been more unassuming. Like a child's drawing of a house, Tom used to say. It was situated as close to nowhere as it is probably possible to get, on a neutral hill near a characterless intersection somewhere in the midst of that vast anonymity of streets no tourist ever drives, and that San Franciscans call the Mission.

I worked as an editor for a leftist magazine that was published by a foundation: a slick magazine to which rich people subscribed out of guilt, but did not read. Tom ran a catering business, and was devoted to the domestic. He could spend weeks searching for just the right toilet brush to match the bathroom fixtures. When I finished showering in the mornings, he'd sometimes wait until he thought I wasn't looking, and then stealthily adjust the towels so that they draped in just the right way.

Once the discovery of a food stain on the bedspread made him freeze in the middle of a kiss, mutter, "I'll just be a second," and pad off naked to the kitchen for spot remover.

You see, this was San Francisco in the late eighties, and many of the people we knew had died.

Two of our neighbors had died. And a Greek man who ran a deli. And the editor of the magazine I worked for. Even our doctor had died.

So I suppose that was why we bought our little house, our "crypto-dream-house," as Tom used to call it, quoting Elizabeth Bishop. By establishing and guarding this shelter, he must have hoped he could protect us both from the stained sheets and fouled toilets and soggy mattresses that are the necessary accessories of death.

Later, when I saw the photographs of Saddam Hussein's atom bomb–proof bunker, with its marble bathrooms and carpeting and candelabrums, I thought, yes, of course—something along those lines.

People in San Francisco talked a lot in those days about "grief management." Now I look back, and it seems to me that grief was managing *us* all that time: grief, the puppeteer, cool behind the curtain.

When, I wondered, would grief pull off its mask, switch on the light, burst into the room in troops, like cops at a stakeout?

I thought it was going to happen one night in 1988. We were getting dressed for the opera when the telephone rang. It was Tom's friend Caroline, and she was calling to tell him that Ernie, with whom he had once lived for half a dozen years, had died an hour earlier.

"Vincent," he said to me, putting the phone down. Nothing more, but I knew. I was in the middle of tying my tie, and I remember that I stopped, the tie hanging half-looped around my neck, like a noose, and without saying a word I walked over to Tom and held him, tightly, and then we just stood like that, me holding him and his body shaking, but he never cried, or said a word. And then we let go of each other; I finished tying my tie. And we went to the opera.

The opera that night was a concert version of *Dido and Aeneas*. A famed soprano stood before us, resplendent in feathers and white satin, and sang Dido's deathbed aria:

When I am laid, laid in earth,
Let my wrongs create
No trouble, no trouble, in thy breast;
Remember me, remember me,
But ah, forget my fate!

So grief sang, in her feathery gown. Bejeweled grief. *Couture* grief. And it seemed that she was looking at us as she sang, and what were we, after all, but two well-heeled faggots in the last decade of a century we had no assurance we would see the end of?

Whose fate, in any case, would doubtless be forgotten?

How can it be that I've neglected to say what he looked like? That is, what he looked like when he was still alive.

Well, he looked like . . . the good faggot. Handsome, in a neutered sort of way. He always clipped the hairs out of his nose. His skin was unblemished, his nails tidy as the *maresciallo*'s.

He was not tall. Gray streaks ran through his black hair—thick, dark hair, a fringe benefit of Italian blood. Whereas I was going bald early.

Of course, the thing about Italian men is that often, no matter how handsome they are in youth, they age very badly. I suppose I should have been alerted to this likelihood the one time I met Tom's father, who was a second-generation immigrant from Sicily. Although he wasn't yet seventy, he had a face like a shar-pei's. His teeth were yellow from smoking. Moles bloomed on his cheeks. Yet his eyes, his mouth, even his nose—these were Tom's.

It was only after we broke up that his looks really started to go—as if inheritance, after waiting in the wings for decades, had suddenly decided to step forward and stake its claim: I gave this to you, I take this from you. The blessing and curse of the genes.

A year had passed during which we had not seen each other—he had just moved to Rome, I had just moved to Düsseldorf—when out of the blue, I got an assignment to work a film festival in Rome. So naturally I called and told him I was coming. He insisted on meeting me at the airport. When I stepped off the plane, a jowly little man ran up to me, holding a bouquet of violets.

I blinked. Could this be Tom? Since we'd last seen each other he'd gained what looked like forty pounds. His hair had thinned in front, and to compensate, he'd grown it long in the back. He had a ratty beard.

A few days later, while I was waiting to meet him near Torre Argentina, I got to talking with an old lady who came there to feed the stray cats. It seemed that she was one of a group of women—*gattaie*, they were called—who had set up a makeshift cat clinic down among the ruins, a sort of squatter's hospital. The city was trying to evict them, she said, because many of the cats had feline AIDS and people were afraid of catching it. ("A ludicrous notion," she added, "since they are separate diseases. But Italians are not very interested in facts.")

A cat approached—fat and white, blind in one eye. She picked him up and handed him to me. "We call him Nelson," she said, "after the admiral."

I smiled at Nelson. His blind eye was clouded and milky, like a piece of Carrara marble. I stroked his neck and he purred. Then Tom appeared, waving at me from across the street. I put Nelson down. "My friend is here," I told the woman.

She peered. "Is that him? He's very ugly," she observed, in that mild, uninflected tone that a Roman adopts when he informs you—meaning no offense—that you've gotten quite a bit fatter since the last time you saw each other.

Bidding her goodbye, I hurried to meet him. "Sorry I'm late," he said. "I got held up by one of my students. Pierluigi." He groaned. "Those double names—Pierluigi, Piergiorgio—they'll get you every time."

"Handsome?"

"*Mamma mia.* And to make matters even worse, a Fascist. I mean, a major Fascist. 'The man I most admire in the world is Jean-Marie Le Pen,' he wrote in his paper. So naturally I failed him. And then his father called. And then . . ."

"What?"

"Well . . . it was all very tiresome."

We turned a corner, and went into a trattoria. In Rome all social occasions with Tom took place in restaurants. "I only just found this one last week," he said. "It's got the best pasta and chickpeas."

The trattoria was stuffy, narrow. We were led to a back table, far from any window. Tom ordered for us—pasta and chickpeas, naturally—and soon enough two bowls of soup arrived, carried by a handsome young waiter with whom he appeared to be on a first-name basis. The first name, in this case, being Enzo.

"Taste that rosemary," he said, his eyes on Enzo's back.

I tasted. Believe me, I know something about cooking, and no rosemary had ever come near that soup.

After a while, the trattoria got busy. A crowd had gathered in the foyer, businessmen and neighborhood shopkeepers, all waiting for tables to open up, while Tom, with a kind of obstinate disregard, remained rooted to his chair even though we had long since finished our meal. The coffee came. He took a long time stirring in his sugar, then asked me about Düsseldorf. Did I have much of a social life there? Were my friends American or German? What was the food like?

Something of a social life, I answered. I had both German and American friends. The food was . . . German.

And my apartment?

I leaned back. I was wondering when he was going to work up the courage to ask the question that was obviously on his mind—that is, was I "seeing" anyone in Düsseldorf—when Enzo appeared, and asked very sheepishly if we might mind paying up and getting out. As we could see, people were waiting.

Tom's neck stiffened. "What? You're asking us to leave?"

"I'm sorry, *signore*, but as you see—"

"That's hardly the way to encourage a regular customer, Enzo. Why, for all you know I might be a journalist, about to write a review of your trattoria for an important American newspaper!"

Enzo spread out his hands. "*Signore*, what can I do? How can I vindicate myself?"

Tom smiled. He pointed to his cheek. "A kiss," he said.

Straightening his back, Enzo laughed, as if in disbelief. Then he looked over his shoulder. Then he bent down and kissed Tom, very quickly, on the cheek.

"Might he have misunderstood what another person said to him, if the other person were speaking Italian?"

Of course, his claims to have no interest in "that sort of thing" begged the important question of what he was doing in that men's room in the first place.

"Well," he said, "you know that whenever I'm in New York I always go to Bloomingdale's. And I was shopping for sheets, when nature called. Normally I would never have stayed, once I'd realized that it was *that* kind of men's room. But then your socks caught my eye."

"My socks?"

"They were all I could see under the door to the stall. Blue and red argyle. I liked them."

"So that was the only reason you went into the next stall? Because you liked my socks?"

"I suppose."

"And if it hadn't been for my socks?"

"I would have left. You know I can't bear that sort of atmosphere."

"But wait a minute . . . that means that our whole relationship—our whole history together—owes to the fact that you liked my socks."

"I guess you could put it that way," Tom said. "Not that I ever would."

It is worth noting that when we had this conversation, we were looking at china. We seemed always to have our most important conversations while looking at china; even that first afternoon, after the men's room, it was to the china department that we drifted, and in the china department that we told each other our names.

"Oh, this is nice," Tom said. "Hand-painted, too."

Because the carnality that had started everything seemed suddenly so remote, I glanced at his crotch.

"The measure of a man," I began.

He blushed. "Oh, please. Do you like Aynsley?"

"I'd like to do more with you. Preferably without a wall between us."

He picked up a teacup. "I know a place in London where you can get this stuff dirt cheap. Seconds, of course. Tiny flaws."

"I'd like to kiss you for about a month."

He smiled with pleasure, looked over his shoulder. "Ssh," he said. "People will hear you."

Spode. Wedgwood. Royal Doulton.

We had our picture taken together. Tom framed a copy, and put it on the desk in the kitchen, the one on which he worked out the menus for the dinners he catered, and wrote the children's books he could never get published.

His devotion amazed me. Nineteen manuscripts, hundreds of rejection letters, and still he persevered, claiming that he derived enough satisfaction from the mere act of writing, and enough pride from the pleasure the books gave to the children he knew.

For they all read his books in manuscript, those Justins and Sams and Maxes. Their mothers read them too. "Those New York publishers are absolutely crazy not to take these," Gina said once. "If they did, they'd make a fortune."

But not even his friend Mary, whose brother worked at Simon & Schuster, ever offered to help him.

He asked her once. I don't know how, but somehow he mustered the wherewithal to ask her. If she could mention him to her brother, mention his books . . .

Mary's mouth tightened. "But my brother works in the marketing department," she said. "Probably he doesn't know anyone in children's books."

That *probably*. It gave everything away. The truth was, she wanted him in his place.

Caterer. Babysitter. Giver of kitchen wisdom. Have I mentioned marriage counselor? If Tom had come into his own, he might no longer have been available.

"Tom, you're so wise!" How often I heard those words, spoken by his weeping married friends. Sitting in our living room, they would sob and vent. Stories would dribble out, of stains and threats and temptations.

And Tom would hand over the box of tissues, pour the tea, and proceed to give the shrewd and reasoned advice for which he was famous.

He was good at it, too. He kept more than one spouse from straying. Unfortunately, it was never his own.

Via in Selci

I'm starting to relax now, to fall into the rhythm of interrogation. Already I've been here for three hours. Once we've gone out for coffee—me, the *maresciallo*, and his deputies. We walked down Via in Selci to Via Cavour, to a bar on the corner, where all three of them bought cigarettes. We ordered espressos. As is the masculine fashion in Italy, the *carabinieri* drank theirs Arabic-fashion, out of shot glasses.

Afterward, they fought over who would pick up the bill. The *maresciallo* won, which probably explains why he is the *maresciallo*. Then we returned to the *caserma*. It was just after eleven o'clock in the morning, the sky cloudless and blue, a perfect backdrop for the Colosseum rising above rooftops. I remembered Tom taking me on one of his typically brisk tours around its periphery. As was his habit, he had pointed out unusual details: the flowers growing in the cracks, the birds who had built nests in the little holes pocking the ancient stone.

"Lovers used to come here for trysts," he'd said. "Remember 'Roman Fever'? Malaria—from the Italian, *mal aria*. Bad air."

Last night, the Colosseum was lit up with bright yellow spotlights. I asked the *maresciallo* why.

"They're lit every time a death sentence is commuted somewhere in the world," he said.

"Whereas in Italy," I said, "even if you find the person who killed Tom, you couldn't sentence him to death."

"Would you want us to?"

"No! I've always thought the death penalty was barbaric."

"You are more civilized than most of your countrymen," the *maresciallo* said.

At the *caserma*, he waves to the guard in his bulletproof cubicle, then leads me down a badly lit corridor, past two empty holding cells, up a staircase, through a storage room, and back into his office. Once again, he takes his place at the gunmetal desk. His deputies, however, change positions. The one who had been typing sits on the corner of the desk. The one who had been sitting on the corner of the desk prepares to type.

"So where were we?" he says, opening his pack of cigarettes. "Oh, yes. You were saying that the professor would never have brought someone home with him when he had a guest staying."

"At least he never did when I was staying there."

"Please forgive me if this is an intrusive question, but when you and he lived together, were you faithful to each other?"

"He was faithful to me."

"As far as you know."

"That much I know."

"Would you describe him as jealous?"

"I made sure he never had occasion to be jealous."

The *maresciallo* smiles. Like his colleagues, he is broad-shouldered and hairy-chested, the first three buttons of his shirt undone to show off the gold chain around his neck. When I first arrived here, I felt anthropological, as if I were a member of some tribe whose habits the experts interviewing him found fascinating but bizarre. In Italy examples of the "out" homosexual are still rare. Much more common is what one might call the *situational* homosexual, the man who, though he might go now and again to the park on the Monte Caprino, or even to the bar just up Via in Selci from the *caserma*, would never in a million years identify himself as a *frocio*. Perhaps the *maresciallo* himself went around that block a few times, when he was doing his military service, before he got married . . . Yet the idea that Tom and I, beyond youth and very publicly, should have chosen to make this thing the center of our lives—even to forge a sort of marriage—this was the part I feared the *carabinieri* would never get their minds around.

The surprise, however, is that the hours we've spent together have revealed unsuspected common ground. If nothing else, the *carabinieri* recognized that my life wasn't really all that different from theirs. For instance, the reluctance to sleep on the sofa of someone with whom you once shared a bed—that they could understand. Or the sly evasions of the disloyal spouse.

"Let's move on to another matter," the *maresciallo* says, lighting another cigarette. "Did the professor ever speak to you of a friend called Pepe?"

"A few times."

"Do you know his last name?"

"I never met him. I only heard about him."

"Did he ever happen to say how he met Pepe?"

"I think they were neighbors when Tom first moved to Rome."

"When he was living in Monti."

"Exactly."

"How old is Pepe? Do you know what he looks like? Have you ever seen a photograph of him?"

"I haven't. I'm sorry."

"Do you know if the professor ever had sexual relations with Pepe?"

"The way he talked about him, it seems unlikely. My impression was that they just went out together. That they were friends."

The deputy reads: "The professor had an acquaintance called Pepe, who had been his neighbor when he first moved to Rome and was living in the Monti area. As far as I know, he never had sexual relations with Pepe, though they went out together."

"Might Pepe have been a person the professor approached if he hoped to procure a sexual partner for money?"

"It's possible."

"Was the professor in the habit of offering money in exchange for sex?"

"Certainly not when we lived together. In Rome . . . well, if he was, he never said anything about it."

"Did he ever speak of anyone to whom he was attracted? A student, perhaps?"

I think for a moment. Then I remember our lunch. *Taste that rosemary . . .*

"There was a waiter," I say. "His name was Enzo. He worked at a trattoria—Da Giuseppina, I think it was called—near Torre Argentina."

"But not a student."

"Come to think of it, he did mention a student. Piergiorgio, Piervincenzo: one of those compound names. Tom said he was very good-looking. The only problem was that he was a Fascist."

"And the professor was a Communist."

"He was a Democrat, yes."

The deputy reads: "The professor expressed attraction to a waiter called Enzo, who worked at the Trattoria da Giuseppina, as well as to a student with a compound name, beginning with 'Pier.' However, they were of divergent political views."

"Anyone else?"

"Only the Dying Gaul."

"The Dying Gaul?"

"Tom always claimed to have a crush on the Dying Gaul," I say.

When did it start, his passion for marble? Certainly there was no evidence of it in our San Francisco days. I don't remember anything about marble from our San Francisco days. Back then Tom had other passions: cooking, chiefly. He also collected baseball cards. Though this may have been more for the sake of his many godsons.

As for me, I went to night school. Foreign language courses. I was lucky; fluency came naturally to me. For most people new languages are buffeting, even brutal oceans. I dived into them without hesitation. Although timid in English, I found my voice when speaking these stepmother tongues, deriving a gastronome's pleasure from words: *tendresse, Zitronen, geniale.*

Already I spoke French, German, and Italian. Now, three nights a week, I studied Russian and Japanese. Later, just for the hell of it, I convinced a woman I knew from Bilbao to give me lessons in Basque. "Vincent is so intellectually curious," Tom would say at his dinner parties. My studying, my lessons with the woman from Bilbao, became his amusing excuse for my being out on the evenings when he gave dinner parties.

The marble, though—it must have come after we broke up, when he was first living in Rome, in that tiny apartment on Via del Boschetto. Not yet the big, dreary apartment in the Olympic Village, in which he was killed. For the moment, his plans were too uncertain to justify furniture. After all, he had moved to Rome on the spur of the moment, in the immediate wake of my deciding to move to Düsseldorf. Tit for tat; or maybe he left in order to feel that he wasn't being left.

In Rome, he let two furnished rooms from a widow who lived on Via Frattina. Like many Romans, she owned pockets of real estate all over the city, none of which she occupied. Instead she rented the apartments she owned in order to pay for the apartment she rented. Recently she had sold her beach house in Fregene, the furniture from which had been moved into Tom's bow tie–shaped flat. Old seaside junk: a rattan sofa with matching armchairs, the wicker uncurling; a wrought-iron dining table with four wobbly chairs; a bed with a headboard shaped like a wave, topped by a crest of white foam.

There was always a smell of salt air in that apartment, which was odd, since it was very dark, its attic windows giving only onto rooftops and balconies and other attic windows. No water, no fishing boats. If you took the pillows off the armchairs, grains of sand scattered onto the floor.

I remember one afternoon we were taking a stroll through the Forum. It had been raining, and the ground was muddy. Tom was talking about the different kinds of marble that the Romans quarried. "That's *africano*," he said, pointing to a paving stone that lay propped against a rusty fence, in tall grass. "Look how it glows, after the rain. As if it's been polished."

I looked. In the gray light, the stony masses that made up the slab glistened green and red and a white like lard. Nearby lay a column, cream veined with purple-brown. It made me think of fudge-swirl ice cream.

"Pavonazzetto," Tom said. "And that one there, that's *rosso antico.* Not porphyry. You can tell because the red isn't speckled. Porphyry is always speckled. It's the caviar of marbles."

"Marmo come lardo," I said, my eyes still on the *africano.* "It's like a poem."

Tom had his eyes on the path in front of us. "If you look carefully, sometimes you see glints of things," he said. "Especially after the rain, the stuff comes up like mushrooms. For instance—there." And he stopped. "You have to use your toe," he added, digging in the mud with his boot.

The path winked. He stepped back.

"Make sure no one's watching," he whispered.

I glanced over my shoulder. In the distance a German family was photographing itself. "Be my lookout," Tom said, and pulled a screwdriver from his jacket pocket. Then he bent down and jabbed at the mud.

The German family put away its cameras and walked toward us. "Tom," I said.

"It's O.K.," he said, stuffing something into his pocket.

"Well, what did you find?"

"We'll see in a minute."

We turned off the path, into a copse of umbrella pines, where Tom took out his treasure. At first I thought it was an ordinary rock, until he scraped the dirt off with his nails. It was the color of red wine, spotted like a duck's egg.

"See?" he said. "Porphyry."

He put it back in his pocket.

"But isn't it illegal to take things out of the Forum?"

"A little crumb like this? Who'll even notice? Anyway, the real crime would be *not* to take it. To leave it there to crumble into tinier and tinier pieces, under the tread of all these tourist feet. Instead of which—think of it this way—I'm saving a piece of history." He took my arm, which one could do in Italy. "Besides, no one ever really *owns* marble. It'll outlive us all. All I'm doing is giving it a home for a few years. Protection from the elements."

How many excuses he had! Nor were most of them unconvincing. After all, as he went on to show me that day, the Forum was already overflowing with relics, more than anyone had the money or resources to catalogue, much less display. In ditches left over from old archaeological digs, in makeshift "temporary" warehouses set up decades ago and never dismantled, bins of marble fragments lay untouched, unsifted. Cats meandered past them, slept on them, peed on them. He was right. What did a little chip like that matter?

A few nights later, though, returning to his apartment after some touring of my own, I tripped over something as I came through the door. The paving stone—the enormous one of *africano*—was sitting on his living room floor.

"How on earth did you get it out?" I asked.

He winked. "I used my toe," he said.

He started to acquire larger and larger pieces. Some of these, he told me, he had bought from a dealer he knew, while others he had won at poker games hosted by his friend Adua. Although by profession Adua was a doctor, her real passion—her only passion—was for marble. "You think I've got good stuff!" Tom said. "Wait until you see what Adua has stashed away!"

I met Adua only a few times. She was a small, heavy-hipped woman in her mid-forties. Her hair was dark, crudely cut. She lived alone, Tom told me, and was a sort of theoretical lesbian, though she had no lovers of whom he was aware. All her friends were men, fellow *marmisti*, or marble collectors. I called them the marble thieves. Around Tom, at least, Adua spoke of little else save her collection.

One morning she took us for a drive along the Via Appia Antica. The air was muggy that day. Outside her apartment building in Monte Verdi, where we met, she opened the trunk of her battered Fiat so that we could put our coats away. An immense block of serpentine sat next to the spare tire, half-covered in plastic.

"From the Temple of Heliogabolus," Adua said.

"Where did you get it?"

"I won it," she said. "The only problem is, I haven't figured out how to get it up the stairs."

"In the old days, at Hadrian's Villa," Tom said in the car, "you could find incredible stuff. All the marble, it was just piled up in these caves the archaeologists had dug out. The caves had metal doors on them, but they were never locked. You could walk in and help yourself."

"And now?"

"Oh, everything's padlocked. I suppose they got wind of what Adua was up to."

He winked. Adua tousled what hair he had left. By now we were out of the city, driving through the *campagna*, a flat landscape of sunflowers and hayricks. Big villas passed us, their high walls studded with hunks of broken glass bottle.

We came to some ruins—old arches and bits of aqueduct. Behind a tall fence, fields of grass and wheat spread out. In the distance I could see sheep grazing against a silhouette of buildings, one of which I recognized as St. Peter's.

Adua parked the car. We got out. It was raining, which should have clued me in on what they had in mind. With a kind of medical authority, as if it were a gland to be palpated, she felt at the metal fence. A sign was tacked to it, explaining in bureaucratic Italian that this was an archaeological zone: no trespassing.

"I think we can get over it," Adua said, fitting her foot into one of the wire squares of the fence. Yet when she hoisted herself up, the fence sagged. She started again. "Push my ass," she commanded, and we did. She hauled herself over, dropping abruptly onto the other side.

Tom went next, then I. As I fell, my jeans caught on the fence, which ripped a hole in them.

"Don't worry," Tom said. "Torn jeans are fashionable this year."

I looked back at the fence. How were we ever going to get back over it? I wondered. Meanwhile, Tom and Adua had set off toward St. Peter's. I followed them. For several minutes we trekked through mud and grass. Very far out, so far that you could no longer see the car, the ground started yielding up marble. The rain had moistened it, making it easier to see. I hadn't noticed before, but both Tom and Adua were carrying backpacks. Very quickly, they began gathering up their booty. "Look, this one's perfect!" Tom said, digging out a hexagonal paving stone.

"Oh, *cipollina*," Adua said, as she yanked a column fragment from the mud. "Look, the surface is striated, like a slice of onion."

After about twenty minutes—by now their backpacks were nearly full—a dog appeared. She was a very friendly, very dirty, brown-and-white sheepdog. I patted her head. Next some sheep rounded a hillock, accompanied by an old man carrying a stick. All of them gazed at us.

Immediately, Tom and Adua put down their backpacks.

"Good morning," Adua said to the old man. "Are these your sheep?"

"They are."

"What are you raising them for? Ricotta?"

"Ricotta, pecorino."

She smiled confidingly. "It's not too easy now, finding a really fresh ricotta in Rome. Not like in the old days."

"Everything was better then," the shepherd agreed.

Rather disingenuously, I thought, Adua touched Tom on the shoulder and pointed toward the skyline. "Perhaps you can help us," she said to the shepherd. "I've brought my American friends here so that they could get a view of the city from a distance, and we were wondering if that building was St. Peter's."

"Yes, it's St. Peter's," the shepherd answered. "And that one's San Paolo fuori le Mura."

"Of course! I didn't recognize it from here."

The shepherd now proceeded to give us a telescopic tour of the great Roman monuments. Adua asked him how long he had been working these fields. All his life, he said. Seventy-eight years.

"Well, we'd best be heading back," she said after a few minutes, and offered her hand. "It's been a pleasure."

"*Arrivederla, signora,*" the shepherd said, moving away with his dog.

Adua and Tom picked up their backpacks, and we started moving back toward the fence.

"Incredible, isn't it?" Tom said. "Sheep and shepherds—yet we're still inside the city limits."

"I hope he didn't notice what you were up to," I said.

Adua laughed. "Don't worry," she said. "He's not interested in marble. He's only interested in his ricotta."

After that, Tom became a fixture at Adua's poker games. The other players, he told me, were "lunatics" like him. He had "gotten the disease." He sent me letters in Düsseldorf describing his winnings: a slab of *giallo antico* from Ostia, some perfect tesserae of green *serpentino* from the baths of Caracalla. "Adua's had a lot of her pieces put into the floor of her apartment, like tiles," he said. "Only she keeps them covered with a carpet. She lives in terror of the *carabinieri* coming after her."

Via del Boschetto, he told me, was getting too expensive, so he had decided to sublet the apartment of a friend of Pepe's, on Via Bulgaria, in the Olympic Village. "Far out from the center, but the place is huge, and has a terrace. And compared to Via del Boschetto, I'm paying nothing. Practically nothing."

"But isn't it a problem getting to work?"

"Why? The fifty-three bus stops right outside my door."

I visited him only twice on Via Bulgaria. Even by the grim standards of the Roman *periferia*, the Olympic Village was ugly to the point of inspiring a kind of interior desolation: what Eastern Europe must have looked like before the wall came down. Long ago the habitations of 1960s athletes (designed, no doubt, according to sound principles of architectural rationality) had been converted into public housing: long, low rows of apartment blocks, constructed from umber-colored brick and raised up on pylons. A bramble of antennas sprouted on the roofs, and though there was space beneath the pylons for plenty of shops, almost all were vacant, only the most basic—a tobacconist, a grocery store, a pharmacy—having proved capable of flourishing in such meager soil.

Most of Tom's neighbors were elderly. They trod up and down the pedestrian walkways, daughters of seventy leading mothers of ninety. On the door of the pharmacy, to which he took me the first day, a placard announced, AVAILABLE HERE: INCONTINENCE DIAPERS.

As a language, Italian tends to eschew the sort of polite euphemisms in which English glories. Yet Tom, who in San Francisco had always displayed such a need for cheer, here seemed immune to the dreariness of his surroundings. Indeed, as he led me across the so-called park, clotted with weeds and littered with hypodermics, or down dark streets that, because the city had designated this the official zone for driving lessons and driving tests, were always filled with cars screeching to a halt, irritated instructors slamming their feet on auxiliary brakes, he exulted. "This is the real Rome," he said. "You want to eat the way the Romans eat, you want to eat *abbacchio* cooked the Roman way? This is where you'll find it."

As for his apartment—well, as he had promised, it *was* large. Essentially it consisted of a corridor off of which three square rooms opened. The floors were terrazzo, the walls a blinding white, the ceilings lit by naked bulbs. Because he had as yet had no time to shop, there was little in the way of furniture: a table (the one he was tied to) and two chairs in the kitchen, a foldout sofa in the living room, an ugly laminate armoire and a mattress in the bedroom. No lamps, no pictures, none of the decorative frippery to which he had been so devoted in San Francisco. Instead the apartment was dark, especially on those mornings when the sirocco swept down the long, quiet streets, spattering every outdoor surface with Saharan sand. Most of the marble he kept hidden in the armoire, and took out only when he wanted to show it off.

No doubt the apartment's strangest feature, however, was its door, which was padded, covered in what looked like red leather, and buttoned like a chesterfield. It would not have looked amiss in an asylum. Nor would any loud noise—for instance, a scream, or glass breaking—have been likely to penetrate that door. For what reason, I wondered, had Pepe's friend had it installed?

His new apartment made me frightened for Tom, much more frightened, even, than I'd been the day I'd gotten off the plane and he'd walked up to me, so changed that I barely recognized him. Everything about the move seemed contrary to his spirit—or perhaps I should say, contrary to the spirit he had displayed when we lived together. And why did he need so badly to save money? We had just sold the house, so he had some cash. Was it because he was spending everything he earned on marble? Or on something else?

It occurs to me, sitting in the *caserma*, that perhaps I ought to mention the poker games to the *maresciallo*. Only if I do, I might get Adua in trouble—assuming they haven't already found her. No doubt *her* number was in Tom's Filofax.

So did they just show up at her door, leading her, for an instant, to believe that her day of reckoning had come at last, and that her marble was to be confiscated? That she was to be fined, jailed, ruined? Probably. Until they explained the real reason for their visit. Tom was dead.

Something else I hadn't thought of: after the murder, when the *carabinieri* searched his flat, they must have found the paving stone. The one in *africano*. Not to mention the obelisk—a poker game winning. And God knows what other contraband.

Oh, how complicated it's all getting! Such a proliferation of motives! If Gina knew, she'd be thrilled. Yes, she'd say, it had to be one of those marble thieves. An intrigue. Killed for the sake of some *cipollina rossa.* Or a fragment of *frutticoloso*, so called because its many component colors suggest a basket of fruit, and, according to Adua, the rarest of the rare.

If they ask me, I'll tell them. I'll tell them everything I know. As long as they don't ask me, though, I'm keeping my mouth shut. This was something I learned to do in San Francisco, when I was cheating all the time on Tom: always tell the truth, but never volunteer anything.

Wool Street

Would things have gone better for us if we'd behaved like all the other faggots we knew, and had what was known as an "open" relationship? If Tom had been the sort of man who, upon surprising his lover in bed with someone else, didn't get mad, but got undressed . . . well, would we be living on Wool Street still? Sitting on a fortune in real estate? Still together? Tom still alive?

No, no. The scenario's too simplistic. For just as easily as it might have liberated me, the knowledge that Tom, too, was getting up to "that sort of thing" could have provoked in me a jealousy equal to his own. Or the lifting of the onus might have defused the thrill of adultery altogether. When transgression is divorced from subterfuge, the illicit becomes banal. The pleasure of cheating, it's in the scam, not the payoff—right?

So I took his loyalty for a ride. He never found out. Discord overwhelmed us, and we parted.

Oh, everything went so wildly, so perversely out of kilter! None of this was supposed to happen: not the Olympic Village, not Düsseldorf, not the patrol car nosing its way stealthily around the corner of Wool Street as I stand gawking at the house we used to own. For suddenly I'm there again—no longer in the *caserma* at all. The policeman slows, lowers his sunglasses. And what am I but a loiterer, a ne'er-do-well, just the sort of rabble he's paid to scare away?

Of course, if I wanted to, I could explain my presence to him. "I used to live here," I could say. "This neighborhood used to be my neighborhood. I used to shop at the grocery store on the corner." But I don't want to. Instead I smile, walk back across the street, and climb into my rental car. Switch on the ignition. Drive away.

It's all my fault. I squandered what I should have cherished. I took for granted Tom's reliability, the fact that every day, at every hour of the day, I knew where to find him: mornings in the kitchen, writing or cooking; from noon to one, the gym; afternoons back in the kitchen, or babysitting. More crucially, on those rare occasions when he veered from his routine, he always made a point of calling to tell me. "I'll be at Gina's until three-thirty," he'd say. "Then I'm going grocery shopping. Then I have to meet Mrs. Roxburgh to plan a lunch. I should be home by seven, unless I hit traffic—"

"That's fine," I'd say.

"Let me give you the number at Mrs. Roxburgh's," he'd say.

"That's all right. I don't need it," I'd say.

"I just don't want you to worry," he'd say.

As for me, I gave him no outward cause for anxiety. I kept all my ducks in a row. Only sometimes I'd call half an hour before one of his dinner parties and say that I couldn't come. "I forgot that we have a test this week. My Urdu class."

How feeble was the noise he made on these occasions, disappointment thudding in the echo chamber of purported indifference.

Sometimes I wondered if he ever got suspicious. I rather hoped he might. I rather hoped he'd make inquiries, and discover that indeed, an Urdu class *was* being offered at San Francisco State on Thursday evenings. For my deceptions were artful. I knew Tom well enough to know that once he found out the course existed, he would never check whether I was actually enrolled in it. Instead, shame at having distrusted me in the first place would swamp him, inducing that superfluity of regret that in his case almost always took the form of an urge to bake: something creamy and sticky, which I would find waiting for me when I got home.

It was on these nights—sitting in our kitchen in the aftermath of some carnal misdeed—that I would experience most deeply the giddy relief of the liar. Nor is this delight so remote, in the end, from artistic ecstasy, the pleasure of seeing a well-crafted thing work well.

All my ducks in a row.

* * *

Or perhaps I have it wrong, and it was Tom who was playing *me* for the fool. Perhaps, the whole time, he too was getting up to "that sort of thing"; in which case his pledges of fidelity, his insistence on keeping me abreast of his many activities— all this was as much a needless vaudeville as my Thursday night Urdu class.

Needless—unless what he needed was to feel that he was getting away with something.

I tried to remain faithful, if not to him, then to his fear, to his largely unspoken conviction that only by being "good" might we hope to avoid the sort of fate so many others had suffered. For he seemed to perceive our coming together as a covenant, the terms of which required us to give up, in exchange for health, the very life implied by the place where we had come together. Only by retreating from a septic world, as the storytellers in the *Decameron* had done, might we save ourselves, save each other.

According to this way of thinking, to look for sex outside your marriage was not merely to betray the person you loved, but to bring rabies into England—as if a vow of loyalty were the same thing as a vaccination.

In lying there is often this lie: that we do it to protect other people.

Keeping him in the dark was never very difficult, I think in part because, without even being aware of it, he wanted to be kept in the dark. Also, the combination of my language classes and Tom's devotion to his friends' children left me with large amounts of time for which I wasn't accountable, especially on those weekends when he would volunteer to babysit for some couple who were going off to Lake Tahoe to save their marriage. He'd move himself into their house, sleep in their bed, and take care of their kids.

During those weekends, what seemed most important to him was that he establish, with those Justins and Samuels and Maxes, the very camaraderie of boys from which, as a boy, he had been excluded, thanks largely to his inability to throw a ball, his high voice, in short, his stubborn adherence to all the classic attributes of the good faggot. For despite the cruelty that had marred his childhood, still, he longed to be treated as a boy by boys, which was why, even as he baked, he collected baseball cards, and was always trying to get me to go to the park with him to play catch.

Now he was not so much the adult to whom children looked up as the secret playmate whose grown-up bearing and possessions (a credit card, a driver's license) brought certain enviable and forbidden attractions within reach. With Tom, his young charges could eat the things they weren't supposed to eat, see the movies they weren't supposed to see. In this regard Tom fit perfectly the clinical profile of the pedophile . . . except that he was not a pedophile. Sexuality had nothing to do with it; to him those boys were not emblems, they were not "the boy" whose allure must wither as he himself blooms. Instead he loved them simply and individually, as well as loving the ease with which they loved him, their love reliable and pure of complication, and remote from the bristly, fitful love of adult for adult.

And yet in the background, there always lurked a certain unease, a skittishness on Tom's part to match the volubility with which his friends avowed their trust in him.

For instance, I remember a dinner once—it was an occasion dinner, though I can't recall which occasion: Thanksgiving, perhaps. Tom had done all the cooking, of course. There were children, and two or three of the couples, and only one other queer: his former boyfriend Ernie, whom he had invited only because he was alone, and dying. Visibly dying.

I mean, you could see the patches of foundation make-up that he had rubbed onto his face to hide the KS lesions.

A husband—this was Tony, who was married to Gina; typically, he worked in the computer industry—was talking about his boyhood. About all the "macho crap" he'd had to put up with, coming of age in the fifties. Of late Tony had joined a men's group, the members of which went on camping trips, and danced around a wood fire, and wept together over paternal cruelties.

"When Justin grows up," he said, "I want him to be at peace in his masculinity. That way he'll be a better father than I am. A better husband, too."

Gina picked up her napkin and dabbed at the corner of her eyes. Reaching across the table, she squeezed his hand.

A silence fell. I remember there was a big bowl of tangerines and walnuts in the center of the table. Ernie took a walnut and cracked it between his teeth. "All well and good," he said, "but what if Justin grows up to be queer?"

Tony, who was taking a gulp from his wineglass, spluttered onto the tablecloth, then looked anxiously toward his son, who was playing with Lego blocks.

He appeared to regard Justin's fixation on the Lego blocks with relief.

"You see?" Ernie said. "The very idea terrifies you. And yet who's to say he won't grow up to be queer? I did. Tom did."

"Ernie, please," Tom said.

"Look, I understand your point, and I respect it," Tony said, "only in the case of Justin, it seems fairly obvious—"

"Why, because he plays baseball? I played baseball. For Christ's sake, I was pitcher on the varsity team."

"What Tony means," Gina interjected, "is that we just want our son to grow up to be happy and well adjusted. To be a good partner and a good parent."

"So you're saying you won't mind if he turns out to be queer?"

"Please keep your voice down."

"Well, that proves my point. Suddenly *queer*'s a dirty word. And if that's how things are in your house, then no matter what Justin does, he's fucked for life. For all your sanctimonious good intentions, you're making it clear that you expect him to grow up a certain way. In a sense you're ordering him to."

"Justin, why don't you go to the other room?" Tony said. "The grown-ups need private time."

"No," said Justin.

By now Tom was nearly apoplectic. He hated it, he told me later, when his dinners were spoiled. And what had spoiled this one?

"Conflict," he replied, plunging a steel pan into scalding dishwater.

"But Ernie only said what he felt."

"He didn't have to be so confrontational. He offended Tony."

"Tony offended him."

"Tony didn't mean to offend anyone. A guy like that, it's not easy for him to open up. For once he was feeling at ease, like he could really say what was on his mind. Now he'll always be on his guard with us."

"He offended me," I added after a moment.

"I just don't see why Ernie had to be so holier-than-thou. It's as if he thinks being sick means he isn't obliged to be civil."

"Was he being uncivil?"

"He should have watched his language. Also, his timing was terrible. He upset everybody, especially the children."

"The children weren't listening."

"How do you know?" Tom asked.

What seemed imperative to him, during those years, was a certain kind of forgetting: to do one's duty, to pay one's dues, and then at the end of the day to return to a place from which illness—even the mention of illness—was effectively barred.

And because sex was for him so intimately bound up with illness, this had to be a place from which sex, too, was barred—virtually barred.

So once a week—it seemed to be part of that bargain he had struck, altruism in exchange for a life sentence—he volunteered at the AIDS hospice that his friend Caroline ran. Sometimes I accompanied him. I liked the hospice, which was in many ways far more cheerful than our own crypto-dream-bunker. It was located in a small, sunny house at the end of a cul-de-sac around which children rode their bicycles with unusual ferocity. We would bring food, and if it was spring, fresh flowers—irises and tulips—and I remember that one morning Tom was arranging the flowers in vases, when one of the patients called out, "Caroline, could you come here for a moment? I think John just died." Caroline went, and it was true: John had died. No one seemed overly upset. The police were summoned. They did not, as I'd heard they had early in the epidemic, when no one knew anything, pull a gun on the corpse. ("If you'd feel better about it, you can tie him up," the distraught widower is reputed to have remarked on one of these occasions; "it wouldn't be the first time.") A doctor arrived to sign the death certificate, an ambulance to take away the body. Quiet prayers were said, and lunch was made.

"Around here," Caroline said, "death is never an emergency. The only emergency is pain."

We stayed for lunch—corn chowder, chicken with almonds, chocolate pudding. Comfort food, all made by Tom. Then the roommate of the man who'd died called Caroline over to his bedside and whispered something to her. "He wants to speak to you," she said.

"Who? Me?" asked Tom. "Why?"

"I don't know."

We walked over to the man's bed. He had a tube in his nose. He could barely lift his head.

There was a chair next to the bed, and Tom sat down in it.

The man lifted his lips to Tom's ear. "Don't you remember me?" he asked.

"I'm sorry," Tom said. "I . . ."

"I'm a friend of Ernie's. Keith Musgrave. Don't you remember that weekend in Lake Tahoe? We rented a cabin— you and Ernie and Steven and I. Four boys and only one bed."

Tom blushed. "Oh, of course. How are you?"

"How am I?"

"Sorry," Tom said, "I didn't mean . . ."

"It's O.K. So how's Ernie doing these days? Are you two still in touch?"

"Ernie? Oh, well, he's . . . passed on. Just a few weeks ago."

"Ah. So I'll be seeing him soon." Keith looked up. "Or on second thought . . ." And he looked down.

Tom stood. "I'm afraid we have to go," he said. "It's certainly been a pleasure."

"The pleasure was all mine," Keith answered, turning to look out the window. And we headed out the door.

It had started raining by the time we left the hospice. I remember Tom's silence in the car, his pale and vulnerable profile: chiseled sideburn, protruding nose, watermelon-colored lips. His hand gripping the wheel. One half-obscured, blinking brown eye focused, urgently, on the road. We had no plans for the rest of the weekend, and I was desperately trying to think some up, running in my head through an ever shorter list of friends on whom we could still count for company . . . but Mary's baby was sick, and Gina and Tony were at Disneyland, and Joan's best friend was dying. Suddenly a car made an illegal left turn in front of us, Tom honked the horn, smashed on the brakes, we skidded in the rain and nearly collided with a 94 bus. "Fuck," he said, in a voice that suggested he was sorry we hadn't, then, righting the car, lugged us back into traffic.

"Was the problem that you didn't recognize him?" I asked.

"Who?"

"Keith."

"Oh, him. No, at first I didn't."

I stretched my arms behind my head. "So I guess it mustn't have been a very good weekend."

"And what's that supposed to mean?"

"Nothing. Just . . . that if it had been a good weekend, you'd have remembered it."

"We didn't do anything unsafe, O.K.?"

"What does that have to do with anything?"

"Well, clearly that's what you're wondering . . . and if that's the case, you can rest assured. I've been completely up front with you so far as my history is concerned. You've got nothing to worry about."

"Of course I've got nothing to worry about. We never have sex."

"Oh, so we're back to that again—"

"We're not back to anything."

"Why won't I just have the test and be done with it."

"I never mentioned the test. You brought up the test. All of this is in your head, not mine."

We arrived home. The rain had gotten worse. I remember that I was correcting proofs, and Tom was sitting at his desk, drawing endless concentric circles with a protractor, when I felt a drop of water hit my head and, looking up, saw a patch of paint on the ceiling bulging like a tumor, rainwater collecting underneath. Tom noticed it the same moment I did, a pregnancy gathering there, and then before we could do or say anything the fragile membrane broke, and water fell to the floor, as before a birth. He jumped up, grabbed a box of tissues, and dropped to his knees before the spreading gray stain on the carpet.

"Call a plumber!" he screamed, but I just watched as he piled tissues on top of tissues to soak up the water.

"But, Tom, a plumber can't—"

"Are you just going to stand there? Aren't you going to help at all?"

"O.K., O.K."

"You don't need to use that tone of voice. There's really no justification for that tone of voice. And bring some paper towels."

I went into the kitchen, where we kept the phone books. I called a plumber, though I could not fathom what he was supposed to do. In crisp tones, he informed me that a weekend visit would cost $55 off the bat, plus $35 an hour, plus parts. "Whatever," I said, hung up, and went back into the living room, where Tom was still crouching over his soggy pile of tissues.

"I've called the plumber. He's on his way."

"You're so slow. Three minutes I've been waiting here for you to bring me paper towels. And now that I think about it, it's probably been three minutes every day since we started living together—at least. That's twenty-one minutes a week, eighty-four minutes a month, over a thousand minutes a year. Which means that in ten years, I've lost a hundred and sixty days—something like five months—just waiting for you. Now give me the damn paper towels."

"I forgot the paper towels."

Tom looked up at me. I sat on the sofa.

"I can't stay here anymore," I said. "I'm going crazy. You're driving me crazy."

"Are you saying you're leaving me?" he asked, his voice low, as if he'd been expecting it.

"Not you. This." I pointed to the rug, to the sopping pile of tissues.

"I knew you'd do this one day," Tom said. "You're a coward. You think you can run away from pain. Soon enough you'll find out, though. No one can."

He quieted, and I turned to watch where the rain was falling against the window, so thickly sheeted that for a moment it seemed to be flowing upward.

"Just don't expect me to be waiting for you when you come back," Tom said. He was rubbing his hands together, gathering the white clots of tissue into a ball.

"I wouldn't expect that."

Suddenly our voices were calm, we were talking like normal human beings. "Where are you planning to go, anyway?" he asked, as casually as if I were a friend planning a vacation.

"I thought Düsseldorf."

"Düsseldorf!"

"There's a job in Düsseldorf. I saw it posted at school. For an interpreter."

"Oh, that sounds grand! Now I know why you were taking all those language courses."

I hadn't known myself until then.

He threw a vase at me. I remember feeling a certain detached curiosity, because no one had ever thrown anything at me before, and the vase was the same color as the water, and suddenly, everywhere, there were pieces of vase, and water, and flowers.

I put on my jacket, even though my shirt was soaked with the stinking water the flowers had been rotting in. "Vincent!" I heard him call as I went out the door, but his voice was distant already, as if I'd never see him again. I got into my car. He was standing by the window, looking out at me. Silent. The heavy rain against the glass made him look as if he were melting.

Via in Selci

Is it only thanks to what happened afterward—to that shadowing of motive with which retrospect tints the past—that I remember Tom, the last time I saw him, as somehow both sullen and brazen, withdrawn and at the same moment broken-bottle sharp, as if he had decided to throw off once and for all that wadding of gentility in which most of our intercourse sheathed itself? Not surprisingly, the occasion was dinner. The Morgue. Across a marble table the metaphorical ironies of which would only become apparent later on, we peered at each other—or rather, I peered at him and he peered over my head, over my shoulder, at a new waiter who had started the day before. Since the episode with Enzo and the pasta and chickpeas—not suprisingly, he had never gone back to Trattoria da Giuseppina—this matter of Tom and waiters had become a source of worry, and not only to me but, I learned later, to all his Roman friends. "Look at those forearms," he said, and I did—hairy and dark, the requisite gold bracelet slung low on the wrist. The hands that gave us our pizzas were blunt-fingered, with clean, moon-colored nails.

"Noontime shadow," Tom said.

"Noontime what?"

"That type would never make it to five o'clock."

It was typical of his jokes. "He looks like Tony," I said.

"Does he?" Tom put on his glasses, which of late he'd taken to wearing on a cord around his neck. "No, he doesn't. He doesn't look anything like Tony."

We ate our pizzas quickly, and without saying much. Later, I would try to explain to the *carabinieri* the peculiar impression I took with me as we left the pizzeria, of something having changed in Tom . . . and yet my Italian wasn't up to explaining just what that something was. Now I've had time to consider the matter, and I think I can fairly say that what had changed was his attitude toward love. Somehow it was both harder and sharper than it had once been, vulnerable and rapacious at once, like a can with a rusty edge. When we'd lived together, I'd often thought that Tom perceived love the way dogs did, that the idea was for us to be a warm lap in which he and I could curl up; love, in other words, as sleep. Only I hadn't played along. I'd left, and in doing so robbed the crypto-dream-house of its lazy, cozy, dull, lovely dream.

All this I try to tell the *maresciallo* and his typing deputy, who takes down every word. Even so, I fail, at least in my own mind, to get the idea across in all its raggedness. Any student of language knows that limit. They are silent while I speak, and I speak for a long time. Then I stop speaking. The deputy stops typing. "Yes," he says.

The other deputy coughs; interrupts. "Excuse me," he says, "but may I ask if the professor ever expressed any resentment, after you left him?"

I shake my head. "Not a word. He never rebuked me, or threatened me, never even tried to convince me to come back. In fact, the only thing he said was that he respected the choice I had made, and wanted to do everything he could to make sure we stayed friends."

The deputy types: Tom's nobility, his humility, glow green against that black screen. And yet even as I extol him, I'm doubting myself. After all, for whom else but me could he have been performing the last night at the Morgue, when he stared so brazenly at the waiter? Not merely undressing him with his eyes, but tearing into him with his eyes, the rusty edge of his eyes—as if to say, because of you, Vincent, I am brought this low. This is my revenge. There is no better way to hurt someone else than by hurting yourself.

The interview is almost over. Across from me, the *maresciallo* regards his folder; says, "Bah-bah-bah"; drums his fingers against the desk. "Let me see if there's anything else . . . Oh yes, the waiter at the Morgue. What did he look like?"

"Well, he was tall. Dark."

"The classic Mediterranean?"

"I suppose you could say so."

"Thin?" interjects the typing deputy.

"No, quite well built."

"Hairy?"

"Quite."

"Hairy like me," the *maresciallo* asks, "or like my colleague?" And he points to the deputy at the corner of the desk.

I glance from one chest to the other. Both men have the first several buttons of their shirts undone, and both have abundantly, one might even say exuberantly hairy chests . . . which Tom, it was true, always admired. I don't have a hairy chest. In fact, I wasn't his type at all, nor was he mine.

And yet I don't go along with the pornographic joke, I don't, as Tom, in his last days, might have done, say, "Well, I'm not sure. Perhaps if you took your shirts off . . ." For Tom is dead, and I must not be nearly so bad a faggot as I have pretended, for I simply tell the *maresciallo*, "I would have to say hairy like your colleague," and then look away, as if it's no business of mine.

The *maresciallo* gets up from his chair. "Thank you," he says. "I believe we're finished now."

"Are we?"

"All that's left is to print out your statement. You can read it and see if there's anything you'd like to change or delete . . . or add. Then you need merely to sign the document and you're free to go."

"But who killed him?"

He laughs. "If we knew that, we wouldn't have dragged you here from Düsseldorf, now would we?"

Pages spit out of a printer and are handed to me.

"My name is Vincent Burke," I read, "and I first met Thomas Carlomusto in New York in 1985 . . ."

The story of our lives, then. Yet who would have guessed it would have been written here, and in such exceptionally elegant Italian?

After the interview's over—after I've signed the statement, shaken the hands of all three *carabinieri*, and been treated, against my will, to yet another coffee—I walk through the Forum to the Colosseum, and then down Via San Giovanni in Laterano, until I reach the church of San Clemente. The church has just reopened. No one's there except for a young seminarian, perhaps an assistant to the sacristan, who has come to remove the guttered candles. Through the gloomy church light he looks at me; across pews and frescoes and acres of marble, those intricate floors by which Tom was so bewitched.

Was it him, then? He could not resemble the *maresciallo* less: a beanpole of a boy, with narrow shoulders, squinting eyes, a fat nose out of which hairs grow. Like a grotesque figure in some Renaissance painting . . . and yet, as he gathers the dead candles, he gazes at me, and his gaze is unwavering.

Was that what got Tom, then: the allure of the uniform? The rough belt loosened, and then, all at once, his mouth inside the cassock, sucking in the odor of wool and sweat?

The seminarian's hands clutching his head, like a bobbing pregnancy?

Well, it's possible. Anything's possible. It could have been the Fascist student, or an offended waiter, or a marble thief. Or a Romanian hustler—an *extracommunitario*—picked up at the station men's room, the one with the glass partitions. Or a fellow English teacher. Or it could have been me. Really, there's no reason at all why it couldn't have been me.

You'll never know. The case will never be solved. In a few months the folder with Tom's name on it will be shut, taken off the *maresciallo*'s desk, and deposited in that storage room through which I was led on the way to his office. Filed away with others of its kind.

Twenty-two others, to be precise.

I approach the seminarian. "*Buon giorno,*" he says.

"*Buon giorno,*" I say, and feed a 500-lire coin into a black metal slot. There is an echoey clangor as it hits the dark bottom of the collection box. Then I take a fresh candle and light it; set it down amid all the other votives; form my lips around Tom's name.

I walk away. I have no idea if the seminarian is watching me, if he is lifting a monstrance or an obelisk to smash against my skull. Instead I have my eyes on the floor. These Escher-like interlardings of color really do create the most peculiar illusion of depth . . . and yet if you fell into them, they would break your nose. You couldn't lift it off, once you'd been spread out on that table, and the marble quilt had been drawn over your eyes.

A NOTE ON THE AUTHOR

David Leavitt is the author of several novels, three story collections, and, most recently, *Florence, A Delicate Case*, from Bloomsbury's series The Writer and the City. He lives in Gainesville and teaches at the University of Florida.

A NOTE ON THE TYPE

The text of this book is set in Bodoni Book. Giambattista Bodoni designed his typefaces at the end of the eighteenth century. The Bodoni types were the culmination of nearly three hundred years of evolution in roman type design. Bodoni is recognized by its high contrast between thick and thin strokes, pure vertical stress, and hairline serifs.